GW01607272

SLAVE SHIP

This major novel of the slave trade annihilates the myths of black African docility and white humanity on an unforgettable voyage.

Aboard the slave ship *Jubilation* is Captain Horneby, a quietly lethal man for whom slaving is a way of life and a chance to play God. Below decks, in a hold overflowing with degradation and death, is Osai Adoko, a proud Ashanti warrior who waits to prove that chains do not make a man a slave. And there is Dunbar, a journalist who intends to expose the atrocities of the trade, but is forced to become the owner of a beautiful slave.

The action moves swiftly, from a ruinous jungle slave factory to an opulent African court, from a bizarre shore leave to a bloody sea battle and to rampant depravity aboard the ship. The book builds towards a brilliant, horrifying climax.

Also by the author:

Slave

The Long Tattoo

Prelude to Civil War: Kansas-Missouri 1854-1861 (nonfiction)

SLAVE SHIP

by Eric Corder

W. H. ALLEN · LONDON · 1970

First British edition, 1970
Printed and bound in Great Britain by
Butler & Tanner Ltd., Frome and London
for the publishers
W. H. Allen & Co., Ltd.,
Essex Street, London WC2.
ISBN 0 491 00304 8

For Fredi

and for Ron and Laura

with love

Money? Why, I'd plow the sea to porridge to make money.

—*Simeon Potter* (Rhode Island shipowner and slave merchant)

The Negro is a beast, but created with articulate speech, and hands, that he may be of service to his master—the White man.

—*Charles Carrol* (author)

We shall have our manhood. We shall have it or the earth will be leveled by our attempts to gain it.

—*Eldridge Cleaver* (black militant and author)

BOOK I

BOOK I

THERE was a scream—a dog, a colicky child, something dying shrilly in the forest; Osai Adoko stirred on his woven sleeping mat. The scream was worth no more.

But the second one was, and he came fully and instantly awake, lunged up and toward the corner of the room where the long spears stood and the heavy-bladed sword rested on twin pegs of wrought gold. His right hand seized the handle of the sword, his left closed around the shafts of two spears. He ran into the night.

It was not dark. A three-quarter moon washed pale light down through thin black clouds. But more, there was a thick yellow glow rising from the home of Okomfo Kenoyo. The thatched roofs of the small buildings were burning fiercely.

Osai Adoko slashed empty air with his sword. The

Ashanti were king. When they fought, when they made war, which was often, it was the *Ashanti* who dictated the time and place. No one attacked an Ashanti village, even one this small and this far from the center of the nation. Osai Adoko would more readily have believed that a household slave would relieve himself upon the personal fetish of the Asantahene of all Asantahenes. Both acts were equally unthinkable.

The brightness of the spreading fires overwhelmed the moonlight and Osai Adoko saw figures struggling in silhouette. He raised his sword and raced to battle on long, well-muscled legs. They would pay, whoever they were. They would pay with their blood and with the blood of their children and with the blood of their cousins and of their cousins' cousins. They would pay with their bound bodies delivered over to the white slavers, and the foul-smelling ships. They would pay with their severed heads on flat stones, with their slaughtered animals left for the carrion scavengers, with their homes reduced to dust and ashes. They would pay until nothing remained to prove that they had ever lived.

Osai Adoko saw the sons of Okomfo Kenoyo and that good man's slaves. They were well armed and they were fighting intelligently, banding together, presenting solid resistance to the superior numbers of the enemy. Shouts from behind told Osai Adoko that his own brothers and the slaves of his father had reacted as quickly as he, and, in midstride, he bloomed with joy and pride and easy, vengeful confidence.

He could see the invaders now. Fanti, treacherous pigs! They were near brothers of the Ashanti, sharing a language and customs whose difference was no more than that in the sound produced by striking a drum slightly left of center, then slightly right. Brothers did not enslave brothers, not, at least, among the Ashanti and Fanti.

A musket boomed and one of the raiders somersaulted backwards. Adoko's great rashness, to the thinking of his fellows, was that though he valued firearms for others, knew fully that no tribe, no nation, could survive, much less triumph, without them, he preferred wood and cutting edges; and he had won much glory because of it.

A group of Fanti were closing a circle around a party of Ashanti. Adoko came lightly to a halt, cocked his arm, bellowed, and skewered one of the enemy through the back. The man fell, breaking off the iron head and the few inches of wood that had ripped through his chest, then quivered on the ground, dying, sending tiny vibrations through the shaft that rose from between his shoulder blades.

Half a dozen raiders whirled and rushed Adoko. He thrust left-handed with his remaining spear and opened the stomach of the first man. He took out the eye of the second man in the same fashion. Then his sword whistled down and lopped off an arm at the elbow. His other assailants leaped upon him, and he fell under their combined weight. His head and chest were struck heavily. Someone was trying to drive a knee into his groin. His weapons were useless in such quarters. He let them slip from his hands. He began to bite and claw and squeeze. His fingers plunged into a mouth; he hooked them and pulled. The man atop him shrieked, his cheek ripped apart nearly to the ear.

The bodies lifted suddenly and blood spilled warm upon him.

"Up, Adoko, up!" A hand jerked him to his feet. It was one of his brothers. Two of the household slaves were with him, red with the life juice of the Fanti lying dead at their feet.

Adoko rejoined the fight. Yellow and orange light flickered and glimmered on faces and sweat-sheened bodies as the fires spread. The hot air was difficult to breathe, and pounding feet raised clouds of dust that scraped and spasmed the lungs. The Ashanti had one advantage. The raiders were forced to curtail their use of deadly force; corpses could not be sold. The Ashanti labored under no such restraint. They could and they did kill freely, striking with ferocity at any man within range. They held their ground for several vicious minutes, but then sheer numbers began to batter them down and they were forced to draw back. Grudgingly.

Something rolled across the ground and bumped against Adoko's foot. He looked down and saw the head of Okomfo Kenoyo. Blood was spurting from the neck. The lined face of the venerable old man was scratched and bruised. The eyelids fluttered, opened wide, then closed. The mouth tightened, and Okomfo Kenoyo's head became garbage for the pigs.

Adoko was driven to the buildings of his father's house. He saw one of his sisters spitted as she tried to wield a sword much too heavy for her. Adoko felt pride. There would be few slaves taken tonight. He split open the face of an oncoming Fanti. A thrown club caught him on the temple. He went to his knees. A raider came howling at him. Adoko thrust with his spear. The point went into the man's open mouth, cut upward, and penetrated his brain. The butt of the spear was wrenched from Adoko's grasp when the man fell. Adoko regained his feet and gripped his sword with both hands. His back was against the wall. He spun to parry a blow from his left. He saw his son, Osai Tola, who was five years old and one of the most wiry and clever of the village children. Tola's lips were pulled back from his even white teeth. He held a ceremonial dagger over his head and tried to drive the blunt ornament into the back of a Fanti who was clubbing a fallen man. The Fanti sent the boy sprawling with a backhanded slap.

Adoko was smashed in the kidney by a musket stock. He

twisted with pain. He was kicked in the stomach. He swung his sword; bone crunched. He was tripped with the shaft of a spear. They were on him before he fell. Strong hands locked his wrists, pinned his ankles together. Choking fingers dug into his throat. He bit. His teeth went through flesh and muscle and joined each other. He shook his head like a dog, tearing. There was a crack on the top of his skull, and brilliant white fingerlets fractured his vision. He bit again. His head exploded twice more. The fourth time the club struck, Adoko raged at his own weakness, and then he knew nothing more.

The corpses were heaped into three large careless piles. An equal number of heads, young and old of both sexes, lay on the blood-sodden earth a few feet away. The executions had begun at dawn, as soon as there was sufficient light for the Fanti to weed out captives so severely wounded that the white slavers would not purchase them. There were many, but the victors were efficient and the process consumed little more than an hour.

Adoko, who had awakened with ringing ears, chained, saw his father brought forward. The Osai of the house, the father of the family's fathers, the Osai of the village's four Fathers, shook off the hands he found so offensive, walked without faltering, as if the two deep and crusty wounds in his chest were of no concern and the foamy blood hemorrhaging on his lips were natural, and then—refusing to go to his knees—dropped to sit cross-legged, inclined his head, and said, "Strike, land snails!"

Two cuts of the sword were needed. The head finally fell into the Osai's own lap. He sat erect, ludicrously, headlessly, until a Fanti kicked him over. Adoko watched in expressionless silence. He prayed briefly for his father. Then a sense of anxiety rose in him. The family was now fatherless.

Something should be done. His brothers and sisters should consult. A new Osai should be selected. A family needs its father. Under other circumstances he would have been his kinsmen's choice. This was not pride, but simple recognition of fact. Osai Adoko was without peer in valor. Osai Adoko, in the interludes of peace, made the family business, the merchanting of the stimulating kola nut, prosper in a way equaled only by his father. Osai Adoko was frequently sought by his brothers and sisters and others of the household for counsel.

Because it was necessary, Osai Adoko, sitting in chains, took it upon himself to become *the* Osai of his family. It was a question of survival.

"Get up! Get moving!" The Fanti were using sticks and leather straps to rouse their captives and set them on the march. There were groans and the clinking of chain links.

A supple rod stung Adoko's shoulders. He clenched his jaw and pushed himself to his feet. His body ached; there was a sharp pain in his skull. He accepted. Pain was something to be borne. Standing, he looked at his manacled wrists. A ring was set in one of the cuffs and through it ran a heavy chain that fastened Adoko to the other males in the coffle. Iron round his flesh! He shook his hands furiously and strained against the metal until the muscles of his shoulders and arms threatened to rupture.

In moments he gave it up and consciously relaxed himself. Action now was futile. The time would come, perhaps soon, more likely not, but it would come, eventually, and then he would act. Not before.

The coffle started forward. The Fanti had taken only some eighty prisoners, including women and children. That from a village of more than three hundred. Adoko felt satisfaction. Ashanti were not slaves. He searched the women, who, like the men, were nearly all of them naked, the attack having jerked everyone in the village from sleeping mats. The women were shackled in pairs, right wrist to left wrist, and were not joined together by a chain. Adoko filed this away; it might later prove crucial. Neither of his two wives was among the female captives.

They were dead, then. Some, a handful or two of the women and probably a few servants, would have escaped into the forest. But not Adoko's wives. Their character was not such. Adoko entered a period of formal sorrow. They had been good women, both of them, dutiful wives and careful mothers. Eama, the first, had also about her a gentleness that sprang from strength and confidence and that was the foundation of her seemingly limitless patience. Tui, the second, barely out of girlhood, had a quick and full smile. Where Eama succored and restored, Tui swept like gales to heights of dizzying excitement. He hoped they had died without ignominy. Perhaps later he could find someone able to tell him.

There were only a dozen and a half children. They were tied to each other with a light cord, which was circled in a noose around each little neck. His son Tola was there. The boy, his oldest, Eama's child, was walking with his back straight, his face stony. Adoko was proud. Clasping Tola's hand and waddling alongside with her thumb in her mouth was Lianu, Adoko's first child from Tui. She was the youngest in the coffle, and her presence was surprising; the price she would bring was hardly worth the effort of carrying her along. Maybe she had been spared because of her chubby health, a profitable item after all. Or one of the raiders might have softened with his sword suspended above her. That did not seem likely. No others her size had survived. And all the infants, including two that were Adoko's flesh, had either been massacred or had burned, helpless where they lay, when the flaming roofs collapsed upon them.

Four dead from the seven that had been his own small family . . . He swept the coffle again, counting. His father's family, with thirteen slaves, had numbered eighty-four. He found, including himself and his two children, only nineteen. He mourned the many dead. Then he exulted in the courage the house of his father had shown.

Instinctively he embraced all the captives as his new family. It was natural. It was essential.

Should this family, in time, elect someone other than him to be their Osai, he would abandon the responsibility and give all support and loyalty to the new father. For now, though, he must act, feel, and think solely for their benefit.

There were two dozen Fanti guarding the coffle, all heavily armed. Ordinarily, less than half that number would have been sent to shepherd so few slaves. But these were Ashanti and could be expected, if they thought they had the slightest chance of success, to fight even though chained. That most would die would not deter them. The only real safeguard was to provide so many warriors that no attempt would be made. The majority of the guards carried muskets along with their swords and daggers; a few had unwieldy large-bore pistols, as well. Many wore rings and bracelets and robe ornaments of worked gold which they had stolen from the conquered village. But they were glum and sour-faced. The attack had cost them dearly, and several had begun to think of the consequences. They treated their prisoners with increasing harshness, trying as their confidence slipped to reassert their supremacy, their sense of control.

The Ashanti suffered the sticks and straps and the occasional flesh-ripping bite of a whip in silence. But when a guard shouted insults at one of the captives, the man began an angry reply.

Adoko called sharply, "That is not to our good. Hold your words."

The Fanti, because of their uneasiness and growing fear of retribution, misunderstood, interpreting Adoko this way: *Quiet, defy them and you will only worsen the treatment they give us.* The acquiescence relieved them.

But the rebellious Ashanti knew instantly what Adoko meant, and he shut his mouth. It is unforgivable to antagonize an enemy, particularly one holding the superior position, for no reason other than personal satisfaction. Such behavior only heightens his alertness and therefore diminishes your chances of success. One taunts an enemy only when such insults might move him to an anger which will cause him to act rashly, carelessly.

They were marching south, toward the coast, but also swinging wide to the west, away from Ashanti territory. The Fanti wanted no chance encounter with the tribesmen of their captives. Adoko studied the guards carefully. They were all strong, blooded warriors, and they worked with smooth efficiency under a leader who was vigilant and perceptive. Every man's musket was charged; hammers rested at safety cock. Swords looked clean and well cared for and were in easy reach. If the Fanti were weary from last night's fighting, they displayed no sign of it. The guards were heaviest around the male captives, close enough to move in and strike quickly, yet not so near that they could be grabbed by a sudden lunge. Adoko could find no vulnerable point.

For the moment.

The column halted when the sun was a little past its peak. The guards had the women build small fires. Yams and plantains were cooked, and after the Fanti had eaten, small potions were doled out to each captive. Slight murmurs, like soft breezes in a growth of ferns, swept over the prisoners. No one spoke aloud. There was only the shifting and rearranging of posture, a few whispered syllables, barely perceptible gestures. But information was being gathered. It began when one of Adoko's brothers looked at him with his features saying: *What do we do?* Adoko leaned forward to pick a piece of hot yam from a palm leaf and said, "Weapons?"

The question was passed through the Ashanti ranks, to the women, too, and the answer came back negative. Adoko then sent out a request for any weaknesses that had been noted in their captors.

None.

Are anyone's bonds defective? Is there a chance of single escape to bring help?

No.

Is anyone seriously wounded?

A daughter of Okomfo Kenoyo. She is hemorrhaging up blood from her lungs. But she is swallowing it to keep the pigs from knowing.

Help her as you can.

Adoko assimilated what he had learned. There was nothing that could be done. But they had turned to him. They had accepted him as their Osai without hesitation. He was responsible for them.

He said: *We must—*

The Fanti began kicking and rod-lashing the captives to their feet. There were several groans, for the rest had caused bruised muscles and joints to stiffen anew.

"Your tongues will feast insects! Your skulls will gleam on trees!" Besu, one of Adoko's older brothers, hurled himself at a guard. The chain caught him up short, dragging the men before him and behind him to the ground, but his straining fingers still managed to bunch up the Fanti's robe. Besu and the guard sprawled down together. Besu butted the top of his skull into the man's chin. He raised his manacled hands for a nose-crushing blow, but the butt end of a spear chunked against the back of his head and he pitched to the side, stunned. The chained Ashanti line shifted forward.

"Back! Get back, or you all die here!" the Fanti leader cried.

The guards brought their muskets to bear pointblank on naked chests. Fingers curled around triggers.

The line hesitated.

Adoko breathed once, deeply. He took a step backward, then another.

The Ashanti sighed, and followed him.

The guards remained poised while three of their number freed Besu. He was too dazed to comprehend, and he stumbled drunkenly as they hauled him off the trail. He muttered to himself while they tied his hands with a rope. The other end was tossed over a branch. Two of them pulled on the free end, jerking his arms up sharply and lifting him a few inches off the ground. The pain returned his senses to him. He looked at his kinsman and his captors, his face vacant.

The Fanti leader signaled. A guard uncoiled a long black whip with a splayed end and paced off a few feet from Besu. The Fanti's arm swung forward, snapped back at just the right moment. The whip doubled on its own arc, too fast for the eye to follow.

Crr-rack!

A red line split Besu's back.

The guard was expert. In a few moments twelve raw wet wounds had been cut into Besu, each deep and each separated from the others by an inch or two of unmarred skin. The slash across Besu's shoulders had exposed muscle. The muscle was gray. At a second signal Besu was cut down and led back to the coffle.

No sound has passed his lips; his expression had not changed. But his face was plagued by half a dozen little tics, and he walked unsteadily because his legs were trembling. There was admiration in Adoko, but it paled in the face of his anger. Besu had failed his family on three counts. First, he had made the taking of the guards by surprise that much more difficult. Second, he had caused his own strength to be reduced, and that strength was necessary to the community, was the *property* of the community. Third, his failure and punishment might well have demoralized those among them of wavering resolve.

When Besu had been rechained, Adoko sent out the message: *We must wait for the right time. All else is folly.* Had it not been Besu, no rebuke would have been necessary. This was typical of his brother; Adoko should have foreseen it. Though unarguably courageous and a brother deserving of love, Besu had always been impulsive to the point of danger, had never fully mastered the self-restraint a man should have.

The Fanti leader addressed them. "No one will attempt such foolishness again. The penalty will be death. Slow and humiliating death."

It was the prospect of humiliation that gave major impact to the threat.

The march was continued. The Fanti used their rods and straps liberally; every captive paid for Besu's assault.

There was this problem: By tomorrow's nightfall the coffle would have arrived at the coast. There the Ashanti would truly become slaves. And no matter whether they were loaded directly onto a ship or locked into barracoons, escape would be many times more difficult.

The move should be made as soon as possible. But there was no opportunity. Each step jarred Adoko's aching head. Wait. Wait.

In the late afternoon they came to a small stream. The

guards had water bags, but the only moisture the Ashanti had tasted during the long, hot day had been that in the yams and plantains and whatever spittle they could work up by chewing leaves into green pulp. Now they were allowed to go down on their hands and knees and scoop drinks from the stream. Tiny white creatures darted with mindless panic in the water Adoko's hands cupped. He drank. It was cool. It tasted good.

They marched in deepening darkness for some time after the sun set. Then they made camp. Adoko went to sleep immediately. If the guards grew lax, they would do so in the early hours of the morning. There was no point in staying awake now.

He opened his eyes a few hours later, orienting himself in the first moments of consciousness. His head hurt terribly, but he had slept deeply and his body felt stronger. Pools of moonlight spilled through holes in the twisted green canopy above them and whitened small patches of the ground. Two fires were burning. Some of the guards were asleep around them. Others were sitting up, talking and gambling, glancing at the sleeping captives every few moments, weapons close at hand. Small movements in the shadows on the periphery of the coffle told him there were guards there also.

It was useless.

He lay on his back, flexing his arms to dissipate the stiffness brought by the manacles. A swift night-bird cut through the air on whirring wings.

He prayed to his ancestors and to the Obosoms favored by his house. Then he prayed to the Supreme Spirit from whom all lesser divinities flowed.

> You, Odomankoma, I honor you:
> Who created the Thing,
> Hewer-Out, Creator,

You created the Thing.
What did you create?
You created Order.
You created Knowledge.
You created Death
Which is the quintessence.
You, Odomankoma, I honor you.
You who made Death eat poison.

And he prayed to Onyame, who was another part of Odomankoma.

Onyame, the Earth, the Mother,
You need not be pointed out to your children.
You are the end as well as the cause
Of All things.
You need not be pointed out.
There is no escaping Onyame's destiny.
Onyame, the Earth, the Mother,
You are the end as well as the cause.

And he prayed to Nyankopon, who was another part of Odomankoma and Onyame.

Nyankopon, drink for thirst,
Food for hunger,
I look up and cannot see you,
Yet you are here.
If living man empties my goblet of wine
Or my body of blood,
You will refill it.
Should all things conspire
To destroy you,

You will not perish.
If all men suffer you,
You will suffer them to suffer nothing else.
Nyankopon, I look up and cannot see you.
I am falling downward.
Catch me in your strong arms!

He felt better for having prayed. He had a sense of continuity, and some peace was his, some comfort. Awake, he rested. Someone among the women was moaning softly. He worried about the girl with the injured lungs. His listened more carefully. No, there were two voices, not one. That was good, the guards would pay less attention. Some of the children were whimpering in their sleep. That also was good. Most were too old to permit such sounds to pass their lips when they were awake. Yet the whimpers were within them, and in the darkness, in their sleep, they could express themselves without shame.

A while later he heard retching sounds. A guard swore and went to the women. He shouted. The Fanti headman and three others rushed over. Adoko sat up. The guards dragged two women away from the others. Both were in pain and were vomiting profusely. "Clay," Adoko heard the headman say. "The bitches ate clay." He kicked one. A guard went to the side of the fire and returned with a pouch. The headman took something from the pouch and forced it past the lips of each girl. He held their mouths locked shut until they had swallowed. The purgative was strong. They would have rid themselves of the clay without it, but now their stomachs heaved with massive violence. When, some minutes later, it was over, they lay exhausted and sobbing. The headman turned two of the guards loose on them with straps. The beating went on for a long time.

The captives were told at dawn they would be allowed no water today. An explanation was not necessary. All the Ashanti knew of the attempted suicides. The two women were haggard, and their bodies were welted and bruised.

The headman was true to his word. Smarting under blows, the captives were made to run across the three shallow streams they encountered that morning, feet splashing up droplets which glinted brilliantly in the bright sunlight, and stirring clouds of grainy sediment that eddied in the slow current, ribboned, then vanished.

At a little after midday one of the captives cried out in surprise. The guard nearest him called a halt, unsheathed his sword, and lunged forward. He chopped the earth, then impaled something on the sharp point and raised it into the air. The decapitated body of an emerald-colored snake twisted and coiled around the sword. The Fanti's face screwed up in disgust. He flung the creature into the brush. The Ashanti had been bitten. The headman took out a knife and slashed a deep X across the twin punctures. Then he tied a thong tightly around the man's leg, a little below the knee.

Adoko knew it was not going to work. The man knew it, too. His eyes said he was already dead, and on his mouth, just faintly, there was an intimation of happiness.

The afternoon meal was again plantains and yams, which had been cooked the previous day. This time they ate without stopping. The journey was taking longer than expected, but the Fanti still hoped to reach the coast by nightfall. The man who had been bitten could not hold his food down. He was beaded with perspiration, and his breathing was difficult. His eyes were taking on a yellowish hue.

The afternoon lengthened. They were nearing the coast. Trails became more frequent, and they were better used, easier to travel than they had been farther inland. The Fanti headman ordered the coffle into a paced run. The guards were happier now that their goal was within reach. They did not strike their captives except to hurry along laggards.

The man dying of snakebite stumbled, slowed the line, then was dragged several yards when the guards whipped the men ahead of him on. He regained his feet only when the man behind him, running, seized him under the shoulders and helped him up. His arms flapped raggedly at his sides, his feet tangled in themselves, and he lost his balance frequently, but somehow he managed not to fall. For a while.

The second time he went down, a whip was used on him, and it cut the arms and chest of the man who again helped him. The third time was the last. The Fanti headman gave a command. The nearest guard unsheathed his sword without breaking stride and hacked through the man's arms between wrists and elbows.

He rolled to the side of the trail. The coffle ran by, the severed forearms bobbing in their manacles.

Adoko considered slaughter. He ached with the need of it. That he and his kinsmen should live, was that of real importance? What joy there would be, even in death, ripping the Fanti apart. What ecstasy. He made fists of his hands. The iron that bound him was heavy. It could crush skulls. And the long chain could garrote, brutally. But even as he thought about this, he was watching Besu, afraid his brother would launch an attack and knowing that this time the others would probably follow. And as he watched he realized that he would not give the signal. It was not yet time. So he forced the images of vengeance from his mind. Since he could not act, he was only tormenting himself.

They came at last to a river. It was broad and swift.

Water leaped and crashed around great rocks. Logs and bits of flotsam spun crazily in cross-currents. The coffle trekked a mile upstream to a fording place. Here the bottom was gravel and the water no higher than a man's knees. But the current was strong and crossing was not easy. A handful of guards helped the women. A few more uncoiled a rope to which the children clung. One guard swung Lianu, Adoko's small daughter, up on his shoulders. The child laughed wildly. She thought it was a fine game. Water broke against legs and surged in white foam up to waists. Pebbles were torn from beneath feet. A hundred strong and insistent hands tugged at ankles and calves. Many of the captives and a few of the guards stumbled and disappeared momentarily. The slaves were beaten and kicked until, sputtering and gasping, they regained their feet.

Adoko had nearly reached the opposite shore when Lianu screamed. He turned and saw the guard upon whose shoulders she was riding finish his headlong pitch into the water. The man was up in an instant, spitting water and shaking his head. Lianu was no longer on his back.

"There she goes! Get her!" another guard shouted.

The man scanned the water, spotted Lianu, who was being carried speedily downstream, fat little legs and arms thrashing above the surface, and started after in a sluggish, shambling parody of a run. He was cursing. He fell, went under, came up again with a furious scowl, and continued the chase. Lianu was far ahead of him, and the gap between them increased each moment. The dark little body was rolling over and over across the surface, approaching the deeper water. A rock loomed in front of her. Water geysered angrily over its top. Lianu was flung up hard against it and pinned there several moments. Then the water worked beneath her unmoving body and lifted her up and over. She was a brief black flash on the swirling surface, then she disappeared. The guard who had pursued her made a gesture of tired capitulation.

Adoko closed his eyes. When the moment came, there was much to be repaid.

At the end of another hour the forest began to thin. The sky, increasingly more visible, was turning scarlet. There was a sound like distant, muted thunder. The guards were jubilant. The pace of the run was increased. It was grueling. The undergrowth disappeared. Trees grew farther apart. And the thunder became ever louder. Then, in one abrupt and disorienting instant, the forest was behind them and the full dome of the sky, fired by the setting sun, rose over them while, lower, lay the limitless expanse of the sea, only slightly less red than the sky.

The guards danced and clapped each other on the back.

They were on high ground overlooking a beach of yellowish-white sand. At the forest's edge was a cluster of weathered buildings. Great white-capped breakers were booming in; near deafening. Farther out, two ships stood at anchor. And behind them, in the distance, the sails of a third could be seen.

Some of the guards fired muskets into the air. The Fanti laid into their captives and the coffle went streaking to the beach, slaves tripping and falling, dragging each other down, whipped to their feet again. Figures moved out from the buildings and walked toward the approaching column in a casual, leisurely fashion. It was difficult running in the sand. Adoko fell, and when he rose there was a sharp grittiness in his mouth. He saw that three men had come to meet them. One was a white, flanked by a pair of huge broad-shouldered blacks who carried whips.

Two other men were wheeling a small cannon a little way

onto the beach. They positioned it with its muzzle pointing out to sea.

Boooom!

"Come in," Horneby said.

A seaman opened the door. He remained in the companionway holding his cap deferentially in both hands. "Begging your pardon, sir, but we've had a signal from shore."

"Good!" Horneby pushed back his chair from the table. "What about the frigate?"

"She's moving in again, sir."

The captain grunted. The British warship had appeared three days ago. He had ordered the Stars and Stripes run up. The British had left them alone, but had boarded and searched the Portuguese slaver anchored nearby. Finding no slaves, the frigate drew back. She stood out to sea through the day, then, as night fell, moved in close enough to observe any loading that might be attempted under cover of darkness. She retired again at dawn. It was mostly harassment, which had meant nothing to Horneby. But now with the coffle arrived it became irritating. "Tell Mr. Knye to lower a boat and stand by. I'll be there directly."

"Aye, sir."

Still standing, Horneby dregged out the last of his wine, then wiped his lips with a linen napkin. "Mr. Wilkes, Mr. Petersen. When you've finished, be so good as to report to me topside. I want to get this settled tonight."

The Chief Surgeon and his assistant nodded.

To his first mate Horneby said, "Mr. Meredith, detail two men to my cabin to transport the money. Issue them arms."

"Yes, sir. Are we going to fight?" He sounded hopeful. "She's only five guns and a small crew. We could send her to the bottom in pieces."

"No."

“Very good, sir.” Meredith said, and left.

Horneby stared at the bulkhead and lightly stroked his jaw. He did that often when he was thinking. Sometimes he touched his forehead or his cheek, softly, as a woman would if she wanted to comfort without intruding. It was an incongruous habit. He was a tall, sharp-featured man whose face was furrowed rather than lined—so deep were the depressions—and whose thin lips were perpetually drawn tight. If anyone found anything humorous in this caressing hand, he had never mentioned it to Horneby. People sensed anger in the renegade English captain, savagery. But they were wrong. Horneby was indeed a lethal man and capable of wreaking great destruction. But he was rarely angry. If insulted, Horneby might well crush the offending party, yet only because he had a very clear sense of the order of things and had interpreted the assault as a dissonance. Some dissonances had to be removed because they threatened equilibrium and structure, but others were simply curios, irrelevant, and could therefore be ignored. No one, not even Captain Horneby, could predict which he would view as irksome and which as irrelevant. This made him all the more intimidating.

While the captain stood and thought, the men remaining in the officers’ mess sat in uncomfortable silence, looking wistfully at their food.

After several minutes Horneby said, “You’ll excuse me, gentlemen. Please don’t rise.”

He went to his cabin and removed the strongbox from the wall locker at the head of his bed. He began counting out enough gold to purchase one hundred slaves. One hundred Ashanti, which meant, of course, that the price per head would be substantially higher than that he’d paid for the Ibos, some two hundred of whom were already stretched out on the slave decks.

Horneby's ship was the *Jubilation*. During her eight years as a slaver, though, neither her bow nor her stern had borne any name. She would answer to the name *Jubilation* if her American papers of registry were presented. She would also, according to either her Spanish or Portuguese papers, answer equally well to the name *Jubilación*. And on her Danish papers was a name Horneby could barely pronounce, but which, he supposed, was the Danish equivalent of *Jubilation*. He didn't know if any of the registrations were legitimate. But his crew was predominantly American and the capital behind the ship was American, and so, for Horneby, the *Jubilation* was American.

He could not tolerate the sophistry of which his New England employers were so fond.

Meredith had been correct. They could easily send the frigate to the bottom. Horneby was one of the perhaps two dozen fighting captains left on the slave run. Earlier, sea battles had been common with pirates and with other slavers, who looked upon hijacking as a cheaper and speedier way to fill their holds. Then the British interdicted the trade and there were the warships of His Majesty's African Squadron to contend with. But in the next three decades the emphasis shifted from armament to speed. The British ships were slow, and it seemed much more sensible to most funding combines to outrun the patrols than to stand and fight. There was also this benefit: The faster you made the trip from the shores of Africa to Brazil, to the West Indies, to Cuba or to the illegal depots in Texas, Florida, and the South Carolina coastal rivers, the fewer the slaves who died en route. And the fewer black bodies tossed overboard, then obviously the larger the profit. This was the kind of logic that Yankee merchants found irresistible. Profit was everything. So a new kind of sleek-hulled vessel with smartly raked masts began to appear on the slaving lanes. They had been designed in Baltimore and were called clippers, and now, for every one engaged in legitimate trade, there was another slicing westward and home, the stench of its black cargo carrying an easy two or three miles downwind.

But the British managed, with three ships, to box and capture the streamlined clippers often enough to cause some slavers to question their advantage. And design made them impractical to arm. Horneby wanted no part of clippers. The *Jubilation* was a good, solid three-masted ship of traditional design, one of the best he had ever seen, and certainly the best he had ever commanded. With a fair wind and a full spread of canvas she could show her heels to nearly any ship—excluding the clippers—who wanted to try her. She was sturdy, too. In bad weather, with light sail and a good hand at her helm, she could plunge through seas like a bull through a canebrake.

If Horneby could outdistance the patrols, fine. If not, then he would fight. Twice, once as a mate and once as a captain, his ships had been overhauled and taken to the Prize Court at Sierre Leone. The tribunal condemned both ships. Since neither was judged fit for appropriation, the vessels were burned. Their frightened cargoes were turned loose in Freetown, to be supported by the British government for a year, then left to shift for themselves. As a mate, Horneby had been fined and then languished on the coast six months, nearly dying of fever, before he found a loaded slaver ready to return to Cuba and in need of an extra hand. As a captain, the heavy fine destroyed most of his savings, and he spent a year in a damp and fetid prison cell.

He did not intend to let the British rob him again. Nor did he intend to surrender his body to them for imprisonment behind stone and iron. He no longer accepted commissions on ships that were not armed, and over twelve years he had fought five times, twice with privateers turned pirate and three times with ships of His Majesty's African Squadron. He had sunk one pirate and beaten off the other and the three warships. The *Jubilation* had been armed at his direction when he took command of her four years ago. She carried nine guns, four six-pounders, four eight-pounders, and a murderous carronade swivel-mounted on the quarterdeck. Instead of a gun deck, which would have consumed a disproportionate amount of valuable space, the cannons were sunk into pits cut into the topdeck. They squatted on platforms whose backs were unenclosed, over which the guns could slide in snubbed recoil, and under which slaves could be jammed. Firing ports were worked into the bulwarks. They would not be noticed until they were raised. The keynotes were economy and concealment. Horneby had achieved both. He had yet to fight the *Jubilation,* but her readiness afforded him a certain necessary peace of mind.

Only the carronade, which was always kept loaded, had been fired. Once. Horneby had been asleep in his cabin. The ugly, stubby-barreled monster ripped apart his dreams with a tremendous roar. He leaped to his feet, grabbed pistol and cutlass, and raced up the stairs. A melon-breasted black girl shrieked in his abandoned bed, and in her terror she urinated on Horneby's sheets. Naked, the captain burst into the cool night air. Armed members of the watch were rushing toward the forward hatch. The bosun came down from the quarterdeck at the stern. He was pale and he was trembling.

"I—I had to do it, Captain. They were boiling out like ants. There wasn't time for anything else."

Horneby walked several yards forward, to the hatch. Maybe twenty blacks were sprawled around it. All were mutilated, most dead. A few, dying, groaned their agony. Blood and pieces of gore were everywhere. The deck and mainmast were gouged. Some of the lower rigging had been shot away. The two sailors guarding the hatch had been stuporously drunk and the slaves had somehow worked loose their shackles and forced the hatch cover. They had butchered the drunken sailors and taken their muskets and cutlasses. Then they'd seized handspikes, boathooks, and barrel staves, anything they could reach. Someone had shouted an alarm. The bosun took in the scene with one quick glance and made his decision. He primed the carronade and yanked the lanyard. The short-range battering gun, bored for a thirty-pound shell, was loaded with bolts, nails, and junk metal. It had butchered the rebels, killed one seaman and wounded two others.

Loud, hollow wailing was issuing from the hold when Horneby arrived. He ordered the slaves quieted. Seamen beat on the hatch grating with musket stocks and the flat sides of cutlasses, shouting. They accomplished nothing.

"Pour hot water on them," Horneby said. "Not scalding, mind you—you don't want to damage their hides—but hot. They'll understand soon enough."

"Aye, aye, sir."

He walked aft with the bosun. "You did well, Mr. Prentiss. You most likely prevented a massacre."

The man was immensely relieved. "I'll find out how those men got into the rum, sir. And if anyone else was involved, you'll have their names."

"Yes, you do that. Good night, Mr. Prentiss."

"Good night, Captain."

Horneby stopped. "Oh. I'll speak to the owners when we make port. You deserve a bonus for tonight's work, Mr. Prentiss.

"Thank you, sir!"

Horneby went below. His groin was throbbing by the time he reached his cabin. It had nothing to do with the girl quailing in the corner of his bed in wide-eyed fear. It sprang from death, from the grinning skeleton who had stalked the deck with his sharp scythe, sniffing Horneby's blood. It sprang from the defeat of death, who had clattered into a pile of harmless bones because an essentially simple man had retained enough presence of mind to fire a carronade. It had nothing to do with the black girl who watched the captain approach, who saw his aroused sex and took hope from it, feeling secure in the familiar and knowing that this, at least, would not hurt her.

He hovered over her. She licked her lips and opened her arms and her thighs to him. A piercing, multi-voice screech came from the slave decks. The girl jerked, but was reassured when Horneby lowered himself and penetrated deeply and easily. The wailing diminished, but did not stop, and minutes later there came a second screech. The wail was not resumed. But by this time Horneby was focused only on the hard root of his masculinity as it slid in the warm, yielding wetness. He rode the girl with exhilaration. He was embuggering Death, whom he had rendered helpless. That was triumph.

After setting aside the money to buy the Ashanti, Horneby returned the strongbox to the locker and changed into his dress uniform—tight white breeches, knee-high well-polished boots, a linen shirt starched to stiffness, a scarlet ascot and a long coat of matching color whose tails were flared, whose cuffs were wide and whose brass buttons gleamed. He cut a severe and impressive figure as he came onto the topdeck. Immediately behind him was an armed seaman with a leather carrying bag, heavy with gold, slung over his shoulder. Following was another sailor, musket at port arms. The longboat was already in the water, manned by eight seamen. They held their oars aloft, waiting for the captain. Horneby paused at the head of the Jacob's ladder and looked out to sea, at the British frigate looming larger, moving in to her night berth.

He watched several minutes, and he stroked his jaw.

When the signal pennant was hoisted, an hour after dawn, the first of the loading canoes put out from shore and moved to do battle with the terrible surf. Virgil Dunbar was high above the deck, bare feet on the catline beneath the arm of the fore topgallant sail. He was bent forward, stomach resting on the stout arm itself. He and three others were shaking out the canvas.

He paused and looked at the canoe. *It rose and pitched,* he wrote in his mind, *as must the slim spar to which Odysseus so desperately clung while the wild and cruel sea, whipped to a frenzy by the angry Poseidon, raged about him. However, nothing daunted the strong backs and sure paddles of these savages, these consummate overlords of the pounding breakers, who are called Krumen. On they flew, straight as the loosed arrow, with their hapless cargoes. . . .*

"Aiiii!" He cried out in terror as the catline twanged viciously beneath his feet, destroying his balance. He clawed at the arm, got purchase and hung there, heart pounding and stomach twitching.

Eight feet away, Jamey O'Brien laughed with huge guttural roars. O'Brien was a black-bearded pillar of a man with tight curls of hair matting his chest, arms, shoulders, and back. He had stomped the catline intentionally. On the opposite side of the mast, their two companions on the yardarm looked on with mild curiosity. Dunbar flopped and twisted until he regained his position.

"You're learning, boyo," O'Brien said. "If I'd thought to do that a month ago, you'd o' been squashed flat dead on the deck."

Dunbar said nothing. He couldn't, even if he'd been able to think of a reply; his throat was constricted. He wanted to weep. The fear was that strong. This last week he had begun to think they were going to leave him alone. But they weren't, they weren't!

Virgil Dunbar was not his real name. That was Virgil Carey, and it was familiar to thousands of Americans. He doubted when he had undertaken this trip that anyone on board would have recognized it, but certain precautions did have to be taken. It had been dramatic then to think he might be murdered if his true identity or his intent were known. It was no longer so. No one knew who he was, but he was liable to be killed anyway . . . simply because the crew saw him as a fledgling seaman, and a poor one at that. They hazed him as a matter of course, the way upperclassmen hazed freshmen at colleges and universities. But their brand of harassment could prove lethal, a fact that didn't concern them at all.

Dunbar, for that is the way he would continue to think of himself until he was safely off this ship, trembled for his life.

He was a journalist whose literary reports on the Black Hawk War, in which the Fox and Sauk tribes had been crushed and butchered across two states and one territory, had thrilled the eastern seaboard. Some of his more colorful passages were quoted by politicians, clergymen, and society matrons. Barely out of his teens, he found himself famous. Everyone thought he was quite grand, and he believed them. He struck out to the frontier and did moody, semi-heroic pieces on mountain men and buffalo hunters. He returned to New York in time to cover the great hospital scandal. His personality sketches of the major figures involved in the Panic of 1837 secured his position as one of the top freelance journalists in the country.

He was the perfect choice for the New England Abolition Society.

Ezra Pearson was the man who, in a rather severely appointed office in Boston, completed the arrangements. Pearson was a short man with milk-white skin. But his handshake was firm, his tone brusque, and his manner indicated that he had little patience with frippery.

He came directly to the point. "Basically the situation is this. Despite its illegality, the slave trade is still rampant on the west coast of Africa. And unfortunately a very large part of it is financed by American investors. More than three decades have passed since the British, ourselves, and most other nations outlawed the trade. But only the British have made any real attempt to suppress it. Are you a religious man?"

The journalist shifted uncomfortably. He was not, but obviously Pearson was. "I imagine I'm about as religious as the next man."

"I am quite religious," Pearson said. "And as Thomas Jefferson wrote, I tremble for my country when I realize that God is just. However, as I'm sure you're aware, man often perverts religion, even God Himself. There is in this country a general sentiment that the United States of America is a direct inspiration of God. Any question of our right to do exactly what we please is considered sacrilegious. If some country views us askance, we rattle our swords and begin growling *war, war.*"

Dunbar was not convinced of this, but he thought it politic to agree, so he nodded.

"This penchant is of no special concern to me," Pearson said, "except as it relates to the slave trade. There are now in existence literally hundreds of treaties between Great Britain, ourselves, and the other major powers, and each one qualifies, amends, supersedes, or even contradicts the others. The British African Squadron is greatly restricted. If an officer violates any of these complicated agreements, his punishment may range from heavy fine to revocation of his commission and dismissal from the service.

"Now, the most debilitating restriction is the one that we have imposed. What it comes down to is: if you fly the Stars and Stripes you are safe. You may have slaves stacked on the deck like cords of wood and more lashed to the masts and still more hanging from the bowsprit, but the British cannot touch you. In fact, without *very* good reason, they cannot even request you to heave-to and present your registry papers. The only way to take into custody a ship sailing under the aegis of our colors is to apprehend that ship in the *actual process* of loading slaves."

"That's difficult to believe."

"Mr. Carey, human beings are difficult to believe. We have filled half a warehouse with documentation. You may examine the material any time you so desire."

"That won't be necessary," Carey said, a little offended. But then, lest the abolitionist think he was offering an apology, he added, "For the moment, at least."

Pearson shrugged. "As you will."

"What is it, exactly, that you want from me?"

"For you to sign on a slaver, sail to Africa, load a cargo of slaves, and return with them. Then commit your observations and experiences to a book-length manuscript, which we will publish and distribute."

"Why me?" Carey knew, but he wanted to hear the words.

"Because you have ability to sway people, to arouse them. They are deaf to the lamentations of hundreds of thousands of black voices crying out from the slave decks, but they will listen to your voice—because you are their darling, because you entertain them, and because you are white."

Carey bristled and began a retort, but checked himself. He had written nothing spectacular for a year and he was beginning to fret; his name was not mentioned in the appropriate circles as often as he would have liked. And he recognized that here, in the right hands, *his* hands, was an assured *cause célèbre*. He allowed himself to go this far. "I sympathize with you, Mr. Pearson, but regrettably my sympathies alone would not be sufficient recompense for the time I'd have to spend on this project."

"Naturally," Pearson snapped. "We are prepared to pay you an outright fee of five thousand dollars. And for each book we distribute we will pay you a royalty of one-half dollar. If your literary rendering is up to its usual standard, we project a distribution of some one hundred thousand copies within the space of two years. Your earnings, as you'll see by a simple process of arithmetic, will be considerable."

Carey said nothing. The money was incredible.

"What is your answer? I must know now. If you decline, I will begin other arrangements."

"I accept."

"Good." Pearson rose, came around the desk, and when Carey stood, took the journalist firmly by the shoulder and guided him to the door. "You will see my assistant, Mr. Hastings, tomorrow morning. He will have the contract for your signature and will explain all the necessary particulars."

Carey decided he would be quite happy if he never had to face this man as an enemy. He shook the hand Pearson proffered. "I must say that you don't very much resemble other abolitionists I've known."

"When you are fighting a war, Mr. Carey, you accept aid from whatever quarter it is offered."

"A variation on 'The end justifies the means'?"

"Not really. Good day, Mr. Carey."

The journalist found himself on the street. And he admitted to himself that he was relieved to be out of Pearson's office.

So Virgil Carey, journalist, became Virgil Dunbar, apprentice seaman, and off he went to South Carolina with the fervent hopes and blessings of Mr. Hastings, who was an efficient but nervous and naive man, an earnest embodiment of all that the journalist considered worst in moral crusaders. You accept aid from whatever quarter it is offered, Pearson had said. Well, that must explain Hastings.

Hastings had told him that finding a slaver would be as easy as falling off a log. He was wrong. It was easier. There were nine ships in the Charleston harbor, two of them slavers. The astonishing thing was that everyone *knew* they were slavers, and no one cared. The largest, the *Jubilation,* a three-master with a black hull, was sailing within the week. Virgil Dunbar, apprentice seaman, made inquiries and discovered that there were still a few berths open aboard her. After buying drinks for a red-haired, foul-mouthed fellow who was the *Jubilation*'s first mate and who was too drunk to stand alone, Dunbar went on board and was given ship's articles to sign.

Now he was on the other side of the ocean, shirtless under a relentless and glaring sun that had bronzed his skin and lightened his hair, far above a holystoned deck, shaking out canvas, only a few moments past a near fall that would have broken most of his bones and had him dumped into the water off this God-abandoned continent to be munched upon by fish and small, clumsy crabs. The sail dropped and began flapping in the wind, as the crew on deck hauled on the sheets and braces.

Below them the bosun cupped his hands to his mouth and shouted. "All right. To the deck now, and quick."

Dunbar seized one of the backstays, swung out into the

air, and went sliding down. It wasn't nearly as difficult as it looked, and it was a flamboyant way to descend, far more impressive, visually, than backing down the ratlines. It was a gesture meant to regain some of the status he had lost on the arm. The crew had left him pretty much alone since the first slaves had been loaded; they focused on the niggers, and Dunbar wanted to keep it that way. So he slid down, wanting to resemble his fellow sailors as much as possible, wanting not to be noticed.

"Cargo approaching, Captain," the first mate called.

Horneby stood at the bulwark, hands clasped behind his back. "Put over the Jacob's ladder, Mr. Knye."

"Aye, aye, sir." The rope ladder was flung over the side.

"Mr. Meredith," Horneby said, "man the deck pumps if you will."

"Aye, sir." The first mate ordered seamen to the pump handles.

"Dunbar, O'Brien, Santiago," the bosun said, "draw cutlasses and stand by the pumps. Escort and shackle the first ten."

Dunbar, with O'Brien and Santiago, went to Mr. Randall, the second mate, who was dispensing the heavy, sharp swords as they were needed. The weight of the weapon was more than one would have thought, but there had been a time, during the Black Hawk War, when the journalist had wielded a cavalry saber, and so he carried it easily. More proficiently, he noted, than O'Brien. This fact had not escaped the hairy Irishman, and Dunbar was pleased.

A long, narrow canoe came gliding in abreast of the ship. Only a few inches separated it from the hull. She was expertly manned by ten jet-black muscular Krumen. This one-time coastal fishing tribe had, during the centuries of the trade, turned into a kind of craft guild. Hardly a slave was conveyed through the pounding surf that was not carried in the long canoes of the Krumen. No one could cope as well with the wild white water. There were twenty male slaves chained in the canoe. One of the Krumen looked up at Horneby and asked, "Send 'em over-on now, huh?"

The captain nodded.

The Krumen freed two of the slaves, started them up the Jacob's ladder, and kept them climbing with bites of a whip and goosing paddle-jabs. Seamen stood by on deck with boathooks and ropes, ready to retrieve any slaves who might leap into the sea. The first two were hauled over the rail and pushed to the pumps. The Krumen started the next pair up.

"Mr. Meredith," Horneby said. "A sail check, please."

Meredith turned to the bosun. "Mr. Knye?"

The bosun picked up a small megaphone and directed his voice up to the top spar of the mainmast. When the seaman posted there replied, his voice was thin and distant: "Clear sea to the horizon."

The captain was informed. He was pleased. He had negotiated with his counterpart aboard the Portuguese ship last night and had made the man a payment of $750. At dawn the warship pulled back, and when it was well out to sea the Portuguese slaver unfurled her sail and made a run for it. As Horneby expected, the British thought the Portuguese had managed to load slaves undetected during the night, and the frigate gave chase. When both ships had topped the horizon and disappeared, the *Jubilation* had signaled to shore and the first loading canoe put out from the beach.

Dunbar stood with his cutlass poised. These blacks bothered him. They weren't like the last bunch, cowed, cringing, and frightened. They stood tall and with dignity, and though it seemed to the journalist impossible under the circumstances, they were clearly defiant. You could see it in the narrowed eyes, the thrusting jaws, the downturned mouths, hands clenching into fists. O'Brien and Santiago felt it, too; they gestured menacingly with their cutlasses more than was necessary to keep the blacks in a tight group. Four sailors were seesawing the handles of the two pumps. Two more held the hoses from which cold seawater was spurting. Each slave was doused from head to foot. The first six had come aboard naked. The seventh wore a loincloth. A hoseman ripped it off and flung it away; even the skimpiest rag could support vermin; slaves were transported naked.

When ten blacks had been washed, Dunbar, Santiago, and O'Brien prodded them toward the first of the two holds. Dunbar brought up the rear. He stepped down through the hatch. A scuffle broke out behind him. He looked back. One of the slaves, a man with open whip wounds on his back, had shoved or struck a seaman. The Negro was surrounded instantly. Two cat-o'-nine-tails slashed into him. He was kicked, he was punched. He was brought to his knees. He bellowed rage and flailed out. They turned the butts of the whips on him and cracked him over the skull. Someone brought a belaying pin into play. He slumped to the deck, scalp bleeding.

"Chain that one," Horneby said. "Hands and ankles."

Dunbar went down into the hold. There were seamen, some with muskets, guarding, others to do the placing and securing. There were three slave decks, built out from both sides like shelves, a narrow passageway running lengthwise down the center. The slaves were positioned with their heads to the ribbing, their feet to the center. A shackle was fastened with a peened bolt around each man's left ankle. A ring curled from the iron, and through this was passed a heavy chain, ends locked into thick support beams, binding the slaves together in groups of thirty.

Dunbar breathed as little as possible. The air was foul. There was no place on a slaver free from the stink of its cargo. You adjusted to that after a while. But the holds were enough to make a man vomit. He was relieved when he returned topside, and he stood a moment taking deep breaths.

The last of the males were being hosed down, and the first pair of females had just come over the railing. They were young, uncertain, and apprehensive. They were naked from the waist up. Their breasts were small, hard black buds. There was some hooting and cheering, but mostly the seamen were quiet. They stood in place rubbing and scratching themselves, shifting nervously. Gomez, a dark Spaniard with a single gold earring and a scarlet neckerchief, took his knife from its belt sheath. He flicked his wrist. Sun glinted on the blade. One of the girls screamed and leaped back, her loincloth split. It fell away. A hairline of blood marked the girl's thigh. Dunbar glimpsed a small pubescent triangle of hair at the junction of her legs, then the girl covered herself with pressing, humiliated hands.

"Hey-eee, pussy!" someone yelled.

Sailors guffawed and shouted. A seaman slapped the girl's bottom. She spun. Gomez jammed his fingers into the crack between her buttocks. She shrieked, like an animal about to be butchered. A crewman ripped the covering from the second girl.

"Mr. Meredith," Horneby said. "Direct those girls to the pumps, please."

"All right, you swollen cocks!" Meredith roared. "Break it up and move 'em on. Lively there!" He laid into the nearest sailors with a length of rope.

"Slave for the sea! Slave for the sea!" The warning cut across the deck like a whiplash.

A black from the last group of males was sprinting toward the seaward bulwark. A seaman caught him from behind. The Negro whirled and chopped him down with a blow to the head, then ran again. A sailor racing in at an angle dove forward and slashed desperately with his cutlass. The blade bit above the ankle, and the black went sprawling down.

"Mr. Wilkes," Horneby said. "See to him, please."

The rotund surgeon, a fringe of natty gray hair hanging over his ears, went to the slave and examined the wound. "The tendon's cut," he said. "He's hamstrung."

Horneby nodded. "Over the side with him."

Meredith selected two men who lifted the slave and heaved him over the railing. He plunged down, splashed into the sea, was gone a moment, then broke the surface. He kept himself afloat with awkward butterfly motions of his arms and began making his way around the ship. Blood billowed thinly behind him. A seaman climbed a little way up the shrouds to watch. When the slave had circled the ship and made some twenty or thirty yards toward the coast the sailor called: "Five points off the starboard!"

Crewmen rushed to the rail. Four dark fins were slicing across the surface. One outdistanced the others, closed rapidly, and hit the slave from behind. Water boiled and sprayed. It was over in moments, and then there was nothing visible but a spreading red stain. The seamen turned away.

Dunbar tried to write the episode in his mind, but failed. It wasn't that he was unable; he just didn't want to.

The seaman who had cut the slave was apologizing to the captain. "I only meant to stop him, sir," he finished. "I didn't realize what I was doing."

"I'm sure of that," Horneby said. "Nevertheless, you destroyed a valuable piece of merchandise." He called Meredith over. "After evening mess this man is to receive fifteen lashes, and make note that the price of the slave is to be deducted from his pay when we reach port."

"Very good, sir."

Horneby dismissed the sailor, and the man returned to his duties slump-shouldered and with scuffling feet.

There was darkness in the hold. But there was a blacker and more bitter darkness in Adoko's heart. He had failed his people. His shame and self-loathing were great. They were slaves now, and slaves of a kind the most twisted mind would not have been able to imagine. In the nation of the Ashanti, and in other nations Adoko knew, slavery was something vastly different. There, the difference between slave and master was one mostly of wealth and social privilege. Slaves had legal rights. They could acquire property. They were treated more or less as members of the master's family. Their children were born free, and it was considered no stigma or shame to be descended from a slave. Indeed, the father of Adoko's father had been a slave.

But this! Pigs would be treated better. The slaves were lying on their backs on rough, unfinished planks. There were only males. Adoko did not know what had been done with the women and children. The shoulders of each man pressed against the shoulders of the men on either side of him, and again there was iron on his flesh. Another deck was built two feet above them; it was impossible to sit up. It was impossible, actually, to do anything but lie where one had been placed. There were small portals every dozen feet, but what they accomplished toward ventilation was feeble. The hold was hot and the air rank with body smells and the pungency of urine and the thick odor of excrement.

They were slaves.

There had been no possibility of escape, but still Adoko felt he should have found one, and he thought perhaps it might have been better if he had led them against the Fanti. This, certainly, could not be called life. He felt neither anger nor resentment toward Maliyo, his cousin, who had gone to the sea. Or toward Besu for attacking the white man. With the disappearance of hope each man had been free to make his choice. Soon others would follow Maliyo. Maybe Adoko himself would be among them.

Someone called his name.

"Yes?" he answered.

"Adoko, what do we do?"

He was silent several moments. He listened. From the other slaves, the ones who had been here when the Ashanti were led down into the hold, the ones whose tongue he could not understand, came many moans and some weeping. Adoko's people were soundless. This was as it should be. There was rightness about it. Pride returned to Adoko. And with it purpose. And a forgiving of himself. And the will to live. To triumph.

"We will wait," he said. "We will wait today and we will wait tomorrow. We will wait, if we must, until we are old men. We will wait because someday there will be a time, a moment, when action is right. And then we will act. And then we will be victorious."

Besu snorted. "You will wait until you are toothless and too weak to lift a sword. We are already dead. It is better to be rid of these shells, these bodies, now. So long as we can kill some of those who have killed us."

"Besu, Besu my brother," Adoko said gently. "We are not dead. *You* are not dead. Your muscles are still strong, the blood flows in your veins. But what is more important, the fires rage in your heart. How can you speak of being dead when the vengeance hunger, the killing lust, runs so strong in you?"

"I will not continue this way. I can not, Adoko."

"Wait with us, Besu. Please. We need your mighty arm, your boundless courage."

Besu did not answer.

"Wait," Adoko said.

The slaves heard muted shouts above them and a dull clanking and scraping; there were small vibrations in the planking they lay upon. Tiny breezes began to blow through the portals a short while later. The slaves felt motion.

The *Jubilation* was under way.

"Three kings," Dunbar said.

There were five of them sitting in a circle. Dunbar and Harris were the only ones left in this hand. The other three had folded when Harris' final up-card had given him two pairs showing.

"Ahh, shit!" Harris tossed his hole cards down. "I couldn't fill it in."

Dunbar scooped up the pot. The money wasn't much, and it meant nothing to him. Actually, he would rather have lost, and he'd thought Harris was holding a full house. He wanted to be alone. He had joined the game, an hour earlier, strictly as a tactical move. If they would let him, it would be good to try mixing with them. It had gone well. Nobody, not even O'Brien, was interested in baiting him.

A three-quarter, aseptically white moon rode above the ship. It made the night seem unreal. Most of the crew were here on the forward deck, off duty and riotous. The fo'c'sle had been given over to female slaves and children, a thin partition between the two. The seamen could have slung hammocks in the supply hold if they wished, but that was stuffy and intolerably hot. So they slept on the foredeck in the open. There were tarps nearby to raise as shelters if the weather turned foul.

A couple of these had been tossed over lines to make small tents, which were used by seamen with a sense of modesty. Most didn't bother with them; they took the black girls into the nearest dark corner. There had been a fight the night before. One of the sailors had carried a candle behind a coil of line, where a sweating man was plunging up and down between a pair of ebony thighs. The sailor tipped the candle and dripped hot wax on his comrade's pumping buttocks. The burned man did not see the humor in this. The sailors had their fingers dug into each other's throats and were strangling one another when Mr. Randall, the second mate, broke up the fight by clubbing them unconscious.

Randall was responsible for the black girls. He had one of the two sets of keys that would open the fo'c'sle; the other was in Horneby's cabin. Randall oversaw the removal and return of the females, and kept a strict head count, limiting the number on deck at any given time to six. He took his duties very seriously.

Dunbar had a losing hand. He bet it heavily.

There was a scream, and one of the tarps shook, was punched from within by arms and legs. Muttering, Randall strode over to it and gave it a kick. "Goddamn it!" he yelled. "Who's in there? Barnes?" He received a muffled reply. "Well, what the hell are you doing? You wreck that little bitch and her price'll come out of your pay."

"He ain't gonna hurt nobody, Mr. Randall," someone called. "He couldn't. Not with that little fishhook of his."

There was general laughter. Randall glared at the shifting, bumping tarp a few moments, then walked off, still muttering.

Dunbar lost another hand. He stretched. "That's about as much as I can afford tonight. Better deal me out."

"Want a marker against your pay?"

"Nah. I get back to port with nothin' left, and I'll have to ship right out again."

"That's what it's all about, brother."

"Not tonight it isn't."

The dealer shrugged and flicked out the cards, skipping

the journalist. Dunbar rose, stretched again, then sauntered aft. He was pleased. He knew O'Brien didn't like him, and that he would have to be careful around the Irishman, but the rest of the crew, with the exception of the first mate, Meredith, who seemed to hate everybody, were no longer threatening. He walked past the middle hold entrance. Instead of a solid hatch there was a stout iron grating. Dunbar instinctively held his breath. The stench was fiercest around the gates. And there was always a low moaning issuing from the hold. Two armed seamen were on guard duty. One of them said, "Hey, Virgil. You take my watch for me? I'll stand the next two for you when you're on."

"Sure, Tom. Just like you did last time."

"Well, can't blame a man for tryin'."

"No, guess not."

Dunbar stopped between the mainmast and the mizzenmast. He leaned his elbows on the bulwark and looked at their wake, a long trail of green phosphorescence. Santiago had once explained it to him. There were delicate and tiny creatures in the water, or tiny plants (Santiago seemed to think they were a little of each), that ruptured when the ship passed over them. And dying, they became luminous. It sounded as plausible as anything else. Dunbar liked the phenomenon. Somehow, looking at it gave him a sense of solitude, which, aboard ship, was a luxury. The journalist was moody. Increasingly he was avoiding his work. Or rather, he was losing the desire to work. He excused himself by saying that he was too tired, promising he'd get to it later. He couldn't keep notes—that was dangerous—but he could fix background and incidents in his mind with a fair degree of precision by writing mental paragraphs. He was doing little of that now.

It had begun well enough, and through the first week out of Charleston he was intrigued and enthusiastic. He had never met a man before who held *nothing* sacred. In every professional soldier, mountain man, buffalo hunter, killer, brigand, and convict he had known he had been able to find something that was sacrosanct. Perhaps a simple or even ridiculous thing like personal word or a childhood memory, but something. Not so among the sailors of the *Jubilation*.

Then, because his jargon wasn't quite right, because a rope splice he made gave way, because he slipped on the rigging, because there was awkwardness in most of what he did, the men began to break the tedium of the voyage by making sport of him. Some things, like a loosened hammock rope that crashed him to the deck and knocked out his breath, were relatively harmless. Others, such as the day three sailors stepped back from a taut winch, which caused the handle to tear from his grasp and spin wildly, threatening to break his arms or crush his skull, were not. The seamen did not seem to differentiate between the fatal and the nonfatal. Only O'Brien, though, actively disliked him. The rest were simply marking time.

When the *Jubilation* passed its midpoint on the way to Africa, excitement swept the crew. They became more animated. And as they neared the coast a palpable tension appeared. They moved with quick, snapping motions. Their speech was curt and edged. Fights broke out, and the mates and bosun had to swing short stout lengths of rope across backs and shoulders.

There was a killing a week before the *Jubilation* reached its first anchorage. Stapelton, a big stupid Swede, quarreled with Billy Mays, a sailor with a pockmarked face and ferret eyes, over which of them was to scrub a final section of deck. They kicked aside their buckets and holystones and charged. Stapelton broke Billy Mays' arm. Billy sank his knife into Stapelton's heart. Wilkes, the surgeon, set and splinted Mays' arm. Then the sailor, who wasn't much more than a boy, was put in irons and chained alone on an empty slave deck. Horneby had the crew assembled and he officiated at Stapelton's funeral, speaking a few somber words, to which neither he nor anyone else listened. Then the board on which the Swede rested was tipped up. The corpse, stitched in canvas, slid away. There was a moment of silence —broken by the screeching gulls wheeling above—and a splash.

"Dismiss the men, Mr. Meredith," Horneby said.

The *Jubilation* sailed on, the sea bubbling at her sides.

Seven days later a lookout high above the deck shouted, "Land ho! Off the larboard beam!" There was a rush to the side. Dunbar had expected cheering, backslapping. But there was only a tightening and swelling, as if the crew had collectively drawn its breath and was holding it. Anticipation was evident in the glitter of eyes, the set of shoulders, and hands clenched so strongly that knuckles blanched. Looking about, Dunbar grew inexplicably frightened.

All but the main and topsails were furled, and a reading was taken on the sextant. A slight course correction was made. The coast loomed nearer, and details began to emerge. There were champaigns beyond the white strip of sand, and small rolling hills heavy with vegetation. There were wild groves of limes and oranges. They saw a village surrounded by a high mud wall. Fresh rivers appeared here and there. There were marshes and great mangrove swamps. The clean smell of the sea vanished, the air grew hot, humid, and oppressive. Even small movements brought forth beads of sweat. Shirts were cast aside.

They were off the west coast, the White Man's Grave. Like a mad apothecary, Africa stocked a multitude of plagues and diseases that could destroy white men with the same unfeeling ease with which arsenic curls colonies of ants into brittle shells.

Within an hour the ship was nosing leisurely into a broad bay whose water was a murky yellow. It proceeded to the mouth of the Old Calabar River, where a large, fortified town was built on both sides of the bank, and then, at Horneby's order, the anchor was dropped. Two other slavers were there, sails furled and tied.

Wilkes, who had been the only man to treat Dunbar from the beginning with friendliness, stood with his hands clasped behind his neck and a dour expression on his face. "With two ships ahead of us we'll be here a month," the surgeon said. "We'll lose approximately six of the crew."

"What do you mean?"

"Oh, they'll get the flux, or any one of a hundred varieties of fever, or the rot, or parasites, or they'll go blind, or their stomachs won't accept any food and they'll starve to death. Six if we're lucky. I hate landfalls like this. They always mean dead men."

One of the ship's two longboats was lowered and manned. Horneby came on deck, in spotless and impeccable full-dress uniform. It was as if he were not even aware of the sweltering heat; the crew hated him a little for that. Billy Mays was brought up, still chained, from the slave deck. His eyes were glassy, and he was haggard. His arm was not healing properly.

"Into the boat with him, Mr. Knye," Horneby said to the bosun.

Billy Mays jerked away when Knye laid hands on him. "You can't put me off here," he screamed. "You can't! I'll die and you know it."

Horneby looked up, a little amused. "Would you prefer being brought back and tried for murder?"

"Go ahead. Bring me back and tell them I killed a man on a slaver you captained. You do that, Horneby!"

The captain turned away. Billy Mays started to shout again, but Meredith stepped forward and struck him hard in the mouth. The sailor crumpled to the deck, blood welling from his mouth. When the longboat pulled toward shore, he lay limp and unconscious on the bottom, an oarsman's bare feet planted on his chest.

The boat returned two hours later, *sans* Billy Mays, but with two new seamen, the only ones among the three or four dozen slowly rotting in town that Wilkes had considered fit for duty. One was a Dutchman, nearly as big as the towering O'Brien, and with a jutting slab of a jaw. Incredibly, the Dutchman seemed to have thrived during his stay on shore. The second was a short, leather-skinned, wiry old Englishman. He had been wasted by fevers once, but had survived. He was hard and tough, without excess flesh, and his small black eyes manifested a maniacal will to survive. His name was Crawford. Wilkes was pleased with them both.

The captain returned to his cabin, and the results of his palaver with the traders spread quickly through the crew. The only part the seamen considered pertinent was that they would be in port at least three weeks. Meredith said shore leave was effective immediately, and cheering broke out. A skeleton crew which would be relieved in three days was picked to watch the ship. The second longboat was lowered and the seamen jostled and wrestled for the first positions in line, hilariously good-spirited.

"Like morons happily readying to jump off a cliff," Wilkes said. "Dunbar, use your head, lad, stay aboard. You'll find naught but your own coffin on land."

But Dunbar had to go; he owed it to his readers. And, though he didn't admit it, the emotion of the crew was infectious; he was excited.

He saw the town with Santiago and a somewhat retarded man named Renner. Actually, he only saw a part of it. When the longboat bumped against the loading dock, it pushed aside the bloated corpse of a white man, which went bobbing up against the mossy pilings, stinking. Large pieces of flesh were missing, and the edges around these wounds were ragged, as if things had been feeding. Dunbar clapped his hand to his mouth and gagged. Renner giggled. Santiago said, "Sleep tight, mate. *Buenos sueños.*" Then he put a brown hand under Dunbar's arm and helped the journalist onto the dock. "Up you go, *amigo.*"

The *Jubilation*'s seamen moved down the old pier in a solid block. They were set upon by half a dozen skinny white men in ragged and dirty seamen's trousers.

"Hey, mates, how 'bout a couple of coppers, eh?"

"Talk to your captain, lads, he needs another hand. I know he does! And there's not a better man in Old Calabar than me."

Their ages were indefinite, and they were all of them, Dunbar supposed, dying. One, whose eyes were yellow, whose lips were black and split, and whose fingernails were long, filthy claws, grabbed at the sailors. "What ship are you?" he wailed. "Is there a Tom Henderson among you? Tom Henderson. Please. He's my brother. My own dear brother. And he's coming to get me. Please. He's going to take me home. Tom?" He snared O'Brien and thrust his face close to the Irishman's. "Tom?" O'Brien hit him on the side of the head. He reeled back, tottered on the edge of the dock, then went over into the water. The crewmen laughed. Santiago pulled Dunbar on. "*Vámanos, compadre.*"

The streets were hard-packed earth, and they were narrow. The tiny houses were built of mud and had thatched roofs. Doors and windows were simple holes; few of the openings were masked by cloth. Naked children ran and screamed everywhere. Dogs, goats, and chickens wandered freely. Flies abounded. The heat was stifling. They went through a market square where piles of over-ripe vegetables and fruit bled juices onto straw mats and wooden stalls and hunks of sickly bluish meat hosted swarms of insects. It stank of waste and rot. Once they crossed a broad avenue. "The royal palace," Santiago said, pointing. A large three-story building with arches and portals and balconies squatted, colorless and simple, at the end of the avenue. Guards in bright red robes flanked its entrance, wicked scimitars in their hands.

The area to which they went was one of crooked streets and strewn garbage. There were no children here. Walls of buildings were cracked and broken. Some of the roofs had fallen in. Seamen from one of the slavers anchored in the bay sprawled drunkenly on the ground. Dunbar had to step over one to enter the bar Santiago wanted to visit first. The journalist drank himself staggering in less than an hour. No man could stand against two months' abstinence, the heat, and the raw, throat-searing whiskey that was served.

He did not have a clear thought until the next morning, when he was awakened by the brightness and heat of the sun streaming through a glassless window onto his face. He grunted; consciousness hurt. Several moments passed before he was willing to open his eyes, and many more before he turned his head. He was in a cramped and littered hut, on the floor. A few feet away was a sleeping black woman. She was fat. She was on her back and her huge, spongy breasts fell in opposite directions, lolling heavily over her arms. Her mouth was open. She had no front teeth. A slick line of spittle ran down her check to a little pool on the floor. She was breathing with hoarse, bubbling sounds. She stank. He stank. Everything stank. Unbearably.

Dunbar closed his eyes. Direct thought was too painful, maybe even impossible. But by sliding sideways, he began to remember some things. Vague, dreamlike scenes. He had drunk much, and in many places, all of which blended together, confused and jumbled in his mind. There had been a contest, some kind of contest. Not with alcohol, but it had made him drink more. He remembered an argument, and breeches . . . being opened. Oh, my God! Yes, breeches opened, and pallid, funny-looking organs laid out on a table and the owner of the bar with a measuring stick. Santiago, the winner, a giant among men. And later, someplace else, the man from the Cuban slaver, hearing of Santiago's endowment, challenging. They had got a girl, hadn't they? a girl who, *Christ,* who had no pupils, whose eyes were pure unbroken white, and she touched everybody with her hands because she could not see them, and they cleared a space for her in the middle of the floor and Santiago and the Cuban went at her for what seemed like hours while she laughed and clapped her hands and drummed her heels. They had been in the marketplace, too, roistering and spreading havoc until the black guards, or policemen, or whatever the hell they were, drove them back, roughly but without injury; these were, after all, the white benefactors. In darkness, later, there had been a large brawl between the crews of the three slave ships. As he remembered, Dunbar touched his face. Parts of it were swollen and tender to his fingers. The journalist gingerly tested his nose and was relieved to discover it was not broken. There was something about O'Brien, too, but that escaped him completely. He didn't care. He remembered more than enough already.

He eased himself up on his elbows. He groaned. He ached, everywhere. He saw that he was naked, and he looked around for his pants. He found them and put them on, slowly and with care. They were torn and dirty. He buckled the belt, noticing that his knife sheath was empty. He considered this, and then he went rigid. He shook his head, but denial could not be obtained through a simple gesture. He leaned against the wall.

He had murdered O'Brien.

He had been stumbling down a street with Santiago and Renner, singing, heading someplace or another. And Renner tripped over a big seaman. " 'S O'Brien," Renner said, still on the ground, close to the Irishman. "He'sh dead, all dead."

"Whoopee," Dunbar said in a little voice.

"No." Santiago shook his head with exaggeration. "Nothing kill him. *Nada en el mundo.*" He got down on his knees and took one of the Irishman's ears in each hand. "O'Brien! O'Brien, *abre los ojos!*" He shook O'Brien's head up and down, whacking the man's skull against the hard earth.

The Irishman belched and licked his lips but did not awaken.

"Borracho," Santiago said with pride. "See? Just drunk." He stood up and helped Renner to his feet. The two of them went staggering down the street.

Dunbar stayed behind, looking down at O'Brien. "You nearly kill me . . . killed me," he said. "Make everybody laugh at me. Made me wet myself! Well . . . you're not so fuckin' tough now. Too bad, you bastard."

"Dunbar," Santiago called from the blackness.

"Bye, O'Brien," the journalist muttered. He reached behind him for his knife, but he felt only the empty sheath. Okay, he'd use O'Brien's own knife then. He bent over to get it. But then his stomach clutched in on itself and he vomited. The sour liquid splashed over the Irishman. Dunbar sobered a little. His face screwed up with horror.

"Duuunbarrr," Santiago called again.

The journalist ran away.

Thank God, thank God! Dunbar laughed and tears squeezed from his eyes. He hadn't killed O'Brien! He felt very weak. If O'Brien were to die, he, Dunbar, would certainly not mourn him. But to stick a knife into a helpless, drunken man, that was too much to bear.

Dunbar left the hut without another look at the snoring mountain of black flesh on the floor, made his way shakily back to the wharf, and promised a Negro two coppers to row him out to the *Jubilation*.

He went ashore only once more during the month the ship was in port—when the two coffles designated for the *Jubilation* arrived from the interior. Dunbar was one of the men assigned to row the captain, Wilkes, and Wilkes's assistant, Mr. Petersen, to the dock. It was early in the morning. The king's chief caboceer met them at the barracoons with a phalanx of armed and whip-carrying guards. The caboceer unlocked the heavy log gate, and the party entered. Gibbering and wailing rose from the penned slaves.

The first thing Dunbar saw was a number of black bodies hanging from the ridgepole of the rain shelter. The caboceer screamed in rage, then issued a rapid series of orders. The dead slaves were taken down and heaped in a pile. There were sixteen of them. Next, a detachment of sleepy, blinking, and frightened guards was hauled into the pen. So far as Dunbar could gather, these men had been on duty the previous night and had neglected to secure the newly arrived slaves to the ground chains, which would have prevented the suicides. The guards were beaten, then whipped in with the cowering slaves and themselves chained. The caboceer sulked, obviously wanting to put the guilty men to death. But sixteen slaves had been lost, and the books had to be balanced as best they could.

A slave was seized and dragged to the surgeons. The rest

of the Negroes set up a great howling. The guards' slashing whips could not quiet them. "Tell them they're not going to be eaten," Horneby said to the caboceer. The black man glowered; he did not like to be told his business. Nevertheless, he had been negligent. A seaman beside Dunbar shifted the tobacco wad in his mouth and spat brown juice. "Jesus, they're stupid," he said with disgust. "Every nigger what lives more'n fifty miles from the coast thinks we're cannibals. Shee-it! Hogs got more sense."

The linguists delivered the message in several dialects. Gradually the uproar subsided. The slaves had no real reason to believe what they were told, but they desperately wanted to believe, and so, with only a little reluctance, they allowed themselves to be convinced.

The first man trembled before the corpulent surgeon. Wilkes cocked his head and ran a quick, professional glance over the black. "Mhmm." He stepped forward. The slave retreated, and was pushed roughly back by a guard. Wilkes pulled the lower eyelids down, examined them, pinched out the upper eyelids and looked them over. The slave whimpered. Wilkes peered in both ears, then put his fingers in the man's mouth and pulled open the jaw. "Teeth sound," he said to himself. He felt under the man's armpits and tested the articulation of shoulders, elbows, and fingers. He poked and probed the belly and abdomen. He took the man's scrotum and penis and worked them briefly with his fingers. Next he had the man squat. "Knees and ankles all right," he said. He investigated the soles and the spaces between the toes. "No parasites." He told a guard to turn the man and bend him over. He spread the slave's buttocks and scrutinized the pink bud of the anus. "Grease," he said. Petersen extended a jar. Wilkes dipped two fingers into the lubricant. "Hold him steady." The guard gripped the slave around the shoulders and locked him into his bent position. The surgeon thrust both fingers into the rectum. The black screamed and tried to jerk free. Wilkes worked his fingers around. "No tumors," he said. "Finished. Put him over there."

The slave was taken away.

"That's how it's done," Wilkes said to Petersen, who was making his first run on a slaver. "The whole process should take only three or four minutes. Keep an eye out for all the things I mentioned to you. If you find anything out of the ordinary, let me know."

Two more slaves were brought forward. Wilkes worked with quiet proficiency and without wasted motion. Petersen performed his examinations with an expression of consummate loathing. When nine other slaves had joined the first, Wilkes had the ten run twice around the perimeter of the barracoon at full clip. Then he stood watching their chests heave and listening to them breathe. He punched each one hard on the breastbone. Satisfied, he said to Horneby, "All of them healthy, Captain."

"Thank you, Mr. Wilkes." The captain bent his head together with the caboceer.

In the end, some two hundred slaves were deemed fit. Nearly thirty were rejected—some because they had been wracked by coughing fits when their chests were punched, others because they had rheumy eyes or the backs of their thighs were sticky with the evidence of dysentery, a few who were burning with fever, one because there were only three teeth in his mouth, another because of badly infected battle wounds. The one who brought bile up Dunbar's throat, though, was a female with worms. When her buttocks were spread, the thin white creatures could be seen wriggling there in the pinkness. Petersen made the discovery, and he announced it by spinning around, grabbing his stomach, and vomiting. The caboceer was violently indignant over each refusal, and he stormed with great theatricality when Horneby indicated the group that was not to be purchased.

"Come, now," the captain said. "You know as well as we do that those slaves are faulty."

"Little problems!" the caboceer ranted. "You blind. All good. All! We hurry, sell 'em twice as much quick to next ship."

"Go ahead."

"Right away. We most exceedingly honest. Not like you traders with bad exploding guns and water-whisky and pewter-silver, fake stuff. Right away, I tell you!"

"Fine. But in the meantime let's settle on a price for the ones *we* are taking."

Horneby walked off with the caboceer, the black man's hands beating the air in vehement protest.

"What will happen to the rejects?" Dunbar asked Crawford.

The wizened little Englishman looked at Dunbar as if he could not believe the stupidity of the question. "They'll kill them," he said.

The crew had been rounded up and brought back to the ship two days before the purchase so they could be dried out and restored to some semblance of fitness. Wilkes had not been far wrong. Two were missing, one was dead, and six more were sick. Of the latter, the surgeon expected only two to recover.

The black males were loaded first. The sailors made Dunbar uneasy. They had lost weight, were thin and bony. Some of their sea-tan had vanished, and a strange pallor underlying what remained suggested dissolution. Their faces were sharp, and they carried themselves tautly. The journalist decided that the stay in port had boiled away everything but the distilled concentrate of their basic ferality. Something within him quavered. The slaves came over the rail, were hosed down, herded together, taken into the hold, and chained. And Dunbar, watching, understood that there was more to slaving than money, something that would sustain the trade even if it were a far less profitable business.

It was the power.

Here were all these black-skinned people for you to do with as you pleased, short of destroying their market value. Instinctively, Dunbar believed the Negroes were inferior. It was a self-defining condition; a man could not be made a slave, the journalist felt, unless there were some essential flaw in his character. But this business of their being some high species of ape, that was all cant and rubbish, and regardless of what was said, only a few, like Wilkes, actually believed it. They were human, that's what made them so seductive: you couldn't get this kind of pleasure by playing God over, say, cattle.

Tongues darted out and wetted seamen's lips; quick and reasonless little smiles curled their mouths; they breathed with rapid doglike pants. And the hands, always and everywhere the hands. Whips and clubs were used only for difficult problems, otherwise—hands. Hands taking hold of arms and shoulders when a gesture would have sufficed, hands touching necks and cheeks, rubbing coiled hair, cupping breasts, sliding over wet rounded bottoms and backs and thighs during the hosing, hands pushing, hands patting, hands lingering on a calf after the manacle had been closed, white hands moving over black bodies, all parts of which seemed equally voluptuous, regardless of age or sex.

It was first contact. It was a preliminary. It was a teasing of self, the initial light and delicious caress given by a lover to his mistress's breast while it was still encased in silk. It spoke and promised of all that was, in time, in due and luxurious time, to follow.

It horrified Dunbar. It also thrilled him, and his hands, too, touched.

He grew giddy, and he sensed, with fear, that he was reaching the heart of some primal truth, something philosophers and theologians had been able to postulate in only the most feeble and oblique way.

That was three weeks ago. Now the second lot was aboard. And they were different. Dunbar, like the rest of the crew, was angry, and the slaves had suffered during the loading.

More troublesome, though, was the journalist's own confusion and unhappiness.

Above the slap of canvas and the creaking of timbers came the sound of approaching footfalls. It was Wilkes, waddling toward Dunbar with moonlight gleaming on his bald pate.

"Evening," the surgeon said. "No carousing for you tonight?"

"Evening, Mr. Wilkes. I wanted to think awhile, is all." Wilkes was a valuable find. The man was a dedicated raconteur and possessed an apparently inexhaustible knowledge of the trade, its history, and the blacks. He was affable and good-natured and at least basically literate. Dunbar found him a relief after the coarseness of the crew. Wilkes seemed to like him, too, and of course was happy to have a new and willing listener.

"Thinking about anything in particular?"

"The niggers we loaded this morning," Dunbar said. "They don't carry themselves like the others."

"Naturally. They're Coromantees, or Ashanti, if you prefer."

"From Cormantine, the port?"

"The same."

"Why didn't we buy them from the port, then?"

"Precisely because they *are* Coromantees. They don't sell their own kind." Wilkes lighted his pipe. "Years ago," he said, "they were an inland tribe, very warlike and proud, but not organized and therefore prey to their neighbors. Europeans wanted slaves, and niggers were willing to hand over their fellows in exchange for guns and other stuffs, but mostly guns. Guns meant military superiority, which of course protected you from being enslaved yourself. On the other hand, the only way to get guns was to enslave the people around you. The Coromantees had the natural ability; all they needed were the weapons, which they got. The story holds for all the black empires—slaves, guns, slaver, slaving nation.

"These Coromantees, though, magnificent animals! The most impressive niggers in Africa . . . and the most troublesome. For example, over fifty percent of all slave revolts have been led by them."

"Then why bother with them?"

Wilkes shrugged. "Partly out of perversity, I imagine. You know, the wilder the beast the stronger the desire to break it. And partly because, when they *can* be tamed, they make truly superior slaves—overseers, warehouse managers, that sort of thing. Almost impossible to get these days. The captain had to work like hell. I predict heads'll be rolling in that stinking jungle for months." Wilkes laughed. "I had a cousin once, on the moneyed side of the family, who used to breed dogs. You know, niggers are much more fascinating than dogs."

"I guess so," the journalist said sharply. He found the surgeon's last statement not to his liking, particularly because he was somewhat in agreement.

Wilkes, responding, fell into an uncharacteristic silence.

The two men stood looking out at the luminous wake and listening to the water foaming past the sides. They were under three-quarter sail and tacking against the wind. After several minutes Wilkes said, "May I be candid with you, Dunbar?"

Virgil cringed. He was certain the surgeon would say something he didn't want to hear. Something personal. Something naked. "Sure, sure." He deliberately gruffened his voice.

Wilkes was not deterred. "I don't want to presume," he said humbly, "but you're an intelligent man and you seem to have a good deal of understanding. I thought . . . that is, if you wouldn't mind . . ."

For Christ's sake, get it over with! Dunbar thought. "No, go ahead," he muttered.

"Well, the thing is, you see, I'm not, and, uh, I never was a very good surgeon. Oh, I'm competent, but just competent, and for this job only. It's always been like that. When I was a boy I was barely competent at being a boy. My parents used to point to my cousin. He seemed to excel in everything. I tried. But I just wasn't very good, at anything."

Dunbar squirmed. Wilkes didn't notice. He was talking as much to himself as he was to the journalist.

"I'm fifty-eight years old and I've never worked at anything but slaving in my life. One thing, though, I enjoy slaves. I mean, like my cousin did his dogs, or other men horses. But it's not much of a life, is it? And I won't even have that in a year or two. I'll have to retire, it's getting to be too much for me. What's been gnawing at me is: What was the point of it all? What will I have to show for my life?"

This last was choked. Dunbar was sure the man was fighting back sobs. The journalist was outraged. What right did Wilkes have to subject him to this? And he was scornful. He had seen broken men before, and men who had wept. But they had been men smashed by monumental blows of fate, men whose legs had been torn away by cannonballs, whose bodies had been rotted by terrible diseases, whose vast fortunes had been swept off by the changeling winds of investment and trade. . . . Always there had been an element of the epic, the immense, involved. And that was the key: ruin in the face of Irresistible Force. That justified despair, even ennobled it. But this!

Dunbar felt something else, too, small, but as stubborn as a root forcing through a tight crack in a rock. He looked at the fleshy surgeon and experienced a glimmer of compassion. "Come on, Mr. Wilkes," he said. "There aren't any world-shakers, not in reality, at least."

Wilkes tried unsuccessfully to smile.

"There are Alice and Alicia," Dunbar ventured.

"Yes," Wilkes said somberly. "Yes. There are." His face took on a wistful look. "If there is a point to it all, then they are that point. When I'm with them, my—well, it may seem terribly sentimental, but my heart is full. I have joy." The surgeon reached beneath his shirt and drew out a locket that was suspended from a thin chain round his neck. It was old-fashioned, but finely crafted of filigreed gold. He opened it and stared lovingly. "Would you like to see them again?"

Dunbar nodded. The locket contained two enamel miniatures, portraits of Wilkes's daughters. The girls were twins, fourteen years old, and it would have been impossible to tell them apart had not Alice worn a red ribbon in her hair and Alicia a green one. Their smiling faces were deeply dimpled. Their eyes were large and blue and their long hair was golden.

"They're lovely," Dunbar said with honesty.

"Yes." Wilkes looked at them one last time, smiling, then closed the locket and replaced it. "I have them to be proud of and to be thankful for." He slapped his big belly, signaling the return of his spirits. "Not many men have that much."

"Right."

"Well, I have things to do, and I'd best be at them. Dunbar?"

"Yes?"

"Thank you, lad."

"Sure, Mr. Wilkes."

"Good night."

"Good night."

The surgeon left. Dunbar put him out of mind. The journalist was unhappy, but he was not certain why. He considered the stench and rigors of the ship, the harshness of his circumstances, the fear, the necessary deception, even the Negroes themselves, and it was none of these. No, it was . . . it was as if, very subtly, he were coming apart, losing his shape and form, like a freshly cast plaster statue in a rainstorm, softening, slipping, a kind of erosion. He didn't understand it. It made him afraid.

Virgil Dunbar, under his other name, was viewed by many as an insufferable narcissist. Dunbar himself was in partial agreement, although he did not consider himself insufferable. But in truth Dunbar lacked the requisite ego. Regardless of what anyone else thought, he *knew* his writing had no real depth. He was a highly skilled technician, nothing more. He knew how to build a scene, he knew what words to use, he knew what nerves to tweak to obtain the desired response. But it was all artifice. Though his articles screamed outrage or choked pathos, and moved his readers to the same, Dunbar had never felt anything about his subjects; they remained just that—subjects, tools, like quills or sheaves of paper.

And since he could feel nothing for anyone else, he became himself the focus of his own emotion, lover and beloved, mover and moved. Thus a narcissist, insufferable to some.

Strangely, though, his readers were closer to the truth than he was. Dunbar was indeed a man of keener than average sensibilities. However, they terrified him. To feel compassion toward, to empathize with, is to become horribly vulnerable. It is to risk devastation. The possibilities were too frightening for Dunbar, and he had begun at quite an early age to erect barricades, to become sufficient in himself. His writing was a useful and efficient device. Consigning things to paper sucked them dry of their life juices, made him safe, made him master.

Most of this was unknown to Dunbar, and so he was unable to recognize the change that had begun: His walls were being breached. They still held, but the first inroads had been made. He did not know what was happening, but he sensed terrible danger.

Matthew Hollister's cabin was small, nicely appointed, and not, unless you had a touch of claustrophobia, uncomfortable. The young man did not care, would not have cared if he had been on the rolling plains west of Missouri and Iowa, or if he had been in a cramped prison cell. It was all the same to him. Nothing mattered to Matthew Hollister—and this was partly why he was aboard the *Jubilation*.

His family name was something to be reckoned with in Rhode Island. It meant wealth and political power; it meant proud lineage. The original Hollisters had arrived in New England several decades before the Constitution of the

United States was framed. The present paterfamilias was a man of iron will and iron body named Peyton Quartus Hollister. He was Matthew's father, and he despised his son, which the son knew, but about which the son did not care.

Matthew's cabin was dark. He rarely lit the lamp. When it was day, then the cabin was light. When it was night, the cabin was dark. It worked quite well, and he saw no reason to make any alteration. He had drawn a chair to the small leaded windows that looked out the stern. The windows were open, and a light breeze freshened the room. He sat, letting it blow upon him, and looked out into the night. At nothing in particular. Soon he would go to bed. And sometime after that, it would be morning again and he would get up. It was all easy enough.

Peyton Hollister took pride in his son, as he took pride in anything he owned or produced, but he believed children were the exclusive province of their mothers until the age of five, at which time a man could begin to reason with them and to shape them. This was eminently satisfactory to Madeline Hollister and to little Matthew. Madeline was a warm and loving woman with prodigious maternal instincts. Matthew was a marvelously happy baby, who only dimly understood, and did not especially resent, the fact that he had a father. Peyton was up and out of the house before Matthew woke, and usually did not return until long after the infant was in bed. Peyton was the man Matthew called *Sir* on weekends, the man who treated Matthew amenably, the man to whom people doffed their hats and paused to pay respects on Sunday, the day *Sir* and Mother and Matthew went to church.

Madeline Hollister was found cold in her bed by a maidservant one morning when Matthew was three. A little blood vessel had burst in her brain during the night. It was called apoplexy.

Matthew, after the hysteria had passed, was numb with shock. No one had ever told him that the world could be destroyed. Peyton Hollister was enraged by his wife's death. He had placed all his trust in her, and she had betrayed him. And she had deprived him of the other children who would, eventually, have been his. He could not and would never forgive her.

He didn't know what to do with Matthew, so he did nothing, relegating responsibility to various housekeepers and tutors over the next several years. Then he set out to make a man of the boy. Since he conceived of Matthew as a youthful copy of himself, he treated him accordingly. When the boy did not manifest the same fervor and enthusiasm for the intricacies of mercantilism that had over the years secured his father's position as one of the eastern seaboard's most influential magnates, Peyton was baffled. At first. Then he became angry, and finally he settled for disgust. What had begun, to Peyton's thinking, as Matthew's inexperience, grew into Matthew's ineptitude, into Matthew's complete lack of interest . . . in anything.

Peyton found this intolerable. He looked upon it as an insult to God and nature. Any other man he would have driven from him as anathema. But Matthew was, biologically, his son. So Matthew remained in Peyton's house, and the father in his thoughts declared his son dead, dug a grave, lowered in the corpse, and then returned to his many and difficult businesses.

Someone rapped on the door of Matthew's cabin. He sat in silence. The rapping came again. "Matthew? Matthew, are you awake?" It was the surgeon, Wilkes. Matthew breathed with a slow and steady rhythm. Through the windows he saw starlight twinkling on the water. The surgeon tried once again, then gave it up and went away. Matthew listened to the footsteps receding down the companionway.

Matthew understood his father; Peyton was not a complicated man. Matthew did not hate him. Nor did he love him. He neither loved nor hated anyone, including himself. During the years following his mother's death he had been a *de facto* if not a titular orphan, and those in charge of him, all competent and above reproach, understandably had no reason to love him. When his father finally came to him he had been overjoyed. But tariffs and market gluts, theory of price determination, vehicles of cost stability, and the laws of marginal and secondary production are not of natural interest to a twelve-year-old boy. Nor are they capable of sustaining, much less enhancing, his life. They are all but incomprehensible, no matter how strong the desire to master them and thereby win approval, gain a father, a place, a self.

And behind them all stood a man of iron. And iron will always overwhelm simple flesh and blood.

Except for vague memories of some other time, there seemed to be nothing but pain. So, piece by piece, Matthew Hollister withdrew from pain until, at the age of eighteen or nineteen, he had neutralized himself.

Once he considered suicide—as he might have considered a choice of two shirts, a matter of form more than anything else. It was clear, though, that there was no reason for self-destruction. One could not help but realize that it would all take care of itself in the end. Like day and night, there was a cycle, and in due course night would come.

Peyton was responsible for Matthew's presence on the *Jubilation.* The elder Hollister owned a one-third interest in this voyage, and Horneby was hardly in a position to refuse when Matthew arrived in Charleston with a letter from his father.

There were two reasons behind Peyton's decision. First,

it served admirably as yet another expression of paternal displeasure. And second, on the anniversary of his wife's death Peyton felt a twinge of guilt, and so he exhumed Matthew's corpse for one last attempt to break through the boy's lassitude. A slaving voyage was ideal on both counts.

Horneby did not like to carry supercargo; but there was a small cabin empty and so long as Matthew did not get in the way, the captain would tolerate him. To the surgeon, who was garrulous and suited for the job, Horneby passed on Hollister's request that an attempt be made to draw the boy out of himself in any manner possible.

Matthew opened his eyes. The night had darkened. Thin clouds stained the moon. He realized he had been asleep. He sat a while longer, then he got up, stripped off his clothes, and went to bed. Soon he was asleep again, without dreams.

Leana pushed as far from the woman with the huge belly as she could. It was only a matter of inches, and then she was pressed hard against the woman on her other side. But now even inches were valuable. There was a baby inside the woman from whom Leana was trying to escape. The baby must be hurting her, for the woman was groaning and thrashing her head. The baby might be trying to get itself born. Leana did not want that.

Leana was young. A white man with gray whiskers and fat lips had paused over her, undecided as to whether she should go with the children or with the women. He finally put her with the latter. At home Leana would have thought it her due and would have been pleased by this recognition of her newly acquired status. But here in the dark, where she could hardly move and scarcely breathe the fouled air, she was frightened and she wished she had been put with the children. She felt like one.

She had seen babies press out between spread and muscling thighs before and there was nothing in it that was unreasonable; it was even interesting. But here the blood would puddle and stay, and the purple thing that came afterward would slip and slide across them all with the motion of the ship. And already Leana's small breasts and her belly were slick with her own vomit. And there was a soft warm paste on her buttocks and thighs. And how could they cut the cord and make the little thing live? It was all corruption. They were being smothered in the spew of their own bodies. Leana could stand no more.

The girl whimpered. Her body was bruised. In the village she would have been married in another year or so. Boys had touched her and it had been good. But, when she had come onto the ship, the white men had been waiting. They were hideous to look at, their skin colorless and sickly. And their bodies were hairy, like animals'. She looked at them and could see nothing but giant, nightmarish maggots. They had put their hands all over her, and one of them, a man with red hair, had hurt her and she screamed. He laughed, but at least he did not touch her again.

Leana wanted to be dead. If only she could move. If only the darkness weren't smothering her. If . . . She covered her face with her hands, bent her back, and drew her legs up as best she could. The muscles of her jaw ached; her lips were quivering. She pressed her hand to her mouth to hold her lips, then, jerkily, her thumb went between her teeth. She closed her lips round its base and began to suck. Her other hand drifted without conscious thought down her body and lodged softly between her thighs. She stroked herself. In a while her loins tautened. She sucked hard on her thumb, eyes squeezed shut, and pushed her fingers into herself. She rocked, and the movement grew stronger and her breathing intensified until finally she pressed her knees together, yanked her thumb from her mouth and went *aaahhhh!*

And for a moment there was peace, happiness, too, and fine, wonderful scenes of home in her head. But they did not stay with her long, and in a little time Leana was sobbing. Heavy, strangled sounds that tore from deep within her chest.

BOOK II

BOOK II

A SEAMAN was beating a drum. Another was playing a kind of bellows, stretching and shortening it between his hands. Naked slaves were jumping and whirling to the beat. Adoko had been mystified when he and half the males had first been brought to the topdeck. But gestures had shown them what was expected, and whips ensured compliance. It was a form of exercise. Adoko saw no sense in it. It did little against the stiffening and weakening of the dark holds; it did not make sick men well; it was not the kind of sport that pleased their captors. The jumping caused the shackle on his ankle to scrape his skin. He saw little lines of blood. He didn't mind, for the iron was a kind of spur, and when it was removed, the white men would die and his people would be free. Adoko decided the exercise was good. The more willing the slaves were to perform this silly dance, the more the whites relaxed, and the more the whites relaxed, the sooner they would be dead.

The music stopped. The slaves could do as they wished now, within limits. The black children had the run of the entire deck, while females were restricted to the fore- and mid-decks, and males to the mid-deck only. There was not much activity today. The seas were heavy, spray splashed over the bulwarks, and the ship was pitching strongly. Many of the slaves were sick.

Adoko sat with two of his kinsmen at the base of the mainmast.

"There is always a man by the big gun," one of them said angrily. "We can do nothing!"

"Smile, Kiuky," Adoko said. "Your face must never look menacing. We must not give them cause for suspicion."

"We will slit your throats, you white slugs," Kiuky sing-songed. Then he laughed, as if he had just told the punch line to a joke.

Adoko said, "Quiet, you fool!" A slave with chest tattoos was looking at them fearfully. "There are some among the others who speak our tongue. You will alarm them."

"Let them choke on their own tongues. They have the hearts of slaves."

"No," Adoko said. "It is only their fear."

"They are nothing to us."

"They are slaves and we are slaves."

"We are Ashanti."

"Yes, but they are more like us than they are like the whites."

"We owe them nothing," Kiuky insisted.

"Perhaps."

"They will not help us."

"Some will, and more will join when they see we are winning."

"How can we win, Osai Adoko, when, as Kiuky observes, the great gun remains?"

None of them looked up to the quarterdeck, but all felt the weight of the huge carronade. It was trained on the mid-deck, where the males were, each moment of the day. Though the slaves had never seen a gun like this fired, clearly it could kill a great number of them with a single, deafening roar.

"A way will be found. That is not our concern at the moment. Was anything taken today?"

"One of the wooden clubs they use to tighten their ropes."

"Nothing more?"

"This was your son's prize."

"Who has it now?"

"Gyase."

"Tell him to hide it as the others have been hidden."

With the club their arsenal—or tool store, for each implement would serve a dual purpose—held eleven pieces: one club, two files, one length of stout rope which was twice the height of a man, two pieces of flat metal, and, miraculously, three long spikes and two knives. Planks had been pried loose from the slave decks, and the treasures hidden beneath them.

"If only we could get a musket or a sword," Kiuky said longingly.

"If one comes easily, good. Otherwise, the risk is too great."

A guard approached, armed with pistol and cutlass. Though it lacerated his soul, Adoko grinned and bobbed his head up and down. This was the supreme sacrifice. He could more easily have undergone torture by fire. *Convince them you too think as they do, that they are gods,* he had told his people. *Then more easily may we topple them from their thrones.* It was difficult; belly-crawling did not come naturally to his kinsmen. The white seaman smirked at him, and walked on.

Kiuky and the other man averted their eyes several moments; then Kiuky said softly, "You are stronger than we, Osai Adoko. Forgive us."

"Forgiveness is for strangers—it is not needed in the family."

The third man said, "Again I smelled alcohol on the breath of the one with the scar and the beard."

"That is four times now," Adoko said. "He drinks much. Good. He will be one of the first. His weapons will be helpful."

"The one by the nearest water barrel is still negligent," Kiuky said. "He is bored."

Adoko nodded. "He will die bored. The drunken one and the bored one together. We are fortunate. They stand close by each other. When we strike we will not be divided, and our backs will be to the rail."

"Their leaders are not fools," Kiuky said. "It will be difficult to surprise them."

"It is more difficult to be a slave. The one in the fine coat who stands on the high deck is the most dangerous, I think. He is the leader of their leaders, and not without reason. His eyes miss little. His mind is quick. He does not have the arrogance of the others, but neither, I believe, does he know fear. If he cannot be killed instantly, then it will be best to wait until he is not present."

"I would be cautious of the one with the red hair, too," Kiuky said. "He has the look and the senses of a hunting cat."

Adoko glanced at Meredith, the first mate. "The one who likes to hurt. Yes, he is dangerous. But he can be trapped.

He cannot resist pain. He will come to it like the crushing snake to the staked pig."

A sailor strode toward them, cat-o'-nine-tails unlimbered.

"This one thinks we have been together too long. Laugh, my brothers."

The three slaves guffawed. Then the sailor was on them, growling in his incomprehensible language, laying into them with the whip, scattering them. Adoko scrambled away and held out his hand, as if in supplication. He knew his words would be only so much jabber to the white man. What he said was: "Show him fear." Kiuky managed a whine. Adoko knew the sound had cost him much. "Thank you," he called.

He couldn't locate Tola in the area he was free to roam, so he stopped another child and asked him to find the boy. Across the deck a guard grabbed a girl, forced his hand into her crotch and pressed her to him, mouth working against hers. She did not resist; that would have meant even more pain. Adoko closed his eyes. He saw this same ship, but manned now by him and his people, proud in their robes and ornaments, armed and free, guarding a deck that teemed with white men, who were chained and who were humiliated by their pale nakedness and gibbering with mortal fear. He heard them scream as the whips fell upon them. He saw them weep and crawl and beg. He saw the soul-destroying sickness in their eyes as proud black men threw their white, unclothed, and defenseless women down, bent them over casks and rails, and filled them with black, stiff organs. Weep, white men, weep! Cry for your children, your wives, your homes! Die your living deaths! Walk in hopelessness and terror!

Adoko opened his eyes in time to see the seaman release the girl and push her from him. The man's face was flushed. He pushed his hand under his waistband and scratched his genitals. It gave Adoko pleasure to know that some would die with their loins throbbing. The women would come to them, when the moment was at hand, and the black fingers would touch and fondle those despised white man-stalks for the final time. In his hip-thrusting heat the white man would suddenly find the black woman gone, and in her place would be a black man with steel, and white guts would come spilling onto the deck in the bright sun.

That would be good. Adoko would be happy.

Tola was there. He took his father's hand. Adoko looked down. Was the boy really that small? He swept Tola up in his arms and hugged him tightly several moments, then set him down. "Kiuky tells me you have stolen a club."

The boy nodded.

"I am proud of you."

Tola smiled, a little shyly. "Will you use it to kill the white men?"

"Yes."

"Can I help you?"

"There will be killing for all of us. My heart will know joy to have you with me."

"I will be there. I will be a warrior with you."

Adoko kissed the boy on his forehead.

"And when it is done," Tola said, "will we go home then?"

"Yes."

"How will we know where it is?"

"We will know. I will find a way for us."

"Good. I miss our home."

"All of us do, Tola. We will return."

The boy believed him. He had no reason not to. His father had never lied to him before. Two boys called to Tola. He looked at them but didn't respond. "Go," Adoko told him, "we will talk later." The boy obeyed, and Adoko watched the three of them walk away. He longed to hear laughter from them.

As usual, Besu was sitting alone, glowering at the white men. The fat, bald healer had put some kind of poultice on Besu's back, and the wounds were closing nicely. But his head and shoulders were marked with bruises and small cuts. He had offered no overt resistance since the day he had been beaten unconscious, but he made no effort to conceal his hate, and the sailors abused him frequently. Besu had always had a haughty spirit, and Adoko knew that bondage had struck him the most severely. Each day ripped another piece of his heart away. Besu was dying, and Adoko feared that what small restraint his brother still possessed would disintegrate soon and that Besu would strike for his freedom no matter the cost or the odds. Adoko was helpless. At first Besu had listened patiently and then, ignoring everything that had been said, asked "When do we move against them?" Now he would no longer listen, and he had not spoken to Adoko for two days.

Adoko decided to try once again. Besu saw him coming, and slowly and deliberately turned his back.

Dunbar, sprawled across a slave shelf in the number two hold, gagged. His stomach had been empty several minutes, but the reflex would not stop.

A dozen feet away Crawford cackled like a gleeful and malicious spinster.

"Give 'er another twenty years, matey. It'll get so's you can't live without this 'ere stink. Go ashore an' you'll keep sniffin' the wind, lookin' for it, like a dog for 'is favorite tree."

They were part of the work gang scrubbing down the shelves. Females and children were brought topside daily. Only half the males could be accommodated at any given time, so each black man was brought up every other day. When the *Jubilation* was fully loaded, the males would be aired every third or fourth day. As the decks were emptied, seamen were sent down to clean. They scoured the raw wood with stiff wire brushes and a solution of vinegar, water, and soap. Pails of pure vinegar were placed at intervals, and musket balls heated a shimmering red in braziers were dropped into them. The vinegar boiled and hissed, and its vapor fumigated the enclosed space.

Dunbar stripped himself naked like the others when he entered the hold; the filth would ruin a pair of trousers. He took his brush and bucket and squirmed onto a shelf, bumping his head and scraping his back at first because he tried to crawl on his hands and knees. There wasn't enough room. He had to lie flat . . . in the soft feces . . . on the tacky urine . . . in the doughy vomit. Several times he thought he would faint, and he scuttled to one of the tiny portals, pressed his face to it and, in panic, sucked in the sea air until his head cleared. He felt that if he passed out here he would die.

The shift was only forty-five minutes long; that was the most a man could stand. Toward the end Dunbar was almost hysterical. He was praying, something he hadn't done since he was ten years old. *Please, God, get me out. I love you. God, help me. Please get me out. I don't want to die. Please, God!* And then, finally, when he knew his collapse was only minutes away, Meredith came down and yelled, "All right, shit-lovers! Fun time's over. Topside."

Dunbar tipped over his bucket in his scramble to back off the shelf. He fell to the bottom of the passageway, pushed himself up, and stumbled down the length of the hold to the ladder. Crawford came directly behind him, going, "He-he-he-he-he-he."

"Your breech-clout, Dunbar," the mate said. Dunbar

grabbed the cloth, tied it round his waist then clawed up to the deck. Nakedness was for the animals; the sailors wore at least breech-clouts. Except, of course, when they were copulating with the animals, but even then they were liable to simply push their trousers down around their knees. On the deck Dunbar staggered to the railing and stood gasping clean air, trying to regain control of his stomach and his mind. Then he walked to the foredeck where the others of his shift were washing themselves down. His gait was unsteady; his face was haggard. But no one laughed at him. It was foul duty and few men, except for old oddities like Crawford, got through it easily.

Dunbar scrubbed himself from head to foot with a rough cloth and a bar of crude brown soap. Then he scrubbed himself again, and then a third time. He still did not feel clean. He toweled dry and put on his trousers. Forty-five minutes in the hold was followed by an hour of off-duty time. Dunbar had consumed half of that bathing. Now he sat on a coil of rope and, calmer, took out a cigar. He watched the slaves.

Wilkes was right. They *were* animals. Certainly no man could survive those shelves. For that matter, not many animals, either. The niggers must be among the hardiest things in creation. Dunbar marveled at them. *It's horrible,* he thought. Then he muttered to himself and savagely struck the ash from his cigar. A feeling of compassion had shot through him. He suppressed it. *Poor black bastards,* he thought. And he was more comfortable with this. He sat and he smoked, studied the slaves with a kind of gruff sympathy, and he regained his equilibrium and was happier.

The *Jubilation* was moving west along the windward coast. They had lost only ten slaves so far, four to suicide, three to melancholy and three to fever. There were no signs of dengue or smallpox or the flux or contagious fevers. Twice the ship anchored to barter with small independent black traders, which resulted in the taking on of fifty more heads. The lookout had warned of sail on the horizon half a dozen times, but only two ships had come close enough to turn a glass on, and both were slavers. It was a good voyage.

As Horneby figured, it was another day to the factory of Uriah Richardson, three more to Hyak, capital of the slaving Jaffi nation, and two to ben-Ahmen's factory. He expected full barracoons at each stop. So, eliminating waiting time, supposing a total of three days for loading, and adding another day in the Bay of Lycosu, the *Jubilation* could, barring a run-in with the British, turn homeward in ten days.

There was a knock.

"Come in."

A seaman opened the door. "Mr. Meredith wants to inform you, sir, that there's a smoke signal from shore."

Horneby consulted his charts. He had not been topside for several hours, but if course had been maintained and the wind had held, they should be . . . his finger stopped on a small lagoon.

"Fine," he said. "Tell Mr. Meredith to fire a signal shot and heave-to. I'll be up directly."

"Yes, sir."

When Horneby arrived on the quarterdeck, seamen were aloft on the yards reefing canvas, and the *Jubilation* was swinging into the lagoon. A sailor on the bow was taking soundings with a marked line and a lead weight. He called out the fathoms, which were relayed by the bosun to the helm.

There was a party of blacks on shore, fifteen or so tied

and seated, four others guarding them with trade muskets and swords.

"Just this one bunch, Captain," Meredith said.

"You're sure?"

"Yes, sir."

Horneby asked for the glass. He put it to his eye and turned slowly, scrutinizing the foliage. "Very good. Instruct Mr. Knye to ready a seizure party."

The bosun selected a small group of seamen and armed them. The traders on shore loaded their merchandise into a canoe and struck out for the ship. Horneby came down from the quarterdeck and stood by the Jacob's ladder. The first man over the rail was an overweight, round-faced black in seaman's pants and a red silk shirt. He wore a stovepipe hat and carried a fine, inlaid sword of Sheffield steel, a British officer's sword. He picked out the captain instantly and said, "Top grade slaves, Cap'n. Mighty finest you see anywhere. Healthy, strong like two men each one."

"Bring them up and I'll have my surgeon examine them, Mr . . . ?"

"Honest Jack, you bet." He shouted down to his companions, who whipped the slaves up the ladder and then followed.

The slaves were a bedraggled, broken-spirited bunch, all males. They had come from several different tribes. Some were marked with tattoos and one had longitudinal scarification lines on his chest and forehead. Another, whose hair was long and matted with filth, had sharp, filed teeth. He looked ferocious, but cringed when anyone raised his voice or moved suddenly. The sailors found him hilarious and clapped their hands behind him, belly-laughed when he leaped away in fear. While Wilkes went over them, Honest Jack chattered their merits to Horneby.

The surgeon finished and said, "They're run down, Captain, and they could use some food, but they all seem more or less sound."

"One musket each," Honest Jack said. "One musket, two knives and seventy-five dollars Yankee. Excellent good price, Cap'n. Not find such excellence with other traders. Right? Very much certainly. White captains sirs know Honest Jack give—"

"Mr. Knye," Horneby said.

The bosun made a short, chopping gesture. Seamen lunged for Honest Jack and his three comrades. Honest Jack screeched, jumped back and drew his sword. A sailor kicked him in the stomach. Another cracked a belaying pin over his wrist, and the sword went clattering to the deck. Honest Jack was dragged down. His arms were twisted behind his back, a knee was jammed into the curve of his spine. The other traders were immobilized before they could gather their wits.

"Take them below," Horneby said.

"Treachery pig!" Honest Jack screamed. "Mud spawn! We get revenge! We kill—" A sailor clubbed him unconscious.

Virgil Dunbar became a slave owner the following night. He had been six hours on duty at one of the hatches, the low moaning of the slaves washing over him with the same enervating ceaselessness of waves foaming thinly up a beach, receding, foaming up again . . . The sound had taken him gently away, swept him into a place of thick darkness where he was alone, where he was frightened, and where, if some tiny part of his brain had not remained aware of the man on duty with him, he might have whimpered.

He hated Pearson, that self-righteous little bastard of an abolitionist who sat so securely and untouchably in the correct and unassailable Bastille that was his Boston office. Dry, bloodless objections to slavery, pompous theories. What right did *he* have to hate slavery? What did he really *know* about it, safe and inviolate amid his numbers and his documents? Dunbar hated him—for the misery that was Dunbar's, and for the nights he tossed in restless, troubled sleep while moans, not unlike those from the holds, slipped past his lips.

It was late when he was relieved, and most of the crewmen were asleep. Dunbar flung himself down on his pallet, exhausted. There was a commotion by the fo'c'sle. Dunbar rolled over on his stomach and tried to get comfortable. A girl screamed.

A man near Dunbar cursed, sat up, and threw something. "Belay that, you bastards!"

"Up yours, mate," Jamey O'Brien replied.

The man lay back down. "For Christ's sake," he muttered to himself. "For Jesus bleeding Christ's sake. You can get more sleep in hell."

"Ow! The little bitch *bit* me."

"Oh, she's a game one, she is."

"Watch her foot there. He-he, you almost lost your nuggets, Gabe."

Scum! Dunbar thought. He tried hard to go to sleep, which was, of course, impossible.

"Hold her. Hold her, you ape!"

"Yiiee! My face."

"After her!"

Bare feet pounded across the decking. "Take her from the side. Cut her off by the mast."

Somebody's feet struck Dunbar's. He rolled to his side and saw a black figure falling atop him. She was small, but she landed with force, and the journalist grunted. She clawed at him, and he caught hold of her wrists. She tried unsuccessfully to ram her knee into his groin. "Hey, stop that now!" he said.

She went limp. Dunbar stared at her. She was only a girl, slim, with small, conical breasts, and thighs that were just beginning to round into womanhood. Beneath long, coarse hair was an oval face. Her nose was broad, her lips thick. But it was her eyes that drew the journalist's attention. They were quite large, and their pupils were a deep, bottomless black. Although he had occasionally alluded in his writing to the look in the eyes of a hopelessly trapped animal, he had never really seen it. Now he did, and it devastated him.

The sailors who had been in pursuit surrounded Dunbar and the girl. "Damn me for a rebel," O'Brien said, "if she didn't run straight for old Sea-King here."

Gomez fingered his earring. *"Está suyo*. He catch her. He has first."

O'Brien took the girl's hair in his thick fingers and hauled her to her feet. "Ah, but I've an ache in me tender heart for her, and Dunbar likes the boys best anyhow. Isn't that so, laddie?"

The journalist rose. "She's just a girl," he whispered. "A terrified little girl."

"Right, matey." O'Brien clapped him on the back. "And very soon she'll be a little woman. Over to the hawsers, then, and I'll surrender my place to anyone who can best me in a fair fight."

There were no takers. They led the girl away. Dunbar watched them. "No," he said softly, "no, you can't do that to her." Then everything became quite clear and he shouted, "NO!" and spun and raced aft. He heard from the foredeck:

"She's off again!"

"What the hell, Jamey?"

"She's a goddamned monkey!" O'Brien boomed. "All right, it's ring-around-the-ship then. Run her till she drops, boys, but keep her way from the railings!"

Thank you, God, Dunbar thought. *Oh, thank you*. He

banged open the door that led to the officers' rooms beneath the quarterdeck and went down the steps two at a time, missing his footing once and bouncing off the wall, regaining his balance, then coming to the bottom. He lurched to a halt in front of Horneby's door and beat on it with his fist. "Captain, Captain. Please, Captain!"

The door swung open. Horneby was there in his undershorts, face puffy with sleep, one cheek reddened and marked by his pillow. But his eyes were alert, and there was a cocked pistol in his hand. "What is it?" His glance flicked over Dunbar, then past him, looking for trouble.

"There's a girl, Captain. Please, forgive me. I—"

"A *girl?*"

"Yes, sir. It's . . . I'm sorry for waking you like this. I know it's . . . but . . ."

"Stop stammering, man!"

It occurred to Dunbar that the probable outcome of his intervention would be a flogging. He didn't care. He had to try. If he couldn't get what he wanted from Horneby, then he would go back and kill O'Brien. He'd kill them all if he had to. "Some of the men," he blurted. "They have a girl on deck. She's only a child! They can't hurt her. You can't let them!"

"Mr. Randall sees to it that none of the cargo is damaged." Horneby narrowed his eyes. "Are you drunk, seaman?"

"You don't understand." Dunbar's hands moved up as if to seize the captain's shoulders. Horneby raised his pistol. The journalist forced his arms down and took a step back. "Captain, I want that girl. I want her now. I've got to have her, sir!"

A door several paces away opened, and Meredith, dressed in a nightshirt, appeared. Instinctively he leveled his own pistol at Dunbar. "Trouble, Captain?"

"This man seems either to be drunk or to have gone mad. Put him in irons. I'll deal with him in the morning."

"Please!" Dunbar shrieked. "I want to buy her. I want her for myself." He went down on his knees. "For the love of God, Captain! I must have her. *I must!"*

Meredith's hand fell roughly on the journalist's shoulder. "Let's go, you."

Horneby was stroking his face. "Wait," he said quietly. "Return to your room, please, Mr. Meredith. I'll call if I need you."

Meredith scratched his head. "Whatever you say, Captain." He walked away.

Dunbar, kneeling, bowed his head. "Please."

"Stand up," Horneby said sternly.

Dunbar did. He looked at his feet.

"Why do you want this girl?"

Dunbar raised his palms helplessly.

Horneby's hand was still moving softly across his own face, caressing his cheeks, his mouth. "How do you propose to pay for her?"

I have money, Dunbar almost said, *more money than I can use. I'll give you any amount*. He stopped himself only because he knew this would have sounded like lunacy. "I'll put all my pay against her, Captain."

"That wouldn't be enough."

"My pay as a deposit then. I've saved some money. It's in a bank. You'll have it as soon as we're back home."

"You are, in a way, her slave, aren't you?" Horneby said in an abstracted tone.

I no longer exist, Dunbar thought. *I do not know who I am or what I am doing*. "Yes."

Horneby nodded. "You're the apprentice, Dunbar, correct?"

"Yes, sir."

"What is your first name?"

"Virgil."

"Wait here." The door closed part-way. The captain was gone a minute, then he returned with two pieces of paper and a writing quill. "Sign this," he said. "You understand that you will receive no portion of your pay at all and that if you fail to deliver the balance of her purchase price, your deposit will be forfeit."

"Yes, yes, I do." Dunbar scrawled his signature.

Horneby took the document and gave over a simple handwritten bill of sale. Dunbar clasped his hand strongly. "Thank you, Captain. Thank you. God bless you!" He ran down the hall.

Horneby stood in his door several moments, touching his face. Meredith poked his head into the corridor. "Everything all right, sir?"

"Yes," the captain said crisply. "Good night." He went back inside and closed the door.

Dunbar ran across the deck shouting, "Wait! Stop!" and clutched the bill of sale as a condemned man, moments from the gallows, would clutch a royal pardon.

They had the girl far forward, near the base of the bowsprit, where the forestays were secured. She was on her back, blood running from her nose and from a cut on her lip. Her eyes were closed. Gomez held her shoulders, and each of her ankles was trapped by another seaman. O'Brien was between her legs. His naked buttocks were heavy twin globes, pale in the moonlight. "Can't bust her," the Irishman grunted, straining. "She's got a cherry like canvas."

Dunbar threw his shoulder into a watching sailor and knocked him out of the way. His foot lashed out, caught Gomez in the back and sent him sprawling. "Let go of her. She's mine!"

O'Brien surged to his feet, his swollen sex bucking from

D

his loins. He curled his hands into fists the size of sledges. Gomez was crouched, hissing, and his knife was in his hand. Mr. Randall, who had been hovering fretfully by, cautioning the seamen not to do any lasting damage, rushed into the center of the three-man triangle. "Here, here! None of this now. Gomez, put that knife away. Put it away, I tell you, or you'll have the hide flogged from your back! Stand easy, O'Brien." He turned to Dunbar. "What in God's name is the matter with you, man?"

"The girl. She's mine. I bought her. Here!" He thrust the paper at Randall.

"What's this, eh?" The mate held it at an angle to catch light from a nearby lantern. "Hhm! Well, I'll be damned." He scratched his armpit and said to the sailors, "It's a bill of sale, is what it is. All proper and signed by the captain hisself. He's right, boys. He owns this girl. If he don't want you bangin' on her, then it's no bangin'."

O'Brien snatched the document. "Give that here." He puzzled out the words laboriously, then said, "Shee-it! What can you be makin' of that?" He gave the title back to Dunbar, and the look on his face was one of befuddlement rather than anger. "Well. All right then, though I never heard the likes of it before." He hitched up his pants. "Come along, boys. It's looking in other places for our sport we're having to be."

The journalist waited until they had gone. The girl was still on her back, legs spread. "Come, get up," Dunbar said, and then felt foolish; his words were only so much babble to her. He tried to make his expression reassuring. He gestured for her to rise. She stared at him and did not move. "I'm not going to hurt you," he said gently, hoping she could understand from his tone. "You're safe now. Nobody will hurt you. I've seen to that." She sat up and pressed her legs together. "Please." He pointed. "We can go over there where no one will come, and I'll try and make you understand." She remained motionless. "Well . . . then I'll sit down with you." When he made to do so, she scuttled away, sprang to her feet, and poised to run. Dunbar did not attempt to go after her. Cross-legged, he patted the place next to him. She looked at him mistrustfully and frowned, trying to discern the ruse. "I can wait," Dunbar said softly.

She approached tentatively, inches at a time, with long pauses between, muscles taut, jerking back whenever he shifted to a more comfortable position, and nearly half an hour passed before she lowered herself into a kind of hunkering squat, a little less than a yard away. He tried to explain to her, using an earnest tone and exaggerated movements of his body, like a second-rate Shakespearean actor, that she would not be harmed, that he was her protector and . . . what else? What else could he do for her? He was going to set her free when they reached the United States, and he had vague ideas of seeing that she was returned to her home, but how could he get that across to her? He was not sure, actually, that he had managed to communicate anything.

"Come," he said. "I'm sorry, but I can't keep you here with me."

She followed a few paces behind while he hunted out Mr. Randall. The mate turned the key in the fo'c'sle lock, then reached for the girl. She sprang away and pressed in close to Dunbar. Dunbar laid his arm lightly around her shoulders. She trembled, but did not try to escape.

Randall laughed. "Jesus, this beats it all. Come along, looks like she won't go unless you're with her."

The lantern Randall carried cast a swaying, orange glow over the naked black bodies, making them ripple and heave. When Randall pointed, the girl slipped away and went, eagerly it seemed, to her place. Her large eyes stared at the journalist, then she turned her head away, and Dunbar was no longer able to single her out from the others.

It was quiet when he settled back onto his pallet. There was the wind, and the gurgling wake, and the snap of canvas, but the crew was asleep and Dunbar was glad of that.

The momentum was gone now, and he had a chance to reflect on what he had done.

He did not understand. He realized only that he was no longer the conscious director of his life. It was both a horrible and an exhilarating discovery.

Nothing short of madness could have propelled him to Horneby's door like that. Horneby? Had Horneby really agreed? It made no sense.

Dunbar, glad to focus his mind on something specific, considered the captain.

The journalist knew a fair amount *about* the man, but nothing *of* the man. It was intriguing.

Horneby was English, the son of a slaving captain who had sailed from Liverpool when the trade was still legal, during the days when that city was a monument to the institution. The Town Hall was embellished with great statues of chained black men, jewelers advertised SILVER COLLARS AND LEASHES FOR DOGS AND NEGROES, and most conversation revolved about the economics of the trade, or anecdotes of past voyages. Such was the atmosphere in which Edward L. Horneby spent his childhood. He shipped aboard his first slaver, with his father as captain, when he was fourteen years old. One year later, with two trips behind him, Parliament outlawed the trade. Horneby interpreted the interdiction as a personal assault. He liked slaving, and he was excited by it. He quarreled with his father, who had a strong sense of King, tradition, and law, and who refused to participate in the business illegally. Horneby left home, worked for the Spanish, and for the

Brazilians when that South Amercian nation became independent, then finally for the Americans.

Dunbar knew the captain had once been imprisoned by the British, and he knew that Horneby was capable of very cold and sudden brutality. He was known as one of the most savage captains on the slaving lanes, but his voyages were always profitable and thus he had no difficulties signing a crew.

Why had he given Dunbar the girl? *Why?*

The journalist, afraid of the dreams that might come if he closed his eyes, worried and sniffed about the image of Horneby until the stars faded and the sky began to lighten, which brought the bosun striding into the midst of the sleeping crewmen, kicking them awake.

The sea had been bad three days running, and there was no place on the topdeck free from spray. During the day, at least, work was a distraction, but at night the water was torment; it drove sleep away with stinging little drops and spread across the skin, a clammy, inescapable film, like syrup. The tarps were useless. Within half an hour of pulling one over himself a man, choking, steamed by his own sweat, would throw it aside in rage.

No one except Horneby, who was responsible for the final economics of the voyage, gave any thought to the slaves in the holds. The ship was pitching too wildly to allow them on deck, and the foaming sea had forced most of the ventilation ports to be closed. They were dying down there, and Horneby, understandably, was disturbed. But the sleepless and irritable sailors could not have cared less.

Captain and crew were equally pleased when the helmsman turned the *Jubilation* toward a narrow opening in the dense, green forest that had been the coast these last few days. The soundings dropped from twelve fathoms, down through ten, to eight, to six, alarmingly to little more than four, then back to six, and held steady there until the ship had entered a small crescent-shaped lagoon. The rough sea was left behind, its anger and its roar smothered by the lush vegetation that fringed the harbor.

Uriah Richardson's factory was situated on the tip of the west horn, a complex of weathered dwellings, barracoons, and warehouses. A single broad dock set on huge mossy pilings jutted into the water. When the fathom call lowered again, the *Jubilation* dropped anchor. The ship swung about in the slight breeze, and Horneby ordered a light kedge dropped from the stern. The heat was sweltering.

A party of blacks led by a single white man came down to the water. The white man walked to the end of the dock and stood with his hands on his hips.

The captain ordered a boat lowered. The crew gathered in expectant groups around the tackle of the other boats.

Meredith called to them from the quarterdeck, "No shore time today. The captain wants the niggers aired, all of 'em, in shifts, and the holds washed top to bottom. Each man'll have six hours ashore tomorrow."

There were groans and angry shouts from the sailors. "What the hell does he think we are?" someone yelled. "Animals? By God, we're not gonna—"

Horneby nodded, and the bosun, who had moved up behind the rebellious man, clubbed the sailor to his knees and kicked him in the kidneys. "Ten lashes, sir?" Knye asked.

Horneby nodded again, then went over the side. He had with him the second mate, Mr. Wilkes and Mr. Petersen, and a rowing crew. When the boat bumped against the dock, the sailors shipped their oars and reached for the pilings. The white man signaled forward two of his blacks, who wore fezzes and red cloths wound round their waists, reaching almost to their ankles; they ran forward on bare feet, caught and secured the lines that were cast to them, then stepped back. The white man helped Horneby out of the boat.

"You're Captain Horneby? And your ship is the *Jubilation?"*

"Yes. Where's Richardson?"

"Up at the house. I'll take you to him. I'm Gregory Mueller, his clerk."

"What happened to Adams?"

"Fever. He died two months ago." Mueller gnawed his lower lip. He was dressed in soiled pants and a shirt from which the buttons had been torn. His hair was uncombed, there was a three-day stubble of graying whiskers on his cheeks, and his fingernails were rimed with dirt. Old whisky was sour on his breath.

"You have something on your mind?" Horneby asked.

Mueller scratched his stomach, deciding. "No." He led Horneby off the dock and up a small incline.

The clearing in which the factory rested was not very well attended. Ferns, creepers, and hardy, thick-stalked plants had penetrated far in from the perimeter. Two buildings, or rather, what remained of two buildings, had already been reclaimed by the jungle; one had to squint to make out the shapes of those few rotted boards still standing. Garbage, old broken and rusted tools, and empty bottles were strewn everywhere.

They came upon a white man lying on his back in the sun. The man was wearing a dirty nightshirt which was hiked up around his swollen stomach. His eyes were closed; his face was flushed and slack. Spittle dribbled from the corner of his mouth. He was mumbling to himself.

"I would have expected Martin here to go before Adams," Horneby said.

Mueller prodded the man with his foot. Martin groaned

and flung himself over. "He won't last too much longer, I don't guess," Mueller said.

Near the house was a stout, boxlike cage built of heavy bamboo and pieces of scrap iron. Within it was a young, lowland gorilla weighing in, Horneby estimated, at close to two hundred pounds. As they approached, the beast ran to the side of the cage nearest them, pressed his black, humanoid face to the bars, stretched out a beseeching arm and went: "*Ah*-oo! *Ah*-oo! *Ah*-oo!" A pile of half-rotted fruits and vegetables lay beyond his grasp.

"King Henry the Eighth," Mueller said. "He helps pass the time." He rattled something in dialect to one of the blacks who were following.

The man shouted at the gorilla. The beast quailed. Its call assumed a plaintive note. The black man rushed to the cage, seized a pole and jabbed at the animal, who had retreated to the far end and was trying to squeeze into a corner. "Yah! Yah!" the man yelled. The animal screeched in terror. Mueller gave another order. The black withdrew the pole. The gorilla huddled in the corner, hugged itself, and rocked back and forth. Mueller scooped up some of the vegetables and flung them into the cage. The gorilla scuttled over to them and began stuffing them greedily into its mouth.

"Usually don't feed him 'less he does what we want," Mueller said. "But we don't want the bastard starving, do we?"

Richardson's house was two stories tall, and once it had been attractive. Now only a few patches of stubborn paint still clung to the weathered wood. Half the balcony that ran around the second floor had collapsed. Most of the window frames were empty. Whole planks were missing from the porch. The building sagged, seeming to yearn for the day when it could surrender and settle peacefully into the earth.

As Horneby entered, the stairs creaked and threatened to

give way. Other than sections illuminated by the brilliant shafts of sunlight slashing through the windows, the two-story living room was in gloom. There were few furnishings and they were in disrepair. There was an odor of mildew and decay.

"You here already, Captain . . . Captain . . . Horneby? Yes, Horneby. Already?"

Horneby raised his eyes to the gallery. Uriah Richardson stood leaning over the railing, a bottle of rum in his hand. Richardson wore only undershorts. They looked as if they had not been changed in weeks. His skin had a faint copperish hue, and swatches of his hair and beard were missing. There were wet chancres on his face. "Welcome, welcome to Paradise Regained," he said.

He weaved his way around the gallery, stopping twice to lean against the wall and take a drink, then he started down the stairs. He missed the fourth step and was suspended a moment, arms beating circles in the air; then he pitched forward and came to a sprawled halt on the landing.

"Mr. Mueller," Horneby said. "My surgeon should be near at hand. Call him, please, and tell him he's needed."

Mueller shrugged, left, and returned a few moments later with Wilkes. Horneby was still standing where he had been when Richardson had fallen. The surgeon went to Richardson's side.

"Drink, Captain?" Mueller asked.

"No."

"Christ in heaven, he stinks!" Wilkes said. "Worse than a nigger." He probed the factor with evident distaste. "How long has he been drinking?"

Mueller laughed. " 'Bout eight years, I'd say."

"This time, man!"

Mueller sneered. "I don't know. A few days, a few weeks. Does it make any difference?"

"How come you're still sober?" Wilkes asked.

"Who says I am?"

Wilkes turned his head to the side and spat.

"Where's McClaine?" Horneby inquired.

"Dead."

"Mr. Wilkes, how long will it take to dry that man out?"

"Well, nothing's broken, and if we can get a couple of niggers to sweat him in hot water a few hours, I suppose he'd be able to carry on a conversation sometime tomorrow morning."

"You're in charge, then," Horneby said to Mueller. "Is there any reason why we can't examine your merchandise now?"

"None at all, Captain."

"Good. Instruct your boys to carry Mr. Richardson upstairs and bring him round to some semblance of sobriety."

Mueller went to the door and barked out a couple of sentences. Two blacks came running in, lifted Richardson without apparent effort, and carried him up the stairs.

"Captain," Mueller said. "Can I speak to you alone for a minute?"

"Mr. Wilkes," Horneby said. "Please get Mr. Petersen and Mr. Randall and go to the barracoons. I'll be along directly." When Wilkes had gone, Horneby said, "Now," and waited.

Mueller ran his tongue over his lips. "You, uh, you have a reputation for being a, uh, shrewd bargainer, Captain. And I've heard it said—not to your discredit, oh no, on the contrary, with admiration—that . . . how do I say it? that you have at times been involved in, uh, unorthodox dealings."

"Get to the point."

"Yes. Of course. I know you've dealt with Richardson

before and that you'll probably . . . I mean, I, uh, wouldn't suggest anything that'd interfere."

"I'm out of patience, Mueller."

"Wait, Captain! Wait, wait, please. It's this." He worked his jaw a moment, then plunged. "Two nights ago there was a break-out and thirty prime males escaped. I think, with luck, if you'd be interested, I just might be able to recapture them and deliver them to you—uh—two hours' sail up the coast." Mueller looked everywhere but at Horneby's eyes.

"At a lower price than I'd have to pay here for them."

"Of course! Uh, there'd be, uh, one other thing, too."

Horneby said nothing.

"I've been a long time on this coast. I want to go home. So, uh, as part of the deal, you'll, uh, carry me as supercargo to your port of destination."

"From which you will immediately dispatch a bank draft to Mr. Richardson covering the sale of his runaways."

"Wha—! Oh, yes, certainly. Without delay. Do you . . . find the proposition interesting?"

"Mm-hm. Let's go see your niggers."

"Yes, sir!"

The blacks were in two crude barracoons. Wooden palisades with sharpened tops enclosed pits that were ten feet deep. Only the smallest children were not chained. There was no shelter from the glaring sun, and the pits had not been cleaned in some time. The stink was unbearable. Most of the blacks were sluggish and bleary-eyed. Maggots squirmed in the refuse of their food and in the festering piles of their wastes. Guards set ladders into the pits and went down with Wilkes and Petersen. The slaves did precisely as they were told; they no longer cared what happened to them.

Horneby did not observe the examinations. He stayed only a little while at each of the barracoons, eyes moving over the females. This did not escape Mueller, who said, "Looking for something in particular, Captain?" Horneby did not bother to answer. He walked away, sat down on a crumbling log, lit his pipe, and sat staring at the jungle.

Wilkes came to Horneby when he had finished. Petersen went straight to a well, stripped down, and splashed and scrubbed himself repeatedly. "It's a goddamn miracle," Wilkes said. "The guards tell me they've been in there two weeks. By all rights they should have been hit by the flux or smallpox, any one of a number of things, but they weren't. How, I'll never know. I count seventy-nine acceptable, Captain. Eight rejects."

Horneby's fingers were flat against his cheek, moving in a slow, circular pattern.

"Captain?"

Horneby turned his head toward the surgeon and blinked.

"I said we have seventy-nine acceptable, sir."

Horneby nodded. "I had hoped for more, but we can fill out later."

"I gave the count to Mueller. He can inform Richardson when Richardson is coherent again."

"Fine."

"We'll be returning to ship now?"

"You go on with the others. Send a boat for me in two hours."

"Is anything wrong, sir?"

"No." Horneby stood up. "I just want to walk awhile." He moved off slowly toward the forest.

At first Leana thought they were angry at *her,* because she was slapped and kicked, and twice sailors hit her with pieces of rope. Soon, though, she saw that the others were being treated no differently, some even worse, particularly the males. The whites, then, were angry at all of them. Why?

There seemed to be no reason. But then, perhaps there didn't have to be a reason. The whites were not human. It was senseless trying to understand them.

She looked for the man who had claimed her that night when the others had brought her on deck and hurt her, when the big one with the beard had made her bleed, trying to force his huge organ into her. Leana did not understand what had happened. For all she knew, she might be married now to the man who had rescued her. Did these whites have such things as women? She had never seen one. Maybe that was why they took the black women. Possibly it was just some game the man had been playing, some kind of sport she could not understand.

She didn't think so. His face and his voice had been so serious, so earnest. He had wanted her to understand him, which of course was impossible. She thought he desired something from her. If that was the case, why didn't he simply take it? Did he want something that could not be taken? That was absurd. What could she, what could any of the slaves have, that did not already belong to the white men?

But she looked for him, because he had protected her and she felt that, for whatever reason, he would do so again. She did not see him anywhere on the deck. She watched a gang of seamen who had dragged bodies of dead black men up from the holds and stacked them in a pile by the bulwark, and who were now heaving them over the side. The scene was quite unreal; then it became too real, and she turned away.

There were men up in the great logs and cross-woods and ropes doing things with the huge pieces of cloth that evidently had much to do with the movement of the ship. She found the man she was looking for and she sat, staring up at him, waiting for him to come down. He noticed her after a while and he smiled and waved his arm, but it was some time before he descended.

On the deck, he walked over to her, stretched and grunted, and sat down. He looked pleased. He said things to her. Not knowing what she was supposed to do, she did nothing. He shook his head, but the corners of his mouth were lifted. He pointed to his chest and mouthed a word, the way one might do for a child, which angered her. She was not a child. He repeated the gesture and the word several more times.

She said, "Duhbar."

He grinned and nodded vigorously.

"Duhbar," she said.

He reached out and she shrank back. He withdrew his hand, but looked saddened, and she regretted having withdrawn. Maybe he had not meant to hurt her, maybe it was something else. She told him so. He cocked his head and arched his eyebrows. She pointed to her own chest, between her small naked breasts, and said, "Leana."

He pointed at her. "Li-yana."

Her lips opened a little way in a smile. It was so funny, him trying to pronounce her name. He moved again, and this time she remained still, though it was hard to do. He patted her hand, that was all. She wanted to cry.

"Li-yana," he said.

"Duhbar."

Both of them grinned.

There was a loud, harsh voice. Leana looked up and saw the big, hairy man with the beard standing over them. A sound of fear escaped her, and she inched backward. Duhbar's hand clamped down on her arm. He said something to her in a tone that was firm, but not threatening. Then he said something to the big man. The big man said something back. They talked together a few minutes, Duhbar's face looking friendly at the big man. The big man scratched his stomach and one of his armpits as he spoke. At last he shrugged his massive shoulders, shook his head, and exploded in laughter, a tearing kind of noise, like that made by large trees when they fall. Then he went away.

Duhbar and the big man were friends. Leana was bitter. She pulled her arm from his grasp, folded her hands in her lap, and stared down at the deck. She did not want him to touch her. He talked to her, and there was a coaxing sound in his voice, but she would not raised her eyes to his face.

A man called Duhbar. He answered, was told something, and stood up. He spoke to her, then walked off. Leana sprang to her feet and followed. She didn't want him to leave her alone. A few sailors pointed and laughed. Duhbar, too, seemed to find it amusing. She did not. At the entrance to the hold Duhbar picked up two buckets. His face was twisted in such a way that Leana knew he was about to do something he did not want to do. He started down the ladder into the hold. She followed, but another white barred her way and shook his head. She tried to get around him. The white man called Duhbar. Duhbar's head reappeared. Duhbar's voice was strong, and he shook his finger at her. Clearly, he did not want her with him. All right, then she would wait for him. She sat down.

A while later the big man went by. He stopped to look at her. She did not like the way he was doing it; it reminded her of that first night. At different times a few others ran their eyes over her in a similar manner, and she bent over and tried to make herself small, but she did not leave.

When Duhbar came up, dirty and gagging, face strained, she was still there.

Richardson was awake by midmorning. He was famished, and he ate ravenously, with the inevitable result, as Wilkes had warned, that he regurgitated his first meal in total. However, his second breakfast stayed down, along with a prodigious amount of black coffee. It did not occur to him to make apology, nor did Horneby expect one. As soon as Richardson had finished eating, the factor and Mueller sat down on one side of a table and Horneby and Meredith took chairs on the other side.

"All right," Richardson said. "We have one hundred and seventeen top-quality slaves on hand. I know you were looking for more, Captain, but that's all we could get. Sorry. But—"

"Excuse me, Mr. Richardson," Mueller said. "We only have eighty-seven in the pens."

Richardson frowned. "Did you sell the rest? Was there another ship in? I don't remember . . ."

"No, sir. I'm sorry to report that, uh, there was an escape." He glanced nervously at Horneby.

"What the hell are you talking about! What escape? When?"

"Two nights ago. They forced the chains somehow and dug under the palisade."

"Just like that? And simply walked away!"

"No, sir. There was a fight. I took a clout on the head. Two of our boys were killed, and so was McClaine."

"McClaine's dead?"

"Yes."

"Huh. Wondered where he was. Dead, eh? I'll be damned. Poor bastard. Huh." Richardson slumped back in his chair. "Thirty goddamned niggers."

"Some of the boys are still trailing them. But they're probably long gone by now."

"Thirty niggers. Son of a bitch." Richardson slammed his fist on the table. "Thirty of the bastards!"

"It happens sometimes," Horneby said.

Mueller exhaled with almost a sigh.

"How did the rest shape up?" Richardson asked.

"We'll take seventy-nine of them."

"Well, at least that's something. Thank God for little favors and all that shit, eh?"

They came to agreement within the hour. A third of the purchase price was to be paid in trade goods—knives and copper pots, Manchester cotton, salt, various trinkets, cheap muskets that, exploding, killed their users as often as they did the enemy, and whisky, half a dozen cases of raw, head-splitting stuff for the black traders, and half a dozen more of good Irish and Scottish liquor for Richardson's personal larder.

The slaves would not be loaded until nightfall. One of Richardson's lookouts had reported sail not far off the coast. It had been confirmed as British. Its course was erratic, and apparently it was working a box trap with other, unseen warships.

Behind the main area of the factory stood several sheds and one-room buildings. These housed the black guards and their wives and their whores, and a few unclaimed women as well. The seamen of the *Jubilation* spent their promised shore time here, some of them buying a few hot moments between sweaty black thighs, which seemed ridiculous to the others since the same thing could be had at no cost on board ship, and all of them paying outrageous sums for bottles of the searing trade whisky. Richardson insisted that Horneby and his officers dine with him and Mueller, which they did, and the meal was a surprisingly good one with a variety of vegetables, a mixed meat stew, roast pig, and small birds whose delicate bones were sucked clean, then used to pick teeth. Horneby supplied a few bottles of French brandy from his private stock. Richardson, who was half drunk before the meal began, consumed a bottle of wine during the dinner, and made heavy inroads on the brandy after. He tipped over his chair when he rose from the table. The sores on his face were wet. He used his napkin to wipe them. "Gentlemen," he said, "if you'll come upst— *outside* with me, I think I can show you something the lipes—*likes* of which your eyes have never laid eyes on before."

With an arm around Mueller's shoulders for support, he led them into the darkness and around to King Henry VIII's cage. "Light some torches," he ordered one of the guards, "and get coals for the brazier. Turn out as many as them—of them sailors as you can. Tell 'em they're goin' t' see a show, an' the drinks are on Uriah Richardson!" He waved an arm in a circle above his head.

Blacks brought flaming brands and jammed them into the ground around the cage. One wheeled an iron brazier close to the bars. Another brought red coals and dumped them into the bowl. King Henry VIII screeched and ran furiously back and forth in his cage.

The first of the sailors appeared, whooping with drunken cheer, and Richardson gave another order. Two blacks sprinted off and returned a few moments later with heavy leather harnesses and some slender iron rods; they pushed the ends of the latter into the burning coals. Seamen pressed around the cage, swaying, jostling each other, singing, laughing, asking what the hell was going on, and saying let's get to it, and passing bottles back and forth. The factor waved to his blacks. A dozen of them closed in on the cage, carrying poles, ropes, and the harnesses. King Henry VIII jumped to the top of his cage and clung there with both hands and both feet, gibbering. The blacks beat him down and then prodded and jabbed and maneuvered him while trying to snare him with ropes and secure the harnesses to his arms and chest. It took a while, and they succeeded only by threatening him with the red-hot tips of the iron rods and backing him against a wall, holding him there while the first arm harness was fastened. After that, it was easier. There was the smell of burnt hair. The harness traces were drawn tight and hitched around spikes driven deep into the ground outside the cage. The gorilla's movement was effectively limited to a little less than a foot in any direction.

"Gentlemen!" Richardson shouted. "Gentlemen and scholars! Quiet, please!" When the hubbub died down, he said, "Are you ready to see a sight that not even monarchs and potentates the world over can ever hope to see? A sight that no beast in the whole of God's bleeding animal kingdom other than our own inestimable King Henry the Eighth can give you?" There were whistles and footstamps, loud applause and cheers. "Then let the show commence!"

The door to King Henry VIII's cage was opened. The gorilla moaned. Two of Richardson's guards appeared, carrying a low, broad bench. A woman, one Wilkes had rejected this morning because of a tumor in her armpit, was strapped to the bench, legs spread wide, a wooden block under her buttocks raising her pudendum. The sailors jumped up and down, hooted and pounded each other on the back.

"She's in heat," Richardson said to Wilkes. "We saved her special for this. The son of a bitch won't do a thing—even if we burn him to death—unless he can smell cunt-blood."

The woman's crotch was shoved up against the beast's loins. The gorilla stamped his feet and strained backwards. The woman threw her head from side to side. Both of them were screaming.

Richardson took a long drink from the brandy bottle he held, belched, then said to Horneby, "Makes a funny duet, doesn't it?"

A man behind the animal was prodding it, aiming for the anus, trying to force the hips forward.

Richardson yelled, "Come on, one of you black mothers, stroke ol' Henry and get him interested . . . That's it, keep it up . . . Uh-huh, uh-huh . . . Shift her around there . . . Well, shit, use the hot iron on him if he won't work . . . Righto! Give it to him again. Burn his ass off! . . . Now you got him! . . . Hold up, easy now, easy . . . That's it, that's it, by God! . . . Ram her down, King Henry!"

The sailors broke into a roaring ovation.

"Incredible," Wilkes said. "I wouldn't have believed it possible."

"Took us eight bloody months, it did," Richardson said. "He's a stupid bastard. We're trying to teach him to bugger one now, but the dumb shit won't have any part of it. We'll get him, though, sooner or later. Or we'll damn well burn his hide off in the process."

Only a handful of the seamen turned away from the spectacle and went reeling off into the darkness. One was too drunk to walk. He went on his hands and knees mumbling, "Oh God. Sweet Jesus. Oh Christ. Oh."

Nobody noticed him.

At dawn no sign of the British warship could be found. Richardson, who was nearly as drunk as he had been when the *Jubilation* arrived, accepted payment for his slaves, managed to slur out *Go'speed, safe voyage,* then returned to his bed, taking with him a fresh bottle. Mueller handed Horneby a small hand-drawn map, showing a promontory marked with an X, and struck out into the jungle. The slaves were loaded in an hour and a half. Canvas was unfurled, billowed in the light wind, and the *Jubilation* slipped down the harbor, through the narrow channel and out to the open sea.

The waters were calm and sun-dazzled. The sky was an

enameled blue, spotted here and there by puffy white clouds. The slaves were being danced on the maindeck. Wilkes was surprised to see Matthew Hollister watching them from the quarterdeck; Hollister did not often leave his cabin. The surgeon climbed the stairs and stood off to the side. He studied the young man. Hollister's interest appeared mild, but it was interest nonetheless. Wilkes walked over to the boy's side, folded his arms, and gazed down. He did not want to risk speech; each time he had tried to engage Hollister in conversation, Hollister had left.

After several moments the boy said, "Most of them just accept it, don't they?"

"Most."

"They're really not human."

"No."

"Pity."

"What?"

"I mean, it would seem such an admirable quality in some cases, that kind of acceptance."

"Well . . . yes, I guess maybe it would."

"Niggers are funny."

"They're interesting. I've been studying them most of my life."

Hollister, to the surgeon's disappointment, said nothing more. But neither did he move away. They watched in silence.

An end was called to the dancing when the meal bell rang. The slaves formed lines leading to two huge kettles that simmered over twin hearths bricked onto the deck. These contained the slabber sauce that was cooked daily and that would constitute their complete diet until they reached port. Horse beans and lard were its foundation, on top of which were added a few chunks of old beef, some slivers of salt fish, and a little rice. Water was poured in, the sauce stewed to a thick hot paste, then sprinkled with cayenne pepper. Finished, it was ladled into deep copper bowls, one of which was allotted to every three slaves. As the blacks received their portion they moved off to the side, sat down with the bowl between them, and scooped the paste into their mouths with their hands.

"They are very simple and stupid creatures," Hollister observed.

Wilkes was about to agree, but he sensed a possible opening, so he said, "No, on occasion they can be quite complicated."

Hollister gave a little laugh.

"I'll show you sometime."

"Show me?"

"Yes. When we have time. But you'll excuse me now, won't you? There's a seaman with a sprained wrist I have to check."

He walked away and was quite pleased with himself. He had handled it well, he thought. If Hollister did have any interest, then it would be heightened by having to wait for an explanation. As Horneby had pointed out, Wilkes was under no obligation to do anything whatever with Hollister. But the surgeon knew that any efforts in that direction would be appreciated, and it disturbed him to see anyone that young—the boy couldn't be more than twenty—so phlegmatic and uncaring.

"Mr. Wilkes." A seaman touched his arm. "Mr. Meredith, he says to tell we got another one what won't eat."

"Where?"

"Up by the number two hatch."

"All right. Find Mr. Petersen and ask him to bring me my bag."

Wilkes went forward and found Meredith and two sailors with a lanky slave stretched out on the deck. The slave's eyes were closed. He lay perfectly still. He was bleeding from his nose, and large swellings were beginning to appear on his face. "Is he conscious?"

"Sure," Meredith said. He kicked the black in the ribs. "Aren't you?"

The slave opened his eyes, looked at the white men, then lowered his lids again.

"Do you know how long he's been without food?"

"Nah, we just noticed him this morning."

Wilkes palpitated the black's stomach, put an ear to the thin chest, and felt the limbs. "Two, three days possibly."

"Here's your bag, John." It was Petersen. And behind him, to Wilkes's surprise, was Hollister, looking as if he had come against his better judgment.

Wilkes fingered the slave's cheekbone; he thought it might be broken. "You tried to persuade him to eat?"

"Sure," Meredith said. "He acts like he doesn't even feel it."

Hollister edged forward. "Why won't he eat?" he asked quietly.

"Melancholy," Wilkes said. "He doesn't want to live anymore, so he's starving himself to death."

"Really? Is that possible?"

"Mm-hm. Hand me the speculum oris, Dan."

Petersen rummaged in the surgeon's black bag and withdrew an instrument resembling a pair of calipers. Each of its legs ended in a chisel-like shape, and at its opposite end, where it was joined, was a threaded metal pin and a wingnut.

"Let's try one more time," Wilkes said. He knelt over the man and slapped him hard on both cheeks. The black opened his eyes. The surgeon held a bowl of food above his face. "Now eat this, you bloody fool!" The slave turned his head aside. Wilkes shook him violently. "Come on! You're going to do it one way or the other, so you might as well make it easy on yourself."

"Hell," Meredith said. "I've already tried that, and if I couldn't get him to do it, you're not."

Wilkes sighed. "All right."

"Want the hammer?" Petersen asked.

Wilkes nodded. He screwed the wingnut up until the legs of the speculum oris were flat against each other.

"I prefer coals," Meredith said.

"You would."

"Coals?" Hollister asked.

"Yes," Wilkes said. "They use them on some ships. When a slave won't open his mouth like this, they put live embers against his lips."

"That changes their minds pretty fast." Meredith said.

"Not always," Wilkes said to Hollister. "It's a stupid practice. Sometimes they'll let their lips be burned to cinders. I've seen them with nothing left but a charred hole. Half of all coal burns on the mouth become infected. Then the slave dies, and you've lost your investment."

Wilkes pushed the speculum oris past the slave's lips. He butted the chisel tips flush against one of the bottom front teeth, just under the upper incisors. He took up the hammer, tested its weight, aimed and brought it hard against the butt pin: *Kack!* Then: *Kack! Kack! Kack!* The tooth broke at midpoint and the tool was through, into the mouth cavity. Hollister leaned over, his lips pursed.

"Here," Wilkes said. "Work the screw. There's nothing to it. Just turn it down. It spreads, and the mouth opens. Couldn't be simpler."

Hollister knelt. His hands moved up slowly. He touched the metal, paused, then gave the nut a quarter-turn.

"Go on," Wilkes said.

Hollister did, with deliberate, sectioned motions. The slave's jaws were forced open. Wilkes dabbed blood away from the gums with a piece of cotton. "No, don't stop yet. A little more," the surgeon said. "You've got to get some tension there so he can't move it. Good, that's it."

Hollister rocked back on his heels, forearms resting on his knees, and stared at the slave. The black had not uttered a sound and had made no attempt, other than trying to keep his jaws closed, to resist. "Sit him up," Wilkes said to the sailors, "and hold his arms so he can't pull it out. That's the way."

The surgeon took a funnel from his bag and pushed the spout far back into the slave's throat. He poured the slabber sauce into the funnel's mouth, then pressed the paste down through the spout with his hand. The black gagged. Sauce, flecked with blood, dribbled from the corner of his mouth. Wilkes loaded and emptied the funnel three times more. "There. Well, we got some of it down him, anyway. Watch him," he said to the sailors. "If he throws it up, let me know right away."

"What do you do about his next meal?" Hollister asked.

"If we're lucky, he'll take it himself. If not, then we force-feed him again, and every day thereafter until we reach port." He added, in a low conspiratorial tone, as if he were afraid the slave might understand and act upon the information, "In some cases it doesn't work. Even if we can get food down them, they still die."

"Why?"

Wilkes spread his hands, palms up. "They just seem to will themselves dead."

Hollister looked back at the slave, from whose mouth Petersen was removing the speculum oris. "I would like," he said, "to know more about niggers."

By midday the *Jubilation* was standing off the promontory Mueller had indicated. Horneby ordered one of the cannons fired, and the shot was answered from shore a few minutes later by a column of white smoke. The sea was calm, the surf was modest, and Knye assured the captain they could transport the slaves in the longboats with little difficulty. Horneby had Knye select and arm a party of sixteen men. Meredith was put in charge of the operation. He commanded the first boat and Knye the second.

The *Jubilation* positioned herself just outside the surf and the boats were lowered. Sailors lounged against the bulwarks and watched them make their way to shore. Figures moved from the jungle and onto the beach. The slaves were clustered tightly together, tied by their necks. Mueller led the column, and with him were six black guards from Uriah Richardson's factory. The slaves were made to sit. Mueller paced up and down, waiting for the longboats to beach. Meredith's pulled in ahead of Knye's. The mate went over the side in water up to his knees and strode toward the coffle, his long red hair whipping in the breeze. Mueller came to meet him, hand extended. Meredith whipped a pistol from his belt. The seamen on the *Jubilation* could not hear the report; but they saw the pistol buck in Meredith's hand, and they saw Mueller knocked backwards to the sand. Mueller's blacks swung their muskets to bear. But Meredith's men had already leveled their own weapons. Puffs of gray smoke appeared on the beach, and the guards dropped, their muskets spinning away. Knye's men came running up. They surrounded the cowering slaves, hauled them to their feet, and got them moving toward the boats. Meredith's crew bent over Mueller and his guards. Sun flashed from a cutlass as a coup de grâce was administered.

The slaves loaded, the boats struggled through the white water and returned to ship without mishap. Horneby was waiting at the top of the Jacob's ladder. "Well done, Mr. Meredith."

"Thank you, sir."

"They are all dead?"

"Yes."

"And the slaves are in good order?"

"They seem so. We have one casualty. Turner took a ball in the shoulder."

"Have Mr. Wilkes attend to him. Mr. Petersen can examine the slaves. When you've seen to that, please join me in my cabin for a glass of brandy."

"Yes, sir."

Full sail was set and the *Jubilation* turned west-northwest toward the Bay of Lycosu.

Besu's wrists as well as his ankles had been chained from the first day. He walked with difficulty, hobbled and unable to swing his arms for balance.

Adoko watched him approach, and he grieved. They had made his brother a cripple as well as a slave. They had indeed killed him.

"Adoko," Besu said. "We have not talked in some time."

"I have missed you."

"And I you."

"I understand, Besu. I have regretted, but I have not been angry."

"Do you smell the forest? The wind is blowing off the land."

"Yes, such days bring pain."

"Let us go to the side and look."

They went to the rail, Besu shuffling. A seaman watched them suspiciously, and after a few minutes Besu, who had been standing in silence, said, "Come. I do not like that dungheap's eyes on us."

They moved back to the center of the deck. "What do you want, my brother?" Adoko asked.

"That you can give me? Your love."

"You have always had that."

"Do you remember the time our father made us sit before him? He said to me, 'Besu, listen to Adoko. He can help you to see with more eyes than you have, listen with more ears, feel with more hearts, understand with more minds.' And he said to you, 'Watch Besu. You can learn strength from him, and suddenness. He can teach you the transcendence of action, the value of decisiveness.' "

"He said that if we were one we would have been a man more than any man before."

Besu stretched out his hands. Adoko took them in his own. They gripped each other strongly. "We have learned much from each other, but sadly we have not learned enough, I think."

"Besu—"

"I am thirsty now, my brother. More thirsty than I have ever been. I leave you now, and I go to drink."

Besu turned and walked away with short, chain-snubbed steps. His back had healed well. The whip wounds had closed into long, red wales. He went to the water barrel nearest the mainmast, where a slave was scooping out a drink with a dipper. A couple of blacks fell in behind Besu. The seaman assigned to this barrel was a few paces away, leaning against the butt of the mast, his musket propped at his side. The first black finished drinking and stepped aside for Besu.

Adoko looked at the guard. It was the one Kiuky had

said was bored and negligent. Suddenly he understood and he opened his mouth to shout. But he had no time and he did not know, nor would he later be able to decide, what he would have shouted.

Besu plunged his hands into the water barrel and pulled out and held high a dripping cutlass. He spun, took two hopping steps, and split open the head of the sailor leaning against the mast. He tossed the cutlass to a waiting slave, and snatched up the dead seaman's musket and blade.

Two blacks leaped upon the next closest guard, bludgeoned him down with belaying pins, and seized his weapons.

A passing sailor shouted a warning, drew his cutlass, and rushed forward. Besu shot him.

There were five in revolt. Not enough, not near enough. Adoko started for them, was kicked in the knee from the side, and went down. A white man stood over him, menacing him and the other immediate slaves with a musket.

Whites were running to the scene, shouting, clubbing slaves with musket stocks and slashing at them with swords. Besu lopped off the hand of a sailor. One of Besu's followers shot another. A dark seaman with a gold earring came sliding down a rope, struck the deck and threw a knife, which sunk to the hilt in the stomach of one of the rebels. A musket ball ruptured the throat of another. Then the tall red-haired white man was among the sailors, screaming and pushing aside their aimed muskets. Whites carrying long boathooks moved in and formed a circle under the direction of the man with the red hair, forcing Besu back against the mast and his two remaining men against the rail. With the slaves thus pinned, other whites advanced, slowly and warily. One of the blacks tried to go over the side. Two whites sprang forward in unison. The fugitive was dragged back onto the deck. Besu and the other man were overwhelmed in an instant.

Adoko lowered his head. It had not been much of a drink for one so thirsty as Besu. He hoped, knowing better, that his brother would at least be favored by a quick and merciful death.

The rebels had been dragged up to the quarterdeck so that the rest of the slaves, jammed below on the main and foredecks, could have as unobstructed a view as possible. There was a woman with the three men and the two corpses. Through Honest Jack as interpreter, mass floggings had been threatened unless the whites were given some explanation as to how the cutlass had been hidden in the water barrel. Two terrified females had named this plump brown woman, and she had been seized.

Horneby delivered a short and unemotional address to the assembled slaves and told them why Besu and the others were being punished. What they were about to see he said, was mild by comparison to the fate awaiting any others who attempted to revolt. Honest Jack restated the captain's words in three languages, and the slaves then translated for each other into another half-dozen tongues and dialects.

"All finish, Cap'n sir," Honest Jack reported. "Them black bastards pretty damn sure not gonna try this for certain again. Pissin' down they legs right now, you bet!"

"Proceed, Mr. Meredith," Horneby said.

Meredith gave Honest Jack a knife and told him what to say to the first of the bruised and slump-shouldered rebels who was pushed forward.

Horneby felt very little toward the condemned black men. He was enraged, though, with the two seamen whose slovenliness had permitted the revolt. You expected slaves, particularly Coromantees, to have impulses in this direction. But so long as each man aboard did his job properly the wish could never become reality. Horneby regretted that the two sailors had been killed. Their deaths under his order would have been as good an example to the crew as the execution of the rebels would be to the slaves.

Honest Jack handed the knife over and pointed to one of the black corpses. The naked slave to whom the weapon had been given looked down dumbly at the cadaver. He shook his head and began backing away. Meredith, smiling, laid into him with a cat, striping his back from left to right, driving him forward again.

Horneby did not like Meredith, but he valued him highly. The pleasure the mate drew from inflicting pain was, so long as Horneby kept it reined, a useful tool. The captain was not a brutal man. It was simply that he understood brutality as the most efficient and expedient means to any end. He had been sailing with Meredith for five years; they were a formidable team. But when the day came, as Horneby knew it would, on which Meredith overstepped himself and brought about his own destruction, Horneby would not really grieve.

The slave fell to his knees beside the cadaver, and Meredith kept at him with the cat until the man dimpled cold black flesh with the knife point. It was hard work, splintering apart the ribs, and Meredith spurred the slave on with a few lashes whenever he seemed to falter. At last the Negro had it, and he stood up, trembling, holding away from his body the clotted heart he had taken from the corpse.

"Tell him to eat it," Meredith said.

Honest Jack translated.

The slave grunted and threw down the heart.

"Don't think we can whip 'im up to it, boss sir," Honest Jack said. "He pretty strong taboo on that."

"Right. Well, we're ready for that." On Meredith's order several seamen grabbed the slave, and one thrust the heart back into his hand, held it clenched there. Meredith knelt and slipped a set of thumbscrews over the man's big toes. "Tell him all he has to do to stop the pressure is to begin eating." He turned the screws. The slave screamed when the swollen flesh around his nails split and blood spurted forth like juice from a burst grape, but it wasn't until the bones had been crushed that he frantically tore off a piece of the heart with his teeth and swallowed. "Tough bastard," Meredith said, admiringly.

The knife was given to the second rebel, who was instructed to kill his comrade. He refused. Meredith took up the cat again, but didn't need it. The first black held out his arms imploringly to his comrade. They exchanged a few quiet words. Then the man with the knife laid a hand gently upon the other's head . . . and drove the long steel blade straight into the throat.

Meredith seemed disappointed when, without being told, the slaves removed the heart of the man he had just killed, ate part of it, then stood and handed the knife to Besu.

Besu took it, spun and drove the blade at Meredith. The mate had anticipated this and was ready. He stepped lightly to the side and chopped the cat's wooden handle across Besu's wrist. The knife clattered on the deck. Seamen dragged Besu down. Meredith smiled.

Adoko watched without expression. It was good that he had no weapon. He would have used it to grant Besu an instant death, no matter the consequences.

The woman was dead. Besu was bloodied, and from the way his right arm hung it was evident that his shoulder was broken. They had whipped and beaten him, burned him with coals, and peeled off strips of his skin. But he had refused to raise a hand against either the remaining black man or the fleshy brown woman. The tall red-haired white had become frenzied, but Besu had withstood everything done to him, and the white stopped just short of killing him; he did not want Besu dead yet.

The other slave was butchered with a single stroke of a cutlass. The woman was tied to the lower rigging. A burly seaman whipped her to death, and by the time they cut her body down, her ribs and her spine could be seen, and the dark purples and grays of some of her organs.

A rope was positioned over one of the crossarms of the rear mast. They were going to hang Besu. Adoko had seen this form of execution once before, at a garrison of English soldiers. He was surprised. The English soldier had died in seconds. Adoko had expected the white men on the ship to use a more painful and a slower method. He did not bother to puzzle over it, he was simply glad Besu would not linger.

The red-haired man made a noose and slipped it over Besu's head. This was not what Adoko remembered. There had been a large knot that time, which rested at the back of the prisoner's neck, and the criminal had stood upon a platform, through which he had fallen when a lever was moved, breaking his neck. Two whites stood off to the side holding the other end of the rope. They pulled a little, tightening the noose. The red-haired man motioned for them to stop.

Besu skimmed the crowded slaves with his eyes and found Adoko. He smiled.

The red-haired man took a grip on the rope with the waiting sailors, and they pulled. Besu's chained feet lifted into the air. Leisurely, hand over hand, they hauled him up above the planking, then snubbed the rope fast.

Now Adoko saw the difference. His brother would be garroted by his own weight. It would not be a sudden death.

Besu's ankles crossed each other. He locked his fingers together. His eyes were squeezed shut. Adoko knew he had resolved to die without giving sport to the whites. Adoko approved. His respect and his love were great.

But Besu's body would not permit his victory. After several moments, in which he turned a lazy circle, his feet began to snap up and down. A redness suffused the ebony of his face. His cheeks puffed. His eyes bulged open. His arms strained as he attempted to keep his hands locked together. But the fingers sprang open as if by their own accord, then closed, flexed again, closed . . . He kicked, and the chain joining his ankle shackles rattled. His muscled belly rippled and heaved. His mouth gaped. His hands went to his neck, clawed at the rope, and his fingernails dug bloody furrows into his throat. He jerked. His tongue protruded. He arched his back and lashed his feet out. His hands beat against his chest and his head. His bladder and bowels emptied themselves. Then, gradually, his struggles subsided. He hung quivering, turning in the breeze.

The red-haired man twanged the taut rope.

Besu shuddered.

The red-haired man plucked the rope a second time.

Besu was still.

My brother, Adoko thought, *I will eat his heart for you. I will do that for you. I promise.*

A day had passed since the bodies of the rebels had been heaved over the side, but Dunbar still felt numb. He had no words for the execution, nor did he think he ever would have. And he did not care. He was deadened. He was afraid not to be.

The slaves hadn't changed—that was the incredible thing. They behaved no differently than they had before. Hadn't the executions affected them at all? He did not think this was so. It occurred to him, rather, that the blacks were masterful dissemblers, that it was near to impossible to determine what they were actually thinking and feeling. This made him apprehensive. There were so many of them.

He looked for Li-yana, and he could not find her. He was a little worried about her. He had had to loosen his protection a little. There would have been trouble otherwise. Mostly the crew had looked upon it as a big joke. They thought Dunbar some kind of lunatic, and what the hell, every man is entitled to his private madness. But a few of them had begun to glance at her in more than a casual way. The journalist realized that by removing her from their grasp and branding her inviolate he had added a new dimension of desirability to the girl. Men want most what is forbidden them. If he, Dunbar, remained rigid in his rights of ownership, then it was quite possible that some of the crew, like O'Brien or the drooling Renner, would focus upon her and eventually decide their need to take was stronger than Dunbar's singular privilege. They would have Li-yana, and they would be violent. She would suffer.

Dunbar did not know what to do.

The seamen were ugly and excited after the revolt. It was O'Brien who brought it to a head. Dunbar was coating a rope splice with hot tar. Li-yana was watching him. The girl yelped, and Dunbar turned. O'Brien had come up behind Li-yana, snared her with one big arm, and cupped one of her breasts. She squirmed. He laughed and nuzzled her neck. She went limp and looked expectantly at Dunbar. O'Brien moved his eyes to the journalist and waited.

Dunbar considered the possibilities rapidly. Horneby might well back up the journalist's sovereignty, but the captain would soon weary of the business and would not be pleased by Dunbar's importuning him at regular intervals. Dunbar could order O'Brien to leave her alone, and the Irishman probably would . . . this time. The same for a fight. A quick swipe across the face with a brush of hot tar would take the guts out of O'Brien, but again it would be only a temporary victory, and sooner or later the Irishman would be back. There was, really, only one feasible answer.

"Ah, Jamey," Dunbar said, "you never get enough, do you?" He chuckled and went back to the splice.

O'Brien laughed. "Boyo, there's not enough in all the world." He whacked Li-yana's bottom and sauntered off, whistling.

The tension eased from Dunbar's shoulders. If he could convince them that he wasn't going to be belligerent about it, then with luck they'd be satisfied with pats, pinches, a little fondling, and the girl would be safe.

"Li-yana . . ." he said.

But she was gone.

Five small rivers emptied into the Bay of Lycosu. The shoreline was scalloped with inlets and backwaters, and there were nearly a hundred islands of varying sizes, as well as floating bogs, many large enough to support thick trees and colonies of small animals. The bay was a favorite haunt of ships waiting to be slaved. It offered a multitude of hiding places from the British.

The *Jubilation* nosed into Lycosu a little after daybreak. Seamen who had sailed under Horneby before knew that a day's layover was ahead of them. They supposed the captain liked to drink a social glass with the officers of other ships, many of whom were his long-time acquaintances. He never, though, remained aboard another vessel much more than an hour. Whatever his reason for stopping, the crew was happy enough. There wasn't much that had to be done while the *Jubilation* slipped about the bay under quartersail. Only the oarmen assigned to the longboat grumbled. While crews from different ships might mingle ashore, they were a closed and tight little fraternity on water, and they resented the intrusion of strangers. So the sailors from the longboat clustered together in out-of-the-way places on the decks of the other ships and fidgeted uncomfortably until Horneby was done.

Horneby was aboard a Spanish barque when two muffled cannon shots sounded from across the bay. The Spanish captain, who was new to the trade, raised his eyebrows.

"Do you have American papers, *señor?"* Horneby asked.

"Yes, but . . ."

"That was a courtesy warning from one of the other ships. The British have entered these waters."

"I am correct in assuming my American papers will protect me?"

"Yes, if they're valid, or a reasonable facsimile thereof."

"I think they will be acceptable."

"Good. You have nothing to worry about, then. Just insist on your rights."

"I will do so."

"You'll excuse me now, *señor*. I'd best be getting back to my own ship."

"Por supuesto. Of course. I am sorry you did not find what you are looking for."

"Yes. Well . . . Thank you. Goodbye."

"Goodbye, *capitano. Buena fortúna."*

"Muchas gracias."

Meredith had sent lookouts high up the mainmast when the cannons sounded. He was at the rail to meet Horneby.

"Report, Mr. Meredith?"

"Sail movement around the islands, sir. Two ships showing no colors have broken for open water. No sign of the British yet."

"Run up the American flag."

"Yes, sir. Shall I have the slaves put below?"

"Not necessary. His Majesty's navy won't bother us."

The lookouts reported warships off the starboard. Horneby and Meredith went up to the quarterdeck, where Horneby turned the glass on the British. There were three of them—two frigates and a paddle-steamer. They had strung themselves out across the mouth of the bay and were moving in. Horneby swore. The British were no threat to the *Jubilation,* but they had effectively prevented him from searching the slave complements of the other ships in the bay. There remained, then, only Balmallah and ben-Ahmen. He closed the telescope savagely.

He had been searching nine years, and the fear, irrational, but no less real for that, had been growing in him that if he could not bring his long quest to a successful close soon, he would never be able to do it.

"Set three-quarter sail, Mr. Meredith," Horneby said, "and lay in a course for Hyak. Tell the helm to keep us straight and easy. We don't want one of those warships to think we're running and send a ball through us."

"Aye, sir."

It took the better part of an hour to close with the British. During that time both the slavers that had tried to flee were boxed and boarded. One of them carried cannon, but was so obviously outgunned by the three warships that it offered no resistance.

"Steamer approaching," the lookout called.

The paddlewheeler, gouting heavy black smoke from her stack, had veered off from her sister ships. She carried only six guns, but two were massive thirty-pounders.

"Maintain course," Horneby ordered.

The paddlewheeler ran up signal flags ordering the *Jubilation* to heave-to.

"Sir?" Meredith asked.

Horneby said nothing.

The blacks rushed to the rail and jostled each other for a

look at the steamer. When the seamen whipped them back, they stood on their toes, craned their necks, pointed, and jabbered.

One of the warship's guns roared. Water spouted high into the air off the *Jubilation*'s bow.

"All right, goddamn them," Horneby said. "Bring her around, Mr. Meredith."

The ship swung to meet the oncoming British. Sailors manned the steamer's cannon. Marines in bright red and blue uniforms and flat-brimmed hats lined her rails, muskets at the ready. The block letters on her prow read *H.M.S. PEREGRINE*. The British lowered a longboat. A navy Leftenant in blue dress tunic stood in its bow, hand resting on the hilt of his sword. Nearing the *Jubilation* he picked up a megaphone and shouted:

"Throw over a ladder there. We're coming aboard."

Horneby cupped his hands to his mouth and replied, "You have no right to board an American ship."

"We want to examine your papers of registry."

"On what grounds?"

"Suspicion."

"That is insufficient."

"If you do not permit us to board, then we must assume you are not an American ship and demand your surrender. If you resist, we will open fire."

Horneby stroked his jaw. His face was stony. "Drop the ladder, Mr. Meredith."

The Leftenant climbed aboard, followed by two marines. Horneby had not come down from the quarterdeck to greet him. The slaves had run to the far side of the deck when the *Peregrine* fired her single round. Now they stood and stared at the British in silence. The Leftenant, who was young and who had an air of intense dedication about him, the kind bordering on fanaticism, looked back at them grimly.

He made a snapping turn on his heel, strode quickly to the stairs, and mounted to the quarterdeck. The marines double-timed after him.

"Leftenant Michael C. Hastings, His Majesty's Navy," he said with a little inclination of his head.

Horneby sent Meredith below to get the papers, then stood looking out to sea, ignoring the officer until the mate returned. Meredith handed the folio with its wax seal and flourished signatures and trailing red ribbons to the Leftenant. The young man scrutinized them several minutes, then said with ill-concealed reluctance, "Your papers are in order, Captain."

Horneby turned. "Quite. And the next member of the Royal Navy who tries to board without provocation will be looked upon as committing an act of piracy and his head will be blown off."

The Leftenant stiffened to attention. "Standing orders require me to offer my courteous thanks for your cooperation. I hereby do. Personally, though, I should welcome an attempt by you to blow my head off. It would give me an excuse to sink you and send you to hell, which I would find most gratifying."

"The only gratification you'll ever get," Meredith said, "will come from pulling your pud."

"I will see you hang," the Leftenant spat.

"Not bloody likely. Now you best be toddling along and leaving us men to our work."

The Leftenant left the quarterdeck. He paused at the Jacob's ladder and looked back at the slaves. His face was pale. He wiped the back of his hand across his eyes, gave a little cry and struck the rail hard with his fist. Then he went over the side, followed by his escort.

The seamen of the *Jubilation* hooted and jeered as the longboat pulled back to the steamer.

"Bring us about again," Horneby said. "There are slaves waiting in Hyak." His hand was stroking his cheek.

The woman had her baby. She began to groan and twist not long after the females had been shut in for the night. Leana pressed away from her. The loudness of the woman's voice and the violence of her movements increased steadily for two hours. When she screamed, a few other voices answered in the darkness, some angry, telling her to be quiet, others comforting. Mostly, though, there was no response; everyone was locked in her own private misery.

The woman was saying something. Leana could not understand her. The ship rolled and the woman was thrust against the girl. Leana shrank back, and the woman babbled and clutched at her. Leana put out her hands, touching heavy, spongy breasts, and pushed as hard as she could.

She put her fingers in her ears. *Stop it, stop it.* But the woman did not, and her screams turned to shrieks. She beat her head against the planking; her limbs flailed. Between shrieks she made a choked, sobbing kind of sound. Leana could stand it no longer. She raised her hand to strike, but when the woman's hand slapped against her own, Leana seized and held that hand and drew it to her. She locked her fingers with the woman's and pressed her lips against the sweaty skin. She touched the woman's wet brow and murmured, "That's all right. You're going to be all right. Don't worry now. Please. I'll take care of you."

The sound seemed to quiet the woman somewhat. Leana moved closer until her body was resting against the woman's side. "I'll help you. I'm here. I'll take care of you."

The woman moaned.

"It's all right," Leana whispered.

The girl maintained a gentle flow of words, bracing herself when the contractions came, so the woman could pull against her, and, in an hour, amid screams and wild thrashing and what seemed a limitless amount of hot, sticky blood, the baby was born. Gasping, the woman tried to reach it, and when she could not, she began to chitter and lash out. Leana squirmed and twisted and probed with her hand and finally touched a soft, wet thing that was a tiny arm and she drew the baby up, cut the cord with her teeth, tied a quick, simple knot, and struck the baby twice. It coughed, whimpered, then cried. The woman heaved and clawed at Leana, and calmed only after the girl had laid the baby upon the pendulous breasts. The woman made a soft, weary sound and began to rock slowly back and forth.

Leana snuggled into the woman's side, exhausted. Comforted by the feel of flesh against hers and soothed by the rocking, she fell asleep in moments.

She was awakened in the morning by the sailors who came to bring them out to the deck. The flesh against which she rested was cold. One sailor stopped another, said something, and pointed to the woman. Leana pushed herself up on one elbow. The woman's mouth was open. She was not breathing. Neither was the baby, who was locked in the dead woman's crossed arms, face buried in the space between her great breasts.

Leana moved away. Much blood had crusted between them during the night and it stung when the girl separated herself from the corpse. Neither the woman nor the baby seemed real to her. It had been different in the darkness, but now with light streaming through the ventilation ports and through the open fo'c'sle door, they looked like carved wooden figures. She could not believe that she had had anything to do with them.

On the deck a seaman motioned her to the pumps. She saw two whites carry the dead woman up and walk with her to the railing. The baby was still clutched to the woman's chest. The sailors threw them into the sea.

The men at the pumps turned the hoses on her. She scrubbed away the dried blood with her hands. One of the whites tickled the juncture of her thighs with his fingers. She submitted.

Her thoughts of Duhbar were bitter. She did not know who he was or what he was, or the nature of his relationship to her. But it had seemed that he was going to protect her, and she had begun to trust him. She had even felt herself liking him, in a shy and wary fashion. But he had only been playing. And now he was tired of the game. He didn't care about her at all. He didn't stop any of the others from putting their hands on her. Sometimes he even laughed with them.

She hated Duhbar.

Wilkes was dreaming of a desert. It was a hot, unfriendly land of jagged stones and shimmering sands and stunted, spike-ridden bushes. It was a dead land, and he was tossing in his bed, tangling in the sheets.

There was a knock on his door and he woke to it with a sense of relief. He put on a thin cotton dressing gown. Horneby and Meredith were in the companionway. "Yes, Captain?"

"Mr. Wilkes, we have a patient who requires medical attention."

"All right, just a minute." Wilkes drew the cord of his gown tight, lit his lamp, and checked the contents of his bag. "Who is it, and what's the matter with him?"

Horneby and the mate stepped into the cabin. Meredith closed the door behind them. Horneby said, "Sit down a minute, John."

Wilkes looked at him curiously and sat on the edge of his bed. Horneby folded his hands, in the manner of a cleric. "John, we have passengers aboard whose presence, in consideration of their safety and of shipboard harmony, has been known to date only to Mr. Meredith and myself."

"Oh?"

"Are you familiar with Mount Celestial, the foundlings' home outside of Charleston?"

"I've seen it. It's a foul place."

"Yes. One of the worst. Well . . . we are carrying five of the unfortunate waifs from that place."

"What do you mean, *waifs?* Why? What are you going to do with them?"

"Girls, from twelve to fourteen years of age. We're bringing them to ben-Ahmen."

"To ben-Ahmen! Why . . . why . . . My God, Horneby! You're going to make whores of those children. You're going to give them to black animals! I don't believe you. It's—it's—*unthinkable.* It's sacrilegeous!"

"Hold on, John. First, they are *not* going to the niggers. As you well know, you can't even give a white woman to a black merchant, let alone sell her. And even if it were possible, I'd agree with you; it would be disgusting. So no problem exists here.

"Now, consider the lives of these girls in the orphanage. They are unwanted, abused, and despised. Their lot, since they are of no value to anyone, is certainly far worse than that of a slave. Ben-Ahmen will sell them to Moorish potentates, who find white concubines highly desirable. The girls will be treated like queens. They'll enjoy luxury and comfort such as few Western women will ever know. And they will be honored and protected all their lives."

Horneby went to the surgeon's side and clapped him on the shoulder. "Come, John. You know the truth of what I'm telling you. We've rescued these girls from a life of squalor and ugliness. We are, in a certain sense, their saviors."

"I . . . I don't know. I don't like it."

"Well, can you refute anything I've said?"

"No, it all *sounds* correct. It's just that . . . it just doesn't seem right, that's all."

Horneby gave the surgeon a friendly shake. "That's only because you were taken by surprise. Give it some time. Mull it around. You'll see that I'm right."

Wilkes shook his head slowly.

"Of course you will," Horneby said. "But you're needed now. You'd better attend to your patient."

The girls' cabin was at the end of the corridor, just the other side of Horneby's. It was secured by an iron bar, which was padlocked into place. Horneby turned a key in the lock, removed it, and drew the bar free. The room was small, and five narrow bunks had been built one atop the other against a wall. Four of the girls were crouched around the bottom bunk, where the fifth one lay. They stood up when Horneby, Wilkes, and Meredith entered, revealing thin but pretty faces.

"Girls," Horneby said, "I'd like you to meet Mr. Wilkes, our surgeon."

"Are you going to make Holly better?" the tallest one asked. The other three pressed around her.

Wilkes swallowed hard. "Yes. Yes, that's why I'm here." He tried to sound cheerful. "And what's your name?"

"Millicent."

"That's lovely."

"Do you think so?"

"I certainly do."

The girl smiled. "This is Anne, and this is Grace, and this is Cheryl."

"How are you all?"

They answered in unison, "Fine, thank you, Mr. Wilkes. We hope you are well, too."

The swish of the headmistress's rod could be heard behind the singsong; the surgeon shuddered. "I am, thank you."

"Mr. Wilkes," Horneby said. "If you please . . ."

Wilkes nodded. "Will you move over a bit, girls, so I can take a look at Holly? There. That's fine." Holly's long black hair was spread out across the pillow. Her eyes were open, but they were glazed and she was not aware of her environment. Her skin was gray and moist. Wilkes took her pulse. It was rapid and weak. Her hand, in contrast to her face, was warm, even hot. Wilkes pulled back the sheet and lifted the girl's shift. Only Millicent remained, peering down with an intent face, when Holly's body was uncovered. The other three blushed and turned away. Wilkes touched Holly's abdomen. The child cried out. Wilkes nodded to himself, lowered the girl's shift and pulled the blanket back up around her neck. "How long has she been sick?"

"Three or four days," Millicent said. "But like this only since this morning."

"Has she been throwing up?"

"She started yesterday. A lot."

Wilkes turned to Horneby and Meredith. "Have you given her anything?"

"I thought she was stopped up. I gave her a cathartic last night," Meredith said.

"A cathartic! You goddamn fool, you've probably—"

"Holly's going to *die,*" one of the girls wailed.

"No, no, she's not," Wilkes said quickly. "Come here, Anne. Anne? It is Anne, isn't it? I thought so." He hugged the girl to his chest and patted her back. "Holly's going to be all right. She's pretty sick now, but I'm going to take care of her and make her well again." He raised the child's face and brushed the tears from her cheek. "Do you believe me?" Anne sniffled and nodded. "Good. So I don't want any of you worrying. I'll make her well."

"How soon?" Anne said.

"Well, that's a bit of a problem, I'm afraid. It's going to take some time. I'm going to move her to my own cabin so I can keep my eye on her until she's better."

"Your cabin?" Horneby said. "I don't know if—"

"Please, captain," Wilkes said without looking up. "It's absolutely necessary."

"There's no other way?"

"None."

"All right, then. Mr. Meredith, carry the girl to Mr. Wilkes's room. Remain with her until Mr. Wilkes returns."

"Yes, sir." The mate went to the bunk and picked the girl up. She whimpered. Surreptitiously he laid his hand across her mouth and carried her out.

"Will you visit us?" Anne said. "And tell us how Holly is?"

"Yes, I will." Wilkes laughed. "You know, you are the prettiest girls I've ever seen, along with my own daughters, of course."

"You have daughters?" Grace asked.

"Two of them."

"And they're prettier than we are?" Anne pouted.

"Now, I didn't say that. I said that you and they are *all* pretty."

"What do they look like?" Cheryl said.

"I'll show you." Wilkes took the locket from under his robe, opened it, and held it out for the girls' inspection.

"But that's two pictures of one girl," Anne protested.

"Those are twins, silly," Millicent said.

"What are twins?"

"Two people who look just the same."

"That's right," Wilkes said.

"They *are* pretty," Cheryl said.

"What are their names?"

"How old are they?"

"They're called Alice and Alicia, and they're about your age."

"Whose age?" Anne demanded. "I'm eleven. Millicent is the oldest. She's fourteen and a half. Holly's only one month younger than Millicent. Grace and Cheryl don't know how old they are."

"Well, they're just a tiny bit younger than Millicent."

Millicent looked pleased.

"Are you proud of them?" Grace asked.

"I'm the proudest father in the world."

"I never had a father," Anne said, and her lower lip trembled.

"Of course you did," Millicent said authoritatively. "Everyone has to have a father. What you mean is that you don't have one now."

"No," Anne insisted. "I never had one. But . . . but I want one!" And she began to cry again.

"Hush, hush that now," Millicent said. She took the girl in her arms.

Wilkes coughed. "Uh, do you girls know, uh, I mean, are you happy you're not at Mount Celestial anymore?"

Horneby frowned, but the surgeon ignored him.

"Oh, yes!" Grace cried.

The others nodded.

"They used to beat us," Cheryl said. "And there were maggots in the bread and—"

Grace shivered.

"—and we had to go to church every day and memorize the Bible, and we had to work in the gardens all the time, and we could only play on Saturdays, just for two hours, and . . ."

Anne bounced out of Millicent's arms. "But that's all over! Do you know where we're going?"

"Uh, yes, I think so. But why don't you tell me?"

Anne slapped a hand to her mouth and looked guiltily at Horneby.

"It's all right," the captain said. "Go ahead."

"Well, we're going to another land, where they have princes and kings and everything and funny-looking castles, all pointy. Captain Horneby showed us drawings. And we're all going to live there. There'll be swimming pools for us and flowers and all different kinds of food, as much as we want. We're going to wear beautiful silks and things and we'll have jewels and gold and servants of our very own. Just think!"

"That sounds wonderful," Wilkes said. He smiled and kissed Anne on the cheek.

She grinned at him. "Maybe you can come and visit us there, too."

"I'll try," the surgeon said. He stood up. "Now, though, I think I should go take care of our friend Holly."

"You'll come see us again, real soon?" Grace said.

"Tomorrow."

"Promise?" Anne said.

"Yes."

In the hall, Horneby replaced the bar and the padlock. "You see?" he said.

"You neglected to tell them about the harems."

"Don't be petty. They'll get over that in a few days. Moors are not animals, you know. They can be quite sensitive. In America those girls would have lead lives of misery."

"Mmmmhm." It was a noncommittal sound.

"Will the girl be healthy by the time we reach ben-Ahmen's?"

"Healthy?" Wilkes snorted. "She'll most likely be dead by morning."

Horneby stopped. "Then what was that nonsense you were speaking back there?"

"Captain, those are children. Did you want me to tell them their friend is dying? I had her moved so they wouldn't see it, but I'll be damned if I'm going to tell them about it. When I visit, which I am going to do, every day, I'll make up little stories about Holly. There's no reason for them to know."

"You can't do anything?"

"If you had come to me the first day, maybe. It's her appendix. It was going bad, and that stupid cathartic Meredith administered caused it to rupture. She's filled with poison, and on top of that she's in severe shock. Every hour she lives is a boon, depending upon your point of view."

Horneby was silent.

"What's she worth, Captain? Six slaves, a dozen?"

"Eight."

Wilkes spat.

They came to the surgeon's cabin. Wilkes turned the latch and pushed open the door. He reeled against the jamb, as if struck, and he gasped.

Holly was on his bed. Her shift had been pulled up to her neck. Meredith was bent over the girl, his hands on her body.

"You swine!" Wilkes screamed. "You scum-sucking swine!" He seized a footrest, hurled himself across the room, and struck the mate across the shoulders. Meredith was knocked against the wall. Wilkes hit him again, and Meredith went to his knees. The surgeon brought the footrest down a third time. It splintered in his hands and he began kicking at Meredith. Horneby grabbed him from behind and pinned his arms back. "That's enough. That's enough, Mr. Wilkes!"

Meredith was bleeding from a scalp wound. He reached to his belt and yanked his knife from its sheath.

Wilkes struggled to throw Horneby off. "Drop it!" the captain roared. "Drop it and get the hell out of here!"

Meredith rose to his feet, still holding his knife.

"Mr. Meredith," Horneby said coolly, "if you do not leave this cabin immediately, I will personally tie the knots that secure you to the bowsprit and you will remain there until you are dead."

The wavering knife caught the light of the lantern and flashed. Meredith was breathing deeply. He was flushed, and the muscles of his jaw were working. He shook his head angrily, then stalked out of the room.

Horneby allowed Wilkes to pull free. The surgeon went directly to Holly, examined her to make sure the mate had not harmed her, then pulled her shift down. "Someday someone's going to kill that man," Wilkes said. "And take great pleasure in doing it."

"Probably. It's regrettable, and I'm sorry it happened, but it's over and it's best forgotten. Stay with her, see if there's anything you can think to do. If not, then notify me when she dies."

Wilkes nodded.

"Good night then, John, and thank you."

The surgeon did not answer. The captain left, and Wilkes bolted the door behind him.

It was a long night. Wilkes did what he could for the girl. He kept her brow dry. He dosed her with quinine and rubbed her down with alcohol, trying to control the fever. He forced brandy down her in an attempt to strengthen her heartbeat. And while he worked he could think of nothing but his own daughters. Nor did he *want* to stop thinking of them. Tears ran down his cheeks.

He loved them that much.

He saw the night begin to lighten outside his windows. Above, the watch called five bells. Holly died.

BOOK III

BOOK III

T'KOMO, standing with his back to the double doors, said, "I announce his Eminence, and you fall on faces. Except you, Captain. You stand with head lowered. No one looks until I say. Understand?"

Horneby nodded. Wilkes and Meredith said yes, as did Hollister, who had asked permission to accompany them. The rest of the crew was still aboard ship, which was at anchor in Hyak's harbor.

"You sure these men all necessary, Captain Horneby?" T'Komo obviously disapproved of their number. He had reminded them that only men of status and rank were permitted into the royal chamber. "Your red-haired man looks like animal. If he offend His Majesty, his life end."

"I would not insult His Majesty by bringing a lesser being into his presence."

Meredith glowered.

"Yes." T'Komo did not look convinced. He was a tall man who carried himself with overweaning pride. He wore robes of a deep, rich red. Gold hoops hung from his ears, and a gold chain from his neck. He carried a staff which was circled with a carved snake and tipped with a brass leopard's paw. The doors behind him were of wood, cut with bas-reliefs depicting the advance of the Jaffi nation from its predatory hill-tribe origins to its present position, one of the most powerful slaving empires on the coast. The preponderant figures were members of other tribes, dead or dying, or, most frequently, bound and chained and marching under the lash.

T'Komo stood with one hand on his staff, the other resting on his hip, and openly studied the white men until a slave wearing an iron collar with the leopard-paw emblem came padding up to him with a message.

"His Eminence receive you now." T'Komo pursed his lips, straightened Wilkes's tie, then turned and drove the staff against the floor three times.

A muted voice from behind the door asked, "Who wishes entrance?"

"The honored Captain Horneby of the ship *Jubilation,*" T'Komo replied. "And three companions."

"Who brings them?"

"I, T'Komo, High Minister of the People, Faithful Right Arm of our Lord, King and God Balmallah."

"Enter."

The doors swung open. The portal was blocked by a dozen black warriors in leather armor. They carried cocked muskets, and swords hung at their sides. T'Komo raised his staff. The warriors divided into two groups and withdrew to stand against the walls. T'Komo led the white men down a long, wide, windowless corridor illuminated by torches.

"Is that someone coming? Are you white? Can you speak English? Please, for God's sake!"

Matthew Hollister looked around in puzzlement. He could see no one. And the others either had not heard, which seemed impossible, or . . . were not surprised.

"Yes. I can hear 'em!" It was a new voice.

Then a second and a third, and still more, a clamoring in English, French, Spanish, and Portuguese.

"Help me!"

"Buy me out, Captain!"

"I'm dying, please, *please!*"

"My brother's an Earl, he'll pay you ten times my ransom!"

It became a babble, each voice trying to outshout the others, demanding, pleading to be heard.

Hollister came to a stop and stared. "Christ!" he whispered. Set into the wall was a tiny cubicle, faced with iron bars. Behind those bars, in a space barely large enough to accommodate him, was a filthy, naked white man. The man stretched out his arm: "Mate, if you got any soul at all, *help me!*"

Hollister was stunned. He realized, suddenly, that T'Komo and the others were several paces ahead. He hurried to catch up.

"Rot in hell!" the caged man screamed. "Burn, burn, burn!"

They passed ten such men, all hoarse desperate voices and grasping hands. Save for the last. He was an old bent man with a ragged white beard and a mane of twisted gray hair. He looked at them with craftiness, absorbed in some sly fantasy, then broke into wild giggles, grabbed himself and began masturbating.

The corridor turned abruptly to the right. A second detachment of guards was stationed here, before another set of doors. T'Komo passed Horneby's party through the guards, repeated the litany of identification to open the doors, then ushered the white men into a high-ceilinged chamber filled with the whispering of many black attendants and court functionaries. Little notice was taken of their entrance. T'Komo led the way down a lush carpet. He stopped some twenty feet from a three-leveled dais, upon which rested two ebony wooden stools and one, the highest, of intricately carved ivory inlaid with gold. "You stand here," T'Komo told them. "Talk if you want. It is permitted." Then he walked away to consult with a dour courtier.

"Goddamn monkey," Meredith muttered. "Who the hell do these niggers think they are?"

"People with enough power to remove your head if the fancy strikes them," Horneby said.

Meredith nodded toward T'Komo. "Well, I'd like to have a few of 'em aboard ship. I can tell you that I would."

"And I would like to see *you* in one of those cages," Wilkes said. "You belong there."

"Christ, are you still on that? What's the matter, did she remind you of your 'daughters'?"

"Don't ever mention my daughters! I won't have their names befouled in the cesspool of your mouth!"

"Leave it, both of you," Horneby said sharply.

Hollister looked from Wilkes to Meredith. He had never known much about passion. But now he saw that it could make men go to lengths that were quite ridiculous, and he was rather intrigued. He waited, expecting the mate or the surgeon to say something further. But it seemed that Horneby had ended the argument. He was disappointed. "Captain," he said. "Why are niggers permitted to put white men in cages?"

"It's not a matter of permission. It's one of power. Here,

they have it all. And each of those men is a ship-jumper, or a criminal."

"But they're white."

"Offer them my congratulations."

Hollister was silent several moments. Then he said, "I thought niggers all lived in grass huts and ran around killing and eating each other."

There was a sudden hush. T'Komo mounted the first level of the dais. He waited for complete silence, then bellowed a long series of phrases, each accentuated by a blow with his staff.

"The introduction," Wilkes whispered to Hollister. "He's reeling off Balmallah's titles, which are various and wonderful."

T'Komo finished. Two men with elephant-tusk horns came to the front of the dais and blew a single, low note.

The more important members of the assemblage, and Horneby, lowered their heads. Those of lesser rank prostrated themselves upon the carpet. Several moments passed. There were scuffling sounds from the dais, a grunt, and a loud creaking from the wooden platform. T'Komo barked a few words.

"We can get up now," Wilkes said to Hollister.

Balmallah dominated the room; it was impossible to look elsewhere. He was a monstrously obese man whose features blurred and were lost in the great black expanse of his face. Neither chin nor neck were visible, only a spongy horse collar of flesh that spread heavily across his round shoulders and his chest. His forearms, extending from the sleeves of his robe, were the thickness of a man's thigh. His legs were twin pillars of fat. He obscured the stool upon which he sat.

He was flanked by two tall men in loincloths, each of

whom carried a headsman's axe. A dwarf sat at his feet. A leather strap fixed with a dagger angled down across the dwarf's chest. The pinch-faced creature surveyed the court with suspicious and hostile eyes.

T'Komo occupied the bottom stool, and an elderly adviser with hands that twitched in his lap sat between T'Komo and the king. Balmallah spoke to T'Komo.

"Captain Horneby," the minister said. "Two steps forward. So. King Balmallah, he say he examine gifts in the trunks your men bring and he accepts them."

"Tell His Highness I'm pleased he finds them worthy. Also, I have with me additional tokens of our esteem, which I wished to deliver to him personally."

T'Komo translated. Balmallah raised a hand. The dwarf leaped up, scampered down the levels of the dais, and thrust out a demanding hand. Horneby handed him an envelope containing a draft from an English bank in the amount of £500. Balmallah did not trust American banks. The king glanced at the draft, then handed it to his adviser. The old man studied it, nodded, and passed it on to T'Komo. The minister approved, and it was returned to the king.

"His Highness thanks you," T'Komo said.

"He is welcome. And these are for his amusement." He snapped his fingers, and Meredith stepped forward with an oblong box of hand-rubbed walnut.

The dwarf brought the box to Balmallah, who opened it and smiled. He lifted one of the matched pair of exquisitely crafted French dueling pistols and turned it over. He cocked the weapon, raised one arm, and sighted down the barrel at T'Komo. The minister did not flinch. Balmallah pulled the trigger. *Click*. The king laughed, the great rolls of his body quivering and shaking, and returned the pistol to the black velvet of the box. He rattled off a few sentences.

T'Komo said, "King Balmallah say the pistols very fine.

He regret, after such good gifts, he have to tell you no slaves here for you. Maybe, he say, a week. Not much longer."

"We agreed during my last trip," Horneby said evenly, "that one hundred and fifty slaves would be waiting for me this month."

T'Komo translated. Balmallah slapped a hand against his knee and replied, gutturally. The dwarf's gnarled hand drifted to the hilt of his dagger.

"His Highness not need to be made reminded of agreements," T'Komo said. "He make exception for you because you are old friend, otherwise penalty most painful."

"You will thank His Highness for me," Horneby said. "The slaves in the waterfront barracoons have been promised to other ships, I presume, in agreements that predate mine?"

"That is correct."

"And of course His Highness, the value of whose word is known throughout the world, could not violate those agreements by giving me one hundred and fifty of the slaves he has on hand."

"Of course." T'Komo smiled . . . as did the king's adviser, and Balmallah himself.

"Of course," Horneby repeated.

Balmallah spoke, and when he finished T'Komo said, "The king, he say the city of Hyak at the pleasure of your crew. And he looks with happiness for the joy of you and officers for feasting at palace tonight."

"Tell His Highness my crew is grateful and that I and my officers will attend him this evening."

T'Komo nodded. "You may go."

The white men were ushered out.

The family was distintegrating. Kiuky had fallen in upon himself. He spoke only in monosyllables and spent long periods staring at nothing. He did as he was told. As he was told by anyone—white man, black man, child. He no longer cared. Kiuky was the worst, but the sickness was spreading. The others were listless, and Adoko sensed a crumbling of spirit, a blunting of their need and love for each other.

This frightened him. Man alone was nothing. Does a wing severed from a bird have meaning? May a branch stand without a tree? There was neither significance nor even existence outside the family. And the family was dying.

Were they, then, to cease being? Adoko could not accept this.

The worm was in his heart, but he would not yield; he would find the slimy thing and he would crush it.

Horneby rather enjoyed the feast. The hall was crowded with members of the court and captains and officers from the several slavers moored in the harbor. Food was plentiful and excellent, a great variety of spiced vegetables and meats served in stews and steaming pastes and garnished roasts, all to be eaten with the fingers from long, low tables, in front of which the guests sat cross-legged on the polished and immaculate floor. Servants were everywhere, spaced along the walls methodically swishing broad-bladed fans, swatting flies and beetles that had managed to squirm though the protective netting over the glassless windows, replacing platters of food, and pouring French wine, English ale, and a potent local palm wine. Horneby liked the heat of the food on his fingers, and the juices running down his hand and his chin. Occasionally he glanced up at Balmallah. He had a certain admiration for the gross king, who was hard, tough, and shrewd. It would be no shame to lose to him. But Horneby was confident of success; he understood the king's boundless greed.

At the end of the meal the guests were invited into an adjoining hall, where there were numerous tables, styled upon European lines and equipped with padded armchairs. Baccarat was offered, and poker, sixes, twenty-one, chemin de fer, scattered dice tables, and several indigenous games, the most volatile and treacherous employing hexagonal chips of wood and weighted feathers. Blacks from the royal household with crude proficiency in several languages kept the play moving. The hall filled quickly with cigar and pipe smoke. Captains and officers slipped off their jackets, loosened their ties, and rolled up their sleeves. The sustained murmur of voices was broken now and then by shouts and laughter.

Horneby wandered, sipping brandy, making an occasional bet, but not, in contrast to most of the players, for more than a few dollars. At one table an American captain half rose from his chair as a baccarat card was flipped to him. He read it and slumped back.

"I am sorree," the dealer said, and scooped away the pile of banknotes from the center of the table.

The American stood up. He looked at Horneby with a stupid expression. "I lost better than ten thousand of my backer's money," he said. "What am I going to do?"

Horneby took a glass of brandy from the tray of a passing slave and handed it to the man. "Have a drink," he said, then strolled off.

Two hours passed before the king's scowling little dwarf tugged at Horneby's sleeve. He accompanied the creature to the head of the hall where Balmallah sat, flanked by his bodyguards and attended by T'Komo. The minister said, "His Highness notices you do not play. He wish you to have a good time. He wonder if you like a private game with him, few others."

"Thank His Highness for me. But tell him I think not. I'll be returning to my ship soon. I want to get a good night's sleep. We'll be sailing in the morning."

"In the morning? With no slaves?"

"Yes. I can't afford to wait. I'll have to buy them elsewhere."

T'Komo translated rapidly. Balmallah's smile faded. He instructed T'Komo, who said, "The king, he say few days not make much difference for you. The slaves coming are very fine, worth the time."

"I wish I could accommodate him, but I'm under strict orders from my investors. Tell His Highness we appreciate his efforts and we are sorry it all came to nothing. Perhaps next time we'll be able to do business." He bowed his head, turned, and walked away.

He had gone only a few steps when T'Komo called, "Wait!"

Horneby walked back slowly. Balmallah was working his mouth. He resembled a great, bloated pig scenting a refuse heap. "Yes?"

Balmallah uttered a few harsh words. T'Komo said, "His Highness value his earlier business with you. He willing to sell you tonight twenty-five excellent slaves he have set apart for the palace."

"That's very generous of him, but it would still leave me one hundred and twenty-five short."

T'Komo discussed this with Balmallah, then took Horneby's arm, led him off to the side, and spoke in a low, conspiratorial voice. "Captain, you see little Portuguese sloop in harbor?"

"I have."

"Very cheap captain in charge, small crew. Cannot pay

port price so he offer tax to His Highness for permission to go up-river, trade himself with villages, and bring slaves back."

"So?"

"Gone three weeks now. Runners say returning, only half day from city tomorrow morning. Seventy, eighty slaves, not many guards. His Highness, he say tax they pay not enough, rude, inferior men. He say he would not be upset if something happen to Portuguese, and he say Captain Horneby might be happy to find seventy, eighty slaves someplace. So happy he make payment to His Highness in thanks for hospitality. Yes? And he say if you still need more, he arrange for 'nother twenty-five. Then Captain Horneby sail pleased with full cargo for only one day's wait."

Horneby looked at Balmallah, who was smiling. "Tell His Highness he is a most resourceful man. My faith in him is renewed and amplified. Of course, should anything unfortunate occur to the Portuguese who are bringing these slaves down-river, I would never suspect him of any involvement, nor he me, I am sure."

T'Komo spread his hands. "Could it be otherwise?"

"If something *were* to happen, I would speculate it would go this way: A man or two of this kingdom would meet a party of piratical villains at dawn and lead them up-river to a place suitable for an ambush. And once the slaves were in the hands of these villains, then a payment of twenty dollars per slave would be made to the guides. Do you agree?"

"Yes, except for price. I do not think guides do this for twenty dollars each slave. I think thirty dollars."

"Twenty-five, possibly."

"No. Thirty still much less than villains pay here."

"You are probably right, thirty dollars."

"Yes, that would be fair."

The dwarf was turning handsprings, making Balmallah laugh.

They set out while the sky was still dark, with only a thin arc of gray beginning to spread across the rim of the eastern horizon. There were twelve of them, armed with muskets and cutlasses. Meredith led the sailors, but followed the two silent black men.

My God, oh my God, what am I doing? Dunbar thought. He had begun recently, needfully, to believe in God. Something had to offer assurance, mercy, hope. Clearly, none of these were to be obtained on earth; therefore he had to turn to the supernatural, or go mad.

He had witnessed and written about battles—even, infrequently, participated in them when his life hung in the balance. But then he had fought against voluntary combatants, and the killing had been formalized and absolved because it occurred under circumstances rendered acceptable by being called war. And even the few times he had taken up a weapon he had still felt himself more a detached observer than anything else.

Now he was carrying a gun, and he was on his way to commit murder.

His companions, though cursing the difficulty of the trek, were in generally good spirits. They would each receive a five-dollar bonus for this venture.

It was chilly. Fog suffused the jungle, limiting visibility and dampening clothes. It was quiet, except for the grunts of the men, a few bird calls, and odd scurryings in the brush. Huge silk-cotton trees with trunks fifteen and twenty feet in circumference towered into the air, their peaks only dimly visible. Thick lianas drooped from the uppermost branches, sometimes coiling all the way to the ground.

Broad-leaved ferns rose to twice the height of a man, and creepers and thick, vigorous stands of bushes abounded.

As the sun rose, the fog was burned away, and for a while it was a relief to be free of the night's cold and the large droplets that fell incessantly and with such stinging force from the branches far above. But then a slow heat enveloped the men, increased, and soon the jungle was sweltering and steaming, and breathing became difficult. They were following the course of the river. The first few miles out of Hyak, the going had been difficult; now, deeper into the jungle, it was grueling. Save for a few flat mudbanks, the vegetation grew to the very edge of the river, if not a few inches into it.

The sailors were drenched by their own sweat. Sword arms grew leaden as they hacked through the brush, chopped vines thicker than cable-ropes, slashed in frustration at skin-tearing, nettly branches. Clouds of insects buzzed about their heads. Birds screeched and unseen animals snuffled and coughed in the foliage to the side. Once a man screamed and fired his musket. The others turned quickly and saw him frantically trying to reload. Poised on a branch above him, tail flicking, was a leopard. The large cat hissed, then turned, leaped to another branch, and disappeared. The black guides laughed. The sailor drew his cutlass and shook it menacingly. Meredith strode back and hit him on the side of the head, then the march went on.

On the mudbanks they encountered crocodiles sunbasking, waiting for movement in the water that meant prey. Mostly these beasts slithered into the river when the men approached. But twice huge old bulls stood their ground and roared a challenge. The black guides advised circling. The scaly reptiles were hard to kill and could do much damage before their lives were ended. Once a tribe of angry, howling monkeys pelted them with sticks and retreated only after two of their number had been shot.

Dunbar was beyond thought. He could do little more than stagger along, dizzy, head pounding, watching his numb arm rise again and again to cut through the endless barriers the jungle threw against him. Climbing over a fallen tree trunk, whose height was greater than his own, he broke through its rotted surface and sank to his thighs in decayed pulp that was crumbly and doughlike. He did not have the strength to free himself, and he called out weakly for help. Meredith came to him, reached up, caught hold of his shirt, dragged him out, then let him fall to the ground. Dunbar lay there several moments before he pushed himself up, and rising seemed to him one of the most impossible things he had ever accomplished.

The blacks called a halt in the early afternoon, and one of them said, "Here."

The seamen dropped down, and several of them were asleep in minutes, a sleep made fitful by too deep an exhaustion, by the relentless insects that burrowed and bit and sucked.

Meredith went with the guides to reconnoiter. The river bent in an L here, and was narrow and shallow in the bend itself and for several yards farther downstream. The seamen were on the short leg of the L. They would not be seen until it was too late. The water could be waded, which meant that if any of the canoes capsized, the slaves would not be drowned. Meredith approved. The guides moved upstream to scout for the Portuguese, and Meredith returned to his men, lay down, and closed his eyes.

By the sun, two hours passed before the blacks returned. They shook Meredith awake. "Be here fifteen minutes," the one who spoke English said. They had been running, and their bodies were slick with sweat, but neither of them was winded.

"How many canoes?" Meredith asked.

"Five."

"White men?"

"Ten."

"Good. This'll be a turkey-shoot."

"You pay now. We go."

"Not on your life, mate. You get your money as soon as we have the slaves. Not one second before."

The blacks shrugged, drew off to the side, and hunkered down to wait. Meredith roused and positioned his men. The rest had drained off the worst of their weariness; and the knowledge that they would soon be in canoes, would complete their trip in what, compared to the first part, would be sheer physical luxury, gave them more than enough incentive to concentrate on the job at hand. "Hold your fire until I signal," Meredith instructed them. "Then one volley, all together. After that, into the water and secure the canoes and the slaves. Use your cutlasses to finish any of those Portuguese still alive." He assigned two men to fire on each canoe and designated two more to pick off any targets missed by the volley. The seamen stood behind trees and crouched behind bushes.

Several minutes passed. Then, faintly, they heard voices nearing. The canoes turned the bend. They were bunched fairly close together. A white man sat in the bow and in the stern of each one. There were roughly a dozen slaves paddling each craft, bound to one another by a rope that ran between neck loops.

Dunbar's target was the first white in the third canoe. His sights zeroed in on the man's chest automatically, and he marveled at this. Logically, he knew he could have aimed almost anywhere, but here were his sights set on a stranger's chest.

"Fire!" Meredith screamed.

There was a rattle of musketry. White men collapsed and fell into the water. Dunbar saw one of the canoes roll over. The journalist rose from his crouch. His aim did not waver, but neither did he fire. His man was reaching for a gun. Surely one of the others would see him and kill him. But there was no shot. The man in the canoe looked directly at Dunbar and raised his weapon.

Dunbar squeezed the trigger. The stock punched into his shoulder, and smoke spurted from the muzzle. He saw the Portuguese pitch backward out of the canoe. The sailors of the *Jubilation* splashed into the river, shouting, cutlasses high.

Dunbar did not move. It was so simple to commit murder.

He could not believe how simple it was.

He watched his comrades grabbing hold of canoes. He saw them pull up slaves who had been thrown into the water by the capsized canoe. He saw cutlasses flash down and strike wounded, floundering men. Wavering red ribbons striped the river.

"Gimme a hand, for Christ's sake!" a man shouted. He had hold of the prow of a canoe and was pulling it toward shore. The slaves had bunched in the stern, cowering.

Dunbar let his musket slip from his fingers. He waded out from the bank and helped the man.

When the canoes were beached, the black guides quieted the slaves. It was not hard. They understood that this was merely a change of ownership, which they easily accepted, especially since none of them had been hurt. Many had been captured far inland, had been slaves more than a year, and had been passed from trader to trader seven or eight times. *Who* owned them no longer mattered. Meredith assigned his men to the canoes, took a precise head count of the slaves, and paid off the guides.

The two black men were gone before the raiding party pushed off from the bank.

The current was not swift, but it was steady, and, with the slaves bending their backs to the paddles, the canoes skimmed along at a fairly good pace. The sailors hooked their legs over the gunwhales, trailed their hands in the water, smoked, called jokes to each other, and forgot the tortures of their earlier march through the jungle.

Several times Dunbar picked up his musket and turned it over in his hands. The man he shot had looked neither surprised nor fearful, only angry in that brief moment before he toppled over into the water. Dunbar remembered that look, and he told himself, *He was a slaver, he had forfeited his right to live.*

Is that what he, Dunbar, had come to? Did he believe slavers had no right to life? That, were it possible, they should all be executed?

Yes!

Because Virgil Dunbar was a slaver, because all men were animals, because life was horror, because Virgil Dunbar was a murderer, a mass of quivering, whimpering meat rolling over and over in its own filth without hope of salvation . . . and death, at least, would mean an end to pain.

They were attacked in the late afternoon, and Virgil Dunbar discovered that he wanted to live.

What had worked for the men from the *Jubilation* worked almost as well for those who ambushed them, the only difference being the latter's poor marksmanship. The fusillade raked the canoes just after they had rounded a blind bend not dissimilar to the one at which the Portuguese had been struck. Dunbar was in the stern. The man in the prow jerked around violently, the side of his throat torn open. He collapsed against the nearest slave, who shrieked and shoved him away.

Dunbar threw himself over the side. He meant to swim underwater as far as his breath would carry him, but it was too shallow and his dive scraped his face and chest against the rocky bottom. He staggered to his feet. The assault party, which was black, was rushing into the river to finish the job with swords. Dunbar made for the far shore. The water resisted him. He lunged forward, stumbled, flailed out with his hands, and half swam, half crawled toward the bank, choking as water splashed into his gaping mouth. He reached the thick roots of a large tree and began pulling himself up . . .

Something smashed into the back of his skull. His consciousness exploded into blinding heat, and then he knew nothing.

A white and scarlet bird with a high crest and a long bill was studying him with great seriousness. He stared back at it, confused. Then he groaned. The bird ducked its head up and down, as if it had received some kind of confirmation, then turned, waddled a few steps, leaped into the air, and flapped leisurely away on large wings.

Pain cleaved Dunbar's head, and helped clear his mind. He was hanging above the water, doubled over a taproot like a sack of flour, arms and legs trailing down. He tried to move, but could not; his limbs were numb. He remained still, trying to force feeling back into his extremities. After a while he stirred again slowly, because it hurt and because he was weak. He was able to pull himself onto the bank. He touched the back of his head. A large area of his scalp was torn, the hair and ragged flesh matted with crusty blood. It must have been a grazing musket ball—a sword stroke would have split his skull. Curiously, it had saved his life. Hanging there, limp, head torn and bloodied, he had been ignored as dead.

He remembered his panic, the incredible hysterical fear. Had it been that way for the Portuguese? He did not want to think of it.

Now there was the problem of survival. He knew he could not push through the jungle. He had no strength left. He would fall and lie there until he died, or until some hungry, foraging animal found him. It had to be the river, then. There were still a few hours of daylight left, for which he was grateful. But he was weaker than he had thought—once he fainted and was unconscious awhile—and the sun was setting by the time he was ready.

He had lashed two logs together with vines, then placed a third one across them as a cross-arm for balance. He found a stout stick which he thought he could use to pole himself along. But after launching his raft he laid down in its shaft to rest, holding the ends of the cross-arm so he would not fall off, closed his eyes, and fell into a stupor. The pole slipped from his grasp.

Many hours later, just outside Hyak, a child playing at the side of the river called his mother. She in turn called her husband, who summoned two of his friends. The three black men waded up to their chests in the river and caught hold of a log raft that, trapped in a backwater, was turning in slow circles. There was, unbelievably, a white man on this raft, a white man who was probably dead.

They brought him to shore and laid him on his back. Then one of them knelt and pressed his ear to the white man's chest. He was alive. The black men were pleased. There would likely be some little reward from the palace.

Happily, the largest of them slung the white man over his shoulder, then started with his companions off to the city proper.

In the morning Horneby went alone to Balmallah's court. The king had cost him men and a good deal of money, but he wasted neither time nor emotion on futile schemes of vengeance. Actually, the fault was his own. He had attempted to manipulate Balmallah. Instead, the black man had manipulated him. Balmallah was a man of high craft and cunning, a man who succeeded. Horneby admired him.

Still, there was the cost—$2520 had been paid to the guides, for eighty-four slaves. The remaining $480 Meredith carried had been lost in the attack of the *Jubilation*'s party. Write off $3000. And nine seamen. Three had returned. Meredith, bruised and scratched and nearly insane with rage, was now locked in his cabin lest he make some mad attempt to exact retribution from Balmallah. Allison was another. The edge of his palm had been struck by a ball which then continued on to smash nearly every bone in his hand. Wilkes and Petersen had been arguing, when Horneby left the ship, as to whether or not the hand should be amputated. And Dunbar, who was suffering from shock, exhaustion, and a bad scalp laceration, but who, according to Wilkes, should be fully recovered in a few days. Horneby would have to buy half a dozen of Balmallah's captive seamen. The *Jubilation* could function well enough without the nine who had been lost, but there were bound to be a few more fatalities before the ship reached her home port, and he would need extra hands then.

Horneby was ushered into the royal chamber. He knew

immediately that something was seriously wrong. He paused, but a moment later his intuition told him it had nothing to do with the *Jubilation*. He folded his arms and looked about. There was heavy tension in the air; some of the blacks were obviously upset. Their gestures were curt, their voices hollow with forced attempts at naturalness. Most, though, seemed as ignorant as Horneby. Even T'Komo looked puzzled.

The minister announced the king. When Balmallah had settled his bulk onto the royal stool, Horneby was told to step forward. "His Highness," T'Komo said, "is unhappy to hear men of your ship meet such trouble. He makes sympathy."

"Such are the fortunes of . . . business."

"Yes. He wishes to tell you good news, too."

"Which is?"

"Unexpected coffle arrive last night. He offers these slaves to you so you do not have to sail empty."

"How many slaves were in that coffle?"

"Eighty-four."

"If a man had paid a holding price of thirty dollars each, that would amount to . . ."

"Two thousand five hundred and twenty dollars."

Balmallah beamed at Horneby.

"What price is His Highness asking?"

"Captain, I am surprised. You know the Hyak price. Ninety dollars each head."

"I thought there might perhaps be a reduction, in view of the circumstances."

"Circumstances? I do not understand."

"No, of course not. However, certain financial losses have cut into my capital, and I simply cannot meet the price. If His Highness, in view of our longstanding relationship, could find another sixteen slaves and accept eight thousand even for the lot of one hundred, I could make the purchase."

T'Komo consulted with Balmallah, then said, "His Highness value your association. He accepts."

Horneby tended his thanks. Balmallah said something to T'Komo. The minister looked nonplussed. "His Highness, he say he have farewell gift for you."

"Oh?"

Balmallah stared at T'Komo. The minister frowned and began to fidget. Balmallah clapped his hands. A slave stepped forward with a silver platter, on which rested an object covered by a green silk cloth. Balmallah nodded. The servant whipped away the cloth, revealing a severed black head. T'Komo recoiled, and then screamed.

The doors to the chamber burst open, and a squad of soldiers rushed in. One of Balmallah's giant bodyguards bounded down the dais and seized T'Komo. There was scuffling behind Horneby. He turned. The soldiers had taken into custody nearly a dozen black courtiers and noblemen. One of them drew a pistol from beneath his robe. A quick sword slash opened his belly and spilled out grayish ropes of intestines. He fell with the weapon still uncocked.

The king's dwarf shrieked, drew his dagger, and ran at T'Komo. The bodyguard holding the minister fended the little man off with one long arm. The dwarf shrilled his rage and stabbed at the empty air. Balmallah's other guard walked down and, scooping the dwarf off his feet, held him in the crook of his arm like an infant. The king remonstrated with the dwarf and gradually the stubby creature subsided, resumed his accustomed place at Balmallah's feet, but refused to sheath his dagger, and glowered at everyone who moved.

A nervous young man stood before the dais and addressed the court in Jaffi. There were gasps and flurries of whispering. When he concluded, he pointed to the head and said to Horneby, "This King Balmallah's cousin. Plot murder on His Highness with T'Komo and others. Some die. But king say rest be your slaves. T'Komo, nine, ten more. King say he like this. They try highest, end lowest. King happy. You take them as presents. Sell them worst masters you know. Yes?"

"Tell His Highness I accept his present with gratitude, and that the men will be disposed of as he wishes. Also, congratulate him on his continued and proper good rule and health."

The young man translated. Balmallah waved a fat hand and inclined his head, dismissing the captain.

The slaves were brought aboard the *Jubilation* that afternoon. Matthew Hollister was on deck, contemplating the Jaffi noblemen, particularly T'Komo.

There was a small outbreak of the bloody flux, which the sailors hated as much as they hated anything. The discharge was repulsive, blood and thick mucus. Stricken slaves were packed together in a feeble attempt at some kind of quarantine, and their deck was scrubbed daily. The heat in the holds was savage, and the planking, at the height of the epidemic, was slick with the foul emission. Cleaning, the seamen added their own vomit to the filth. Mr. Petersen fainted once while administering to the slaves and had to be carried out. He refused to return to the hold, convinced he had narrowly missed death by some kind of osmotic corruption. Horneby spoke to him. The assistant surgeon did not relate his conversation with the captain to anybody, but was obviously shaken, and the next day he was performing his duties again.

Wilkes fretted much more over Millicent and the other girls than the slaves, although the children themselves seemed pleased with their situation. Horneby is right, the surgeon thought, they'll be far better off than they would have been at home. But his dreams were haunted by visions of lascivious and depraved Moors, and he thought often about Alice and Alicia. He would have forgotten Hollister entirely if the young man had not sought him out. The first time, the surgeon was anxious to visit the girls and give them a progress report on Holly, complete with funny little things she had said, and so he put Hollister off. But Hollister returned the next day, and his persistence roused Wilkes's sense of responsibility. He had, after all, said he would try and reach the boy. And he was afraid that if he rebuffed him a second time, there would be no further opportunity.

"You told me," Hollister said, "that you would show me something, something about the niggers."

Seeing Hollister's slowly awakening interest in the slaves, it had been Wilkes's original intention to encourage the boy in thinking that blacks were all stupid, primitive, and simple. Then, when he felt Hollister held this conviction firmly, he intended to present to the young man evidence contradicting this notion. It had been the surgeon's experience that one of the surest ways to involve a man was to present him with a paradox. He would work like the devil to resolve it. This was particularly true of youth. He had little idea as to whether or not this approach would work with Hollister, and even if it did, what its eventual outcome would be, but it was worth trying. This present inquiry seemed to indicate success.

"Let me check something. I'll get back to you in an hour," Wilkes said. He went to see Horneby, then got sidetracked cutting a long splinter from a sailor's arm. When he returned to the quarterdeck, where Hollister could usually be found, looking down at the blacks for hours at a time, he said, "After mess, the captain would be happy to see you for a brandy in his cabin."

"The captain?"

"Yes, he can explain it better than I."

Following dinner that evening, as the officers were filing out, Horneby said, "May I have the pleasure of your company in my quarters, Mr. Hollister?"

"The pleasure would be mine, sir."

"Mr. Wilkes?"

"I believe I'll pass, if you don't mind, Captain. There are . . . some young females I'd like to look in on."

"I understand. Go right ahead."

The captain took Hollister down the companionway and into his cabin. When the door opened, there was a flurry of wings and a twittering. Hollister waited at the door while Horneby turned up the lamp. The room was not large by landside standards, but it was three times the size of Hollister's cabin, big enough to accommodate four leather armchairs, a desk, a couple of footrests, and three large ironbound sea-chests, stacked one atop the other, as well as a wide bunk and a wall locker. "Sit down," Horneby said.

Hollister did, and looked curiously at the small, brightly colored birds flitting about in their twin cages, two dozen of them. Horneby unstoppered a decanter, poured brandy into two snifters, and handed one to Hollister. Walking around behind his desk, the captain thumped each cage on its top by way of greeting. The birds fluttered madly, then settled down and hung on the bars closest to him. Horneby took a piece of bread from a drawer, broke two pieces from it, and put one in each cage. The birds swarmed to the bread.

"Parakeets?" Hollister asked, a question of why, rather than of recognition.

Horneby nodded. "Mr. Wilkes tells me you wanted to see me. About blacks."

"Well, I, uh, Mr. Wilkes was going to show me something. He said you could probably do it best."

Horneby inserted a taper into the flame of his lamp and used it to light his pipe. "What do you think of the blacks, Hollister?"

"Oh . . . I don't know. Maybe they're animals. Maybe they're poor specimens of men. Maybe they're something in between."

"Mm-hm. What about Hyak?"

Hollister shifted uncomfortably. Horneby's manner stirred in him memories of his father. "It was a surprise. I didn't know they could build a city like that."

"Not a city, an empire. An empire that rules four or five million people. Here, give me a hand with these." He went to the sea-chests and with Hollister's help set them out in a row. He took a key-ring from his pocket, turned the locks, and laid back the lids. "Look at these."

He held up first a heavy metal plaque, cracked around the edges, and somewhat discolored. It was a three-dimensional scene of a royal family and retinue. The lines were straight and clean, the balance of mass and space nearly perfect, the detail work extremely fine. "This," Horneby said, "is from Benin, it's bronze, and it's more than two hundred years old. It was cast from wax in a process as sophisticated as any known in Europe."

He set down the plaque and lifted a delicate woodcarving of an antelope head. The basic shape consisted of three conjoined and complementary curves, inlaid with tiny blue and black stones that seemed endless and cyclic restatements of the three fundamental lines. Next the captain handed Hollister a small spring-worked jewelry box of wood and glazed ceramic. This was followed by a funeral mask that had been *cast,* not overlaid with thin sheets, of pure gold. And there were masks, and bas-reliefs from temples and palaces, and carved authority sticks of ivory and ebony . . . It was a large and varied collection and the pieces were of uniformly superb quality.

Horneby went back to his desk and sat down. "We are told by the arbiters of such things," he said, "that art is one of the most important criteria in evaluating a culture. If that is so, then blacks, Hollister, are the equals of whites."

Hollister returned to his chair, picked up his brandy snifter, and rotated it slowly between his palms.

"It makes no difference to me," Horneby said, "whether you live or die. It makes no difference to me whether *any* man lives or dies. But your father asked a favor of me, and your father has invested a good deal of money into my voyages over the years. So I will tell you anyway."

"Don't bother," Hollister said bitterly, and he rose to leave.

"Sit down!" Horneby roared. "If you want to spend the rest of your life with your thumb up your ass whimpering to yourself, all right. But not until I've finished."

The boy sat down. His face was sullen.

"First, niggers," Horneby said. "They're what started this, and they're as good an example as I can think of. Hollister, there were complicated and flourishing black civilizations on this continent when your ancestors and mine were groveling in their own muck like pigs in a sty, and while some of our more far-flung antecedents were still living in caves and painting their bodies blue. There are several empires in existence at this moment—the Mandingoes, Coromantees, Jaffi, Dahomians, half a dozen more. They have systems of law and government that are the equal of half the nations of the Western world.

"These are men, Hollister, no better nor worse than we are."

"They spend most of their time warring against each other, Captain, and white men do not sell each other into slavery."

Horneby rose and began to pace back and forth. "You cannot name for me a single year in the history of man in which one tribe or nation of white men was not slaughtering another. And slavery? I give you Greece and Rome. But we can come even closer, a time shortly before the African trade began: Did you know, Hollister, that one Pope excommunicated the entire city of Venice for repeatedly capturing and selling their Christian brothers into slavery? And that another excommunicated nearly every merchant in Genoa for the same reason? And have you ever seen an indentured servant? An indentured servant is a slave without the name."

"Niggers are our slaves, Captain, we are not theirs. This alone proves the inferiority of the black man."

Horneby spun and thrust his arm out at Hollister. "Here you have the crux of it! Not just between blacks and whites, but of all life—*power!*" He slammed his fist into the palm of his other hand. "If a man is seven feet tall, he is more powerful than a man of five feet, and he may do as he wishes to the smaller man. But if the smaller man obtains a gun, then he is more powerful than the larger man. *We had the power; the blacks did not.* And that is the reason they are our slaves. Everything is power, Hollister. Power is the ruling principle of nature." Color spread through Horneby's cheeks. "The large prey upon the small, the strong upon the weak. It has always been this way, it is now, and it always will be. No man can deny this."

Hollister bent forward. His elbows were on his knees, and his hands were on his temples. "But . . . with animals, yes, but there are factors such as religion, ethics . . ."

"Inventions of the weak, Hollister! Attempts to curb the power of the strong. Give any man power and see how long he continues his pious prattling."

Hollister shook his head slowly. "I . . ."

Horneby sat down on the edge of his desk. He was tired. He looked at the parakeets. There was silence in the cabin for several moments, then Hollister said, "I think I'd better go now, Captain."

"Leave, then."

"Yes. I will. Uh, thank you."

When Hollister left, the captain was sitting with his back to the door. He had inserted his hand into one of the cages, and some of the birds had come to perch on his finger and his wrist. The sound was so low that Hollister couldn't be sure, but he thought the captain was talking to the birds.

"Voilà!" Wilkes said. He whisked the checkered cloth from the plate and revealed half a dozen pastries. He had given the cook a dollar to make them. The dough was gummy, the fruit dry, and the sugar glaze haphazardly applied, but they were recognizable pastries nonetheless, and the girls squealed in delight. Even Millicent, who was very conscious of her age and tried to maintain her poise at all times, could not contain herself.

"For us?" Cheryl said. "All for us?"

"Actually, no," the surgeon said. "I just brought them down so you could look at them. When you're done, I'm going to take them back upstairs and feed them to the gulls."

"Oh," said Cheryl.

"He's just kidding, silly," Grace said, then added uncertainly, "Aren't you, doctor?"

"Of course I am! But if you don't dig in right now, my feelings will be hurt immensely, and I will indeed feed them to the gulls."

The three youngest lunged forward. Millicent stood daintily behind, waiting.

"What," said Anne with her mouth full, "are we going to do with the two that are left over?"

Millicent took hers. "Thank you, doctor."

"Well, Mr. Wilkes gets *one* of them," Grace said.

Anne gulped down the last of the pastry. "And we split up the one that's left over!"

"Right," said Wilkes.

"But what about Holly?" Cheryl cried.

The surgeon flushed. "Well, she, uh, she can't have sweets yet. It wouldn't be any good for her."

Anne was torn. Her hand was suspended over the last pastry. "And she'll get a treat as soon as she's better? I mean, if we eat this, we won't be cheating her or anything."

"No, you won't. I promised her as many sweets as she can eat, the very day she gets well."

"Lucky Holly!" Anne broke off a quarter of the pastry and popped it into her mouth.

Millicent was looking at the surgeon oddly. He could not meet her eyes.

Life at the orphanage had been bleak and simple, and the girls exhausted their anecdotal resources during his first two visits; so it fell to Wilkes to provide the bulk of their dialogue. This, since he liked to talk anyway, and since the girls were such excellent listeners, he found a thoroughly enjoyable business. Mostly they wanted to hear of his daughters. He told them tale after tale, drawing long-forgotten incidents from his memory. And he told them about his house, which was set high up on the slope of a hill, overlooking the water, on one of the Bay Islands off the coast of Honduras. There was a wrought-iron balcony where they sat in the evenings taking tea and watching the sunset. He remembered all the warmth and the happiness there, as he spoke to the girls, and he missed his home and his daughters very much. He did not consciously make a decision, it happened spontaneously when Grace asked, "Don't you want to be with them? Why do you keep going back to sea?"

"Yes, I do want to be with them," he said. "This is going to be my last voyage. I'll retire when it's over. Then Alice and Alicia and I will be together all the time."

"But how can you come and visit us if you're retired?" Anne said. "You said you'd come. You did!"

Wilkes mussed her hair. "And I will. There's nothing to prevent me from taking a pleasure voyage, is there?"

"Will you bring Alice and Alicia?"

"I'll certainly try."

"I'd like to meet them."

"I'm sure they'd like to meet you, too."

He played two word games with them, then said he had to go.

"Doctor," Millicent said.

"Yes?"

"What is your first name?"

"John. Why?"

The girl lowered her eyes. "If it's not impertinent, sir, may we call you . . . Uncle John?"

The others screamed *Yes. Oh yes. Please.*

Wilkes's throat tightened. "I'd like that."

Anne bounded into his lap, threw her arms around his

neck, and kissed him. Then Cheryl and Grace were on him. Millicent stood a little way off. Wilkes held out his hand to her. She rushed to him, eyes wet, but smiling.

Dunbar's heart was joyous. This voyage was his road to Tarsus. Like St. Paul, he had been toppled from the horse of his complacency and ignorance and sent crashing to the ground. But there, in the midst of his agony, he had received illumination. And he gained his feet a new man, a whole man.

Upon his return, he would join the Abolition Society, and he would work as long and as hard for them as was necessary until the trade was finally suppressed, and after that until the institution of slavery was outlawed.

With this resolution had come a tremendous sense of relief. He was sure he would survive the voyage. There was a point to it now; it was all fuel for the blast furnace of his future campaign.

He was grateful, too, that Li-yana no longer seemed to hate him. He did not know what had been responsible for her anger, but he was happy to see it end. She had not resumed following him about like a puppy, which he had enjoyed in a way, but neither did she spin away from him when he tried to approach her. Still, he was disappointed. He did not want gratitude from her, but he wished she would give him some sign that he had made her happy.

Wilkes was in foul temper the morning the *Jubilation* edged behind a reef and dropped anchor off a palace that was the only building of purely Moorish design on the West Coast. It was the home of Yussef Abd ben-Ahmen, an exquisite structure of slender towers and scalloped walls and porticoes. Horneby was below, preparing the girls for debarkation, and Wilkes, winding a bandage around a seaman's sprained ankle, was in the grip of a futile rage. He drew the bandage savagely tight.

"God!" the sailor yelped. "You're gonna tear the bloody foot off, Mr. Wilkes."

"Shut up, just shut up," Wilkes said, and finished.

Pain twisted the sailor's face. He limped away, using a boathook as an awkward crutch, muttering and cursing to himself.

Wilkes went to the side. He placed his forearms on the rail and gazed at the palace. It would be the girls' home . . . for a while, and they would be treated well. Then they would be purchased. Wilkes did not want to think beyond that. He glowered at the rowdy seamen who were crowding around the longboats, awaiting permission to go ashore. The palace of ben-Ahmen, or more precisely the outlying community of the palace, boasted some of the most refined and exotic diversions on the West Coast. Ben-Ahmen had at one time been the largest slave dealer in Mozambique. Grown haughty and overconfident, he attempted to seize power from the emir who governed the province. But the merchant had overestimated his own resources; he was roundly defeated and had to flee for his life. His personal fortune survived, though, and by the liberal and judicious placing of bribes he managed to have the bulk of it brought out of the country. Yussef Abd ben-Ahmen relocated on the West Coast, and within a decade, relying heavily on a well-armed black army of mercenaries, had established himself as the ruler of a small but quite comfortable and satisfactory kingdom. He had most of what he wanted and he was beginning to feel the inroads of old age, so he withdrew from the general slave trade and became a specialist. He dealt exclusively with concubines. He bought girls of any color and nationality, and he sold them to buyers of any color and nationality.

The man whose ankle Wilkes had bound was hobbling about in agony. The surgeon repented. He went to the seaman and said, "Here, sit down a moment," then loosened the bandage and rewound it properly.

"Thanks, sir. I was going out of my head, I was."

Someone shouted, "My God! Look at that!"

Horneby and Meredith had appeared on deck with the girls, who were freshly scrubbed and garbed in simple cotton dresses.

There was a quick, loud gabbling from the crew, followed by a silence that was strange and threatening. The girls stared at the dirty, half-naked seamen and shrank back against the captain and the first mate. Wilkes was thankful there were no niggers on deck. Since most of the crew was to be given shore time, the slaves had been kept in the holds.

Anne saw him. "Uncle John! Uncle John!"

"I'll be right there," he answered.

The injured seaman grinned. "Uncle John . . . well, blow me over. Reckon you had yourself just a fine trip."

Wilkes kicked him in the ankle. The sailor fell, howling, and the surgeon went to the girls. "Good morning," he said cheerfully. He gestured at the crew. "Motley lot, aren't they? We'll be on shore in a few minutes, and things will be much nicer there."

Grace wrinkled her nose. "It smells awful up here, much worse than it did in the cabin. What makes it stink so?"

"This is a slave ship, isn't it?" Millicent asked gravely.

"Uh, yes, we *are* bringing some slaves back with us," Wilkes said.

Millicent nodded.

Anne's eyes widened. "Are we going to be slaves, Uncle John?"

"Now who ever heard of such a preposterous idea? Slaves are all big and black."

"That's right," Cheryl said. "Don't you know anything, silly?"

Seamen were pressing nearer, open hunger on their faces. Their voices were low, but much of what they said could be heard. Millicent was the only one old enough to understand the words. She paled.

"Boat's ready, Captain," the bosun said.

They loaded under the stares of the crew, and Wilkes was relieved when they pulled away from the *Jubilation.* Grace and Cheryl and Anne were chattering excitedly, but Millicent sat in the bow, silent and frowning.

When the physical examinations were over, a guard led Wilkes to a cool and multiwindowed chamber in which ben-Ahmen, Horneby, and Meredith were lounging on silken pillows around a low table of food. The merchant's physician had verified the girls' virginity. There was nothing for Wilkes to do, but he had insisted on being present. The investigation had confused and humiliated the girls, except Millicent, who submitted quietly and with tightly compressed lips, which shamed the surgeon beyond endurance. But it was good that he had stayed. He had told the girls that ben-Ahmen was concerned about their welfare and merely wanted to make sure they were in good health. They believed him and were comforted by his presence. He was filled with contempt for himself.

Horneby and Meredith were drinking. Ben-Ahmen was smoking a hookah. The king eschewed alcohol, but was fond of mild amounts of hashish. Wilkes had tried the drug once, and his response had been violently negative and frightening. But in ben-Ahmen it seemed to produce nothing more than a heightened conviviality. Wilkes sat down. His guide spoke to ben-Ahmen in Arabic, then left.

"I am informed that all the girls are in good order," ben-Ahmen said.

Horneby nodded.

"Now," the Moor said, "I presume you wish to discuss price. They are young; they are attractive. There is no sense in haggling. I will offer you five girls of your choice for each one."

Horneby shook his head. "Ten."

"Ah, Captain. You are not being reasonable. I would barely make a profit."

"My friend, you would make a profit at fifteen."

"At such a rate I would be impoverished within a year. Allah is my witness. I could perhaps offer six."

"Nine is the lowest I can go."

"Seven, but definitely no more."

"Eight."

"No, that cannot be done."

"Let's say an even thirty then, for the four of them."

Ben-Ahmen pulled deeply on the hose of his water pipe, closed his eyes, and held the smoke in his lungs several moments, then exhaled and said, "Agreed."

"I'll make the selection this evening."

"What's the matter, Wilkes?" Meredith said. "You don't look so good."

The surgeon's hands clenched tightly, and his fingernails dug into his palms. "I am . . . quite . . . well."

Meredith laughed. "Good, good. Glad to hear it."

A servant burst into the room.

Ben-Ahmen beckoned him forward, listened to the man's whispering, and surged to his feet. Horneby, Meredith, and Wilkes rose, too.

"One of your girls has mutilated herself," the king snarled.

They hurried through a series of corridors and into the girls' room. Grace, Anne, and Cheryl were huddled in a corner whimpering. Millicent lay on the floor. Her dress was stained dark red around her waist, and blood had soaked into the carpet. Ben-Ahmen's bearded physician stood nearby holding a candle, which was also discolored with the girl's blood. He conferred with the Moor, who then said, "She destroyed her own maidenhood. She is useless to me."

Millicent emitted a high, strained laugh. "You can't make me a whore now," she gasped. "I stopped you, I stopped you."

Horneby kicked her in the stomach. Wilkes sprang forward and pushed him away. "Captain, no!" He went to his knees beside the girl and cradled her head in his lap. "Millicent, Millicent," he crooned. Tears slid down his cheeks.

She pulled away. "Don't touch me!" she hissed. "You lied to us. You knew all the time." She spat at him, then raked his face with her fingernails. He held his hands out to her, and she clawed him again. "Millicent . . ."

"Get away from me!"

Wilkes stood up. He looked helplessly at the other three girls. "I didn't . . . I . . ." His shoulders slumped, and he bowed his head.

"You understand that she no longer has any value," ben-Ahmen said to Horneby. "I will dispose of her for you."

The captain looked at him with narrowed eyes. "That's not necessary. I'll take care of it right here." He reached into his jacket pocket and his hand came out with a derringer.

"Wait!" ben-Ahmen said. "It is possible that I might find a client not so elevated as my usual customers. One who desires—how is it said?—a bargain."

Horneby lowered the derringer's hammer and returned the weapon to his pocket. "I thought that might be the case."

"Obviously, though, her worth has been greatly diminished."

"Twenty-five for the lot."

"That is acceptable."

The king ordered Millicent confined and watched. The other three girls shrank from Wilkes when he tried to approach them. Anne began to cry. They had only a vague understanding of what had happened, but they knew that Millicent considered the surgeon guilty of something horrible. Outside, in the corridor, Wilkes was drawn and pale. He asked Horneby for permission to return to the ship, which the captain granted. Horneby and Meredith then retired, at ben-Ahmen's invitation, for baths, rubdowns, and ministrations of the palace's skilled houris. They were feasted at sunset.

Horneby was depressed. This was the last stop, and the *Jubilation* would turn back to America when she weighed anchor. Again, he had failed.

He drank heavily. Later they went to the courtyards, to choose the concubines for ruddy Southern slave owners from the young and pretty black virgins who were ben-Ahmen's stock. The captain had consumed enough alcohol to send him staggering, under normal circumstances. But still, disappointingly, he was not drunk. He experienced only a sluggishness of his emotions. Nevertheless, he picked the girls slowly and carefully, with the exaggerated caution of a man who believes himself sober, but who does not disallow the possibility that he is not. Petersen, whom Wilkes had sent ashore, examined the slaves and pronounced them all sound.

"You will linger here and enjoy our hospitality a few days?" ben-Ahmen asked.

"Thank you, but I don't think so. We'd best be setting sail in the morning."

Ben-Ahmen looked disappointed. "I had hoped to arrange a more meaningful and effective presentation. But we must accept what is, mustn't we?"

"Yes." Horneby barely heard him. The coast of Africa was dead to him now. He was thinking of the time that would be eaten by the voyage to the Bay Islands, the sale of his cargo and the settling with his backers, the weeks required to stock provisions and make repairs, the return trip and then, then the new hope that would leap in his heart when the lookout called down the first sighting of the steaming coast. It was not all that long, really, just a few months . . .

"Would you please come with me, Captain?"

Horneby nodded and followed the king through a maze of passageways and up spiraling steps. They were nearing ben-Ahmen's private quarters, as was attested to by the increasing number of heavily muscled guards in bright silks. The king led him into a small, voluptuously appointed chamber and asked him to wait.

Horneby looked about and wondered why he was here, trying to remember what the Moor had said. Something about acceptance and a presentation?

"Captain."

Horneby turned. There was a girl with ben-Ahmen. He reeled, and a rush of blood inflamed his face. He could not breathe. "Sylas," he whispered. "Sylas, oh God!"

Ben-Ahmen held a yellowed piece of paper, the circular Horneby had given him years ago. He raised it and compared the drawing to the girl. "The ears were larger on the original," he said, "and this one's forehead is a bit higher, and her chin not quite so pronounced. But all aspects considered, I think you will agree that the resemblance is truly remarkable."

Horneby did not hear him. He sank to his knees before the girl and pressed his cheek softly against the bare mound of her belly. She stood rigid. Ben-Ahmen gave her a reassuring look. "I found you, Sylas," Horneby whispered.

"Her name," ben-Ahmen said, "is . . ."

The captain was crying. Ben-Ahmen studied him a few moments, curious, then silently left the chamber. He summoned a guard, telling him to wait by the door and to notify him when the captain emerged.

He walked away, hands clasped and lips pursed, reflecting, briefly, on the wondrousness of life, and speculating as to how much the captain would be willing to pay for the girl.

"Balmallah," T'Komo said, "he begin to believe he really a god. He feel there nothing he not able to do. Take bigger share of money than law says is king's. Make slaves of some of noblemen's cousins." Sitting across from Hollister in the small cabin, T'Komo shrugged and sipped his whisky. "Make many enemies."

Hollister marveled at him. Like the other male slaves, the tall man was naked and wore a shackle around his ankle. Yet he was able to sit and speak without self-consciousness, as if he were still the High Minister of Hyak, the right hand of Balmallah. That was dignity! And presumption. In the presence of God himself, Hollister thought, this man would retain his arrogance. Hollister had been studying him with fascination. T'Komo held himself aloof from the slaves. When, infrequently, he mingled with other blacks, he restricted himself to the half-dozen Jaffi noblemen Balmallah had also sent to the ship in chains. And even with them he employed an imperious attitude.

One thing, though, Hollister noted with slow pleasure. T'Komo avoided the seamen at all times. He was not clumsy, and he managed to give the impression that drifting away was a whim of his own, unrelated to the approach of a sailor. But Hollister was not deceived. And he understood.

He had seen Gomez lay into T'Komo with a leather strap one afternoon, and the black man had trembled—not with rage. Once T'Komo had been cored with unbending iron. But he had lived too long in luxury, and now, Hollister suspected, rust and corrosion ran deep.

T'Komo had been wary of Hollister at first. But before too long he let himself believe that the young man was truly interested and a little in awe of him. After years as High Minister, T'Komo found this quite natural. So when the white man offered him food from the officers' mess, brought him to the cabin and gave him the most comfortable chair, poured whisky, and spoke to him with deference, T'Komo accepted it as more or less his due. He began to think of returning to Hyak after this interlude aboard the *Jubilation,* which was unpleasant but which would also be brief, regrouping his supporters, and deposing Balmallah.

"Three weeks, maybe four more, we would have be enough powerful. But the wife of one man thinks to gain favor, to become rich. Her husband is weak. She tell him Balmallah too strong, we all die. She frighten him." He made a sound of disgust. "He betray us. Next time, no weak men." He raised a fist. "None!"

"There won't be a next time," Hollister said amiably. His heart was beating rapidly. *Power,* Horneby had said, *power.*

T'Komo smiled. He leaned forward and said, as if he had misunderstood, "Please?"

"There will be no next time." Hollister's palms were perspiring. T'Komo wore iron and was naked. He slept in filth and ate slop that was little better than garbage, but still he believed that not only was he a free man, but a man to whom homage and supplication were due. "You're a slave. We're going to sell you. You'll be a slave until you die."

T'Komo's face went cold.

Hollister imagined that the High Minister had looked thus countless times in the past . . . just prior to ordering a beating or proclaiming the death sentence. The black man was a full head taller than Hollister, broad-shouldered and well muscled. He could kill the youth easily. Except for . . . *power*. Hollister had the will to dominate. So did T'Komo. And the black man had the physical strength to triumph, so the advantage to T'Komo. But court life had undermined the High Minister. He valued his life too much. And at this moment, the question of life or death did not exist for Hollister, only the throat-clutching thrill of the contest.

Hollister's voice was unsteady. "Say 'I am a slave,' " he whispered.

T'Komo glared at him.

"Say it!"

"You are scum!"

Hollister fumbled open a drawer in the table next to his bunk. He withdrew a double-barreled pistol. Power, power. His throat was dry. His hand shook, but he managed to cock both hammers and keep the wavering muzzle pointed at T'Komo's chest. "Say it."

T'Komo smiled savagely. "You kill property? No. Lose money that way."

Hollister squeezed the first trigger. Flame and smoke exploded from the muzzle. The roar, in the confined space, was deafening. T'Komo slapped his hands to his chest, screamed, and toppled backward in the chair. Hollister emitted a thin, staccato laugh.

Everything was still for several moments. Then T'Komo pushed himself up from the floor. He looked at the powder burns on his chest, then up at Hollister. There was terror in his face.

"I did not put a ball on top of the charge in the first barrel," Hollister said. "However, there is one in the second barrel." He extended the pistol, finger curled around the rear trigger.

T'Komo shuddered. "I . . . I . . . am a . . . slave."

"Very good!"

The sailor on guard at the end of the corridor burst into the room, musket at the ready. "What's going on? You all right, Mr. Hollister?"

"Yes. Just fine, thanks. The weapon discharged accidentally. You can take him away now."

The sailor grasped T'Komo by the arm and shoved him toward the door. "Come on, you."

T'Komo spun suddenly and spat. The viscous fluid splattered across Hollister's face. "Aha!" Hollister cried with glee.

The sailor smashed his knee into T'Komo's groin. The High Minister doubled with a groan. The sailor clubbed him behind the ear with the musket stock, then began kicking him when he fell.

"Wonderful, wonderful," Hollister breathed.

The seaman, who was grunting with exertion, did not hear him.

It was immediately obvious to ben-Ahmen that, in the space of an hour, Horneby had undergone a drastic change. The white man was abstracted, distant-voiced; he moved slowly. And there were other, more subtle, differences, the cumulative effect of which gave the captain an air of . . . helplessness.

Ben-Ahmen turned away. He found Horneby's condition distasteful. Also, he added $2500 to the price he had intended to ask for the girl. "You find her satisfactory?" he said.

"She is the one. Yes."

"Your joy is mine."

"Thank you," the captain said humbly.

"There is, if you will permit me, the matter of her purchase."

"I'll buy her."

"Seven thousand five hundred dollars," ben-Ahmen said bluntly. "In gold."

"Yes. Sylas is mine."

The Moor cursed silently. He could have had ten thousand, possibly more. "It is a bargain, then. May I have accommodations readied for you?"

"Accommodations?"

"For the night."

"No. No, I'll be going back to the ship now."

"As you will."

"I can take Sylas? I'll send the gold as soon as I'm aboard."

The old Captain Horneby would neither have bothered, nor have needed, to ask. "Certainly."

A skiff returned Horneby and the girl to the *Jubilation*. The captain went directly to his cabin, counted out the gold, and sent Randall ashore with it. The girl stood silently against the bulkhead, head lowered, hands clasped tightly. She wore golden earrings, a silken vest which was joined with a single strand of silver and which afforded tantalizing glimpses of her moderate breasts, ballooning pants of a fine translucent material, and sandals. Her costume was a gift from ben-Ahmen. It was handsome, but it was not what Sylas had worn. He had offered Sylas a multitude of garments, including some of the finest gowns of Europe, and she had occasionally played with these, like a small girl, but for daily apparel preferred simple skirts of bright Manchester cotton. Bare-breasted, she wore them knotted high on one hip and slung low across the other, an unintentionally saucy effect that Horneby had always enjoyed. Tomorrow he would dress her in such a skirt.

Some of the parakeets were chirping. The girl raised her head, and Horneby motioned. "Come here. They're yours, come and see them."

She advanced obediently.

He opened one of the cage doors and inserted his hand. A bird perched on his finger. He drew it out. "Here. Hold your finger straight. Like this. That's right. Now press it alongside mine." The bird hopped to the girl's finger and cocked its head. She smiled. Horneby placed a seed between his lips and leaned forward. The bird gauged the distance, then snatched it away. Horneby offered the girl a seed, which she took, and which the bird took from her. She laughed and said something to Horneby.

"I can't understand you," he answered.

She pointed to the bird. He decided she was asking its name.

"I don't know. He hasn't any, actually. None of them do. Sylas had names for them, but they all died over the years. These are their successors. I've never named them. You can do that." She raised her eyebrows. Horneby indicated the birds in the twin cages. "They're all yours. Because they're pretty and you like them. That's why I got them in the beginning. Because you liked them and they made you happy."

She listened with an attentive, intelligent expression.

"We used to let them out, remember? We had muslin over the windows so they couldn't escape. We let them fly for hours." He got up suddenly, went to the door, called a seaman and ordered him to bring down a bolt of muslin, tacks, and a hammer. He paced nervously while he waited. "Of course, you have to understand that these are not the same birds, Sylas. They've never been out. And though there's ample room in the cages, their wings are probably not very strong. They'll get better, with exercise."

The girl's eyes followed him back and forth across the cabin.

"I do understand that you're not really Sylas, you know. But then *really* is just a word, isn't it? And if you look like Sylas and act like Sylas, then you are, for most purposes, Sylas. You see, we were together three years. I've been alone now eight years. You don't know what it's been like; no one does. I had come to . . . feel very strongly about her. When I lost her, I think I went a little mad. That's when I had those posters printed. It was— But you know, don't you? I feel that somehow you know."

She smiled at him.

The sailor arrived. Horneby took the material and dismissed him. "Just a minute now," he said to the girl. "Wait, it won't take me long. We'll get this tacked on good and tight, and then they can all fly, they can all be free. We'll like that. It will be like before."

He worked feverishly, ripping the cloth into rough squares and tacking the edges to the frames of the open windows. "There!" He rushed to the cages.

The girl had been watching him closely, trying to read his intention. Now she understood. She joined him, and together they released the birds. Some had to be coaxed and shooed out, but soon all of them were streaking about the cabin, whirring wings, blurs of color. The girl was laughing. Horneby began to laugh, too. He sat down behind his desk and guffawed hugely. He laughed until his jaw muscles hurt and tears were wetting his cheeks. He leaned forward and rested his head on his arms. Gradually his laughter subsided, and when it was over he felt drained, exhausted.

He raised his eyes to look at Sylas. There was a bird

perched on her head, another on her shoulder, a third on her finger. She was trying to coax others to her. Delight suffused her face. He watched her for several minutes, then he said, "We have to put them back now."

He closed his hand gently around one of the birds and returned it to its cage. She understood, and she helped him. When all the parakeets had been captured, he went to his bed and began undressing. The girl immediately removed her own clothes. She finished before him, and she lay down, on her back, expectant. Horneby snubbed down the lamp, pitching the cabin into darkness, and entered the bed beside her. He kissed her lightly on the lips. She returned the pressure firmly and wrapped her arms around his neck. He extricated himself. "No, Sylas," he whispered. "Not tonight. I'm weary. I feel as if I've never slept in my life."

She made no move to embrace him again.

"What you can do," he said, "you can do this for me." He raised her to a sitting position, then he lay back down so that she was leaning over him. He took her hands and he placed them softly on his face. "Like this. Lightly, just ever so lightly." He guided her hands in slow, circular stroking motions. "Yes. That's it. That's good. That's *so* good. Sylas used to do that. God, how I've missed it. So good. So very good, Sylas."

He fell asleep murmuring his pleasure.

Horneby, in the old days, had been a lusty man. His crews used to joke about him, claiming that by the time they reached home port the captain would have topped nearly a third of his female cargo. It was exaggeration, true, but not in the extreme. Then he found Sylas, a jet-black girl whose shyness and timidity had, on a night he was a little drunk and somewhat melancholic, stirred in him a certain gruff tenderness. The girl had been terrified, and she felt a consummate gratitude when he did not abuse her. He woke in the morning to find her staring at him with a gaze that was nearly worshipful.

Horneby was embarrassed, another fairly unique experience for him. He ignored her, dressed, left the cabin, and did not give her another thought during the whole of the day. When he returned to his quarters after mess, he was surprised to find her still there. He had, he realized, forgotten to order her taken back to the hold. She shared his bed a second night.

At first he thought it was simply a matter of convenience. She was there, she kept herself clean, she satisfied his body. It was easier than selecting and dealing with a new female each night. So he did not send her away, and he had time to discover in her that quality upon which he eventually became so strongly dependent. Sylas was a near-perfect emotional sounding board. She could register half-tones, quarter-tones, even eighths with an accuracy that verged on the supernatural. She was responsive to his every mood, complementary to and supportive of his satisfied moments, unintimidated and silently assuaging his darker states. She loved him, completely, selflessly.

And Horneby loved her, as much as he was capable of loving anyone, which was only to a moderate degree, and in a selfish way. Mostly it was a matter of need, accentuated by habit.

He killed her toward the end of their third year together. He was master of a Portuguese ship then, and had no American papers of registry. His ship had been only one day on the coast of Africa, was moored in a river mouth, not having loaded as yet a single slave, when a British warship entered the waters and signaled him to stand by for boarding. Horneby had nothing to prove that he had purchased Sylas in any legal market. She was therefore contraband,

and her discovery would mean a cold cell in some damp prison, or a noose.

Expressionless, Horneby watched the British lower two longboats. The sailors of His Majesty's Navy bent their backs, and varnished dripping oars glinted in the sunlight. When the longboats had covered half the distance, Horneby left the quarterdeck and went below. Sylas bathed him in her smile when he opened the door, and she came forward to put her hands on his shoulders. She saw his face and stopped. She looked at him intently several moments, then her entire body seemed to sag, and she lowered her head. Horneby walked stiffly to her, took her arm, and led her to the window. She waited, without moving, without looking at him, while he went to a locker, rummaged a moment, then returned carrying a length of chain.

Muted commands sifted down to them from above. The British were boarding.

Horneby looped the chain around Sylas's neck, trailed it down her torso, wound it twice around her waist, brought it lower and bound her ankles together, securing the free end with a loose but sufficient hitch. He gripped her strongly at the hips and lifted her up to the windowsill. His fingers dug into her upper arms. She raised her face. There was no reproach in it, nor terror, nor pleading . . . only immense and overwhelming sadness.

Horneby stared at her. He began to tremble violently.

He pushed.

Her head and torso vanished, her legs swung up and out . . . and below, there was a splash.

Horneby screamed and staggered back from the window. He stumbled against the night table by his bed, seized it, and smashed it against the bulkhead.

The first mate and the British officers found him wild-eyed and disheveled amid the wrecked furnishings of his quarters. He crouched when they entered, then curled his fingers into claws, and sprang at them with a ragged hideous cry. The first mate rushed to meet him, and the British officers moved to help. Horneby was overpowered and pinned to the floor. The ship's surgeon was sent for. The surgeon forced a strong sedative down the raging man's throat, then Horneby was lashed to his bed.

The British backed apologetically from the cabin, went abovedeck and deployed their men, conducted the search, then, having found no slaves, thanked the mate for his courtesy and departed.

Eight years ago.

But not eight years distant. Now, with the girl from ben-Ahmen's factory beside him, the captain thrashed in his sleep. He was dreaming of an empty window, beyond which the sky was a pale blue, marked by wheeling gulls. Out of sight, objects were splashing into the water, one by one. He saw himself twisting on the floor of his cabin, his bones liquefied, his body opened from breastbone to pudendum, the glistening red cavity empty. And he knew that it was his life, his organs, that were being thrown overboard.

"Sylas, Sylas!" he moaned.

The girl awakened, looked down at him curiously a moment, then stroked his face, his throat, and let her hands drift down to his shoulders where they began working and loosening the knotted muscles. Slowly Horneby quieted.

Ben-Ahmen's females were loaded early in the morning. Several times the captain, on the quarterdeck, became so abstracted that Meredith had to repeat questions to him.

Seamen scrambled aloft to loose canvas, sprinted down the deck hauling on the braces, and strained against the winch that raised the great bow anchor. Full sail was set, and the *Jubilation* slipped away from her anchorage under a cloud of canvas. The spires of ben-Ahmen's palace dropped slowly behind, and with them, Africa. The helmsman swung the ship west, and just a little north, toward the Bay Islands off Honduras, better than four thousand miles distant. The sailors were in good humor. There was much joking and mock roughhouse.

The bosun came loping up to Horneby. "Lookout reports sail on the larboard horizon, sir."

"Identification?"

"None, sir, only her mainmast visible yet."

"Sweep the lee horizon."

"Aye, sir."

Knye was gone a few minutes, then returned to inform Horneby that the lee was clear. Horneby dismissed the sail from his mind. Warships approaching from both sides might have been cause for concern, but pursuit from a single direction, assuming the ship was hostile, was not worth bothering about, not when it was a quarter-day's sail behind.

Gyase had helped him. For that Adoko would always be grateful, even if he lived, a mumbling, toothless old man, to see the children of his children's children.

But now Gyase could not meet his eyes. Was the man ashamed, had he repented his action? "Please," Adoko said to him over the corpse that lay between them. "It had to be done. For the family, Gyase."

Gyase said nothing. *Please* was a word members of the family used with one another out of politeness and respect. Not sprung from the desperate need which had caused Adoko to speak it. That kind of *please* was craven. And if I beg, Adoko thought, am I no longer Osai, am I no longer even a man?

"Gyase," he said angrily, "tell me what you are thinking."

"I am thinking nothing, Adoko."

"Is it that the family exists no more? That we are all destroyed?"

"You have said those words, Adoko, not I."

Adoko looked down at the contorted face of Kiuky. All the while they had been chained in this ship, the shore of their homeland had stood not far away, offering some solace, keeping tiny flickers of hope burning.

But this morning a slave near one of the ventilation ports had noticed the land drawing back, diminishing. Others pressed their faces to the small openings. Anxiety shot through the slave decks, and when, an hour later, the coast vanished, a great moaning went up in the holds, a sound so deep and anguished that it seemed the ship itself, some monstrous water-beast, had just foreseen its own death. There were screams and sobs, a rattling of chains, and dull thuds as heads were beaten in frenzied despair against the planking.

That is when Kiuky died; killing him was superfluous, simply an affirmation of his deeper death.

Kiuky pulled loose a piece of planking and withdrew the knife concealed there. His breath was whistling through his nose and mouth, and he ground his teeth fiercely together. Then he began to rage: He would kill the whites when they came to take the slaves up to be aired. Adoko tried to talk to him, to reason. It was only when Kiuky slashed out at him that he understood. He seized Kiuky's wrist. Even so, the blade opened a long, thin cut across Adoko's shoulder. Gyase grabbed Kiuky from behind. Adoko wrested the knife away. Kiuky began to scream.

"He will not become Kiuky again," Adoko said.

"No," Gyase agreed, "he will not."

"He is gone. What remains can do nothing but harm to itself and to our kinsman."

Gyase nodded.

They had strangled Kiuky.

But if there was no family?

"Please!" Adoko said. Not only to Gyase, but to all the Ashanti chained in the hold.

No one answered. And no one looked at his neighbor. Each was alone.

Adoko bit down on his knuckle. To prevent himself from screaming. As Kiuky had screamed.

There were two of them, and they were definitely in pursuit. The wind had slackened, but evidently to a lesser degree in the area of the pursuers. The lookout had reported the following ship as a barque, and soon after, he had called down the presence of a second, smaller, ship. It was impossible to discern what colors they flew.

There were only two possibilities: pirates or warships. Horneby suspected the latter. He had nothing to fear from the British, legally, but individual captains of His Majesty's African Squadron had been known on occasion, moved by zeal or fanaticism, to take into custody slavers protected by treaty. Though the slaver was eventually freed by the Prize Court in Sierra Leone, months could pass before litigation was settled, and the result was financially disastrous.

Horneby ordered the sails wetted down. The crew grumbled. This was an exhausting job. Men had to string themselves along the deck, up through the shrouds and rigging and across the spars, hanging, waiting for the buckets that were filled by the deck pumps to be passed hand by hand to them, then by them up to the next man, and from him even higher, until they could be sloshed onto the canvas. But the seamen were no more pleased by the prospect of being taken to Sierra Leone than was Horneby, so they set to work with only token murmurs of resentment. The initial dousing required the better part of an hour. It was a continuous process, though, for left alone, the canvas would dry in short order. Sodden, the sails were less porous and managed to get more driving power from the wind they trapped.

Two more knots were coaxed from the *Jubilation.*

The pursuers had neared to within two hours' time of the *Jubilation,* but this was the closest they would come. The wind would be slackening in their own sails any minute now.

The bosun took the stairs to the quarterdeck two at a time. There was agitation on his face. "Captain, lookout reports identification of colors. The barque is American and her companion is British! And the limey's a steamer, sir! The *Peregrine,* or one of her sisters."

Horneby set his jaw. "Thank you, Mr. Knye. Keep the men at it. We'll run through the night this way if we have to."

"Aye, sir."

Horneby recalled the young, angry Leftenant who commanded the *Peregrine.* This sort of tactic suited the man. Confronted by a British and an American warship simultaneously, there were no registry papers in the world that would protect a slaver. However, the game belonged to the *Jubilation.* The Leftenant would lose.

Knye informed him that the *Jubilation* had begun to widen the gap between her and the warships. Horneby nodded. It was as expected. The bosun returned fifteen minutes later to report that the steamer had reefed her sails and fired up her boilers. That, too, was expected, and would do the *Peregrine* little good. She was designed primarily for bay and river work, where maneuverability rather than speed counted. Her shallow draft made her skittish and difficult to handle on the open seas and prevented her from taking full advantage of that speed of which she *was* capable.

The *Jubilation* would leave her behind, and by nightfall, or the end of the next day, depending upon the Leftenant's determination, the *Peregrine*'s paddlewheels would grind to a halt and she would bob alone in the vast and empty sea while her commander brooded, and then finally she would turn her bow back to Africa.

Horneby's expectations were fulfilled throughout the early afternoon; the tapering trail of black smoke from the *Peregrine*'s stack dropped farther and farther behind. Knye appeared again and suggested, since there was no longer any danger of being overtaken, that the slaves be brought up on deck. It was his way of requesting that the seamen be allowed a respite after a grueling day's work. Horneby said no. He did not yet feel comfortable, and was willing to accept the handful of black bodies they would find the next morning as a price worth the guarantee of safety.

Then the wind failed.

The sails flapped, sighed, and drooped, and the *Jubilation* slowed, listed a bit to port, then came to a stop, gently rising and falling on waves that were broad and soft.

Work stopped on the deck and in the rigging. Men turned their heads toward the stern. A bowed column of smoke soiled the sky. The *Peregrine* was steaming on.

The Leftenant, Horneby knew, would be carrying authorization from the American captain to seize the *Jubilation* on his behalf if she presented United States registration. "Mr. Knye," the captain called, "secure your men."

The bosun shouted. The order was passed up through the shrouds and topmasts, and sailors came clambering and sliding to the deck.

Horneby summoned the mates. He instructed Randall to issue muskets, powder, and shot. Meredith was to have the gun pits prepared for action. He, Horneby, was going below. He wished to be notified when the steamer was within twenty minutes of them.

The girl was sitting on the floor of the cabin, absorbed by the colorful illustrations in the old book *Strange Lands and Strange People* he had given her this morning. It had been one of Sylas's favorites. She smiled when he entered. His fingers went to the buttons of his shirt. "They're not going to take you from me again," he said. "Not this time."

The *Jubilation*'s sails hung slack from the arms. Astern, the *Peregrine* was churning steadily forward, less than fifteen minutes away. Horneby addressed the crew from the quarterdeck:

"If this is done properly, we'll come through untouched. I don't want to see a single casualty, and I want not one piece of cargo damaged. The *Peregrine* carries only six cannon, but two of them are thirty-pounders, swivel-mounted on her deck. These are your primary targets. She also ships a complement of marines, whom we can assume to be proficient with muskets. These are your secondary targets. When the *Peregrine*'s cannon and marines have been eliminated, concentrate your own cannon fire on her waterline, and your musketry on any man still alive.

"With the exception of the gun crews, I want all hands on deck as she nears. And I want you looking miserable and dejected, as if you're seeing a prison cell as your home for the next few months. There is to be no show of defiance. Charged muskets will be left out of sight on the deck, and gun ports will remain closed until my signal. Once that is given, fire at will. To your stations, now!"

The seaman scattered under the direction of the mates and the bosun. Gun crews dropped into the cramped pits and readied their cannon. Muskets were loaded and primed and placed close at hand. Then the sailors leaned on the rails and watched the *Peregrine* approach.

"Jordan, you lout!" Mr. Knye shouted. "Wipe that grin off your mouth. You're going to prison, man. Prison! Remember that. That goes for you too, Smith. Christ, what a bunch of morons!"

The *Peregrine* was now a thousand yards astern, bow rising and dipping in the gentle swells, her twin wheels spinning a fine mist into the air that caught the sun in rainbow patterns. She altered course slightly and began to come abreast of the *Jubilation* to starboard. Black-hatted marines in bright blue and red uniforms lined her rail. Sailors manned her deck guns. Her two longboats had already been swung out on their davits, and crewmen were ready to lower them. The Leftenant stood by his helmsman, directing. His face contained only a faint trace of triumph. The paddle-wheels slowed, the *Peregrine* overtook the *Jubilation*, the wheels stopped, reversed their motion, stopped again, and the warship bobbed, stationary, a little less than a hundred yards from the slaver.

Horneby admired the young officer's seamanship.

The Leftenant put a megaphone to his mouth. "Ahoy, the *Jubilation!* Stand by to receive a boarding party. Clear the area around your carronade. At the first sign of resistance, you will be fired upon."

Horneby cupped his hands and shouted back. "Come ahead, you sonofabitch! You know there's nothing we can do!" Then he folded his arms and turned his back.

"They're lowering the boats and loading," said Meredith, who was close to the captain. "Ten marines in each boat. Maybe a dozen left on the ship. Their gun crews are relaxing a bit."

"Tell me when the boats are thirty yards off."

"Pulling away now. That Leftenant is in the first one. Bastard's got his foot planted on the bow like Lord Nelson." Meredith spat. "Eighty yards . . . sixty . . . forty . . . thirty."

Horneby turned. "Open gun ports and commence firing, Mr. Meredith."

"Ports and fire!" Meredith bellowed.

The four ports on the *Jubilation*'s starboard side were cranked up. The *Peregrine*'s gun crews stared dumbly, either failing to understand that the slaver carried cannon, or too startled to react. Then one of the thirty-pounders was brought to bear. The lanyard was yanked, smoke and flame gouted, the ship heeled up on its side . . . and first blood belonged to the *Peregrine*. But it was the blood of slaves; the huge ball had struck to the side of its mark, ripping into one of the slave decks. An eight-pounder fired aboard the *Jubilation* before its port was fully open. The wooden panel exploded into splinters. The ball smashed into the decking at the base of one of the *Peregrine*'s thirty-pounders, and the gun crashed over on its side. Knye screamed orders. Musket fire cut down the crew of the second thirty-pounder. Seamen leaped to the carronade, whose usual load of junk metal had been replaced with a solid ball. Two of them were killed by the *Peregrine*'s marines, and were quickly replaced by other men. A shot from the warship wiped out one of the slaver's gun pits. An answering roar brought down the *Peregrine*'s foremast. Smoke hung thickly between the two vessels. A wild shot from the British punched a large, neat hole through a sail. The carronade thundered its Olympian rage. The thirty-four-pound ball smashed through the iron plating of the *Peregrine*'s boiler. The boiler exploded. Broken men, twisted metal, and torn planking were hurled into the air in the midst of hot, white steam. The *Peregrine* listed heavily to starboard.

The sailors of the *Jubilation* shouted their victory.

When the first cannon had fired, the British Leftenant had ordered the longboats' oars shipped. Still some twenty-five yards from the slaver, the marines were firing up at the seamen. The concussion wave from the bursting boiler had rocked their boats and spilled a few of them into the water, but most had recovered their balance and were maintaining fire. With the *Peregrine* herself out of action the *Jubilation*'s crew turned to the marines in the boat, and the first volley reduced the British by half.

Horneby removed a pistol from his waistband, laid one arm along the rail, and rested the barrel on this arm. He brought his sights to bear on the Leftenant. The officer's face was anguished. His eyes met Horneby's. The anguish was replaced by defiance. The young man drew his sword and raised it, as if about to signal a charge.

Gestures are for literature, Horneby thought, *they have no real meaning.*

Then he shot the Leftenant through the head.

Three balls from the carronade were put into the *Peregrine* just below her waterline. She went down bow first, stern rising momentarily into the air, then slipped beneath the surface, water boiling and churning, forming into a small whirlpool which spun itself out over the span of a few minutes. Horneby wanted no survivors. A boat was lowered to prowl among the wreckage. Only two of the British were found alive, both wounded; they were quickly dispatched.

The sun was setting, and there was still no sign of wind or breeze. Casualties were reported to the captain. Nine seamen had been killed. The *Peregrine*'s first shot had crushed and jellied thirteen slaves. While the dead seamen were stitched into canvas, a work gang hauled up the broken black bodies and pitched them over the side. The crew was assembled for a brief twilight service. The corpses of the sailors were committed to the deep. Horneby congratulated his command, ordered a token watch, and relieved the rest of further duties until dawn. Also, he promised them a homeward-bound party at the end of the first full day's sail.

The wind freshened at three bells that morning. The sails

began to billow and swing, ghostlike in the heavily starred night, then snapped and finally filled. Lines tautened, timbers creaked, and the *Jubilation* moved sluggishly forward. The captain had left orders that he was not to be disturbed. The watch awakened Meredith and Knye. Meredith set the course while the bosun roused the crew. Quarter and studding sails and skysails were reset. The *Jubilation* plunged cleanly and easily through the heightening rollers.

As if to compensate for its previous absence, the wind blew strongly and steadily through the day, driving the ship hard. The *Jubilation* cleaved the froth-tipped sea with an easy, rhythmic pitch. She performed best in open waters, and now she seemed like a sleek racing horse too long penned, joyously stretching out its stiff body on a hard-packed time course. The land-raised slaves who had been brought up to air on deck were sick almost to the man, and work gangs were kept busy sloshing off their spewed vomit from the planking.

Horneby appeared only once, briefly, in the late afternoon, found everything to his satisfaction, and returned to his cabin. The slaves were put belowdecks at the end of the day, all canvas but the mainsails was furled, enabling the ship to be handled by no more than a handful of men, then evening mess was served, following which the alcohol was broken out. There were five barrels of rum, five of beer, and two cases of whisky that Horneby had contributed to the celebration. The restriction concerning the number of females who could be brought on deck at any given time was removed. The seamen were cautioned that whatever their state the next morning, they were expected to be at their duties. Darkness blanketed the ship, and lanterns were lit. It was an uninspired debauch—common drunkenness, brawling, and sexuality; the scale was larger, that was all.

Dunbar drank sparingly. He would have liked to have

Li-yana with him. He had become obsessed with the need to communicate to her the fact that soon she would be free, and would, no matter what the cost, be returned to her home. He was convinced she understood nothing of what he had tried to tell her. To try once again, though, was not the reason he wished her with him this night. He was surrounded by human beings who were either victims or victimizers, and he needed something to blunt that reality. But he couldn't bring her out of the foc's'le. He would not subject her to the sight of what was being done to her black sisters, and, too, he had serious doubts as to whether or not the drunken sailors would respect his rights of property.

It was impossible on deck to avoid the others, so, when he could stand the roistering no longer, he went down the hatchway into the food larder behind the galley, dumped a couple of grain sacks on the floor, and stretched out atop them. He couldn't find a comfortable position, and he rolled and twisted for some time, dozing fitfully, then snapping awake with little twitches, his muscles aching, touching the back of his hand to his forehead thinking he was feverish, trying to ignore the sounds above him, and finally, hours later, falling into a troubled sleep.

Half the sailors drank themselves comatose before midnight. The rest staggered about the deck, singing, shouting exuberant obscenities at each other, colliding with their fellows, and working the black girls relentlessly, trying to push their alcohol-dulled senses into one more fleeting moment of sensation. A Portuguese seaman set to chasing another man with a handspike. There was no anger—it just made such good fun roaring and stumbling around. But the Portuguese slipped, and when he fell, the handspike tore through the fleshy part of his thigh. He sat there, grinning foolishly, then saw the sharp bloodied point sticking through his torn pants, and let out a great bellow. His comrades gathered and held a slurred caucus. Mr. Petersen, drunk, could not be awakened. Therefore, they must summon Mr. Wilkes. Wilkes had kept to his cabin since he'd returned from ben-Ahmen's palace. He had appeared on deck only once, after the battle with the *Peregrine,* ravaged and despondent. He had patched up the wounded men with a detached air, and had spoken to no one.

Koenig was sent lumbering aft to fetch the surgeon. Wilkes, in a nightshirt and carrying his bag, returned with the Dutchman, who had picked up a lantern and was swinging it jauntily in time to some song he was trying to sing. Wilkes knelt, glanced at the wound, and opened his bag. He took out a scalpel. Meredith, in the front rank of the onlooker, said, "Have to cut the leg off, eh, doctor?"

The injured seaman screamed and tried to scuttle away. Meredith and another man shoved him back. "Oh, it don't hurt all that much," Meredith said. "Come on, now, we'll carve you a new one out of a barrel stave."

The Portuguese shook his head and wailed. Wilkes cut open the man's trousers, reached under the thigh to the butt of the spike and pulled it free with a quick yank. The Portuguese looked down and began to laugh. He pointed to the wound and to the cast-aside spike, and beamed proudly at his fellows. Wilkes unstoppered a bottle and sprinkled powder liberally on both openings of the ugly puncture. Then he wrapped a bandage twice around the thigh and knotted it tightly. He returned the bottle and the scalpel to his bag.

"Have a drink, Mr. Wilkes." A seaman thrust out a bottle.

Wilkes pushed it aside, stood, and turned to go.

Another sailor laid a long, strong arm over the surgeon's shoulders. "Aww, come on."

"Goin' home," a third said. "Gotta have a drink for goin' home."

The surgeon hesitated. His self-imposed isolation and the memories of the four little girls he had helped sell into slavery had taken a heavy toll. He was not a man meant for solitude or introspection. He desperately needed fellowship, drunken loud fellowship, but he had worked himself into such a state that he could not make the first move, he had to have an excuse.

The bottle was proffered again. "Here!"

"Well . . . all right." Wilkes took a deep swallow, then rubbed the back of his hand across his lips. "Ahh! To going home, then." He drank again.

"That's the way, doc. Come along."

The surgeon allowed himself to be led forward, where those who still possessed some degree of consciousness were reveling as best their drunkenness would permit. He was well greeted. Someone threw him an unopened bottle, which he barely managed to catch. He hiked his nightshirt over his knees and sat down cross-legged. He clamped his molars around the cork, twisted it free, then spat it a good eight feet. The seamen nearest him cheered. Wilkes upended the bottle and swallowed deeply.

An hour later he was drunk, in excellent spirits, and unable to understand how he had allowed himself to wallow about in such a fetid sinkhole of depression. Only a handful of sailors had not yet succumbed to the lateness of the hour and the alcohol. Wilkes was sitting in the center of them, his tongue tripping over words as he regaled them with funny anecdotes and extended jokes. The men were, to his great gratification, laughing hilariously. The surgeon experienced a strong sense of camaraderie and even, yes, that too, even love. It was overpowering. Tears brimmed in his eyes.

"My friends," he said. "My gu'n'wonn, my good and wonderful friends." He became careful of his words and enunciated with elaborate precision. "A little quiet, please, my fast and true comrades. Thank you. There is something I wish to tell you, which, because of our closeness at this moment, may well, no, will certainly have overtones of sadness. However, I know you will share with me the deeper joy therein contained."

Heads nodded solemnly. "Hear! Hear!" someone shouted.

Wilkes held up his hands. "Gentlemen, this is the final voyage of John Wilkes, Surgeon. When we reach port, I will debark, and never will I sail the white-capped seas again."

"No!"

"I don't believe it!"

"God, what'll we do without you?"

They shook their heads and shouted protests, like children in a school play recognizing and responding to a cue, pleased with their astuteness, attempting to outdo each other.

Meredith, who had begun to sulk earlier and had drawn off a little way to drink alone, shouted, "Hooray!"

No one paid him any attention.

"Yes, yes, it's true, good friends."

"But what are you going to do?"

"Oh, I'll be busy enough watching over my business interests at home, but mostly I will bask in the warmth of my daughters' company."

"Alice and Alicia," a seaman said sagely. There was barely a man aboard to whom Wilkes had not, at one time or another, spoken of his daughters.

"Just so," the surgeon said. "They're growing up now. They need their father to guide them properly into womanhood. And I confess that this old surgeon will find incalculable pleasure in loving and caring for them."

"Christ!" A sailor blew his nose into his hand, then wiped his palm on his pants. "It's wonnerful, it's just goddamn bloody wonnerful."

"Makes a man go all soft inside," said another.

Wilkes drew out his locket and opened it. The seamen pressed in to tell him how beautiful the girls were and how lucky he was.

Meredith stalked over. "What the fucking hell!" he snarled. "This is the biggest bunch of shit I've ever seen."

"Kindly remove yourself and your Philistine soul to some other place," Wilkes said.

The seamen shifted with embarrassment.

"You men just going to sit there and let this fat old wreck make fools outta you?"

"Come on, Mr. Meredith. Doc's a nice guy, let him be."

"What you mean, fools?" Santiago asked.

"His daughters. His goddamn daughters. That's what I mean."

"You're not fit even to speak their names," Wilkes hissed.

"Why, their ghosts gonna haunt me if I do?"

Wilkes gasped. The color drained from his face. A seaman screwed up his face. "Ghosts? Whose ghosts?"

"He doesn't have any daughters, you jackasses. They're dead, been dead ten years!"

"Wh—what are you saying?" Wilkes rose to his feet.

"They were killed in a hurricane," Meredith said to the bewildered sailors. "Remember that big blow down in Nicaragua and Honduras? The one that took down better than a dozen ships? Well, it hit that little island where his house was, and flattened it out just like some giant stomping with a seaboot."

"Shutup," Wilkes said hoarsely. *"Shutup!"*

Meredith laughed. "Smashed his precious little Alice and Alicia like bugs."

"That's not true, not true!" Wilkes shouted.

"I was there," Meredith said. "I saw them, mates, and they were dead as dead ever was. Hell, there was hardly enough left to bury."

"That's a lie," Wilkes screamed. "A horrid, filthy lie!"

"Old Wilkes here is trying to make you as crazy as he is."

"They're alive! Goddamn it, I tell you they're alive. They're not dead!" He lunged for Meredith.

The mate fended him off easily. "They're dead, you lunatic. They're dead and—" He ripped the locket from around the surgeon's neck and hurled it over the side into the blackness and sea. "—they're gone!"

"Alice!" Wilkes shrieked. *"Alicia!"* He stumbled to the rail. He was halfway over it before two sailors dragged him back. "Let me go," Wilkes sobbed. "Let me go. They'll drown. I've got to save them. Please."

"It's all right, Mr. Wilkes," one of the seamen mumbled. "They're all right. That was just the locket."

"You don't understand. I've got to save them. I can't let them die. They'll drown."

"They're home. They're not here, Mr. Wilkes. We're on the ship."

The surgeon calmed. "That's right," he said slowly. "They're home. They are, you know. They're probably asleep now, and dreaming about me."

"Uh-huh."

The sailors were staring at him. Wilkes began backing away. "They're fourteen years old," he said. "It's their birthday next month. They'll be fifteen. I have to buy them something. They'd be very upset if they thought I forgot. A father should remember his daughters' birthdays . . ."

He turned and vanished into the night.

"You shouldn't ought to've done that," a sailor said to Meredith.

"Bastard's had it coming a long time," the mate said sourly.

At dawn the watch discovered John Wilkes hanging from the main yard of the mizzenmast.

Horneby was roused. He stood beneath the surgeon, who was turning in the breeze, nightshirt flapping about stiffened legs. Death had made Wilkes old. Gray flesh sagged and drooped. It was a body that had exhausted itself. Horneby looked away. Wilkes and he had been contemporaries. The captain wondered: When his own muscles were slack with sleep, is that what Sylas saw, an old worn-out man? "Cut him down," Horneby said.

They buried Wilkes at noon. Most of the crew were baffled; a few had blurry and disquieting memories of having been with Wilkes and having witnessed something . . . strange. But they couldn't focus these shadows very well, and, anyway, they had no reason to try very hard; in an hour or two the surgeon was put out of mind.

Dunbar was carried into the dead man's room, and given quinine by Mr. Petersen. The cook had found the journalist moaning in the storehold, face scarlet, lips swollen. There was another seaman also delirious with fever, and they put him in with Dunbar. A third was stricken in the late afternoon. Petersen was angry, and he cursed Wilkes. The newly appointed Chief Surgeon could do nothing to bring the fevers down. Worried by Horneby's warning not to let the infection spread to the cargo, he railed at the dead man's image, as if Wilkes had purposefully and cruelly abandoned him. Isolation of the sick men was the best Petersen could do. He hoped it was enough.

Dunbar burned, sometimes comatose, sometimes raving, for three days. It was on the second night that O'Brien got to Leana.

Several of the crew had hidden away bottles brought aboard from ben-Ahmen's, and more had been stolen from the captain's bounty and secreted the night of the party. One man, drunk in the early morning, had already fallen from the rigging to his death. The crew waited for admonishments from Horneby. None came. The captain, who was rarely seen now on deck, did not seem concerned. And if the captain did not care, then the mates were not going to work themselves into a lather. It came to be understood that so long as the necessary duties were performed, then nothing was going to be said about the drinking.

O'Brien, Crawford, and Renner were half-drunk, on Renner's whisky, by nine bells. They had cut cards to see who would supply the bottle. Crawford stacked the deck awkwardly, but Renner, who was not very perceptive even at the best of moments, did not notice, and so, wondering why it was that he never seemed to win when he gambled, he went off to dig out a bottle from the dirty clothes in his seabag. O'Brien and the little Englishman took him for a second bottle, but when that was finished, he refused to risk a third, complaining he only had one left.

"Well, what'll it be, then?" Crawford said.

Renner rubbed his loins. "How 'bout a little pussy?"

O'Brien waved his hand. "They're all beginnin' to look the same these days, and about as lovely and excitin' as a puff-fish."

"Try one of the bucks' cornholes, why don't you?" Crawford suggested.

"Is it a cesspool cock like yours you think I have?"

Crawford chortled. "Gives me twice as many holes to plug, matey."

O'Brien tipped one of the empty bottles. A single amber drop slipped from it. He made a sound of disgust and threw it overboard, then lay back on the deck and cupped his hands beneath his head. After several moments he sat up and snapped his fingers. "Aha! There's Dunbar's wench. Now there might be some sport."

"I think maybe he wouldn't like that," Renner said dubiously.

O'Brien cuffed Renner on the shoulder. "Now what's there to object to in a little simple wick-dipping, eh, laddie?"

"Got to sneak her by Randall," Crawford said.

"That's simple enough. I'll get her, and when I'm bringin' her through the door, you divert the good and true mate."

They formulated a plan. O'Brien rose and went swaying off to the fo'c'sle. Randall unlocked the door and let him in. Renner and Crawford were crouching in the shadows several yards away. When they saw O'Brien's lantern emerging, Renner sprang up and ran forward. Crawford shouted, "I'll cut your heart out, you damned blackguard!" Knife in hand, he went after Renner.

"It's mine, it's mine," Renner yelled. He skidded to a halt next to Randall and thumped the mate on the shoulder. "Tell him it's mine, sir!"

"Here, now, what's going on?" Randall said crossly.

Crawford came up and menaced Renner with his knife. "You thievin' scum!"

O'Brien passed through the fo'c'sle door, arm tight around a black girl. "Thanks, Mr. Randall," he said, and walked quickly away.

"He stole my silver belt buckle, he did," Crafword said.

"Did not, it's mine."

"Crawford, put that knife away," Randall said. "That's better. Now, can you prove it's yours?"

"Sure, got my initials on the back."

Randall took the buckle from Renner and examined it. "No initials of any kind here."

"Huh?" Crawford craned his neck and peered. "I'll be damned. Sorry, matey."

"I told you so," Renner muttered, carried away. "I sonofabitching well told you so."

"Right. Well, come on, I'll spot you to a bit of a drop." He took Renner's arm. Sulkily, the other man allowed himself to be led away.

"Told you so," Renner muttered.

"Belay that, you idiot. We've done it. O'Brien's got her over by the tar barrel."

"O'Brien?" Renner frowned. Then recollection brightened his face. "Oh."

The Irishman had the girl's arms clamped behind her back. She was grimacing. Blood trickled from two long cuts on O'Brien's face. "She's a hellion, she is. I told you she'd be sport enough for us all. Tried with all her pretty little might to take my eye out. Oh, toppin' you, my darlin' girl, is goin' to be one great pleasure for Jamey O'Brien."

Renner loosened his pants and let them fall around his ankles.

"Right after me, boyo," O'Brien said to him. "But we're going to do it right or not at all. Bleed off some rope from that coil and hand me the end."

"We can hold her well enough," Crawford said.

"It's not for holdin' I'm wantin' it. We're going to wash this nigger shit and animal stink off her with sea water."

"O'Brien, you've a touch of the poet in you." Crawford brought the rope.

Renner giggled and clapped his hands. While O'Brien was fashioning a harness around the struggling girl, Crawford reached out and gave Renner's stiff organ a playful caress. Renner slapped the old man's hand. "Now, stop that!"

Crawford smirked, exposing yellowed stumpish teeth. "In the dark, you wouldn't know the difference."

"Give me a hand, boys," O'Brien said. "Over the side with her."

Leana bit and clawed as they lifted her. "Let her loose," O'Brien said. He played the rope through his hands. Leana descended, bumping and scraping against the side of the ship. O'Brien brought her snub, her feet dangling a little above the foaming water. He held her there a moment, then abruptly let several feet of rope slide free. The girl plunged beneath the surface.

"We baptize you in the name of the Father, the Son, and the Holy Ghost," Crawford said solemnly.

Renner broke into peals of laughter. He pounded his fists on the bulwark.

O'Brien caught the rope up; it tightened, slanting astern, and Leana was yanked to the surface. She twisted and grabbed at the line. The Irishman bounced and skipped her.

"Careful," Crawford said, "you don't want to drown her."

Renner pointed, jumped up and down, and went: "Ah! Ah! Ah!"

"What's the matter with you?" O'Brien said.

Crawford followed the direction of Renner's arm and said, "Shark!"

A long, dark shape was slashing through the water toward the girl. O'Brien strained at the line. Leana was pulled forward, her torso rose into the air . . . then she was out of the water, and O'Brien was hauling her up hand over hand. "Got her!"

The shark knifed up through the foam, glistening slickly in the moonlight. It touched the girl, then fell back with a heavy splash.

Leana screamed.

When they dragged her over the rail, she fell and lay on her back. Her left leg ended at the knee. Blood ran darkly across the planking.

O'Brien stroked his jaw. "Well, now. Darlin's, it looks like we've just bought ourselves a slave."

Crawford kicked at nothing. "Shit! There goes a nice piece of pay."

"Can I have her?" Renner said.

The girl groaned at their feet.

"For what?" Crawford said. "She's half dead."

"But there ain't nothin' wrong with her pussy."

O'Brien clapped Renner on the back. "You're right, lad. By all the saints, you surely are. My own dear mother, rest her soul, used to say, 'Jamey, there's nothin' so bad that some good can't be found in it.' And she was right. Press her shoulders down there, Renner, my boy."

Renner pinned the girl. O'Brien knelt between her legs, shoved his pants down and, after a few moments of effort, managed to force himself into her. There were bubbles of spittle on Leana's lips. Her hands clutched at the air. She thrashed wildly, and her stump beat against the planking and against the Irishman, streaking him with blood.

"Duhbar," she moaned. "Duhbar . . . Duhbar . . ."

O'Brien finished and exchanged places with Renner.

Randall walked by, several paces away. He glanced at them and went on.

Leana screamed.

Randall turned back. "What are you doing to that girl?" When he was near enough to see, he said, "Oh my God!" rushed forward and yanked at Renner's shoulders.

"Lemme alone!" Renner cried. "I ain't done yet."

Randall threw him off. "Christ, you stupid animals, that's the one that belongs to Dunbar."

"Goddamn, goddamn," Renner mumbled. He hunched over, masturbating.

"What?" said O'Brien.

"She's the girl Dunbar bought." Randall was pale with anger. "What did you do to her?"

"We were washing her over the side," O'Brien said. "Shark hit her. Thought as long as we were goin' to have to pay for her, might as well get some use out of her. You sure she's Dunbar's?"

"I'm sure, you Irish moron."

O'Brien scratched his head. "Huh! Couldn't've proved it by me. Why didn't you stop me when I brought her out?"

Randall glared at him. "You," he said to Crawford. "Go fetch Mr. Petersen."

"What for? She's near dead now. Might just as well heave her over the side and let that shark finish up."

"Go on!" Randall swung with a knotted length of rope, and Crawford went scuttling away.

"Dunbar's," O'Brien said meditatively. "Doesn't that beat all."

Renner uttered a rapid series of grunts, and then he sighed.

Randall paced back and forth until Crawford returned with Petersen. The surgeon looked and said, "Put her overboard."

"No," Randall said peevishly. "We can't. She's Dunbar's. She's private property. I don't have the authority to get rid of her, and I'll be damned if I'm going to wake the captain. Do what you can."

"It's a waste of time," Petersen grumbled. He ordered a bucket of embers brought from the galley, and a piece of flat iron. Leana was no longer conscious. Petersen heated one end of the metal until it was a shimmering red, then, with several thicknesses of canvas wrapped around the other end, he removed it from the coals and seared the raw stump closed. Leana shrieked. There was a thick odor of burning meat. Petersen wrapped a wide bandage around the wound and said, "That's it. Put her someplace where that bandage will stay clean."

"Sure," Randall said. "In the ballroom."

"Well, shove her in a corner that's not a dungheap at least. Not that I think she's going to last very long, anyway."

Five sailors were stricken with the fever. Two died. None of the slaves were infected. Dunbar's head cleared at the end of the third day. He had lost weight, and he was weak. He remained in Wilkes's cabin another two days, being fed thick broths and dark bread, then portions of meat that grew progressively larger. No one said anything to him of Leana.

When he emerged on deck, the sunlight was painful, and he had to shield his eyes. His gait was unsteady. Mr. Knye did not order him aloft. Working cut away the bed weariness and the stiffness, and he felt increasingly better as the day progressed. He noticed that men paused a few times to look at him curiously, but he didn't think much about it. He ate with a ravenous appetite that evening, and then he went to the fo'c'sle. "Evening, Mr. Randall."

The mate pursed his lips.

"You want to open up and let me in?"

"Uh, Dunbar, have you spoken to anybody?"

"What do you mean?"

"Well, it's about your slave."

"Open the door."

"Just a minute. I want to—"

Dunbar grabbed the mate by the shoulders. "Open the door, Randall!"

"Easy, lad." Randall turned the key in the lock and followed Dunbar down the narrow passageway.

The journalist held the lantern high over his head. "Where is she? I don't see her. What have you done with her!"

"Over in the corner there."

"Oh, Christ." Dunbar moved forward. "Li-yana, Li-yana. Why is she chained?" he demanded.

There were manacles about the girl's wrists and one around her right ankle. The bandage on her stump was soiled and brown in places, with a crust of dried blood. The orange flame of the lantern flickered in her eyes. There was no recognition in her face, only suspicion.

"Careful," Randall warned.

Dunbar reached out to her gently.

Leana went for his eyes. He caught her. Screeching, she slashed open his cheek with the rough edge of one of her wrist irons. She bit him on the back of the hand. Randall grabbed the girl, shoved her back, and lashed her with a leather strap. "Stay back there!"

Dunbar yanked the strap from the mate's hand. "Don't do that!"

The girl smiled. There was a thread of blood from Dunbar's hand on her lip. She licked it and made a sound somewhere between a purr and a growl.

Dunbar stared in silence several moments, then allowed Randall to lead him away. On deck the mate told him what had happened.

"What was done to them?"

"Oh, they paid, all right. Don't you worry about that. Captain's got them each down for a third of her price. You don't owe anything for her. If she lives—and it looks like she might—she's still yours, though there's probably not much you can do with a one-legged nigger girl. And yesterday they was given ten lashes each."

"O'Brien, Crawford, and Renner," Dunbar said. He moved his eyes slowly around the deck and up into the rigging.

"Wait a minute. You got a right to be upset. Nobody's saying you don't. But it's all been taken care of already. If

H

you're thinking of causing trouble, don't. It'll just fall hard on you."

Dunbar walked away. He found O'Brien with two other men, stoning the rust from a heavy chain and slicking the iron down with oil. The Irishman watched Dunbar approach, tugged his beard a moment, then stood and flexed his broad shoulders. His companions sat back on their haunches to watch. Dunbar stopped, face empty of expression. O'Brien folded his arms. "Well?"

Dunbar did not respond.

"Look, boyo, if it's an apology you're wantin', then okay. Jamey O'Brien is not above apologizin'. It was an accident, was all. And I earned a whip-cut back and a loss of pay for it. But if you'd of shared the little black bitch around in the beginning—"

"O'Brien," Dunbar said evenly, "I'm going to kill you." He turned and started aft.

O'Brien stood looking after him, surprised. One of the seamen laughed. "So that's how it is, Jamey. You're a marked man."

"The devil's ass, you say!" O'Brien roared. He raced after Dunbar, caught him, and threw him to the deck. His huge hands knuckled into fists. "Nobody threatens Jamey O'Brien like that! *Nobody*. Try it again, or even so much as look at me the wrong way, and I swear by the pox-ridden Virgin I'll break you in half and feed you to the fish!"

Fear burst upon Dunbar like a hurtling savage bird, rupturing his anger. O'Brien could break him in half. Effortlessly. And would if he thought Dunbar a threat, or if he felt it was expected of him by the rest of the crew. The journalist's spirit, which had seemed a moment ago so indomitable, so blood-hungry and full of righteous vengeance, collapsed upon itself. He closed his eyes in shame and turned his head to the side.

"That's better," O'Brien said. "Much better." He kicked Dunbar in the side.

The Irishman was gone when Dunbar opened his eyes. Many slaves had clustered around him, though not so close that he could strike them. They smiled and they laughed; they loved to see white men beat each other.

Help me, Dunbar thought. *Help me. Please. You don't understand.*

He sat up. The slaves moved back.

A few sailors were watching. too, some smiling. Crawword was peering down from the mainmast shrouds trying to decide whether or not the journalist's submission had been subterfuge (as would certainly have been the case with Crawford). If not, then he needn't worry about Dunbar; if so, he would be prudently cautious around the man. The wrinkled Englishman had not survived all his years on the slave lanes by blind luck. Crawford decided he had nothing to fear. He grinned at Dunbar.

The journalist saw Renner once that night, and only twice the next day. Brief glimpses. Renner was trying hard to avoid him.

Dunbar's anger bloomed again and focused on Renner, because Renner seemed the only one to be afraid of him. Dunbar did not like himself, but neither could he help himself.

The pleasure that flushed through Hollister when T'Komo said *I am a slave* remained with him through the afternoon. But in the evening he went on deck when the slaves were being slopped and was stunned as T'Komo, catching sight of him, drew himself proudly to his full height, hurled his bowl of slabber sauce toward the young man and shouted, "You are spawn of a goat and pig!"

"Bring him here. Right now!" Hollister ordered. He had

no official status aboard the ship, but defiance provoked in the seamen an instant will to punish, and they appreciated Hollister's quick reaction. Two sailors seized T'Komo and wrestled him forward. Hollister trembled. "You are a slave, T'Komo. Remember? You said so yourself. And slaves do not act in this manner."

"I am no slave." One of the sailors wrenched the black man's arm behind his back, and he grunted.

"Oh, yes, you are! T'Komo, I want you to kiss my feet."

"You kill me first," T'Komo said.

"I hardly think that's necessary. Now, kneel down and kiss."

"Never!"

"Gentlemen, would you be so kind as to bend him, please?"

The sailors applied pressure. T'Komo strained against them. Sweat beaded and sheened his skin, but slowly he was forced to his knees.

"Very good. Kiss, T'Komo, kiss."

"Get children on your mother, white scum!"

Hollister shook his head. "You sadden me deeply." His voice was steady, but his bladder was threatening to empty itself. "Gentlemen, lower his head, please."

A sailor put his knee on T'Komo's neck and bore down. T'Komo stiffened his arms and resisted. The other seaman kicked the black man's wrist. T'Komo collapsed, face mashing into Hollister's boot. "Wonderful," the young man said. He nodded to the seamen. "That will be fine, thank you."

They pulled T'Komo to his feet and shoved him back toward the watching slaves. He staggered several paces and fell. He stared at Hollister with pure hatred.

The youth returned to his cabin greatly unsettled. He had won, yes, but it was an artificial victory—as had been, he now realized, his first encounter with T'Komo. The man had obeyed then only to have his life. This time he had been defeated by brute force. He pondered on this. He had given T'Komo resolve, he had given him the contest, and pride. Not the posturing arrogance of fops and fools, but real pride, buttressed by hate. And now the man would rather die than lose it.

Power, Horneby had said. Yes, well, Hollister had the power. But it was technical and inferior power. You could win by playing on fear or by bringing superior force to bear. But if the fear should be overcome, or the force countered by greater force, then what power did you have? None. The only sure power was total—power freely and mutually validated by the one who exercised it and the one upon whom it was exercised. Not even the *possibility* of refusal should occur to the lesser party.

Hollister wanted that power.

He had heard of plantation owners who used black children as foot warmers during the winter months. That seemed an admirable way to begin. Since Horneby was rarely seen on deck these days, Hollister obtained permission from Meredith to have T'Komo chained in his quarters. The mate had not forgotten T'Komo's insults and was content to see the High Minister humiliated. Meredith sniggered, implying that Hollister wanted the black for a spot of buggery. Hollister turned the idea around, but decided against it, partially because his tastes did not run in this direction, but mostly because he felt that T'Komo would not consider it a sufficient indignity. It would be, therefore, pretty much a waste of time.

He paid the ship's carpenter to sink a ringbolt into the floor on either side of the end of his bed. Then he had T'Komo brought down and stretched across the bed on his back, wrists and ankles chained to the bolts. It was an uncomfortable position. It would become, in a little time, an intolerable one.

Hollister told him pleasantly and without malice, "I am your master. You will do what I say, and you will be happy doing it."

He said nothing else, not one word, recalling, from childhood, the effectiveness of silence. And, as a matter of course, he gave T'Komo no food. He slept soundly and well that night, feet pressed into T'Komo's side. In the morning he woke, stretched pleasurably, yawned, and got out of bed. T'Komo watched him strip off his nightshirt and pour water from a pitcher into a bowl, splash his face, chest, and arms. He brushed his hair. Humming, he walked around the bed, urinated on T'Komo's face, turned, half crouched, and voided his bowels on the black man. He dressed and left the cabin.

It was, in the end, fairly simple, a matter of time and logical progression. On the second day he began taking his meals in the cabin, sitting close to T'Komo so the black man could see and smell the food, eating slowly and with exaggerated relish. He offered T'Komo a little water. He did not want to kill the man, just come close to it. The slave, keeping his silence as well as Hollister kept his own, pressed his lips together and refused.

Two days later he accepted. Just a single swallow, though, as if he resented his need to take even this much. Hollister replaced the flagon and took a scarf from his sea-chest, then knelt and wound the scarf around T'Komo's neck. He gripped the ends tightly . . . and began to pull.

T'Komo lay perfectly quiet the first few moments. But his body overwhelmed his will, and soon he was twisting and choking, lips swelling, tongue protruding, his eyes distending. He lost consciousness. Hollister relaxed the scarf.

T'Komo revived slowly. He coughed and gagged. Hollister waited, looking down affably, then took hold of the scarf again. Alternately, he strangled T'Komo, then allowed him to struggle back to his senses, for nearly an hour.

After four days of starvation, soiling, and strangulation, he added the pin. It was long and sharp and tipped at one end with a pearl. It had been his mother's. He used it beneath T'Komo's fingernails, in his armpits, around his nipples, in his testicles, the channel of his penis, and in the tender pink skin of the anus and rectum. The black man broke his silence—shrilly. The first session left him sobbing uncontrollably, and Hollister was well pleased.

The next night he said, "T'Komo, really, I'm becoming very worried about you. You must eat a little something." He had brought meat and cheese and hot biscuits and a mug of ale.

He freed T'Komo's wrists and helped him to sit, speaking solicitously. T'Komo moaned. His lips were dry and cracked, his eyes dazed. His body, allowed barely any movement by the tight chains, had stiffened. He could do little more than turn his head. He whimpered when Hollister raised him. He could not feed himself, so Hollister placed the food into his mouth. He began to slobber, and he swallowed wolfishly, hardly bothering to chew. When he had finished half the plate, Hollister said, "No, no more. We have to build you up slowly. It's too rich for your system now."

T'Komo mewled.

"There, there, you know I'm right. Back you go." He pushed T'Komo down and locked the wrist chain into the ringbolt again.

"Please," T'Komo rasped. "Please . . . no . . . please."

"I'm sorry, T'Komo, I really am. I don't want to do this. But I think you're beginning to understand. It won't be too much longer." He stood. "I do so want things to be right between us." He locked his hands together, raised them over his head, then brought them down hard on the black man's belly. T'Komo vomited. "Please help me," Hollister said. "I want you to be my friend. You must help me in this."

He left and took a turn around the deck, enjoying the stars. When he returned to the cabin, he gave T'Komo a jovial *Hi,* and then he went to the night-stand and picked up the pin.

They had been on the open sea three weeks when the blind slave was discovered. At feeding time a thin, spindly-legged black shambled into a seaman, spilling hot slabber sauce over him. The sailor felled the slave with a blow to the temple. The black scrambled away, and the seaman followed, kicking. The slave scuttled directly into the bulwark, then sat down, swung his head in panic, and held his arms protectively over his head . . . facing to the side of the white man. The sailor hesitated with his foot upraised, then slowly lowered his leg and frowned. He drew his knife and feinted with it. The black did not react.

The sailor backed away, turned toward the quarterdeck, cupped his hands to his mouth, and shouted, "Blind nigger! Blind nigger here!"

Sailors stopped and turned their heads. Meredith came, and sent for Petersen. The slave cowered against the bulwark while they tested him with hand movements. He saw nothing. Petersen examined his eyes. "I don't know. The inner lid is thicker than it should be, and grainy. There are small secretions in the corners. He's blind. What else can I say?"

"Whether it's infectious or not," Meredith snapped.

"I don't know. The only blind people I've seen have been blind from birth."

"That's just fine. We got a great surgeon." Meredith sucked on his cheek. "Put him over."

Seamen hoisted the slave. He screamed and beat the air with his arms and legs. The sailors heaved him over the side. Meredith summoned Mr. Knye and instructed him to have the men examine the eyes of every slave on deck. He went to report to Horneby. The crewmen were scrupulous. Petersen might not be familiar with the symptoms, but they were: Ophthalmia epidemics were the horror of the slave lanes. Three blacks were set aside, all of whom had full vision, but who, also, displayed thin yellowish crusts in the corners of their eyes. Meredith, on Horneby's orders, had them flung overboard.

Having found only these three and having rid the ship of them, the sailors relaxed, as if, offered sacrifices, whatever god dictated these things would stay his hand.

Petersen, surprised, was now offering Dunbar better than even odds that Leana would survive her amputation, but when asked about her mind he would only shrug. Leana was like a cornered animal. Whenever Dunbar came near enough, she attacked with her teeth and nails. Each time he emerged from the fo'c'sle he did so with renewed passion for revenge. But this was shattered, like a wave upon a jetty, as soon as he came upon the big, capable, and ready O'Brien. And if he approached Crawford, the little man's eyes were on him instantly and the weathered, gnarled hand was not far from his knife hilt. Of Renner Dunbar saw nothing but brief glimpses.

It was by accident that they confronted each other, a few hours before dawn. There was little movement on the ship, and Dunbar, sleepless, was pacing the deck savoring the anger born of his frustration. He was amidship when he caught sight of a man just relieved from watch duty. The seaman's face was momentarily illuminated by a bulwark lantern. Dunbar moved quickly. "Renner!"

Renner jerked to a halt. "Who . . . Dunbar?"

"Yes. I want to talk to you."

Renner's hand went to his knife. He edged back. "I didn't mean no harm. We were just playin', that's all. Just playin'." It was the whine of a child.

The distance was too great for a rush. Dunbar said, "It was your idea, wasn't it?"

"It was not! Whoever told you that's a goddamn liar!"

"It wasn't?"

"No, and you can swear on that, by God."

"Then who?"

"O'Brien. You ask him. He'll tell you. I just went along. We didn't mean no harm. Just some fun."

"O'Brien," Dunbar said reflectively. "O'Brien."

"It surely was."

"You wouldn't try and fool me, would you?"

"No. Mr. Randall will back me up. Hell, I didn't even get to come in her."

Dunbar winced. Evenly, he said, "I see. Well, it seems I've done you an injustice. I'm sorry, Renner." He turned and walked to the rail.

"You're not mad?"

"No, not at you."

Renner took a few tentative steps forward. "You sure?"

"Yes."

Renner came up beside the journalist, smiling. "Let's shake on it then, huh? Boy, I'm glad. I was all confused." He pumped Dunbar's hand. He was like a puppy who, realizing it is not going to be punished after all, rolls in ecstasy at its master's feet. "The thing is, see, it's not really like you lost something or anything. We gotta pay for her and that's a lot of money. And Christ, Mr. Knye swung that whip with a mean arm, too! I got ten lashes. I still can't lay on my back."

They were leaning on the bulwark, looking out to sea. Renner's hands fluttered as he spoke. Dunbar swiveled his head, squinting. He could see none of the watch.

"Hey, I'll tell you what," Renner said. "I got one bottle left. I'll get it and we'll have a drink. I really feel good you're not mad any more. I mean, you never made fun of me or anything like the others do. What do you say, huh? You want a drink with me?"

"Well . . ." Dunbar's arm arced up and down, driving his knife into Renner's back, just below the left shoulderblade.

Renner sagged. His mouth opened, and he made a hoarse coughing sound. His knees buckled. His fingers clawed weakly at the rail. He slid down to a sitting position. He looked up at Dunbar in bewilderment. Then his eyes closed, and he fell over on his side.

"Animal," Dunbar said. "Filthy animal!"

He removed Renner's knife and put it in his own empty sheath. He took the dead man under the arms, hauled him up, and leaned him against the bulwark. He was sweating heavily. He reached down, grasped the corpse's ankles and pulled. Renner did not make much of a splash.

Dunbar scanned the immediate area. No one had seen him. He walked to the fore, toward his pallet, trying to ignore the nausea rising in his stomach.

Renner was missed in the morning, but nothing much was made of it; men were lost from ships occasionally. A few of the sailors looked speculatively at Dunbar. No one, however, said anything. Mr. Knye collected Renner's belongings as the slaves were being brought up on deck. There was nothing left but soiled and torn clothing. Others had been there first.

Renner was quickly forgotten when three more blind

slaves were found. Four more showed symptoms. All went over the side. Horneby ordered teams of seamen into the holds to examine the rest of the males.

The captain, behind his desk, entered in his log: *3 blind & 4 with signs jettisoned this AM.* Ten so far. He was alarmed. Three times, ships on which he had sailed had been stricken by ophthalmia epidemics. In the worst, four-fifths of the slaves had been lost, and full half the crew had been blinded. He had heard of other ships struck even more cataclysmically. He looked up at Sylas. She was sitting on a hassock on the opposite side of the cabin, teaching one of the birds to hop up her fingers as she placed them one above the other, ladderlike.

Meredith's report yesterday had been like a bucket of cold water waking him from a warm sleep. He did not understand at first what the mate was talking about. But then instinct and habit had reasserted themselves, and Horneby, after a brief absence, became again Captain Edward L. Horneby of the slave ship *Jubilation*. Watching the girl, he packed a pipe, lit it, and puffed, leaning back and stretching his legs. He remembered from his childhood a second cousin who had lived in the countryside out of Liverpool. The boy had been born an idiot and at the age of five was still as helpless as an infant. But there was one very eerie thing about him. His father had built a kind of half box and canopy in the yard so the child could take air and yet have some shelter from the sun. In the box the boy was happy. He would smile and gurgle and move his arms and legs about, and a look would come into his eyes which convinced Horneby that the boy, in his mind, was seeing and doing many things. It came to the point where the child would scream and sob inconsolably if removed from the box, and would not—could not—be placated until he was returned. His parents were unequal to the task of caring for him. He was sent to an asylum, where, of course, they had no box in the yard for him. He died, for no discernible reason, within six weeks. Horneby looked about the cabin. This is my box, he mused. He recoiled from the thought. But *I* know the difference. I am master of this ship. I have just made an entry in the log. I am Edward Horneby. Besides, he thought, this ship is a box, the entire world is a box. It is merely a matter of size, that's all, a matter of size.

Sylas looked at him, transferred the bird to her shoulder, rose, went to the liquor chest, poured him a brandy, and brought it to him. He patted her flank, and she returned to the hassock. He warmed the brandy between his palms, swirled it slowly, and inhaled its bouquet. He had not wanted this, but he appreciated her effort. She knew he wished her to read his moods, to react without him having to say anything. She was trying. She had not seemed overly adept in the beginning, but she was improving. He didn't know how talented she would prove. Certainly nowhere near as good as she had—as Sylas, the real Sylas, had been. But even if she did not understand, she could be trained to offer specific responses to specific stimuli. All animals can be trained, and human beings are the brightest of animals. He wondered a little about her, what she thought and what she felt. With Sylas it had been simple. *He* was the center of her being, and little else concerned her. This girl, though, what went on in her dark head? Horneby was curious, but only a little.

What she thought and felt really did not matter. Not at all.

Two cycles had passed since Adoko had seen them discover the blind slave and throw him overboard. Adoko was brought up every third day. Nearly a week, then. Now there were many blind slaves. The white men were afraid and, as always, they made the black men suffer for their fears.

It did not matter to Adoko. He no longer cared. There was no escape from the white man. He was a slave. His people were dead. He was dead. The family had been crushed like grain beneath stones. Each was simply a shard of the husk, black fragments that were so much chaff.

After the exercise period he shuffled to an empty part of the deck and sat down. He hugged his legs and rested his head on his knees. He heard the rich, varied sounds of the ship and the men who made it sail, but he did not listen to them. He thought about nothing. In a while he became cramped, but he didn't move, and in a little while longer his body ceased to be aware of the stiffness.

A hand fell lightly on his shoulder. He let it rest there, thinking it would be removed. It squeezed his flesh. "Father?"

He looked up and saw Tola. "Ho, Tola." He tried without much success to smile.

The boy sat in front of him. He held his father's hand. Tola's features were grave. Adoko wished to say something, but he could think of nothing. He put his head back down on his knees. Tola gently stroked his hair. Adoko shuddered. Then, then for an ecstatic and blissful moment, *he* was the child and Tola was the father, and Adoko was solaced and knew a joy that was exquisite.

"Father, tell me . . . tell how we are going to kill the white men." Tola's voice quavered.

The moment passed.

Adoko breathed deeply, raised his head, and this time was able to lift the corners of his lips a little. "We . . . someday, Tola . . . we . . . home . . . we . . . the white men . . ."

The boy burst into tears and lunged into his father's arms. Adoko clasped him tightly. "It's all right, Tola, it's all right."

It wasn't, and both of them knew it, but something had to be said. Adoko began to weep. The naked black man held his son and wept, rocking back and forth, crooning soothing sounds to the boy.

It was an epidemic. Twenty-seven slaves had been put over the side by the end of the third day, and Meredith reported twelve more afflicted and one seaman whose vision was failing. It was too late to control the infection by getting rid of the victims. Horneby ordered a section of the number one hold partitioned off, an area large enough to contain a hundred slaves. If the number of afflicted blacks rose above that, well, then there would no longer be any sense in attempting to isolate them. Horneby had seen several variations of the disease. Sometimes the sight was only partially damaged. More often, as now, the blindness was total. But the damage was not necessarily permanent, and even complete recovery of vision was not unheard-of. They were three and a half weeks from the Bay Islands. Horneby could only hope.

Randall went blind. Two seamen followed him a day later. Three days' sail pushed the number of stricken slaves past fifty. Dunbar visited Leana. She neither hissed nor curled her fingers into claws when he approached. He stopped, the light of his lantern barely touching her. She squinted from the gloom. Dunbar raised the lantern. Her head followed the motion. He moved the light from left to right. Her face turned with it. He hung the lantern from a peg in a rafter and edged stealthily forward. Her eyes remained fixed on the light. He moved his hand. She didn't see him. "Oh, Li-yana."

The girl screeched and struck out wildly. Dunbar backed away, untouched, shaking his head. He retrieved the lantern and left the fo'c'sle. He said nothing to the seaman on duty at the door, but later in the day he saw them take Leana to the area in which the other blind slaves were being kept.

Two and a half weeks from port Horneby entered in his log: *Epidemic out of control. More than half of cargo blind. Number mounts hourly, impossible and pointless to keep count. Eighteen crewmen now sightless. Ship reduced to three-quarter sail. Seaman Jenkins, blind, fell into galley hold. Leg broken two places. Petersen set it. Nerves shredding. Seamen Duffy & Nassiter beat a slave to death for no apparent reason. Docked pay, ordered ten lashes each.*

One of the blinded sailors, a moon-faced simian man, stumbled around the deck collaring slaves and grabbing seamen by the shirtfronts. "We're being punished," he said. "God is going to kill us. 'Whosoever stealeth a man and sell him into bondage shall be put to death.' The Bible says that. James."

The sailors were gentle with him at first.

"Fall on your knees and repent. 'Prepare ye the way of the Lord, make straight in the desert a highway for our God!' "

Sure, Timmy, sure. We will, they said. And they pried loose his grasping fingers.

" 'There is no peace, saith the Lord, unto the wicked.' "

It's all right now, Tim.

" 'I will feed them with wormwood, and give them water of gall to drink.' "

Take hold of yourself, Tim. Let go.

"We can't hide from God. 'They are the eyes of the Lord, which run to and fro through the whole earth.' My eyes! Oh Christ, my eyes! I want my eyes back! Please, help me. It's written: 'They that wait upon the Lord shall renew their strength . . . then the eyes of the blind shall be opened, and the ears of the deaf shall be unstopped.' "

Tim, stop this. That's enough!

"We're doomed!" he wailed. "All of us. 'We have made a covenant with death, and with hell are we at agreement!' "

They shoved him away.

The blacks stood in motionless terror while he ranted at them, his fingers dug into their shoulders. He worsened, moaning and shrieking, grappling with sailors and trying to force them to their knees to pray for forgiveness. Finally they dragged him to the empty cabin in which the girls had been transported, and tied him to a bunk.

Dunbar was the twenty-ninth seaman to lose his sight. That left a complement of thirty able-bodied sailors. The journalist took his blindness calmly: It was quite proper and expected, the next logical step in the progression. The progression not of the *Jubilation,* its crew, and its cargo, but of Virgil Carey-Dunbar. He had realized what was happening when Leana had gone blind. He was being led to his destruction. He didn't know why, but he was certain that he was to be destroyed. The pattern was clear. It had begun with the letter from the Abolition Society and had escalated steadily. But perhaps it had begun earlier, with the achievement of his first literary successes, or even earlier . . . say, the moment he had been thrust kicking and wet from his mother's womb. But the when of the *beginning* did not really matter; the ending was imminent.

He accepted it. The wheel could not be stopped. He experienced a deep tranquillity, the kind he had seen, and never understood, in men who had surrendered themselves to God.

He had only one real regret. That Crawford and O'Brien had not preceded him into darkness. He would have been able to kill them if they had.

Though his mind was peaceful, being blind was physically

upsetting. Without sight, his sea legs deserted him. The pitch and roll of the ship were vastly magnified, as if some childish giant had taken hold of the vessel and were shaking it. He fell many times in the first few hours and finally had to crawl on all fours. Those struck earlier said it was only a matter of a day or two, that the body adjusted and he would regain his balance shortly. He did not believe it, even though several of them were able to walk haltingly about the deck. At mess he ate with his fingers because it was too clumsy trying to use implements. And he ate little, because sitting in the blackness chewing and swallowing things he could not see made him nauseated. Earlier, he would have sworn he could negotiate the deck blindfolded, but now it was filled with an incredible number of obstacles. He bumped and scraped skin from his head and shoulders. Splinters sliced into his palms and knees. Most curious and disturbing was the continuous sensation of something large and dense directly in front of him, a pricking in the forehead and facial muscles. But when he stretched out his arm and probed, he found nothing but empty air. Worst was the darkness, the unremitting darkness which subverted every attempted action.

The blind sailors engaged each other eagerly in dialogue. They described sensations and they answered: *I know. Yes, yes, that's how it is, that's it all right*. But the bulk of the talk was of other plague ships, of seamen who had regained their sight after a few weeks, a few months, or—and even this, if it had to be, was acceptable—a few years. Dunbar decided that if no more than a quarter of the tales were true, the number of men who had recovered must be legion.

Slaves were no longer brought up on deck in the morning. There were not enough sighted crewmen to work the ship and watch them. Food was carried down and distributed to them on their shelves each evening. No cleaning details descended into the holds, and a thick cloying odor of filth and decay lay over the ship like a smothering blanket.

Meredith reports nearly entire cargo blind, Horneby wrote. *Only eighteen men, including Meredith, Knye & myself still able to see. Hit by squall this AM. Captain and all able-bodied men but one on helm into rigging to reef tops & topgallants. Ship heeling dangerously. No choice but to order half a dozen blind seamen up the shrouds. Two fell and lost. Sailing now under lower tops & mains only. Eyes itch. Rubbed back of hand across them, saw yellow secretion. Week & half from port under normal sail. Maybe three weeks at present rate. Distress pennants flying. Two ships sighted, both distant & passed by.*

Hollister was furious. He beat T'Komo about the head and shoulders until the black man collapsed at his feet, and then he kicked him. "You bastard! You goddamn, miserable black bastard. I ought to kill you!"

T'Komo curled into a ball, trying to protect his stomach. His arms were wrapped around his head. His voice was muffled. "I am sorry, Master. Master!"

"You've ruined it! It doesn't mean anything anymore." He aimed a last savage kick at T'Komo's back, then stalked across the room and sat down on the edge of the bed. He ground a fist into his palm and shook his head. "All for nothing," he said bitterly.

He stared at T'Komo with hatred. He had begun with short nervous testing periods, freeing the black man and having him perform simple tasks, only a few of them humiliating. Hollister discerned not even a flicker of resistance, and, keeping careful watch, he gradually lengthened the periods in which he allowed T'Komo out of chains.

Last night had been triumph. T'Komo had been unshackled three hours. It was time for sleep, and the black man went obediently to the foot of the bed, stretched himself out, and waited for the irons to be clamped on. Hollister began disrobing casually. He said, "I don't think the manacles will be necessary. You'll be a good nigger without them, won't you?"

T'Komo flung himself to the floor and kissed Hollister's feet. Hollister rubbed his head affectionately and laughed. "There, there, that's enough. I told you things would be better in time." When Hollister got into bed, T'Komo lay down on the floor. "No, I still want you at the foot of the bed." T'Komo relocated instantly.

Hollister extinguished the lamp. He was in an agony of apprehension and excitement. There were no weapons within easy reach; it would not have been a valid test if he had at hand the means to subdue T'Komo. He waited. The black was grossly weakened, but still basically stronger than Hollister and able, if he wished, to kill the white man. There was nothing to stop him. However, if Hollister had been successful, then T'Komo would not consider that possibility. T'Komo grunted and rolled over. Hollister started, but forced himself to remain quiet. He was sick with fear.

T'Komo began to snore.

Hollister cackled laughter and buried his face in the pillow.

In the morning he pulled on rough trousers and a soiled shirt. He was angry with Horneby and intended to speak with his father about the man. He knew things would be different between him and his father. He felt he understood Peyton now, and he was sure that Peyton would be pleased with him, and would demonstrate his goodwill by censuring Horneby on Matthew's behalf. The captain had ordered Hollister to work on deck from dawn until dusk. Hollister was not interested in the blindness. This was not his ship, the slaves were not his property, and the crew meant nothing to him. He regarded their affliction as outside his concerns. He had not been stricken; he did not believe he would be stricken; there simply was no relationship between him and the *Jubilation*. Soon they would be in port, he would buy T'Komo and strike out for home, and that would be that. Obviously, the ship was in difficulty, and he admitted that his labor, clumsy as it was, was needed. And he would not have refused. What outraged him was the manner Horneby had used. The man had *ordered* him to work—one simple unequivocal sentence. Then he had turned away without even offering the opportunity of reply. It was intolerable. Hollister felt he should have been *asked*.

Hollister wrestled with the question of T'Komo. Should he chain him through the day, or risk leaving him free in the cabin? He decided to leave T'Komo unfettered.

When he had returned at the end of the day, tired and dirty, he had found T'Komo blind.

Sitting on the bed, Hollister's anger peaked. He seized the glazed dish on which his soap rested, and he hurled it. T'Komo was struck on the side of the head. The dish broke. "What good are you? You have to be a whole man. It's worth nothing if you're blind. Nothing! You have to be whole, it doesn't mean anything now!"

A line of blood stained T'Komo's skin. He wept, and he mumbled broken apologies.

The darkness was hard and seamless, the shell of a tight nut, within which rested the meat, Adoko. He was bound forever. The Adoko who was, had died. The new Adoko lay quietly upon the damp and filthy planking through the blind hours turning over memories of that Adoko who had been, marveling at the life that had been led by the man who no longer was. The mythic man in the mythic land, each throbbed with strange and energetic juices; there were screaming passions and wild joys, pains, a thousand textures beneath the fingers and against the skin, rich odors whorling in the nostrils, and a riot of colors that caused the mind to stagger under their impact.

Ah!

Adoko luxuriated in his dreams as he had, a child, in the magic tales of the original Osai, and the other heroes of his people. They enraptured not because their strength was so prodigious or their deeds beyond the doing of other men, but because they were of another, earlier, time and of another, unique, flesh: They were remembered.

Adoko was hardly aware of the white men. They came once a day and they could be heard scraping their great kettle of food down the aisle between the shelves, filling bowls and thrusting them onto the lap of every third slave. Sometimes there were fights over the food; other times, none of it would be touched. There were many corpses. The whites had not bothered to remove bodies in several days; some were beginning to rot, a hint of something overly sweet beneath the general stench. The shelves were quiet, as if the blindness had somehow frozen throats, too, or had made of each man a separate and distinct world, one in which there was no place for sound.

The blind hours succeeded each other, like drops of water, and they were endless.

The seaman's tongue jutted past his lips and moved slowly from corner to corner as he wrote. Horneby was dictating, so at least the sailor did not have to think, but he hadn't held a quill, except to sign his name, since he had been a child, and he found the forming of the letters excruciatingly difficult.

We are all blind now but Summers an Cornish, he wrote.

Too men to sal a ship. Distres flags beeing flown continulously Summers an Cornish speling each other on helm too ships sited today but neether close eenuf too recogneyeze are signal. Saling under mains only imposeble to manetane more canves. I do not no what will hapen to us if Cornish An Summers luse there site. Hope as we draw nerer the coast to intersept a nother vesel.

R. Cornish for Captain Edward Hornabee.

Horneby was terrified. His head ached constantly, and he felt as if his guts were in the grip of a powerful and vicious hand. His legs were given to fits of trembling. He forced himself to spend time on deck reassuring the crew; he did not actually care what happened to them, or even, anymore, to the cargo, but if they were to reach port, or land of any kind, it would depend upon the willingness of the seamen to work as best they could. Horneby could not allow them to despair. But he was terrified: Of the impenetrable blackness, of his overwhelming helplessness, of losing the girl Sylas, and even of the girl herself. The first time he had entered the cabin blind he had held out his hand for Sylas to take. She was still able to see. He waited. She didn't come. He listened. He heard nothing but the creaking of the ship. "Sylas?" There was no response. *"Sylas!"* Nothing. He was sure she would not have left the cabin. She was standing somewhere, then, unmoving, breathing so he would not hear her, studying him. He felt her presence, and it was the presence of a sleek carnivore, tail gently lashing as it estimated the strength of some nervous animal grazing nearby. He began to perspire. *"Sylas!"* He shuffled forward, arms describing slow arcs. He stumbled over something and fell. He heard the sound of bare feet padding toward him. He tightened, expecting the crash of something heavy upon his head, or the quick, searing thrust of a knife. He pushed himself to his knees and forced into his voice as much wrath and authority as he could muster. "Stop right where you are, you bitch!" He rose to his feet. There was silence. He lunged, and he found her where he expected to. He closed one hand round her throat and used the other to rock her head with hard slaps. "Bitch. Bitch. Goddamn bitch! What did you think you were going to do? If you ever, *ever*, try anything like that again I'll kill you. Do you understand? I'll kill you!" When he stopped, she was sobbing. He threw her to the floor. She clasped his legs and wept against his knees. He stood with his hands clenched, breathing stertorously. Sylas lifted her hands to his waist and fumbled with his belt buckle. He folded his arms across his chest and waited . . . She had been obeisant and attentive since then, and had herself gone blind two days later. But Horneby could not forget the shriveling, pulling fear he had felt, blind in the cabin, calling her, knowing she was watching him.

Somewhere in the blackness were Crawford and O'Brien. Dunbar would have sacrificed his life for a moment of sight and a few moments more in which to act upon what he had seen. When Dunbar had learned that the Irishman and the Englishman had gone blind, he began to stalk them. O'Brien's strength and Crawford's ceaseless vigilance no longer mattered. If Dunbar could find them, he could kill them. Both men apparently realized this. They were crafty. Dunbar rarely heard their voices, and when he did, they were at too great a distance for him to attempt anything. At first he had confined his hunt to the night hours so that, should he find and be able to kill one, the likelihood of being seen by one of the few sighted sailors remaining would be diminished. O'Brien was a loud snorer. Unfortunately, so were many others. Dunbar had prowled several nights on his hands and knees among sleeping bodies, but invariably he had bumped over or put his weight down atop a man stretched out between him and the rasping guttural snores toward which he was crawling. Then there would be a brief and noisy altercation. He would mumble apologies and retreat, sulking angrily because he knew the sound of his voice would have alerted O'Brien, if his goal had indeed been the Irishman. Once he had gained his objective and, heart thudding, put his fingers out to gently probe the contours of the man's face. The sleeper woke with a shout and seized his wrist. "What's goin' on, hey?" It was not O'Brien. "Nothing, nothing," Dunbar said. "Just looking for the piss-pot, mate." The seaman told him he'd damn well better look someplace else. Then, as Dunbar was returning to his own pallet, he heard O'Brien. "Dunbar, Dunbar lad, I'm over this way if it's me you're looking for." The journalist turned, knife ready. But the Irishman would be prepared, would be waiting wtih his back pressed against something solid, a weapon in his hands. Dunbar cursed. *Not now,* he thought, *but soon, O'Brien, soon.*

When it had come to the point where only Cornish and Summers were left with vision, Dunbar extended his hunt to the daylight hours. One afternoon O'Brien's laughter boomed close by. He snatched his knife from its sheath, took three quick steps, and stabbed viciously. The sharp blade rent nothing but empty air, and Dunbar, unbalanced, pitched to the deck. He heard O'Brien talking to someone, moving away. The journalist made an animal sound of rage and drove the knife two inches into the planking.

The Osai in him was not yet dead. It stirred a little, it twitched. The two white men had shouted at each other and struck one another. Adoko groaned. Why would not the Osai lie still? The dreams were warm and pleasant. He was happy with them. The white men had dropped the great kettle of food, that was what they had fought about. Adoko tried to quiet the Osai. *Be dead, be dead, Osai, and leave me in my peace.* Oh, the images in his mind were so beautiful, and the life with them was as joyous as any man had ever known. The Osai raised its torso and shook its head. The feeding had been clumsy for days. Why were the corpses not removed? Why had the airings on deck stopped? Adoko grew unhappy. The Osai had no right to do this to him. There was contentment now, hard won, and Adoko did not want to return to his previous torment. The Osai gained its knees. After they had cursed and fought, the two sailors had left the hold, abandoning their kettle and the slopped food, and no others had come with additional food to give to those slaves still waiting to be fed. *No,* Adoko thought. *Don't do this. Leave me. You will only bring futility and pain again. I can stand no more.* But the Osai was not to be stopped. The whites, the whites are— The Osai made fists and raised them to the heavens.

"—are blind!" said Osai Adoko, chained in the hold. His forearms muscled, and he smashed his fists against the shelf above him. "They are blind. The whites are all blind!"

Someone moaned.

"Food, food," a voice called.

"Listen to me! It is Osai Adoko who speaks. The white men are blind. They can see no more than we. They dwell in darkness. Without their eyes, their guns are useless!"

"Do not rant, Adoko."

"Quiet," someone else said. "Have we not suffered enough? They will come and beat us."

"Fools! They have no strength left. Gyase." He gripped the shoulders of the man next to him. "The moment has come. Help me."

"Adoko . . . we are lost. Do not torture yourself."

He struck Gyase. "Are you my cousin? Are you Ashanti? Pah! I spit. You are a woman's slave. Gyase, where are you, Gyase?"

"I do not deserve humiliation," Gyase said quietly.

"You deserve nothing else. You refuse the family."

"The family is dead."

"It sleeps! It remains only to awaken it—and free it!"

"It cannot be done."

"It can, and it will. Do you dishonor the memory of Besu? Do you call yourself the murderer of Kiuky? It is a simple choice: You are dung, or you are Gyase."

"I . . ."

"Say it! The family waits."

"I am Gyase."

Adoko embraced him. "Yes, yes, you are. Now awaken them with me."

"My brothers! Hear me! It is I, Gyase. The family lives. Listen to your Osai. The time is at hand. Our freedom waits, calling like a lover. The spirits of our fathers and of our fathers' fathers grow weary of seeing us in chains. Our slaughtered kinsmen cry for vengeance. Hear your Osai!"

"Our bondage is ended," Osai said. "Take up the tools and weapons we have gathered. We set to the chains at once. Those who can speak other tongues, tell the rest. Persuade, insist, demand. But caution against an outcry, we do not want to alarm the whites."

"We will be killed, Adoko."

"No, their world is as dark as ours. We are six to their one. We will bathe the ship in their blood."

"We cannot pass the metal grate to the deck."

"I will take us past that."

"The great gun points at the hatch. Even without eyes they need only fire it."

"One time perhaps, no more."

There was silence a moment, then: "Glory to Osai Adoko! Eunat fights with his cousin."

"As does Mealaio!"

"And Teali!"

Affirmations layered atop each other: the family was awake. Voices in many languages spread through the hold. Adoko and Gyase took up the stout chain that ran through their leg irons, and began to work on it wtih one of the files. With the Ashanti to lead them, most of the others needed little prompting. The Ashanti military skills were legend; willingness and support were expressed with savagery. But not unanimously. An urgent voice rose and dominated the hold. Then Adoko was called in his own tongue. "Adoko, there is a man here who counsels the others not to join us. He tells them they will suffer Besu's fate. He wants them to summon the whites and inform upon us before it is too late."

"Is that you, Mealaio?"

"Yes, Adoko."

"Do you have a weapon?"

"A knife."

"Kill him. Do it in a manner that will enable the others to hear."

Adoko waited, file poised over the tiny groove he had made in the chain. The man's speech was cut short by a scream. He screamed a second time, a third, then there was silence.

"He is dead," Mealaio said.

"Good. Now tell them what you have done. And make clear that all who do not fight at our side fight against us, and will be killed with the whites."

Mealaio translated.

"Now ask how many there are who will not follow us."

Mealaio put the question, and received no reply.

Adoko and Gyase spelled each other on the chain. When friction heated the metal to a point where it became too uncomfortable to handle, which was often, they cooled it with urine and spittle. It took an hour to cut through one side. Then they had to widen the gap so that the link could be unhooked from the next. The two sections of chain were pulled through the ringbolts of the ankle manacles, and thirty men were free. Adoko told them not to move. He slipped off the planking, handed the file to a man on the next shelf up, then padded down the aisle to consult with and instruct his brothers, his family.

As the other chains were separated, he had two of them cut through again, at the ends, and the twin lengths brought to him. He divided the slaves into four groups, each built around a core of Ashanti. He would lead the first out of the hold and against the big gun on the raised deck at the rear of the ship. The second party was to make toward the women's quarters, remove the bar, and force the padlocked door.

"Why women? Not fight." The speaker was clumsy in Adoko's tongue.

"There are Ashanti among them," Adoko said. "They will fight. They are not chained, and once the door is open, they will be able to help us at once."

The third detachment would proceed to the second hold and use brute strength against the grate, while the last party sought out and smashed open the locked toolboxes which were buttressed against the bulwarks. Hammers and chisels, files, and the two-handed cutting shears were to be brought to the second hold and used to loose the slaves chained there.

Adoko had the two halves of chain joined . . . and they were ready. It must have taken most of the night. He thought about dawn, which no longer existed. There was only night, and the night was endless. Dawn blossomed in other times and other worlds, for which Osai Adoko had no use. He lived in the moment. The moment was enough. He lifted the end of the heavy chain and placed it over his shoulder. Behind him were Gyase and other kinsmen, supporting the chain so it would not rattle against the floor, and behind them were the men Adoko would lead.

Adoko moved to the ladder on the balls of his feet. He climbed slowly and carefully. Gyase followed. Adoko stopped, raised his arm over his head, and searched the air. He ascended the next step. His hand touched the grate. The metal was a little cold, and wet with drops of moisture. He paused. For an instant he wondered if he were mad, and his mind formed a picture of a dozen whites standing in a circle around the grate, smiling, their muskets aimed point-blank at his head. He shrugged; he was committed. He poked a hand between the hatchworked strips of steel. It was slow, exacting work, feeding the chain a few links at a time, wincing when he slipped and the iron clinked against the steel. He ran the chain up through the grate near the hinged side of its frame, across six of the cross-strips, then back down into the hold. Finished, he took both free ends in one hand, backed down the ladder, and went to his knees working toward the side of the ship until he found the huge beam that angled from some deeper area, up through the flooring, and butted supportively against a lateral timber. He brought the ends of the chain around either side of this vertical beam and hooked them together behind it, creating a loop from beam to grating over a distance of some twenty feet.

He inserted three thicknesses of planks into the center of this loop, and then turned the planks, twisting the chain until it tightened. "Carefully now," Adoko said. "One half-turn at a time, evenly done." He and three others manned the lever. A half-turn, a full, then half again, and there came a creaking from the grate. Another turn. There was a sharp splitting noise. Adoko had them wait a full minute. They turned again. Metal wrenched and wood cracked. Adoko was sweating.

"Knife," he said. A man fumbled for his hand, found it and pressed into it a knife, then replaced Adoko on the lever.

Adoko poised himself at the foot of the ladder. "Tear it down!"

There were splitting and tearing sounds above his head, a moment of dreadful silence as if the grate were offering counterpressure, then a loud wrenching followed by falling pieces of splintered wood. "Follow!" Adoko said. He rushed up the ladder. The down-twisted grate blocked his way. He seized it and pulled. It caught somewhere on the twisted frame. "Help me. Quickly!" Two men climbed up to him. Below, slaves grabbed the chain and heaved. The grate moved, springy and resistant, then gave way and crashed down into the hold . . . and Adoko was on the deck, helping up those who followed. The air was chilly and wet upon his skin. He grunted with a hunting animal's pleasure. The whites were stupid. Blind or not, *he* would have posted guards. When he thought a dozen or more men were already with him, he said, "To the gun, now!"

He ran forward in blackness. Bare feet slapped the deck beside him. He tripped, pitched forward, tucked chin to chest, rolled on his shoulders, and came up running, one arm extended stiffly before him.

Summers was dozing with his head against the hub of the wheel and his arms hanging over the spokes. He and Cornish, the only two who could see, had been manning the helm in six-hour shifts for nearly a week; both were on the verge of collapse. The ship had not yet emerged from the dense fog bank into which it had slipped shortly after Summers had come on duty at midnight. With the wheel lashed to allow only a little play, Summers, on the edge of a chair that had been brought up from Wilkes's cabin, had slept on and off during the night.

Some sound awakened him. He groaned and massaged the back of his neck, then stood up and checked the compass. He heard the sound again, like breaking wood. He peered down into the swirling fog, but could see nothing. He decided to ignore the noise; it wasn't very loud, so it couldn't be very important. He untied the wheel, made a nine-degree correction, then snubbed it again. Quite sharply this time he heard something splitting. He frowned and came out from behind the wheel, walked to the rail, and looked down at the maindeck. What in Christ's blue hell was going on? He gnawed his lower lip, wondering if he should rouse Mr. Randall or Mr. Meredith. If one of the masts were going . . .

"Oh God, no!" He reeled back. Naked black men were bursting from the fog, rushing the quarterdeck.

He stumbled to the bell and set it clanging furiously. "The niggers are loose! The niggers are loose!" he screamed. Three sailors, the titular watch, were sleeping at the rear of the quarterdeck. Summers ran back and kicked at them, shouted them awake. He snatched up one of the muskets and dashed to the head of the ladder connecting the quarterdeck with the maindeck. A slave armed with a spike, hand brushing the railtop for guidance, was halfway up the stairs. Another black was directly behind him, and more were converging.

Summers shot the first man in the head. The watch seamen came up lurching and bumping behind him. Sightless, they snapped their heads back and forth, faces panicky. Summers seized a second musket from one of them. "Cutlasses!" he yelled. "Hack up anything that touches you." He fired hastily, missed, grabbed the third musket, and shot a slave who was only two steps away. "Jesus!" Summers said. "The carronade. The bastards are still probably coming out of the hole." He sent two men stumbling back to prime and fire the gun, while he held the head of the stairs, swinging a musket by the barrel, with the third seaman standing behind him, cutlass high, legs trembling.

Adoko's hand encountered a wall. He was unable to stop his rush fully; he struck and bounced off, moved to his right where he knew the stairs were. A bell was ringing. He collided with a naked man; someone pressed in behind him; his foot found the first step. There was a shot. He moved up the stairs. A second musket was fired, close, then a third, and a man fell against him, chest warm and sticky. Adoko pushed him aside, and went on. A body blocked the way. He crawled over it. He was struck a numbing blow on his shoulder. He threw himself forward. He was hit on the back, then his arms wrapped around legs, legs covered with cloth, white man's legs. The white man fell on top of him. Adoko stabbed. The white man shouted, but more in anger than in pain, and his struggles did not abate much. Adoko had not cut anything vital. He stabbed again. He was stepped on by bare feet, fallen over. "The gun!" he shouted. "Turn the gun!" He stabbed again. The white man shuddered and then lay still. He was kicked by someone struggling on the deck in front of him. He ignored the fight, gained his feet, and went forward as quickly as he dared move, arms stretched out and searching.

Gyase did not know how many whites there were. He didn't care; he wanted only to reach the gun. He heard the sounds of conflict to his left and turned in that direction. He came up hard against cold, moisture-streaked metal. "I have it. Here!" he shouted. Three or four others were with him in moments. "Find pins, wheels, levers," he ordered. "Turn them, remove them." Adoko said the gun could be shifted, but that it was locked into place, and first the locking devices must be freed. Gyase moved hand over hand down the thick barrel until he came to the muzzle. He put his shoulder to it. It wouldn't move. "Hurry," he said. Voices chattered in excitement and frustration. Each time something was successfully moved, a man cried out happily. But Gyase, bucking and lunging against the muzzle, was unable to swivel the gun. There was the sound of chopping, and a man screamed. The gun budged a little. "It's free!" Gyase said. "Help me." Slowly the barrel began to swing. The tendons in Gyase's neck grew swollen with the effort. It was turning, turning . . .

The universe exploded. Gyase's shoulder and half his head vanished. He was lifted from his feet and hurled backward, then slammed into the seaside bulwark, which snapped his spine; his feet swung up, and he somersaulted over the rail.

Adoko, working his hands feverishly in the jagged gears, sprang to his feet when Gyase called, "It's free," and threw his weight against the barrel. He heard men on either side of him grunting with similar effort. The gun turned and he was about to tell them enough, the blind whites would not be able to re-aim it. But the gun was fired. The roar deafened him and the concussion sent him spinning away, face peppered with tiny specks of burning powder. His hand fell upon a rail and he used it to keep from falling. He wiped his hand across his face. He shook his head. His ears were filled with a high-pitched ringing, but beneath it he could still hear a little. He was not sure of his position. He leaned over the rail. He heard shouting below. He was facing the maindeck then, not the sea. "Draw back," he called into the blackness behind him. "There is nothing more for us to do here. Make for the second hold." He vaulted over the rail. It seemed momentarily that nothing, absolutely nothing, existed but darkness and that he should fall within it through eternity. But then the shock of the deck, sooner than he expected it, crumpled his legs and made him drop his knife. He scraped his hands across the planking, found the weapon, got to his feet, and moved forward. He ran into someone and was knocked back a little. A tight voice said something questioning—in the white tongue. Adoko slashed with his knife. A miss. Wind feathered against his face. The white had stabbed down, with equal lack of success. Adoko moved away, then continued toward the hold. It was not yet time to fight the sailors, not unless they were obstacles to freeing the rest of the slaves.

There was shouting ahead and to the side. He also heard a chant: "Ho! . . . ho! . . . ho! . . . ho! . . ." He turned to the sound and came up against a wall of naked bodies. The slaves were ringed around the grating, heaving at it in time to the chant. "Mealaio!"

"Here, Adoko."

"Where are the tools?"

"We have nothing useful. Some of the wooden pins, some of the short turning implements. We couldn't force the locks with them."

Loud shouting broke out on the other side of the grate. There were sounds of grappling and of blows. "The whites from the front of the ship," someone cried. "Many of them."

"Attack," Mealaio ordered. "Everyone! Attack!"

Adoko moved with the general surge. He was enclosed on all sides by bodies. He thrust out his hand; when he felt cloth, he struck. He was buffeted, he was gouged with elbows and knees, clawed by fingers. A club broke some of his teeth. He spat the fragments, and blood. A knife sliced across his forearm, shallowly, was disregarded. There was a frenzy to it all, a fear he had never felt in battle before, born of the blackness, the ignorance as to whether the flesh touched was that of friend or enemy. For a few moments he ran amok and he hacked at any living meat he could reach.

The whites were driven back. They were vastly outnumbered by the slaves, and, Adoko thought, they had not planned the attack, merely responded in confusion to the alarm, and stumbled across the blacks. There were high, female screams just beyond where he supposed the sailors to be. The women had been released, then. Good, But he hadn't planned them to be separated from the men. They were not organized yet, and too weak. The whites would butcher them. "Mealaio!" he shouted. "Are you hurt?"

"No, Adoko."

"Then lead a party to the women. They must be joined with us."

He heard Mealaio gathering men and sending them forward. Adoko turned back to the grate. The locks and hinges were too strong. The stripping gave some, but still clung to its frame. Adoko stabbed at the metal in fury.

"The locks, where are they?" someone said. "We have bars from the tool chests."

Adoko pushed to the speaker, took one of the bars, was directed to a lock. The implement he held was long and thick, its end split and curved. He inserted the end through the lock's hasp. "Three men on each bar," he said. More blacks arrived, announcing shears, rasps, hammers, chisels, saws. . . The tools were distributed. Four hands shared the bar with Adoko's. Six arms knotted. The man beside Adoko grunted. The lock snapped open. A voice heralded the demolition of the second lock. The grate was flung back. Adoko ordered men and the appropriate tools into the hold, then went down the ladder, ears battered by the frightened and bewildered din of the chained slaves.

Horneby sat up, rubbed his eyes, then opened them. He saw nothing, and he cursed himself. Habit was constantly at odds with this new, lightless world. Muskets? Dull reports, a couple of them. Or had he been dreaming?

The carronade was fired.

He swung his legs to the floor, lifted a pistol from the nightstand and shuffled as quickly as he could to the door. He touched the bulkhead. *Goddamn, goddamn!* He hated his blindness. He found the door and went through it. Meredith was somewhere in the corridor calling, "Hello? Hello? What is it?"

"You heard?"

"What the hell do you think?" Meredith said. The mate had been badly shaken when he lost his vision, and had become as loud and snappish as a spoiled child.

"You armed?"

"Yes."

"All right. Stay here. I'll go . . ." Horneby laughed brittly. "I'll go *see.*" He made his way down the corridor and climbed the stairs to find that the door, which opened outward, was blocked. He heard shouting on the other side. He pushed. It opened somewhat. He leaned his weight against it. Grudgingly, it swung out. He stepped forward and his foot came down on flesh. He knelt. Blood on the flesh. Naked. Tightly coiled hair on the scalp. His jaw dropped. He stood. The voices mounted in number. Some were shouting in English. More in African dialects.

No. It simply could not be.

"No!" he bellowed. "You couldn't have. You can't, you black bastards, you can't!" His cheeks flushed and tightened.

"No!" He fired his pistol at nothing, lusting for an answering scream, but none came.

He turned and went back down the stairs.

"Captain?" It was Randall.

Horneby brushed by him. "The niggers broke loose. Get to the arms chest. Meredith, you sonofabitch, bring your key and break out the arms."

A door opened. "Captain Horneby," Hollister said. "What is the meaning of this?"

Sightless, Hollister was insufferable. T'Komo's blindness had angered him; his own was sheer outrage. He would not tolerate its effrontery. Somehow he would destroy it. Though he walked in darkness, he could not believe he was blind. That was for the others.

Horneby went to the sound of Hollister's voice, reached, touched the youth's nightshirt, bunched it in his hand, and flung him down the corridor. "The niggers are trying to take the ship," he said. "And they just might do it."

"Well stop them, for God's sake!"

"I intend to. Meredith's breaking out weapons. Carry as many muskets, shot, powder, and cutlasses up to the deck as you can."

"I'm a passenger, not a member of the crew. It's your duty to protect me. This isn't my affair."

"When they come for your balls with a knife, it will be very much your affair. Now move, or I'll kill you myself."

Hollister muttered angrily but he obeyed, because he believed Horneby would kill him.

Horneby went into his cabin and pulled on a pair of trousers. Naked, he had felt unbearably vulnerable. Then with Hollister and the two mates he gathered up muskets and swords, pouches of shot, and boxes of paper cartridges. They made their way awkwardly up the stairs. A musket slipped and clattered to the floor. Meredith cursed. They gained the deck and Randall said, "It sounds like a slaughterhouse."

"It is." Horneby cupped his hands to his mouth. "Lads! This is the captain. Rally to the quarterdeck companionway! We have weapons here. Rally to us, lads!"

"What good are guns," Hollister whined, "if we can't see to aim them?"

Meredith said, "If you don't want one, you don't have to use one, you stupid bastard. And I hope the sharks like the taste of you."

"Summers!" Horneby called. "Cornish! Summers, where are you? Cornish!"

A voice came thinly from mid-deck. "Here, Captain. It's Cornish."

"Don't fight!" Horneby shouted. "Protect yourself. Stay out of it. We need your eyes!"

Someone was drawing near, panting.

Horneby aimed a pistol at the sound. "Identify yourself!"

"Thompson, Captain. Johnny Thompson."

Horneby reached, found the seaman, and pulled him in. "Meredith, give him a musket and cutlass. Thompson, up on the quarterdeck. Start loading the carronade."

"Aye, Captain. But they're at the number two hold already. The carronade's covering number one."

"Get to it. Cornish! Hurry, man! We've got to train the carronade on them!"

Seamen came stumbling in singly and in pairs, a few wounded. Horneby sent two of them below for more arms. Cornish arrived, and Horneby ordered him directly up the stairs to the quarterdeck. At the top he called down, "Summers is here, Captain. He's dead."

Horneby had expected as much when Summers failed to answer, but still he swore.

"How many men do we have left?"

A pause. "Thirty, thirty-five."

"How many on the quarterdeck already?"

"Maybe thirty. Uh! Gibson just caught it."

"Fire the carronade as soon as you're ready," Horneby said.

Three more sailors reached them and were given weapons. The cannon thundered. Cornish whooped joyously. "We cut down at least fifteen of them, Captain!"

Horneby told him to maintain fire. He sent Randall and Hollister up, and Randall had orders to direct the seamen to pour musket fire into the mid-deck area. Any black that luck allowed them to hit would be one less they had to fight.

Teams of blacks with chisels and pry bars attacked the beam-set metal plates to which the chains were bolted. Adoko and others were cutting through the ringbolts on leg shackles.

The great gun fired. Adoko heard scerams. Two bodies fell into the hold with heavy thumps.

"Adoko," someone called. "We're lost! They can see!"

"No," he said savagely. "You know from the fighting they cannot. They shoot blind. Only chance gives them victims."

He was furious with himself. He had been stupid thinking all he need do was turn the gun. He should have left men to hold it.

There was a victory cry; one of the chains had been loosened. Thirty more men were free.

The thunder sounded again.

The gun would have to be taken. It would be a costly assault.

Adoko abandoned the shears and went up out of the

hold to the deck. He called questions and learned there had been no contact with whites for several minutes. Eunat thought they had all converged on the deck that held the cannon. Adoko agreed. Muskets popped sporadically from the rear of the ship. Balls could be heard whistling through the air, thwacking into wood; occasionally a man screamed. A small form stumbled into Adoko's legs. "Tola," he said. But the child moved away without answering. Adoko called his son once more. The boy did not respond. Adoko drew around him as many of his kinsmen as could be located and told them what had to be done, and that they must make as many of the slaves move with them as possible. The gun roared again. There were cries of agony nearby, and something wet and sticky slapped across Adoko's face.

Cornish was giddy. He was God, hurling murderous thunderbolts with divine impunity, and he was neither able nor disposed to stop giggling. He would aim the carronade and jerk the lanyard. And below on the maindeck black bodies would be flung down bloodied and broken. While he waited for the gun to be swabbed and recharged he was handed loaded muskets. By taking just enough time to draw a decent bead, he could squeeze off seven or eight shots before it was time to return to the carronade. That meant seven or eight dead or wounded slaves. When he missed, he was furious. The slaves were beginning to gather around leaders. Wonderful. He aimed the carronade, pulled the lanyard, and a cluster of black bodies was hurled down like tenpins. He took a musket, pressed the butt to his shoulder and his cheek to the wood. His eyes widened. "Well gohh-*damn!* You bastards won't believe this, but two o' them blind bucks got wimmen down on the deck an' they're pumpin' hell out of 'em. He-he-he-he-he." He shot one of the coupling men; the impact of the bullet rolled the slave off the female. He took another musket and shot the second man, who, disappointingly, merely slumped atop the woman.

"Hold your fire!" Cornish shouted. "Load up and stand. Looks like they're gettin' ready to charge. Yes, that's it, by God! That's what they're goin' t' do."

Horneby ordered men in mass to the head of the stairs. He had the rest string themselves out along the rail, muskets at the ready, cutlasses leaning at their sides. "How many will be coming?"

"Two hundred, maybe," Cornish said quietly, realizing he was neither immune nor invincible after all.

"Weapons?"

"Most of them—knives, spikes, belaying pins, boathooks. . . ."

"Direct our fire."

"They're at the mainmast. Aim for the mizzenmast area."

"Hold your fire for Cornish's signal!"

Cornish rolled the lanyard between his fingers and ran his tongue across his lips. Scattered shouts rose from the slaves, increased in number, climbed to a great and unnerving caterwaul, then . . .

"Here they come!" Cornish yelled. "Steady . . . steady . . . *fire!*"

The carronade belched flame and smoke and punched a hole in the impacted black wall. The musketry dropped not more than a dozen, who, falling, tripped the men behind them and then were lost from Cornish's sight as the slaves came on. There was no time for another volley. Blacks were pushing and shoving each other up the stairs and leaping for the vertical posts of the railing. The sailors screamed and hacked wildly with their cutlasses. Blood was everywhere. It spouted from severed limbs and headless torsos. Swinging blades sent thick drops spraying into the air. It slicked the deck. The men at the stairs had chopped up the impetus of that rush and were now holding the blacks to a standstill. But slaves were close to breaching the rail. At least four seamen were dead. Black hands wrested cutlasses from white ones. A sailor was dragged over the rail and thrown to the slaves below.

Cornish grabbed his cutlass with both hands and rushed forward. He opened the belly of a slave who had topped the rail. The man fell backwards and down. He slashed a throat. A black hand clamped on the rail. He lopped it off. A sailor with a bleeding arm and hysterical face threw away his cutlass, pushed Cornish aside, and went stumbling to the bulwark, which he mounted clumsily and from which he then dived into the sea. A black woman bore down a seaman. Cornish cut halfway through her neck. The whites were forced back, then their line collapsed, and slaves came streaming onto the quarterdeck. The small area filled with bodies, living and dead, and movement became difficult.

A cutlass near the end of its arc caught Cornish directly across his eyes. He shrieked, dropped his weapon, and covered his face. No, no, no! He shook his head, blinked, and there was nothing but redness. He held his hands out, palms up, fingers spread, as if asking why, why now? A groping hand found his shoulder, clamped down, and a moment later Cornish's skull was split open by a hatchet blow.

He had escaped the quarterdeck, which seemed to him not a little incredible. His nose was broken and part of his right ear was gone, but that was all. Had O'Brien escaped? He shouted the Irishman's name, but there was no answer.

When Horneby had yelled for them to scatter, to save themselves as best they could, Dunbar had gone over the rail to the maindeck, knocking two naked bodies to the planking, killing one with his sword, managing to break free of the other's clawing hands. He would have remained on the quarterdeck dumbly swinging his cutlass until his death overtook him were it not for the thought that O'Brien might still be alive. He could not surrender until he knew the Irishman was dead.

Crawford he was sure of. Answering the alarm bell and finding the slaves at the second hold Dunbar had heard Crawford raging lunatically as he grappled with a black. Then the Englishman had screamed, and the scream had ended in a gurgle.

But O'Brien still lived . . . perhaps. Dunbar had to know with certainty. He ripped off his clothes and flung them aside. Nakedness might shield him awhile. He kept close to the bulwark, creeping toward the bow, cutlass poised, ears straining for the sound of the Irishman's voice. He heard a seaman screaming for help. A female shrieked savagely from the same place. The sailor stopped screaming. He collided with someone. A hand pressed against his naked belly. He touched the man, who was also without clothes. Something was said to him in guttural dialect. Dunbar replied with a grunt, and waited. He was not struck. He moved on. Most of the clamor was behind him now; he guessed there were not many seamen left, and that those who had survived were being methodically brought to bay and slaughtered.

He found O'Brien on the foreside of the fo'c'sle. He heard the deep, unmistakable voice whisper, "It's to one of the boats we've got to get. We'll cut her loose, then follow her over the side."

"I don't know, Jamey," his companion said. "I don't think we can make it."

"They'll be findin' us soon, you bloody fool, and then there's nothing you'll be able to make."

Dunbar raised his cutlass and leaped forward. *"Die!"* he

screamed. *"Die, you pig!"* He felt the heavy blade cut through flesh and muscle, jar against bone. He struck again, and the Irishman went down. He straddled the man and hacked at him in frenzy, the sound of his blade that of butcher's cleaver cutting meat. He stopped only when his arms were too tired to lift the cutlass any more. He knelt, ecstatic, and touched the body. It was naked. "Saved you from the blacks, but not from me, eh Jamey, 'boyo' old boy?" He moved his hand up the trunk. The flesh was wet and split. He reached the face, which was clean-shaven. *"No!"* He touched the hair. It was long and straight. He had killed the Irishman's companion. He seized his cutlass and sprang to his feet. "O'Brien, you whore's son! O'Brien, you can't get away! I'm coming for you. Do you hear? I'm coming for you!"

The boats. He'd be making for the boats. Dunbar started off in a shambling run.

He was struck on the shoulder by a club. He turned, thinking O'Brien had been lying in wait. He was grabbed, by more than one pair of hands, and thrown to the deck. Slaves. He was confused. How did they know he was white? They hadn't touched his hair. The apical spike of a boathook tore into his arm. He screamed. "No, no, wait!" he cried. Another spike ripped his chest. "You don't understand." The spike was withdrawn from his arm, then furrowed his neck. "I love you. Stop! I want to save you. I love you!" The spike plunged into his belly, was pulled free, plunged, was pulled free . . . He tried to speak, to explain, but blood was bubbling in his mouth, choking him, and he slumped to the side, feeling the continuing impact of the stabbing spikes, but no longer any pain, and he died.

Leana watched them kill Dunbar with the long poles, and pleasure keened from her throat. She was above the deck, at a height twice that of a man, clinging to the cross-ropes. The bandage round her stump was half unraveled and new blood was soaking through it. The pain demanded white death. The pain was insatiable.

She had never been fully blind like the others. At their worst her eyes could still distinguish points of light in the darkness. Then, while her left eye went on to die completely, her right began to rally. She could see. Colors at first, blurry shapes next, and finally, though everything had a tendency to shimmer, her vision in the one eye was almost as good as it had been before.

The women had screamed and moaned and beat their breasts when, amid the shouting, the door leading to their quarters was attacked. Then the door splintered, and men, naked black men with weapons, ran inside and began to pull up the women and push them out to the deck, telling them that the whites were dying, that they had to help kill the whites.

Leana, who was the only one chained, was left alone. "I can see!" she cried. "See! Free me. I can help kill! I can tell you where they are! Free me!" She crawled as far as her chain would allow, and she beat upon the floor with her fists, shouting for them to come. At last someone did, two dark men who hesitated at the door, listening, then moved inside, hands pressed against the walls to guide themselves. They used a cutting tool to loose the chain from her shackle. They spoke softly to her and did not believe she could see. But she made one of them hold up his hand and she told him how many fingers he raised. Excited, they carried her out to the deck and found one of the Ashanti, who told them to help her up into the ropes, from which vantage point she could direct them in hunting down the scattered whites.

The girl yanked on the ropes and went "Mmm-mmm-mmm-uh!" each time one of the sailors was cornered, dragged to the deck, and butchered.

Then she saw the big one, the one with the ragged beard who had lowered her over the side. He wore no clothes. He carried an axe in his hands and was moving in a stumbling run from the front of the ship toward her. She jabbed her finger. "Him! Him! *Kill him!*" But none of the slaves moved to intercept him. Leana screeched furiously, realizing that no one could see her pointing. She was about to scream instructions when Duhbar broke into view.

The big one was merely an animal, while Duhbar was a devil and a betrayer; she needed his death first. She shouted to the slaves nearest him. They moved, found him, beat him down. She watched him die, and it was joy.

The big man had not been stopped. He had run into a slave, but had broken him with his axe. Now he was nearly beneath her. Leana loosened her grip on the ropes, waited, then dropped. She fell on the big man's back and they crashed to the deck. She hissed with the pain from her stump. The white man had lost his axe. One of his hands went around her throat, and with the other he began hammering at her head. His testicles bobbed before her. Dazed, she grabbed them with both hands and squeezed. He gasped, and his hands fell away from her. She curled her fingers as hard as she could. The big man screamed. He went over on his back. His body flopped against the deck, and his fingers clawed at empty air. Leana rose to her knees. She was crushing her palms together and yanking, as if she could tear the man apart. He vomited. "Help me!" the girl called. "Here. I have a white!" She ground his testicles between her hands. He writhed. Black men with clubs and swords drew in around her. They found the man, and they beat him and cut him until he was dead.

Leana released him. She looked down at the bloodied corpse, smiling like a coy little girl.

Hollister woke up groaning. It was as if someone had driven a spike into the center of his head. He had been forced back to the stern rail of the quarterdeck, bleeding from cuts on his arms and chest. He remembered that Horneby had shouted for them to scatter, and he remembered thinking blankly: How? And then . . . then he must have been struck unconscious.

He was lying on his back. He listened. There was still shouting, but not as loud as before; it was erratic now, as if there remained only moments of excitement. And he heard, not too far away, men talking to each other. They were speaking in no language he recognized. He heard children.

Angry, he struggled to a sitting position, then pushed himself to his feet. Head throbbing, his anger burgeoned into rage.

"Horneby!" he shouted. "Where are you, you bastard? Where's your power now, Horneby? Answer me! Where is it, damn you!"

A small form hurtled into him. He staggered back, but brushed the child aside. "Horneby! Answer me! You lied, lied!"

There was a clamor of young voices. Diminutive hands grasped at him. A monkey-like figure leapt on his back and thin arms went around his throat, choking. His legs were tugged at. He toppled over and was swarmed upon by half a dozen little bodies. He was kicked and punched and bitten. One of them was thumping a club against his head. Something sharp drove into his leg. Fingers scratched for his eyes. A thumb went into his nostril and tore open the side of his nose. Teeth ripped flesh from his arm.

"Horneby!" he raged.

There were two knives now, stabbing into his belly and his chest.

"Horneby!"

His throat was cut open.

Two men formed a kind of chair with their locked hands and carried her, her arms around their shoulders. Adoko and several others circled around her. She directed them to the whites, who were in hiding, and they flushed the sailors out and killed them. Adoko had ordered one taken prisoner; the rest were of no use.

"Ask her again," he said to a man who could speak both Ashanti and the girl's language, "if she does not see the one with the red hair anyplace."

The man translated, and answered, "No. She will tell us if she does."

They took her down into the first hold. She told them there was nothing there but the bodies of slaves who had already been dead when their chains were cut. But there were two in the second hold, hiding far back on the shelves. Black men slid onto the planking and went after them. The whites heard death inching toward them, and shrieked in fear. They did not have long to shriek. Another was discovered in the place where the whites cooked their food. He resisted ferociously and managed to kill one black and wound another before he was cut down.

The girl spoke just after they had passed the mast closest to the front of the ship. The man who translated said to Adoko, "The red-haired one is here. She says he looks dead. His stomach is open."

"Where is he?"

Adoko went too far, and the girl called him back. He

dropped to his hands and knees and crawled until he came upon the man. He laid his hand on the man's chest. There was still some life left. Adoko straddled the man and slapped his face back and forth and shouted at him. The white moaned, then mumbled something. "That is good," Adoko said. He lifted his hatchet and chopped down on the man's breastbone. The man screamed. Adoko said, "Ah!" He struck three times more, then thrust his hands into the gaping wound. The body beneath him jerked and twitched. Adoko's fingers dug further, tearing through the tissue around the heart. He seized the organ and, needing all his strength, pulled it free. The man shuddered for several moments, then went limp. Adoko raised the dripping heart above his head.

"Besu!" he called. "I keep my promise!"

Horneby fell backwards down the stairs to the officers' quarters. His pistol did not discharge, and he was unhurt.

He heard Gomez shout *"Hijos de putas, ardes en infierno!"* and fire his pistol. Webster screamed—they'd caught him then. Horneby got to his feet and moved backwards down the corridor, weapon leveled. After several minutes of strained listening in which they decided there were no slaves close to them he had crept out of hiding with Webster and Gomez toward this sanctuary. He couldn't understand how the blacks had come upon them—it was almost as if they could see.

"Captain," Gomez called. "Captain?"

Horneby was at his door. He threw it open, stepped into the cabin, slammed it closed and shot home the bolt.

"Captain!" Gomez shouted. "Don't leave me alone. They're coming. Please, Captain, *por el amor de Díos,* don't leave me alone!"

Horneby backed away from the door, keeping his pistol trained upon it. He winced when Sylas said something. "Shut up," he rasped. "Shut up, you stupid bitch."

He heard the doors to other cabins being banged open, furniture tossed around. Gomez screamed. Horneby's hands were shaking. His door was tried. He ran his tongue over his lips. The door was hit. It creaked. Horneby could scarcely breathe.

Sylas drove a knife into his back.

He grunted and fell forward to the floor.

The door splintered.

Horneby raised his head and widened his eyes, but still he could see nothing.

The door crashed inward.

Horneby jammed the pistol barrel into his mouth and pulled the trigger.

Leana missed again and threw down the musket in anger. She could not make the guns shoot where she wanted them to. There were four whites left in the ropes high above the deck. She had told the Ashanti, the one who had led them, about the sailors much earlier. He chose to ignore them until the last white on deck had been ferreted out and killed. Then he had had a chair brought out for her, and loaded muskets. He told her how to hold the guns, how to point them at the men she wanted to kill, making the little post at the front of the barrel fall into line with the V that was near the hammer, both of them resting on a white body.

The first time she fired, the wooden part of the gun jumped from her shoulder and struck her jaw. She paid no attention to the pain, was only angry that the white man was still clinging to the ropes. Next time she held the gun more tightly. It did not kick her jaw, but neither, again, did it make the white man fall. After many shots she managed to hit one of them. He jerked, let go of the ropes, and came down, turning lazy somersaults in the air until he struck the deck with a loud, dull thud. Leana clapped her hands. But her happiness was short-lived. She tried again and again for what seemed a very long time, but was unable to kill any of the remaining seamen.

"I can't do it. I just can't do it!" she sobbed.

The man next to her translated for the Ashanti. The Ashanti said something she could not understand, but his voice was low and comforting, and he patted her softly.

"He says do not be upset," the translator told her. "You have done much already. He says they will die up there, anyway, or that they will come down for water and then we will kill them."

That was true, but Leana wanted to kill them herself.

The first thing was to clear the bodies from the deck, and some of that was done. White and black corpses were thrown over the side indiscriminately. Soon the water below was boiling and frothing as sharks moved in to feed. Wounded blacks were lifted gently and carried to the mid-deck area; seamen who were not yet dead were thrown over the side with the bodies. But bottles were found, and liquor casks, and barrels of salted pork and sides of dried beef, and the liberated slaves lost interest in unburdening the deck and they gulped great swallows of alcohol and stuffed their mouths with meat. Some, their systems shocked by the unaccustomed richness, became ill. Others merely passed out. Men and women dropped down beside dead bodies and joined with fierce greediness.

Eunat, who was one of the handful of Ashanti who had survived, found Tola and then brought Adoko to his son.

The boy was lying on his back. His forehead was beaded with sweat. "Where are you injured?" Adoko asked.

"My side." The boy's voice was taut.

Adoko touched his son's shoulders, then trailed his fingers lightly down the small body. A little above the hip, he touched a wide opening, through which warm things from the boy's belly had pushed. Tola gasped. "It will be all right," Adoko said. "It will heal." He knew it would not.

He sent someone off to find cloth, as clean as could be had. He sat feeling helpless, holding Tola's hand.

"Father?"

"Yes."

"I fought. I killed one of them for you."

"You are a man of courage and strength."

"You never called me a man before . . . I'm going to die, aren't I?"

"Today you became a man, that is all. No, you are not going to die. I am bringing you home with me."

"Do you promise?"

"Yes."

"Will it take long?"

"It won't be tomorrow or the next day, but I do not think it will take very long."

"I will be glad to go home."

"I, too. And my gladness will be even greater because we will go home together."

The cloth arrived. Adoko ripped it and tied it into a single long strip. "Your body may want to cry out against the pain," Adoko told his son. "Let it. There is no shame in that." He pushed the things from Tola's belly back inside the wound, then wound the bandage three times round the narrow waist and knotted it. The boy whimpered, but did not scream. Adoko picked him up. "I will bring you down below the deck," he said. "And you will rest in a bed that belonged to one of the white leaders."

The boy's agony made him pant. Adoko crossed the deck and descended the stairs with great care, not wanting to fall or to jostle the child. He placed the boy softly on a bed and said, "I will find a woman to come and care for you. I will visit you when I can."

"Wait," Tola said. "Father . . . I am not sure I killed the white. I cut at him with a knife many times, but then I was knocked away. I could not swear he was dead . . . am I still a man?"

"There are few I would be as sure of as you. You are a man."

"You will be proud of me, I promise."

Adoko left. His son *was* a man. He would miss him. The whites had stolen much. He was sorry they could not have died in a less hurried fashion.

He knew from the nature of the heat and the patches of coolness that were shadows that the sun must be close to sinking. There was much to do, and to him and the others it no longer mattered if the sky were light or dark, but he was weary, and there was little chance of stopping the revelry or raising men from their stupors. The habit that told him night was for sleeping was still strong, so he went to the raised deck at the rear of the ship, found an empty place, lay down, and shut his eyes.

There were four of them by the wheel, which was still lashed as Summers had left it the previous morning: Adoko, Eunat, T'Komo, and a white man. The white man was in chains. A musket cracked below. Leana was trying again to shoot the whites from the ropes; one of them had fallen during the night. The remaining three had tied themselves so they wouldn't slip off in their sleep.

"Tell him," Adoko said, "we will let him live as long as he does what we want him to."

There was a long silence.

"Well?" Adoko said.

T'Komo's voice trembled with deference. "I am a slave. He is white, a master."

"You are no longer a slave. None of us are. We are free, T'Komo. We fought the masters and we killed them."

"I did not fight. I hid. I was afraid."

"That means nothing. Tell him. He is *your* slave."

"They will come back."

"No, I promise you no one will be your master again."

T'Komo spoke to the white man. His tone was unsteady and lacked conviction. The sailor answered at length, eager and ingratiating.

T'Komo said to Adoko, "He will do anything we ask. He says we are only two, three days at the most, from land. He will steer the ship there."

"No, he will take the ship back to our homes."

T'Komo translated, heard out the white man, who seemed alarmed, then replied, "He says that is impossible. It is a long journey, as long as we have been on this water already. There is not enough food. And many men are needed to make the ship sail. We would not even have time to starve, he says. The water would destroy the ship and make it sink. We would all drown."

"Tell him we will eat the food that is left, and when that is gone we will take fish from the sea. We have lived on garbage, and the fish will be as a feast for us. He will tell us what must be done for the ship, and we will do it."

Words were exchanged. T'Komo said, "He says you do not understand. You cannot understand. His people spend many years learning how to work on ships. And even then they are often killed and the ships lost. He can bring us to the near land, but if we do not let him, then we will all die. That is certain."

"That is *not* certain," Adoko said angrily. "But it will be so if he brings us to his land." He stretched out his arms and walked forward until he encountered the rail. He shouted:

"Ashanti, my people! Friends and comrades of the Ashanti! Hear me. Hear Osai Adoko." He waited for the murmur from the deck to subside. "We are close to land. But it is a white land. If we set foot on it, we will be killed, or we will be made slaves. If we try to return to our homes we may die . . . or we may rejoin our people and our families. I, Osai Adoko, will never be any man's slave again. *Never!* What is in *your* hearts?"

Shouts of *Home, home!* rose. Excited voices rattled translations, and soon the deck was booming with chanted words and phrases Adoko could not understand. At his side, T'Komo said, "I hear no one calling for the white land."

"And you?"

"I will do whatever you want," T'Komo said humbly.

"No!" Adoko slapped him hard across the face, then seized his shoulders and shook him. "You are not a slave. What do you want, *you!*"

"I . . . home. Yes, I want to go home, Osai Adoko."

"Then tell the white pig that is what we do." The chanting from the deck roared in his ears.

The white was chained to the wheel. Adoko has listened patiently to all the reasons why they could not return to his homeland. He understood few of them and was swayed by none. Determination of direction was simple. Before, the sun had risen behind them and over their right shoulders, traveled across the sky, set in front of them and over their left shoulders. They would merely position the ship so that this process would be reversed. The sailor would tell him what had to be done, and Osai Adoko would see that it was done. The girl, Leana, would be eyes for all of them. It was understood that if they discovered the white trying to deceive them, they would cut out his tongue and fill his mouth with burning embers.

Adoko led men into the high ropes again and again through the day. The white man claimed that the great cloths would have to be manipulated in various ways if they were to have any hope of success. T'Komo said that this was true. Adoko attempted nothing with the cloths that day, but he wanted men to learn how to climb the ropes, to overcome their fear. Only a few refused to leave the safety of the deck, and Adoko ordered no punishments. Most were willing, and the one thing the blacks possessed in more than sufficient quantity was manpower. Some, maybe even ten, Adoko was not sure, fell to their deaths. But this did not discourage the others. The younger ones, the boys who were almost men, were the most adept and seemed even to enjoy it. In the first few hours, moving according to directions Leana shouted up to them, they hunted and killed the three white men who had hidden so high, and glory was earned.

Once Leana reported a ship passing by. Adoko ordered them all down from the ropes, but it was a needless precaution. Leana said the ship remained a good distance away, and it made no move toward them.

The deck was crowded, and it was not possible to walk very far without bumping into someone, but it seemed to the blacks a world of spaciousness and they would not, not one of them, venture down into the holds in which they had been chained. What food there was would, Adoko estimated, last several days. He ordered that everyone be given as much as they wanted. They had gone hungry long enough, and fish, he was told by those who had lived near the water, were not hard to catch.

The next day they managed to unfurl and secure one of the huge cloths, the one hanging from the second cross-wood on the great pole nearest the front of the ship. It was only one of three the white man wanted strung thus, and the job had consumed the entire morning. But Adoko was proud of their accomplishment, and when Leana announced that they were finished, cheering broke out.

Adoko came down from the ropes and went to see Tola. The boy was feverish and could keep no food down. Adoko did not think he would live more than a day or two. He told him in detail how they had managed the cloth. Tola seemed to like the story.

Eunat came to the cabin. "There is a ship, Adoko. The girl says it has turned in our direction."

Adoko went up to the deck. "What do you see?" he asked Leana.

"A ship," said the translator. "Not as large as ours. Only two of the poles that carry cloth. It was almost by us then it began to raise flags, and in a little while it turned, and you were sent for."

T'Komo, whom Adoko had summoned, said, "The whites use flags and banners to talk to each other when they are on ships. We have not answered, and they are probably coming to find out why. They must see that our ship does not look as it should."

"How far are they?" Adoko asked.

The girl answered that they were not far, yet not near.

"They will be looking at us through their telescopes," T'Komo said.

Adoko did not understand.

"Tubes that make things seem closer. They will see that there are no whites with us, and they will capture us. We would make a fine prize."

"If they are slave traders," Adoko said.

"If they are, they will make us slaves again. If they are not, they will put us to death for having killed the other whites."

There was a booming sound. The slaves, massed on the deck and not yet aware of the other ship's presence, were suddenly silent.

Leana told T'Komo that the ship had fired a gun, and that the ball had landed in the water ahead of their own vessel.

"A warning," T'Komo said to Odoko. "Now they will begin to fire at us."

"Come," Adoko said. "I will tell our people what is happening, and that we must fight again."

"We cannot win, Adoko."

"We will not be slaves!"

"Yes," T'Komo said sadly. "Yes, we will."

"No, we will kill them, and we will not be slaves. I will tell you how."

They went to the raised deck. Adoko had just begun to shout when three cannons, not far way, thundered. Moments later, there was the sound of splitting wood, and screams. A wild clamoring swept the deck. Adoko could not make himself heard. "The girl," said the man next to Adoko, "says they are running about, falling over each other. Many are taking up weapons, but they don't know where to turn. Others are jumping into the water."

The cannons fired again, and the tumult among the blacks intensified. "Soon," T'Komo said, "they will be close enough to use their muskets, and then when they have killed enough of us, they will come aboard and make the rest of us slaves again."

Adoko reached out to find the white man chained to the wheel.

Adoko had to use a knife on the white before the man would tell him what he wanted to know. And when they left him, the sailor was slumped at the base of the wheel, gasping and crying out in agony. Adoko, T'Komo, Eunat, and a handful of others went, carrying Leana, to the storage space behind the galley. They brought up four large barrels and rolled them back to a small trapdoor set in the deck near the rear of the ship. The cannons of the approaching craft fired several more salvos, crushing bodies and splintering large sections of the deck, then fell silent. "There are whites with muskets all along the side," Leana said. "They will be upon us very soon now."

Adoko lowered himself through the opened trapdoor into a small chamber in which he was barely able to stand erect. The others handed down the barrels to him, and he stacked them alongside the two dozen casks already stored in the chamber. A rattle of musketry sounded. Shrieks and screams swept the deck. Eunat gave Adoko a hatchet and a pistol. Adoko chopped through the top of one of the large barrels and tipped it, spilling pungent oil across the floor. Then he split open one of the small casks, which contained gunpowder.

"Adoko," T'Komo said. "I . . . I am not a slave. May I take your place with the pistol?"

There was a moment's silence. Then Adoko said, "Come." T'Komo dropped into the hold. Adoko gave him the pistol and placed his hand on the open powder cask. Musket fire was crackling steadily. Adoko pulled himself up on deck. T'Komo spoke to Leana.

Adoko stood a moment, listening to the gunfire and to the screams. Then he said, to all of them, "Goodbye." And he turned and made his way toward the rear of the ship, pushing milling bodies to the side.

He went down the stairs, entered the cabin, worked his arms beneath his son, and lifted the boy as gently as he could. "Tola, we are going home."

"Now?" the boy said. "Already?"

"Yes."

Tola was in much pain. He gasped with each step Adoko took. Adoko climbed the stairs and went directly toward the side opposite the approaching ship. He was knocked to one knee by a running figure. The boy screamed.

"We are almost there," Adoko said. "Just a moment longer." He encountered the rail. He swung first one leg over it, then the other, and balanced a moment.

"Are you coming with me?" Tola asked.

"Yes, we are going home together."

He clasped his son tight to his breast, leaned forward, pushed against the side of the ship, and went arcing out toward the water.

"They're beside us," Leana said, "throwing iron hooks, trying to catch hold. One of them is swinging across on a rope. Now, now! *Kill them!*"

Below her, in the small chamber, T'Komo cocked the pistol. He held it inches from the ruptured powder cask, and he pulled the trigger.

Adoko drove deeper beneath the surface. Contentment and peace spread through him. He realized, dimly, that his legs had fallen still. He did not care. He was happy. He was going home. With Tola, who was pressed softly and yieldingly to his chest, no longer clinging, no longer . . . no . . . longer . . . no . . . home . . .

Some distance above, the *Jubilation* exploded. The concussion wave reached Adoko and his son in moments and rolled them head over heels, rolled them again, and then passed on, leaving the two black bodies to sway from side to side as they sank, slowly, through the darkening depths.

GW01607177

ArtScroll® Series

Rabbi Nosson Scherman / Rabbi Gedaliah Zlotowitz
General Editors
Rabbi Meir Zlotowitz ז״ל, *Founder*

THE INZELBUCH FAMILY EDITON

Rav Nosson Tzvi

Published by

ARTSCROLL
Mesorah Publications, ltd

Speaks

שיחות רבי נתן צבי

INSIGHTS ON CHUMASH
FROM THE BELOVED MIR ROSH HAYESHIVAH

FIRST EDITION
First Impression ... April 2022
Second Impression ... August 2022

Published and Distributed by
MESORAH PUBLICATIONS, LTD.
313 Regina Avenue / Rahway, N.J. 07065

Distributed in Europe by
LEHMANNS
Unit E, Viking Business Park
Rolling Mill Road
Jarrow, Tyne & Wear NE32 3DP
England

Distributed in Australia & New Zealand by
GOLDS WORLD OF JUDAICA
3-13 William Street
Balaclava, Melbourne 3183
Victoria Australia

Distributed in Israel by
SIFRIATI / A. GITLER — BOOKS
POB 2351
Bnei Brak 51122

Distributed in South Africa by
KOLLEL BOOKSHOP
Northfield centre, 17 Northfield Avenue
Glenhazel 2192, Johannesburg, South Africa

ARTSCROLL® SERIES
RAV NOSSON TZVI SPEAKS

ITEM CODE: RNTSH
ISBN 10: 1-4226-3128-1
ISBN 13: 978-1-4226-3128-7

Typography by CompuScribe at ArtScroll Studios, Ltd.
Printed in the United States of America.
Bound by Sefercraft, Quality Bookbinders, Ltd., Rahway NJ

מה זרעו בחיים אף הוא בחיים

In honor and loving memory of our dear father

ר' חיים מענדל ב"ר משה זאב הכהן טרויבע זצ"ל

Reb Chaim Traube זצ"ל

He lived a life of dedication to Torah, was steadfast to his mesorah, and personified humility, modesty, and *simchas hachaim*. He displayed a deep devotion to *avodas Hashem* and true care and compassion for others.

His most cherished possessions were his children and grandchildren, who attempt to follow in his noble ways. He taught them by example how to live as Torah Jews.

זכור ה' לדוד

In honor and loving memory of our dear brother

הרב דוד זלמן ב"ר חיים מענדל הכהן טרויבע זצ"ל

Harav Dovid Traube זצ"ל

In his too-short life he achieved great heights toiling in Torah and *avodas Hashem*. His devotion to his *ruchniyus*, coupled with his dedication to his family and his *aishes chayil* תחי', serve as a prime example of what it means to be a true *ben aliyah*.

His presence elevated everyone around him, and he was a genuine חבר טוב to all who knew him.

בן יכבד אב

In honor of my dear parents

Mr. and Mrs. Michael and Michelle Inzelbuch עמו"ש

To whom I owe the deepest debt of gratitude for guiding me on the path that led me to the Mir Yeshiva.

May they continue to see *nachas* from their children and grandchildren.

Azriel and Aleeza Inzelbuch

ישיבת מיר ירושלים

YESHIVAS MIR YERUSHALAYIM

Founded in Mir 1817. In Jerusalem 1944 | ע״ר 580037638 | בס״ד נוסדה במיר בשנת תקע״ז. בירושלים בשנת תש״ד

RABBI E.Y. FINKEL
DEAN

הרב א.י. פינקל
ראש הישיבה

בס״ד　　　　　　　　　　　　　　　　אדר שני תשפ״ב

מה נכבד היום בעלות על שולחן מלכים הספר הנכבד והמיוחד **שיחות רבי נתן צבי** על עניני תורה ומוסר, מתורת אאמו״ר ראש הישיבה הגאון המופלא רבי **נתן צבי פינקל** זצוק״ל מגדולי מרביצי התורה ומענקי התורה והרוח בדורנו, אשר עמל ויגע בעמלה של תורה ומסר שיעורים ושיחות לאלפים בכל מקצועות התורה.

וזה כמה שנים אשר ספר זה יצא לאור עולם, ורבים נהנו לאורו, ועתה זכינו לאור גדול עם צאת הספר מכבש הדפוס מתורגם ללשון המדוברת לבני חו״ל, לפתוח שערי תורה ומוסר ולזכות את הרבים המשתוקקים וצמאים לתורתו בדבר נאה מתוקן ושוה לכל נפש.

אמינא לפעלכם טבא, יישר חילכם על העבודה הגדולה והטירחה העצומה, יהי ה׳ עמכם להרבות חיילים לאורייתא ללמוד וללמד לשמור ולעשות, ויהא כבוד שמים מתרבה על ידכם להגדיל תורה ולהאדירה.

בברכת התורה

אליעזר יהודה פינקל

הרב אליעזר יהודה פינקל
ראש הישיבה

3 Beth Israel St. P.O.B 5022 Jerusalem 9105001 Tel. 02-5410999 Fax. 02-5323446 ● 580037638 ע״ר 02-5323446 פקס. 02-5410999 טל. 9105001 ירושלים 5022 רח. בית ישראל 3 ת.ד.

Table of Contents

Sefer Vayikra ❖ ספר ויקרא

Sefer Bamidbar ❖ ספר במדבר

Sefer Devarim ❖ ספר דברים

Publisher's Preface

It is a great privilege for us to present this volume to the Jewish public. Few people in our time have had such a profound influence on adults and *talmidim* as HaGaon HaRav Nosson Tzvi Finkel *zt"l,* Rosh Yeshivah of Mir-Yerushalayim. That an "American boy from Chicago" could not only become the head of a great yeshivah, but make it the largest Torah institution in the world would be astounding enough. But that he did so while delivering *shiurim* and despite a severe physical handicap is what made him one of the most beloved and inspiring Torah leaders in the world.

This volume is a collection of his Chumash *shmuessen* to *talmidim* of the yeshivah. They are profound and illuminating. There is no doubt that they will be discussed and repeated by all who read them.

We are grateful to the Rosh Yeshivah and *hanhalah* of Mir-Yerushalayim for choosing us to publish this brilliant work and thereby enable many more thousands of our fellow Jews to become his *talmidim.*

Rabbi Gedaliah Zlotowitz / Rabbi Nosson Scherman

Menachem Av 5782/ August 2022

Foreword

All who were privileged to attend the Rosh Yeshivah *zt"l's* Erev Shabbos *shmuessen* understands that it was much more than a simple *parashah shiur.* The experience for every English-speaking *bachur* was that of the warmth and love of a father sharing his love of Torah.

With that same *ahavas haTorah,* the Rosh Yeshivah's late son, Hagaon Harav Yitzchok Finkel *zt"l,* transcribed and faithfully recorded each of the *shmuessen,* which were later compiled and published in *lashon kodesh* by his son-in-law *ybl"c* Hagaon Harav Ahron Kessler *shlita.*

Rabbi and Mrs. Yanky Perkal of Targumasters, together with their family, dedicated hundreds of hours throughout the days and nights translating and faithfully preserving the nuances, voice, and message of the Rosh Yeshivah *zt"l.*

A very special thank you to Reb Gedaliah Zlotowitz and his staff at ArtScroll for lending their considerable expertise to ensuring the success of this project.

No Mir publication is complete without the talented and creative flavor of R' Baruch Mordechai Wenger and his team at Artech Marketing. Thank you for your help and guidance on this sefer.

As with every special project that happens in Yeshivas Mir Yerushalayim, Chanoch Zundel Herskowitz and Uri Stern have their fingerprints all over this *sefer's* success.

Our sincere thank you to our dear friends, Azriel and Aleeza Inzelbuch, who so graciously and proudly seized the opportunity to sponsor the *sefer* in memory of Reb Chaim Traube *zt"l* and Harav Dovid Traube *zt"l,* forever linking the memories of Mrs.

Inzelbuch's father and brother *z"l* with the Rosh Yeshivah *zt"l's* Torah. May it be a *zechus* for the entire family and may they see *doros yesharim u'mevorachim oskim baTorah.*

Acharon acharon chaviv — our heartfelt thank you to the Rosh Yeshivah *shlita,* his mother Rebbetzin Leah Finkel *tichyeh,* and the entire Finkel family for their support and encouragement in bringing the vision of this *sefer* to life.

Yeshivas Mir Yerushalayim

ספר בראשית
Sefer Bereishis

פרשת בראשית
Parashas Bereishis

⁂ *The Sudden Plummet*

וַיְהִי מִקֵּץ יָמִים וַיָּבֵא קַיִן מִפְּרִי הָאֲדָמָה מִנְחָה לַה׳. וְהֶבֶל הֵבִיא גַם הוּא מִבְּכֹרוֹת צֹאנוֹ וּמֵחֶלְבֵהֶן וַיִּשַׁע ה׳ אֶל הֶבֶל וְאֶל מִנְחָתוֹ. וְאֶל קַיִן וְאֶל מִנְחָתוֹ לֹא שָׁעָה וַיִּחַר לְקַיִן מְאֹד וַיִּפְּלוּ פָּנָיו . . . וַיֹּאמֶר קַיִן אֶל הֶבֶל אָחִיו וַיְהִי בִּהְיוֹתָם בַּשָּׂדֶה וַיָּקָם קַיִן אֶל הֶבֶל אָחִיו וַיַּהַרְגֵהוּ.

After a period of time, Kayin brought an offering to Hashem of the fruit of the ground. And as for Hevel, he also brought of the firstlings of his flock and from their choicest. Hashem turned to Hevel and to his offering, but to Kayin and to his offering He did not turn. This annoyed Kayin exceedingly, and his countenance fell ... Kayin spoke with his brother Hevel. And it happened when they were in the field, that Kayin rose up against his brother Hevel and killed him (*Bereishis* 4:3-8).

The sequence of events recounted in the Torah indicates that Kayin brought his offering first and was then joined by Hevel. The words: וְהֶבֶל הֵבִיא גַם הוּא, *And Hevel also brought,* imply that Hevel was second to Kayin and followed his lead, after

Kayin conceived and initiated the spiritual concept of *korbanos* in this world, as the Ramban notes (v. 3): "These people understood the great secret of *korbanos* and *menachos*." It wasn't until after Kayin presented his offering to Hashem that Hevel was inspired to do the same.

Kayin brought his *minchah* from a lofty plane of spiritual appreciation, intuiting the secret of *korbanos* from his own mind and heart. Nevertheless, Hakadosh Baruch Hu did not accept his offering, since it was sorely lacking in quality, as Rashi interprets the words *mipri ha'adamah* to mean *min hagarua* — from the worst.

The Rosh Yeshivah, Rav Chaim Shmulevitz, observes that at this point in history, the only inhabitants of the world were Adam HaRishon and his wife and children, while the world itself was replete with a virtually endless array of the finest and most succulent fruits, grains, and produce. Adam and his family couldn't possibly have consumed even a tiny fraction of the great bounty that flourished all around them, and abandoning all the excess produce in the fields would leave it to rot. What prevented Kayin from offering the cream of his crop to Hashem, especially when it was he who originally grasped the exalted secret of *korbanos* and felt inspired to offer a gift to Heaven?

Rav Chaim explains that this is the innate nature of man. Even when a person is blessed with all the bounty and goodness in the world, he is reluctant to part with his possessions or share them with others. Furthermore, even when a person does share his wealth, he tends to be stingy and give with an *ayin ra'ah*. The attribute of *nesinah,* giving from the heart, is so challenging for a human being to master that even when a person engages in this lofty spiritual form of giving — offering a *korban* to Hakadosh Baruch Hu — his nature would be to do so frugally, with an *ayin ra'ah.*

If someone were to present low-grade produce as a gift to his friend, the friend would surely be offended. Why, then, was Kayin so shocked and dismayed that Hashem did not accept his *korban*?

Kayin's reaction stemmed from the same negative trait of stinginess that underpinned his offering. It is so difficult for a person to give genuinely from himself that even when he gives the bare minimum, he feels that he parted with everything he owns, and that others owe him appreciation for his magnanimous gift! Kayin presented the worst of his produce to Hashem, yet he still believed that his offering would be accepted graciously and with desire — because in his mind, he had given everything in the world. This is why the rejection of his *korban* caused him deep distress.

The Gateway to Spiritual Degeneration

The Torah continues: וַיֹּאמֶר קַיִן אֶל הֶבֶל אָחִיו וַיְהִי בִּהְיוֹתָם בַּשָּׂדֶה וַיָּקָם קַיִן אֶל הֶבֶל אָחִיו וַיַּהַרְגֵהוּ, *Kayin spoke with his brother Hevel. And it happened when they were in the field, that Kayin rose up against his brother Hevel and killed him.*

While the Torah does not specify exactly what Kayin said to Hevel, it is clear that their dialogue sparked a conflict that led Kayin to "rise up against his brother and kill him." *Targum Yonasan ben Uziel* states that Kayin and Hevel discussed why Hevel's *korban* had been accepted with desire, while Kayin's had been rejected. In the course of their argument, Kayin declared, "There is no justice and no Judge; no World to Come, no reward for the righteous, and no punishment for the wicked."

Hevel argued, "There is justice and a Judge; there is a World to Come, and there is reward for the righteous and punishment for the wicked." The *Targum* continues, "About these words they fought, and then Kayin rose up against Hevel his brother and threw a rock at his forehead and killed him."

How is it possible that an intense spiritual discussion regarding matters of faith impelled Kayin to slay his brother so ruthlessly? Moreover, how did Kayin, who had attained the exalted spiritual level that enabled him to innovate the concept of *korbanos,* plummet so rapidly and dramatically to this base level of denying the central tenets of *emunah* and brazenly proclaiming *"leis din v'leis Dayan* — There is no justice and no Judge"?

This answer,[1] as evident once again from the sequence of the *pesukim,* is that this episode occurred immediately after Hakadosh

---

1. See *Sichos Mussar, MeIgra Rama L'Bira Amikta.*

Baruch Hu's rejection of Kayin's offering, which left him crestfallen. When a person is in a state of shock and distress, he can easily lose control of himself and his emotions. At that moment, he can stumble right into the trap of the *yetzer hara* and plummet all at once to a spiritual abyss. His lack of control can even lead him to the point of severe transgressions that he would never dream of committing when in a state of *yishuv hadaas*, when he is in control of himself, his thoughts, and his emotions. The ill-fated discussion between Kayin and Hevel took place when Kayin was in an emotional state of *naflu panav* and *vayichar me'od* — his countenance fell and he became exceedingly annoyed — which caused him to utterly lose himself and commit the cardinal sins of murder and heresy.

Responsibility: The Foundation of Proper Living

This lesson underscores the fundamental obligation to improve and strengthen one's *middah* of *achrayus*, responsibility. Everything we do, every word we speak, and every action we take must be with forethought, as otherwise, in a brief fit of anger, shock, or distress, one is liable to utterly lose his judgment and discretion and destroy his life and the lives of others. Every hour and day must be measured and planned.

The path to acquiring the *middah* of *achrayus*, which allows a person to remain in full control of himself and take responsibility for his actions even during times of challenge and adversity, is learning *mussar* and davening constantly to Hashem. Society today is sorely lacking in responsibility and prudence. People act rashly and impulsively, without exercising discretion or stopping to calculate if something is necessary, if it's a priority, and if it's worth the time and effort. People act on instinct instead of logically evaluating their course of action. They do whatever strikes their fancy at the moment without reflecting upon future ramifications or consequences.

Achrayus is the secret to success in every realm. Our primary aspiration in life is to achieve *gadlus baTorah* and spread the Torah's radiance throughout the world, but one cannot be *marbitz Torah* — become a rosh yeshivah, *mashgiach,* or rebbi — without fully mastering the *middah* of *achrayus*. Only someone who hones this *middah* in his youth will be capable of positively influencing others later in life.

Beyond the requirement to act with responsibility and fulfill our personal obligations in this world, the *middah* of *achrayus* also encompasses the precept of *"Kol Yisrael areivim zeh bazeh* — All Jews are guarantors for one another" (*Shevuos* 39a). People are constantly observing, evaluating, and learning from our behavior, and we are destined to provide a full accounting for our conduct throughout life. This was the crux of Hevel's response when he insisted that there *is* justice, there *is* a Judge, there *is* a World to Come, and there *is* reward and punishment.

In contrast, Kayin's declaration of *"leis din v'leis Dayan"* repudiated the need for *achrayus* and denied the ultimate accounting that a person is destined to give. This false conception led to his downfall.

What emerges is that there are two motives that should compel a person to enhance his *middah* of *achrayus*: The first is that lack of responsibility bars one from achieving success in any realm, be it *emunah,* Torah, or an occupation. The second is that the *neshamah* will one day render an accounting in the Heavenly Court regarding how well he fulfilled his responsibilities, and woe unto the one forced to stand before the Throne of Glory and admit to a life lived with carefree impulsivity.

One who internalizes the knowledge that there will come a day when he will stand before the Heavenly Tribunal and provide an accounting for each and every action will automatically exercise better judgment and refrain from frittering precious moments away. We must evaluate our every word and action and conduct ourselves in a measured manner that enables us to enhance our *limud Torah* and *yiras Shamayim,* which will in turn benefit Klal Yisrael on both the collective and individual level.

פרשת נח
Parashas Noach

◆ *Sharing the Burden of a Friend*

כִּי מֵי נֹחַ זֹאת לִי אֲשֶׁר נִשְׁבַּעְתִּי מֵעֲבֹר מֵי נֹחַ עוֹד עַל הָאָרֶץ.
For [like] the waters of Noach this shall be to Me: Just as I swore that the waters of Noach would never again pass over the earth (*Yeshayah* 54:9).

Why is the Mabul called *mei Noach* — the waters of Noach? Chazal explain that the *navi* refers to the Mabul as "Noach's waters" because he did not daven to save his generation from the flood after learning that he and his children would be spared (*Zohar, Bereishis* 7:1).

This statement of Chazal is puzzling, in light of Noach's incredible selflessness, as the Midrash describes (*Tanchuma* 58:9):

> R' Levi said: Throughout all those twelve months, Noach and his children did not sleep, as they were compelled to feed the beasts and the wild animals and the birds. Rabbi Akiva said: Even twigs for the elephants and glass for the ostrich they brought with their hands in order to sustain them. There are animals that eat at two hours into the night, and those that eat at three hours. [I can] prove to you that they did not taste sleep, as R' Yochanan taught in the name

of R' Eliezer son of R' Yossi HaGelili that once, Noach was delayed in feeding the lion, and the lion bit him. After that, he limped, as it is written: וַיִּשָּׁאֶר אַךְ נֹחַ, *Only Noach survived* (*Bereishis* 7:23). *Ach* implies that he was incomplete and not fit to offer a *korban*; therefore, his son Shem offered it in his stead.

Throughout the many months that Noach and his family dwelled in the *teivah*, they devoted themselves exclusively to sustaining creation, laboring arduously and indefatigably to feed the animals, to the extent that they did not sleep for even a moment.

Furthermore, Radak teaches (*Bereishis* 9:4) that the reason Noach was ultimately permitted to eat meat from the flesh of animals was that "he toiled with the beasts and wild animals and insects and birds, to sustain them in the *teivah*." These intensive efforts were not for his own sake or even on behalf of his children, who surely had no need for all the various animal species. Had Noach been absorbed in his own needs and desires, he could have justifiably allotted himself several hours of rest and peace of mind each day, instead of busying himself day and night with the needs of the animals. It is obvious that Noach's efforts were spurred by noble intentions to sustain the world, so why did he fail to daven on behalf of the people of his generation and thereby prevent their annihilation?

Upon learning of the imminent destruction of Sedom, Avraham Avinu petitioned Hashem repeatedly to spare the city even on behalf of only ten righteous individuals, as the Torah states: וַיֹּאמֶר אַל נָא יִחַר לַאדֹנָי וַאֲדַבְּרָה אַךְ הַפַּעַם אוּלַי יִמָּצְאוּן שָׁם עֲשָׂרָה, *So he said, "Let not my Lord be annoyed and I will speak but this once: What if ten would be found there?"* (*Bereishis* 18:32). When Hashem replied that even ten *tzaddikim* could not be found in Sedom, Avraham stopped davening.

Chazal explain that Avraham Avinu saw that "in the generation of the Mabul there were eight [*tzaddikim*], and the world was not saved in their merit" (*Bereishis Rabbah* 49:13). Since the merits of eight righteous people in the era of Noach had not spared the world from destruction, Avraham grasped that this was not a sufficient *zechus*, and he did not attempt to daven that Hashem spare Sedom for the sake of eight *tzaddikim*.

If Avraham Avinu was not faulted for stopping to daven when he reached only eight *tzaddikim*, it stands to reason that Noach knew that his prayers on behalf of his generation would be ineffective. Why, then, was he held accountable for failing to daven?

A Life of Yissurim Is Better Than Death

Rav Chaim Shmulevitz (*Sichos Mussar, Mei Noach*) writes that upon seeking ways to weaken Bnei Yisrael's influence in Egypt, Pharaoh declared: הָבָה נִתְחַכְּמָה לוֹ, *Come, let us outsmart it* (*Shemos* 1:10).

The Gemara expounds (*Sotah* 11a): "Three individuals were involved in offering that counsel to Pharaoh: Bilam, Iyov, and Yisro. Bilam, who counseled Pharaoh to drown the Jewish babies, was slain; Iyov, who was silent, was punished by having to undergo suffering. As for Yisro, who fled, his descendants merited to sit in the Chamber of Hewn Stone in the Temple as members of the Sanhedrin."

While Bilam's crime was far more severe than Iyov's silence, Iyov seems to have received a harsher punishment. Bilam was simply condemned to death, but Iyov was subjected to lifelong adversity and suffering. Chazal relate (*Kesubos* 33b) that Chananyah, Mishael, and Azaryah were able to withstand the *nisayon* of bowing down to an idol because they were threatened merely with death; had they been subjected to torture, they could not have withstood the agony, and would have succumbed. This implies that torture is worse than death. If so, why was Iyov punished more harshly than Bilam?

The respective punishments of Iyov and Bilam highlight the supreme value of life. Even a life filled with unimaginable misery and adversity is preferable to death, because as long as a person lives, he is able to draw closer to Hashem, attain loftier heights of *ruchniyus*, and elevate his *neshamah* with merits. Even if, on a personal level, death is easier than a lifetime of agony — as demonstrated by the case of Chananyah, Mishael, and Azaryah — the actual punishment of death and the forfeited opportunity to achieve *dveikus* to Hashem is infinitely worse. This is why Bilam was condemned to death, while Iyov received the lesser punishment of *yissurim*.

Noach Was Not Pained by the Destruction

The grounds for Iyov's punishment are still unclear. Had he attempted to protest Pharaoh's evil plot, his objections would have been dismissed, as is evident from the fact that Yisro fled without sounding a protest, since he knew it wouldn't help. Why, then, was Iyov punished so severely for his silence?

Rav Chaim answered that the purpose of *yissurim* is not only to punish a person for his sins, but also to indicate to the person how he sinned and to show him the proper path so he will not sin again. This is the essence of *middah k'neged middah*, which prompts a person to take stock of his *aveirah* and evaluate where and how he faltered.

Human nature is such, the Brisker Rav observed, that one who is suffering cries out in pain even when he knows his cries won't help. When it hurts, you cry! And if a person doesn't cry, that indicates that he is not in great pain. Iyov's silence in the face of Pharaoh's evil decree proved that he did not feel Bnei Yisrael's suffering as he felt his own. The intense *yissurim* that he endured underscored that even if all his protestations would have fallen upon deaf ears, he should still have sounded a cry of bitter anguish against the cruelty.

The same can be said regarding Noach and the Mabul. Although Noach dedicated himself wholeheartedly to sustaining the world inside the *teivah*, he was still held accountable for failing to daven to save his generation. Noach knew that without the merits of ten *tzaddikim*, the world could not continue, yet he should nevertheless have prayed, shed copious tears, and sounded an agonized cry upon the annihilation of humanity and the destruction of Hashem's beautiful world, just as he would have grieved his own personal destruction. Since Noach did not daven, it is clear that he did not sufficiently feel the pain or mourn the indescribable loss. Therefore, he was faulted for not davening, and the Mabul was called *mei Noach* as if he, himself, had brought it upon the world.

Feeling Another Person's Pain as Our Own

This great level of concern and empathy is expected of all of us as well. We are all required to genuinely sympathize and feel the pain of a fellow Yid. Every person must possess a sense of *achrayus* toward Klal Yisrael and feel the pain of the *klal* as if it were his personal *tzarah*. Each one of us is responsible for everyone!

This is true in yeshivah as well. When a *bachur* is in yeshivah, which is a *makom tzibbur*, he bears responsibility for the entire *tzibbur*, and he must be aware that his every action will impact the *klal*. Even a personal act of his that is unrelated to the *tzibbur* may still affect the *klal*, and he must therefore be exceedingly careful with even the minor details of his behavior.

The obligation to share the burden of others pertains not just to the *klal*, but to individuals as well. The Gemara teaches (*Berachos* 12b): "Rabbah bar Chinana the elder said in the name of Rav: Anyone who has the opportunity to beseech God for mercy on behalf of his fellow and does not beseech Him is called a sinner…. Rava said: If [the person who is in need of mercy] is a Torah scholar, one is required even to make himself ill on his behalf."

For a person to pray sincerely for his friend, and certainly for him to become sick with concern for his friend, he must first feel the person's pain deeply, as if it were his own. A person who prays for another without experiencing his pain cannot daven with emotion and sincerity, and his *tefillah* emerges vacant and ineffective. In contrast, one who truly sympathizes with another person's anguish, and feels his loss, need, and hardship, automatically sounds a genuine cry of anguish and weeps on his behalf. This intensity and passion have the power to work wonders on the friend's behalf and generate his salvation.

Davening for Another Jew Benefits Him Spiritually

One who prays for his friend while feeling his pain can benefit him also in matters that we would not generally consider subject to being changed through *tefillah*. The Chazon Ish (*Orach Chaim, He'aros*) writes that one is permitted to daven for his friend to do *teshuvah*. It may seem, he elaborates, that a person should not daven for this, since *teshuvah* is contingent upon a person's *bechirah*, and Hashem's help would seem to negate that *bechirah*. Yet we know that a person may compel his friend to serve Hashem, whether by force or through positive incentives. This is not regarded as negating his *bechirah*, since the Jewish people are considered "one man with one heart," so the person is regarded as if he made the choice using his own *bechirah*. The same applies to one who davens for his friend to do *teshuvah*. When Hashem draws the person close, it is considered as if he came close of his own will, not that his *bechirah* was overridden.

The Alter of Slabodka epitomized feeling another person's pain and davening for him, and this attribute was emulated by his son, the Rosh Yeshivah Rav Eliezer Yehudah Finkel. When either of the two would see a *bachur* in yeshivah faltering in his learning, they would daven fervently, and even fast, so he would succeed in *ruchniyus*.

What led them to achieve this exalted devotion to their *talmidim*? It was the feeling that their *talmidim* were a part of them — their sons, themselves! So potent was the love and commitment that these *tzaddikim* felt toward their *talmidim* that they truly experienced their pain and challenges as if they were their own. Filled as they were with such powerful emotions, it is no wonder that they were able to daven with all their might and even fast until their *tefillos* were answered.

My rebbi, Rav Chaim Kamil, taught (*Imrei Chaim, Koach HaTefillah*) that a person must daven both for his own success in learning as well as for the success of all *lomdei Torah*. Obviously, a prerequisite to davening sincerely for the success of others is to acutely feel pain over what they lack.

We are now on the brink of a new *zman* — a time of renewed Kabbalas HaTorah. From this *parashah,* we gain a powerful insight into how to merit *hatzlachah* in Torah: Each of us should share the pain of our friends and feel their needs, in both the spiritual and material realms, and pour out our hearts in prayer on behalf of others.

In the merit of feeling the pain of others and davening for them, may we all receive the *yeshuos* we need, as the Gemara teaches (*Bava Kamma* 92a), "If anyone prays for mercy on behalf of his fellow, when he himself needs that very same thing, he is answered first."

פרשת לך לך
Parashas Lech Lecha

⚜ The Path to Greatness: Dedication to the Klal

וַיֹּאמֶר ה׳ אֶל אַבְרָם לֶךְ לְךָ מֵאַרְצְךָ וּמִמּוֹלַדְתְּךָ וּמִבֵּית אָבִיךָ אֶל הָאָרֶץ אֲשֶׁר אַרְאֶךָּ. וְאֶעֶשְׂךָ לְגוֹי גָּדוֹל וַאֲבָרֶכְךָ וַאֲגַדְּלָה שְׁמֶךָ וֶהְיֵה בְּרָכָה . . . וְנִבְרְכוּ בְךָ כֹּל מִשְׁפְּחֹת הָאֲדָמָה.

Hashem said to Avram, "Go for yourself from your land, from your relatives, and from your father's house to the land that I will show you. And I will make of you a great nation; I will bless you, and make your name great, and you shall be a blessing ... and all the families of the earth shall bless themselves by you" (*Bereishis* 12:1-3).

The Midrash elaborates (*Bereishis Rabbah* 39:11):

R' Levi said: A person did not finish assessing the value of a cow that he wished to purchase from Avraham before the person would be blessed, and Avraham did not finish assessing the value of a cow for one who wished to sell him the cow before the seller would be blessed from his association with Avraham. How great was the power of his blessing? Avraham would pray for barren women and they were granted a child, and he would pray for the sick and they were granted relief.

R' Huna said: It is not only that when Avraham would go to the sick person he would be cured; rather, the sick person would simply see him and improve.

R' Chanina said: Even ships that were crossing the great ocean in stormy weather were saved in Avraham's merit....

R' Berechyah said: It is already written earlier in the verse: וַאֲבָרֶכְךָ, *and I will bless you*; why, then, does the Torah state again: וֶהְיֵה בְּרָכָה, *you shall be a blessing*? Rather, God was saying to Avraham: "Until now I needed to bless those in My world who deserved blessing Myself. Henceforth, the blessings are entrusted to you. Whoever appears deserving to you to be blessed, bless!"

When Hakadosh Baruch Hu blessed Avraham, he acquired the power to bless others. This transformed him into the source of blessing, and from then on, all *berachah* was channeled into the world in his merit. Indeed, regarding the words: וְנִבְרְכוּ בְךָ כֹּל מִשְׁפְּחֹת הָאֲדָמָה, *and all the families of the earth shall bless themselves by you*, the Midrash states (*Bereishis Rabbah* 39:12): "Rain is in your merit; dew is in your merit."

The marvelous *koach haberachah* that Hashem conferred upon Avraham Avinu was rooted in his sense of responsibility and his desire to benefit the public. Avraham Avinu excelled in this regard, as evidenced by his passionate *tefillos* and pleas on behalf of the people of Sedom (in contrast to Noach; see previous essay). This quality propelled him to the pinnacle of spiritual elevation and closeness to Hashem. The entire world was therefore sustained by his merits, and he became the source of blessing in the world.

Composer of People

The Alter of Slabodka was a paradigm of taking responsibility for the generation. Someone once asked his son, the Rosh Yeshivah R' Eliezer Yehudah Finkel, why he never spoke about his father or shared stories or lessons from him.

Upon hearing the question, R' Eliezer Yehudah's face reddened, and his body began trembling. His voice thick with emotion, he replied, "In the merit of my holy father, Klal Yisrael merited two or three generations of Torah. How dare I speak about him?"

Similarly, the Chofetz Chaim praised the Alter of Slabodka by saying, "I am a *mechaber sefarim*, but the Alter of Slabodka was a *mechaber bnei adam* — he composed people." In his wisdom, the Alter of Slabodka intuited how to build the *nefesh* of every *talmid*, and by doing so he laid the foundations for generations of Torah and *talmidei chachamim*. By developing his disciples, he caused the world to be sustained and blessed. This ability to serve as a source of blessing to the world drew from his willingness to selflessly shoulder the burden of the *klal*, and from his profound sense of *achrayus* toward the building of Klal Yisrael.

His son R' Eliezer Yehudah likewise carried the burden of the *klal*, devoting his heart and soul to promoting the spiritual growth and success of *lomdei Torah* everywhere. He would sit and listen patiently to *chiddushei Torah* from any yeshivah student who approached him, whether his *chiddush* related to the *masechta* that was being studied in the yeshivah or to any other *sugya* in Shas. When the yeshivah was studying the *sugya* of *yiush shelo midaas* (*Bava Metzia* 21b), R' Eliezer Yehudah attested that he had heard 243 *chaburos* on this *sugya* alone — and could repeat the *chiddushim* he had heard from every individual.

A group of accomplished *bachurim* once approached him to complain about a particular *bachur* who was not behaving properly. They requested that the Rosh Yeshivah expel this *bachur*, but R' Eliezer Yehudah refused. When the *bachurim* declared that if this *bachur* would remain, they would all leave, the Rosh Yeshivah replied that it was more important to him to keep this *bachur* within the walls of the *beis midrash*, even on account of losing the others. He explained that he had no doubt that they would continue learning Torah wherever they were, whereas expelling this particular *bachur* from the yeshivah would likely lead him to spiritual ruin. This, he maintained, was sufficient grounds for allowing him to stay.

What an incredible display of *achrayus*! R' Eliezer Yehudah was prepared to sacrifice the reputation and success of the Mir Yeshivah by bidding farewell to some of his leading *talmidim,* in order to preserve the spiritual health and future of a single troubled *bachur*. This devotion to others was the attribute of Avraham Avinu, which made him worthy of becoming a source of *berachah* and radiating goodness to all the inhabitants of the world.

The primary impediment to becoming a greater person by taking responsibility for others is *negios,* personal interests. People are concerned primarily with themselves, and their choices reflect what they believe will benefit them and bring them the most prestige. Yet a person who constantly places himself first can never come to devote himself to the good of the community. The more a person focuses on benefiting the *klal,* the greater he becomes, whereas one who is motivated exclusively by his own interests earns less respect, and his actions are regarded as petty.

Your Blessing Precedes Mine

Each day in *Shemoneh Esrei,* we describe Hashem as: אֱלֹהֵי אַבְרָהָם אֱלֹהֵי יִצְחָק וֵאלֹהֵי יַעֲקֹב, *the God of Avraham, the God of Yitzchak, and the God of Yaakov.* The source of this description is the following Gemara (*Pesachim* 117):

> R' Shimon ben Lakish said: וְאֶעֶשְׂךָ לְגוֹי גָּדוֹל, [*Hashem said to Avram...*] *I will make of you a great nation* — this teaches that we say, "the God of Avraham"; וַאֲבָרֶכְךָ, *and I will bless you* — this teaches that we say, "the God of Yitzchak"; וַאֲגַדְּלָה שְׁמֶךָ, *and I will make your name great* — this teaches that we say, "the God of Yaakov."

Midrash Tanchuma (*Lech Lecha* 4) adds that the words וֶהְיֵה בְּרָכָה, *and you shall be a blessing,* mean that "your blessing precedes My blessing": First, we recite the *berachah* of *Magen Avraham,* and only afterward do we recite the *berachah* of *Mechayeh HaMeisim,* which indicates that Avraham's *berachah* was so exalted that it precedes even Hashem's *berachah*!

R' Yerucham Levovitz (*Daas Torah, Biurim*) explains that the phrase *the God of Avraham, the God of Yitzchak, and the God of Yaakov* cannot be interpreted as a praise of Hakadosh Baruch Hu, for if it were, then both the *berachah* of *Magen Avraham* and the *berachah* of *Mechayeh HaMeisim* would be extolling Him — so how could He say that Avraham's blessing precedes His?

It must be that this *berachah* is lauding Avraham for his being the first person to recognize that Hashem is the Creator and Sovereign of the world. Avraham's raison d'etre was to crown Hashem as King of the world and increase *kevod Shamayim*, to the point that "Avraham" and *"Melech Ha'olam"* merged into one concept, and Avraham's entire existence reflected his revelations of the conduct of the King of the universe.

The attributes of *Elokei Yitzchak* and *Elokei Yaakov*, as well, are rooted in Avraham Avinu's *berachah*. R' Yerucham adds that everything mentioned in this first *berachah* is based on Avraham Avinu's actions and traits; for example, the phrase הָאֵל הַגָּדוֹל, *the great God*, alludes to the promise of וְאֶעֶשְׂךָ לְגוֹי גָּדוֹל, *And I will make of you a great nation*. Accordingly, we can understand why the first *berachah* is called "your blessing," since this *berachah* revolves around Avraham Avinu's revelation of Hakadosh Baruch Hu as King of the universe, which reflects the extent of the revelation of His Kingship in this world until the End of Days.

Examining Avraham Avinu's actions, we see that they were primarily geared to benefiting the public — whether through his heartfelt supplications on behalf of the wicked people of Sedom, through his *hachnassas orchim*, or through his teaching others to have faith in Hashem. All these actions led him to attain the level of *kevod Shamayim* at which his *berachah* could precede Hashem's *berachah*.

The only way to generate *kevod Shamayim* is through acting on behalf of the *tzibbur*, without personal interests. An action that is motivated by self-interest does not increase Hashem's honor in the world. Since Avraham Avinu's distinguishing trait was that all his actions were performed for the benefit of the public, these actions increased Hashem's honor in this world, to the point that he was granted an incredible power to bless others.

Elevating Yourself and the World

The Midrash teaches (*Devarim Rabbah* 3:3):

> R' Shimon ben Shetach bought a donkey from a certain Ishmaelite, and his disciples found a precious stone hanging from its neck. They said to him, "Rebbi! *It is the blessing of Hashem that enriches*" (*Mishlei* 10:22). R' Shimon ben Shetach replied, "I have purchased a donkey; I have not purchased a precious stone." He went and returned the stone to that Ishmaelite, who declared, "Blessed is Hashem, the God of Shimon ben Shetach!"

The seller's response seems puzzling. Shouldn't he have commended Shimon ben Shetach for his integrity in returning his precious stone, rather than blessing his God?

Through his actions, a person can either sanctify the Name of Hashem, or, *chas v'shalom*, desecrate it. The more one acts for the sake of Heaven, without personal interests, the more Hashem's honor is increased through his actions. Shimon ben Shetach, whose every action was done *l'shem Shamayim*, merited to reveal Hashem's honor through his behavior, which is why the seller blessed his God.

It is not only lofty *tzaddikim* who are capable of acting in a way that benefits the public — regular people can do so as well. Anyone who endeavors to help the *tzibbur*, without regard to his personal benefit, becomes a greater person.

Chazal tell us that "*Kol Yisrael areivim zeh bazeh* — all Jews are guarantors for one another" (*Sanhedrin* 27b), and this obligation of *arvus* applies to each and every Jew, without exception. The only way for a person to become a guarantor for Klal Yisrael is by growing in Torah and *yiras Shamayim*, which causes the world to be supported by him and elevated along with him.

פרשת וירא
Parashas Vayeira

◆§ *Spiritual Challenges Are Harder Than Physical Challenges*

יֻקַּח נָא מְעַט מַיִם וְרַחֲצוּ רַגְלֵיכֶם וְהִשָּׁעֲנוּ תַּחַת הָעֵץ . . . וַיְמַהֵר אַבְרָהָם הָאֹהֱלָה אֶל שָׂרָה וַיֹּאמֶר מַהֲרִי שְׁלֹשׁ סְאִים קֶמַח סֹלֶת לוּשִׁי וַעֲשִׂי עֻגוֹת . . . וַיִּקַּח חֶמְאָה וְחָלָב וּבֶן הַבָּקָר אֲשֶׁר עָשָׂה וַיִּתֵּן לִפְנֵיהֶם וְהוּא עֹמֵד עֲלֵיהֶם תַּחַת הָעֵץ וַיֹּאכֵלוּ.

Let some water be brought and wash your feet, and recline beneath the tree ... So Avraham hastened to the tent to Sarah and said, "Hurry! Three se'ahs of meal, fine flour! Knead and make cakes ... He took cream and milk and the calf which he had prepared, and placed these before them; he stood over them beneath the tree and they ate (*Bereishis* 18:4-8).

The Gemara expounds (*Bava Metzia* 86b):

> In reward for three things that Avraham did for the angels, the Jewish people merited three things: In reward for the *cream and milk* that he gave them, the Jewish people merited the *mahn;* in reward for *and he stood over them,* they merited the Pillar of Cloud; and in reward for *Let some water be brought,* they merited the Well of Miriam.

The Maharsha notes, however, that elsewhere (*Taanis* 9a), Chazal teach that the Well was provided in the merit of Miriam, the Pillar of Cloud in the merit of Aharon, and the *mahn* in the merit of Moshe — which seems to contradict Chazal's statement that this was in the merit of Avraham Avinu.

A similar question can be posed regarding the conflicting reasons given by Chazal for why Bnei Yisrael were granted the mitzvah of *tzitzis*. After the Mabul, Noach drank wine and became inebriated. The *pasuk* states (*Bereishis* 9:23): וַיִּקַּח שֵׁם וָיֶפֶת אֶת הַשִּׂמְלָה ... וַיְכַסּוּ אֵת עֶרְוַת אֲבִיהֶם, *And Shem and Yefes took a garment ... and covered their father's nakedness*. Rashi notes that the verb *vayikach* is singular, indicating that Shem exerted more effort for the mitzvah than Yefes, which is why Shem's descendants merited the garment of *tzitzis*. R' Eliyahu Mizrachi (ibid.) points out that this contradicts the following statement of Chazal (*Chullin* 88b): "As a reward for Avraham Avinu's having said [to the king of Sedom]: אִם מִחוּט וְעַד שְׂרוֹךְ נַעַל, *If so much as a thread or a shoestrap* (*Bereishis* 14:23), his descendants merited two mitzvos — the thread of *techeiles* and the strap of *tefillin*."

To resolve these contradictions, we must first clarify what constitutes a *nisayon* in Hakadosh Baruch Hu's eyes.

What Were the Ten Nisyonos?

Pirkei Avos states (5:3): "Avraham Avinu was challenged with ten *nisyonos*, and he withstood them all." There are two opinions regarding what these ten *nisyonos* were.

Pirkei D'Rabbi Eliezer (Ch. 26) enumerates these challenges as: (1) Avraham's hiding underground for thirteen years; (2) his being imprisoned for ten years and then being cast into the furnace; (3) the commandment of *lech lecha*; (4) the famine in Eretz Yisrael, and Avraham's descent to Mitzrayim; (5) Sarah's being taken to Pharaoh's palace; (6) the war of the kings; (7) Avraham's believing the prophecy of אָנֹכִי מָגֵן לָךְ שְׂכָרְךָ הַרְבֵּה מְאֹד, *I am a shield for you; your reward is very great* (*Bereishis* 15:1); (8) the mitzvah of *bris milah* (9) Avraham's banishing Yishmael from his house; (10) Akeidas Yitzchak.

The Rambam, in his commentary on the above Mishnah (*Avos* 5:3) presents a separate list: (1) the commandment of *lech lecha;* (2) the famine in Eretz Yisrael; (3) Sarah's being taken to Pharaoh's palace; (4) the war of the kings; (5) Avraham's marrying Hagar; (6) the mitzvah of *bris milah;* (7) Sarah's being taken by Avimelech; (8) Avraham's banishing Hagar after she bore him a son; (9) his banishing of his son Yishmael; (10) Akeidas Yitzchak.

Closer analysis of these two lists reveals that the fundamental difference between them lies in whether a physical challenge that results in increased *kevod Hashem* in the world is regarded as a *nisayon,* or whether only challenges that are spiritual in nature qualify. If someone sacrifices his body in order to increase Hashem's honor in this world, is he considered to have withstood a *nisayon,* or does overcoming a *nisayon* involve not sacrificing the body but rather conducting oneself according to the will of Hashem?

Pirkei D'Rabbi Eliezer lists *nisyonos* in which Avraham Avinu endured physical peril for the sake of Hashem's honor and his belief in Him, such as by hiding for thirteen years and enduring imprisonment for ten years. The Rambam, however, counts only spiritual conflicts that were supremely difficult, such as Avraham leaving his father's house and his banishing his wife and child. The Rambam's list of the *nisyonos* faced by Avraham Avinu includes those that reflect the value of בְּכָל דְּרָכֶיךָ דָעֵהוּ, *Know Hashem in all your ways.* Avraham embodied this dictum in every aspect of his life, conducting himself even in challenging situations according to the path Hashem set for him. In this regard, it has often been said that living *al kiddush Hashem* is more important than dying *al kiddush Hashem.*

These divergent approaches shed light on the differing opinions regarding the specific *zechus* that earned Bnei Yisrael their three gifts in the Midbar, and the mitzvah of *tzitzis.*

Avraham Avinu's request to Sarah, "Knead and make cakes," and his returning all the booty of war to the king of Sedom, were physical *nisyonos* in which Avraham sacrificed material wealth for the sake of a mitzvah. Since some maintain that physical challenges can also be regarded as *nisyonos,* there are grounds to state that it was in the merit of acts like these that Bnei Yisrael were rewarded with the *mahn*, the Pillar of Cloud, and the Well of Miriam, as well as the mitzvah of *tzitzis*.

Others maintain that these challenges of Avraham Avinu do not qualify as *nisyonos*, and Bnei Yisrael were granted the *mahn* and other gifts only in the merit of Moshe Rabbeinu's actions, which were spiritual in nature. Similarly, because Shem ben Noach performed a spiritual act to spare his father disgrace, his descendants were rewarded with the mitzvah of *tzitzis*.

At the crux of this dispute is the idea that a physical challenge is limited, and its significance is therefore likewise limited. There is an end to the pain and distress that a person can feel, a limit to the financial loss he can incur — and the greater the loss, the greater the reward he will garner for withstanding the *nisayon*.

Surmounting a spiritual challenge — such as when Avraham believed the prophecy and fled from sin — is immeasurably greater, however, since there is no limit or boundary to spiritual actions.

Oblivious to Adversity

A person whose life revolves around *ruchniyus* can surmount any *nisayon*, since he is capable of soaring to lofty spiritual heights, to the extent that he ceases to feel hardships and adversity — even physical suffering. Many a story is told of *gedolei Yisrael* who underwent surgeries or painful treatments without anesthesia, while delving into a halachic *sugya* or enveloping themselves in *dveikus* to the point that they didn't even feel the scalpel cut into their flesh.

Even today, we find *talmidei chachamim* who immerse themselves wholly in Torah learning, even if they are plagued with terrible *yissurim*, such as a sick child or extreme poverty. During the hours of the yeshivah's *sedarim*, they are engrossed completely in learning, and all their troubles seem to disappear, as they delight in their *chiddushei Torah* and *yegiah*.

The primary reason why Avraham Avinu was tested with the ten *nisyonos* was so he would not receive his reward freely, but rather as a result of struggling to overcome these challenges. Similarly, Hakadosh Baruch Hu sends each and every one of us *nisyonos*, and our task is to work on overcoming these challenges and hardships so we can reap reward. The harder the *nisayon*, the greater the reward; and although reward is granted for every word and moment of Torah study and for every mitzvah, the main *schar* we receive is for withstanding our *nisyonos* and exerting ourselves for the sake of each mitzvah.

As *bnei Torah*, our primary *avodah* is to immerse ourselves in Torah study with intense effort — and indeed, we see that those who learn Torah despite hardship and adversity merit to attain the loftiest spiritual heights.

The Rosh Yeshivah ended with the following message:

This Motzaei Shabbos, I will be traveling to America *b'ezras Hashem*. Though everyone is concerned about this upcoming trip, the circumstances compel it, and I have no choice... I request that every one of you make sure *tzu ligen in lernen* — to immerse yourself in learning, to daven and conduct yourselves with *middos tovos*, and surely, in the *zechus* of these actions, we will merit *siyata diShmaya*.

פרשת חיי שרה
Parashas Chayei Sarah

Good Middos: The Basis of Spiritual Achievement

וְאַבְרָהָם זָקֵן בָּא בַּיָּמִים וַה׳ בֵּרַךְ אֶת אַבְרָהָם בַּכֹּל. וַיֹּאמֶר אַבְרָהָם אֶל עַבְדּוֹ זְקַן בֵּיתוֹ הַמֹּשֵׁל בְּכָל אֲשֶׁר לוֹ שִׂים נָא יָדְךָ תַּחַת יְרֵכִי. וְאַשְׁבִּיעֲךָ בַּה׳ אֱלֹהֵי הַשָּׁמַיִם וֵאלֹהֵי הָאָרֶץ אֲשֶׁר לֹא תִקַּח אִשָּׁה לִבְנִי מִבְּנוֹת הַכְּנַעֲנִי אֲשֶׁר אָנֹכִי יוֹשֵׁב בְּקִרְבּוֹ. כִּי אֶל אַרְצִי וְאֶל מוֹלַדְתִּי תֵּלֵךְ וְלָקַחְתָּ אִשָּׁה לִבְנִי לְיִצְחָק.

Now Avraham was old, well on in years, and Hashem had blessed Avraham with everything. And Avraham said to his servant, the elder of his household who controlled all that was his: "Place now your hand under my thigh. And I will have you swear by Hashem, God of heaven and God of earth, that you not take a wife for my son from the daughters of the Canaanites, among whom I dwell. Rather, to my land and to my kindred shall you go and take a wife for my son for Yitzchak" (*Bereishis* 24:1-4).

Eliezer, the servant of Avraham, was a man of lofty spiritual stature, as the Torah attests with the description: הַמֹּשֵׁל בְּכָל אֲשֶׁר לוֹ, *who controlled all that was his,* which the Midrash

(*Bereishis Rabbah* 59:8) interprets to mean *"shalit b'yitzro kemoso* — he ruled over his *yetzer hara* like him [Avraham]." Avraham trusted Eliezer implicitly, and Eliezer would draw from his master's Torah wisdom to teach others — *"doleh u'mashkeh"* — which is why the Torah calls him "Damesek Eliezer" (*Yoma* 28b).

If Avraham placed absolute confidence in his servant, entrusting him with both his material possessions and his spiritual teachings, why did he suddenly lack faith in Eliezer's integrity, as evidenced by his request that Eliezer swear that he would not take a wife for Yitzchak from the daughters of Canaan?

R' Eliyahu Lopian explains, in *Lev Eliyahu*, that the task of building a Jewish home is unlike any other. Shlomo HaMelech states (*Mishlei* 14:1): חַכְמוֹת נָשִׁים בָּנְתָה בֵיתָהּ וְאִוֶּלֶת בְּיָדֶיהָ תֶהֶרְסֶנּוּ, *The wise among women, each built her house, but the foolish one tears it down with her hands.* A woman wields immense power in building her home, and she carries a massive responsibility: With her wisdom, she can build a splendid palace worthy of the *Shechinah*, and with imprudence, she can demolish the very foundations of her home. The importance of choosing a worthy wife for Yitzchak, the woman who would serve as matriarch of all of Klal Yisrael, was inestimable. Selecting the one with the wisdom and stellar character to build this home was beyond human ability, and therefore, while Avraham Avinu trusted Eliezer with all his household needs, in this case, his regular trust was insufficient, and he required Eliezer to make a vow and perform a physical action to affirm his commitment.

Recognizing the gravity of his mission, Eliezer set out to seek a wife for Yitzchak, and davened to Hashem to guide him to identify the maiden who would serve as Yitzchak's life partner. He entreated Hashem for a sign: When he would ask the girl to tip her pitcher so that he could drink, she would reply, "Drink, and I will also give your camels to drink."

Eliezer's request raises many questions. While such an offer surely indicates sterling *middos* and exceptional generosity, it fails to offer any indication regarding the maiden's righteousness or fear of Heaven. Why did Eliezer suffice with a demonstration of good *middos* before ascertaining that Rivkah possessed the level of *yiras Shamayim* required for her to wed Yitzchak? The question is compounded by the fact that Rivkah was the daughter of Besuel and the sister of Lavan, known idol-worshippers and swindlers, which was fair reason to suspect that she might be inclined to follow their ways.

After Avraham Avinu withstood the last of the ten *nisyonos*, Hakadosh Baruch Hu commended him: כִּי עַתָּה יָדַעְתִּי כִּי יְרֵא אֱלֹהִים אַתָּה, *for now I know that you are a God-fearing man* (*Bereishis* 22:12). The ultimate purpose of the ten *nisyonos* was to evaluate Avraham Avinu's fear of Heaven; indeed, the primary focus of a person's *avodah* is to *attain yiras Shamayim*. How could Eliezer test only Rivkah's *middos*, without assessing whether her values, beliefs, and lifestyle were compatible with those of Avraham and Yitzchak?

What to Look for in a Spouse

R' Eliyahu Lopian derives a powerful lesson from this incident. Although a person's primary focus in *avodas Hashem* is to develop *yiras Shamayim*, if someone possesses refined character and good *middos*, but has not yet attained fear of Heaven, he will eventually seek that virtue, since good *middos* are the basis of all spiritual achievements. A person of corrupt character will never acquire *yiras Shamayim*, however, even if he invests enormous efforts to do so, and any *yiras Shamayim* he works to achieve will be unsustainable.

Therefore, a person who is seeking a spouse should first and foremost search for good *middos* and a refined, gentle nature. Even if the woman in question does not yet possess the desired level of *yiras Shamayim*, ultimately, her good *middos* will prevail and she will attain it. Many a time, I've been asked by *bachurim* what attributes they should seek in a prospective wife, and I always respond that the primary focus should be *middos tovos* and *yiras Shamayim*. This *parashah* teaches that even if the woman has not yet attained fear of Heaven, if she has good *middos*, she will eventually attain it. (Obviously, even if she does not yet possess full *yiras Shamayim*, she must still appreciate its necessity, because without the recognition of this value, she will lack the motivation to work toward it. But if it is clear that she is prepared to work on achieving greater *yiras Shamayim*, then this is sufficient, and her good *middos* will propel her to attain it easily.)

Chazal advise (*Bava Basra* 110a) that before marrying a woman, one should examine her brothers. They do not state that one should assess the level of her brothers' *yiras Shamayim*, as that offers no proof regarding their sister. Chazal's intention is that one should evaluate the brothers' *middos*, since it is likely that children who were raised in the same home will exhibit similar *middos*, which typically pass from parent to child. If the brothers are well-bred and model superior *middos*, their sister will presumably follow the same mold. And the converse is true as well: If the brothers display poor *middos*, it is unlikely that their sister's character traits will be any more admirable.

This sheds light on why Avraham Avinu adjured Eliezer not to take a wife for Yitzchak from the Canaanites, who were known to be depraved and corrupt, descending as they did from Cham, who purposely disgraced his father, Noach. Cham bequeathed his immoral, wicked traits to his descendants for all generations, and their characters were intrinsically flawed, which led Noach to curse Cham and his children with the words: אָרוּר כְּנָעַן עֶבֶד עֲבָדִים יִהְיֶה לְאֶחָיו, *Cursed is Canaan; a slave of slaves shall he be to his brothers* (*Bereishis* 9:25).

The descendants of Cham are forever locked in slavery, never worthy of attaining the status of free men. A free man has the liberty to act at will, which is why it is dangerous to enable an entire nation of corrupt, dissolute people to do as they wish. Noach cursed the children of Canaan, marking them eternally as slaves for their own benefit, as this binds them to the will of a master rather than freeing them to act upon their evil, licentious whims, which would inevitably lead to destruction.

In seeking a partner for Yitzchak and laying the foundations of the Chosen Nation, Avraham Avinu could not allow even the faintest character flaw to mar the perfection of Klal Yisrael. Therefore, despite his absolute faith in Eliezer, he did not feel secure sending him to find a wife for Yitzchak without entreating him to swear that he would not take a woman from the daughters of Canaan.

The words of Chazal on this *parashah* illuminate just how deeply an innate character flaw can affect a person. Before departing to Padan Aram, Eliezer asked Avraham: אוּלַי לֹא תֹאבֶה הָאִשָּׁה לָלֶכֶת אַחֲרַי אֶל הָאָרֶץ הַזֹּאת הֶהָשֵׁב אָשִׁיב אֶת בִּנְךָ אֶל הָאָרֶץ אֲשֶׁר יָצָאתָ מִשָּׁם, *Perhaps the woman will not wish to follow me to this land; shall I take your son back to the land from which you departed?* (ibid 24:5). Chazal expound that "He was sitting and weighing whether his daughter was worthy or not worthy. [Therefore] he said, 'Perhaps she will not wish [to follow], and I will give him my daughter [as a wife]. He [Avraham] said to him [Eliezer]: 'You are cursed, and my son is blessed; and one who is cursed does not cleave to one who is blessed'" (*Bereishis Rabbah* 59:9).

As noted above, Eliezer had attained an exalted spiritual plane akin to that of Avraham, and even taught his Torah. In truth, Avraham saw no reason why Eliezer's daughter wasn't worthy of marrying his son Yitzchak, other than the fact that she descended from a cursed nation. Considering the virtues of Eliezer's daughter, and those of her father, she was indeed a good match for Yitzchak. Yet the character deficiency of the Canaanites was so profound that Avraham feared that it would ultimately impact her, too, and she would lose her stellar qualities. For this reason alone, Avraham refused to allow her to marry Yitzchak.

In contrast, while the family members of Avraham's nephew Besuel sorely lacked *yiras Shamayim*, they still possessed the capacity to acquire it by virtue of their *middos*, as Rivkah indeed demonstrated. Her outstanding character would enable her to develop deep *yiras Shamayim*, which is why Avraham Avinu specifically chose to link his son's fate with Besuel's family.

Deplorable Middos Are Hereditary

This concept is also reflected in the Torah's harsh view of Amalek, which is the only nation that Bnei Yisrael are commanded to utterly annihilate, as Hashem commands: תִּמְחֶה אֶת זֵכֶר עֲמָלֵק מִתַּחַת

הַשָּׁמָיִם לֹא תִּשְׁכָּח, *You shall wipe out the memory of Amalek from under the heaven — you shall not forget!* (*Devarim* 25:19). Similarly, the Torah states: מִלְחָמָה לַה׳ בַּעֲמָלֵק מִדֹּר דֹּר, *Hashem maintains a war against Amalek, from generation to generation* (*Shemos* 17:16). No other nation is described in such strong terms.

Nevertheless, if a descendant of Amalek wishes to convert to Judaism, he is accepted as a convert and welcomed into Klal Yisrael like any other ger (see *Rambam, Hilchos Issurei Biah* 12:17). Yet male descendants of Ammon and Moav, who did not harm Bnei Yisrael as Amalek did, are eternally barred from marrying into the Jewish people, as the Torah states: לֹא יָבֹא עַמּוֹנִי וּמוֹאָבִי בִּקְהַל ה׳ גַּם דּוֹר עֲשִׂירִי לֹא יָבֹא לָהֶם בִּקְהַל ה׳ עַד עוֹלָם. עַל דְּבַר אֲשֶׁר לֹא קִדְּמוּ אֶתְכֶם בַּלֶּחֶם וּבַמַּיִם בַּדֶּרֶךְ בְּצֵאתְכֶם מִמִּצְרָיִם, *An Ammonite or Moabite shall not enter the congregation of Hashem, even their tenth generation shall not enter the congregation of Hashem, to eternity, because of the fact that they did not greet you with bread and water on the road when you were leaving Egypt* (*Devarim* 23:4-5).

It would seem that, if anything, Amalek should be the nation whose potential converts are not accepted. Amalek possesses the ignominious trait of chutzpah and was the first nation who dared to diminish Bnei Yisrael's status and fear among the nations by engaging them in war, thereby desecrating Hashem's Name. In contrast, Ammon and Moav never actively engaged Bnei Yisrael in war; they merely failed to greet Bnei Yisrael with food and water after they left Mitzrayim. Why does this crime warrant their eternal rejection, to the point that they can never marry a Jew?

The fundamental difference between Amalek and Ammon and Moav is that Amalek is described as *"lo yarei Elokim"* (*Devarim* 25:18). The Amalekites did not fear Hashem, which is why they dared to attack Bnei Yisrael and cool the aura of glory and fear surrounding them. Yet if at any point in time their descendants would seek to accept the yoke of Heaven upon themselves and become God-fearing, they would be no different from any other potential convert.

Ammon and Moav, on the other hand, were innately corrupt. Chazal explain (*Bereishis Rabbah* 41:3) that the grievance against them is that they forgot the great kindness that Avraham Avinu had performed for their ancestor Lot by sparing him from death in Sedom. Both these nations should have recalled this favor and greeted Avraham's descendants with bread and water upon their departure from Mitzrayim — but rather than displaying gratitude, they went so far as to hire Bilam to curse Bnei Yisrael. Since deplorable *middos* are passed down from generation to generation, even if a descendant of Ammon or Moav acquires *yiras Shamayim*, he will ultimately lose it due to his deep-rooted character flaws, which is why these nations are forbidden to marry into Klal Yisrael.

Reaping Reward Already in This World

With this in mind, we can understand Rashi's summation of Sarah Imeinu's life. The *pasuk* states (*Bereishis* 23:1): וַיִּהְיוּ חַיֵּי שָׂרָה מֵאָה שָׁנָה וְעֶשְׂרִים שָׁנָה וְשֶׁבַע שָׁנִים שְׁנֵי חַיֵּי שָׂרָה, *Sarah's lifetime was one hundred years, twenty years, and seven years; the years of Sarah's life*, and Rashi comments: "The years of Sarah's life — they were all equally good." This is a truly astounding statement, for how can a person attain such a lofty spiritual level that every period of his life is regarded as equally wonderful?

Only a person who possesses stellar character traits and *derech eretz* lives in a way that all his years are equally good. Such a person can conduct his life calmly, with peace of mind and serenity, reaping his reward already in this world. But one who possesses poor *middos* and displays negative traits such as anger, arrogance, and lust is never at peace. He is constantly distracted and anxious, as *Pirkei Avos* teaches (4:21): "Jealousy, the desire for pleasure, and the craving for honor remove a person from the world." Sarah Imeinu, who possessed exemplary character traits, enjoyed a consistently good and full life.

The Power to Change

Now that we have established that good *middos* are the prerequisites to *yiras Shamayim* and spiritual perfection, we must address the question of how to permanently acquire superb *middos* and perfect our qualities of patience and consistency.

In this context, R' Eliyahu Lopian cited the following account of the Gemara (*Bava Basra* 16a):

> Iyov sought to exempt the entire world from judgment. He said, "Master of the Universe! You created an ox with split hooves. You created a donkey with closed hooves. You created Gan Eden; You created Gehinnom. You created righteous people; You created wicked people. Who can stop You?" What did Iyov's friends answer him? *"Certainly, you will mitigate fear [of Heaven] and diminish prayers to God"* (*Iyov* 15:4). Hakadosh Baruch Hu created the Evil Inclination, He created the Torah as its antidote.

Rashi explains that Iyov's intention was to spare the world from judgment by arguing that all people are compelled to transgress, for their base nature causes them to sin, and they cannot change those impulses. Just as Hakadosh Baruch Hu created every creature with its unique identity — an ox with split hooves, a donkey with closed hooves — so, too, Iyov argued, a *tzaddik* and a *rasha* were created as they are, and are unable to alter their nature or disposition.

This is wrong, however. While oxen and donkeys cannot change their physical forms, a person can adjust his actions and choose a different path, for Hakadosh Baruch Hu imbued him with the wisdom to recognize the need to rectify his character failings.

Iyov drew a parallel between man and animal in his attempt to exempt all of humanity from accountability for their sins, arguing that a person possesses innate character traits, just as an animal is born with natural instincts. In truth, however, perfecting one's character does not require uprooting natural traits, but rather overcoming the tendency to surrender to one's nature — just as animals can be trained to rein in their wild nature.

Iyov's friends seem to concur with his claim, yet they remind him that Hakadosh Baruch Hu created Torah as the antidote to the *yetzer hara*. Torah study empowers a person to overcome the *yetzer hara* and mitigate its influence, and therefore a person cannot argue that he was compelled to sin.

Torah study is the only remedy for negative character traits

— and without Torah, a person's own strategies will not help him to overcome the *yetzer hara*. Even if one is certain that he managed to transcend his baser nature, the character failings will remain ingrained in his soul.

Only through learning *Torah lishmah*, with *amal* and *yegia*, can we successfully work on our *middos*. Without it, we can never succeed, as the Gemara teaches (*Yoma* 72b) that if a person learns Torah with improper motives, it becomes a drug of death for him.

What emerges, then, is that we must invest intensive effort to refine our character, for good *middos* are the basis of a person's spiritual development, and without them we cannot attain the spiritual heights we aspire to.

May Hakadosh Baruch Hu help us to improve our *middos*, our spiritual core, and may each person find his proper *zivug*, a person with *middos tovos*, at the right time, and merit building a *bayis ne'eman b'Yisrael*.

פרשת תולדות
Parashas Toldos

◆§ *The Divergent Paths of Yaakov and Eisav*

וַיִּגְדְּלוּ הַנְּעָרִים וַיְהִי עֵשָׂו אִישׁ יֹדֵעַ צַיִד אִישׁ שָׂדֶה וְיַעֲקֹב אִישׁ תָּם יֹשֵׁב אֹהָלִים.

The lads grew up and Eisav became one who knows hunting, a man of the field; but Yaakov was a wholesome man, abiding in tents (*Bereishis* 25:27).

Rashi interprets the words *ish sadeh* to mean "an idle man who hunts animals" and the words *yoshev ohalim* as a reference to the tent of Shem and the tent of Eiver.

Yaakov and Eisav represent the divergent paths that people traverse throughout their lives. The first path is taken by one whose concern is his future in Olam Haba, and who immerses himself in Torah, *tefillah, yirah,* and *mussar,* like Yaakov Avinu. The second path is chosen by one who is absorbed in the pleasures and luxuries of this world, without ever reflecting upon the future. This is the path of Eisav, the *ish sadeh* who was innately drawn after physical desires and idol worship.

Every Jew is granted the choice to pursue the route of ascent taken by Yaakov Avinu, which leads to Olam Haba and spiritual completion, or to follow the lead of Eisav and choose Olam Hazeh, with its plethora of physical indulgences and base pleasures.

The core disparity between Yaakov and Eisav lay at the root of their *neshamos* and was evident already at the moment they exited their mother's womb into the world. The *pasuk* says (v. 25): וַיֵּצֵא הָרִאשׁוֹן אַדְמוֹנִי כֻּלּוֹ כְּאַדֶּרֶת שֵׂעָר וַיִּקְרְאוּ שְׁמוֹ עֵשָׂו, *The first one emerged red, entirely like a hairy mantle; so they named him Eisav.* Rashi explains that Eisav received his name because he was born complete with all his body hair. The next *pasuk* relates: וְאַחֲרֵי כֵן יָצָא אָחִיו וְיָדוֹ אֹחֶזֶת בַּעֲקֵב עֵשָׂו וַיִּקְרָא שְׁמוֹ יַעֲקֹב, *After that his brother emerged with his hand grasping on to the heel of Esau; so he called his name Yaakov.* Rashi explains that Yitzchak called his son "Yaakov" because of the grasping of the heel.

Spiritual Complacency Spawns Misery

Eisav, who was formed as a complete entity, lacked aspirations to advance. One who does not yearn for more, who does not strive to move ahead, will not get anywhere in life. The Rosh Yeshivah, R' Chaim Shmulevitz, actually expressed that he "abhorred" complacent people who lack aspirations and ambition to grow.

Yaakov symbolized the diametric opposite. From the moment of his emergence into the world, he was already grasping onto Eisav's heel, demonstrating his desire to constantly attain more in life. The name "Yaakov" derives from the word "*eikev*, heel," for one who perceives himself as a heel — the lowest part of the body, which we step on constantly — regards himself as incomplete and is constantly endeavoring to reach higher. This is what inspired Yaakov to become a "*yoshev ohalim*" — a *mevakesh Hashem* who seeks Him out at every opportunity. Indeed, *Targum Yonasan ben Uziel* renders these words as "*tava ulpan min kadam Hashem,* searching for Torah before Hashem."

R' Chaim Shmulevitz highlighted this distinction between Yaakov and Eisav to emphasize that one does not embark on his path of life once he is already complete, but rather grows slowly, step by step, as he overcomes one obstacle after the next. He compared this process to the clothing a person wears throughout the stages of life. A young boy wears short-sleeved shirts and short pants. When he gets a little older, he wears long shirts and pants. As an adolescent, he proudly wears a hat and jacket like his peers, and when he is of marriageable age, he dons a respectable suit, tie, and hat. Eventually, when he has attained the requisite level of wisdom, he will dress in a rabbinic frock and hat. The natural progression of life is one of growth, of honing one's intellect and perfecting one's character as befits his age and capacity. In contrast, one who has no desire to advance and starts out life convinced that he is flawless and has no room to improve will never achieve spiritual completion. On the contrary, he is destined for destruction.

Eisav's essence was one of completion and complacency. He lacked spiritual aspirations, and his interests and desires focused on the pleasures of Olam Hazeh. Ironically, a spiritually complacent person is never satisfied with his lot, because even the sweetest of material indulgences dissipates quickly.

Yaakov, on the other hand, epitomized the incomplete person who is constantly lacking, yearning, and "grasping onto his brother's heel" in order to advance further. He thirsted for spiritual attainments, which filled him with joy but simultaneously left him craving more and yearning to ascend ever higher. There is no one happier than a person like this, for he experiences gratification that fills every fiber of his being and imbues him with zest, and this motivates him to strive for more. As he matures, his inner joy and satisfaction grow, due to the spiritual wealth that he has amassed through learning Torah and fulfilling mitzvos optimally. We ourselves can see elderly *gedolim* and *talmidei chachamim* whose faces glow with radiance and tranquility, while others in their stage of life, who have not acquired Torah and *yiras Shamayim,* become increasingly impatient and irritable with age.

What is the difference between them? Our *gedolim* know that they can always move forward and accomplish, at any stage in life, whereas elderly individuals who lack Torah to guide and inspire them feel that they have already completed their life's work and have nowhere left to grow or advance. A person who has no goal or destination inevitably plummets to despair and forfeits his *tzuras ha'adam.*

Based on this, we can appreciate a subtle difference in Rashi's portrayal of Yaakov and Eisav in their mother's womb. Rashi comments that when Rivkah passed by places of Torah study, Yaakov would run and toss about to leave the womb — *ratz u'mefarkes latzeis*, whereas when she passed temples of idol worship, Eisav would toss about to leave the womb — *mefarkes latzeis*. Rashi adds the word *"ratz* — ran" only in regard to Yaakov, who embodied passion and determination to serve Hashem. Eisav, in contrast, was in no rush to achieve.

The Deceiver Versus the Wholesome

The Torah relates (v. 28): וַיֶּאֱהַב יִצְחָק אֶת עֵשָׂו כִּי צַיִד בְּפִיו, *Yitzchak loved Eisav for game was in his mouth*, and Rashi explains that Eisav would ensnare Yitzchak with his mouth and deceive him with his words.

Yaakov, however, is described as *"ish tam,* a wholesome man," which Rashi interprets as one who is not skilled at deception — "as is his heart, so is his mouth." Yaakov's essence was that of a *ben aliyah,* who continually strove for *ruchniyus* and perceived the world only as a corridor to Olam Haba. One who does not view this material world as his ultimate purpose sees no reason to deceive others in order to gain material assets. His heart and mouth are aligned, and he is trustworthy. Eisav, who spurned spiritual aspirations in favor of indulging in the pleasures of this world, used his mouth to deceive others in order to satisfy his base desires.

The next *pasuk* states: וַיָּזֶד יַעֲקֹב נָזִיד וַיָּבֹא עֵשָׂו מִן הַשָּׂדֶה וְהוּא עָיֵף, *Yaakov simmered a stew, and Eisav came in from the field, and he was exhausted*. The Gemara expounds (*Bava Basra* 16b): "That scoundrel, Eisav, committed five sins on that day: He had relations with a betrothed maiden; he murdered someone; he denied the fundamental belief [the existence of God]; he denied the doctrine of the Resurrection of the Dead; and he belittled the birthright."

Of these five sins, why does the Torah explicitly mention only Eisav's rejection of the *bechorah*, which is the least significant of the five, and only hint to the other, cardinal sins that he committed on that day?

In recounting this episode, the Torah is conveying Eisav's core essence, depicting him as the epitome of physicality, a person who was profoundly connected to the pleasures of Olam Hazeh and lacked any spiritual aspirations. Only someone who is utterly detached from spirituality can ask: הַלְעִיטֵנִי נָא מִן הָאָדֹם הָאָדֹם, *Pour into me, now, some of that very red stuff* (v. 30), as an animal would be fed. Similarly, although Eisav had rejected the core tenets of faith, he sounded "an exceedingly great and bitter cry" upon learning that Yaakov had taken the *berachos*, because these were material blessings, which he was not prepared to surrender.

The Contemporary Choice Between Two Worlds

If someone were to ask me whether I would choose life in this world or life in the next, I would answer that I choose life in Olam Haba — but when we say this, our mouths and our hearts frequently do not correspond. It is virtually impossible to choose the path leading to Olam Haba to the exclusion of all else, without desiring at least a small taste of Olam Hazeh. Therefore, while we face two diverging roads, each one leading in a different direction, it is hard for us to make a definitive choice. Instead, many of us seem to opt for life in this world as well as life in Olam Haba.

If we were given the opportunity to choose *only* Olam Hazeh or Olam Haba, would we actually choose the latter?

The world today abounds with material pleasures and indulgences, offering an endless array of food, clothing, and devices. When I first came to yeshivah in Eretz Yisrael, there was nothing to be had! Many homes didn't have gas or even a refrigerator. All everyone had equally was poverty! Even in *chutz la'aretz*, where the economic situation was far better, people struggled to earn a living. Under such circumstances, the choice of a glittering Olam Haba over a wearying, poverty-stricken Olam Hazeh is self-understood.

Today, we live in a world of plenty, showered as we are with both spiritual and material bounty. Everyone has a home and every device necessary for a home. In the past, someone who owned even one of these gadgets was considered wealthy. Today, anyone who doesn't own a cell phone is regarded as practically barefoot. How, then, are we expected to choose between Olam Hazeh and Olam Haba?

Every Yid in every generation has the choice to dwell in the tent of Shem, like Yaakov, or set out into the big world to hunt game, like Eisav. Is it possible that in this generation, we no longer have to choose between the two worlds, and we can choose a third course that encompasses both?

Yaakov's Derech — Choosing the Ikar

I once heard from a distinguished woman that a person who knows how to differentiate between the *ikar* and *tafel,* the core versus its external trappings, and to seize that core has great potential to succeed in life. Even if he also acquires the *tafel* along the way, he will succeed, as long as his primary focus is on the *ikar*.

In our world today, it is virtually impossible to live without any grasp on Olam Hazeh, for even luxuries have become necessities.

"The principle of the matter," writes the *Mesillas Yesharim* (Ch. 1), "is that man wasn't created for his circumstances in Olam Hazeh, but for… Olam Haba, although his circumstances in Olam Hazeh are the means for his Olam Haba, which is his ultimate purpose." Here, the *Mesillas Yesharim* expresses that the function of the bounty that we enjoy in Olam Hazeh is to enhance our *avodas Hashem*. Olam Hazeh, then, is the tool that enables us to attain our ultimate goal in life.

Our task is to distinguish between *ikar* and *tafel,* to appreciate our essence and role in this world — and this is the manifestation of *bechirah* in our generation. Do we regard *limud Torah* as fundamental and everything else in life as the tools and external trappings that enable us to acquire it? Or does the endless *gashmiyus* surrounding us constitute the focus of our lives?

This is the essence of *bechirah* — the choice to follow Yaakov's path to Olam Haba or to traverse Eisav's path as an *ish yodei'a tzayid.* Two people may dress identically and learn shoulder-to-shoulder in the same *beis midrash;* they may live in the same type of home, and their lives may follow similar courses. Yet one may be following the path of Yaakov, and the other, the path of Eisav — since the former considers Torah the *ikar* and views everything else merely as a means of acquiring Torah, while his friend's aspirations revolve around Olam Hazeh, and he regards *limud Torah* merely as another task in life.

Yitzchak's Berachah Gave Yaakov Tools to Attain Olam Haba

Yitzchak instructed Eisav to prepare delicacies for him in order to elevate his spirits and enable him to bless him prior to his death. Then, when Yaakov brought him the meal that Rivkah had prepared, Yitzchak asked him to approach, and he felt him to ensure that he was really Eisav.

The Beis HaLevi (*Shu"t, Drush* 3) asks why Yitzchak specifically wished to bless Eisav when, as their father, he must have known deep down what each of his sons represented. Why, of the two, did he choose Eisav to be the recipient of all the blessings?

He explains that Yitzchak wanted to bequeath to Eisav all of Olam Hazeh and leave Yaakov with Olam Haba exclusively, so Yaakov would have no association at all with materialism that could potentially lure him away from spirituality, as the Torah states: וַיִּשְׁמַן יְשֻׁרוּן וַיִּבְעָט, *Yeshurun became fat and kicked* (*Devarim* 32:15). Yitzchak's intention in conferring the *berachos* of Olam Hazeh upon Eisav was that Eisav would support Yaakov and his descendants, while Yaakov would merit Olam Haba through his exclusive pursuit of *limud Torah*.

Moreover, Yaakov himself was wary of seizing the *berachos* of Olam Hazeh, preferring to remain with Olam Haba, as Chazal teach (*Tanna D'Vei Eliyahu Zuta* Ch. 19):

> When Yaakov and Eisav were in their mother's womb, Yaakov said to Eisav: "Eisav, my brother, we are two [sons] to our father, and there are two worlds before us — Olam Hazeh and Olam Haba. Olam Hazeh encompasses food and drink, commerce and trade, marriage and bearing children; but Olam Haba has none of this. If it is your will, take Olam Hazeh, and I shall take Olam Haba."

Yaakov made this offer to Eisav since he knew that Olam Hazeh is replete with spiritual pitfalls that could cause him to falter.

Rivkah Imeinu, however, who received the prophecy of *the elder shall serve the younger* (*Bereishis* 25:23), knew that Yaakov was the one who required the *berachos* of Olam Hazeh in order to properly serve as master over Eisav. Rivkah was not concerned that Yaakov would lose himself in material indulgence, but rather hoped that Eisav would enjoy the pleasures of the world while providing for all of Yaakov's needs.

This demonstrates that it is possible to draw upon the best of both worlds and simultaneously enjoy Olam Hazeh and Olam Haba, although it is essential to discern the *ikar* from the *tafel*. As long as one identifies and chooses the path of Olam Haba as the *ikar*, he qualifies as a *yoshev ohalim*, even if he simultaneously draws pleasure from Olam Hazeh.

If we look at the world around us, we'll see that even though Yaakov seized the *berachos* of Olam Hazeh, it is the nations of the world who wallow in worldly desires and pleasures, while Yaakov's descendants suffice with meeting our basic needs and express our gratitude to Hakadosh Baruch Hu for all that He grants us. Our power to do this stems from our forefather Yaakov, who took the *berachos* of Olam Hazeh from Yitzchak only in order to merit Olam Haba. This is why he was able to make do with the minimum, leaving the superfluous pleasures and luxuries of this world for Eisav to enjoy.

A famous story is told of a wealthy man who once visited the home of the Chofetz Chaim and was appalled by his humble abode and meager furniture, which consisted of little save for a table, several rickety chairs, a low bed, and sagging bookshelves of *sefarim*.

"Rabbi," asked the man, "where are all your furniture and belongings?"

The Chofetz Chaim responded with a question: "And where are all of yours?"

"I am a guest," replied the man, "so I brought along only my bare necessities. But at home, I have a mansion filled with riches."

The Chofetz Chaim answered, "I, too, am a guest in Olam Hazeh, and my treasure houses await me in Olam Haba."

Choosing Both Worlds — the Key to a Joyful Existence

We cannot expect anyone to live as a guest in this world, like the Chofetz Chaim, as we are far removed from his exalted level. But let us at least recall what is primary and what is secondary in life.

An *avreich* once approached me to ask about installing air conditioning in his home. He explained that his apartment is very hot in the summer months, and his wife suffers from the heat. Is air conditioning a necessity, he asked, or a luxury?

Had this question been posed to the Chofetz Chaim in his times, the answer would have been clear. Today, however, air conditioning — like many other amenities — is a necessity, not a luxury. Yet again, we must remain focused on what is the *ikar* and what is the *tafel*.

One who chooses to follow this course will enjoy a happier, better, more fulfilling life. In previous generations, when many people lacked for food, they still enjoyed happy, full lives. Yet today, when we are showered with limitless material bounty, people tend to lose sight of the *ikar*. Confused as to what is truly important and meaningful in life, they lack *menuchas hanefesh* and *simchah*, and any time anything goes awry, they hurry to consult with psychologists and therapists. Why is this?

The answer is that people don't know how to live simultaneously in two worlds. Instead of viewing one world as *ikar* and the other as *tafel*, they elevate both to the pedestal of *ikar* and fall into a vicious cycle of pursuing everything at once, which ultimately leaves them hungry, joyless, and dissatisfied. If we can only learn to properly distinguish between these two realms, designating one as the goal and the other as the means with which to achieve it, then we will attain our goal — and with it, the *simchah* and peace of mind that we crave. One who leads his life in this way is the quintessential *ben aliyah*.

Torah Gladdens the Hearts

Dovid HaMelech teaches: פִּקּוּדֵי ה׳ יְשָׁרִים מְשַׂמְּחֵי לֵב, *The orders of Hashem are upright, gladdening the heart* (*Tehillim* 19:9).

The Radak explains: "For the wise one shall rejoice with his intellect; and when he overcomes his physical body and guides it in the way of the intellect, there is no joy in the world as great as this." Indeed, there is no greater *simchah* or satisfaction than surmounting the test of the *yetzer hara*. Even today, when one who opts for a life of Torah must nevertheless acquire the material items that society deems necessary, the *ben aliyah* does not derive his true pleasure and satisfaction from those physical pleasures. He is choosing the path of Yaakov Avinu — and the pursuit of Olam Haba brings unmitigated pleasure even in this world.

This pleasure is not reserved exclusively for one who fought a mighty battle against his *yetzer hara* and emerged triumphant, but can also be accessed by one who successfully overcame temptation even for a single moment. Often, a battle with the *yetzer hara* is momentary, because as soon as the *yetzer hara* sees that he cannot prevail, he disappears.

The Gemara teaches (*Succah* 52a):

> "In the future, Hakadosh Baruch Hu will bring the *yetzer hara* and slaughter him in front of the righteous and wicked. To the righteous, he will appear as a tall mountain, and to the wicked, he will appear as a strand of hair. These cry, and these cry. The righteous cry and say, "How were we able to conquer a mountain as great as this?" And the wicked cry and say, "How were we unable to conquer this strand of hair?"

At the End of Days, *reshaim* will realize that all they needed to do was surmount the *yetzer hara* for several moments, yet they failed to do so.

The Rosh Yeshivah concluded:

I apologize if I am speaking unclearly, but I will say this one point: We live in a perilous, frightening generation when the *yetzer hara* lurks at every corner, waiting to trap us and tempt us with every imaginable desire. There are three cardinal sins that compel a Yid to sacrifice his life rather than transgress — *avodah zarah, giluy arayos*, and *shefichas damim*. The lust for murder does not exist in these times, and neither does the *yetzer hara* for *avodah zarah;* yet the desire for *giluy arayos* is rampant.

Some people recognize the severity of idolatry and murder, but view immorality as a personal matter, *bein adam l'atzmo,* and therefore do not consider it so bad.

We must remember that *giluy arayos* is one of the three cardinal sins for which a person must sacrifice his life! It is also the most powerful *yetzer hara* in our generation; the entire world shouts of this desire. The way people dress is shocking, and it impacts us, too!

Today, the talk is all about phones. If we would forbid a yeshivah *bachur* to walk around with a television, which contains all the filth of the street, no one would be surprised. So why is it permissible for him to walk around with a television in the device in his hand?

Even if a person promises that he won't view any forbidden sights, he is still carrying a television on him! All it takes is a few clicks, and who can guarantee that he will never succumb?

A person should not try to justify owning such a device by claiming that he can also perform mitzvos with it, such as calling a friend to wish him *mazel tov,* calling his wife to lift her spirits, or calling his parents to wish them *"gut Shabbos"* — because it's all a pack of lies. A phone is a television! In a single glance, in the briefest moment, one can destroy generations! Vision is an unparalleled power and gift, which is why a blind person is considered dead; yet it also has the potential to cause a person to plummet into a spiritual abyss.

Even "kosher" devices cause terrible *bittul Torah*. It's a disgrace! An *avreich* can be sitting and learning in the *beis midrash,* and suddenly his phone starts ringing in his pocket. How can we allow this? It's an affront to his learning and disturbs the *tzibbur*. I ask you, I beseech each one of you — please refrain from bringing a cell phone into any of the *batei midrash*. Please! It is a *bizayon* to the *klal*. How is it that a person isn't ashamed to stop and say, "Hello?" in the middle of learning? Is it *pikuach nefesh?*

Under no circumstances may anyone keep a phone in the *beis midrash*. In this *zechus*, may we enjoy the pleasures of both this world and the next, and merit to bask in the aura of the *Shechinah*.

פרשת ויצא
Parashas Vayeitzei

◆§ *Preparing to Face Challenges*

וַיֵּצֵא יַעֲקֹב מִבְּאֵר שָׁבַע וַיֵּלֶךְ חָרָנָה. וַיִּפְגַּע בַּמָּקוֹם וַיָּלֶן שָׁם כִּי בָא הַשֶּׁמֶשׁ וַיִּקַּח מֵאַבְנֵי הַמָּקוֹם וַיָּשֶׂם מְרַאֲשֹׁתָיו וַיִּשְׁכַּב בַּמָּקוֹם הַהוּא.

Yaakov departed from Beer Sheva and went toward Charan. He encountered the place and spent the night there because the sun had set; he took from the stones of the place which he arranged around his head, and he lay down in that place (*Bereishis* 28:10-11).

Rashi notes that the words וַיִּשְׁכַּב בַּמָּקוֹם הַהוּא, *and he lay down in that place,* indicate limitation: He rested *in that place,* yet throughout the previous fourteen years in the *beis midrash* of Eiver, he did not sleep at night, for he was engaged in Torah study.

Yaakov Avinu was sent from his parents' home to the house of the wicked Lavan, about whom the Haggadah says: "*Lavan bikesh la'akor es hakol* — Lavan wished to uproot everything." Yaakov knew exactly where he was headed; he was keenly aware that he was about to enter a place of *nisayon,* as it is virtually impossible to dwell in close proximity to a *rasha* for an extended period without being influenced by his evil ways. Yet despite this fear, he fulfilled the mitzvah of *kibbud av va'eim* and journeyed to Lavan's house.

Learning in Yeshivah Gives Strength to Withstand Nisyonos

Why wasn't Yaakov concerned that dwelling near Lavan would cause him to falter spiritually and forfeit his Olam Haba? Why did heeding his parents' command justify placing himself in a position where he would be prone to sin, especially after he had just spent fourteen years studying Torah and developing *yiras Shamayim* in the *beis midrash* of Eiver?

The simple answer is that this is precisely why Yaakov went to the yeshivah of Eiver first. Yaakov knew that a yeshivah was the only place where he could prepare himself and acquire tools to surmount the formidable *nisyonos* that he would surely encounter. He also recognized that a year or two of learning in yeshivah was by no means sufficient, and he required a full fourteen years of continuous Torah study in order to build a spiritual fortress strong enough to withstand temptation in the house of Lavan. Only after fourteen years of study did Yaakov feel ready to continue onward.

Many parents are content with sending their son to learn Torah in yeshivah for a year or two, convinced that this is sufficient to prepare him for a lifetime of *nisyonos* in the big world. They are gravely mistaken, because two years is nowhere near enough time, as we clearly see from the example of Yaakov Avinu. In order to contend with a lifetime of challenges, one must first sit and learn Torah for many years in the *beis midrash* and invest one's heart and efforts wholeheartedly into his learning.

Preparing for *nisyonos* involves two elements. The first is the actual years of learning and growing in the *beis midrash*, and the second is immersion in Torah study — investing every ounce of energy into the learning and delving into each *sugya* with mind, heart, and soul, to the exclusion of all else. Only after such intensive preparations and effort did Yaakov feel equipped to fulfill his parents' command and continue his journey to Lavan's house.

The Baal HaTurim (*Bereishis* 28:10) notes that *Parashas Vayeitzei* is a *parashah stumah* — a *parashah* with no section breaks (*stumah* meaning closed, or hidden), which indicates that Yaakov's escape was concealed from others. It also hints that Yaakov's sojourn in the yeshivah of Eiver was also kept secret, since Yaakov Avinu took refuge in Eiver's home, cutting himself off from the world and hiding for fourteen years while immersing himself in an ocean of Torah. Only after these intensive preparations did he feel equipped to fulfill his parents' command and face the *nisyonos* that awaited him in the house of Lavan.

Torah Creates a New Person

Chazal teach (*Kiddushin* 30b) that Hakadosh Baruch Hu tells the Jewish people, "I created a *yetzer hara*, and I created Torah as its antidote. If you engage in Torah, you do not fall prey to his hands." Our holy Torah is the only remedy, our only means of subjugating the *yetzer hara*, as it encompasses a unique quality that is not found in any other wisdom of the world — the power to change a person.

One who studies math, astronomy, geography, or any subject is not affected deep inside, and his accumulated knowledge and understanding does not initiate any change in his heart or character traits. Yet one who learns Torah is touched at his very core, and is so deeply affected that he evolves into an entirely new entity.

The world is filled with *nisyonos*, and our *avodah* is to overcome them. The *Mesillas Yesharim* writes (Ch. 1): "The essence of man's existence in this world is only to fulfill mitzvos, to serve Hashem, and to withstand tests." We are presented with challenges in order to grow and elevate our souls through *avodas Hashem*; and the way to achieve this spiritual elevation is by learning Torah to the exclusion of all else. This changes the person's very essence and imbues him with new strengths that enable him to overcome any *nisayon*.

Gauging Zehirus

Regarding the words, וַיִּפְגַּע בַּמָּקוֹם וַיָּלֶן שָׁם כִּי בָא הַשֶּׁמֶשׁ, *He encountered the place and spent the night there because the sun had set*, Chazal state (*Bereishis Rabbah* 68:10): "This teaches that Hakadosh Baruch Hu caused the sun to set not at the designated time, in order to speak to Yaakov Avinu privately."

The *nevuah* that Yaakov Avinu received was so vital that

Hashem shortened the day in order to cause him to lie down at the future site of the Beis HaMikdash, where He appeared to him in a dream. Nevertheless, when Yaakov awoke, he regretted having slept in that place, as he said: אָכֵן יֵשׁ ה׳ בַּמָּקוֹם הַזֶּה וְאָנֹכִי לֹא יָדָעְתִּי, *Surely Hashem is present in this place and I did not know* (28:16). Rashi explains that he meant, "Had I known, I would not have slept in a place as holy as this."

Why did Yaakov regret sleeping on Har HaMoriah, if Hakadosh Baruch Hu went so far as to alter the laws of nature in order to cause him to go to sleep, and then revealed Himself to him? What was there to possibly regret?

The next *pasuk* continues: וַיִּירָא וַיֹּאמַר מַה נּוֹרָא הַמָּקוֹם הַזֶּה, *And he became frightened and said, "How awesome is this place!"* What was Yaakov afraid of? Certainly, he could not be faulted or punished for sleeping in this place, as Hakadosh Baruch Hu had just promised him in his dream: וּשְׁמַרְתִּיךָ בְּכֹל אֲשֶׁר תֵּלֵךְ, *I will guard you wherever you go* (v. 15).

Yaakov's *nevuah* and Hashem's revelation were parts of a test measuring how Yaakov would react upon discovering that he'd lain down and slept in a holy site. There are two types of *nisyonos*: The first is temptation, to test whether a person will rebel against Hashem by failing to do a mitzvah or by transgressing a prohibition. The second, which is a loftier level of *nisayon*, does not involve explicit *aveiros*, but gauges a person's level of caution, to see if he can discern that he has done something that he should better have avoided.

Hashem challenged Yaakov with this second category of *nisayon* to test if he would sense that there was anything wrong in sleeping in this holy place. And indeed, when Yaakov awoke, he regretted having slept there, even though, as the Alter of Slabodka teaches,[2] Yaakov Avinu's sleep was on a spiritually elevated plane, not the type of sleep that regular people experience. Indeed, regarding the words (v. 16), וַיִּיקַץ יַעֲקֹב מִשְּׁנָתוֹ, *Yaakov awoke from his sleep (mishnaso)*, the Midrash teaches (*Bereishis Rabbah* 69:7): "Rabbi Yochanan said, '*mimishnaso,*' from his learning."

---

2. *Ohr HaTzafun* Vol. 1, *Maamar Derech Eretz Kadmah LaTorah, Os* 3.

Hakadosh Baruch Hu revealed himself to Yaakov in a dream, and Yaakov was elevated to an extraordinary spiritual height at that time. On the other hand, Yaakov had chosen to go to sleep at that time, which demonstrated a spiritual shortcoming for someone on his level, as he should have known to conduct himself with greater *derech eretz*. Yaakov therefore expressed that it would have been better if he had not slept at all, even if it would have meant forfeiting his *nevuah* and the *giluy Shechinah*.

The Difficulty of a Challenge Depends on Our Perception

Later in the *parashah* the Torah says: וַיַּעֲבֹד יַעֲקֹב בְּרָחֵל שֶׁבַע שָׁנִים וַיִּהְיוּ בְעֵינָיו כְּיָמִים אֲחָדִים בְּאַהֲבָתוֹ אֹתָהּ, *So Yaakov worked seven years for Rachel and they seemed to him a few days because of his love for her* (*Bereishis* 29:20).

Seven years is an exceedingly long time, yet Yaakov's love for Rachel was so deep that the years melted away and appeared to Yaakov as but a few days. When a person works and toils for his own benefit, the pain and effort that he invests feel like the opposite of his goal. Even if he is aware that shouldering the burden is a necessary stage to achieve his goal, he resents the actual work, which often feels long and drawn out.

When a person works for another person because he loves him, however, his exertion and suffering do not conflict with his goal. On the contrary, they are the highest expression of his love, proof that he is willing to work hard and sacrifice on the other's behalf. The efforts are therefore extremely satisfying, and time flies.

Every person faces constant challenges throughout life. When presented with a particularly grueling challenge, one should recall that the pain and adversity are only temporary, and Hakadosh Baruch Hu will ultimately transform them to joy and celebration. Every *nisayon* has a purpose, and when a person focuses on that purpose, he gains the strength to overcome it. If love of a human being can cause seven years of physical toil to feel like mere days, then this is all the more true with regard to *ahavas Hashem*. If we would only place Hashem's honor and our goal of *dveikus* at the forefront of our minds, and recall that the difficulties we confront along the path of *avodas Hashem* are for the sake of His holy Name, then it will be so much easier for us to surmount these challenges, even if they sometimes last a very long time.

Avoiding Places of Danger

The fourteen years that Yaakov spent in the *beis midrash* of Eiver constituted spiritual preparation for entering the house of Lavan and confronting whatever challenges awaited him there. We learn from this that our ability to overcome our *nisyonos* depends on our spiritual preparation — and obviously, the more we prepare ourselves, the easier it will be for us to withstand the *nisyonos* of life.

Yet fortifying ourselves to meet our challenges does not grant us license to willfully enter a *nisayon* or a place of danger, as the Gemara teaches (*Shabbos* 13a): "We tell the *nazir*, 'Go around, go around. Do not approach the vineyard.'" A Yid must do his utmost to distance himself from danger and *nisayon*. Even Yaakov Avinu, who was forced to travel to Lavan's home to fulfill his parents' command, did not approach Aram until he had shielded himself with fourteen years of spiritual preparation.

Every person must continually contemplate the question, "When will my actions reach the actions of my forefathers Avraham, Yitzchak, and Yaakov?" (*Tanna D'Vei Eliyahu Rabbah* Ch. 23). We must reflect upon the actions of our holy *Avos* and learn from them how to contend with the challenges of life. Every *nisayon* is a priceless opportunity to elevate ourselves and draw close to Hashem, and if we properly withstand even one challenge with the understanding that it came from Hashem, then we have already attained a higher spiritual plane. Yet we must also remember that we are forbidden to place ourselves into a place of danger, whether physical or spiritual, and that our principal *avodah* is to strengthen ourselves in *tefillah*, Torah, and *yiras Shamayim*.

May Hashem help us to strengthen ourselves in these areas, and in this *zechus*, may He lead us all along the proper path.

פרשת וישלח
Parashas Vayishlach

The Advantage of Serving Talmidei Chachamim

וַיֹּאמֶר אִם יָבוֹא עֵשָׂו אֶל הַמַּחֲנֶה הָאַחַת וְהִכָּהוּ וְהָיָה הַמַּחֲנֶה הַנִּשְׁאָר לִפְלֵיטָה.

For he said, "If Eisav comes to the one camp and strikes it down, then the remaining camp shall survive" (*Bereishis* 32:9).

The Gemara teaches (*Sanhedrin* 39b): "R' Yitzchak said: Why did Ovadiahu merit prophecy? Because he hid a hundred prophets in the cave, as it is written (*I Melachim* 18:3): *It was when Izevel was decimating the prophets of God, that Ovadiahu took a hundred prophets and he hid them, fifty men in a cave*. Why did he choose to hide them fifty men to a cave? R' Elazar said: He learned from Yaakov, as the verse says, *then the remaining camp shall survive*."

Why, asks the Maharsha, does the Gemara assume that Ovadiahu learned this strategy from Yaakov Avinu? Perhaps he used his own logic to devise this plan, just as Yaakov did.

The Gemara (*Sanhedrin* 11a) relates a story about Rabban Gamliel, who instructed: "Bring me early tomorrow morning seven *dayanim* to sit on the *beis din* [to decide if this year should be a leap year]." The following morning Rabban Gamliel arrived early at the *beis din*, and upon finding eight *dayanim* present he announced, "Whoever came without permission should descend."

Shmuel HaKattan rose and said, "It was I who ascended without permission, yet I did not come to establish the leap year, but to learn practical halachah regarding how to set a leap year."

Rabban Gamliel then replied, "Sit, my son, sit. It is worthy that all the calendars should be set together with you. Chazal, however, taught that a leap year may not be established by anyone other than the *dayanim* who were summoned for this purpose, and because you were not summoned to sit on this *beis din*, you cannot take part in it."

The Gemara subsequently explains that Shmuel HaKattan had been summoned to join the *beis din*, but implicated himself in order to avoid shaming the *dayan* who had come uninvited.

In a similar incident, Rebbi was once sitting and lecturing to his *talmidim* in the *beis midrash* when an unpleasant odor filled the room. "Whoever ate garlic should exit," he announced. R' Chiya immediately rose and exited the *beis midrash*, prompting everyone to rise and follow him outside.

The next morning, Rebbi's son R' Shimon met R' Chiya and asked, "Are you the one who distressed my father?"

R' Chiya replied, "Heaven forbid! I would never eat garlic before coming to the *beis midrash*, but I walked out in order to avoid humiliating the one who did. Seeing that I left the *beis midrash*, everyone rose and left after me, so no one knew who was the one who ate garlic."

The Gemara notes that R' Chiya learned this practice from R' Meir. Once, a woman entered the *beis midrash* and declared, "One of you betrothed me through cohabitation, and now he must either marry me or divorce me." In order to avoid humiliating the *talmid* who had perpetrated this disgraceful act, R' Meir immediately wrote a *get* and gave it to the woman. Seeing that R' Meir had done this, all his *talmidim* immediately followed suit and wrote *gittin* to the woman, allowing the perpetrator to divorce her quietly, without suffering public humiliation.

The Gemara adds that R' Meir was following the example of

Shmuel HaKattan, who abandoned his seat on the *beis din*. Then, the Gemara goes on to say that Shmuel HaKattan learned this from Shechaniah ben Yechiel, who wanted the nation to confess to marrying gentile women and to repent. In order to avoid embarrassing those who had stumbled in this sin, he included himself in this confession (*Ezra* 10:2). The Gemara continues that Shechaniah ben Yechiel learned this from an incident involving Yehoshua, in which Hashem chastised the entire nation to avoid embarrassing the transgressor (*Yehoshua* 7:10-11).

Another opinion maintains that Shechaniah ben Yechiel actually learned this from Hashem's reprimand to Moshe Rabbeinu after the *mahn* was collected on Shabbos. Although only two people sinned, the nation was castigated collectively for their crime, to avoid embarrassing them (*Shemos* 16:28).

Each of these noble actions could have easily been performed on its own, without a prior example to inspire it. Our holy Amoraim possessed the finest *middos* and profound sensitivity; each one could surely have performed such an act of kindness and empathy for a fellow Jew on his own, by exercising simple logic and common sense. Why does the Gemara present the entire sequence of events, implying that without a previous model to follow, the Amoraim would not have known how to act?

Furthermore, each person mentioned in this account of the Gemara learned the practice from his own spiritual mentor. R' Chiya learned it from R' Meir, who learned it from Shmuel HaKattan, who learned it from Shechaniah ben Uziel, who learned it from a *pasuk* about either Yehoshua or Moshe Rabbeinu. If so, why couldn't all these Amoraim have drawn their example directly from the *pesukim*? Why did they need to observe someone else who modeled this behavior?

Proper Conduct Is Relayed Through Mesorah

R' Chaim Shmulevitz[3] derived from here a beautiful and essential lesson for life. A person, he taught, cannot adopt a new behavior

3. *Sichos Mussar, Shimush Talmidei Chachamim I*

or practice independently, based on his own logic and reasoning. Even the decision to perform a kind, compassionate action, such as taking responsibility for another person's mistake, cannot — and must not — be made in a vacuum. A person is not authorized to draw his own conclusions from the Torah regarding the ideal way to act. Rather, he must consult and learn these behaviors from a rav — and not just any rav, but a rav from his generation with whom he shares a close relationship.

This concept is expressed in the very first mishnah in *Avos*: "Moshe received Torah from Sinai and transmitted it to Yehoshua; and Yehoshua to the Elders; and the Elders to the Prophets; and the Prophets transmitted it to the Anshei Knesses HaGedolah." This mishnah delineates the clear progression of our *mesorah* — how the Torah was passed down through the generations, from rebbi to *talmid*, and how, conversely, a *talmid* receives the Torah from his rebbi, who received it from his rebbi, and he from his rebbi, going back through the generations until the times of Yehoshua and Moshe Rabbeinu.

To illustrate this in contemporary terms, if R' Akiva Eiger issued a *psak*, and the *gedolei hador* of our time ruled differently, we would be bound by the ruling of today's *gedolim*, not that of R' Akiva Eiger, since a Yid is obligated to uphold the *piskei halachah* of the *gedolim* of his generation.

Shimush of the Yeshivah

Every individual is required to follow the practices and rulings of his rebbi, so that his actions perpetuate the actions and legacy of his rebbi's own rabbanim. The best way for a *talmid* to absorb the ways and intention of his rebbi is through *shimush*, serving him, as the Gemara states (*Berachos* 7b): "*Gedolah shimushah shel Torah yoser milimudah,* as it says, *Elisha ben Shafat who poured water over Eliyahu's hands* (*II Melachim* 3:11). It does not say that Elisha learned from Eliyahu, but rather that he poured water over his hands, to teach that serving [*talmidei chachamim*] is greater than learning [from them]."

Furthermore, the Gemara adds that even if one has learned *kol haTorah kulah*, if he did not serve *talmidei chachamim*, he is still regarded as a layman and cannot be included in a *zimun* (ibid. 47b).

The reason why *shimush* of one's rebbi is greater than learning Torah from his mouth is that when learning, the *lomed* learns only what he is taught; but during *shimush*, the *lomed* also learns *why*. He understands why his rebbi delivered a particular *psak* in one case and a different *psak* in another. He has the opportunity to delve deeper into his rebbi's meaning and intentions. And he learns to apply from one situation to another and rule accordingly. The ability to quote one's rebbi verbatim does not make one a *talmid*, for only after he has served his rebbi, understood his reasoning, logic, and analysis, and ingrained his rebbi's qualities and *derech* deep within himself to the extent that he can rule in his *derech*, does he earn the title "*talmid*."

Two *bachurim* with similar talents and abilities may learn beside each other in the same *beis midrash*, and ultimately only one merits to become a great *talmid chacham* and *marbitz Torah*, while the other does not. Indeed, Chazal teach that "One thousand people enter to learn Torah, and only one emerges to teach" (*Koheles Rabbah* 1:28).

The difference between the two lies in the fact that the first is *meshamesh* his rebbi; he absorbs and ingrains his rebbi's essence and *derech* deep in his heart, and eventually becomes a *doleh u'mashkeh* who draws forth his rebbi's teachings and disseminates them to others. The second *bachur*, in contrast, only learned his rebbi's Torah, but never actually served him and thus never attained the level of a genuine *talmid* who can relay his rebbi's teachings to the next generation.

R' Baruch Ber Leibowitz often described the profound reverence and *hisbatlus* that he felt toward his rebbi, R' Chaim Soloveitchik, and this, I believe, is what led him to attain an incredibly profound understanding of his Torah. Not only do the *shimush* and *hisbatlus* that a *talmid* manifests toward his rebbi enable him to absorb his Torah in the most meaningful way, but the rebbi likewise receives a special dose of *siyata diShmaya* that enables him to teach and imbue knowledge and wisdom in his *talmid*. R' Chaim Shmulevitz would often say that a chassidic Rebbe receives his bounty of *ruach hakodesh* only because his chassidim submit themselves to him entirely.

This clarifies why the Gemara states that Ovadiahu followed the example of Yaakov Avinu by dividing the prophets into two camps. Ovadiahu did not attain his level of prophecy by his own merit, but by doing *shimush* — learning from Yaakov Avinu how to act in his situation.

R' Chaim added that in our times, the title of "rebbi" applies to the yeshivah. *Shimush yeshivah* means being an intrinsic part of the yeshivah — davening Shacharis in yeshivah and strictly maintaining all *sedarim* — both regular *seder* and *mussar seder*. *Shimush* in yeshivah is even more important than learning in yeshivah, because only one who attaches himself to the yeshivah and makes himself an indistinguishable part of it can merit the crown of Torah. I believe it was the Alter of Slabodka who once expressed that his outstanding growth and achievements in Torah were all rooted in the fact that he was very careful about maintaining his *sedarim* in yeshivah.

Someone once approached R' Chaim Kanievsky to ask if he could learn independently, or if it is necessary to learn with a *chavrusa*. Rav Chaim replied that while he may learn on his own if he wishes, he must still discuss his learning with others in a yeshivah framework, since this is the only way that one can attain the quality of yeshivah-style learning and, with it, the indispensable aspect of *shimush*.

Utilizing Every Moment of Time

Unfortunately, today there is a terrible dearth of *emunas chachamim*. The honor we accord *talmidei chachamim* is sorely lacking, and very few people merit to achieve the lofty level of *shimushah yoser milimudah. Baruch Hashem*, we are learning well, formulating *chiddushei Torah*, and being tested on what we learn, but we do not expend sufficient effort to achieve that degree!

When I was a *bachur* learning under R' Nochum Partzovitz, we completed sixty *blatt* of *Maseches Yevamos* in a single *zman*! Today, our *gedolim* decry the paltry amount that we learn, but there is no one heeding their call.

Why is it that when a person suffers a challenge or tragedy, *lo aleinu,* he runs to *gedolei Yisrael* to seek their counsel, but when the very same *gedolei Yisrael* appeal and demand that we learn more, we carelessly dismiss their words?

If Ovadiahu could draw a lesson from Yaakov Avinu, we must likewise learn from our *Avos* and rabbanim. The solution to all this is *nitzul hazman,* utilizing every moment of time for learning. Our rabbanim took advantage of every moment, viewing each second as more precious than gold, which is how they attained spiritual greatness. If we would only utilize our time properly, we would also see how much more we can do and achieve.

Improvement in this area can come only from the *bachurim* themselves — those who yearn to learn more, to cover more ground, and absorb the *limud* faster — and the aspirations of these select few will impact many. If only a few *bachurim* would resolve to learn more, to learn faster, to accomplish more, it would surely affect everyone. Once there is increased desire and demand, nothing will stand in the way of our *hatzlachah* in learning. Hakadosh Baruch Hu should help that in the *zechus* of accepting the *ol haTorah,* we should be *zocheh* very soon to the *geulah sheleimah*!

פרשת וישב - חנוכה
Parashas Vayeishev — Chanukah

◆§ *Inner Peace Comes From Ameilus BaTorah*

וַיֵּשֶׁב יַעֲקֹב בְּאֶרֶץ מְגוּרֵי אָבִיו בְּאֶרֶץ כְּנָעַן.
Yaakov settled in the land of his father's sojournings, in the land of Canaan (*Bereishis* 37:1).

Rashi comments: "Yaakov wished to dwell in tranquility; the incident of Yosef was sprung upon him. [When] *tzaddikim* wish to sit in peace [in this world], Hakadosh Baruch Hu says: 'Is it not enough for *tzaddikim* that which awaits them in Olam Haba, that they also wish to sit in peace in this world?'"

Yaakov Avinu craved a life of peace and harmony — yet for what purpose? Only to grow spiritually, and to sit and learn Torah with peace of mind. Learning Torah in a calm frame of mind does not require any special material conditions. A learner doesn't need a fancy house or splendid furniture; all he needs is to enter the hallowed halls of the *beis midrash*, leave his troubles and distractions outside, and delve into the *blatt* Gemara with the age-old melody as he delights in the words of Chazal and the Rishonim. Aside from this, he needs nothing at all; anyone who has ever experienced this has tasted true *shalvah*, ultimate tranquility.

The Greatest Tranquility Is Toiling in Torah

I recall the joyous occasion when my rebbi, R' Chaim Kamil, celebrated the birth of his only daughter, several years after his marriage. At the time, I was learning with him *b'chavrusa*, and on the day that his wife returned home from the hospital, he asked that we learn in his home in the Zichron Moshe neighborhood in Yerushalayim, instead of in the yeshivah as we always did.

When the taxi pulled up outside with the new mother and infant and assorted bundles and packages, R' Chaim rushed outside to greet his wife and baby and help them into the house. R' Chaim trekked up and down the steps several times to bring in all the packages, glowing in elation upon the birth of this long-awaited child. Still, whereas others would have surely dallied and chatted excitedly about the great *simchah*, he hurried to arrange the items quickly in the house and then immediately returned to the living room to resume learning in the same peaceful tune that we learned every day. This is true *shalvah*! R' Chaim greeted his wife and daughter with *simchah* and *shalvah*, and then returned to his learning, his lifetime passion, with the same calm, elevated frame of mind. Watching this unfold, I reflected that one who has never felt tranquility like this has never experienced real *shalvah*!

I can still envision the Rosh Yeshivah, R' Chaim Shmulevitz, learning in the *beis midrash* on Shabbos after davening. While we'd all troop down the steps to the yeshivah dining room for *Kiddush*, he'd sit down beside the right window facing the *Mizrach*, remove his frock, and delve into the Gemara. So absorbed was he in his learning that he wouldn't even notice someone standing right beside him! He was utterly engrossed in his learning, immersed in the sweet sea of Torah, and wreathed in a magnificent aura of pleasure and peace of mind. This was *shalvah*!

Every *ben Torah* knows that there is nothing sweeter in the world than this *shalvah* — the incredible *menuchas hanefesh* of sitting with a *shtender* and learning a *blatt Gemara*, of resolving a *kushya* of Rabbi Akiva Eiger. (Personally, I don't believe that it's possible to resolve any one of Rabbi Akiva Eiger's *kushyos*, although there are times when we dare to imagine that it is possible!) This is the experience of *shalvah,* and it was this *shalvah* that Yaakov Avinu yearned to experience throughout his life.

I hope that it will not sound like I am boasting, but I was once privileged to enjoy six weeks of true *shalvah* in my life. At the time, I was learning the famous *sugya* in *Maseches Kesubos daf tes* with a *chavrusa,* and together, we plumbed its depths with the *Shev Shmaatsa, Shaarei Yosher,* and *Shaar HaMishpat.*[4] We were utterly enveloped in the *sugya,* and the peace of mind and satisfaction that we felt during those weeks was indescribable. I did this only once in my life, but at least that one time, I tasted genuine *simchah shel Torah.*[5]

Many ask why R' Nochum Partzovitz merited that his *divrei Torah* would be discussed and analyzed in *batei midrash* around the world. There are several possible answers, but I will highlight one: When Rav Nochum offered a *sevarah* in learning, he radiated *simchah* and *shalvah,* and anyone who possesses this wonderful attribute can grasp Rav Nochum's Torah. Similarly, the Chofetz Chaim always spoke softly and serenely, living every day with *shalvah* and *menuchas hanefesh* — and his *sefarim* are today fundamental works in every Jewish home.

Achieving Shalvah in Olam Hazeh

Yaakov Avinu sought a life of tranquility, yet Hakadosh Baruch Hu responded: "Is it not enough for *tzaddikim* that which awaits them in Olam Haba, that they also wish to sit in peace in this world?"

A person's efforts and toil in this world are rewarded: *"Lefum tzaara agra."* The harder it is to withstand the lure of the *yetzer hara,* the greater the reward one will reap in Olam Haba for his efforts to surmount it. Moreover, the toil and hardship involved

4. The Rosh Yeshivah noted that he does not actually recommend this method of learning, but that he was simply telling the story as it occurred.

5. The Rosh Yeshivah related this story with trademark modesty, although we all know that his entire life was devoted to immersion in Torah amid true *mesirus nefesh.*

in overcoming each *nisayon* are a prerequisite to reward in Olam Haba, as our mission in the world is to fulfill Hashem's will despite the hardships that we face.

As explained above, true *shalvah* in this world is attained only through *amal baTorah*, and therefore, a person should not ask for *shalvah* that obviates the need for effort and toil. Indeed, we see that the *shalvah* and *simchah* attained by our *gedolim* were only the results of their ceaseless efforts to toil in Torah.

Hakadosh Baruch Hu's response to Yaakov Avinu was that *shalvah* without effort and toil can occur only in Olam Haba, where all that exists is pure pleasure from the aura of the *Shechinah*. Olam Hazeh, in contrast, is a place of work, of striving and exerting ourselves to the maximum in order to accomplish more and more. This — and only this — is what allows us to attain *menuchah* and *simchah*.

There are those who might view this as paradoxical, as we find that people who work long, hard hours are often embittered and prone to anger or impatience, and certainly lack joy and peace of mind. Yet this is true only with regard to the pursuit of material wealth, and does not apply to toiling in Torah, which imbues a person with joy and serenity.

Chazal teach (*Kiddushin* 30b):

> Even a father and his son, or a rebbi and his *talmid*, who are studying Torah together in one gate, at first become enemies of one another, but they do not move from there until they become devoted friends of one another, as it says (*Bamidbar* 21:14): אֶת וָהֵב בְּסוּפָה, *[Therefore it will be told in the book of God's wars] of that which He gave on the Red Sea.* Do not read this as *"besufah"* (on the Red Sea) but rather as *"besofah"* (in the end).

Imagine that two *bachurim* are debating a *sevarah*. Their voices rise heatedly, and their cheeks redden in zeal. Their eyes spark with passion and fervor as they loudly defend their respective lines of reasoning. One who observes the pair from the side may easily mistake them for two opponents, yet this is how these *chavrusos* clarify their *sevaros* and attain the *emes* of Torah. This is the way they reach a mutual *derech* and come to accept and respect the other's opinion, which leads them to a unique place of *shalvah.* The *pilpul* and vigorous debates that turned them momentarily into adversaries draw them close together, and they do not leave the *beis midrash* until they are friends again.

This is the way we attain *simchah* and *shalvah* in this world!

If *limud Torah* does not gladden a person's heart, it is obvious that his *limud Torah* is lacking something. A *bachur* who feels sad or depressed despite his *amal baTorah* is missing a vital element in his *yegiah.* Everyone is capable of acquiring *shalvah* in this world, and the way to do it is by withstanding *nisyonos* and hardships in *amal haTorah.* Just as Yaakov Avinu was reproved for requesting *shalvah* in *limud Torah* and was immediately forced to contend with the tragedy of Yosef's disappearance, each and every one of us is likewise obliged to cope with our challenges in *amal haTorah* — as this is our ultimate *avodah* in this world.

Completing a Mitzvah

We draw another essential lesson from this *parashah* from Yehudah, who took a stand to save Yosef's life, by saying: מַה בֶּצַע כִּי נַהֲרֹג אֶת אָחִינוּ וְכִסִּינוּ אֶת דָּמוֹ. לְכוּ וְנִמְכְּרֶנּוּ לַיִּשְׁמְעֵאלִים וְיָדֵנוּ אַל תְּהִי בוֹ כִּי אָחִינוּ בְשָׂרֵנוּ הוּא, *What gain will there be if we kill our brother and cover up his blood? Come, let us sell him to the Ishmaelites — but let our hand not be upon him, for he is our brother, our own flesh* (*Bereishis* 37:26-27). Ultimately, Yehudah's brothers scorned him for this, [saying that once he saw that they were accepting his proposal, he should then have suggested that they bring Yosef home to Yaakov] which caused him to wander afar and marry the daughter of Shua, who bore him Er, Onan, and Sheilah, two of whom perished. From here, Chazal derive that "one who starts a mitzvah and does not complete it, buries his wife and two sons" (*Tanchuma, Eikev* 6:6).

Why is that? Isn't dispensing entirely with a mitzvah worse than starting it without finishing it? Why is one who began a mitzvah but did not complete it punished more severely than one who didn't think to start it at all?

Leaving something unfinished demonstrates a lack of appreciation for its significance. One who values a task or mission remains involved with it until the very end, whereas one who starts something and abandons it partway conveys an attitude of derision. This cannot be said about one who never started the task at all, because it is possible that had he started it, he would have completed it.

A *bachur* or *avreich* who arrives early to *seder* is beginning a mitzvah, and it is up to him to ensure that he continues learning with fervor until the end of *seder*. This requirement is even more compelling for him than for a *bachur* who comes late to *seder* and does not learn properly.

One who starts learning early and interrupts it in the middle demonstrates a gross lack of appreciation for the mitzvah of *limud Torah*. In contrast, one who completes each *seder* displays incredible appreciation for learning and earns massive merit. Aside from the boundless reward that awaits him for the learning itself, he also sanctifies Hashem's Name by demonstrating the awe and love he feels toward the mitzvah of learning Torah.

The Chashmonaim: "Oskei Torasecha"

We are just starting the radiant days of Chanukah, and I want to share with you a thought that occurred to me in the midst of reciting the *tefillah* that was composed to thank Hashem for the miracle of Chanukah. Mattisyahu and his sons were intrepid warriors who stood courageously against the many hardships and challenges of the time; yet we find that the *tefillah* of *Al HaNissim* refers to them only as *tzaddikim* and *oskei Torasecha,* stressing their constant devotion to Torah. I've mentioned on numerous occasions that an *osek baTorah* is one who makes Torah his *eisek,* his business in the world that occupies him completely, and the Chashmonaim personified this. Moreover, they devoted themselves to their mission of purifying the Beis HaMikdash until they completed the task one hundred percent. They started and ended the mitzvah, demonstrating how valuable it was to them.

Chanukah is the ideal opportunity to strengthen ourselves in Torah study, following the example of Mattisyahu and his sons, who did not abandon their *eisek baTorah* even at the height of war. It is so painful to see how *limud Torah* weakens during the days of Chanukah, which is a time auspicious for soaring in learning and immersing ourselves exclusively in *amal haTorah*. I am certain that those who utilize these days of Chanukah properly will grow in Torah and attain the spiritual level at which they can experience the special *shalvah* reserved for those who toil in Torah.

May Hashem help us to achieve this special *shalvah,* and to utilize each of these days of Chanukah for *aliyah* in Torah and *yiras Shamayim.*

פרשת מקץ
Parashas Mikeitz

◈ *Nekius: Integrity*

וַיַּעַן יוֹסֵף אֶת פַּרְעֹה לֵאמֹר בִּלְעָדָי אֱלֹהִים יַעֲנֶה אֶת שְׁלוֹם פַּרְעֹה.

Yosef answered Pharaoh, saying, "That is beyond me; it is God Who will respond with Pharaoh's welfare" (*Bereishis* 41:16).

On the word בִּלְעָדָי, Rashi comments: "The wisdom is not mine; rather, *it is God Who will respond* — He will place the response in my mouth for Pharaoh's welfare."

Pharaoh's actions seem astounding. The king of Egypt takes a young man — a former slave who has just been released from prison, and who comes from the land of the Hebrews, who were despised by the Egyptians of that era — and, seemingly on a whim, declares him viceroy, with powers second to no one but Pharaoh himself! What exceptional qualities did Pharaoh discern in Yosef that spurred him to spontaneously appoint him as ruler of his country?

The Rosh Yeshivah R' Chaim Shmulevitz explained[6] that it was precisely one word that allowed Yosef to earn Pharaoh's unqualified trust: "*Biladai.*"

6. *Sichos Mussar, Shleimus HaMaaseh* I.

When Yosef HaTzaddik stood before Pharaoh, he knew that he had not been redeemed from prison and taken to the king's palace without a reason; clearly, someone had praised him effusively to Pharaoh, as Pharaoh himself attests (v. 15): וַאֲנִי שָׁמַעְתִּי עָלֶיךָ לֵאמֹר תִּשְׁמַע חֲלוֹם לִפְתֹּר אֹתוֹ, *Now I heard it said of you that you comprehend a dream to interpret it*.

Yet instead of highlighting his rare power, Yosef categorically denies his talent and answers, "*Biladai* — it is not my strength or power, but the wisdom and help of Hakadosh Baruch Hu." He does not demand honor or even request minor credit for his remarkable ability to interpret dreams, professing that it is all *siyata diShmaya*! A person like this — who does not request anything for himself and demonstrates an utter lack of self-interest — is someone who can surely be trusted.

Yosef HaTzaddik again demonstrates this quality in the next *parashah* when he sends wagons to bring Yaakov to Mitzrayim, as the *pesukim* say: וַיִּתֵּן לָהֶם יוֹסֵף עֲגָלוֹת עַל פִּי פַרְעֹה, *And Yosef gave them wagons by Pharaoh's word* (ibid. 45:21) and וַיִּשְׂאוּ בְנֵי יִשְׂרָאֵל אֶת יַעֲקֹב אֲבִיהֶם . . . בָּעֲגָלוֹת אֲשֶׁר שָׁלַח פַּרְעֹה לָשֵׂאת אֹתוֹ, *The sons of Yisrael transported Yaakov their father ... in the wagons which Pharaoh had sent to transport him* (ibid. 46:5).

Yosef HaTzaddik was the *mishneh lamelech*, yet he never acted without obtaining Pharaoh's express permission. Since Egyptian law prohibited sending wagons out of the country without the royal stamp of approval, Yosef made sure to ask Pharaoh, and never once infringed upon his word, as the Torah attests on numerous occasions. This is the model of a person who acts with *nekius* (integrity), taking nothing for himself — and this is a person who is deemed trustworthy. When Pharaoh discerned this exceptional quality in Yosef HaTzaddik, he immediately determined that this is a person whom he could trust to serve as his viceroy.

Eliezer the servant of Avraham also demonstrated this trait of *nekius* when he traveled to Besuel's house to request Rivkah's hand in marriage for Yitzchak. In fact, his very first words upon greeting Besuel were עֶבֶד אַבְרָהָם אָנֹכִי, *I am the servant of Avraham* (ibid. 24:34).

R' Chaim explains that Eliezer said this because his features bore a strong physical resemblance to those of Avraham Avinu (*Bereishis Rabbah* 60:7). When Lavan first saw Eliezer, he was certain that he was, indeed, his relative, which was why he greeted him with the words: בּוֹא בְּרוּךְ ה', *Come, O blessed of Hashem* (v. 31). Eliezer therefore hurried to correct him and replied, "I am the servant of Avraham," as he did not wish to benefit even momentarily from honor or a welcome that was not intended for him. How apt, then, is Chazal's observation that "the conversation of the servants of the forefathers is more beautiful than the lessons taught by the sons" (*Bereishis Rabbah* 60:8).

The Severity of Lack of Nekius

The importance of acting with *nekius* and avoiding even a hint of self-interest is evident in the Gemara's account (*Avodah Zarah* 18a) of how R' Chanina ben Tradyon's daughter was extricated from the terrible fate of being relegated to a brothel, which the Roman authorities had decreed upon her. The Gemara explains that this punishment befell her because she had once been walking before several Roman leaders and had overheard them remarking, "How beautiful are this maiden's footsteps." Upon hearing their words, she took care to refine her gait even more.

The *Mesillas Yesharim* (Ch. 16) elaborates that R' Chanina ben Tradyon's daughter was exceptionally modest, a quality evident even in her gait, and it was this modesty that the Roman officers noticed and praised. R' Chaim Shmulevitz adds, based on the *Mesillas Yesharim*, that the extra care she took to enhance her gait was in order to reach an even higher level of *tznius*, and yet she was punished severely for this, because she felt praised by the words of the Roman officers and drew pleasure and pride in this practice.

What flaw did R' Chanina ben Tradyon's daughter exhibit in attempting to walk with extra modesty? Her reaction reflected some self-interest and lack of integrity that was not appropriate for a person of her caliber. Therefore she, the very paragon of modesty, was still punished harshly.

A similar example in the Torah is that of Nadav and Avihu, who were punished for the sin of: וַיֶּחֱזוּ אֶת הָאֱלֹהִים וַיֹּאכְלוּ וַיִּשְׁתּוּ, *They gazed at God, yet they ate and drank* (*Shemos* 24:11). Nadav and Avihu reached the consummate *madreigah,* at which they were able to "gaze" at Hashem, as it were, and yet they sinned by deriving personal pleasure from the experience, which is why the Torah describes it as if they had eaten or drank. The momentary ecstasy they experienced caused them to lose the exalted level they had attained during their moment of closeness to Hashem, and this resulted in their deaths.

We find that even angels were punished for drawing personal pleasure while fulfilling a directive of Hashem. Chazal teach that the angels who were sent to rescue Lot from Sedom were banished from Hashem's midst for 138 years after they declared (*Bereishis* 19:13): כִּי מַשְׁחִתִים אֲנַחְנוּ אֶת הַמָּקוֹם, *for we are about to destroy this place* (*Bereishis Rabbah* 50:9). Although they expressed in the very same *pasuk,* וַיְשַׁלְּחֵנוּ ה׳ לְשַׁחֲתָהּ, *so Hashem has sent us to destroy it,* they are faulted for taking credit for destroying Sedom.

We mere mortals cannot fathom what it means that these angels "sinned," but we *can* learn from here how vital *nekius* is, for even a *malach* who takes an iota of credit for an action that should be attributed exclusively to Hakadosh Baruch Hu is punished severely.

The Reward of Nekius

Conversely, one who acquires the *middah* of *nekius* attains a lofty spiritual level and will reap infinite reward.

Chazal teach (*Avos* 6:4): "*Kach hi darkah shel Torah* — this is the way of the Torah: Eat bread with salt, drink water in measure, sleep on the ground, and live a life of hardship — yet toil in the Torah. If you do this ... you are fortunate in this world, and it is well for you in the World to Come."

The only way to earn this vast reward is by making do with the bare minimum and drawing no pleasure from Olam Hazeh. A person who possesses more than the proverbial bread and salt has already taken more than the bare necessities, and this is not the way of Torah, about which Chazal proclaim, *"Ashrecha ba'olam hazeh vetov lach la'olam haba."*

In this vein, the Gemara teaches (*Taanis* 24b): "Each day a *bas kol* descends and declares, 'The entire world is sustained because of my son Chanina, and my son Chanina suffices with a measure of carobs from Erev Shabbos to Erev Shabbos.'"

The simple explanation is that the entire world is sustained in the merit of R' Chanina, who sufficed with virtually nothing. Yet the Gemara may also be imparting a far deeper lesson, which is that what made R' Chanina worthy of sustaining the entire world was his *histapkus b'muat* — making do with a measure of carobs all week. This quality is so commendable that its presence in one person alone — R' Chanina — was enough to sustain the entire world!

Hashem commands Bnei Yisrael: קְדֹשִׁים תִּהְיוּ, *You shall be holy* (*Vayikra* 19:2), which Chazal interpret as *"Perushim tihiyu* — you shall be separate" (*Toras Kohanim* ibid.), and *"Kadesh atzmecha b'mutar lach* — Sanctify yourself with that which is permissible for you" (*Yevamos* 20a).

With these lessons, Chazal underscore the importance of the *middah* of *perishus*, not partaking of worldly pleasures more than one needs. That abstention is what enables a person to reach loftier levels of *kedushah*.

Similarly, regarding the *pasuk*, קְדֹשִׁים תִּהְיוּ כִּי קָדוֹשׁ אֲנִי, *You shall be holy, because I am holy*, Chazal ask (*Vayikra Rabbah* 24:9): *"Yachol Kamoni?* Can you be as holy as Me?" Pointing to the words *ki kadosh Ani*, they answer, "My Holiness is greater than your holiness."

We learn a marvelous *chiddush* from these words of Chazal, which express that had the Torah not informed us that we cannot reach the level of Hashem's *kedushah*, we could have assumed that a person who abstains from all worldly pleasures and takes only the basic necessities from this world can attain such a lofty level of holiness that his *kedushah* could parallel that of Hashem.

To reach this level of *perishus*, a person must possess absolute self-control and avoid taking any action before carefully evaluating whether it is necessary. Then, after weighing his every action to see if it is right and acquiring the level of *histapkus b'muat*, he can attain exceedingly lofty spiritual levels.

Two Additional Years in Prison

Chazal teach (*Bereishis Rabbah* 89:2-3) that Yosef was punished with an additional two years in prison because he twice asked the Sar HaMashkim to mention him to Pharaoh, as he said *"Ki im zechartani"* and *"Vehizkartani"* (*Bereishis* 40:14).

The famous question asked on this Midrash is: Why was Yosef punished for performing what could surely be considered basic *hishtadlus* to gain his freedom? Why did an extra word result in the harsh sentence of an additional two years in prison?

The answer becomes clear when viewed from the perspective of *histapkus b'muat.* A Yid has no reason to draw any more pleasure from this world than those he requires in order to live — each person on his own level. Hakadosh Baruch Hu dealt stringently with Yosef HaTzaddik for adding a superfluous word because he possessed the exalted *middah* of *nekius*, as he subsequently displayed in the dialogue with Pharaoh when he answered him, *"Biladai."* Since Yosef had attained the spiritual level at which he recognized that nothing in the world belonged to him, the addition of the word *"vehizkartani"* was regarded as an attempt to take more from the physical world than necessary, and therefore he was punished for this.

One Who Takes From This World Cannot Be a Mashpia

R' Eliyahu Lopian shared a sharp story highlighting the importance of not partaking of worldly pleasures more than necessary:

R' Aharon Shulevitz, a *talmid* of R' Yisrael Salanter, founded and served as Rosh Yeshivah of the Lomza Yeshivah. When it came time to appoint a *mashgiach*, he asked the Chofetz Chaim to recommend a suitable candidate.

The Chofetz Chaim suggested a man who was one of the rising

stars in that era, a Torah genius who possessed deep sensitivity, passion, and other admirable traits that made him qualified to fill the position.

Several days later, the Chofetz Chaim dispatched an urgent letter to Rav Shulevitz retracting his recommendation and advising him against hiring the man as *mashgiach*. The Rosh Yeshivah noticed that the letter had been written on Chol HaMoed, attesting to its critical nature.

Rav Shulevitz immediately returned to Radin to ask the Chofetz Chaim what had triggered this change of heart. The Chofetz Chaim replied that while he had originally believed that this man was the right person for the position, several days after their meeting, the person had visited him and bemoaned his difficult financial plight. "One who complains about his *gashmiyus* is not fit to be a *mashpia ruchani* in a yeshivah," he concluded.

This episode underscores the magnitude of the *middah* of *nekius*. A person who is unable to dissociate from his own self-interest and from all connection to Olam Hazeh — besides the share that he has been granted — cannot educate *talmidim* or serve as a spiritual example to them, even if he has personally attained an exalted spiritual level.

May Hakadosh Baruch Hu guide us all to acquire the *middah* of *nekius*, which is a foundation to all other spiritual attainments, and may we merit to soar in *yiras Shamayim* and all *middos tovos*.

פרשת ויגש
Parashas Vayigash

◆§ *Responsibility: The Cornerstone of Majesty*

וְעַתָּה יֵשֶׁב נָא עַבְדְּךָ תַּחַת הַנַּעַר עֶבֶד לַאדֹנִי וְהַנַּעַר יַעַל עִם אֶחָיו.

Now, therefore, please let your servant remain instead of the youth as a servant to my lord, and let the youth go up with his brothers (*Bereishis* 44:33).

The *Tosefta* recounts a discussion between R' Akiva and a group of Sages (*Berachos* 4:16):

> "Why did Yehudah merit royalty? They answered, "Because he confessed regarding Tamar." He asked them, "Is one rewarded for a sin?" They answered, "Rather, why did Yehudah merit royalty? Because he saved his brother [Yosef] from death, as it is written: וַיֹּאמֶר יְהוּדָה אֶל אֶחָיו מַה בֶּצַע כִּי נַהֲרֹג אֶת אָחִינוּ וְכִסִּינוּ אֶת דָּמוֹ, *Yehudah said to his brothers, 'What gain will there be if we kill our brother and cover up his blood?'* (*Bereishis* 37:26)." He told them, "[Rescuing Yosef] was only enough to atone for the sale." [They continued:] "Rather, why did Yehudah merit royalty? Because of his humility, as it is written: וְעַתָּה יֵשֶׁב נָא עַבְדְּךָ תַּחַת הַנַּעַר עֶבֶד לַאדֹנִי וְהַנַּעַר יַעַל עִם אֶחָיו, *Now, therefore, please let your*

servant remain instead of the youth as a servant to my lord (ibid. 44:33)." He said to them, "Did he not serve as a guarantor for him, and a guarantor is obliged to fulfill his pledge? Rather, why did Yehudah merit royalty? Because he sanctified the Name of Hakadosh Baruch Hu, and when the *shevatim* stood at the sea, one saying, 'I am entering [the sea],' and another saying, 'I am entering [the sea],' the *shevet* of Yehudah leaped up and entered first, sanctifying the Name of Hakadosh Baruch Hu."

The *Tosefta* presents four reasons why Shevet Yehudah was deserving of royalty. R' Chaim Shmulevitz explained[7] that the spiritual levels a person attains depend on his level of *achrayus*, his sense of responsibility. One who does not take any responsibility for his actions is an utter fool; while the more accountability one manifests for his actions, the higher levels of greatness he will attain. Based on this premise, we infer that the person most suited for majesty and for ruling his nation is the one who accepts the highest level of responsibility.

Each of the four explanations of why Yehudah merited royalty is rooted in *achrayus*. Yehudah surpassed his brothers in this trait, and since *achrayus* is the foremost *middah* required for *malchus*, it was he who was awarded the crown.

Yehudah Accepted Eternal Servitude

In the *Tosefta* above, Chazal dispute whether Yehudah's declaration to Yosef, "Now, therefore, please let your servant remain instead of the youth," was an expression of his humility, or whether he was merely fulfilling his obligation after guaranteeing to Yaakov Avinu Binyamin's safe return.

On the surface, the second opinion seems correct, as Yehudah himself says in the previous *pasuk*: כִּי עַבְדְּךָ עָרַב אֶת הַנַּעַר מֵעִם אָבִי לֵאמֹר אִם לֹא אֲבִיאֶנּוּ אֵלֶיךָ וְחָטָאתִי לְאָבִי כָּל הַיָּמִים, *For your servant took responsibility for the youth from my father, saying, "If I do not bring him back to you then I will have sinned to my father for all time."* With these

7. *Sichos Mussar, Achrayus I.*

words, Yehudah willingly assumes eternal servitude in order to fulfill his pledge to his father.

Why does the first opinion in the *Tosefta* see this as evidence of Yehudah's humility, if he was simply fulfilling his promise to Yaakov?

Yehudah could surely have found a way out of his promise, which compelled him to display extreme *mesirus nefesh* and accept a lifetime of servitude. Yet instead of evading responsibility, Yehudah looked past his own needs and self-interest. His supreme humility empowered him to accept full responsibility to redeem Binyamin at the cost of his own freedom and surrender to a future of lifelong adversity and disgrace.

We find another example of Yehudah's profound humility in *Parashas Vayeishev,* when he publicly confesses to his role in the episode with Tamar with the words "*Tzadkah mimeni*" (*Bereishis* 38:26). By admitting his misdeeds, despite the terrible shame and ignominy it brought upon him, Yehudah accepted full responsibility for his actions and proved himself the consummate *baal achrayus.*

Yehudah Refused to Allow His Brothers to Kill Yosef

A third reason offered by the *Tosefta* for why Yehudah merited *malchus* is that he challenged his brothers' plan to murder Yosef: וַיֹּאמֶר יְהוּדָה אֶל אֶחָיו מַה בֶּצַע כִּי נַהֲרֹג אֶת אָחִינוּ וְכִסִּינוּ אֶת דָּמוֹ, *Yehudah said to his brothers, "What gain will there be if we kill our brother and cover up his blood?'* (ibid. 37:26). Rashi interprets the words *mah betza* as *mah mammon* — what financial gain?

Yehudah does not seem to actually object to the murder of Yosef, but merely labels it unprofitable — which, on the surface, seems no more laudable than the *shevatim's* intention to kill him. Besides, why did the *shevatim* accept his objection after they had formed a *beis din* and ruled that Yosef was deserving of death? Their considerations in executing Yosef were never financial to begin with, so why did Yehudah's argument cause them to change their minds and sell Yosef to the Yishmaelim instead of killing him?

The core of Yehudah's objection is found in his last three words — וְכִסִּינוּ אֶת דָּמוֹ, *and we will cover up his blood*. Rashi interprets these words to mean "we shall conceal his death."

A *psak din* delivered in a *beis din* is legitimate only if the *dayanim* are willing to accept full responsibility for their ruling and are prepared to respond to any argument or objection against it. Without this ability to defend a *psak*, it is invalid; this was Yehudah's point when noting that the *shevatim* intended to conceal Yosef's death. Their reluctance to assume responsibility for the *psak* that they had issued in their impromptu *beis din* proved that it arose from personal *negios*, which negated its validity. Accordingly, this objection underscores the remarkable trait of *achrayus* and integrity that Yehudah possessed.

Shevet Yehudah Was the First to Enter the Yam Suf

This *middah* of *achrayus* was so dominant in Shevet Yehudah that it impelled them to be the first to enter the Yam Suf. When Bnei Yisrael stood terrified on the banks of the sea, flanked on one side by the raging water, while the Egyptian army advanced on the other, Hakadosh Baruch Hu commanded Moshe: דַּבֵּר אֶל בְּנֵי יִשְׂרָאֵל וְיִסָּעוּ, *Speak to the Children of Israel and let them journey forth* (*Shemos* 14:15). Despite this explicit order, no one was eager to be the first to jump into the sea — until Shevet Yehudah rose and leaped into the sea, publicly sanctifying the Name of Hashem.

While all of the *shevatim* inherited the trait of *mesirus nefesh* from our holy *Avos*, Shevet Yehudah also inherited the virtue of *achrayus*. Had any of the *shevatim* been commanded to sacrifice their life for Hashem's sake, they would have surely done it. At the sea, however, Bnei Yisrael were commanded not to sacrifice their lives, but to enter the water very much alive — to walk in it with their families and all, as if the water had turned to dry land. This challenge was beyond their ability.

All but Yehudah.

With his innate sense of responsibility for Klal Yisrael, Yehudah took the initiative to leap into the sea and carry out Hashem's formidable command. This act ultimately culminated in the final stage of Klal Yisrael's redemption from Egyptian bondage, and for this Yehudah was rewarded with *malchus*.

The Foundation of Achrayus Is Humility

At the core of Yehudah's supremacy above his brothers was an exceptional sense of *achrayus*, which brought him to such an exalted spiritual level that he was deemed worthy of *malchus*. What is so remarkable about this *middah* that it has the power to carry a person to such heights, and how can we work to attain it?

The *Tosefta* implies that the foundation of *achrayus* is *anavah*, humility, as a humble person does not demand anything for himself and is free of personal *negios*. His humility enables him to perform any action for its express purpose without accounting for his own needs or calculations; it also empowers him to take responsibility for himself and for others and confers validity upon his *piskei din*.

Chazal (*Sifra, Bechukosai* 7:5) expound the words, וְכָשְׁלוּ אִישׁ בְּאָחִיו, *They will stumble over one another* (*Vayikra* 26:37), to mean "*ish b'avon achiv* — each man will stumble over the sin of his brother. This teaches that *kol Yisrael areivim zeh bazeh* — every member of Klal Yisrael is responsible for the others."

Achrayus Benefits the Person First

When Yosef finally revealed himself to his brothers, he did not rebuke them for selling him to Mitzrayim, but merely uttered two words: אֲנִי יוֹסֵף, *I am Yosef* (*Bereishis* 45:3). The *pasuk* continues: וְלֹא יָכְלוּ אֶחָיו לַעֲנוֹת אֹתוֹ כִּי נִבְהֲלוּ מִפָּנָיו, *But his brothers could not answer him because they were left disconcerted before him*. Regarding the words כִּי נִבְהֲלוּ מִפָּנָיו, Rashi comments, "due to the shame."

R' Chaim Shmulevitz noted that on the surface, Yosef's words do not seem to contain any reprimand, and certainly not of the sort that would cause the *shevatim* to suffer deep shame or fear. Genuine *tochachah*, however, involves revealing a person's mistakes to him and indicating where he went wrong, which was Yosef's message to his brothers.

The declaration *"Ani Yosef"* showed the *shevatim* that the *psak din* they had rendered so many years earlier had not only been a grave mistake, but had actually brought about the fulfillment of his dreams — which were not mere dreams, but prophecies. This point, which completely overturned all that the *shevatim* had held to be true for twenty-two years, highlighted their flawed reasoning, which caused them to feel such intense shame that they could not face Yosef.

The *shevatim's* original intention to conceal their *psak din* proved that their conduct throughout the judicial proceedings was not rooted in a sense of *achrayus*, but rather from personal *negios*. This blatant lack of integrity motivated Yehudah to object to the *psak* and propose that they sell Yosef instead of killing him. Years later, it also brought deep mortification upon them and nearly caused them to die of shame.

From here, we see that conducting oneself with *achrayus* benefits not only others, but oneself as well. Furthermore, one who demonstrates *achrayus* has clearly mastered the *middah* of *anavah*; he is not motivated by his personal *negios* and can identify the core of an issue, which is why he rarely errs.

The quality of *achrayus* encompasses all aspects of a person's *pnimiyus*, to the extent that one who acquires this trait reaches a supremely lofty spiritual level and is worthy of royalty. In contrast, one who lacks this trait possesses a grave character flaw that is akin to lacking intelligence and proper judgment.

This underscores how essential it is for us to weigh every action carefully, spurred by the knowledge that every action has consequences and that we will, one day, be called to task for it. One who acts without forethought or logic, while motivated by personal inclinations and whims, will invariably err and will ultimately experience the profound humiliation that the *shevatim* felt when Yosef proclaimed *"Ani Yosef,"* refuting with two simple words everything they had held to be true. The holy *sefarim* teach that when Mashiach arrives, he will look every person in the eye and immediately discern their actions and sins, which will cause them to melt in shame and anguish.

Chazal teach (*Berachos* 32b): "Four activities require strengthening, and these are they: Torah, good deeds, prayer, and pursuing a livelihood." It is incumbent upon us to strengthen ourselves by increasing our *hasmadah* and intensifying our *kavanah* in *tefillah*.

There are *bachurim* in the yeshivah who possess a talent for uniting the *tzibbur*, and I request that they make the effort to rally the *bachurim* to strengthen themselves in learning by committing to extra hours and *sedarim*, undertaking *kabbalos*, and increasing *hasmadah*. If we all unite in this effort, *k'ish echad b'lev echad*, then surely the combined *koach hatzibbur* will enable us to reach heights far greater than those that can be attained by an individual.

When one acts on behalf of the *tzibbur*, he ultimately works for himself as well, because the yeshivah's collective effort to *shteig* touches him and inspires him to *shteig* as well and reach unimaginable heights.

One who endeavors to elevate the spiritual level of the *tzibbur* is a *nogei'a b'davar*, yet this is a commendable *negiah*, one that catapults him to higher levels of *ruchniyus*! This is the greatest *chizuk* that can result from our gathering here, and although we are but a small group, the message will surely spread to all.

May Hakadosh Baruch Hu grant that all our actions should be driven by a profound sense of *achrayus*, as opposed to personal *negios*, so that we should never come to err or sin, and we should merit *siyata diShmaya* in all our endeavors!

פרשת ויחי
Parashas Vayechi

◆§ *The Attributes of the Shivtei Kah*

כָּל אֵלֶּה שִׁבְטֵי יִשְׂרָאֵל שְׁנֵים עָשָׂר וְזֹאת אֲשֶׁר דִּבֶּר לָהֶם אֲבִיהֶם וַיְבָרֶךְ אוֹתָם אִישׁ אֲשֶׁר כְּבִרְכָתוֹ בֵּרַךְ אֹתָם.

All these are the tribes of Israel — twelve — and this is what their father spoke to them and he blessed them; he blessed each according to his appropriate blessing (*Bereishis* 49:28).

Strength in Unity

In *Parashas Vayechi,* Yaakov Avinu assembles his children in order to bless them before his passing. The *mefarshim* explain that he wished to bless each *shevet* with the unique *berachah* that would suit his respective attributes, strengths, and path in *avodas Hashem.*

The Gemara teaches: "There are only three who are called *Avos*" (*Berachos* 16b). No human being is capable of achieving the exalted spiritual level of our *Avos Hakedoshim* and meriting the title "*av*" other than our forefathers Avraham, Yitzchak, and Yaakov. Yaakov Avinu recognized that none of his children could attain the spiritual stature of the *Avos,* and he therefore sought to bless each one in a way that would enable him to realize his maximal potential in *avodas Hashem*, and thereby enable his children collectively to attain the spiritual level of the *Avos*.

No matter how high an individual can ascend in *ruchniyus*, he will never achieve the level that can be reached collectively by the *tzibbur*. When a *tzibbur* strives to grow in a unified effort, they can soar to the pinnacle attained by our *Avos Hakedoshim*.

Teshuvos HaGeonim (*Shaarei Teshuvah* 178) describes how Rav conducted himself piously in ten different realms. One manifestation of his extreme piety was that he never lifted his eyes — to the extent that he could identify his *talmidim* only by the sound of their voices. This practice was later emulated by his *talmidim* Rav Yosef and Rav Sheshes. Another manifestation was that if he was upset after being hurt by a fellow Jew, he would personally go to apologize and appease that person, a practice that was adopted by his *talmid* Rav Zutra ben Rav Nachman. The *Teshuvos HaGeonim* continues with a detailed description of Rav's ten extraordinary practices, each of which was adopted by one or a small cluster of his *talmidim*, since no individual was capable of emulating them all. Rav's *talmidim* realized that even if no single individual could uphold their rebbi's legacy fully, the collective effort of all the *talmidim* to emulate their rebbi, each one according to his own spiritual stature and ability, would perpetuate his hallowed ways after his passing.

Obviously, one can benefit from the *koach hatzibbur* only if he links himself to the *tzibbur,* which allows him to draw from its colossal power and binds him to its special qualities. This is one of the core foundations of our yeshivah — the unification of individuals into a precious whole that enables everyone to soar to loftier spiritual levels.

Based on this, we can better understand Chazal's famous statement that Yaakov Avinu did not die (*Taanis* 5b). After Yaakov Avinu departed from this world, there was no one person who could ever attain the spiritual stature of the *Avos*. Yet the *koach hatzibbur* that he bequeathed to Klal Yisrael empowers us to collectively reach his spiritual level, and this is how Yaakov Avinu lives on eternally.

Koach HaTzibbur Brings Spiritual Growth and Protection

My rebbi, R' Chaim Kamil, related[8] that the Rosh Yeshivah R' Chaim Shmulevitz would often quote R' Yisrael Salanter, who declared that if someone would tell him that the Vilna Gaon had ascended alive to *Shamayim*, he wouldn't believe it. Yet if they would say the same thing about the three *tzaddikim* of Reisin, *talmidei haGra* who resolved to serve Hashem together through special *kabbalos*, he would believe it.

What advantage did the *tzaddikim* of Reisin have over their master, the Vilna Gaon? What made them worthy of this phenomenal praise? Undoubtedly, the Vilna Gaon achieved a more exalted level of *ruchniyus* and Torah than his *talmidim*, yet the three *tzaddikim* of Reisin possessed something that their rebbi did not — *koach hatzibbur*, and this enabled them to climb to unfathomable heights.

R' Chaim illuminated the *pasuk* (*Tehillim* 95:7), וַאֲנַחְנוּ עַם מַרְעִיתוֹ וְצֹאן יָדוֹ, *And we can be the flock He pastures, and the sheep in His charge*, based on the Gaon of Portova's understanding of the Gemara's statement that that one cannot have a *chazakah* on animals (*Bava Basra* 36a). The Rashbam (ibid.) writes that having a sheep in one's possession is not proof to his assertion that "*Lakuach hu b'yadi* — I bought it, and it is mine," since it is common for sheep to wander off in the marketplace, and they could easily enter any person's house on their own.

Nevertheless, the Gemara notes that in Nehardea, possession of sheep did constitute ownership, since the city was filled with Arab thieves, and owners would not allow their sheep to frolic unattended.

When the *pasuk* describes Bnei Yisrael as *tzon yado* of Hakadosh Baruch Hu, it is expressing that we are like sheep under the constant watch of our Master. This ongoing connection ensures that *daas Torah* will forever prevail among Klal Yisrael, as our bond with Him is continuous and eternal. R' Chaim Kamil added that Hakadosh Baruch Hu closely guards Bnei Yisrael specifically

8. *Imrei Chaim, Maalas HaRabbim.*

because we are a *tzibbur*, a cohesive unit working in unison to fulfill His will, and this earns us Divine protection, as well as the *daas Torah* that enables us to continue fulfilling His will. *Koach hatzibbur* is so potent that it draws Hashem's *shemirah* upon us.

The Power of Learning and Davening With the Tzibbur

Koach hatzibbur gifts us with another level of *shemirah* from Hakadosh Baruch Hu, as well.

The Midrash expounds the verse, הַקֹּל קוֹל יַעֲקֹב וְהַיָּדַיִם יְדֵי עֵשָׂו, *The voice is Yaakov's voice, but the hands are Eisav's hands"* (*Bereishis* 27:22), to mean: "When Yaakov lowers his voice, Eisav's hands dominate ... and when he raises his voice, the hands are not the hands of Eisav; Eisav's hands do not dominate" (*Bereishis Rabbah* 65:20).

The Midrash adds:

> R' Abba bar Kahana said: There were no philosophers in the world like Bilam ben Be'or and Avnimus of Grad, before whom all the idol worshippers gathered and said, "Tell us that we can prevail over this nation." He said, "Go and visit their shuls and *batei midrash*. If you find young children chirping aloud, you cannot prevail over them, for their forefather promised them, 'The voice is Yaakov's voice.' When Yaakov's voice is found in shuls, the hands are not Eisav's hands; but if it is not, the hands are Eisav's hands, and you can overpower them."

When Bnei Yisrael lift their voices collectively in Torah and *tefillah*, the non-Jews cannot prevail over us, and we are saved from those who seek to harm us.

Koach HaTzibbur Depends on Achdus

Koach hatzibbur exists primarily in the *beis midrash*, which is our place of communal gathering. It is here that we achieve maximal unity — that of וְיֵעָשׂוּ כֻלָּם אֲגֻדָּה אַחַת, *and they will all form a single assembly* — and attain the exemplary level of *"K'ish echad b'lev echad,* as one man with one heart."

When striving together in unity, *talmidim* can achieve spiritual levels that surpass even that of their rebbeim, as illustrated by the generation of R' Yehudah bar Ila'i, when six *talmidim* would gather under a single *tallis* to learn Torah. Despite the harsh conditions and discomfort, when every person made an effort to ensure that his friend had a place beneath the *tallis,* they collectively achieved an exalted level of Torah and *yiras Shamayim.*

Our duty is to join together as a *tzibbur. Baruch Hashem,* our yeshivah boasts many *batei midrash.* Even though we do not all sit and learn in a single location, and every *beis midrash* has its own unique *tzibbur* and flavor, we are all unified under the name "Yeshivas Mir," and all the yeshivah's *batei midrash* are part of this one exceptional *beis midrash.* When *bachurim* from around the world unite as part of the Mir Yeshivah, that enables each individual to draw from the tremendous *maalos* of the yeshivah.

Every *bachur* and *avreich* must make an effort to be part of the *tzibbur,* and not to separate himself from it. If he binds himself to the *klal,* he will surely see great *siyata diShmaya* in his learning and all his endeavors.

ספר שמות
Sefer Shemos

פרשת שמות
Parashas Shemos

◆§ *The Value of Life*

הָבָה נִתְחַכְּמָה לוֹ פֶּן יִרְבֶּה וְהָיָה כִּי תִקְרֶאנָה מִלְחָמָה וְנוֹסַף גַּם הוּא עַל שֹׂנְאֵינוּ וְנִלְחַם בָּנוּ וְעָלָה מִן הָאָרֶץ.

Come, let us outsmart it lest it become numerous and it may be that if a war will occur, it, too, may join our enemies, and wage war against us and go up from the land (*Shemos* 1:10).

The Gemara expounds (*Sotah* 11a): "Three individuals were involved in offering that counsel to Pharaoh: Bilam, Iyov, and Yisro. Bilam, who counseled Pharaoh to drown the Jewish babies, was slain; Iyov, who was silent, was punished by having to undergo suffering. As for Yisro, who fled, his descendants merited to sit in the Chamber of Hewn Stone in the Temple as members of the Sanhedrin."

Bilam and Iyov were both involved in this scheme, yet each received a different punishment. Bilam, who proposed the evil plot, was killed, while Iyov, who remained silent, was punished with terrible suffering. The Rosh Yeshivah R' Chaim Shmulevitz pointed out[1] that although Bilam's crime was far worse than Iyov's

---

1. *Sichos Mussar, Osher HaChaim.*

silence, Iyov received a harsher sentence. Bilam met his death in an instant, but Iyov endured lifelong *yissurim*.

Evidence that physical torture is worse than death can be derived from the story of Chananyah, Mishael, and Azaryah, who refused to bow down to an idol even when threatened with death. The Gemara notes, however, that had they been physically tortured, they would not have withstood the challenge (*Kesubos* 33b). If torture is worse than death, why was Iyov deserving of harsher punishment than Bilam?

Life: A Matnas Chinam

From this, R' Chaim deduced a fundamental principle: Life in Olam Hazeh is the greatest conceivable gift, a *matnas chinam* from Hakadosh Baruch Hu unparalleled by any other. Every moment of life is infinitely precious and irreplaceable, and if a person would only learn to feel the joy intrinsic to life and to appreciate the vast treasure that he possesses, he would experience life differently.

Even a life riddled with misery and adversity, like those suffered by Iyov, is valuable, as the *pasuk* teaches: מַה יִּתְאוֹנֵן אָדָם חָי, *Of what shall a living man complain?* (*Eichah* 3:39). Rashi explains (*Kiddushin* 80b): "Why should a living man complain? Why should man be incensed by the events that transpire in his life, after all the *chessed* that I do with him, that I gave him life and did not bring death upon him?" The gift of life suffices to fill a person with supreme joy, and if he chooses to focus on that joy, he will no longer feel his *yissurim*.

This can be compared to a person who discovers that he just won the lottery, and while on his way to the lottery office to submit his winning ticket, he stubs his toe. So exhilarated is he by his big win that he won't even feel the throbbing pain! This is precisely how a person should regard *yissurim* relative to the colossal gift of life that he receives each day anew, gratis.

At times, a person is so enveloped in pain and suffering that he is incapable of focusing clearly on this thought, which is why Chazal teach that had Chananyah, Mishael, and Azaryah been subjected to physical torture, they would have been sucked into a mire of confusion and pain that would have blinded them and caused them to kneel before the idol. Yet there is no question that death — which means absolute and final disconnection from the wick of life — is immeasurably worse than a life replete with suffering.

This clarifies why the death sentence meted out to Bilam was inestimably worse than Iyov's lifelong adversity. Bilam, who proposed the wicked plot to kill all male infants, lost his most valuable possession — life itself; while Iyov, who remained silent and refused to actively participate in a plan to kill others, received his life as a gift in return.[2]

This is a profound lesson, and who was more suited to teach it to us than R' Chaim, who cherished every moment and strove to utilize each second to the maximum! This is an awe-inspiring *chiddush*, an excellent approach to life, and we must each reflect on it constantly!

Man's purpose in life is to learn the Torah and fulfill the mitzvos, yet from the *pasuk* (*Vayikra* 18:5), וּשְׁמַרְתֶּם אֶת חֻקֹּתַי וְאֶת מִשְׁפָּטַי אֲשֶׁר יַעֲשֶׂה אֹתָם הָאָדָם וָחַי בָּהֶם אֲנִי ה׳. *You shall observe My decrees and My laws, which man shall carry out and by which he shall live — I am Hashem*, the Gemara (*Yoma* 85b) derives that one may violate prohibitions in the Torah — including those punishable by death and *kareis* — even in a situation of possible danger to life. We, see, then, that the value of life is immeasurable.

One Who Does Not Appreciate Life Forfeits Life

Not everyone recognizes the value of life. There are many, even among those who sit and learn in the *beis midrash*, who take life for granted and fail to appreciate the incredible value and potential in every moment. Only when they face physical danger, Heaven forbid, do they suddenly wake up, realize what they are about to lose, and make every effort to stay alive.

A person who does not sufficiently value life can so easily lose it!

2. See *Parashas Noach*, "Sharing the Burden of a Friend."

The *Daas Zekeinim MiBaalei HaTosafos*, citing Chazal, states (*Bereishis* 47:8):

> When Yaakov said: מְעַט וְרָעִים הָיוּ יְמֵי שְׁנֵי חַיַּי, *Few and bad have been the days of the years of my life* (ibid. 9), Hakadosh Baruch Hu said to him: "I spared you from Eisav and from Lavan; I returned Dinah and also Yosef to you; and you complain about your days that they were few and bad? I swear that the number of words from וַיֹּאמֶר פַּרְעֹה אֶל יַעֲקֹב כַּמָּה יְמֵי שְׁנֵי חַיֶּיךָ, *Pharaoh said to Yaakov, "How many are the days of the years of your life?* until בִּימֵי מְגוּרֵיהֶם, *in the days of their sojourns*, shall be deducted from your years, so that you will not live as long as your father Yitzchak." These are thirty-three words, and this amount was subtracted from Yaakov's life, as Yitzchak lived 180 years, and Yaakov only lived 147.

While we are unable to comprehend the harsh punishment that Hashem brought upon Yaakov Avinu, we do glean from the Midrash that although Yaakov Avinu suffered greatly throughout his life, he had no right to express a grievance against Hakadosh Baruch Hu. His complaint about the life that Hashem had granted him was regarded so severely in *Shamayim* that he was punished with losing years of life.

The thirty-three words for which Yaakov was punished included not only his response to Pharaoh, but also the previous *pasuk*, which contains Pharaoh's question: וַיֹּאמֶר פַּרְעֹה אֶל יַעֲקֹב כַּמָּה יְמֵי שְׁנֵי חַיֶּיךָ, *Pharaoh said to Yaakov, "How many are the days of the years of your life?"* Even if Yaakov was punished for complaining, why was he held accountable for Pharaoh's question?

The *Daas Zekeinim* explains that Pharaoh's question was prompted by Yaakov's white hair and beard, which lent him a very elderly appearance, and Yaakov's reply clarified that although he was not particularly old, the suffering and adversity that he'd faced throughout life had aged him. Yaakov was punished for Pharaoh's question because his physical appearance reflected the emotional suffering that he had allowed himself to feel in his heart. Had he regarded his suffering as immaterial relative to the gift of life that he was granted, and not brooded over it, Yaakov would not have aged so significantly, and Pharaoh would have never asked his question.

A Life of Mitzvos in Olam Hazeh

Elaborating on this concept, R' Chaim cited the Mishnah's statement (*Avos* 4:17): "One moment of pleasure (*koras ruach*) in the World to Come is better than an entire lifetime of pleasure in this world." We cannot fathom what the *koras ruach* of Olam Haba is, but we are taught that this is not the actual pleasure of Olam Haba; rather, it can be compared to a person standing outside a gala banquet who is refused entry and can only inhale the aroma of the tantalizing foods inside. All the pleasures and satisfaction of this world, from the beginning until the end of time, cannot compare to a single whiff of Olam Haba!

Yet this statement of the Mishnah is preceded by the words: "One moment spent in repentance and good deeds in this world is better than an entire lifetime in the World to Come." This is surprising, for here the Mishnah refers not merely to the *koras ruach* ("whiff") of Olam Haba, but to life in Olam Haba itself — which involves infinite and eternal pleasure — and asserts that a single moment of *teshuvah* in Olam Haba surpasses all that!

Indeed, there is no way to describe or measure the significance of a single moment of *teshuvah* or good deeds in Olam Hazeh!

What is so special about a life lived with *teshuvah* and good deeds?

Life in Olam Haba is eternal and infinite, and life in Olam Hazeh is our only path to achieving that perfection in Olam Haba. Since every moment of life in this world equals another opportunity to enhance the quality of our eternal life in Olam Haba, each moment in this world is greater than a moment in the World to Come, where the opportunity to grow and achieve more no longer exists.

It is known that when the Vilna Gaon lay on his deathbed, he grasped his *tzitzis* and wept copious tears. When asked by his *talmidim* why he was crying, he replied that he was departing a world where he could acquire eternity by fulfilling a mitzvah like *tzitzis* that cost pennies, and once he would pass on to Olam Haba, he would no longer be able to acquire eternity, for all the riches in the world.

R' Preida's Sacrifice

The Gemara relates (*Eruvin* 54b) that R' Preida would teach and review material with his *talmid* four hundred times, until he understood the text. One day, a *gabbai tzedakah* approached R' Preida regarding an urgent matter, interrupting him in the course of his lesson. The *talmid* was distracted and failed to understand the material even after his rebbi had repeated it for the four hundredth time. R' Preida didn't lose patience, and taught his *talmid* another four hundred times until he understood. At that moment, a *bas kol* emanated from heaven and asked R' Preida whether he preferred to live an additional four hundred years, or whether he preferred that he and his whole generation should be rewarded with Olam Haba. R' Preida chose the latter, and Hakadosh Baruch Hu replied, "Give him this and that."

The Gemara implies that R' Preida received extra reward because he selflessly chose Olam Haba for all the people in his generation, rather than reap the benefits of another four hundred years of life for himself. But what is surprising about his choice? Wouldn't anyone choose eternal reward over temporal life in this world?

Delving deeper into the choice, we see that R' Preida's decision reflected supreme altruism. Had his choice been based on his own needs and benefit, he would have surely requested an additional four hundred years of life — which, for a *tzaddik* of his caliber, would translate into infinitely greater eternal life. R' Preida recognized the value of life, knowing that each moment in this world offers endless opportunities to acquire greater eternity, in keeping with Chazal's statement that "one moment spent in repentance and good deeds in this world is better than an entire lifetime in the World to Come." Another four hundred years of utilizing this world to its fullest would have allowed him to improve his lot immeasurably in the *Olam HaEmes*. Nevertheless, he willingly sacrificed this opportunity in order to guarantee eternal life for all his contemporaries, and was ultimately rewarded for this choice when Hashem granted him both rewards.

The Pleasure of Friendship: Unique to This World

R' Chaim highlighted another aspect of how a life lived properly in this world is superior to all the pleasures of Olam Haba.

The Midrash (*Shemos Rabbah* 52:3) recounts the story of R' Shimon ben Chalafta, who was destitute and once had no food for Shabbos. In his anguish, he exited the city and davened fervently to Hashem, until a precious jewel miraculously descended from heaven. R' Shimon exchanged the jewel for money and purchased all that was needed for Shabbos. When his wife asked how he had obtained all this, he responded, "Hakadosh Baruch Hu provided for us."

"If you do not tell me where it is from, I will not taste a morsel," she declared.

R' Shimon explained that he had davened for salvation, and a jewel had descended from heaven. Aghast, his wife proclaimed that she would not taste anything until her husband would promise to return the stone after Shabbos. "I do not want your table in Olam Haba to be missing, and your friend's table to be full," she said.

R' Shimon went to Rebbi and related what had happened, and Rebbi replied, "Go and tell her that if your table is missing anything, I will fill it from my own."

When R' Shimon repeated Rebbi's message to his wife, she asked that he escort her to Rebbi's *beis midrash*. "Rebbi," she inquired, "does one see his friend in Olam Haba? No! Each and every *tzaddik* has his own world there, as it is written (*Koheles* 12:5): כִּי הֹלֵךְ הָאָדָם אֶל בֵּית עוֹלָמוֹ, *so man goes to his eternal home*. It does not say *'olamim*, worlds' but rather *'olamo*, his world.'" Upon hearing this, R' Shimon ben Chalafta stretched out his hand to return the jewel, and a *malach* descended from *Shamayim* to retrieve it.

Although we cannot possibly fathom the workings of Olam Haba, this Midrash illustrates the fundamental difference between our present life in Olam Hazeh and our future existence in Olam Haba: In Olam Haba, every person dwells in his private Gan Eden, basking alone in the pleasure of the *Shechinah* and cleaving to Hakadosh Baruch Hu, and there is no one else present to share his world. In contrast, in this world it is impossible to live without *dibbuk chaveirim.* Even Adam HaRishon, who resided in Gan Eden — the apex of spirituality — required a life's partner, as the Torah attests: לֹא טוֹב הֱיוֹת הָאָדָם לְבַדּוֹ *It is not good that man be alone* (*Bereishis* 2:18). One who lives alone can never attain true happiness.

The *Kuntres HaSefeikos* (*Ketzos HaChoshen* Vol. 2, preface) cites the Mahari Moscato, who writes that if a person were given the opportunity to experience the height of pleasure, on condition that he wouldn't tell his friends what he had observed and experienced, his joy would be incomplete. Even if he could soar to the heavens and watch the ministering angels ascending and descending as they bask in the pleasure of the *Shechinah* — an experience so joyful and fulfilling that it cannot be expressed in words — he would not be able to fully enjoy it.

Why is this?

At the time of Creation, Hakadosh Baruch Hu created a reality called *dibbuk chaveirim*, which compels man to live within a society in order to enjoy life and its blessings. A *ben Torah* who formulates a *sevarah* or *chiddush* cannot experience true joy until he shares it with another person. Yet this need for *dibbuk chaveirim* — and the profound happiness that it brings — is exclusive to Olam Hazeh, and ceases to exist in Olam Haba.

I once experienced this on a personal level when a philanthropist donated a huge sum of money to the yeshivah — on condition that I wouldn't tell a soul. It was exceedingly difficult to keep the news inside and not share it with others, and I really felt that my *simchah* was incomplete.

On another occasion, R Chaim vividly described the incredible joy of *dibbuk chaveirim* in this world, as opposed to the solitude of Olam Haba. At the time, one of the storefronts in the Beis Yisrael neighborhood belonged to a shoemaker, who would place the shoes he repaired on a shelf outside so they would dry in the sun.

Several times, R' Chaim was seen stopping near the store and gazing for a long moment at tiny shoes intended for a toddler taking his first steps. Finally, a *bachur* summoned the courage to ask the Rosh Yeshivah what interested him so much about these shoes. He replied: "I am looking at these little shoes and imagining the overflowing joy in the heart of the mother who purchases her child's first pair of shoes. I'm inspired by the thought that this wondrous feeling — a mother's love and devotion to her child — can be found only in this world, but never in Olam Haba."

Only in Olam Hazeh can a person share his friend's joy and celebrate together with him. In the World to Come, however, he is unable to share in his friend's *simchah*, and basks only in the pleasure he has earned through his efforts in this world.

When we speak of the vast spiritual wealth available in our world, it might sound prosaic, but this is only because we have grown so accustomed to the opportunities around us that we fail to appreciate them. When a person rises each morning and proclaims, *"Modeh ani lifanecha,"* his heart should fill with gratitude to the Ribbono Shel Olam for restoring his *neshamah* to him, for enabling him to continue to do mitzvos and learn Torah, and for creating other people to share life with, in times of both joy and sorrow.

The life of a *ben Torah* is enriched with an additional, special element of *simchah*, as we recite every day in davening: כִּי הֵם חַיֵּינוּ וְאֹרֶךְ יָמֵינוּ וּבָהֶם נֶהְגֶּה יוֹמָם וָלָיְלָה, *For they are our lives and the length of our days, and in them we shall engage day and night.* A *ben Torah* who labors in Torah day and night has the best, happiest life possible, and there is nothing that compares to his joy! His happiness grows when he shares his learning with his friends, to the extent that there is no one in the world happier than he.

Only in the *beis midrash* does true friendship exist, between *lomdei Torah.* The secular world has unfortunately come to embody the description, "people swallow each other alive" (*Avos* 3:2), while in the *beis midrash*, "even a father and son or a rebbi and *talmid* who are studying Torah together in one gate at first become enemies of one another, but they do not move from there until they become devoted friends of one another" (*Kiddushin* 30b).

We must learn to appreciate the great gift of life that Hashem has granted us and seize every moment of life!

The Rosh Yeshivah concluded with the following message:

I would like to propose an idea for how we can gain appreciation for every moment of life. Each day throughout the next two weeks, a hundred *bachurim* will come to the *beis midrash,* in alphabetical order, to spend an hour learning before *Shacharis*. This system will teach us all to value time, especially those "dead" hours when so much time is wasted, and this will surely bring great *chizuk* to all those in our *beis midrash*.

I learned this idea from my eldest son's rebbi in *cheder*. When he wanted to teach him the value of time and model how it is possible to utilize every spare moment of time for *limud Torah,* he would arrange to learn with him *b'chavrusa* on Friday afternoon right after *licht bentching,* or at 2 a.m., or at any hour that is usually wasted, to teach him that it is possible to learn during any spare moment.

פרשת וארא
Parashas Va'eira

Staying Inspired

וַיְדַבֵּר ה׳ אֶל מֹשֶׁה וְאֶל אַהֲרֹן וַיְצַוֵּם אֶל בְּנֵי יִשְׂרָאֵל וְאֶל פַּרְעֹה מֶלֶךְ מִצְרָיִם לְהוֹצִיא אֶת בְּנֵי יִשְׂרָאֵל מֵאֶרֶץ מִצְרָיִם.

Hashem spoke to Moshe and Aharon and commanded them regarding the Children of Israel and regarding Pharaoh, king of Egypt, to take the Children of Israel out of the land of Egypt (*Shemos* 6:13).

אמר רבי שמואל ב״ר יצחק, על מה ציום, על פרשת שילוח עבדים. ואתיא כההיא דא״ר הילא לא נענשו ישראל אלא על פרשת שילוח עבדים (ירושלמי ר״ה פ״ג, ה״ה).

R' Shmuel bar R' Yitzchak taught: About what did he command them? About the subject of freeing slaves. This follows the opinion of R' Hila, who said: Bnei Yisrael were punished [with exile] only because of the matter of freeing slaves (*Yerushalmi, Rosh Hashanah* 3:5).

Chazal's words reveal that the mitzvah of *shiluach avadim* (freeing slaves) was transmitted to Moshe and Aharon approximately a year before Yetzias Mitzrayim, at the time when they were first commanded to approach Pharaoh and lead Bnei Yisrael out of his land. R' Hila adds that since this mitzvah was given before Yetzias Mitzrayim, Bnei Yisrael were punished more severely for violating it than for all other mitzvos in the Torah.

The *navi* Yirmiyah states this explicitly: כֹּה אָמַר ה׳ אֱלֹהֵי יִשְׂרָאֵל אָנֹכִי כָּרַתִּי בְרִית אֶת אֲבוֹתֵיכֶם בְּיוֹם הוֹצִאִי אוֹתָם מֵאֶרֶץ מִצְרַיִם מִבֵּית עֲבָדִים לֵאמֹר. מִקֵּץ שֶׁבַע שָׁנִים תְּשַׁלְּחוּ אִישׁ אֶת אָחִיו הָעִבְרִי אֲשֶׁר יִמָּכֵר לְךָ, *Thus said Hashem, God of Israel: I sealed a covenant with your forefathers on the day I took them out of the land of Egypt, from the house of slaves, saying: At the outset of the seventh year, each of you shall send forth his Hebrew brother who will have been sold to you* (*Yirmiyah* 34:13-14). At the time of Yetzias Mitzrayim, the *navi* says, Hashem established a special covenant with Bnei Yisrael regarding the mitzvah of freeing an *eved Ivri* after seven years, and He punishes Bnei Yisrael severely for their failure to uphold it, as the *pasuk* continues (v. 17): לָכֵן כֹּה אָמַר ה׳ אַתֶּם לֹא שְׁמַעְתֶּם אֵלַי לִקְרֹא דְרוֹר אִישׁ לְאָחִיו וְאִישׁ לְרֵעֵהוּ הִנְנִי קֹרֵא לָכֶם דְּרוֹר נְאֻם ה׳ אֶל הַחֶרֶב אֶל הַדֶּבֶר וְאֶל הָרָעָב וְנָתַתִּי אֶתְכֶם לְזַעֲוָה לְכֹל מַמְלְכוֹת הָאָרֶץ, *Therefore, thus said Hashem: You did not hearken to Me to proclaim freedom, every man for his brother and every man for his fellow; behold, I proclaim you to be free — the word of Hashem — for the sword, for pestilence, and for famine; and I shall make you an object of horror for all the kingdoms of the earth.*

The timing of the commandment of *shiluach avadim* seems perplexing, since the halachah is that the laws of *eved Ivri* apply only at the time when Yovel is in force (*Gittin* 65a), and the mitzvah of Yovel was not actively instituted until after the conquest and division of Eretz Yisrael. Consequently, the mitzvah of *shiluach avadim* did not become relevant until after the Land was conquered and divided, fifty-four years after Yetzias Mitzrayim. Why, then, did Hashem give this command a year before Yetzias Mitzrayim, instead of waiting until Mattan Torah to give it along with the rest of the mitzvos? Other mitzvos that Bnei Yisrael were commanded before Mattan Torah — such as Shabbos, *parah adumah*, and the *dinim* taught in Marah (see *Sanhedrin* 56b, and Rashi, *Shemos* 15:25) — all went into effect immediately. In contrast, the mitzvah of *shiluach avadim* did not become applicable until many years later, so what was the purpose of commanding it so early? Moreover, why was Bnei Yisrael's negligence in this area regarded so gravely that they were punished with *galus* as a result?

The Complete Kabbalah

The Rosh Yeshivah R' Chaim Shmulevitz explained[3] that the ideal time to command Bnei Yisrael regarding the mitzvah of *shiluach avadim* was when they were slaves in Mitzrayim. At the time, they still suffered the burden and oppression of Egyptian bondage and felt the intense yearning for freedom. There is no one who can sympathize with a slave's humiliation and his craving for liberation like a fellow slave. Therefore, when Moshe and Aharon first approached Bnei Yisrael to inform them of their impending freedom, Bnei Yisrael were overcome with joy, and were able to accept the mitzvah of *shiluach avadim* willingly, filled as they were with empathy for the *eved Ivri*.

This is why Yirmiyah noted that Hashem had established this covenant with His people "on the day I took them out of the land of Egypt, from the house of slaves." The day that Bnei Yisrael emerged from bondage was the time when they could deeply appreciate the importance of this mitzvah, and this feeling obligated them to fulfill the mitzvah in the future.

A similar idea is expressed regarding the prohibition to oppress a convert, as the Torah states (*Shemos* 23:9): וְגֵר לֹא תִלְחָץ וְאַתֶּם יְדַעְתֶּם אֶת נֶפֶשׁ הַגֵּר כִּי גֵרִים הֱיִיתֶם בְּאֶרֶץ מִצְרָיִם, *Do not oppress a stranger; you know the feelings of a stranger, for you were strangers in the land of Egypt*. Here, the Torah again links the mitzvah of not oppressing converts to the feeling Bnei Yisrael experienced when they were foreigners in Mitzrayim, as there is no comparison between one who fulfills a mitzvah from a place of understanding its root and reasons to one who fulfills it without this appreciation.

With the passing of generations, the inspiration that Bnei Yisrael originally felt upon receiving the mitzvah of *shiluach avadim* faded, and people neglected to liberate their slaves, as Yirmiyah described. Since their original acceptance of the mitzvah had been

3. *Sichos Mussar, Yesh Koneh Olamo B'Shaah Achas.*

wholehearted and enthusiastic, Bnei Yisrael were held accountable for their failure to observe this mitzvah and were punished severely, with *galus*.

From this we can glean the converse, as well: When a person appreciates the *shoresh hamitzvah,* he naturally fulfills it with greater desire, enthusiasm, and love. The emotions that he feels breed a connection to the mitzvah, and he invariably strives to perform it on a higher level. On the other hand, if for some reason he is unable to fulfill the mitzvah, he feels a deep sense of loss and sadness.

Living the Learning

This concept applies to *limud Torah,* as well. When a person delves into a *sugya,* analyzes it with the Rishonim and Acharonim, and reviews it repeatedly, it becomes part of him, ingrained deeply within him. Authentic *limud Torah* means focusing one's mind, heart, and soul on a *sugya* until he can extract every point in halachah, every *chiddush*, and every *nafka mina*. Some people learn the *Shulchan Aruch* without delving into the relevant *sugyos* in the Gemara, and while they may know the halachah presented in the text by heart, they can't infer practical halachah from it, especially regarding cases that aren't expressly addressed in *Shulchan Aruch*. In contrast, one who learns a *sugya* of the Gemara in depth, along with the *shittos* of the Rishonim and Acharonim, understands the roots of the *sugya*. Then, when he learns the *Tur* and *Shulchan Aruch,* he acquires an even deeper understanding. His *Choshen Mishpat* is not the same *Choshen Mishpat;* his *Even HaEzer* is not the same *Even HaEzer.* These portions of *Shulchan Aruch* become his — because he toils to master them and acquire the knowledge and capacity to innovate *chiddushim* and rule regarding cases that are not mentioned explicitly in *Shulchan Aruch*. This *Shulchan Aruch* is *his*!

Limud Torah doesn't mean learning and reviewing — it means *living* Torah! It means experiencing the *sugya* and feeling every *sevarah* in one's bones and muscles, as we declare in *Tehillim* (35:10): כָּל עַצְמוֹתַי תֹּאמַרְנָה, *All my limbs will say*. Earlier in *Tehillim* (1:2), the *pasuk* states: כִּי אִם בְּתוֹרַת ה׳ חֶפְצוֹ וּבְתוֹרָתוֹ יֶהְגֶּה יוֹמָם וָלָיְלָה, *But his desire is in the Torah of Hashem, and in His Torah he meditates day and night*. Rashi notes (*Kiddushin* 32b) that at first, the Torah is called *Toras Hashem*, but when the person learns and reviews it, it becomes *Toraso* — his Torah. Toiling in Torah leads one to acquire it as his own and internalize it, until it becomes an indistinguishable part of him.

Fulfilling Mitzvos With Shleimus

In order to achieve *shleimus*, whether in Torah study or mitzvah observance, a person must *live* the mitzvah! One who is aware of the roots and reasons for a mitzvah can appreciate it more deeply and fulfill it with emotion and *chiyus*, rather than by rote, as a "*mitzvas anashim melumadah*" (*Yeshayah* 29:13). One who endeavors to understand the reasons behind the mitzvos, to do the mitzvos with *chiyus*, and to learn each *sugya* comprehensively, will merit to fulfill the Torah and mitzvos with *shleimus*.

At different points in life, every person experiences special moments of inspiration, and these spiritual highs motivate him to strive for more. Yet inevitably, the ecstasy fades, and he falls back down to earth and routine. A human being is never stationary; he is constantly either on an incline or on a decline, and if he doesn't make a concerted effort to climb, he will invariably fall — in both the realm of *bein adam laMakom* and that of *bein adam lachaveiro*. Therefore, in order to facilitate *avodas Hashem* and spiritual growth, it is critical to preserve these moments of inspiration and ensure that their effects are felt in the long term.

The mitzvah of *shiluach avadim* teaches that a *kabbalah* that a person accepts upon himself during an exalted moment of *hisorerus* encompasses a certain *shleimus*. The way to ensure that we preserve those moments and stay inspired is by accepting upon ourselves positive, practical, maintainable *kabbalos* precisely when the inspiration strikes. During these moments, our hearts surge with genuine desire to improve our *avodas Hashem*, and the *kabbalos* that we accept at this time are therefore especially pure and lofty.

Yet *kabbalos* themselves, while commendable, are not sufficient. We learn this from *Parashas Noach*, where Hashem states (*Bereishis* 9:14-15): וְהָיָה בְּעַנְנִי עָנָן עַל הָאָרֶץ וְנִרְאֲתָה הַקֶּשֶׁת בֶּעָנָן. וְזָכַרְתִּי אֶת בְּרִיתִי אֲשֶׁר

בֵּינִי וּבֵינֵיכֶם וּבֵין כָּל נֶפֶשׁ חַיָּה בְּכָל בָּשָׂר וְלֹא יִהְיֶה עוֹד הַמַּיִם לְמַבּוּל לְשַׁחֵת כָּל בָּשָׂר, *And it shall happen, when I place a cloud over the earth, and the bow will be seen in the cloud, I will remember My covenant between Me and you and every living being among all flesh, and the water shall never again become a flood to destroy all flesh.* This seems repetitive, as Hashem already promised Noach, several *pesukim* earlier (v. 11): וַהֲקִמֹתִי אֶת בְּרִיתִי אִתְּכֶם וְלֹא יִכָּרֵת כָּל בָּשָׂר עוֹד מִמֵּי הַמַּבּוּל וְלֹא יִהְיֶה עוֹד מַבּוּל לְשַׁחֵת הָאָרֶץ, *And I will confirm My covenant with you: Never again shall all flesh be cut off by the waters of the flood, and never again shall there be a flood to destroy the earth.* Furthermore, why do we need the sign of the rainbow at all? Surely there is no need to remind Hashem of His promise never to bring a flood again upon the earth!

R' Chaim Shmulevitz (ibid.) explains that Hakadosh Baruch Hu wished to teach us how to preserve inspiration and maintain the commitments we take upon ourselves. Every time the thought rises in Hashem's mind, as it were, to destroy the world due to the sins of its inhabitants, He paints a rainbow in the heavens. This conveys that when a person accepts positive *kabbalos* upon himself, he should make himself a sign to ensure that he remembers his promise and maintains those *kabbalos* permanently.

Hakadosh Baruch Hu Himself teaches us to create a tangible sign to preserve our *hisorerus*, so that when we are faced with a challenge that might prevent us from keeping our *kabbalah*, we can relive the original moment of inspiration, and that will prompt us to maintain it.

Seizing the Moment

The Gemara (*Avodah Zarah* 17a) relates the famous story of R' Eliezer ben Durdaya, a habitual sinner who once even crossed seven rivers in order to perform an immoral act. In the midst of his sin, his companion remarked that an evildoer like him would never be allowed to repent. Her words struck a chord in his heart, and he immediately experienced a massive spiritual awakening. R' Eliezer went and sat in a mountain range and beseeched Heaven for mercy. When he realized that no one would help him, he declared, "It is up to me!" He then laid his head between his knees and wept bitterly, until his soul departed. At that moment, a *bas kol* proclaimed, "R' Eliezer ben Durdaya has now been readied the life of the World to Come."

This Gemara reveals that in a moment of inspiration, one can soar from the depths of a spiritual abyss to exalted heights, climbing from a place where all attempts of *teshuvah* are rejected to a place of extreme closeness to Hashem.

Upon hearing this, the Gemara continues, Rebbi wept and said, "There is one who acquires his world [to come] in many years, and there is one who acquires his world in a single moment."

Every person has moments like the one experienced by R' Eliezer ben Durdaya, times when he is spurred to draw close to Hashem and serve Him; yet only one in a thousand actually seizes that moment and capitalizes on the sacred opportunity to acquire eternity. Rebbi was not weeping for those who acquire their Olam Haba in an instant, but rather for those who squander those special moments, which are then lost forever.

The Rosh Yeshivah concluded:

Baruch Hashem, we are *zocheh* in the yeshivah to many moments of *hisorerus*, yet we must add to them and strengthen ourselves to seize those moments. Chazal teach: "*Ein mechazkin ela hamechuzakin, v'ein mezarzin ela hamezurazin* — We strengthen only those who are already strong, and we urge only those who display alacrity" (*Bamidbar Rabbah* 7:7); and "*Divrei Torah tzrichim chizuk* — words of Torah must be reinforced" (*Berachos* 32b).

This applies not only to learning Torah, but also to *yiras Shamayim* and *middos*, and it is incumbent upon us all to introspect and reflect upon how we can improve in these realms. Sometimes, giving a *chaburah* can spur a person to innovate *chiddushei Torah*, and these *chiddushim* have a powerful effect on *limud* throughout the entire *zman*.

Hashem should help that we should all be inspired to strengthen ourselves in *limud Torah* and *avodas Hashem*, and to preserve our special moments of *hisorerus* by committing to — and keeping — *kabbalos*.

פרשת בא
Parashas Bo

⁂*Yichud HaLev*

וַיֹּאמֶר ה׳ אֶל מֹשֶׁה בֹּא אֶל פַּרְעֹה כִּי אֲנִי הִכְבַּדְתִּי אֶת לִבּוֹ וְאֶת לֵב עֲבָדָיו לְמַעַן שִׁתִי אֹתֹתַי אֵלֶּה בְּקִרְבּוֹ.

Hashem said to Moshe, "Come to Pharaoh, for I have made his heart and the heart of his servants stubborn so that I can put these signs of Mine in his midst" (*Shemos* 10:1).

When Hashem brought the first five *makkos* upon Mitzrayim, Pharaoh himself hardened his heart and refused to send Bnei Yisrael from his land. After the *makkah* of *shechin* (boils), however, Hashem hardened his heart so he would not free Bnei Yisrael (*Shemos* 9:12). The *pesukim* imply that at this point, Pharaoh would have surrendered and set Bnei Yisrael free, yet Hashem hardened his heart in order to punish him. What was it about *makkas shechin* that would have caused Pharaoh's change of heart and convinced him to finally let Bnei Yisrael go, had Hashem not intervened and hardened his heart?[4]

4. See *Sforno* (*Shemos* 9:12).

The Miracle of Shechin

The *makkah* of *shechin* opens with this description: וַיֹּאמֶר ה' אֶל מֹשֶׁה וְאֶל אַהֲרֹן קְחוּ לָכֶם מְלֹא חָפְנֵיכֶם פִּיחַ כִּבְשָׁן וּזְרָקוֹ מֹשֶׁה הַשָּׁמַיְמָה לְעֵינֵי פַרְעֹה, *Hashem said to Moshe and Aharon, "Take for yourselves handfuls of furnace soot, and let Moshe hurl it heavenward before Pharaoh's eyes"* (ibid. v. 8).

Regarding the words "and let Moshe hurt," Rashi comments: "Something that is thrown with force is thrown with one hand. Behold, there were many miracles. The first was that Moshe's fist held both his and Aharon's handfuls, and another was that the soot spread across the entire land of Mitzrayim." Rashi's explanation indicates that only these two elements were regarded as miraculous, yet the fact that Moshe was capable of throwing the soot to the heavens was considered natural, similar to anyone's throwing a rock or ball with force.

The Sifsei Chachamim notes that had this been a miracle, Moshe would have tossed the soot lightly into the air using both hands instead of throwing it forcefully with a single hand. The fact that he threw it upward with all his strength indicated that Moshe intended it to reach the heavens naturally, without a miracle occurring.

How can this be? How can a human being throw something with enough strength for it to touch the heavens?

Latent Strengths

The Rosh Yeshivah R' Chaim Shmulevitz[5] teaches a fundamental lesson regarding a person's strength, willpower, and capacity to achieve. Chazal teach (*Sanhedrin* 38b) that Adam HaRishon was originally created large enough that he filled the world from one end to the other, yet after he sinned, Hakadosh Baruch Hu diminished his size. Obviously, Chazal are not referring to Adam's physical height or weight, but to the vast strengths that Hashem imbued within him — the capacity to dominate the world and utilize it for

5. *Sichos Mussar, Yichad Lev.*

his needs, as the *pasuk* states: תַּמְשִׁילֵהוּ בְּמַעֲשֵׂי יָדֶיךָ כֹּל שַׁתָּה תַחַת רַגְלָיו, *You give him dominion over Your handiwork, You placed everything under his feet* (*Tehillim* 8:7).

Even after Hakadosh Baruch Hu diminished Adam's strength and power in the world, Adam still retained tremendous dormant strengths that far exceeded his physical capabilities; and the pre-condition for exercising these strengths was unifying the heart, mind, and will.

Man was created with the capacity to achieve all of his physical and spiritual goals effortlessly, just as a fetus in its mother's womb has all its physical needs met and is taught the entire Torah (*Niddah* 30b). After the *cheit*, Hashem told Adam that he would be forced to toil in order to obtain what he desires: בְּזֵעַת אַפֶּיךָ תֹּאכַל לֶחֶם, *By the sweat of your brow shall you eat bread* (*Bereishis* 3:19). Accordingly, Chazal elaborate, "If a person tells you, 'I toiled but I did not find,' do not believe him; 'I did not toil, and I found,' do not believe him" (*Megillah* 6b). The requirement of toil applies to both material and spiritual pursuits, and therefore, one who does not exert effort cannot achieve his goals. In contrast, one who makes a concerted effort to attain something fulfills the requirement of "by the sweat of your brow," and can obtain what he desires just as Adam HaRishon did before the *cheit*.

Realizing Aspirations Through Yichud HaLev

R' Chaim Shmulevitz proves this based on Rashi's description of how Yaakov Avinu lifted the boulder off the well in Charan: "like a person removes a cork from a bottle" (*Bereishis* 29:10).

Chazal surely did not intend to convey that Yaakov Avinu possessed exceptional physical strength, especially after he spent fourteen years in Eiver's *beis midrash* learning Torah — which, the Gemara teaches (*Sanhedrin* 26b), depletes the body's strength. Rather, their intention was that Yaakov Avinu unified his heart and willpower to accomplish something that he regarded as important, and this infused him with strength and vigor that surpassed his natural capabilities and allowed him to attain his goal. This concept is expressed in *Tefillas Geshem*, as we say: ... יִחֵד לֵב וְגָל אֶבֶן מִבְּאֵר מַיִם בַּעֲבוּרוֹ אַל תִּמְנַע מָיִם, *He unified his heart and removed the stone ... for his sake, do not withhold water*. Yaakov executed a near-impossible physical feat by mustering all his willpower to remove the stone, and we entreat Hashem that in this merit, He should grant us rain.

Another example of someone who mustered her strength to accomplish a task is the daughter of Pharaoh, who, Chazal say (*Sotah* 12b), stretched out her hand to pull Moshe from the water, and her arm extended until it reached him. Chazal do not mean that her hand physically grew and then reverted to its natural size, but rather that she was overcome with such passion to save the crying infant that she unified her heart and willpower, which enabled her to accomplish a supernatural feat and draw the *teivah* close from a distance. This, in fact, is why Moshe Rabbeinu was ultimately known by the name given to him by Bisya, Pharaoh's daughter, as this name symbolized the colossal strengths that a person can muster when he unifies his mind and heart to achieve a goal.

R' Chaim added that Chazal expound the *pasuk*, וַיִּשְׁכַּב בַּמָּקוֹם הַהוּא, *And [Yaakov] lay down in that place* (*Bereishis* 28:11), to mean: "He slept in that place, but throughout the fourteen years that he learned in the *beis midrash* of Eiver, he did not sleep" (*Bereishis Rabbah* 68:11). Going without sleep for fourteen years is physically impossible, yet Yaakov Avinu focused his full mind, heart, and willpower to learn Torah each night, and this enabled him to transcend his natural capacities.

Revealing Latent Strengths

Chazal teach that we do not rely on miracles (*Pesachim* 64b). How, then, could Yaakov Avinu and Pharaoh's daughter rely on a miracle occurring? The answer is that their successes were not outright miracles, but outgrowths of the dormant powers that Hakadosh Baruch Hu instilled in them that could only be activated through *yichud halev* and concerted effort. With a person makes such an effort, he can achieve the level of כֹּל שַׁתָּה תַחַת רַגְלָיו, *You placed everything under his feet.*

This also explains how Moshe Rabbeinu was able to throw the soot until it touched the heavens, and why this was not regarded as a miracle. Moshe Rabbeinu unified his heart and willpower, mustering all his energies to fulfill Hashem's command. He threw the soot with all his might, using one hand, in the manner of one who attempts to throw to a distance. His intense efforts enabled him to tap into the colossal strength deep within him, and the result was that he threw the soot with such force that it was propelled until the heavens.

When Pharaoh observed what Moshe Rabbeinu was capable of accomplishing through *yichud halev,* he acknowledged the enormous strength contained within each and every Yid, and the greatness they can achieve. This recognition terrified him, and he realized that it was in his interests to banish them from Mitzrayim. When Hakadosh Baruch Hu saw this, He hardened Pharaoh's heart so that he could be punished for his crimes.

It's Up to Me

R' Chaim further expressed that a person should feel ashamed of any suffering or trial that afflicts him, because he has the ability to make a concerted effort to summon all his strength with *yichud halev,* to overcome this challenge.

Many *gedolim* throughout the generations surpassed human limitations and achieved phenomenal feats through the force of *yichud halev*. It is said that the Divrei Yisrael of Modzhitz required surgery to amputate his leg. As he lay in the operating room of a Berlin hospital, his gaze flitted to the window, where he glimpsed the great city of Berlin in all its glory, and then recalled the destruction of Yerushalayim and how it lays barren until this day. With this thought, he composed his famous melody *"Ezkerah,"* focusing intently on the words and thereby obviating the need for anesthesia or painkillers during the surgery.

A person who recognizes the incredible latent strength within him can withstand serious challenges and intense pain. The more he seeks to utilize these dormant strengths, the more he can grow and accomplish, surpassing his physical capacities.

The Power of Yichud HaLev

Tanna D'Vei Eliyahu teaches (Ch. 25): "A person is obligated to say, when will my actions reach the actions of Avraham, Yitzchak, and Yaakov?" This conveys that everyone must aspire to attain the level of the holy *Avos*; if Chazal describe this as mandatory, then it must, indeed, be possible for us to attain it.

Can a person actually reach the level of the *Avos*? Elsewhere, Chazal imply that this is impossible: "If the early ones were sons of angels, we are as sons of men; and if the early ones were sons of men, then we are like donkeys" (*Shabbos* 112b). How can a simple person ever dream of attaining the awesome spiritual levels of the *Avos*?

The answer is that every person can achieve far more than what he is naturally capable of by unifying his heart and willpower through *yichud halev*!

Chazal are revealing that a person's capacity to achieve all that he desires applies not only to physical desires, but to spiritual aspirations as well. Every *bachur* and *avreich* harbors the potential to reach the level of "sons of angels," and must recognize that if he aspires to become a *talmid chacham* like R' Akiva Eiger, he *can*! Many Acharonim, and even contemporary *gedolim*, attained exalted spiritual levels worthy of the generation of the Chasam Sofer or even greater. Even in contemporary times, every individual can achieve outstanding spiritual accomplishments — as long as he musters his heart and willpower for that express purpose.

The Mishnah teaches (*Avos* 3:5): כָּל הַמְקַבֵּל עָלָיו עֹל תּוֹרָה מַעֲבִירִין מִמֶּנּוּ עֹל מַלְכוּת וְעֹל דֶּרֶךְ אֶרֶץ, *Anyone who accepts the burden of Torah upon himself, the burden of serving the government and the burden of earning a livelihood are removed from him*. The term "*maavirin*" implies that the person will not necessarily surmount his hardships and challenges; rather, Hakadosh Baruch Hu Himself will remove them so that they no longer block his path. One who undertakes to learn Torah and unifies his heart, mind, and willpower toward that goal will be rewarded by having Hashem eliminate all obstacles and pitfalls from his path, empowering him to reach exceedingly lofty levels in Torah.

The Midrash teaches (*Yalkut Shimoni, Devarim* 32:948) that the Torah uses the phrase בְּעֶצֶם הַיּוֹם הַזֶּה, *in the middle of the day,* in connection with three events: Noach's entry into the *teivah* (*Bereishis* 7:13), Yetzias Mitzrayim, and Moshe's passing (*Devarim* 32:48). In all three instances, people tried to block the event from occurring, so Hakadosh Baruch Hu arranged for these events to happen in broad daylight, to show the world that nothing can stand in the way of His will.

While it is understandable that the *reshaim* of Noach's generation would have barred his entry into the *teivah,* and that the Egyptians would oppose the redemption from Mitzrayim, why did Bnei Yisrael think they could prevent Moshe Rabbeinu's death?

The laws of nature dictate that human beings cannot avert death, yet had Bnei Yisrael unified their hearts, minds, and will collectively to prevent Moshe Rabbeinu's passing, they could have actually achieved this phenomenal feat despite their human limitations! All that prevented them from keeping Moshe alive was a special decree by Hakadosh Baruch Hu that no one could delay or avert his death. This is why Hashem took Moshe's *neshamah* specifically *b'etzem hayom hazeh* — to reveal His infinite power and prove that no creation could prevent Moshe's death, even with *yichud halev.*

Force of Necessity

Every Yid possesses untold strength and capabilities, yet many of us are unfortunately unaware of them since we do not direct our minds and hearts to search for them or draw them out. Even those of us who are aware of our latent strengths do not sufficiently endeavor to exercise them and realize our potential. One exception is at a time of danger, when people suddenly exhibit astounding strengths that far surpass their natural abilities, to the extent that they themselves often cannot believe what they accomplished. Generally, however, people do not concentrate all their strengths and willpower into their actions because they don't deem it necessary. Only when they face physical peril, *chas v'shalom,* do they suddenly see the necessity of gathering all their strength, so they summon all their energies, smashing through human boundaries and limitations to achieve incredible results.

A *bachur* or *avreich* who aspires to grow in Torah must gather all his strength and resolve to realize his latent potential. He should never think he is incapable of achieving in Torah because he lacks the mental capacity or emotional strength to do this, as such thoughts are merely the workings of the *yetzer hara,* which is committed to deceiving and weakening him. If the person only knew that his entire life was contingent on his decision to learn and achieve in Torah, if he would only feel that failing to learn places him in actual physical peril, then he would surely channel the immense strengths inside him to climb and achieve greatness in Torah.

This lesson is an invaluable gift to every *ben Torah.* Many *bachurim* and *avreichim* mistakenly think, "How can I relate to R' Akiva Eiger? Rabbi Akiva Eiger was a brilliant *amkan,* an unrivaled *lamdan.* I can never achieve a fraction of what he did." Yet this mindset is patently false, for every *ben Torah* can and must aspire to greatness, asking himself, "When will my actions reach those of my forefathers? When will my achievements mirror those of R' Akiva Eiger and all other *gedolei Yisrael*?"

A *bachur* or *avreich* who feels that his very life depends on his *gadlus baTorah* and who unifies his mind, heart, and willpower to continually toil and strive in Torah is guaranteed that he will achieve exalted levels of Torah, as Chazal teach, "I toiled and I found — believe him." Any time we see a *gadol b'Yisrael,* we should recall that the foundation of his success was his overpowering *need* to grow and strive, and that his spiritual attainments result from his desire and concerted efforts.

This concept applies both to *limud Torah* and to all spiritual endeavors. People often feel that they are unable to reach lofty levels of Torah; when they stumble, partway along the path, they despair of ever trying again. Yet a person should never forget that by continually striving and exerting himself to the maximum, he reveals the latent strength within him that propels him to the pinnacle of Torah and *ruchniyus*!

May Hakadosh Baruch Hu help us focus our hearts and desires to grow steadily in Torah and mitzvos, and may He grant us strength to strive and toil in Torah night and day, so we can ascend to supreme heights of Torah and *yiras Shamayim*.

פרשת בשלח
Parashas Beshalach

✎ *The Root of Evil*

וַיַּרְא יִשְׂרָאֵל אֶת הַיָּד הַגְּדֹלָה אֲשֶׁר עָשָׂה ה׳ בְּמִצְרַיִם וַיִּירְאוּ הָעָם אֶת ה׳ וַיַּאֲמִינוּ בַּה׳ וּבְמֹשֶׁה עַבְדּוֹ. אָז יָשִׁיר מֹשֶׁה וּבְנֵי יִשְׂרָאֵל אֶת הַשִּׁירָה הַזֹּאת לַה׳ וַיֹּאמְרוּ לֵאמֹר אָשִׁירָה לַה׳ כִּי גָאֹה גָּאָה סוּס וְרֹכְבוֹ רָמָה בַיָּם. עָזִּי וְזִמְרָת יָהּ וַיְהִי לִי לִישׁוּעָה זֶה אֵלִי וְאַנְוֵהוּ אֱלֹהֵי אָבִי וַאֲרֹמְמֶנְהוּ.

Israel saw the great hand that Hashem inflicted upon Egypt; and the people revered Hashem, and they had faith in Hashem and in Moshe, His servant. Then Moshe and the Children of Israel chose to sing this song to Hashem, and they said the following: I shall sing to Hashem for He is exalted above the arrogant, having hurled horse with its rider into the sea. The might and vengeance of God was salvation for me. This is my God and I will build Him a Sanctuary; the God of my father and I will exalt Him (*Shemos* 14:31, 15:1-2).

From Ruach HaKodesh to Shaky Emunah

Bnei Yisrael witnessed spectacular miracles and experienced an unprecedented revelation of the *Shechinah* at the Yam Suf, as Chazal teach, "A maidservant saw at the Sea what

Yechezkel and the other prophets did not see" (*Mechilta D'Shirah* Ch. 3). Upon bearing witness to these heart-stopping events, Bnei Yisrael achieved an exalted level of *yiras Shamayim* and *emunah* that earned them *ruach hakodesh* and inspired them to sing *shirah* to Hashem.

Yet just a short while later, upon arriving in Refidim and thirsting for water, Bnei Yisrael displayed a shocking lack of faith in Hashem, as the Torah states (*Shemos* 17:2-4): וַיָּרֶב הָעָם עִם מֹשֶׁה וַיֹּאמְרוּ תְּנוּ לָנוּ מַיִם וְנִשְׁתֶּה וַיֹּאמֶר לָהֶם מֹשֶׁה מַה תְּרִיבוּן עִמָּדִי מַה תְּנַסּוּן אֶת ה׳. וַיִּצְמָא שָׁם הָעָם לַמַּיִם וַיָּלֶן הָעָם עַל מֹשֶׁה וַיֹּאמֶר לָמָּה זֶּה הֶעֱלִיתָנוּ מִמִּצְרַיִם לְהָמִית אֹתִי וְאֶת בָּנַי וְאֶת מִקְנַי בַּצָּמָא. וַיִּצְעַק מֹשֶׁה אֶל ה׳ לֵאמֹר מָה אֶעֱשֶׂה לָעָם הַזֶּה עוֹד מְעַט וּסְקָלֻנִי, *The people contended with Moshe and they said, "Give us water that we may drink!" Moshe said to them, "Why do you contend with me? Why do you test Hashem?" The people thirsted there for water, and the people complained against Moshe, and it said, "Why is this that you have brought us up from Egypt to kill me and my children and my livestock through thirst?" Moshe cried out to Hashem, saying, "What shall I do for this people? A bit more and they will stone me!"*

How did Klal Yisrael plummet so swiftly from believing wholeheartedly in Hashem and Moshe Rabbeinu to complaining bitterly, arguing with Moshe Rabbeinu, and testing the Ribbono Shel Olam? Bnei Yisrael's *emunah* became so fragile that they were no longer certain that Hashem dwelled in their midst, as the Torah states (ibid. v. 7): וַיִּקְרָא שֵׁם הַמָּקוֹם מַסָּה וּמְרִיבָה עַל רִיב בְּנֵי יִשְׂרָאֵל וְעַל נַסֹּתָם אֶת ה׳ לֵאמֹר הֲיֵשׁ ה׳ בְּקִרְבֵּנוּ אִם אָיִן, *He called the place Massah U'Merivah, because of the contention of the Children of Israel and because of their test of Hashem, saying, "Is Hashem among us or not?"*

Chazal teach (*Shemos Rabbah* 26:2) that Bnei Yisrael's doubts regarding Hakadosh Baruch Hu's Presence among them is what brought Amalek upon them; this was meant to remind them of the miracles and wonders that Hashem had performed on their behalf. How did Bnei Yisrael, who had only recently sung the words *"zeh Keili v'anveihu"* on the banks of the Yam Suf, degenerate so rapidly, to the point that they could not sense Hashem's presence in their midst?

A Lapse in Limud Torah Leads to Spiritual Degeneration

The root of Bnei Yisrael's drastic fall is evident from their punishment — the war with Amalek. The Torah relates: וַיָּבֹא עֲמָלֵק וַיִּלָּחֶם עִם יִשְׂרָאֵל בִּרְפִידִם, *Amalek came and battled Israel in Refidim* (*Shemos* 17:8), and Chazal teach that the name "Refidim" alludes to Klal Yisrael's weakening (*rifyon*) in Torah. This weakness is what made them vulnerable to attack — "for the enemy comes only when they are weak in Torah" (*Mechilta* ibid.). The beginning of Bnei Yisrael's spiritual decline, which is what ultimately led them to this grave lapse in *emunah*, was neglecting *limud Torah.*

The phrase "*Rafu Yisrael yedeihem m'divrei Torah* — Bnei Yisrael's hands weakened from words of Torah," indicates that Bnei Yisrael did not utterly abandon the Torah, but were weak and lazy in their learning. The Ohr HaChaim (ibid.) writes: "They were indolent in Torah, which is compared to water and fire, as it is written: הֲלוֹא כֹה דְבָרִי כָּאֵשׁ, *Behold, My word is like fire* (*Yirmiyah* 23:29), and they did not engage in the battle of Torah. Therefore, [Hashem] punished them with thirst, corresponding to water, and with the fire of war with Amalek."

The Ohr HaChaim isolates the precise point of Bnei Yisrael's abandonment of the Torah: They failed to engage in *milchamtah shel Torah,* the battle of Torah. They did not labor to debate Torah concepts with others, with *iyun* and *pilpul,* which Chazal (*Avos* 6:6) list as one of the fundamental means of acquiring Torah. This omission led to Bnei Yisrael's spiritual decline, as they lost the exalted level they had achieved upon leaving Mitzrayim and witnessing the miracles at the Yam Suf. As soon as they stopped fighting the battle of Torah with vigor and passion, they began descending a slippery slope, which resulted in their testing Hakadosh Baruch Hu and doubting His Presence in their midst.

We learn from this episode that as soon as Bnei Yisrael falter in the "battle of Torah," Amalek gains the power to fight and vanquish us. We also see the immense significance of *milchemes haTorah,* of learning with *pilpul* and with *dibbuk chaveirim,* as Chazal express: "Just as fire does not ignite from a single [piece of wood], so, too, the words of Torah are not retained by someone who studies on his own" (*Taanis* 7a). They further state, "A sword upon the enemies of such Torah scholars, who engage in Torah study on their own" (ibid.).

Milchemes Amalek Is Directly Linked to the Battle of Torah

The Ohr HaChaim (*Shemos* 17:9) adds that this was the reason that Moshe Rabbeinu sent Yehoshua bin Nun to choose warriors to fight Amalek: "Moshe recognized that the sin was related to neglecting the battle of Torah, and he said, 'The one who is worthy to set out to war is Yehoshua, about whom it is written (*Shemos* 33:11): *He would not depart from within the Tent* — from engaging in Torah. Therefore, he told him to choose men similar to himself, for this was how they would overcome [Amalek], and so it was." Since Amalek is empowered by weak, lethargic *limud Torah*, the ones best suited to fight and conquer Amalek are Klal Yisrael's spiritual giants, who exhibit strength and might in *milchemes haTorah* and can vanquish Amalek with the force of their *limud*.

Chazal teach: "Hakadosh Baruch Hu vowed that His Name is not complete and His Throne is not complete until the name of Amalek will be utterly obliterated; and when Amalek's name is erased, His Name will be complete and His Throne will be complete" (cited by Rashi, v. 16). The world can only achieve its full *tikkun* once Amalek's name and memory have been wiped off the face of this earth. Since Amalek's powers draw from Bnei Yisrael's weakness in *limud Torah*, it follows that true *tikkun olam* and the revelation of Hashem's glory in the world are all directly linked to *milchemes haTorah*. How great is our responsibility, as *bnei Torah*, to strengthen ourselves in *limud Torah* with *dibbuk chaveirim*, so that we can fight the sacred *milchemes haTorah*!

The Root of All Evil

Amalek is the fundamental source of evil and adversity in Olam Hazeh. Just as Bnei Yisrael's spiritual lapse and laziness empowered Amalek to attack them three thousand years ago in the Midbar, so, too, in every generation, Klal Yisrael's weakness in *limud Torah* leads to the empowerment of evil in the world.

Furthermore, just as the only way to vanquish Amalek in the Midbar was with the force of *lomdei Torah* engaging in *milchemes haTorah*, so, too, our pillar of strength throughout the generations has always been, and will always be, those who toil in Torah. Their Torah study must be with *hasmadah* and perseverance, without interruption or distraction, just like that of Yehoshua, whom the Torah describes as one who "would not depart from within the Tent."

This also explains why, when Hakadosh Baruch Hu commanded Yehoshua bin Nun to lead Bnei Yisrael into Eretz Yisrael and conquer its inhabitants, He commanded him (*Yehoshua* 1:8): לֹא יָמוּשׁ סֵפֶר הַתּוֹרָה הַזֶּה מִפִּיךָ וְהָגִיתָ בּוֹ יוֹמָם וָלַיְלָה לְמַעַן תִּשְׁמֹר לַעֲשׂוֹת כְּכָל הַכָּתוּב בּוֹ כִּי אָז תַּצְלִיחַ אֶת דְּרָכֶךָ וְאָז תַּשְׂכִּיל, *This Book of the Torah shall not depart from your mouth; rather you should contemplate it day and night in order that you observe to do according to all that is written in it; for then you will make your way successful, and then you will act wisely*. The principal way for Bnei Yisrael to conquer their enemies is through constant *limud Torah*: וְהָגִיתָ בּוֹ יוֹמָם וָלַיְלָה.

The Chofetz Chaim (*Sefer Chofetz Chaim al haTorah, Shemos* 17:9) proves from the *pesukim* describing the war with Amalek that *ameilus baTorah* is the only way to overcome the *yetzer hara*. The Torah states (ibid. 17:11): וְהָיָה כַּאֲשֶׁר יָרִים מֹשֶׁה יָדוֹ וְגָבַר יִשְׂרָאֵל וְכַאֲשֶׁר יָנִיחַ יָדוֹ וְגָבַר עֲמָלֵק, *It happened that when Moshe raised his hand Israel was stronger, and when he lowered his hand Amalek was stronger*, and the Chofetz Chaim notes that the Torah employs the future tense in the words יָרִים and יָנִיחַ, which implies that the same *zechus* of *ameilus baTorah* that served as a protective shield to Bnei Yisrael in the Midbar will remain with us throughout the generations. Any time adversaries rise against our nation, the most effective weapon we have is to intensify our *ameilus baTorah*.

Tragically, in recent generations, we have borne witness to the steady rise of evil in this world. This evil derives from Amalek and is surely a result of Bnei Yisrael's weakened *limud Torah*. Our sacred responsibility is, therefore, to increase our *limud Torah*, which is our only means of vanquishing evil. This obligation must be shouldered primarily by those who are privileged to dwell in the tent of Torah and can personally emulate Yehoshua, the quintessential *ben Torah* who "never left the tent."

An Annoying Fly

Amalek's expertise is finding a tiny breach and widening it. All it takes is a fleeting moment of weakness for the *yetzer hara* to enter and destroy everything in its path.

The Midrash (*Yalkut Shimoni* 262), in this *parashah*, compares Amalek to a pesky fly that buzzes around until it finds an open wound, and then zeroes in on it to suck the person's blood. The *Kli Yakar* (*Shemos* 17:8) explains this based on the following statement of the Gemara (*Berachos* 61a): "Rav said: The *yetzer hara* resembles a fly and sits between the two gateways of the heart, as it says: **זְבוּבֵי מָוֶת יַבְאִישׁ יַבִּיעַ שֶׁמֶן רוֹקֵחַ**, *Flies of death corrupt and putrefy perfumed oil* (*Koheles* 10:1). But Shmuel said that it is like wheat, as it says: **לַפֶּתַח חַטָּאת רֹבֵץ**, *Sin crouches at the door* (*Bereishis* 4:7)." Rav compares the *yetzer hara* to a fly that seeks out the smallest wound and widens it in order to suck out blood, while Shmuel adds that the *yetzer hara* will wait patiently outside for an opening as small as a single kernel of wheat, and when it finds that opening, it will expand it until it manages to cause the person to sin.

This is why it is so crucial to guard ourselves against any breach in *limud Torah*. The *yetzer hara* exhibits tremendous patience, and as soon as it detects even a slight lapse, it is prepared to pounce and unleash all its venom against the person.

Imagine if we were to send one *bachur* from yeshivah to fight Amalek and inform him that the final victory against Amalek is dependent on him. Surely, he would concentrate all his energies, thoughts, and willpower to fight our nation's greatest enemy and subdue him.

This is not just a *mashal*, but our daily reality! Our victory against Amalek, and our triumph over all forces of evil in the world, depends entirely on each and every *lomed Torah*, which is why we must all invest all our energies into Torah study, and learn without interruption or distraction.

It is likewise essential to know that our fortress of *kedushah* is breached by Amalek and its armies not only when we transgress prohibitions, but also when we do things that are technically permissible but nevertheless inappropriate for *bnei Torah*.

Before giving the Torah on Har Sinai, Hakadosh Baruch Hu exhorted Klal Yisrael: וְאַתֶּם תִּהְיוּ לִי מַמְלֶכֶת כֹּהֲנִים וְגוֹי קָדוֹשׁ, *You shall be to Me a kingdom of priests and a holy nation* (*Shemos* 19:6). The Ramban (*Vayikra* 19:2) expounds that the essence of this mitzvah is to abstain even from permitted indulgences, to avoid becoming overly entrenched in the desires of Olam Hazeh. Without this mitzvah, a person could easily sink into a mire of worldly temptations until he becomes a "*naval b'reshus haTorah.*" The commandment to be a "kingdom of priests and a holy nation" was a prerequisite to Kabbalas HaTorah, because one who is submerged in Olam Hazeh cannot wholeheartedly accept the Torah. The obsession with worldly pleasures constitutes the perfect gap that the *yetzer hara* eagerly awaits, and it worms itself through this crack and then exploits it to send the person plummeting into a spiritual abyss.

Seeing Only the Present

At times when we suffer spiritual lows, we may be overwhelmed by waves of despair, to the extent that we lose all hope for change. Yet we must know that focusing exclusively on the darkness of the present without looking toward the future can lead us to spiritual devastation.

This lesson can be gleaned from the beginning of the *parashah*, which describes how Hakadosh Baruch Hu leads Bnei Yisrael along a circuitous route, for the following reason: פֶּן יִנָּחֵם הָעָם בִּרְאֹתָם מִלְחָמָה וְשָׁבוּ מִצְרָיְמָה, *Perhaps the people will reconsider when they see a war, and they will return to Egypt* (*Shemos* 13:17).

What exactly was the concern that spurred Hakadosh Baruch Hu to extend Bnei Yisrael's journey in the Midbar? Bnei Yisrael had just emerged from Mitzrayim after 210 years of slavery and oppression, during which they longingly awaited redemption. After all they had endured in Egypt, and after experiencing the miracles of Yetzias Mitzrayim and Krias Yam Suf, why would a minor skirmish with the Pelishtim cause them to turn tail and return to the bondage of Mitzrayim? Klal Yisrael of that era were the *Dor Dei'ah*, not simple-minded people who would easily forget the terrible troubles of Mitzrayim.

We learn from this that human nature is to focus primarily on the present, without contemplating the consequences of their actions. Hakadosh Baruch Hu knew that upon seeing the battle with the Pelishtim, Bnei Yisrael would immediately demand to return to Mitzrayim, without considering the long-term ramifications of their choice.

A Yid must look beyond his narrow circumstances and reflect upon the future consequences of his actions and choices. Our *gedolim*, whose opinions constitute *daas Torah*, are indeed characterized by their broad, far-reaching vision. One who invests all his energies into *limud Torah* trains himself to analyze an issue from every angle, examine it with greater breadth and depth, and envision all potential outcomes.

The Rosh Yeshivah R' Eliezer Yehudah Finkel embodied this quality of long-range vision. Every *talmid* who approached him immediately discerned that his penetrating gaze enabled him to see what others didn't and to answer questions on any topic, whether related to Torah or to their personal lives. The Rosh Yeshivah reflected intensely on every issue presented to him, and his answers invariably revealed far-reaching wisdom, for in-depth Torah study opens a person's eyes to look beyond a single, narrow perspective and examine a subject from all possible angles.

Looking Heavenward

Regarding the verse (ibid. 17:11), וְהָיָה כַּאֲשֶׁר יָרִים מֹשֶׁה יָדוֹ וְגָבַר יִשְׂרָאֵל, *And it happened that when Moshe raised his hand Israel was stronger*, the Mishnah teaches (*Rosh Hashanah* 29a): "Do Moshe's hands win a battle or lose a battle? Rather, the verse comes to tell you that so long as Israel gazed upward (מִסְתַּכְּלִין כְּלַפֵּי מַעְלָה) and subjugated their heart to their Father in Heaven, they would prevail. But if not, they would fall."

The Maharsha explains that "gazing upward" means directing their hearts to *Shamayim*. While his words seem to reflect the basic *pshat* of the Mishnah, the question is, why did the Mishnah choose the word *mistaklin*, which derives from the same root word as *histaklus*, perspective? It is possible that the Mishnah's lesson is that one should not keep his perspective locked in the present, but should always look up — toward the future, eyeing the results of his actions.

Everyone feels down at times, and these periods can potentially drive a person to despair. Yet if one takes a broader perspective and looks toward the future, instead of brooding over the past or present, he will see that he can emerge from this spell of depression and carry on. This perspective not only enables him to extricate himself from his low, but it also empowers and motivates him to succeed. In contrast, one who is unable to view life with a far-reaching vision and focuses only on the present is deeply affected by every minor blow and spiritual decline. He suffers insecurity, lacks the strength to cope with difficult situations, and can easily fall into despair.

A *ben Torah* must always look to the future. Rather than feel daunted by the *nisyonos* and hardships along his path, he should envisage a better future and draw *chizuk* from that vision. Furthermore, he must internalize the knowledge that all tragedy and pain in the world derive from weakness in *limud Torah*, and that reinforcing *amal baTorah* will prevent those hardships from befalling him.

There is never an excuse for weakness in Torah! Every *ben Torah* is obligated to strengthen himself in *hasmadah, yegiah,* and *dibbuk* to ensure that his Torah is strong, powerful, and enduring! There is no reason to come late to *seder* or not to learn with *hasmadah*! This is not only about benefiting Klal Yisrael as a whole, but also about benefiting each and every individual. If, *chas v'shalom*, we do not reinforce these aspects of *limud Torah*, we place Klal Yisrael in mortal danger!

The Rosh Yeshivah concluded:

Chazal teach that the *yetzer hara* resembles a fly awaiting the slightest breach in order to suck out its victim's blood; this breach can occur either through *aveiros* or through actions that are permissible but render a person a *naval b'reshus haTorah.*

Recently, many new eateries have opened in close proximity to the yeshivah. While the storefronts may proudly feature a *hechsher*, entering these establishments makes a person a *zollel v'sovei.*

Someone once joked that we can build a roof over the entire Beis Yisrael neighborhood and call it Beis Yeshivas Mir, and it's really not a joke at all. The *yetzer hara* is hard at work in our neighborhood, mustering all its efforts to distract our *bachurim* from *milchemes haTorah.* If we are already learning and *shteiging* in the *beis midrash*, he brings the *taavos* of Olam Hazeh directly across the street. They are everywhere we look, as if we were not in a yeshivah, but in the center of the market!

Any *bachur* who enters one of these establishments is akin to one who immerses in a *mikveh* while holding a *sheretz*. When Hashem commanded us *"Kedoshim tihiyu,"* He did not direct His words exclusively to those of lofty spiritual stature, but to each and every individual! These words must be publicized throughout the yeshivah, so this *chillul Hashem* will end at once!

I'm searching for the right words to emphasize the severity of this issue. If I would say that I'm *makpid* on anyone who buys there, people may wonder, who am I to be *makpid* on *bnei Torah*? If I would say that it's prohibited, people may wonder, who am I to decide what is permissible?

The point is that it's up to you! We cannot allow such things in our midst, and we must take a stand against them. If we do not enter these establishments or support them, then Hashem will send *berachah* and *hatzlachah* to us, and these places will close on their own.

Klal Yisrael needs tremendous *rachamei Shamayim*! The tragedies befalling Klal Yisrael compel us to introspect and ask, why is this happening? Who is to blame for all this if not us? If, *chas v'shalom,* we allow a small breach to form, we open the door and invite all forces of evil inside. If, *chas v'shalom,* we are weak in our *limud Torah,* we strengthen Amalek and provoke him to engage us in battle. Yet if we strengthen ourselves in *ameilus baTorah,* we will surmount all the *tzaros* in the world!

Let us all strengthen ourselves to continue fighting the battle of Torah, and Hashem should have mercy on us and send us Mashiach speedily in our days.

פרשת יתרו
Parashas Yisro

☙ *Limud Torah Is Life*

Chazal taught: A pauper, a rich man, and a wicked man face Heavenly judgment. To the pauper they say, "Why did you not engage in Torah?" If he answers, "I was destitute and occupied with earning a livelihood," they tell him, "Were you poorer than Hillel?" To the rich man they say, "Why did you not engage in Torah?" If he answers, "I was wealthy, and I was occupied with my assets," they tell him, "Were you richer than R' Elazar?" To the wicked man they say, "Why did you not engage in Torah?" If he answers, "I was attractive and distracted by my yetzer hara," they answer him, "Were you more attractive than Yosef?" We find that Hillel obligates the poor, R' Elazar obligates the wealthy, and Yosef obligates the wicked (*Yoma* 35b).

Examining this Gemara, we find that the three answers presented by the pauper, the rich man, and the wicked man, respectively, are both credible and justified. How can one demand of a person who toils day and night to support his family to also learn

Torah with *hasmadah*? How can one expect a person who inherited an international company and billions of dollars in assets to delve into the sea of Torah when he is overwhelmed with his finances and busy ensuring that he doesn't suffer any losses? How can one fault a person who is constantly being attacked by his *yetzer hara* and battling to avoid sin for failing to invest his energies in learning?

Despite the seeming injustice of it all, Chazal profess that none of these explanations are accepted before the Heavenly Tribunal. A Yid who did not invest himself fully into *limud Torah* will be called to task for this in the *Beis Din shel Maalah* in spite of any hardship or adversity that he faced on earth.

If we take a closer look at the words of the Gemara, we find that the *Beis Din shel Maalah* doesn't ask a person why he did not *learn* Torah, but rather why he did not *engage* in it. A person is held accountable not only for the quantity of his learning, but also for its quality. In fact, even if a person surmounted his challenges and devoted hours of his day to Torah study, he will still be asked why he did not "engage" more deeply and intensely in Torah.

In this *parashah*, the Ohr HaChaim (*Shemos* 19:2) notes that Chazal frequently employ the term "*osek*" with regard to *limud Torah*, to emphasize that Torah study must entail *amal* and *yegiah*. It is not sufficient to merely "learn" Torah; one must be constantly occupied and engaged in it. Moreover, the obligation of *eisek baTorah* applies not only during a person's younger years, but throughout his life, and at each and every moment. Indeed, we find that *tzaddikim* throughout the generations toiled in Torah day and night, devoting their time and energies to Torah study despite major challenges.

Our Gedolim Oblige Us, Too

Chazal's words seem baffling, as we all know that Hakadosh Baruch Hu judges every person according to his strengths and capabilities, and no one is expected to achieve beyond his abilities. The Gemara teaches: "Hakadosh Baruch Hu does not come with grievances against His creations" (*Avodah Zarah* 3a). How, then, is each and every person — scholar and layman, genius and ignoramus alike — expected to engage in Torah and withstand challenges as daunting as those presented to our *tzaddikim* and *gedolei Torah*, who were gifted with phenomenal abilities and spiritual potential?

The Gemara recounts the poignant story of Hillel HaZakein (*Yoma* 35b) who labored every day to earn a *trepik*, half of which he paid to the guard to allow him entry into the *beis midrash*, and the other half of which he used to support his family. One day, Hillel did not find work, and the guard refused to allow him entry. Refusing to forfeit the opportunity to learn, he climbed to the rooftop and sat on the chimney so he would hear the Torah taught by Shemayah and Avtalyon.

Citing R' Yisrael Salanter, R' Chaim Shmulevitz pointed out[6] that Hillel HaZakein's income was extremely meager. If the guard stationed outside the *beis midrash* collected half a *trepik* daily from dozens of *talmidim* who flocked to the *beis midrash*, it must have been a very small amount, or else he would quickly have become rich. From the reasonable assumption that a guard was not a wealthy man, we can infer that a single *trepik*, which Hillel toiled every day to earn, was a paltry sum, yet even this he willingly divided into two for the privilege of learning Torah in the *beis midrash* of Shemayah and Avtalyon. What an awesome level of *mesirus nefesh* it must have been for him to part with a full half of his earnings, money that could have been used to feed his hungry children, in order to gain entry into the *beis midrash* to learn Torah! How can anyone demand that a regular person emulate such a lofty example? How can Chazal declare that Hillel obligates all paupers?

A similar question can be asked regarding the statement that "R' Elazar ben Charsom obliges the wealthy." The Gemara adds that "R' Elazar ben Charsom's father left him one thousand forests on land and one thousand ships at sea; and each and every day, [R' Elazar] would take a leather bag of flour over his shoulder and travel from city to city and from country to country to learn Torah." How can Chazal expect a regular man of means to sacrifice his wealth and travel continually in order to learn Torah, like R'

---

6. *Sichos Mussar, Bittul Torah.*

Elazar ben Charsom? Who knows how much money he forfeited daily while he was engaged in Torah, at the expense of attending to the needs of his business, and how can anyone demand of wealthy people in our day and age to do the same?

Most astounding of all is the declaration that "Yosef obligates the wicked." The Gemara goes on to recount that Potifar's daughter made frequent attempts to entice Yosef to sin and threatened to send him to prison, to demote him from his honorable position, and even to blind him! How can anyone who is not a tremendous *ben aliyah* like Yosef HaTzaddik withstand such challenges and still engage in Torah?

Wisdom Without Torah

R' Chaim Shmulevitz explains that if learning Torah were merely an "extra" in life, then the question would be understandable. However, Chazal teach us that *limud Torah* is so much more than an "extra"; it is life itself!

Regarding a *rotzei'ach b'shogeg* (someone who kills unintentionally), the Torah states: וְנָס אֶל אַחַת מִן הֶעָרִים הָאֵל וָחָי, *He shall flee to one of these cities [of refuge] and he shall live* (*Devarim* 4:42). Chazal add that the phrase "he shall live" implies, "Do things for him that he should have life" (*Makkos* 10a).

Chazal glean from this that when a *talmid* takes refuge in an *ir miklat*, his rebbi is exiled together with him. The Rambam explains that we are commanded to do things for him so that he should live — "and to those who possess wisdom and pursue it, life without Torah study is regarded as death" (*Hilchos Rotzei'ach* 7:1).

Those who possess wisdom and pursue it — the *baalei hachochmah u'mevakshehah* — know that Torah is not just a nice addition to life, but life's very essence!

Knowing That Torah Is Life

Chazal do not expect a person to overcome *nisyonos* that were appropriate for Yosef HaTzaddik and other illustrious sages, yet a Yid who views *limud Torah* as his very lifeblood, and who lives life guided by this knowledge, will discover the strength inside himself to sit and learn Torah.

The lesson drawn from the examples of the righteous R' Elazar ben Charsom, Hillel HaZakein, and Yosef HaTzaddik relates not to their supreme power to overcome the *yetzer hara*, but to the conviction that *limud Torah* is no less vital than any physical need. The hearts of these *tzaddikim* pulsed with the knowledge that *limud Torah* is not merely a commendable endeavor, but the very core of a Yid's life, and this appreciation is what allowed them to uncover the dormant strength inside themselves to surmount their difficult *nisyonos*. Chazal wish to teach us that the ability to appreciate the existential significance of *limud Torah* is not reserved exclusively for our forefathers and sages, but can be accessed by anyone.

A Yid who internalizes the knowledge that Torah is his lifeblood will reveal colossal strengths within himself that will enable him to engage fully in Torah and withstand life's most formidable challenges. When a person faces a choice of life or death, it makes no difference whether he is a king or a pauper; there is no drive in the world more powerful than the desire to live, and every person will expend the necessary effort to survive, no matter what it takes.

This is what is expected of each and every Yid — to strive to number among the *baalei hachochmah u'mevakshehah*. We must recognize that life without constant *limud Torah* is not life at all, and that one who lives without Torah is as good as dead. This is expressed in the *tefillah* of *Ahavas Olam* that we recite daily: כִּי הֵם חַיֵּינוּ וְאֹרֶךְ יָמֵינוּ וּבָהֶם נֶהְגֶּה יוֹמָם וָלָיְלָה, *For they are our lives and the length of our days, and in them we shall engage day and night*.

Ideally, people should engage in Torah — which is eternal life — more than they engage in earning a livelihood, which sustains them only in this transient world. Yet few are those who have truly absorbed this lesson, which is why they are not as occupied with learning as they are with their material needs.

The Key to Hischadshus

Those who are privileged to number among the *baalei hachochmah u'mevakshehah*, and to genuinely feel that life itself is contingent upon *limud Torah*, develop a deep love of Torah and cherish their learning, as people are naturally inclined to love and value those things on which life depends. This feeling, in turn, elevates their learning so that it is no longer done by rote, infusing them with *hischadshus*, with passion and enthusiasm.

The *pasuk* in this week's *parashah* states: בַּיּוֹם הַזֶּה בָּאוּ מִדְבַּר סִינָי, *On this day they came to the Sinai Desert* (*Shemos* 19:1), and Rashi notes that it would seem more appropriate to use the phrase "*bayom hahu*, on that day" than "*bayom hazeh,* on this day." From the choice of the phrase *bayom hazeh,* Chazal derive that one should view the words of Torah as new each and every day, as if they had just been given today.

The way to feel that Torah is given each day anew is by formulating *chiddushim* while learning. There is nothing that brings a learner greater joy or satisfaction than innovating his own *chiddushim*; indeed, Chazal teach that through *chiddushei Torah*, a person can attain the consummate joy experienced at the time of Mattan Torah, as they state, "And the words were as joyous as when they were delivered at Sinai" (*Shir HaShirim Rabbah* 1:10).

I recently visited America, where I met many wonderful people who are exceptional *baalei tzedakah* and *baalei chessed*, yet I was deeply pained by the rampant *bittul Torah*. One man proudly told me that he is "a *masmid*" in his business. Another person I met discussed a variety of subjects with me, yet the question dominating every part of the conversation was how he could earn more money.

I should have asked these wonderful Jews, "Why didn't you engage in Torah? When it comes to business, you spare no effort to earn more and succeed, but when dealing with the most important commodity in the world — *limud Torah* — you do not try as hard as you should."

We *bnei Torah* have the privilege of sitting in the *beis midrash*, where we toil and engage in Torah, and we must recognize that we possess the true *simchas hachaim*, which is exclusive to those who sit in the *beis midrash*! There is no comparison between the *simchas hachaim* of an *oseik baTorah* and the *simchas hachaim* of someone who is wholly engrossed in business and mundane matters.

How fortunate we are!

We must continually strive to recognize that we have been granted the greatest gift possible — the *zechus* of sitting and learning Torah with joy and love. May Hashem help us to strengthen our *limud Torah,* so that we can learn with greater *hasmadah* and *yegiah* and achieve the *hischadshus* and *simchah* that we felt on the day of Mattan Torah.

פרשת משפטים
Parashas Mishpatim

The Goal of Mattan Torah: Bein Adam LaChaveiro

וְאֵלֶּה הַמִּשְׁפָּטִים אֲשֶׁר תָּשִׂים לִפְנֵיהֶם.

And these are the statutes that you shall place before them (*Shemos* 21:1).

R' Shimon ben Yochai says: Why did the Torah place [monetary] laws before all the other mitzvos? When there is disagreement between one man and his friend there is conflict, but when the law is decided, peace between them is restored (*Mechilta Mishpatim, Masechta D'Nezikin* Ch. 1).

Parashas Yisro presents a vivid description of Mattan Torah and Hashem's revelation to Bnei Yisrael on Har Sinai. *Parashas Mishpatim* then proceeds to list the halachos taught at Har Sinai, beginning with a long list of mitzvos *bein adam lachaveiro*, such as the laws related to damages and neighbors. Chazal teach that Hashem specifically opened with these mitzvos since they are a preface to all the mitzvos in the Torah. Fulfilling the statutes of *bein adam lachaveiro* is also a precondition to receiving the Torah, as the Midrash relates that Moshe told Bnei Yisrael, "Hakadosh

Baruch Hu gave you the Torah only so you shall uphold its [monetary] laws" (*Shemos Rabbah* 30:23).

Prerequisites to Kabbalas HaTorah

The ultimate purpose of Mattan Torah was that Bnei Yisrael would perform mitzvos *bein adam lachaveiro*; this was also a prerequisite to Mattan Torah. Lacking this unity and commitment to fulfill the laws *bein adam lachaveiro,* Bnei Yisrael are unworthy of receiving the Torah. The Torah was not delivered to 600,000 individuals, but to Klal Yisrael as a whole, when they attained the level of *k'ish echad b'lev echad*. This quality of *lev echad,* one heart, does not mean acting kindly or with common courtesy — it means harboring deep-seated love and respect for every Yid, without a trace of hard feelings or ill will.

This principle is illustrated in the mitzvah of *prikah* (unloading a burden from an animal), one of the many mitzvos commanded in this *parashah.* The *pasuk* states: כִּי תִרְאֶה חֲמוֹר שֹׂנַאֲךָ רֹבֵץ תַּחַת מַשָּׂאוֹ וְחָדַלְתָּ מֵעֲזֹב לוֹ עָזֹב תַּעֲזֹב עִמּוֹ. *If you see the donkey of someone you hate crouching under its burden, would you refrain from helping him? — you shall help repeatedly with him* (*Shemos* 23:5). Onkelos interprets the phrase עָזֹב תַּעֲזֹב עִמּוֹ to mean that you should remove the hatred that you feel in your heart toward the person and unload with him. Only once your heart is cleansed of negativity and resentment can it fill instead with sentiments of affection and brotherhood, enabling you to fulfill the mitzvah of *prikah* from a place of friendship and connection.

The Rosh Yeshivah R' Chaim Shmulevitz often remarked that there is a common misconception that people give to those they love and love those who give to them, but really, the converse is true: One who gives to another person grows to love him, and the more he gives to him and invests in him, the deeper and stronger their bond grows. *Sefer Orchos Tzaddikim* (*Shaar HaAhavah*) expresses this clearly: "How can a person come to love every individual? The way is to help him emotionally and financially, to the best of his ability."

The Foundation of Torah

The Gemara relates (*Shabbos* 31a): "A non-Jew once came to Shammai and told him, 'Convert me on condition that you will teach me the entire Torah while I stand on one foot.' Shammai pushed him away with the ruler in his hand. The non-Jew then approached Hillel, and Hillel converted him, saying to him, 'That which is hateful to you, do not do to your fellow. This is the entire Torah, and everything else is commentary; go and learn it.'"

Hillel's reply can be explained according to the above principle, that mitzvos *bein adam lachaveiro* are a prerequisite to receiving the Torah. Only when Bnei Yisrael manifested complete *achdus*, as expressed by the words *k'ish echad b'lev echad,* were they worthy of receiving Torah, and Hillel's message to this non-Jew was if he commits to observing the mitzvah of *v'ahavta l'rei'acha kamocha* then he has already absorbed the foundation of the entire Torah.

Three Fundamental Preparations

The Torah describes Bnei Yisrael's journey to Har Sinai with these words (*Shemos* 19:1-2): בַּחֹדֶשׁ הַשְּׁלִישִׁי לְצֵאת בְּנֵי יִשְׂרָאֵל מֵאֶרֶץ מִצְרָיִם בַּיּוֹם הַזֶּה בָּאוּ מִדְבַּר סִינָי. וַיִּסְעוּ מֵרְפִידִים וַיָּבֹאוּ מִדְבַּר סִינַי וַיַּחֲנוּ בַּמִּדְבָּר וַיִּחַן שָׁם יִשְׂרָאֵל נֶגֶד הָהָר, *In the third month from the Exodus of the Children of Israel from Egypt, on this day, they arrived at the Wilderness of Sinai. They journeyed from Refidim and arrived at the Wilderness of Sinai and encamped in the Wilderness; and Israel encamped there, opposite the mountain.*

The Ohr HaChaim poses several questions on these *pesukim*: First, why does the Torah transpose the sequence of events, describing Bnei Yisrael's arrival in Midbar Sinai and then mentioning their departure from Refidim? Second, why does the Torah repeat that they arrived in Midbar Sinai, using the phrase בָּאוּ מִדְבַּר סִינָי and then וַיָּבֹאוּ מִדְבַּר סִינַי? And third, why does the Torah specify that they "camped in the Wilderness" when it already stated that they arrived in Midbar Sinai?

These questions, explains the Ohr HaChaim, indicate that the Torah's intention is not to relate the sequence of events in Bnei

Yisrael's journey, but to teach that there are three fundamental preparations required in order to receive the Torah.

The first preparation is reinforcing *eisek baTorah,* as alluded to in the words וַיִּסְעוּ מֵרְפִידִים. The Mechilta explains that "Refidim" connotes weakening (*rifyon*) in Torah, which left Bnei Yisrael vulnerable to attack by Amalek. Here, Klal Yisrael departed from Refidim — they repented from this weakness and indolence, and strengthened their *eisek baTorah.*

The second preparation for receiving the Torah is *avodas hamiddos*: refining one's character traits in general, and specifically the quality of *anavah,* humility. This concept is reflected in the words וַיַּחֲנוּ בַּמִּדְבָּר, for Chazal teach (*Eiruvin* 54a) that the Torah endures only in a person who lowers himself to the level of a desert. The qualities of humility and submissiveness are frequently lauded by Chazal, as they exhort: מְאֹד מְאֹד הֱוֵי שְׁפַל רוּחַ, *Be very, very humble in spirit* (*Avos* 4:4). This is echoed by the Ramban in his letter, where he describes the *middah* of *anavah* as "better than all other good qualities."

Middos tovos refer not to the proper manners and etiquette prevalent even among the nations, but to the qualities lauded by the Torah, such as respecting others, valuing them, and performing kindnesses for them. A person who behaves humbly and submissively is not focused on himself, but on others, and the more he puts others first, the more worthy he is of receiving Torah. Regarding Moshe Rabbeinu, the quintessential *mekabel Torah* and *melamed Torah,* the Torah attests: וְהָאִישׁ מֹשֶׁה עָנָיו מְאֹד מִכֹּל הָאָדָם אֲשֶׁר עַל פְּנֵי הָאֲדָמָה. *Now the man Moshe was exceedingly humble, more than any person on the face of the earth* (*Bamidbar* 12:3).

The third preparation is fostering *achdus* among Bnei Yisrael, as the Torah expresses with the words: וַיִּחַן שָׁם יִשְׂרָאֵל נֶגֶד הָהָר, *and Israel encamped there, opposite the mountain.* Rashi famously notes that the word *vayichan,* which is written in the singular form, teaches that Bnei Yisrael were unified *k'ish echad b'lev echad.* This also conveys that Torah scholars must join together and connect with one another wholeheartedly in order to hone their understanding of halachah and *divrei Torah,* until they are transformed into one unit.

If, however, they cannot join together *b'lev echad*, then they will not merit Kabbalas HaTorah!

This underscores that in order to fully receive the Torah, Klal Yisrael must improve their character traits until they unite as one.

Natural Middos Versus Middos Delivered on Har Sinai

Shlomo HaMelech teaches: לֵךְ אֶל נְמָלָה עָצֵל ... תָּכִין בַּקַּיִץ לַחְמָהּ אָגְרָה בַקָּצִיר מַאֲכָלָהּ, *Go to the ant, you sluggard ... she prepares her food in the summer and stores up her food in the harvest time* (*Mishlei* 6:6-8). The *mefarshim* explain that the ant works industriously to store its food before the onset of winter, and no ant steals food from another.

Chazal teach: "R' Yochanan said: Had the Torah not been given, we would learn modesty from the cat, [the prohibition of] theft from the ant; [the prohibition of] adultery from the dove; and *derech eretz* from the rooster" (*Eruvin* 100b).

If it is possible to glean these positive attributes from animals, why does the Torah teach them to us? The answer must be that the good qualities in existence before Mattan Torah differ from the *middos tovos* that Bnei Yisrael were taught at the time of Mattan Torah! The *tznius* that the Torah commands Bnei Yisrael is not the same modesty manifested by a cat; likewise, the *middos bein adam lachaveiro* that the Torah obligates us to develop go beyond the common courtesy and manners of the rest of the secular world.

A Yid in America once told me that he had visited the underwater observatory in Eilat, and as he stood there observing the fish swimming and diving about to catch their food, he reflected, "How am I different from these fish that swim about in endless pursuit of their sustenance? I'm just like them — running from place to place to earn my bread."

He shared his sentiments with his son, who replied, "See what it is to be a Yid! While the fish swim around only to catch their food, we run around to earn money in order to support Torah, so it is not regular money, but *Torahdike gelt*!"

If we take a good look, we will see that the entire world is in a state of conflict, with countries, communities, and individuals all at odds with one another. Yet we, who were privileged to accept the Torah, must conduct ourselves with the *middos tovos* that the Torah instills in us and increase the *achdus* among us. Then, we will merit the *Geulah Sheleimah*.

פרשת תרומה
Parashas Terumah

◆§ *Man Was Born to Toil*

וְזֹאת הַתְּרוּמָה אֲשֶׁר תִּקְחוּ מֵאִתָּם זָהָב וָכֶסֶף וּנְחֹשֶׁת. וּתְכֵלֶת וְאַרְגָּמָן וְתוֹלַעַת שָׁנִי וְשֵׁשׁ וְעִזִּים. וְעֹרֹת אֵילִם מְאָדָּמִים וְעֹרֹת תְּחָשִׁים וַעֲצֵי שִׁטִּים. שֶׁמֶן לַמָּאֹר בְּשָׂמִים לְשֶׁמֶן הַמִּשְׁחָה וְלִקְטֹרֶת הַסַּמִּים. אַבְנֵי שֹׁהַם וְאַבְנֵי מִלֻּאִים לָאֵפֹד וְלַחֹשֶׁן.

This is the portion that you shall take from them: gold, silver, and copper; and turquoise, purple, and scarlet wool; linen and goat hair; red-dyed ram skins, tachash skins, acacia wood; oil for illumination, spices for the anointment oil and the aromatic incense; shoham stones and stones for the settings, for the Ephod and the Breastplate (*Shemos* 25:3-7).

Measured by Toil

In these *pesukim*, the Torah lists fifteen gifts that Bnei Yisrael donated to the Mishkan, the last of which are the stones for the *Choshen* and *Eifod*. Why, asks the Ohr HaChaim, didn't the Torah list these items in descending order of value? Instead, it enumerated the jewels of the *Choshen* and *Eifod* last, even though they were more valuable than all the other materials donated. The tremendous monetary value of even one of these stones is evident from the famous story of Dama ben Nesinah, whom the Sages approached to purchase a replacement stone for the *Eifod* (*Kiddushin* 31a); Chazal debate whether that stone was valued at 600,000 or 800,000 golden dinars.

One answer given by the Ohr HaChaim is that the significance of each gift that Bnei Yisrael contributed to the Mishkan was not measured by its market value, but by the effort and toil that the giver invested in order to procure it. Regarding the words וְהַנְּשִׂאִם הֵבִיאוּ, *And the nesi'im brought* (*Shemos* 35:27), Chazal teach (*Yoma* 75a) that the Clouds of Glory delivered the stones for the *Choshen* and the *Eifod* directly to the doors of the *nesi'im*'s tents; since their bequests required no effort or exertion, the Torah listed it last.

A Gift of Effort Reflects Generosity

The purpose of building the Mishkan was to create a place for Hakadosh Baruch Hu's *Shechinah* to dwell among Bnei Yisrael, as the Torah states:וְעָשׂוּ לִי מִקְדָּשׁ וְשָׁכַנְתִּי בְּתוֹכָם, *They shall make a Sanctuary for Me — so that I may dwell among them* (*Shemos* 25:8). Therefore, when Hashem commanded that Klal Yisrael donate to the Mishkan, He said (ibid. v. 2): וְיִקְחוּ לִי תְּרוּמָה מֵאֵת כָּל אִישׁ אֲשֶׁר יִדְּבֶנּוּ לִבּוֹ תִּקְחוּ אֶת תְּרוּמָתִי, *And let them take for Me a portion, from every man whose heart motivates him you shall take My portion*. Rashi explains that the words וְיִקְחוּ לִי תְּרוּמָה mean "for My Name," and the words יִדְּבֶנּוּ לִבּוֹ connote donating out of goodwill. Here, the Torah reveals that a place as sacred as the Mishkan can only be built of gifts bequeathed with generosity and benevolence.

When a person presents his friend with something that is exceedingly valuable to him, it is a sign that he is giving with a happy heart and love. In contrast, a gift that is not meaningful to the giver manifests little generosity or goodness. There was no better assessment of a person's generosity and desire to give to the Beis HaMikdash than the effort and toil he invested in order to obtain the gift. Chazal teach that a person naturally cherishes the possessions that he worked hard to attain, as they say, "A person prefers his own measure over nine measures of his friend" (*Bava Metzia* 38a). Rashi explains: "His own measure is dearer to him, because he toiled for it." The value of each bequest to the Mishkan was therefore calculated based on the effort the giver expended, which reflected the generosity and goodwill that went into his donation.

The Rosh Yeshivah R' Chaim Shmulevitz adds[7] that this lesson can also be learned from *bikkurim,* which is the only mitzvah in the Torah in which a person is required to prostrate himself before Hakadosh Baruch Hu, as the *pasuk* states: וְהִשְׁתַּחֲוִיתָ לִפְנֵי ה' אֱלֹהֶיךָ, *And you shall prostrate yourself before Hashem, your God* (*Devarim* 26:10).

Bikkurim, more than any other mitzvah, reveals a person's generosity, as a person naturally treasures the first fruits of his harvest, which symbolize the product of a year's worth of labor. Giving Hakadosh Baruch Hu the very first fruit, which is so precious to the farmer, is the highest expression of *nedivus halev,* generosity. At the time that the person delivers these cherished fruits to Hakadosh Baruch Hu, he is worthy of prostrating himself before Hashem, as he expresses his detachment from materialism and his desire to entrust his body and soul entirely in the hands of Hashem.

Love between people involves a similar dynamic, as Chazal teach (*Maseches Derech Eretz Zuta* Ch. 2): "If you desire to cleave to the love of your friend, do business dealings for his benefit." A person feels a deep connection to his money and possessions, so when he gives selflessly to his friend and bestows his gifts upon him, he is actually giving a part of himself to his friend, and this act of giving intensifies the love that he feels toward him.

Love is the result of devotion and giving. This principle is powerfully evident in a mother's love for her child, which is the deepest and most enduring love in the world. If a mother is separated from her child immediately after birth and then reunited with him many years later, the bond may still exist, but by no means will it compare to the love of a mother who raised her child devotedly throughout his childhood and adolescence.

---

7. *Sichos Mussar, Nidvas HaNesi'im.*

Their Efforts Versus Our Efforts

In this *parashah,* the Torah underscores how *amal* and *yegiah* have the power to foster affection. This applies to all realms of life, and to Torah above all else.

Moreover, when a person toils in Torah, the Torah becomes part of him and is attributed to him, as Chazal teach (*Kiddushin* 32b) that "a *talmid chacham* may forgo his honor because the Torah that he learns becomes his"; this is derived from the *pasuk*: וּבְתוֹרָתוֹ יֶהְגֶּה יוֹמָם וָלָיְלָה, *And in his Torah he shall engage day and night*" (*Tehillim* 1:2). Rashi notes that first it is called Hashem's Torah, but when the person studies and reviews it, it is called *his* Torah.

Ameilus baTorah differs from effort that a person invests into any other pursuit. Upon leaving the *beis midrash,* a *lomed Torah* recites a prayer of thanksgiving that includes the phrase: "I toil and they toil; I toil and receive reward, and they toil and do not receive reward" (*Berachos* 28b).

The Chofetz Chaim wonders,[8] Doesn't everyone labor in order to receive payment? No one is willing to work for free!

He answers that one cannot compare the effort that a person expends in order to obtain material wealth to the *amal* that a Yid invests into *limud Torah.* When a person works for pay, it is but a means to an end. Furthermore, if someone hires a laborer to build a building or weave a garment, the laborer will not receive payment until the job is complete, regardless of the effort he invests.

Ameilus baTorah, in contrast, is an integral aspect of the mitzvah of *talmud Torah,* and a Yid receives infinite, eternal reward for every moment he toils in learning. There is even an added advantage to learning Torah without achieving understanding, as Chazal teach (*Gittin* 43a) that "a person does not acquire *divrei Torah* unless he has stumbled in them first." The path to attaining the highest level of Torah is by first toiling without results, which is why Chazal use the words "we toil and reap reward" to describe the effort we invest into *limud Torah.* In contrast, the words "they toil and do not reap reward" are an apt description of effort invested into material

---

8. *Chofetz Chaim al HaTorah, Vayikra* 26:3.

pursuits, which are rewarded only when they yield successful results.

Do Not Believe Him

This principle is also expressed in the Gemara's statement (*Megillah* 6b): "R' Yitzchak said: If someone tells you, 'I labored but did not succeed,' do not believe him. [If he tells you,] 'I have not labored, yet I succeeded,' do not believe him. [If, however, he tells you,] I have labored and I have succeeded,' believe him. This is true of Torah study, but with regard to business, one's success is dependent on assistance from Heaven."

The *mefarshim* explain that it is possible to succeed in business without investing any effort, in which case a person could be believed when he says that he has not labored, yet he has achieved financial success. In material pursuits, a person's efforts are only a channel for the blessing to descend, and if Heaven decrees that a person should have wealth, he will receive it regardless of his effort. When it comes to *limud Torah,* however, the toil itself is the goal, so if a person professes that he achieved understanding in Torah without investing effort, one should not believe him, because his statement is in direct conflict with the essence of *limud Torah.*

We see with our own eyes that the more someone toils and exerts himself to learn, the more he comes to love and cherish Torah. When working to attain material possessions, the goal is the item, not the toil; but in *limud Torah,* the *amal* itself is infinitely precious, and constitutes an end in and of itself. Effort is an indistinguishable, vital aspect of the mitzvah of *limud Torah,* which is why toiling in Torah is so rewarding.

The Gemara proclaims, "Fortunate are you, Torah students, that the words of Torah are extremely beloved to you" (*Menachos* 18a). *Talmidei chachamim* are fortunate because they toil in Torah, which lead them to ascend to lofty levels in Torah and *ruchniyus.*

You Should Toil in Torah!

Regarding the words אִם בְּחֻקֹּתַי תֵּלֵכוּ, *If you will follow My decrees* (*Vayikra* 26:3), Rashi comments: "That you should be laboring in Torah." When a person works hard to achieve something, it becomes very precious to him, to the extent that he is willing to sacrifice himself for it. Furthermore, Hakadosh Baruch Hu's bond with Bnei Yisrael is directly linked to the effort they invest into Torah learning. Since *amal haTorah* is an end in and of itself, the many blessings that the Torah promises to Bnei Yisrael are all contingent on the *amal* and *yegiah* that they invest into *limud Torah.*

This actually comes as no surprise, as man's very purpose in this world is to toil and labor in Torah. Indeed, Chazal teach (*Sanhedrin* 99b):

> R' Elazar said: Every man is created for toil, as it is stated (*Iyov* **5:7**): **כִּי אָדָם לְעָמָל יוּלָּד**, *But man is born for toil.* Now, I do not know whether he is created for verbal toil, or whether he is created for the toil of physical labor. When, however, the verse states (*Mishlei* **16:26**), **כִּי אָכַף עָלָיו פִּיהוּ**, *for he saddled his mouth to it,* you have to say that he is created for verbal toil. However, I still do not know whether he is created for the toil of Torah study, or whether he is created for the toil of conversation about other matters. When, however, the verse states (*Yehoshua* 1:8), **לֹא יָמוּשׁ סֵפֶר הַתּוֹרָה הַזֶּה מִפִּיךָ**, *This Book of the Torah is not to leave your mouth,* you have to say that man is created for the toil of Torah study.

One who does not toil in Torah forfeits his right to exist in this world, whereas one who toils properly in Torah achieves his ultimate purpose and merits all conceivable blessings.

Surmounting Laziness

The main impediment to *amal baTorah* is *atzlus,* indolence. Since a person is created primarily to toil in Torah, he must work hard to overcome the tendency toward laziness.

Shlomo HaMelech advises: לֵךְ אֶל נְמָלָה עָצֵל רְאֵה דְרָכֶיהָ וַחֲכָם, *Go to the ant, you sluggard; see its ways and grow wise* (*Mishlei* 6:6). An ant is the symbol of physical labor and industriousness, which is why Shlomo HaMelech exhorts us to observe it and learn from it to overcome the destructive trait of *atzlus.* Furthermore, Shlomo

HaMelech compared the diligence and alacrity required for *avodas Hashem* to the ways of the ant in order to highlight the essence of *amal haTorah.* Just as an ant spends its life collecting and stockpiling food that it doesn't need — as Chazal teach, "And all its sustenance is no more than one-and-a-half [kernels of] wheat, yet she [still] goes and gathers in the summer all that she finds, wheat, barley, and lentils" (*Devarim Rabbah* 5:2) — so, too, our toil in Torah is not just a means of gaining knowledge of Torah, but also a sacred, vital pursuit in and of itself.

Developing an Emotional Connection to the Korbanos

When one invests effort to acquire something, he feels connected to it, and it becomes dear to his heart. In this week's *parashah* and the coming ones, the Torah presents a detailed description of the Mishkan and all its vessels, and *Sefer Vayikra* discusses the *korbanos* extensively.

Despite the lack of a Beis HaMikdash today, a Yid can still develop a deep emotional connection to these topics by studying them in depth and investing his energies into understanding them.

The Gemara teaches (*Taanis* 27b) that during the *Bris Bein HaBesarim,* Avraham Avinu asked Hakadosh Baruch Hu how his descendants would be able to achieve atonement for their sins at times when there is no possibility of bringing *korbanos*. Hashem replied, "I have already established for them the *Seder Korbanos*. Whenever they read from them before Me, I will consider it as if they had brought *korbanos* before Me, and I will forgive them all their sins."

The Gemara (*Menachos* (110a) makes a similar statement:

> R' Yitzchak said: What is the meaning of that which is written: זֹאת תּוֹרַת הַחַטָּאת, *This is the law (torah) of the chatas* (*Vayikra* 6:18), and וְזֹאת תּוֹרַת הָאָשָׁם, *This is the law (torah) of the asham* (ibid. 7:1)? Whoever engages in the study of the Torah of a *chatas* is regarded as if he offered a *chatas*, and whoever engages in the study of the Torah of an *asham* is regarded as if he offered an *asham*.

By studying these topics, a person becomes connected to the Beis HaMikdash and the *korbanos*, and his toil causes him to be regarded as though he actually offered *korbanos*. Moreover, just as a person's love and connection to *divrei Torah* increase in proportion to the effort and toil he invests in his learning, the more effort we expend in studying these topics, the more meaningful our *korban* will be considered.

Anticipating the Redemption by Learning

Chazal teach (*Shabbos* 31a): "When they escort a person to judgment, they say to him: Did you conduct your business transactions faithfully? Did you set aside fixed times for Torah study? Did you engage in procreation? Did you await the Redemption?" We see that one of the first questions a person is asked by the Heavenly Tribunal is whether he yearned for the Redemption.

Similarly, one of the Thirteen Principles of Faith, based on the Rambam (preface to *Perek Chelek*), is: "I believe in the coming of Mashiach, and even if he delays, I will still anticipate every day that he will come."

An integral aspect of the obligation to believe in Mashiach is to await the *Geulah* every day of life. In previous generations, when people were closer to the era of the Beis HaMikdash, they keenly sensed the lack of *kedushah* in the world following the *Churban*, and desperately yearned for redemption. Recent generations, however, are far removed from those days of glory, and cannot fathom what they are missing or yearn properly for the *Geulah*. How, then, can they be expected to eagerly await Mashiach?

Learning about the *korbanos* and the Beis HaMikdash creates an emotional connection to these topics, and the more effort a Yid invests into studying these topics, the deeper this bond becomes. This emotional connection to that era will open his heart to feel the terrible loss of our Beis HaMikdash and yearn for the coming of Mashiach, the building of the Beis HaMikdash, and the renewal of the *korbanos*.

May Hakadosh Baruch Hu grant us strength to serve Him with

nedivus halev, and may we merit to learn Torah with *amal* and *yegiah,* so that the words of Torah will be precious to us. Let us draw our hearts to the Mikdash and the *korbanos* and yearn for the *Geulah,* and may we see the rebuilding of the Beis HaMikdash speedily in our days.

פרשת תצוה
Parashas Tetzaveh

◊ *The Wisdom of the Heart*

In Honor of the Yahrtzeit of R' Chaim Kamil

וְאַתָּה תְּדַבֵּר אֶל כָּל חַכְמֵי לֵב אֲשֶׁר מִלֵּאתִיו רוּחַ חָכְמָה וְעָשׂוּ
אֶת בִּגְדֵי אַהֲרֹן לְקַדְּשׁוֹ לְכַהֲנוֹ לִי.

And you shall speak to all the wise-hearted people whom I have invested with a spirit of wisdom, and they shall make the vestments of Aharon, to sanctify him to minister to Me (*Shemos* 28:3).

The common belief is that wisdom lies in the brain, and is a function of the mind. The Torah, however, repeatedly refers to "*chachmei lev,* the wise of heart," which connotes that wisdom can also be rooted in the heart.

How is wisdom cultivated in the heart?

Preparing Oneself for Eternity

The Gemara relates (*Tamid* 32a) that Alexander the Great asked the Elders of the Negev, "Who is called 'a wise man'?" They replied, "Who is a wise man? *Haro'eh es hanolad* — he who foresees a future development." Rashi explains that this refers to a person who "understands in his heart what is destined to occur — future events — and is cautious with regard to them."

With these words, the Elders of the Negev taught that wisdom requires more than talents and skills; it also requires *havanas halev,* an understanding heart, which enables one to anticipate the future. *Havanas halev* means feeling the responsibility to contemplate the future, and utilizing one's wisdom to properly prepare for what is to come.

The capacity to foresee future events has practical significance in Olam Hazeh, yet is all the more important for our eternal future in Olam Haba. Man is charged with the formidable task of preparing responsibly for his future and exercising wisdom to know why he was brought into this world and what his mission is, as Akavyah ben Mehallalel instructed (*Avos* 3:1): "Look at three things, and you shall not come to sin: Know from where you came, to where you are going, and before Whom you are destined to give an accounting."

Chazal teach (ibid. 2:9), in a similar vein, that Rabban Yochanan ben Zakkai told his *talmidim*: "Go and figure out which is the proper path to which a man should cling." R' Shimon replied: "*Haro'eh es hanolad* — one who foresees the future." R' Ovadiah of Bartenura explains that this refers to "one who looks at what will be in the future, and as a result, calculates the loss of a mitzvah versus its reward, and the reward of a mitzvah versus its loss." Clearly, then, R' Shimon was referring to contemplating one's eternal future.

Feeling the Future

R' Eliyahu Lopian cites R' Yisrael Salanter's analysis of Chazal's choice of the term "*haro'eh es hanolad* — one who *foresees* the future," as opposed to "*hayodei'a es hanolad* — one who *knows* the future." Taking responsibility for future circumstances compels a person to not only *know* what will occur in the future, but also to feel and actually live the future as if it is unfolding before his very eyes.[9]

Chazal teach (*Berachos* 17a): "A man's end is to die, and an animal's end is for slaughter, and all are poised for death." Most people are conscious of their destiny, and if one were to ask them

---

9. *Lev Eliyahu, Shemos, Eizehu Chacham Haro'eh es Hanolad.*

why they were brought into the world, they would unhesitatingly respond, "to learn Torah and do mitzvos." This knowledge remains external, however, and fails to penetrate the heart, as evidenced by the fact that people spend the majority of their days and years occupied with mundane, worldly matters instead of focusing on fulfilling their spiritual obligations. Rather than search for means to serve Hashem, they seek ways to increase their monetary wealth. This is why Chazal exhort, "One who sees his *yetzer hara* overcoming him should recall his day of death" (*Berachos* 5a). While every person is technically aware of his impending death, if one does not remind oneself consistently of it, the knowledge will not impact his heart or actions.

The same applies to trusting in Hashem with regard to *parnassah*. If one were to ask a group of people if they believe that their livelihood is decided in Heaven, they would instinctively reply in the affirmative. And yet the amount of *hishtadlus* that people invest in order to earn a *parnassah* indicates that this knowledge, while perhaps embedded somewhere in the mind, remains remote from the heart, which secretly still believes that: כֹּחִי וְעֹצֶם יָדִי עָשָׂה לִי אֶת הַחַיִל הַזֶּה, *My strength and the might of my hand made me all this wealth* (*Devarim* 8:17).

A Yid who places unconditional trust in Hashem can rest assured that Hashem will provide sufficiently for his needs, and has no reason to fret about his material future. This does not apply to spiritual needs, however, as Hillel HaZakein expressed, "If I am not for myself, who will be for me?" (*Avos* 1:14). With regard to spiritual matters, a person cannot rely on *bitachon*, and must invest maximum efforts to guarantee his spiritual future by serving Hashem genuinely. In this vein, Chazal (*Berachos* 60a) teach that the *pasuk*, אַשְׁרֵי אָדָם מְפַחֵד תָּמִיד, *Praiseworthy is the man who always fears* (*Mishlei* 28:14), is referring to *divrei Torah*, for a Yid must constantly be concerned about whether he is fulfilling his spiritual responsibilities.

External Torah

It is easy to see when a person is learning Torah in order to live according to its ways and draw from its *kedushah* to straighten his path in life. When one learns with this mindset, the Torah becomes a part of him and impacts him so that he continues along the proper path. In contrast, one who, *chas v'shalom*, learns Torah only as a means of acquiring knowledge, and does not link his learning to his conduct, remains unaffected by the sanctity of Torah.

The Gemara states (*Nedarim* 81a) that when the sages and prophets were asked, עַל מָה אָבְדָה הָאָרֶץ, *For what reason did the land perish?* (*Yirmiyah* 9:11), they could not respond, until they asked Hakadosh Baruch Hu Who replied: עַל עָזְבָם אֶת תּוֹרָתִי אֲשֶׁר נָתַתִּי לִפְנֵיהֶם וְלֹא שָׁמְעוּ בְקוֹלִי וְלֹא הָלְכוּ בָהּ, *Because of their forsaking My Torah that I put before them; moreover, they did not heed My voice nor follow it* (v. 12).

Chazal elaborate that it wasn't that Klal Yisrael of that era failed to learn Torah, but rather that "they did not recite the blessings on the Torah first."

The Ran (ibid.) asks why Hakadosh Baruch Hu punished Bnei Yisrael so severely for their failure to recite *Birchos HaTorah*, and he answers, based on Rabbeinu Yonah: "The Torah was not so important in their eyes that [they deemed] it worthy to recite a blessing over, as they did not engage in it *lishmah*, and therefore they were negligent in [reciting] the *berachah*."

Klal Yisrael during the era of the *Churban* learned Torah day and night, and yet they were condemned for their failure to learn *lishmah*. What was so serious about this omission that it led to their being punished with the *Churban HaBayis* and *galus*? Furthermore, why does the Gemara state that the first Beis HaMikdash was destroyed because Bnei Yisrael failed to recite *Birchos HaTorah*, when Yirmiyah HaNavi rebukes Klal Yisrael repeatedly throughout his *sefer* for transgressing the three cardinal sins of idolatry, immorality, and murder? Chazal also declare that the first Beis HaMikdash was destroyed because Bnei Yisrael transgressed the three cardinal sins (*Yoma* 9a).

R' Eliyahu Lopian explains that the question directed to the sages and prophets did not relate to the actual sin that Bnei Yisrael had transgressed, since it is known that the Beis HaMikdash was destroyed because of the three cardinal sins. Rather, the question was how Bnei Yisrael, who learned Torah day and night, had plummeted to the appalling level that they were capable of violating the three cardinal sins. Unable to fathom the answer themselves, the sages and prophets turned to Hakadosh Baruch Hu, Who explained that Bnei Yisrael had not assigned enough importance to *divrei Torah* and did not learn with the proper intentions. They engaged in Torah consistently, modeling incredible *hasmadah,* yet the *limud* remained external. They *studied* Torah, but did not *learn* it or internalize its sacred teachings, which is why the Torah failed to shield them from sin, and they fell to the spiritual abyss of committing the worst possible crimes.

This can be compared to an ill patient who takes medicine to lower his fever. While he may experience immediate relief, if he does not take the necessary steps to treat the illness, his fever will rise again after several hours. Only if he goes to the doctor to receive a clear diagnosis and the right prescription to treat his illness will he recover.

Klal Yisrael during the generations preceding the *Churban* experienced a drastic spiritual downfall, yet even the sages and prophets of the era were unable to isolate the reason for their fall, and they therefore could not offer the proper counsel to extricate Klal Yisrael from their spiritual mire. Only Hakadosh Baruch Hu was able to clarify that even Torah will not safeguard a person from sin if he learns it externally, *shelo lishmah.* Since Klal Yisrael stumbled in this regard and did not sufficiently value or internalize their *limud*, they sank to the lowest spiritual depths.

Just One Hour

R' Eliyahu Lopian related an awe-inspiring story about the Chofetz Chaim, who would seclude himself every evening in his attic and conduct a detailed *cheshbon hanefesh* regarding the day's events. One night, R' Yerucham Levovitz, who at the time was serving as *mashgiach* in the Radin Yeshivah, and R' Leib, the Chofetz Chaim's son, pressed their ears to the locked door to listen to what was unfolding in the *tzaddik's* sanctum. Listening closely, they heard the Chofetz Chaim recount every action he'd performed throughout the day, hour by hour. At one point, he reached an hour whose precise sequence of events he could not recall, and he began chastising himself sharply for his omission.

"Yisrael Meir! *Where is this hour*? What did you do then?"

R' Yerucham was so shaken by what he heard that he fled, while R' Leib continued listening as his father rebuked himself repeatedly about the "loss of this hour," until he dissolved in tears and wept copiously for the hour that he could never reclaim.

The Chofetz Chaim sought nothing from the material world and even expressed contempt for anything that smacked of physical pleasure. Yet the knowledge that a single hour of his time hadn't been properly utilized (in the Chofetz Chaim's perception) anguished him so deeply that he wept bitterly upon this loss. All his life, he thought only about his eternal future, and worried that he had not fulfilled his obligations. R' Eliyahu Lopian further related that he was once privileged to spend a Shabbos in the Chofetz Chaim's presence. During that Shabbos, he heard him discuss the concept of eternity. While he spoke in his trademark soft tone, everyone present could sense the blazing fire and passion burning within.

If a spiritual giant like the Chofetz Chaim, who was known never to waste a moment, could burst into tears and weep bitterly over a single hour that he could not fully recall, what are the implications for us? Taking responsibility for the present and utilizing our time to the maximum are not exalted spiritual attainments reserved for holy *tzaddikim*, but are incumbent upon each and every Yid! Never should we allow a moment of time to elapse without ensuring that we are fulfilling our mission as *ovdei Hashem*. True, we are lowly people who are frequently ensnared in the trap of the *yetzer hara*, which seeks to distract us from our true mission in life, yet this does not absolve us, now or in the future, of providing an accounting for every week, day, and hour: how we learned, how we davened, and how we served Hashem. It is simultaneously terrifying and awe-inspiring!

A Paradigm of Chashivus HaTorah: R' Chaim Kamil

In the last generation, we were privileged to have in our midst a *tzaddik* who was an exceptional *ben aliyah* and could provide a clear accounting of every moment in his day — my rebbi R' Chaim Kamil, whose *yahrtzeit* falls this Monday (15 Adar II). R' Chaim's *hasmadah* and *yegiah baTorah* were legendary, and he learned and reviewed every *blatt Gemara* again and again as if he were learning it for the very first time! No matter where he was or what time of day it was — during *seder* or *bein hasedarim,* in the middle of the *zman* or during *bein hazmanim,* during the week or on Erev Shabbos, Erev Pesach or Leil Purim, he utilized every hour and day of life to the maximum.

Beyond this, R' Chaim's greatness was perhaps most poignantly expressed in his appreciation and love of Torah, and he manifested that *chashivus* with every fiber of his being. If Rabbeinu Yonah's words above express that the fundamental flaw that brought about the *Churban HaBayis* was a lack of appreciation for *divrei Torah,* I would say that R' Chaim Kamil offset this failing with the supreme significance that he assigned to Torah. His reverence not only for *divrei Torah,* but for anything related to Torah, was astounding to behold. Every *sevarah,* every *kushya,* every *teirutz* was infinitely precious to him.

Shlomo HaMelech describes the pricelessness of the Torah with the words: אִם תְּבַקְשֶׁנָּה כַכָּסֶף וְכַמַּטְמוֹנִים תַּחְפְּשֶׂנָּה. אָז תָּבִין יִרְאַת ה׳ וְדַעַת אֱלֹהִים תִּמְצָא. כִּי ה׳ יִתֵּן חָכְמָה מִפִּיו דַּעַת וּתְבוּנָה, *If you seek it as [if it were] silver, if you search for it as [if it were] hidden treasures — then you will understand the fear of Hashem, and discover the knowledge of God. For Hashem grants wisdom; from His mouth [come] knowledge and understanding* (*Mishlei* 2:4-6).

One who genuinely feels that *divrei Torah* are treasures will surely sit and learn day and night, without interruption or distraction, and this will imbue him with the wisdom to plumb the depths of Torah. This was R' Chaim Kamil's greatness! He was one of the select *tzaddikim* whom Hashem planted among lowly men like us so we could learn and gain wisdom from his saintly ways, and we must indeed draw inspiration and ingrain his spiritual legacy deep inside our hearts.

May these words and resulting *chizuk* be *l'ilui nishmas* R' Chaim ben R' Yaakov HaKohen *zt"l.*

פרשת כי תשא
Parashas Ki Sisa

◆ *The Power of the Tzibbur*

כִּי תִשָּׂא אֶת רֹאשׁ בְּנֵי יִשְׂרָאֵל לִפְקֻדֵיהֶם וְנָתְנוּ אִישׁ כֹּפֶר נַפְשׁוֹ לַה׳ בִּפְקֹד אֹתָם ... זֶה יִתְּנוּ כָּל הָעֹבֵר עַל הַפְּקֻדִים מַחֲצִית הַשֶּׁקֶל בְּשֶׁקֶל הַקֹּדֶשׁ עֶשְׂרִים גֵּרָה הַשֶּׁקֶל מַחֲצִית הַשֶּׁקֶל תְּרוּמָה לַה׳ ... הֶעָשִׁיר לֹא יַרְבֶּה וְהַדַּל לֹא יַמְעִיט מִמַּחֲצִית הַשָּׁקֶל.

When you take a census of the Children of Israel according to their numbers, every man shall give Hashem an atonement for his soul when counting them ... This shall they give — everyone who passes through the census — a half-shekel of the sacred shekel, the shekel is twenty geras, half a shekel as a portion to Hashem ... The wealthy shall not increase and the destitute shall not decrease from half a shekel (*Shemos* 30:12-15).

Rashi explains that the *machatzis hashekel* was used to construct the *adanim* of the Mishkan. The Torah commands each and every member of Bnei Yisrael to donate precisely half a shekel, and "the wealthy shall not increase and the destitute shall not decrease from half a shekel."

What distinguished the *adanim* from all the other elements in the Mishkan? While, as Rashi explains, the *terumah* Bnei Yisrael donated for the Mishkan and its vessels reflected each individual's generosity of heart, the *terumah* for the *adanim* was a fixed amount paid equally by everyone. The prohibition of giving less than a *machatzis hashekel* is understandable, since it ensures the availability of sufficient funds to craft the *adanim*, but why did the Torah prevent the rich person from giving a larger donation — which was allowed for all other parts of the Mishkan?

The Shechinah Rests Among a United Klal Yisrael

The Rosh Yeshivah R' Chaim Shmulevitz explains[10] that the Mishkan, which was the designated resting place of the *Shechinah*, needed to be built by Klal Yisrael collectively. As long as even a single item was donated equally by all, it could be said that the Mishkan had been built by Klal Yisrael. If, however, one person were to donate more than another, the result would be that one Yid's portion in the *adanim* would be greater than another's, which would negate the absolute unity of this donation.

If so, why did this principle not apply to all parts and vessels of the Mishkan? Why were Bnei Yisrael prohibited to give more or less than a *machatzis hashekel* only in the case of the *adanim*?

R' Chaim explains that the Torah was more stringent with regard to the *adanim*, which formed the very foundations of the Mishkan. The qualification that every member of Klal Yisrael must contribute equally toward the *adanim* established the foundation of the Mishkan as one of *achdus* and *ahavas Yisrael*, which are the positive qualities that draw the *Shechinah* upon Bnei Yisrael.

This concept is reflected in numerous sources, in both the Torah and the teachings of Chazal. The *pasuk* states (*Devarim* 33:5): וַיְהִי בִישֻׁרוּן מֶלֶךְ בְּהִתְאַסֵּף רָאשֵׁי עָם יַחַד שִׁבְטֵי יִשְׂרָאֵל, *He became King over Yeshurun when the numbers of the nation gathered — the tribes of Israel in unity.*

Citing the *pasuk* (*Yeshayah* 60:19), וְהָיָה לָךְ ה׳ לְאוֹר עוֹלָם, *Hashem*

10. *Sichos Mussar, Maalas HaKlal.*

will be an eternal light for you, *Midrash Tanchuma* (*Nitzavim* 2) elaborates: "When? When you are all a single assembly, as it is written: חַיִּים כֻּלְּכֶם הַיּוֹם, *You are all alive today* (*Devarim* 4:4). If a person takes a bundle of reeds, can he break them?! But if he were to take only a single reed, even an infant could break it. Similarly, Yisrael are not redeemed until they all become a single assembly, as it is written (*Yirmiyah* 50:4): בַּיָּמִים הָהֵמָּה וּבָעֵת הַהִיא נְאֻם ה' יָבֹאוּ בְנֵי יִשְׂרָאֵל הֵמָּה וּבְנֵי יְהוּדָה יַחְדָּו, *In those days and at that time — the word of Hashem — the Children of Israel will come, they together with the Children of Yehudah*. When they are united, they are able to receive the Divine Presence."

An individual Yid, even a great *tzaddik*, is like a single reed that can be easily bent and broken. Yet when Klal Yisrael are united, they become like a thick bundle of reeds that cannot be broken all at once. The above *pesukim* underscore that the *Shechinah* will only dwell among Bnei Yisrael and the Final Redemption will only arrive after we have achieved this *achdus*, which makes us unbreakable.

Conversely, when friction and disunity fester among us, we expel the *Shechinah* from our midst. Regarding the verse, וַיְהִי בִישֻׁרוּן מֶלֶךְ בְּהִתְאַסֵּף רָאשֵׁי עָם יַחַד שִׁבְטֵי יִשְׂרָאֵל, *He became King over Yeshurun when the numbers of the nation gathered — the tribes of Israel in unity*, the *Daas Zekeinim MiBaalei HaTosafos* comments: "Only when Yisrael are united in brotherhood and friendship does Hakadosh Baruch Hu rule over them. However, in times of discord and strife, they act as if Hakadosh Baruch Hu does not rule over them."

One Among the Klal

R' Chaim added that this alone is sufficient reason for a person to strive to be part of the *tzibbur*, so that the *zechus harabbim* will safeguard him from harm.

Regarding Yaakov's encounter with the *Sar shel Eisav*, the Torah states: וַיִּוָּתֵר יַעֲקֹב לְבַדּוֹ וַיֵּאָבֵק אִישׁ עִמּוֹ, *Yaakov was left alone and a man wrestled with him* (*Bereishis* 32:25). The *Sar shel Eisav* dared to approach Yaakov and engage him in combat only when he was alone. When a person is isolated, the forces of evil unite to harm him in various ways, such as through temptation or difficult challenges, and can easily vanquish him. Therefore, one who is not shielded by the *zechus harabbim* is constantly in a state of peril.

Even angels of destruction are empowered to harm a person only when he is alone, as Chazal teach: "To one, he appears and harms. To two, he appears, but does not harm. To three, he does not appear at all" (*Berachos* 43b). The larger the *tzibbur*, the more it undermines the strength of harmful angels. Consequently, when a Yid endeavors to always bind himself to a *tzibbur*, the *zechus harabbim* will protect him, and the *yetzer hara* will no longer be able to harm him.

The Power of the Tzibbur in Learning

While the power of the *tzibbur* positively impacts the fulfillment of all mitzvos, with regard to Torah study the power of the *tzibbur* is immense, and is, in fact, an essential aspect of *limud Torah*. Regarding the *pasuk*, וַיִּחַן שָׁם יִשְׂרָאֵל נֶגֶד הָהָר, *And Israel encamped there, opposite the mountain* (*Shemos* 19:2), Rashi famously comments: "Like one man with one heart." The Ohr HaChaim adds that this *pasuk* is conveying that *achdus* forms the groundwork for receiving the Torah, and without this vital preparation, Hakadosh Baruch Hu would not have given the Torah to Klal Yisrael.

Chazal frequently highlight the importance of *limud Torah b'tzibbur*. One famous example is this Gemara (*Taanis* 7a):

> R' Chama said [in the name of R'] Chanina: What is the meaning of that which is written (*Mishlei* 27:17): בַּרְזֶל בְּבַרְזֶל יָחַד, *Iron sharpens iron [so one man sharpens another]*? This is to teach you that just as in the case of this iron blade, one blade sharpens another, so, too, two Torah scholars sharpen the minds of each other with their debates in halachah.
>
> Rabbah bar bar Chanah said: Why are the words of Torah compared to fire, as it is said (*Yirmiyah* 23:29): הֲלוֹא כֹה דְבָרִי כָּאֵשׁ נְאֻם ה', *Is My word not like fire, says Hashem?* This is to teach you that just as fire does not ignite from a single piece

of wood, so, too, the words of Torah are not retained by someone who studies on his own.

And this is in essence what R' Yose bar Chanina said: What is the meaning of that which is written: חֶרֶב אֶל הַבַּדִּים וְנֹאָלוּ, *A sword upon those who are alone and they shall become fools*? A sword upon the enemies of such Torah scholars, who engage in Torah study on their own. And not only that, but they become foolish as well, as it is said in that verse: וְנֹאָלוּ, *and they shall become fools*. And not only that, but they sin as well.

All the *talmidim* of the yeshivah were privileged to watch R' Chaim coming to the *beis midrash* every Shabbos after *Kiddush* and learning for many hours together with the *tzibbur.*

The Tzibbur as a Protective Force

If the *zechus harabbim* can shelter a Yid from all evil, then learning Torah *b'tzibbur* — which is an integral aspect of *limud Torah* — causes this *zechus harabbim* to multiply exponentially.

The Gemara teaches: "Rav said: A person should never absent himself from the study hall — even for one moment" (*Beitzah* 24b). On a simple level, this can be understood as an exhortation to the *ben Torah* not to miss any time in the *beis midrash*, lest he may lose out on a *chiddush* that will be presented then. R' Chaim indicated, however, that there is another important lesson to be learned from this Gemara.

When a *ben Torah* sits in the *beis midrash* together with the *tzibbur*, the colossal *zechus* of this gathering of *lomdei Torah* shields him from harm. In contrast, when he learns in isolation, he is not enveloped in the *zechus* of dozens or hundreds of *lomdei Torah*, and even if he invests all his efforts into learning, he will not access the tremendous *zechus* of *Torah b'tzibbur*.

Klal Yisrael bore witness to the phenomenal *zechus* of the Mir Yeshivah during the Holocaust years, when six million of our brethren perished *al kiddush Hashem*. While their families and friends were being tortured and gassed, and entire towns and communities were being wiped out, the Mir Yeshivah was saved practically in its entirety, as its *talmidim* made their way across land and sea to safe shores. It is clear that the merit of their salvation was rooted in the exceptional *limud Torah b'tzibbur*, amid friendship and love, which has always characterized the Mir Yeshivah.

May we all unite in love and brotherhood, which draw the *Shechinah* upon us, and may we merit to accept the Torah "like one man with one heart" and hone each other's minds as we learn together in the *beis midrash* as a harmonious *tzibbur*.

פרשת ויקהל
Parashas Vayakhel

⟫ *Initiative Breeds Success*

וַיָּבֹאוּ כָּל אִישׁ אֲשֶׁר נְשָׂאוֹ לִבּוֹ וְכֹל אֲשֶׁר נָדְבָה רוּחוֹ אֹתוֹ הֵבִיאוּ אֶת תְּרוּמַת ה׳ לִמְלֶאכֶת אֹהֶל מוֹעֵד וּלְכָל עֲבֹדָתוֹ וּלְבִגְדֵי הַקֹּדֶשׁ.

Every man whose heart inspired him came; and everyone whose spirit motivated him brought the portion of Hashem for the work of the Tent of Meeting, for all its labor and for the sacred vestments (*Shemos* 35:21).

Regarding the words וַיָּבֹאוּ כָּל אִישׁ אֲשֶׁר נְשָׂאוֹ לִבּוֹ, *Every man whose heart inspired him came*, the Ramban writes:

> This is referring to the wise ones who performed the labor, for we do not find the concept of *nesius halev* (an inspired heart) attributed to the donors; rather, *nedivus* (generosity) is usually the word used to describe them. The reason [these laborers are described as those] *whose heart inspired him* was to draw them to the labor, for none among them had studied these crafts from an artisan or was trained to perform these skilled labors. Yet they discovered the inherent capacity to do it: וַיִּגְבַּהּ לִבּוֹ בְּדַרְכֵי ה׳, *His heart was elevated in the*

ways of Hashem (*II Divrei HaYamim* 17:6), to come before Moshe and tell him, "I will do all that my master speaks."

An Inspired Heart Versus a Generous Spirit

The two qualities of *nesius halev* and *nedivus* were both expressed in the building of the Mishkan. *Nesius halev* was manifested by those who engaged in building the Mishkan and fashioning its vessels, while *nedivus* was displayed by those who donated their wealth to the Mishkan.

Examining these two qualities, we discern a vast disparity between them. *Nedivus*, generosity, is limited, as even the most benevolent person cannot donate what he does not possess. Only one who owned the required items was able to donate to the Mishkan, as the Torah states (*Shemos* 35:23-24): וְכָל אִישׁ אֲשֶׁר נִמְצָא אִתּוֹ תְּכֵלֶת וְאַרְגָּמָן וְתוֹלַעַת שָׁנִי ... וְכֹל אֲשֶׁר נִמְצָא אִתּוֹ עֲצֵי שִׁטִּים לְכָל מְלֶאכֶת הָעֲבֹדָה הֵבִיאוּ, *Every man with whom was found turquoise, purple, and scarlet wool ... and everyone with whom there was acacia wood for any work of the labor brought it.* Rabbeinu Bechaye explains (v. 20) that "*techeiles* and *argaman* were not ubiquitous among all, and only a few distinguished people possessed them." Similarly, he writes, "There were very few who possessed *atzei shittim*."

In contrast, the quality of *nesius halev*, an inspired heart, is unlimited, and anyone who wished to build the Mishkan and craft its vessels was welcome to volunteer. Bnei Yisrael had just emerged from 210 years of oppressive slave labor and persecution, and none of them were trained in the relevant skills or possessed the knowledge and proficiency to perform these delicate labors. The Ramban (ibid. 31:2) notes that "in Mitzrayim, Bnei Yisrael were encumbered with harsh labor, with bricks and mortar, and they never studied to be silversmiths or goldsmiths or to carve fine stones, and they never even saw these things." Nevertheless, many among Klal Yisrael eagerly volunteered to perform the labor required to build the Mishkan, and they succeeded.

What prompted these individuals to approach Moshe Rabbeinu and present themselves as qualified for the task? None of them had ever tried their hand at such delicate crafts, and they sorely lacked the expertise and finesse to perform these labors effectively.

The answer is a fundamental lesson that is relevant to each and every Yid, every day of life: וַיִּגְבַּהּ לִבּוֹ בְּדַרְכֵי ה׳ — their hearts were elevated in the ways of Hashem! (*II Divrei HaYamim* 17:6) Even if someone lacked artistic skill, having never lifted a silversmith's tools or an embroidery needle and having never been trained to carve wood or hew stone, if his heart was inspired, he could discover the latent talent that would enable him to engage in these sacred labors and succeed.

Taking Initiative

R' Yerucham noted[11] that most of the world's wealthiest entrepreneurs did not inherit their fortunes or accumulate them by scrimping and saving pennies. Rather, they became rich by taking initiative — innovating and developing new concepts and ideas that generated massive revenue. Only a person who believes in himself can succeed, whereas one who lacks initiative and confidence is unlikely to ever become wealthy.

This is the lesson derived from the *pasuk*: וַיָּבֹאוּ כָּל אִישׁ אֲשֶׁר נְשָׂאוֹ לִבּוֹ, *Every man whose heart inspired him came*. Those with the quality of *nesius halev* were inspired to perform the intricate labors required for the Mishkan and its vessels, regardless of their lack of training. They took the initiative and committed to do the job, without knowing exactly how they would do it, and this is why they succeeded at their task despite never having learned the trade and never having acquired the requisite skills.

Here lies a significant difference between earlier and later generations, added R' Yerucham. In earlier times, people took initiative even when they knew the task at hand was beyond their capacity to achieve. Yet this very initiative empowered them to succeed and ultimately catapulted them to greatness. In contrast, people today lack spiritual ambition and don't take sufficient initiative, which is why they remain spiritually weak and flawed.

---

11. *Daas Torah* Vol. 2, *Vayakhel-Pekudei*, *Biurim*.

If we do not rouse ourselves to take spiritual initiative — each person on his level and according to his ability — we will never achieve our goals. A *bachur* who doesn't aspire to master *Sidrei Nashim* and *Nezikin* won't gain proficiency in even one *masechta*. A Yid must constantly strive for the summit of the mountain even when he is still at its base, as Chazal teach, "A person is obligated to say, 'When will my actions reach the actions of Avraham, Yitzchak, and Yaakov?'" (*Yalkut Shimoni Va'eschanan*, 830).

This is not merely advantageous, but an actual obligation, because only if we strive to attain the exalted heights of our holy *Avos* will we at the very least achieve our own potential. Without this ambition, we'll forever be stuck at the foot of the mountain with no way to elevate ourselves.

The foundation of any achievement, whether material or spiritual, is *nesius halev* — the lofty feeling that one is capable and worthy of success. Each and every one of us should commit to attaining more, to climbing higher and higher with no limit, as this is what will guarantee our success and *siyata diShmaya*.

פרשת פקודי
Parashas Pekudei

A Building of Mesirus Nefesh

וּבְצַלְאֵל בֶּן אוּרִי בֶן חוּר לְמַטֵּה יְהוּדָה עָשָׂה אֵת כָּל אֲשֶׁר צִוָּה ה׳ אֶת מֹשֶׁה, וְאִתּוֹ אָהֳלִיאָב בֶּן אֲחִיסָמָךְ לְמַטֵּה דָן חָרָשׁ וְחֹשֵׁב וְרֹקֵם בַּתְּכֵלֶת וּבָאַרְגָּמָן וּבְתוֹלַעַת הַשָּׁנִי וּבַשֵּׁשׁ.
Betzalel, son of Uri son of Chur, of the tribe of Yehudah, did everything that Hashem commanded Moshe. With him was Oholiav, son of Achisamach, of the tribe of Dan, a carver, weaver, and embroiderer, with turquoise, purple, and scarlet wool, and with linen (*Shemos* 38:22-23).

Whenever Betzalel's name is mentioned in the Torah, it is written together with his father's and grandfather's names: Betzalel ben Uri ben Chur. Yet the very same *pesukim* refer to Betzalel's assistant Oholiav merely as "Oholiav ben Achisamach" without ever referencing his grandfather. What was Chur's unique merit that made him deserve this repeated honorable mention in the Torah?

Chazal (*Shemos Rabbah* 48:3) pose this question in connection with the *pasuk* in *Parashas Vayakhel*: וַיֹּאמֶר מֹשֶׁה אֶל בְּנֵי יִשְׂרָאֵל רְאוּ קָרָא ה׳ בְּשֵׁם בְּצַלְאֵל בֶּן אוּרִי בֶן חוּר, *Moshe said to the Children of Israel, "See,*

Hashem has proclaimed by name, Betzalel, son of Uri son of Chur, of the tribe of Yehudah (*Shemos* 35:30).

> Why did he see fit to mention Chur here? At the time when Bnei Yisrael wished to serve idols, [Chur] gave his life for Hakadosh Baruch Hu and did not allow them to do so, and they rose and killed him. Hakadosh Baruch Hu said to him, "I pledge that I shall repay you." This can be compared to a king whose legions rebelled against him, until his general rose and fought against them. He rebuked them, "You are rebelling against your king!" Yet they rose and killed him. The king declared, "Had he given me money, would I not need to repay him? All the more so, since he gave me his soul, what can I do for him? All his children and descendants shall be appointed as dukes and lords."
>
> Similarly, when Bnei Yisrael made the Golden Calf, Chur rose and sacrificed his soul for Hakadosh Baruch Hu. [Hashem] said to him, "I promise you that all the children who descend from you, I will elevate them to have a good name in the world," as it is written, *See, Hashem has proclaimed by name, Betzalel.*

Chur sacrificed his life in his battle to sanctify Hashem's Name and prevent Bnei Yisrael from forming the *eigel hazahav* (*Sanhedrin* 7a), and Hashem rewarded him by imbuing his grandson Betzalel with "wisdom and knowledge of Hashem" to craft the vessels of the Beis HaMikdash. Therefore, wherever Betzalel is mentioned in the Torah, he is always referred to as "ben Uri ben Chur."

R' Eliyahu Lopian writes[12] that Chur was rewarded measure for measure: He acted with *mesirus nefesh* to prevent Bnei Yisrael from fashioning the *eigel*, and his grandson Betzalel later showed *mesirus nefesh* in building the Mishkan and its vessels, which atone for the *cheit ha'eigel.* Indeed, regarding the words וַיַּעַשׂ בְּצַלְאֵל, *and Betzalel made*, Rashi writes, "Because he gave his soul for the labor more than other wise ones, it was called on his name" (*Shemos* 37:1).

We see, then, that the Torah's purpose in repeatedly describing

---

12. *Lev Eliyahu, Hashpa'as HaKedushah - B'Nedivus HaLev.*

Betzalel as "ben Uri ben Chur" is not merely to document his illustrious lineage, but also to convey that Betzalel perpetuated the legacy and merit of his grandfather's *mesirus nefesh*. This quality was transmitted from generation to generation, from Chur, who "gave his soul" for Hakadosh Baruch Hu, to Betzalel, who "gave his soul" for the work of the Mishkan.

The *Meshech Chochmah* adds that this idea is also reflected in the Torah's description of Chur as "of the tribe of Yehudah" (ibid. 35:30). The *Tosefta* states (*Berachos* 4:16): "Why did Yehudah merit royalty? Because he sanctified the Name of Hakadosh Baruch Hu. When the *shevatim* stood at the sea, this one said, 'I am entering [the sea],' and this one said, 'I am entering [the sea].' The tribe of Yehudah leaped up and entered first, sanctifying the Name of Hakadosh Baruch Hu."

The Torah associates both Betzalel and his grandfather Chur with Shevet Yehudah to show that their self-sacrifice was rooted in their holy ancestry, as Shevet Yehudah were willing to give their lives in order to sanctify the Name of Hashem.

The Everlasting Mishkan

Why, Chazal wonder, does Moshe introduce Betzalel to Bnei Yisrael with the unusual statement, רְאוּ קָרָא ה׳ בְּשֵׁם בְּצַלְאֵל בֶּן אוּרִי בֶן חוּר, *See, Hashem has proclaimed by name, Betzalel, son of Uri son of Chur* (*Shemos* 30:35).

The Gemara teaches: "When the first Beis HaMikdash was built, the Ohel Moed [Mishkan], its beams, its hooks, its bars, its pillars, and its sockets were hidden ... under the tunnels of the Temple Sanctuary" (*Sotah* 9a).

The Mishkan built by Betzalel was hidden deep underground beneath the Heichal, and thus was never destroyed or lost throughout the ages. Moreover, it wasn't merely the gold, silver, and copper metals — which can endure for millennia — that were preserved in the depths of the earth; even the wooden *kerashim* never decomposed or rotted, as the Torah states: וְעָשִׂיתָ אֶת הַקְּרָשִׁים לַמִּשְׁכָּן עֲצֵי שִׁטִּים עֹמְדִים, *You shall make the planks of the Tabernacle of acacia wood, standing erect* (*Shemos* 26:15). Chazal teach, "Lest you say that their promise is gone and their hope is ruined, the *pasuk* says *omdim*, standing, for they endure forever and ever"(*Yoma* 72b).

The permanence of the Mishkan is rooted in the merit of Betzalel, who fashioned it with *mesirus nefesh*, with supreme *kedushah*, and with an exclusive focus and intention *l'shem Shamayim*.

Unlike the Mishkan, the first Beis HaMikdash was not built entirely with *mesirus nefesh* and *kedushah*, as the servants of Chiram, king of Tzur, were engaged to chop down the cedar and cypress trees used to build its walls, and Chiram's builders, along with the people of Gival, helped hew the stones for the Beis HaMikdash, as the *pasuk* states, וַיִּפְסְלוּ בֹּנֵי שְׁלֹמֹה וּבֹנֵי חִירוֹם וְהַגִּבְלִים וַיָּכִינוּ הָעֵצִים וְהָאֲבָנִים לִבְנוֹת הַבָּיִת, *The builders of Shlomo, the builders of Chiram, and the Gevalites carved the stones, and they prepared the wood and the stones to build the Temple* (*I Melachim* 5:32). Because the first Beis HaMikdash was not built entirely *l'shem Shamayim*, it could not endure eternally, so it was ultimately destroyed and burned. Similarly, while the sacred vessels used in the Mishkan were hidden along with the Mishkan itself, the vessels of the Beis HaMikdash were stolen by the gentiles and carried into exile to Bavel along with the people. While the vessels of the Beis HaMikdash were sullied by gentile hands, the vessels of the Mishkan were never defiled, because Betzalel had dedicated his heart and soul to ensure that they were crafted with absolute purity and the proper intentions, and this extra element of *kedushah* counteracted any force of *tumah*.

The Torah therefore introduces Betzalel with the unusual expression of רְאוּ, *see*. "Take heed!" the Torah is saying. "See from where the eternal strength of the Mishkan derives! See the timeless impact of the actions of Betzalel ben Uri ben Chur, who sacrificed his life to sanctify Hashem's Name and whose legacy endures forever."

A Mishkan for Hashem's Sake

The permanence of the Mishkan and its vessels is not exclusively in the merit of Betzalel. Rather, the Torah clarifies that the sanctity of the Mishkan preceded his involvement. In the original command to donate to the Mishkan, Hashem instructed, וְיִקְחוּ לִי תְּרוּמָה, *And let them take for Me a portion* (*Shemos* 25:2), and Rashi comments, "for Me, for My Name."

R' Ovadiah of Bartenura (ibid.) elaborates, "For Me, meaning sanctified for My Name." All contributions to the Mishkan and its vessels needed to be dedicated entirely for Hashem's sake. Similarly, regarding the words מִזְבַּח אֲדָמָה תַּעֲשֶׂה לִי וגו׳ וְאִם מִזְבַּח אֲבָנִים תַּעֲשֶׂה לִי, *An Altar of earth shall you make for Me ... And when you make for Me an Altar of stones* (ibid. 20:21-22), Rashi comments, "the beginning of its making shall be for My Name." Every action involved in the building of the Mishkan and its vessels had to be *l'shem Shamayim*, from the very first step of collecting the donations to the final touches of the Mishkan. This sheds light on Chazal's teaching, "Every place where it says לִי, *for Me*, it refers to something that endures forever and ever" *(Sifri, Bamidbar,* 34). Only something that is crafted from beginning to end *l'shem Shamayim* can endure eternally.

The Gemara recounts the famous story of R' Chiya, who is praised for ensuring that Torah would never be forgotten by the Jewish people (*Bava Metzia* 85b). R' Chiya planted flaxseed, and after it grew, he wove it into nets. He used the nets to catch deer, slaughtered the deer, and distributed the meat to paupers, and then used the animal hides to fashion parchment on which he wrote the five Chumashim of the Torah. With this sacred scroll in hand, he traveled to one city, where he taught five children each one Chumash from the text and another six children each one *seder* of the Mishnah by heart. He then instructed each child to teach his friend what he had learned, before continuing to the next city to repeat the process. The Gemara concludes with the praise, "About this Rebbi said, 'How great are the actions of Chiya.'"

Why did R' Chiya go through the entire process of planting flaxseed to fashion the parchment, when he could surely have purchased complete *sefarim*, or at least ready-made parchment for scrolls, or at the very least animal hides, in order to prepare the parchment? This would have saved him months of waiting for the seeds to sprout, and many hours of work cultivating the crop, weaving the nets, trapping and slaughtering the animals, and skinning the hides just to prepare the parchment.

The Maharsha (*Chiddushei Aggados* ibid.) answers: "All these actions done for Torah were done from the beginning solely for the sake of Heaven, with no other intention that was not exclusively for the sake of Heaven. For if he had purchased an animal for its hide, the seller would have had his own interests; but from the very start of growing the flaxseed his intention was for the sake of Torah and mitzvos ... and this is how [he ensured] that Torah would not be forgotten."

To guarantee that the Torah would be preserved eternally, R' Chiya made every effort to ensure that each aspect of his plan would be performed exclusively *l'shem Shamayim*. Even if he had purchased the parchment from a God-fearing Jew, the fact that the seller was profiting from the sale would introduce an element that was not entirely *l'shem Shamayim*, which would taint the purity of his endeavor to teach Torah. R' Chiya therefore resolved to perform every aspect of the labor himself — from planting the flaxseed to teaching the children Torah.

Just as Moshe Rabbeinu announced, "See, Hashem has proclaimed by name Betzalel" to highlight the greatness of actions performed *l'shem Shamayim*, so, too, Rebbi declared, "How great are the actions of Chiya" to highlight the greatness of his efforts to disseminate Torah among Yisrael. The unrivaled dedication and perseverance that R' Chiya manifested to teach Torah *l'shem Shamayim* guaranteed that "Torah would not be forgotten from Yisrael," just like the Mishkan, which, Chazal proclaim, stands forever and ever.

Kedushah Is Sustained

Another lesson taught by R' Chiya is that Torah must be learned from a *sefer* written with *kedushah*. R' Chaim of Volozhin cautioned that one who learns from a *sefer* written by a dishonorable person is unlikely to succeed in his learning. Similarly, the halachah is that a *Sefer Torah* written by an apostate must be burned (*Gittin* 45b), for a *Sefer Torah* written with *tumah* can taint the one who learns it. It goes without saying that studying *sefarim* authored by people with impure *hashkafos* is strictly prohibited, as the messages imbued within the words can wreak grave damage on the reader's *neshamah.*

There was a great *tzaddik* by the name of R' Chaim Leib of Stavisk who refused to allow any newspaper past his threshold, to avoid defiling the purity of his home. Once, when he needed to peruse a printed notice regarding possible *chametz* on Pesach, he asked someone to show him the newspaper through the window so it would not penetrate the spiritual fortress of his home. After reading the notice, he immediately hurried to wash his hands before resuming his learning.

Personally, I do not allow any newspapers, even *chareidi* publications, into this room. There are bookshelves here filled with *sefarim,* and I imagine their venerable authors emerging from their tomes and watching me ... I do not insist on this in the rest of the house, as I have not yet reached the level of that *tzaddik;* but at least here in this room, I will not allow impurity to penetrate.

It is essential to preserve the sanctity of any place where Torah is learned. When we avoid speaking idle words in a *beis midrash,* the place receives a bounty of *kedushah* and the one learning there merits immense *siyata diShmaya* in all his actions. The more he endeavors to sanctify the place, the greater the *kedushah* that will dwell there and penetrate his heart and his learning.

The paradigm of this is Har Sinai, which received an unprecedented, spectacular bounty of *kedushah* at the time of Mattan Torah. While the events at Sinai were historic, the *kedushah* that settled upon the mountain was transient and did not endure (*Shemos Rabbah* 46:3). Immediately after Kabbalas HaTorah, Har Sinai descended from its glory to become one among many mountains, as the Gemara relates (*Taanis* 21b), "We find in regard to Har Sinai that as long as the *Shechinah* hovered upon it, the Torah said: *Even the sheep and the cattle shall not graze next to that mountain* (*Shemos* 34:3). [Yet] once the *Shechinah* departed from it, the Torah said: *When the blast of the shofar extends, they may go up on the mountain* (ibid. 19:13)."

Why was the *kedushah* of Har Sinai so fleeting? Wasn't the heart-stopping event of Mattan Torah and the supreme bounty of *kedushah* that accompanied it powerful enough that it should have been retained eternally on the mountain where Torah was given to Bnei Yisrael?

The *kedushah* that enveloped Har Sinai at the time of Hashem's revelation upon the mountain was spontaneous, occurring without any preparation or groundwork, which made it unsustainable. As soon as the *Shechinah* departed, therefore, the *kedushah* surrounding it dissipated as well. In contrast, a Yid who prepares himself to accept and absorb Torah, and focuses on upholding the Torah and fulfilling *mitzvos l'shem Shamayim*, acquires *kedushah* that remains eternally.

Starting Out With Kedushah

If a person truly wishes to succeed in Torah, not only must he prime himself to absorb *kedushah*, he must also begin his daily *limud Torah* in a state of *kedushah* and *taharah*. The Vilna Gaon, in his commentary on *Sefer Mishlei* (1:23), notes that the desire to speak idle words is even greater than the craving for food. The pleasure that a person has from speaking idle words and *leitzanus* surpasses the pleasure that he derives from committing the worst *aveiros*, even though it involves no physical pleasure.

The reason for this is as follows. For every action that a person does, whether positive or negative, he receives an extra thrust from *Shamayim*, as the Mishnah teaches, "One mitzvah leads to another mitzvah, and one sin leads to another sin" (*Avos* 4:2). When a person does a mitzvah he receives a boost of *kedushah* that causes him to do another mitzvah, and the opposite is true for an *aveirah*.

Chazal express this when they say (*Yoma* 39a), regarding the *pasuk*: וְלֹא תִטַּמְּאוּ בָּהֶם וְנִטְמֵתֶם בָּם, *Do not contaminate yourselves through them lest you become contaminated through them* (*Vayikra* 11:43): "If a person contaminates himself a little, he is contaminated a great deal; if he contaminates himself down below, he is contaminated above; if he contaminates himself in this world, he is contaminated in the World to Come." Conversely, Chazal continue, regarding the next *pasuk,* וְהִתְקַדִּשְׁתֶּם וִהְיִיתֶם קְדֹשִׁים, *You are to sanctify yourselves and you shall be holy*: "If a person sanctifies himself a little, he is sanctified a great deal; if he sanctifies himself down below, he is sanctified above; if he sanctifies himself in this world, he is sanctified in the World to Come."

Rabbeinu Yonah (*Shaarei Teshuvah* 3:14) cites Chazal's statement that "just as the reward for Torah study is greater than that of all other mitzvos, the punishment of one who neglects it is greater than that of all other sins." The greatest mitzvah of all is *talmud Torah,* while its diametric opposite is idle talk and *leitzanus.* Therefore, just as the sanctity that is produced by *limud Torah* is like a flowing fountain, reaching and affecting everything, the same is true of the impurity that is caused by idle words and *leitzanus.*

When a Yid sanctifies himself here in this world, he draws a colossal wave of bounty and sanctity upon himself from on High. The more he endeavors to sanctify himself, the farther away from himself he banishes the spirit of impurity, because *tumah* automatically flees any crack or crevice that *kedushah* enters. While this premise is always true, its expression depends on a person's conduct. If one begins his efforts *l'shem Shamayim,* with *kedushah* and *taharah,* then he will be rewarded with a bounty of *kedushah* from *Shamayim.* If, however, he fills his mind and heart with newspapers, gossip, and heretical works, or uses his mouth to speak idle words whose *tumah* is like a fountain, he will enter the *beis midrash* with his mind and lips brimming with impurity, and he will not succeed in his learning. Aside from plugging up the heart, these profane concepts and words draw a spirit of impurity upon the person that prevent him from connecting to our holy Torah.

There are *bachurim* who complain that learning is difficult and that they don't see *hatzlachah* in their learning. Such a *bachur* should introspect and evaluate his actions before *seder*. Does he speak idle words? Does he peruse inappropriate material? These things sully the heart and prevent one from succeeding in learning.

Kedushah and *taharah* are the prerequisites of *limud Torah*! A *ben Torah's* day begins with *limud Torah,* which is the foundation upon which he builds his spiritual character and his greatness in Torah. Yet the success of his learning depends on its beginning in a state of *kedushah* and *taharah*. If he sanctifies himself little by little from below, then he will be showered with a bounty of *kedushah and taharah* from above.

The Rosh Yeshivah concluded:

We are now only in the final days before *bein hazmanim*, and we must recall that, wherever we are, our sacred duty is to maintain *kedushah* and *taharah* in our conduct and comportment. If someone sees a *bachur* in the street, he should be able to exclaim, "That's a Mirrer *bachur*!" People do not evaluate a *bachur* by asking a *kushya* on what he learned, but by observing his behavior.

The Gemara interprets the words וְאָהַבְתָּ אֵת ה׳ אֱלֹהֶיךָ, *And you shall love Hashem your God* (*Devarim* 6:5), to mean: "The Name of Heaven should become beloved through you. You should learn, review, and serve *talmidei chachamim*, and your dealings with people should be in a pleasant manner. What do people say of such a person? "Fortunate is his father who taught him Torah; fortunate is his rebbi who taught him Torah" (*Yoma* 86a).

One should never, Heaven forbid, conduct himself in the opposite manner, which would cause people to say, "Woe unto that person who learned Torah; woe unto his father who taught him Torah; woe unto his rebbi who taught him Torah" (ibid.).

During the *zman*, when a *bachur* spends his day learning in the *beis midrash*, while exerting extra effort to act with *kedushah, taharah*, and *derech eretz*, this conduct continues naturally even when he is away from the *beis midrash*, as he still carries the sanctity of the *beis midrash* with him. During the days of *bein hazmanim*, however, the streets present a greater challenge because one is no longer protected by the spiritual shield of the *beis midrash*.

I have been gravely distressed to notice a growing phenomenon of *bachurim* and *avreichim* walking outside with their suits and yarmulkes, but without hats. This detracts from the person's identity as a *ben yeshivah*! The difference between one who walks around dressed in the attire of a *ben yeshivah* and one who walks without it is the difference between a *kiddush Hashem* and a *chillul Hashem, chas v'shalom.* The obligation to conduct ourselves with *kedushah* and *taharah* is absolute and unconditional!

Anyone who allows himself to be lax in this regard disconnects himself from the *bnei yeshivah,* and if he does this repeatedly, it becomes permissible in his eyes, especially when he looks around and sees that "everyone else is doing it." To avoid this, it is essential to conduct ourselves with extra caution and *tznius* in these matters, and Hakadosh Baruch Hu should help that in the merit of our extra efforts to conduct ourselves with *kedushah* and *taharah,* the *Shechinah* should rest in our midst.

פרשת זכור
Parashas Zachor

◆§ *Amalek — Cooling the Passion of Avodas Hashem*

זָכוֹר אֵת אֲשֶׁר עָשָׂה לְךָ עֲמָלֵק בַּדֶּרֶךְ בְּצֵאתְכֶם מִמִּצְרָיִם. אֲשֶׁר קָרְךָ בַּדֶּרֶךְ וַיְזַנֵּב בְּךָ כָּל הַנֶּחֱשָׁלִים אַחֲרֶיךָ וְאַתָּה עָיֵף וְיָגֵעַ וְלֹא יָרֵא אֱלֹהִים. וְהָיָה בְּהָנִיחַ ה׳ אֱלֹהֶיךָ לְךָ מִכָּל אֹיְבֶיךָ מִסָּבִיב בָּאָרֶץ אֲשֶׁר ה׳ אֱלֹהֶיךָ נֹתֵן לְךָ נַחֲלָה לְרִשְׁתָּהּ תִּמְחֶה אֶת זֵכֶר עֲמָלֵק מִתַּחַת הַשָּׁמָיִם לֹא תִּשְׁכָּח.

Remember what Amalek did to you, on the way, when you were leaving Egypt, that he happened upon you on the way, and he struck those of you who were hindmost, all the weaklings at your rear, when you were faint and exhausted, and he did not fear God. It shall be that when Hashem, your God, gives you rest from all your enemies all around, in the Land that Hashem, your God, gives you as an inheritance to possess it, you shall wipe out the memory of Amalek from under the heaven — you shall not forget! (*Devarim* 25:17-19).

These *pesukim* contain an unusual command: to obliterate the memory of Amalek, and this command is followed by the exhortation לֹא תִּשְׁכָּח, *do not forget*, which is unparalleled in the Torah. In order to grasp the profound significance of this mitzvah, we must first examine the essence of Amalek's evil, which will lead us to understand the *avodah* that is required of us.

Indifference: The Root of Evil

Following the war with Amalek, the Torah says: כִּי יָד עַל כֵּס יָהּ מִלְחָמָה לַה׳ בַּעֲמָלֵק מִדֹּר דֹּר, *For the hand is on the throne of God: Hashem maintains a war against Amalek, from generation to generation* (*Shemos* 17:16). In this *pasuk*, the word "throne" is written as כֵּס, rather than כִּסֵּא, and Hashem's Name is likewise written in a shortened form (י־ה) instead of as the full Name (י־ה־ו־ה).

Chazal teach (*Midrash Tehillim* 9): "R' Levi said in the name of R' Chama: As long as the descendants of Amalek remain, the Name [of Hashem] is incomplete and [His] throne is incomplete, until the memory of Amalek is obliterated, as it is written: כִּי יָד עַל כֵּס יָהּ. [The *pasuk*] should have read *al kisei Hashem*; and when Amalek's memory is obliterated from the world, Hashem's Name will be complete, and His Throne will be complete."

Until Amalek is annihilated and his memory is obliterated from the world, the world cannot achieve its final *tikkun* and Hashem's sovereignty cannot be revealed fully, since Amalek is the root of all evil in this world.

The Torah describes Amalek's wicked essence with the words: אֲשֶׁר קָרְךָ בַּדֶּרֶךְ, *that he happened upon you on the way. Midrash Tanchuma* (*Ki Seitzei* 9) interprets the word קָרְךָ to mean "he made you cold before others." The Rosh Yeshivah R' Chaim Shmulevitz explained[13] that Amalek's war with Bnei Yisrael cooled the flame of passion for *avodas Hashem* that they acquired upon leaving Mitzrayim, and this "cooling" is expressed as apathy and failure to give proper attention to one's *avodah*.

When Bnei Yisrael left Mitzrayim, the nations of the world were all terrified and awestruck by the spectacular miracles that Hashem had performed on behalf of His nation, as the Torah attests: שָׁמְעוּ עַמִּים יִרְגָּזוּן חִיל אָחַז יֹשְׁבֵי פְּלָשֶׁת. אָז נִבְהֲלוּ אַלּוּפֵי אֱדוֹם אֵילֵי מוֹאָב יֹאחֲזֵמוֹ רָעַד

---

13. *Sichos Mussar, Simas Lev; Asher Korcha Baderech.*

נָמֹגוּ כֹּל יֹשְׁבֵי כְנָעַן. תִּפֹּל עֲלֵיהֶם אֵימָתָה וָפַחַד, *Peoples heard — they were agitated; terror gripped the dwellers of Philistia. Then the chieftains of Edom were confounded, trembling gripped the powers of Moav, all the dwellers of Canaan dissolved. May fear and terror befall them* (*Shemos* 15:14-16).

Amalek was the only nation in the world that remained aloof and uninspired by the incredible wonders that Hashem had performed, and dared to engage Bnei Yisrael in battle. In this way, Amalek spread its indifferent, disdainful attitude — which is the force of its *tumah* — throughout the world.

This, say Chazal, is analogous to "a boiling bathtub that no person was able to enter, until one fool came and jumped inside. Although he was burned, he cooled [the water] for others. Here, too, because Amalek came and clashed with them, although he suffered losses at their hand, he cooled them before the nations of the world" (*Tanchuma* ibid.). Amalek was well aware that the bathtub was boiling hot, yet he deliberately disregarded the consequences of his actions, which cooled the fear and reverence that the nations of the world felt toward Bnei Yisrael. This disrespect and contempt, which are the core of Amalek's impurity, are the root of evil in the world, and as long as this attitude exists in the world, both Hashem's Name and His throne remain incomplete.

Amalek's Strength Is Klal Yisrael's Weakness

Amalek draws its power, along with the capacity to battle Klal Yisrael and sow its impurity in the world, from those moments when Bnei Yisrael are weak and lacking in this regard specifically. Regarding the *pasuk*, וַיָּבֹא עֲמָלֵק וַיִּלָּחֶם עִם יִשְׂרָאֵל בִּרְפִידִם, *Amalek came and battled Israel in Refidim* (*Shemos* 17:8), Chazal teach (*Sanhedrin* 106a) that the name Refidim implies that Bnei Yisrael allowed themselves to weaken (*ripu*) in their Torah study.

Weakness in *limud Torah* stems from a lack of regard for the significance of *limud Torah*. Had Torah study been viewed with the proper esteem, surely no one would have demonstrated indolence, lethargy, or weakness in learning; on the contrary, they would have invested all their energies into enhancing and broadening their learning. When Klal Yisrael failed to focus on the importance of *limud Torah*, they empowered Amalek. Amalek's newfound strength enabled them to engage Bnei Yisrael in war and spread their spirit of impurity, at the core of which is cooling the passion of *yiras Hashem* throughout the world.

Amalek is the source of this deplorable tendency, which must be condemned and utterly uprooted in order to bring the world to its final *tikkun*. The Torah declares that "Hashem maintains a war against Amalek, from generation to generation" and commands Bnei Yisrael to obliterate every trace of Amalek — men, women, and children. Moreover, the Torah adds the warning, "Do not forget!" in order to reinforce the importance of serving Hashem with passion and assigning the proper value to Torah and mitzvos.

If Amalek's impurity is the root of evil in this world, it follows that a cold, unfeeling approach toward *avodas Hashem* and indifference to Torah and mitzvos are what delay the final *Geulah*. Conversely, serving Hashem with emotion and holding every word of Torah and every mitzvah in high regard are what bring Mashiach. Therefore, we must stand tall against the force of *tumah* that Amalek has dispersed throughout the world, to prevent the spirit of apathy from penetrating the sacred walls of our *beis midrash* and weakening our resolve to toil in Torah.

Amalek's Presence in the World Conflicts With Shleimus HaTorah

R' Aharon Kotler writes[14] that Amalek's very existence in the world constitutes a conflict to the Torah's perfection, and as long as Amalek endures, it is impossible to soar to the pinnacle of *limud Torah*.

This concept is reflected in the following words of Chazal (*Sanhedrin* 20b):

> R' Yose says: The nation of Israel was commanded to perform three commandments upon their entrance into the

14. *Mishnas Rabbi Aharon — Purim, Milchamah LaShem BaAmalek Midor Dor; Zechiras Amalek.*

> Land: to appoint upon themselves a king, to eradicate the offspring of Amalek, and to build the Beis HaMikdash ... But I still do not know if the commandment to build the Beis HaMikdash must be performed first or if the commandment to eradicate the offspring of Amalek must be performed first. However, when [the verse] states, וְהֵנִיחַ לָכֶם מִכָּל אֹיְבֵיכֶם וגו׳ וְהָיָה הַמָּקוֹם אֲשֶׁר יִבְחַר ה׳ וגו׳, *And when He gives you respite from all your enemies ... And it shall come to pass that the place which [your] God shall choose ...*, I would say that [since the verse first mentions the elimination of Israel's enemies, including Amalek, and only then the building of the Beis HaMikdash] the commandment to eradicate the offspring of Amalek must be performed first.

This Gemara clarifies that the mitzvah of building the Beis HaMikdash applies only after we have fulfilled the mitzvah of annihilating Amalek.

The Divine Presence in the Beis HaMikdash drew from the power of Torah that radiated from the *Aron* in the *Kodesh HaKodashim*, which held the *Luchos HaBris* and a *Sefer Torah*. Similarly, Hashem's *Shechinah* in this world, even after the *Churban HaBayis*, likewise draws from the force of Torah study, as Chazal teach that "from the day the Beis HaMikdash was destroyed, the only [place] Hakadosh Baruch Hu has in this world is the four cubits of halachah" (*Berachos* 8b). Yet, if the mitzvah to build the Beis HaMikdash is secondary to obliterating Amalek, then clearly, Amalek's existence in the world constitutes a direct conflict to the Torah's perfection. This is why we are required to annihilate Amalek prior to building the Beis HaMikdash, whose ultimate purpose is to serve as a dwelling place for the *Shechinah*, via the force of Torah.

Lack of Kavod HaTorah Leads to Abandonment of Torah

Amalek embodies apathy and disrespect for that which is meaningful. In contrast, the ultimate level of Torah study is achieved by learning with intensity, paying careful attention to every minor detail, and appreciating the Torah's significance. When our learning is not characterized by this careful attention and appreciation, our Torah is lacking.

This idea is reflected in Chazal's teaching (*Nedarim* 81a) that what led to the destruction of the Beis HaMikdash was Klal Yisrael's failure to recite the blessings over the Torah — which, as we explained above (*Parashas Tetzaveh*), means that they did not sufficiently value the Torah. Hakadosh Baruch Hu considers this shortcoming tantamount to abandoning the Torah, as He says: עַל עָזְבָם אֶת תּוֹרָתִי, *Because of their forsaking My Torah* (*Yirmiyah* 9:12).

The cold, contemptuous attitude that Amalek sowed in the world, and in Klal Yisrael specifically, strikes at the core of what the Torah represents. The way to battle and overcome the harm caused by Amalek is by reinforcing our value for Torah and mitzvos. Any time a person feels that learning Torah is challenging, or does not understand the depth of a *sugya,* he should recall that this is all the force of Amalek in this world! If he keeps toiling with all his strength to learn Torah, he will surmount this impurity and see great *siyata diShmaya* in his learning, as the Torah attests: וְהָיָה כַּאֲשֶׁר יָרִים מֹשֶׁה יָדוֹ וְגָבַר יִשְׂרָאֵל וְכַאֲשֶׁר יָנִיחַ יָדוֹ וְגָבַר עֲמָלֵק, *It happened that when Moshe raised his hand Israel was stronger, and when he lowered his hand Amalek was stronger* (*Shemos* 17:11).

Hakadosh Baruch Hu should grant us strength to surmount the force of Amalek's *tumah* in this world and uproot from our hearts all lethargy and torpor in *avodas Hashem*. May He imbue us with appreciation for Torah and mitzvos, so that we can serve Him with emotion and love, and may we merit seeing Amalek's name utterly erased and the coming of Mashiach Tzidkeinu speedily in our days!

ספר ויקרא
Sefer Vayikra

פרשת ויקרא
Parashas Vayikra

◆§ *Listening to the Limud*

וַיִּקְרָא אֶל מֹשֶׁה וַיְדַבֵּר ה׳ אֵלָיו מֵאֹהֶל מוֹעֵד לֵאמֹר.
He called to Moshe, and Hashem spoke to him from the Tent of Meeting, saying (*Vayikra* 1:1).

Rashi comments: The voice [of God] would go, and reach [Moshe's] ears, but all of Israel would not hear it. One might think that there was "calling" at breaks as well, but the verse says, "And [Hashem] spoke," [which implies that] for speaking there was "calling," but not for breaks. What purpose did the breaks serve? To give Moshe an interval of time for contemplation between one section of the Torah and another, and between one topic and another. All the more so for an ordinary person who learns from an ordinary person.

With these words, Rashi is imparting fundamental lessons regarding *limud Torah.*

Several phenomenal events transpired when Hashem spoke to Moshe Rabbeinu from the Ohel Moed. Naturally, sound waves spread from their source and enter the ears of anyone in listening range. The voice of Hashem is particularly loud and powerful, as the verse states: קוֹל ה׳ בַּכֹּחַ, *The voice of Hashem [comes] in power* (*Tehillim* 29:4). Yet in this case, Hashem's voice penetrated only Moshe Rabbeinu's ears, while even those standing in close proximity to him heard nothing at all.

The miracle here was that the voice of Hashem, which was spoken with Godly force, couldn't even be heard by those standing outside the Ohel Moed! Rashi explains that the words וַיְדַבֵּר ה׳ אֵלָיו מֵאֹהֶל מוֹעֵד, *and Hashem spoke to him from the Tent of Meeting,* indicate that the voice of Hashem thundered inside the Ohel Moed, but, inexplicably, was not heard outside.

Midrash Tanchuma (*Vayikra* 1) elaborates that the voice that Hashem used to speak to Moshe Rabbeinu from the Ohel Moed was not merely loud and resonant — it was the same awe-inspiring voice that He used when speaking to Bnei Yisrael on Har Sinai. Still, the voice was unheard by all except Moshe, as Hakadosh Baruch Hu created a special channel that allowed His words to travel directly into Moshe Rabbeinu's ears.

What was the significance of this unusual miracle, and what lesson can we draw from it?

Hearing the Kol HaTorah

After Mattan Torah, Hashem's voice could not be heard by every ear, only by those worthy of hearing it. Only ears as pure as those of Moshe Rabbeinu were privileged to hear this *kol Hashem,* while those who were less pure heard nothing.

Today, as well, not every person is privileged to hear the *kol haTorah*. While Hashem gave Torah to Klal Yisrael as a unit, only a select group among us is truly worthy of hearing the holy voice of Torah. Every morning we beseech Hashem for this special capacity to listen and hear, as we entreat: וְתֵן בְּלִבֵּנוּ בִּינָה לְהָבִין וּלְהַשְׂכִּיל לִשְׁמֹעַ לִלְמוֹד וּלְלַמֵּד, *Instill in our hearts to understand and to elucidate, to listen, to learn, and to teach.*

Even a person who is wise and perceptive may not be capable of "hearing" the Torah's words. The request that we merit "to listen" therefore precedes the subsequent requests that we merit "to learn and to teach," for only if one has the special *zechus* to hear and listen to *divrei Torah* can he truly learn Torah, internalize it, and then relay it to others.

Obviously, in order to have the *zechus* of listening to Torah, a person must ensure that he is worthy of it, like Moshe Rabbeinu, who purified himself and sanctified his heart and soul until his ears were the purest receptacles, worthy of וַיִּשְׁמַע אֶת הַקּוֹל מִדַּבֵּר אֵלָיו, *and he heard the voice [of Hashem] speaking to him* (*Bamidbar* 7:89). Similarly, anyone who aspires to hear the *kol haTorah*, and to allow its holiness to penetrate his ears, mind, and heart, must work on himself, refine his *middos*, and beseech Hashem that his heart should be pure and worthy of listening to Torah, as Shlomo HaMelech entreated: וְנָתַתָּ לְעַבְדְּךָ לֵב שֹׁמֵעַ, *May You grant Your servant a listening heart* (*I Melachim* 3:9). While *hearing* occurs in the ear, *listening* takes place in the caverns of the heart, and a person must therefore beseech Hashem for the capacity to truly listen, hear, and absorb the words of Torah.

No Interruptions

Rashi presents another explanation of the words וַיִּקְרָא אֶל מֹשֶׁה, *He called to Moshe*: "'Calling' preceded every statement, and every saying, and every command. It is a language of affection." Hashem's call to Moshe was an expression of His great love for him, as the Ramban (*Vayikra* 1:1) explains, "He would say to him, 'Moshe, Moshe,' and he would reply, '*Hineni* — I am here,' and this is a way of [expressing] affection."

Rashi teaches that only when Hashem spoke to Moshe was there a call of affection; when a break occurred in the learning, as indicated by a space in the *Sefer Torah*, no such expression of love followed. Although it was necessary to pause between one topic and the next in order to provide Moshe Rabbeinu with ample opportunity to reflect upon what he had learned, these intervals were not followed by a new call of affection.

This underscores that interruptions in *limud Torah* are regarded in a negative light. If Moshe Rabbeinu took "a necessary break" from learning in order to absorb and review what he had acquired, and the consequence was that Hashem did not call to him affectionately afterward, imagine the gravity and loss born of "unnecessary breaks" from learning! Worse yet, who can fathom the calamity of "breaks" that cause *bittul Torah* and distract others from learning!

The Gemara states (*Sanhedrin* 71a): "Whoever sleeps in a study hall, his Torah knowledge becomes tattered, as it is stated (*Mishlei* 23:21): וּקְרָעִים תַּלְבִּישׁ נוּמָה, and a slumberer will wear tattered clothing. Here, Shlomo HaMelech teaches that just as a tattered garment is not regarded as clothing, because it is useless to the wearer, so, too, the Torah of one who frequently starts and stops learning is not regarded as *limud Torah*. This is not only because of the time he squandered, but also because the learning is flawed at its source, for such a habit negates the very essence of Torah.[1]

It is imperative to know that *retzifus* in *limud Torah* is not just a commendable attribute or a higher level of learning, but is the very core of how to learn!

Bein Hazmanim — Time to Reflect and Review

Rashi's comment about the purpose of breaks conveys an important lesson to us, as *bnei yeshivah*. If Moshe Rabbeinu, who learned Torah from Hakadosh Baruch Hu Himself, required occasional breaks between topics in order to reflect upon all he had been taught, how much more so do we, simple people learning from simple people, require occasional intervals to reflect, assess, and review the Torah we have learned.

This explains why our rabbanim have instituted the period of *bein hazmanim* within the yeshivah world. From an outsider's perspective, the concept of a *bein hazmanim* prompts many questions. Isn't the institution of *bein hazmanim* the greatest imaginable *bittul Torah*? Why would rabbanim and roshei yeshivah encourage thousands of *bachurim* to leave yeshivah for weeks at a time?

Actually, the period of *bein hazmanim* features a unique quality.

---

1. The Chazon Ish writes famously regarding this topic: "To learn one hour and stop one hour is upholding emptiness, nothingness, and void. It is like one who plants and then pours water upon it to wash it away. The essence of learning is constancy and consistency. Consistent learning is the secret of holiness, and he who makes his Torah into scraps, has collected wind [emptiness]" (*Igros Chazon Ish* Vol. 1, Letter 3).

Just as only a person who was once trapped in darkness is able to fully appreciate the brilliance of sunlight, a *ben yeshivah* who leaves the hallowed halls of the *beis midrash* for the defined period of *bein hazmanim* is capable of recognizing the incredible value of *limud Torah* with *dibbuk chaveirim* and absolute immersion in learning in the yeshivah.

Bein hazmanim offers us the proverbial "space between topics." Chazal teach that it is crucial to pause and reflect upon the lessons gleaned between *sugyos* and *masechtos,* and *bein hazmanim* is the ideal opportunity to do this. For example, now that we have merited to complete *Maseches Yevamos,* and everyone's minds and thoughts are still absorbed in this *masechta,* it is only natural that we take a break before diving into *Maseches Nedarim. Bein hazmanim* grants us the small window of time between one *masechta* and the next to reflect upon all that we have learned and prepare for the upcoming *masechta.*

Time for Cheshbon HaNefesh

Not only is *bein hazmanim* designated for learning and reviewing, it is also the ideal time for a *ben yeshivah* to conduct an honest personal accounting, assess how much learning he has genuinely done during the *zman,* and determine what else he could have accomplished had he invested more effort. It is a time to assess if one grew spiritually during the last *zman,* or if he could have done better. One who conducts an honest evaluation of the recent months and finds himself lacking should continue striving for growth while gathering ideas and suggestions for spiritual growth.

If we all dedicate the coming days of *bein hazmanim* to conducting an honest *cheshbon hanefesh,* then these days will not be wasted, nor will they constitute an interruption from our *retzifus* in *limud Torah.* Rather, they will serve as the bridge linking the previous *zman* to the coming *zman,* and grant us the opportunity to grow spiritually so that we can merit even greater *siyata diShmaya* during the coming *zman.*

An excellent way to accomplish this is to devote several minutes to personal growth. Find a quiet corner, recite two *perakim* of *Tehillim* quietly, with *kavanah,* and then sit down immediately to learn for a half-hour, with *hasmadah* and *retzifus*. Then reflect upon yourself, your learning, and your growth. The brief *tefillah* coupled with the half-hour of uninterrupted learning is a means of purifying yourself so that you can perform honest introspection and assess your spiritual growth. I recommend doing this at least once a week, and one who does this will not have wasted his *bein hazmanim* or allowed his *limud Torah* to become "tattered."

Even during the days of *bein hazmanim,* it is forbidden to waste time or be *mevatel Torah*. We are all charged with the constant obligation of וְהָגִיתָ בּוֹ יוֹמָם וָלַיְלָה, *You should contemplate it day and night* (*Yehoshua* 1:8), which applies equally during the *zman* and *bein hazmanim*. We must reaccept Torah every day of life with love, and *bein hazmanim* provides the additional opportunity to conduct a *cheshbon hanefesh* and prepare ourselves for the coming *zman*.

May Hashem help us to always utilize our hours and days effectively, which will empower us to start the next *zman* in the right way.

פרשת צו
Parashas Tzav

◈§ *The Power of the Nedavah*

וְאִם נֶדֶר אוֹ נְדָבָה זֶבַח קָרְבָּנוֹ בְּיוֹם הַקְרִיבוֹ אֶת זִבְחוֹ יֵאָכֵל וּמִמָּחֳרָת וְהַנּוֹתָר מִמֶּנּוּ יֵאָכֵל.

If his feast-offering is for a vow or a donation, it must be eaten on the day he offered his feast-offering; and on the next day, what is left over may be eaten (*Vayikra* 7:16).

The Gemara (*Megillah* 8a) differentiates between a *neder* (vow offering) and a *nedavah* (gift offering) as follows: "What is a vow offering? One who says, 'It is incumbent upon me to bring an *olah* offering.' What is a gift offering? One who says, 'This animal is hereby designated as an *olah* offering.' "

In other words, a *neder* is a pledge to bring a *korban*, which requires the person to later choose an animal to offer, whereas a *nedavah* is a spontaneous decision to offer a specific animal as a *korban* to Hashem.

Yearning for Dveikus

The Ibn Ezra differentiates further, explaining that a person makes a *neder* when he is in distress, and pledges a *nedavah* when his heart is inspired to bring a *korban* to Hashem, not as a vow, and not as an expression of thanksgiving. Typically, a person pledges to bring a *korban* when he is suffering, as Chazal (*Bereishis Rabbah* 70:1) teach regarding the *pasuk*, וַיִּדַּר יַעֲקֹב נֶדֶר לֵאמֹר, *Then Yaakov took a vow, saying* (*Bereishis* 28:20): "It is written, אֲשֶׁר פָּצוּ שְׂפָתָי וְדִבֶּר פִּי בַּצַּר לִי, *that my lips uttered and my mouth spoke in my distress* (*Tehillim* 66:14). R' Yitzchak of Bavel said: *And my mouth spoke in my distress* means that he vowed, in his time of adversity, to do a mitzvah. What is indicated by לֵאמֹר, *saying*? To teach future generations that they should make vows [to do mitzvos] during times of distress."

In contrast, the spiritual awakening that inspires one to offer a *korban nedavah* stems from a powerful desire to cleave to Hashem, as a *korban* draws a person close to Him. Indeed, the *Zohar* notes (*Vayikra* 5a) that the word *korban* means "to draw close." As the Ibn Ezra teaches, a person makes a *nedavah* pledge not in order to gain salvation, and not to thank Hashem for saving him from misfortune. Rather, one brings this *korban* simply to come close to Hashem.

This also explains why a *neder* is a commitment for the future, while a *nedavah* is a spur-of-the-moment decision to dedicate a *korban* to Hashem. One who is in a difficult situation longs for salvation and looks forward to the day when he will bring a thanksgiving offering to Hashem for having rescued him from his plight, while one who is inspired to cleave to Hashem does not wish to procrastinate the fulfillment of his desire for even a moment, and hurries to give physical expression to his overpowering emotions by dedicating an animal as a *korban*.

This *hisorerus* and yearning for closeness to Hashem that inspires a person to dedicate an animal as a *korban* is what imbues the *nedavah* with its exceptional quality and power. This is one reason why the entire subject of *korbanos* opens with this offering, as Rashi teaches that the verse at the beginning of *Parashas Vayikra* (1:2), דַּבֵּר אֶל בְּנֵי יִשְׂרָאֵל וְאָמַרְתָּ אֲלֵהֶם אָדָם כִּי יַקְרִיב מִכֶּם קָרְבָּן לַה׳, *Speak to the Children of Israel and say to them: When a man among you brings an offering to Hashem*, is referring to *korbanos nedavah*. Chazal elaborate (*Midrash HaGadol*, *Vayikra* 1:3): "A *korban nedavah* is most cherished, as the Torah opens with it; in this vein, the [*navi*] says, וּנְשַׁלְּמָה פָרִים שְׂפָתֵינוּ, *and let our lips substitute for bulls* (*Hoshea* 14:3)."

Learning About Korbanos

This teaching of Chazal requires further explanation. How do the words *and let our lips substitute for bulls* reveal that a *korban nedavah* is the most beloved to Hashem of all the *korbanos*?

This *pasuk* illustrates that the fundamental purpose of *korbanos* is not the physical act of offering the *korban*, but rather the person's inner craving to draw close to Hashem through the *korban*. With this perspective, we can understand how it is that even today, when we have no Beis HaMikdash, a person can express his yearning to draw close to Hashem by learning the *parshiyos* of *korbanos*, and the act of learning is then regarded as if he physically offered a *korban* to Hashem on the Altar. The meaning of the words *and let our lips substitute for bulls* is that a person can offer *korbanos* through the utterances of his lips.

This idea is also expressed in the following account of the Gemara (*Taanis* 27b), regarding Avraham Avinu's request to Hashem during the *Bris Bein HaBesarim*: בַּמָּה אֵדַע כִּי אִירָשֶׁנָּה, *Whereby shall I know that I am to inherit it?* (*Bereishis* 15:8).

> Avraham said: "Master of the Universe! Perhaps Israel will sin before You, and You will do to them as You did to the generation of the Flood and the generation of the Dispersion." Hashem answered him: "No!" Avraham said before Him: "Master of the Universe! Let me know whereby I shall inherit it [i.e., by what means shall Israel atone for their sins and thereby be saved from destruction]." Hashem answered: "*Bring Me three calves and three goats* etc." [i.e., the offerings will achieve atonement for their sins]. Avraham said before Him: "Master of the Universe! That is fine for the times when the Beis HaMikdash will be in existence, but in the times when the Beis HaMikdash will not be in existence, what will be with them?" Hashem answered him: "I have already established for them the Scriptural section

of offerings. Whenever they read from them before Me, I will consider it as if they had brought [offerings] before Me, and I will forgive them all their sins."

Similarly, Chazal teach (*Shir HaShirim Rabbah* 4:12) that the words כְּחוּט הַשָּׁנִי שִׂפְתֹתַיִךְ (*Shir HaShirim* 4:3) allude to the red string that would turn white to signify atonement, while the subsequent words וּמִדְבָּרֵיךְ נָאוֶה allude to the goat that was thrown into the ravine. The Midrash records this dialogue between Klal Yisrael and Hashem: "Israel said before God: 'Master of the Universe! We have no red string and no goat!' He said to them: 'כְּחוּט הַשָּׁנִי שִׂפְתֹתַיִךְ — the murmurings of your mouth are as precious to me as the red string.' R' Abahu said regarding this: *And let our lips substitute for bulls* — what can we pay instead of bulls and the goat? Our lips."

Tefillah Brings Closeness to Hashem

Even today, when we are not privileged to have the Beis HaMikdash and the *Shechinah* in our midst, a Yid can still draw close to Hakadosh Baruch Hu through sincere *tefillah*, and his earnest prayers are then regarded as if he offered a *korban* to Hashem.

Chazal derive this idea from the same words, *and let our lips substitute for bulls*, as they teach (*Bamidbar Rabbah* 18:21) that Klal Yisrael declare, "Master of the Universe! When the Beis HaMikdash stood, we offered *korbanos* and received atonement. Now all we have in our hands is prayer ... *and let our lips substitute for bulls*."

The essence of *korbanos* is the inspiration to cleave to Hakadosh Baruch Hu, and there is nothing that draws a person closer to Hashem than *tefillah*. When a person stands submissively before Hashem, praises Him sincerely, expresses gratitude for the boundless gifts that he has been granted, and entreats for the future, he reinforces his knowledge and faith that his entire existence depends on Hakadosh Baruch Hu, and truly there is no greater means or expression of drawing close to Hashem than this.

This concept emerges from the Sforno's explanation of the words, אָדָם כִּי יַקְרִיב מִכֶּם לַה׳, *When a man from among you brings an offering to Hashem* (*Vayikra* 1:2): "When he offers from himself, with confession and humility, as the *pasuk* says, וּנְשַׁלְּמָה פָרִים שְׂפָתֵינוּ, *and let our lips substitute for bulls* (*Hoshea* 14:3); and as it says, זִבְחֵי אֱלֹהִים רוּחַ נִשְׁבָּרָה, *The sacrifices God desires are a broken spirit* (*Tehillim* 51:19). For He does not desire fools who bring offerings without first humbling themselves, as Chazal derive from the word מִכֶּם, *from among you*, that this does not include all of you; the apostate is excluded."

Hashem desires *korbanos* that come מִכֶּם, *from you* — *korbanos* that bring a person to view himself as the offering and to subjugate himself wholly before Hashem by confessing his misdeeds and revealing his broken heart. One who offers a *korban* but lacks humility and a broken spirit is a fool who has completely missed the point of *korbanos*. The Sforno emphasizes this by accentuating the word of the *pasuk* מִכֶּם, *from among you*, noting that this excludes the apostate, whose *korbanos* lack submission and sincerity.

Achieving closeness to Hashem through humility and a broken spirit occurs not only by offering *korbanos* and davening, but also through each and every mitzvah, and each act of *avodas Hashem* and *limud Torah*. If a person's *avodas Hashem* is not sourced in humility, then he cannot ascend to the heights of *ruchniyus*. Conversely, the more a person sacrifices of himself to enhance his *avodas Hashem*, the greater success he will see in all his endeavors — both material and spiritual. Material success is also linked to a person's dedication, yet in the spiritual realm this devotion is the basis for all success, and without it a person cannot achieve anything.

פרשת שמיני
Parashas Shemini

◆§ Honoring Our Rebbeim

וַיִּקְחוּ בְנֵי אַהֲרֹן נָדָב וַאֲבִיהוּא אִישׁ מַחְתָּתוֹ וַיִּתְּנוּ בָהֵן אֵשׁ וַיָּשִׂימוּ עָלֶיהָ קְטֹרֶת וַיַּקְרִיבוּ לִפְנֵי ה׳ אֵשׁ זָרָה אֲשֶׁר לֹא צִוָּה אֹתָם: ב וַתֵּצֵא אֵשׁ מִלִּפְנֵי ה׳ וַתֹּאכַל אוֹתָם וַיָּמֻתוּ לִפְנֵי ה׳.

The sons of Aharon, Nadav and Avihu, each took his fire pan, they put fire in them and placed incense upon it; and they brought before Hashem an alien fire that He had not commanded them. A fire came forth from before Hashem and consumed them, and they died before Hashem (*Vayikra* 10:1,2).

R' Eliezer taught: The sons of Aharon did not perish until they rendered a halachic ruling before Moshe, their teacher. What did they teach? וְנָתְנוּ בְּנֵי אַהֲרֹן הַכֹּהֵן אֵשׁ עַל הַמִּזְבֵּחַ, *The sons of Aharon the Kohen shall place fire on the Altar, and arrange wood on the fire* (*Vayikra* 1:7). They said: "Even though a fire descends from heaven, it is a mitzvah to bring [fire] from the layman [as well]." R' Eliezer had one disciple who rendered a halachic ruling in his presence. R' Eliezer said to Imma Shalom, his wife, "I would be surprised if he survives the year," and indeed, he did not survive the year. She said to him: "Are you a prophet?" He said to her, "I am not a prophet, nor the son of a prophet; but I have learned that anyone who rules in halachah before his teacher deserves to die" (*Eruvin* 63a).

Why is rendering a halachic ruling in the presence of one's rebbi regarded as such a serious offense that it warrants such a grave punishment? Surely, this detracts from the honor that one is meant to accord one's rebbi, yet the punishment still seems to far exceed the severity of the crime.

To compound this question, we find that the *Shulchan Aruch* rules: "A rav who forgives his honor ... his honor is forgiven" (*Yoreh Deah* 242:32). Why, then, didn't Moshe Rabbeinu forgive Nadav and Avihu so they would not be punished? The same question can be asked regarding R' Eliezer, who predicted that his *talmid* would perish that very year. If he foresaw the man's tragic fate, why couldn't he forgive his honor and save his *talmid* from an untimely death? This is a serious question, especially considering the Gemara's statement that "one whose friend is punished on his account is not granted entry into the chambers of Hakadosh Baruch Hu" (*Shabbos* 149b). Why did both Moshe Rabbeinu and R' Eliezer insist on upholding their honor rather than forgoing it and sparing their *talmidim* from premature death?

Lacking Authority

The Rosh Yeshivah R' Chaim Shmulevitz explains[2] that the main problem with rendering a halachic ruling in the presence of one's rebbi is not the disrespect that the *talmid* manifests nor even the disgrace that it brings upon the rebbi, but rather the underlying issue of the *talmid's* lack of submissiveness to his rebbi's authority — even if he genuinely respects him.

This principle is reflected in the Gemara's teaching (*Eruvin* 63):

R' Levi said: Anyone who answers a word [i.e., renders a halachic decision] in front of his teacher goes to the grave without a child. For the verse states (*Bamidbar* 11:28): וַיַּעַן

2. *Sichos Mussar, Moreh Halachah Bifnei Rabbo.*

יְהוֹשֻׁעַ בִּן נוּן מְשָׁרֵת מֹשֶׁה מִבְּחֻרָיו וַיֹּאמַר אֲדֹנִי מֹשֶׁה כְּלָאֵם, *Yehoshua bin Nin, the attendant of Moshe, responded and he said, "My master Moshe, lock them up."* And it is written (*I Divrei HaYamim* 7:27): נוֹן בְּנוֹ יְהוֹשֻׁעַ בְּנוֹ, *Non was his son; Yehoshua was his son.* [Scripture does not continue the line after Yehoshua, because he left no sons.]

Since Yehoshua issued a halachic ruling in the presence of Moshe Rabbeinu, he was punished with not having sons. While it would be logical to assume that the problem with issuing a halachic ruling before one's rebbi is that it shows contempt for the rebbi, it is clear that Yehoshua's statement was made out of genuine concern for Moshe Rabbeinu, as Moshe himself responded: הַמְקַנֵּא אַתָּה לִי, *Are you being zealous for my sake?* Therefore, we learn that even if the *talmid's* goal is to uphold his rebbi's honor, issuing a halachic ruling in the presence of one's rebbi still reveals a gross lack of respect and a dismissal of authority, and is strictly prohibited.

Submission: A Symbol of Greatness

Regarding the words וּלְזִקְנֵי יִשְׂרָאֵל, *and to the elders of Yisrael* (*Vayikra* 9:1), the Midrash teaches: "R' Akiva taught: The Jewish people are compared to a bird. Just as a bird cannot soar without wings, so, too, the Jewish people cannot do anything without [consulting] their elders" (*Vayikra Rabbah* 11:8). The Midrash is teaching that Klal Yisrael differs from the other nations of the world in that the nations do as they please without seeking anyone's advice, while Klal Yisrael does not do anything without consulting their elders.

Later in the Midrash (ibid.), we see a marvelous expression of the honor accorded to our elders:

> R' Yose bar Chalafta said: Old age is great! When they are elderly, they are cherished, but when they are youngsters, they are still a bit immature. As R' Shimon ben Yochai taught: Not in one place, and not in two places, but in numerous situations we find that Hashem accorded respect to the elders — at the burning bush; in Egypt; in Sinai; in the Wilderness; etc. Even in the future to come, Hakadosh

Baruch Hu will honor the elders, as it is written: וְחָפְרָה הַלְּבָנָה וּבוֹשָׁה הַחַמָּה . . . וְנֶגֶד זְקֵנָיו כָּבוֹד, *The moon will be humiliated and the sun will be shamed ... and there will be honor for His elders* (*Yeshayah* 24:23).

Throughout the ages, Klal Yisrael has always venerated our elders, and Hashem accords them great honor as well.

Submission to Gedolei Hador

The basis of Klal Yisrael's survival has always been our elders and Torah sages. We draw both physical and spiritual strength from our elders, and our strength depends on our level of submission to them. If, Heaven forbid, we cease to defer to the views of our *gedolim*, we forfeit this strength.

The reason that issuing a halachic ruling in the presence of one's rebbi is viewed with such severity is that this type of behavior causes Klal Yisrael to lose its strength and its ability to survive. Both Moshe Rabbeinu and R' Eliezer were therefore unwilling to forgo their honor, because they grasped that Klal Yisrael's very existence depends on honoring the sages. Moreover, even if they had forgone their honor, they could not have prevented the offenders from being punished.

Tosafos state (*Kesubos* 60b, s.v. *Ki afkirusa)* that if a rebbi forgoes his honor, a *talmid* is permitted to issue a halachic ruling before him, yet surely this does not mean that the *talmid* may rule as he desires. Rather, since the rebbi authorized this, the *talmid's* ruling is merely an extension of what his rebbi taught him, so he is not actually ruling independently.

"Nevertheless," *Tosafos* qualify, "he should not issue a ruling, for his ruling will not be successful, because his rebbi is with him." Even if the rebbi explicitly permits his *talmid* to rule in his presence, it is preferable for the *talmid* to avoid exercising this leniency, since he will not benefit from the *siyata diShmaya* that enables him to arrive at the truth.

The punishment meted out to one who issues a halachic ruling before his rebbi is not actually a punishment for an offense, but rather a direct consequence of his actions. Since his actions caused Klal Yisrael to forfeit their right to exist, he forfeits his right to exist, as well.

R' Chaim Shmulevitz taught that the reason certain chassidic Rebbes possess the power to perform wonders is that their chassidim believe wholeheartedly in them and negate themselves before them without any trace of doubt or disrespect. It is this *hisbatlus* that infuses the Rebbes with the power to perform actual miracles.

This is the power of genuine *hisbatlus!*

Fearing Your Rebbi

Chazal teach: "And your fear of your rebbi shall be as your fear of Heaven" (*Avos* 4:12). The awe that a *talmid* feels toward his rebbi encompasses an aspect of the awe that a person must feel toward Hashem Himself. This can be understood in light of the introductory Mishnah in *Avos* (1:1): "Moshe received the Torah at Sinai, and relayed it to Yehoshua, and Yehoshua to the Elders, and the Elders to the Prophets, and the Prophets relayed it to the Anshei Knesses HaGedolah."

The Rambam, in his preface to his commentary on the Mishnah, expands this list to include all the prominent Torah teachers throughout the generations, until Ravina and Rav Ashi, the final Amoraim, who sealed the Talmud. In truth, it would be fitting to document the entire chain of those who taught Torah throughout the generations in order to demonstrate that every rav received the Torah from his rebbi and then relayed it to his *talmid*, extending the conduit of Torah transmission that began at Har Sinai. Conversely, one who disagrees with his rebbi interrupts the pipeline that transmits Torah to successive generations.

This is why Chazal regard issuing a halachic ruling in the presence of one's rebbi as a severe sin that is punishable with death. Since Klal Yisrael's right to exist depends on *hisbatlus* to our elders, one who scorns the *gedolim* is actually harming himself.

R' Yochanan Could Not Forgive Reish Lakish

The Gemara relates (*Bava Metzia* 84a) that R' Yochanan once polemized with Reish Lakish regarding the precise point when a sword, a knife, and a hunting spear are regarded as finished products, which are capable of becoming *tamei*. In the course of their debate, Reish Lakish spoke disrespectfully to R' Yochanan, who was disheartened by this remark. Reish Lakish immediately took ill and was on the verge of death. His wife, who was R' Yochanan's sister, visited her brother and tearfully beseeched him to forgive her husband.

"Act for the sake of my children!" she pleaded, to which he replied by citing the verse: עָזְבָה יְתֹמֶיךָ אֲנִי אֲחַיֶּה, *Leave your orphans; I will sustain [them]* (*Yirmiyah* 49:11).

"Act for the sake of my [impending] widowhood!" she wept again. R' Yochanan answered with the *pasuk*: וְאַלְמְנוֹתֶיךָ עָלַי תִּבְטָחוּ, *And let your widows trust in me* (ibid.), and Reish Lakish perished.

This Gemara is puzzling on many counts. First of all, why did R' Yochanan refuse to forgive Reish Lakish, who was both his prime disciple and his beloved *chavrusa?* Moreover, even if Reish Lakish had insulted his rebbi and not accorded him the proper respect, how had his wife and children sinned to deserve the terrible fate of widowhood and orphanhood?

The difficulty is compounded by the Gemara's description of the profound anguish that R' Yochanan himself experienced upon the death of Reish Lakish. R' Yochanan ripped his garments and grieved the death of Reish Lakish, who had challenged his every statement by posing twenty-four difficulties, until the subject became absolutely clear due to the resulting give-and-take.

"Where are you, son of Lakish? Where are you, son of Lakish?" shouted R' Yochanan. He was so brokenhearted that he wept and screamed until he lost his mind, and the sages prayed for mercy on his behalf, until he expired.

Why didn't the sages daven that R' Yochanan should recover, instead of merely requesting that Hashem end his misery and take him? It was clear to all that there was no purpose in R' Yochanan's continued existence, since the terrible anguish that he felt upon the loss of his *talmid* and *chavrusa* would have only caused him to lose his mind again. R' Yochanan could not live without the tremendous spiritual boost and breadth of study that he enjoyed while learning with Reish Lakish.

This is all the more surprising considering that R' Yochanan possessed exceptional strength of character, as illustrated by the Gemara's teaching (*Berachos* 5b, *Tosafos*) that after R' Yochanan's ten sons all perished during his lifetime, he took a fragment of bone from his youngest son's body and wrapped it so he could use it to console others who had suffered tragedy. So firm was R' Yochanan's emotional and spiritual fortitude that he was able to calmly show people a piece of his child's bone as a demonstration of his acceptance of Hashem's will and teach them to accept His tribulations with love. Nevertheless, when the loss of Reish Lakish affected R' Yochanan's Torah study to the extent that he could not regain the breadth of Torah learning that he had experienced when dueling in Torah with him, his fortitude failed him, and he lost his mind.

All this serves to intensify our original question: If R' Yochanan so appreciated Reish Lakish's intellectual depth and brilliance and knew that this *talmid* catapulted his own learning to unimaginable heights, to the extent that he could not survive a day in the *beis midrash* without him, why couldn't R' Yochanan find it in his heart to forgive Reish Lakish and avert his untimely death?

R' Yochanan knew that the key to Klal Yisrael's survival is its leaders, and that one who fails to submit to the authority of the rabbanim forfeits his right to exist, as we explained regarding a person who issues a halachic ruling before his rebbi. Such a person loses his own privilege to live and undermines the existence of the entire nation, which is why R' Yochanan could not condone forgiving Reish Lakish for his disrespectful words.

Even the Biryonim Honored the Gadol Hador

It is important for each individual to have his own rebbi, as Chazal teach: עֲשֵׂה לְךָ רַב, *Make for yourself a rav* (*Avos* 1:6). Yet, unfortunately, people often allow themselves to dismiss or even denigrate the words of a different rav, which is categorically forbidden!

We must always remember that while *gedolim* throughout the ages have expressed differing opinions, in no way does this grant people license to insult the rav of a different community or sector or to besmirch his name. This has become a prevalent problem in our generation, when boundaries have become blurred and people do as they please.

The Gemara relates (*Gittin* 56a) that when Vespasian and his army besieged Yerushalayim, R' Yochanan ben Zakkai requested a meeting with the Roman general, but he could not leave the city because the Biryonim and Sikrikim refused to allow anyone to pass through the city gates. To escape from the city, R' Yochanan staged his own death and even placed a decaying animal upon his body to emit a rotten odor while his *talmidim* carried him out of the city for a supposed burial. When they reached the city gates, the sentries wished to stab R' Yochanan's body with their spears to ensure that he was truly dead, but his *talmidim* objected, "They will say that they stabbed their rebbi." The guards wished to at least push him, but the *talmidim* again protested, "They will say that they shoved their rebbi." Upon hearing this, the guards conceded and opened the gates to allow the procession to exit.

If the wicked Biryonim, who did not balk at starving the entire city of Yerushalayim in order to avoid surrendering to the Roman army, could acknowledge the honor that they owed R' Yochanan, how much more so must we — *bnei Torah* who toil in the *beis midrash*! — appreciate our obligation to honor our rabbanim and *talmidei chachamim*.

Sadly, in recent years, we have witnessed a stark deterioration in *hisbatlus* to *gedolei hador*, and this corruption has even spread to our holy yeshivos, where we occasionally hear *bachurim* who speak brazenly and scornfully against great *talmidei chachamim*. Somehow, every *bachur* feels he has the right to an opinion, and even if his rebbi says one thing, he thinks otherwise. How contemptible are those people who rush to their rebbi to request a *berachah* or advice when they are suffering a personal difficulty, but when the rebbi instructs them to mend their ways and undertake a *kabbalah*, they refuse to do so, or ignore his words.

We cannot know for sure, yet I believe that many of the *tzaros* that we suffer today, *Rachmana litzlan,* are born of the terrible disrespect to *talmidei chachamim* and rabbanim, as we know that "one bit of *leitzanus* dismisses a hundred rebukes." Even though our sources all state that evil decrees result from *bittul Torah,* the two issues are really one and the same, since without our rabbanim, there is no Torah, and a lack in *kavod haTorah* is tantamount to *bittul Torah.*

We must all improve in this realm and yield to the authority of our *gedolim* and rabbanim, and may Hashem reward us with the fulfillment of the Midrash that states: "In the future to come, Hakadosh Baruch Hu will honor the elders."

פרשת תזריע
Parashas Tazria

৺ *Outside the Camp*

כָּל יְמֵי אֲשֶׁר הַנֶּגַע בּוֹ יִטְמָא טָמֵא הוּא בָּדָד יֵשֵׁב מִחוּץ לַמַּחֲנֶה מוֹשָׁבוֹ.

All the days that the affliction is upon him he shall remain contaminated; he is contaminated. He shall dwell in isolation; his dwelling shall be outside the camp (*Vayikra* 13:46).

The Mishnah teaches (*Keilim* 1:4): "More stringent than a *zav* is a *zavah,* as she transmits *tumah* to a man who cohabits with her. More stringent than the *zavah* is a *metzora,* as he transmits *tumah* through entry."

With these words, the Mishnah describes the powerful *tumah* of the *metzora,* who transmits impurity to any person or utensil inside a dwelling that he enters. Rashi (*Bamidbar* 12:12) adds that a *metzora* is regarded as a corpse, and just as a corpse renders everything impure upon entry, so too, the *metzora* renders everything impure upon entry. The *mefarshim* explain that since the impurity of a *metzora* is as halachically severe as *tumas meis,* he is regarded as if he were dead.

The Four Regarded as Dead

The Gemara states: "Four are regarded as dead — a pauper, a *metzora*, a blind person, and one who has no children" (*Nedarim* 64b).

What is the common denominator among these four groups that earns them the abysmal description of "*chashuv k'meis*"?

The obvious answer is that a pauper, a blind person, and a childless person endure so much emotional anguish that their lives are not worth living, while the *metzora* suffers so much physical pain that his life is likewise no longer worth living.

There must be a deeper explanation, however, because even one who endures unimaginable suffering is still very much alive, and it cannot be the physical or even emotional *yissurim* of these four types of people that cause them to be regarded as if they were dead. The Rosh Yeshivah R' Chaim Shmulevitz frequently emphasized[3] that even a life riddled with dreadful suffering and torturous punishment in Olam Hazeh is still inestimably superior to the finality of death, for as long as man is still present in this world, he can grow, accomplish, and discover the joy and privileges inherent even in terrible tragedy and pain. Death, in contrast, is permanent and irrevocable, and denies a person the opportunity to ever acquire further, eternal happiness, which he will ultimately enjoy in Olam Haba.

A Metzora Is Not Regarded as Dead Because of His Physical Pain

With this perspective, it is clear that the physical pain of *tzaraas* does not render the *metzora's* life not worth living, since even the worst imaginable *yissurim* are still preferable to death. Indeed, Dovid HaMelech declares gratefully: יַסֹּר יִסְּרַנִּי יָּהּ וְלַמָּוֶת לֹא נְתָנָנִי, *God has chastened me exceedingly, but He did not give me over to death* (*Tehillim* 118:18), and Rashi notes that for six months, Dovid was afflicted with *tzaraas*.

3. *Sichos Mussar, Osher HaChaim*; see *Parashas Noach*, "Sharing the Burden of a Friend," and *Parashas Shemos*, "The Value of Life."

The Gemara elaborates (*Sanhedrin* 107a): "For six months Dovid was afflicted with *tzaraas* ... as it is written, תְּחַטְּאֵנִי בְאֵזוֹב, *Purge me of sin with hyssop* (*Tehillim* 51:9)." Rashi explains that since Dovid prayed to be purged with hyssop, it follows that he was a *metzora*. Yet although Dovid HaMelech was afflicted with the excruciating pain of *tzaraas*, he still thanked Hashem for sparing him from death and allowing him to continue living. This is a clear indication that the pain of *tzaraas* is not tantamount to death.

Why, then, is a *metzora* regarded as dead?

Living Alone

R' Chaim Shmulevitz clarifies that a *metzora* is regarded as dead because the Torah condemns him to solitude, as it states, בָּדָד יֵשֵׁב, *He shall dwell in isolation* (*Vayikra* 13:46). Since a *metzora* is isolated, his life isn't life, and he is thus regarded as dead. Examining the four categories of people who are regarded as dead, we find that the common denominator among them is isolation.

Why is a deaf person not regarded as dead? Elsewhere, the Gemara seems to imply that deafness is actually a worse defect than blindness, as it states (*Bava Kamma* 85b) that if a person blinded someone's eye, he must compensate him for the value of his eye, but if he made the person deaf, he must pay his total value. The Rashba notes that the halachah regarding paying compensation for an eye applies only if the victim was blinded in both eyes, for if he was blinded in only one eye, he is still fit to perform all labors. In contrast, says the Rashba, one who is rendered deaf is compensated with his full value, since he is no longer fit to do anything, and is regarded as dead.

This halachah seems to indicate that someone who is blinded in both eyes is not regarded as dead, and therefore receives only the value of the eye in compensation, while a deaf person *is* regarded as dead, which is why someone who causes another to go deaf must pay the person's full value, and not only the value of his ears. Considering Chazal's statement that a blind person is regarded as dead, how are we to understand this?

When Chazal rule in laws of damages, their objective is always to compensate the victim for the loss he personally suffered, and in this regard the value of the ear exceeds the value of the eye. Indeed, Rabbeinu Yonah writes (*Shaarei Teshuvah* 2:12), regarding the verse: מְאוֹר עֵינַיִם יְשַׂמַּח לֵב שְׁמוּעָה טוֹבָה תְּדַשֶּׁן עָצֶם, *The light of the eyes gladdens the heart; good tidings fatten bone* (*Mishlei* 15:30):

> The eye is a very precious organ, because it enables people to see light, which gladdens the heart. Yet the ear is even more precious, because it enables people to hear good tidings, which fatten bone, [a body part] that cannot feel and cannot be fattened on account of the light of the eyes, but only with more intense pleasure. Our Sages, of blessed memory, also stated that the ear is more precious than the other organs, for if one blinded the eye of his fellow, he pays him only the value of his eye, but if one made his fellow deaf, he must pay his fellow's entire value.

In other words, the value of the ear supersedes that of the eye, since it brings pleasure to the entire body, whereas the pleasure of sight does not affect the whole body.

Rabbeinu Bechaye writes similarly (*Shemos* 4:11): "The sense of hearing is more significant than the sense of sight ... for aside from expanding the heart and bringing joy to it, it also invigorates one's bones. Indeed, the benefits a person derives from his ears surpass those of the eyes."

All this relates to the benefits that a person himself enjoys. Yet if we evaluate which sense is more effective in interpersonal relationships, there is no question that the eyes are of inestimably greater importance than the ears! Vision enables a person to see another person, feel his presence, relate to him, and communicate. Indeed, regarding the Torah's statement, וַיִּגְדַּל מֹשֶׁה וַיֵּצֵא אֶל אֶחָיו וַיַּרְא בְּסִבְלֹתָם, *Moshe grew up and went out to his brethren and observed their burdens* (*Shemos* 2:11), Rashi comments that the words וַיַּרְא בְּסִבְלֹתָם indicate that Moshe "gave his eyes and heart to feel distress for them." Only by using his eyes was Moshe Rabbeinu able to truly feel Bnei Yisrael's terrible oppression and suffering. When he "gave his eyes," the feelings touched his heart, and he was able to share their pain.

In contrast, one who cannot see cannot feel another person's pain or share it. We find that when Yaakov Avinu wanted to bless Menashe and Efraim, the Torah states: וְעֵינֵי יִשְׂרָאֵל כָּבְדוּ מִזֹּקֶן לֹא יוּכַל לִרְאוֹת וַיַּגֵּשׁ אֹתָם אֵלָיו וַיִּשַּׁק לָהֶם וַיְחַבֵּק לָהֶם, *Now Israel's eyes were heavy with age, he could not see; so he brought them near him and he kissed them and hugged them* (*Bereishis* 48:10). The Sforno explains that Yaakov Avinu "could not see well enough that his blessing should rest upon them when he saw them." Therefore, "he kissed them and embraced them — so that his soul would cleave to them, and his blessing would rest upon them."

Had Yaakov Avinu been able to see Menashe and Efraim, that would have bred an automatic closeness between them, and his *berachah* would have come upon them immediately. Yet because his eyes were heavy with age and he could not see them well, he needed to embrace them and kiss them in order to for his soul to cleave to theirs so that his *berachah* to them could take effect.

Based on this, we can explain Hakadosh Baruch Hu's words to Moshe Rabbeinu regarding Aharon: וְרָאֲךָ וְשָׂמַח בְּלִבּוֹ, *And when he sees you he will rejoice in his heart* (*Shemos* 4:14). The Torah attests that when Moshe and Aharon were reunited, their souls cleaved to one another with love, as the *pasuk* states, וַיֵּלֶךְ וַיִּפְגְּשֵׁהוּ בְּהַר הָאֱלֹהִים וַיִּשַּׁק לוֹ, *So he went and encountered him at the mountain of God, and he kissed him* (ibid. v. 27). From the moment that Aharon HaKohen glimpsed Moshe Rabbeinu with his eyes, his heart filled with joy.

This also explains why a blind person is regarded as dead, and a deaf person is not. While a deaf person is profoundly affected by his disability, he is still very much alive, aware, and connected to his environment and the people around him. A blind person, in contrast, is alone and isolated, and cannot forge a deep connection of friendship and love with those around him. His life is not a life, which is why he is regarded as dead.

The Inability to Give

The same concept can be applied to one who is childless. On the surface, it would seem such a person has an easy, carefree life. He is exempt of *tzaar gidul banim*; his burden of *parnassah* is minimal, since he has no dependents to support; and his life should be straightforward and comfortable. Why is he, of all people, regarded as dead?

Embedded in the very fabric of human nature is the powerful desire to give to others, and even stronger and more compelling than that is a parent's deep-seated desire to give to a child. Conversely, the only person from whom one is willing to accept so much is a parent. One who is childless cannot sate this overpowering desire to give, which is an integral part of human nature, and his life is thus not a life.

The power of parental giving is demonstrated in the story of the two women who came to Shlomo HaMelech, each claiming that the living infant was her child, and the infant who had perished was the other woman's child. How could the woman who had lost her child be so cruel as to attempt to kidnap another baby from his mother's arms in order to replace the one she'd lost? She had no doubt that this was not her child, so how could she insist on taking the other mother's child for herself?

This bereaved mother knew that if she would raise this child as her own, he would grow up believing that she was his biological mother and would gladly accept all the kindness and love that she would shower upon him. This would satisfy her maternal instinct and fulfill her innate desire to give.

So intense and deep-rooted is a parent's desire to give to a child that this woman was willing to commit a heinous crime against an innocent woman in order to satisfy this craving. This underscores that when a person cannot actualize the instinct to give, his life is worthless, which is why those who are childless are regarded as dead.

The same rationale applies to the pauper. While a pauper is constantly distressed due to his trying circumstances and may suffer hunger, cold, and deprivation, these difficulties are not the reason he is regarded as dead. What reduces the life of a pauper to one that is not worth living is his inability to give to another. His destitution pervades every fiber of his being and prevents him from reaching out to help his fellow man. The feeling that one cannot give anything of oneself to others is infinitely worse than poverty itself, and this is why a pauper is regarded as dead.

The common element among the pauper, the *metzora*, the blind person, and the childless person is that they lack the opportunity and conditions to connect to others, live with them, give to them, and build relationships, and this is why their life is not life.

פרשת מצורע
Parashas Metzora

⇐§ *The Key to Sealing Our Lips*

וַיְדַבֵּר ה׳ אֶל מֹשֶׁה לֵּאמֹר זֹאת תִּהְיֶה תּוֹרַת הַמְּצֹרָע.
Hashem spoke to Moshe saying, "This shall be the law of the metzora" (*Vayikra* 14:1,2).

"Reish Lakish said: What is the meaning of that which is written: *This shall be the law of the metzora?* This shall be the law of the *motzi shem ra* (defamer)" (*Arachin* 15b).

The Gemara teaches that the label *metzora* reflects this individual's wicked actions; it is a contraction of the term *motzi shem ra,* which literally means "spreading a bad name" about another. The fundamental flaw of one who speaks *lashon hara* is that he cannot coexist peacefully with others. Instead of speaking positively of them and praising their good qualities, he chooses to denigrate and malign them, and the Torah therefore calls him a *metzora.*

A *metzora* is punished with *tzaraas,* as the Gemara (ibid.) states: "R' Yose ben Zimra said: One who speaks *lashon hara, negaim* come upon him." The first example of this in the Torah is Moshe Rabbeinu, who is described as: וְהִנֵּה יָדוֹ מְצֹרַעַת כַּשָּׁלֶג, *And behold, his hand was leprous, like snow* (*Shemos* 4:6). Rashi comments: "With this sign, He hinted that he had spoken *lashon hara* when he said, 'But they will not believe me' (ibid. v. 1); therefore, he was punished with *tzaraas.*"

Miriam HaNeviah was also punished with *tzaraas* for speaking *lashon hara*, as the *pasuk* says: וְהִנֵּה מִרְיָם מְצֹרַעַת כַּשָּׁלֶג, *And behold! Miriam was afflicted with tzaraas, like snow* (*Bamidbar* 12:10). Chazal expound: "*Negaim* come because of *lashon hara*. [When] the righteous Miriam spoke *lashon hara* about her brother Moshe, *negaim* afflicted her" (*Devarim Rabbah* 6:8).

The Torah states, regarding the *metzora*: בָּדָד יֵשֵׁב מִחוּץ לַמַּחֲנֶה מוֹשָׁבוֹ, *He shall dwell in isolation; his dwelling shall be outside the camp* (*Vayikra* 13:46). The Gemara explains: "What is different about the *metzora* that the Torah said, *He shall dwell in isolation; his dwelling shall be outside the camp*? He sowed discord between man and his wife, and between man and his friend; therefore, the Torah said that he shall sit alone" (*Arachin* 16b).

The Rambam further teaches, in his commentary on Mishnayos: "They said about this *tzaraas* mentioned in the Torah that it is nothing but a punishment to one who speaks *lashon hara*, so he will be separated from other people and relieve them of the damages [inflicted] by his tongue" (*Negaim* 12:5).

One who wishes to avoid stirring conflict and friction among others should take heed of Dovid HaMelech's words in *Tehillim*: נְצֹר לְשׁוֹנְךָ מֵרָע, *Guard your tongue from evil* (34:14). The Chofetz Chaim illuminates: "Guarding the tongue from evil includes guarding it from all manners of speech intended to harm or belittle one's friend, such as *lashon hara* and *rechilus*, *machlokes* and cursing, humiliating others and *onaas devarim*" (*Shemiras HaLashon*, *Shaar HaTevunah* Ch. 11). All these forms of negative speech drive a person away from the *klal* and sow discord and disunity between man and his fellow, which is why a person must act with extreme caution to seal his lips and avoid stumbling in these severe prohibitions.

Wanting Good for Another

The Torah commands: וְאָהַבְתָּ לְרֵעֲךָ כָּמוֹךָ, *You shall love your fellow as yourself* (*Vayikra* 19:18), yet is it really possible for a person to love his fellow man as he loves himself? This mitzvah seems to be at odds with human nature.

The Ramban (ibid. v. 17) writes about this mitzvah, "It is an exaggeration, because it is impossible for the human heart to love one's fellow as he loves himself; furthermore, R' Akiva has already taught that 'your life takes precedence over the life of your friend' (*Bava Metzia* 62a)."

If we would try to explain that the mitzvah of וְאָהַבְתָּ לְרֵעֲךָ כָּמוֹךָ is a command to feel love and closeness to another, then it would be clear that the Torah's use of the word כָּמוֹךָ, *as yourself,* is an overstatement, because a person will always feel closest to himself and care more about himself than about another person, and it is also impossible to compel the heart to feel love for another person to the same extent that one loves oneself. Moreover, R' Akiva derives from the *pasuk*, וְחֵי אָחִיךָ עִמָּךְ, *And let your brother live with you* (*Vayikra* 25:36), that when faced with a life-threatening situation, a person is obligated to place his own life before the life of another. How can this halachah be reconciled with the requirement to love one's friend as he loves himself?

The Ramban calls attention to the prefix used in the word לרעך: The Torah says, וְאָהַבְתָּ לְרֵעֲךָ כָּמוֹךָ (literally, "you shall love *to* your friend"), as opposed to the more standard construction, **וְאָהַבְתָּ אֶת** רֵעֲךָ כָּמוֹךָ ("you shall love your friend"). He writes:

> The Torah commands here that one shall love his fellow regarding every aspect of life just as one loves himself regarding all that is good ... Many times a person will have love for his fellow only with regard to specific things, such as that he be graced with wealth, but not with wisdom, or other such things. And even if one were to love his fellow in regard to all things, he will want only that his fellow who is beloved to him attain wealth, property, and honor, knowledge and wisdom, but not that he shall be equal to him; rather, he will always want in his heart that he shall be superior to [his fellow] in all that is good. And so the verse here commands that this defect of jealousy shall not be present in one's heart; rather, one shall love the increase of goodness for his fellow as a person strives to obtain for himself.

The Ramban is explaining that וְאָהַבְתָּ לְרֵעֲךָ כָּמוֹךָ is not a commandment to feel sentiments of love; rather, it relates to the physical actions engendered by those feelings. Since a person loves himself, he automatically wants all the goodness in the world for himself — wealth and prosperity, children, *nachas*, and so on. Yet when it comes to others, not only does a person not naturally desire to see his friend succeeding, he also wants his friend's success to be limited, or at least less than the success he enjoys.

The Torah commands us to eliminate these disgraceful sentiments of jealousy and competitiveness from our hearts, as they cause us to desire that others not enjoy blessing. Instead, it is incumbent upon us to love our friends and desire unlimited goodness for them. When we watch our friend succeed and receive blessing and goodness from Hashem, we should rejoice genuinely with him as if the goodness and blessing were our own!

We fulfill the mitzvah of וְאָהַבְתָּ לְרֵעֲךָ כָּמוֹךָ by loving our fellow man, desiring his success, and banishing any trace of jealousy from our heart. Accordingly, the requirement to love your friend as yourself can be understood literally, and not as an exaggeration.

The psychology underlying this mitzvah is that man is motivated by his personal interests, more so than by thoughts of another person's welfare. Even actions that appear benevolent or altruistic are really spurred by personal considerations. Anyone is willing to stroke and calm a crying infant, and even though the action may seem motivated by love and concern for the infant, it is really done out of self-love. Hakadosh Baruch Hu embedded into the laws of nature a love of children in order to ensure that their needs will be met.

The definition of וְאָהַבְתָּ לְרֵעֲךָ כָּמוֹךָ is eliminating envy from the heart and desiring another person's success as much as we desire our own success. This means that even if one is not blessed with wisdom or wealth, children or success, one should still wish these blessings wholeheartedly on others.

Love Leads to Praise

A person who strengthens himself in this mitzvah by eradicating all sentiments of envy from the heart and implanting in himself a genuine desire for the other person's good will be spared from the grave sins of *lashon hara, rechilus, machlokes,* and *halbanas panim.* This is not a reward, but a natural consequence of his actions, as a person who genuinely loves his friend and desires good for him will automatically guard his tongue against evil speech and also rejoice at every opportunity to praise him, as the Rambam writes, "It is a mitzvah for every person to love each and every Jew as himself, as it is written, *You shall love your fellow as yourself.* Therefore, he must speak in praise of him" (*Hilchos Deios* 6:4).

The Chofetz Chaim writes similarly (*Shemiras HaLashon, Shaar HaTevunah* Ch. 5):

> When we contemplate this, we find that fulfilling the mitzvah of judging one's friend favorably and the attribute of guarding one's tongue are both dependent on fulfilling the positive commandment of "You shall love your fellow as yourself." For if one truly loves his friend, surely he will not speak *lashon hara* about him, and he will seek with all his strength to justify his [actions], just as if it ever happened that he did something improper and people would stand and discuss the matter, and he could justify it — or if it was truly a mistake, or if he had some other reason — how he would long for someone to rise and defend him so he would not be humiliated because of it! So he must do this for his friend in the very same way.

Rectifying one's character traits is a significant aspect of *avodas Hashem,* one that is closely linked to *limud Torah.* Although it seems that intellect is the primary vehicle for acquiring Torah, we also know that "Torah is acquired with forty-eight things" (*Avos* 6:6), many of which are *middos* that relate to *bein adam lachaveiro.* The reason for this is that understanding and good judgment are largely rooted in the heart, as we find that the Rashbam teaches (*Bava Basra* 131a, s.v. *Ve'al tigmeru*): "The judge can only make use of what his eyes see, and this rule applies to anything dependent on logic as well, for all he has is what his heart sees." This means that only a person "with a heart," who can see and understand another person's needs, can truly delve into a *sugya,* analyze it from all angles, and understand what his heart sees.

Who was a greater paradigm of this than the Rosh Yeshivah R' Chaim Shmulevitz, who possessed both a razor-sharp mind and a compassionate, loving heart? His unparalleled genius and astonishing breadth and depth of knowledge, which allowed him to fathom the deepest secrets of Torah, were matched only by his vast heart and keen sensitivity to his fellow man. With his supreme brilliance, he melded these two qualities to form the spiritual perfection that we call *gadlus.*

Emulating his example, we must consistently strive to reach out, care for others, and fill their needs even as we engage in *limud Torah,* for these two realms are really intertwined. It is impossible to excel in *limud Torah* or *yiras Shamayim* without *avodas hamiddos,* and, conversely, it is impossible to acquire a wise and understanding heart without *limud Torah* — because only the Torah teaches us how to perfect our character traits.

Hakadosh Baruch Hu should help us learn and complete many *masechtos* while attaining *shleimus* in our *avodas hamiddos,* and we should always merit to notice our friends' positive qualities, and never their shortcomings.

פרשת אחרי מות
Parashas Acharei Mos

◆§ *Shimush Talmidei Chachamim*

וַיְדַבֵּר ה׳ אֶל מֹשֶׁה אַחֲרֵי מוֹת שְׁנֵי בְּנֵי אַהֲרֹן בְּקָרְבָתָם לִפְנֵי ה׳ וַיָּמֻתוּ.

Hashem spoke to Moshe after the death of Aharon's two sons, when they approached before Hashem, and they died (*Vayikra* 16:1).

The Gemara (*Megillah* 31a) establishes that the Torah portion regarding the death of Aharon HaKohen's two sons is read on Yom Kippur. The Be'er Heitev states (*Orach Chaim* 621:1), citing the *Zohar* and Arizal: "One who mourns the deaths of the sons of Aharon and sheds tears over them on Yom Kippur, his sins are forgiven, and his children do not perish in his lifetime."

Why is mourning and crying over the deaths of Nadav and Avihu so commendable that one who does so is worthy of full atonement and is promised that his children will not die in his lifetime?

The Gemara (*Chullin* 71a) teaches that Ben Azzai said about himself: "Alas that Ben Azzai did not serve R' Yishmael," and Rashi elaborates: "It is a loss and destructive to the world that a veteran disciple like me, Ben Azzai, did not serve R' Yishmael."

The Rosh Yeshivah R' Chaim Shmulevitz notes[4] that elsewhere,

4. *Sichos Mussar, HaChiyuv Lehisalos.*

Ben Azzai declared, "All the sages of Israel compare to me as a garlic peel" (*Bechoros* 58a). If Ben Azzai could confidently assert that he was greater than all his contemporaries, including R' Yishmael, why would the world suffer loss and devastation due to his failure to serve R' Yishmael?

Even if Ben Azzai was, indeed, greater than all the sages of his era, serving a *talmid chacham* of R' Yishmael's caliber would still have propelled him forward, enhanced his spiritual ascent, and enabled him to achieve loftier heights in at least some aspect of his learning. Because Ben Azzai forfeited that potential for growth, the entire world suffered a loss.

Chazal extol the practice of *shimush talmidei chachamim*, as they teach (*Berachos* 7b): "R' Yochanan said in the name of R' Shimon ben Yochai: Attending to [Torah scholars] is greater than studying Torah, as it is stated (*II Melachim* 3:11): פֹּה אֱלִישָׁע בֶּן שָׁפָט אֲשֶׁר יָצַק מַיִם עַל יְדֵי אֵלִיָּהוּ, *Here is Elisha the son of Shafat who poured water on the hands of Eliyahu*. It does not say that he studied Torah, but rather that he poured [water on his hands]. This teaches that attending [to a Torah scholar] is greater than studying [Torah]."

One who serves a *talmid chacham* absorbs not only his knowledge and wisdom, but also his methodology and system of learning. This benefits the entire world, since the disciple then relays what he learned to his own *talmidim*, who transmit it to their *talmidim* and onward, until the whole world reaps the extra wisdom gained from the original rebbi. Conversely, if a *talmid* does not serve his rebbi, he deprives others of these priceless gifts, which is an irreplaceable loss for the world.

A Conduit of Wisdom

Beyond the *derech halimud* that the *talmid* absorbs in the course of serving his rebbi, and the ensuing proliferation of Torah, a *talmid* who serves his rebbi also draws spiritual bounty into the world. A *gadol b'Yisrael* is a pipeline that Hakadosh Baruch Hu places in this world in order to share the bounty of His Torah and wisdom with other sages and disseminate it to all of Klal Yisrael. When a *talmid* serves his rebbi and absorbs the wisdom at his fingertips, he automatically grows spiritually and is thus able to impact and draw greater bounty upon his fellow Torah scholars.

R' Chaim proved this from the description of Eliyahu HaNavi's ascent to heaven in a tempest. The *bnei hanevi'im* said to Elisha HaNavi: הִנֵּה נָא יֵשׁ אֶת עֲבָדֶיךָ חֲמִשִּׁים אֲנָשִׁים בְּנֵי חַיִל יֵלְכוּ נָא וִיבַקְשׁוּ אֶת אֲדֹנֶיךָ פֶּן נְשָׂאוֹ רוּחַ ה' וַיַּשְׁלִכֵהוּ בְּאַחַד הֶהָרִים אוֹ בְּאַחַת הַגֵּיאָוֹת וַיֹּאמֶר לֹא תִשְׁלָחוּ, *"Behold, among your servants there are fifty able-bodied men. Let them go and search for your master; perhaps a spirit of Hashem has carried him off and hurled him onto one of the mountains or one of the valleys." But [Elisha] said, "Don't send them"* (*II Melachim* 2:16). Regarding the words פֶּן נְשָׂאוֹ רוּחַ ה', Rashi comments: "This teaches that from the day that Eliyahu was hidden, *ruach hakodesh* began to be taken from the prophets, and afterward, *ruach hakodesh* was no longer prevalent among the Jewish people." During his lifetime, Eliyahu HaNavi served as the spiritual conduit that channeled *ruach hakodesh* to the prophets of his generation, and from the time he ascended to heaven, all the prophets of his generation experienced a decline in their level of prophecy.

The same applies to Torah wisdom. Every *talmid chacham* becomes a spiritual channel that spreads Torah wisdom to his fellow sages, so every additional aspect of Torah that he acquires benefits the entire world. In contrast, if a *talmid chacham* lacks even a minor aspect of the Torah's wisdom, it is an irreplaceable loss for the entire world. Perhaps this is the reason why Chazal instructed that "your fear of your rebbi should be as your fear of Heaven" (*Avos* 4:12) and instituted the halachah exempting a *talmid* from leaning at the Pesach Seder in the presence of his rebbi (*Pesachim* 108a), out of his reverence for him. Moreover, a *talmid* who sits and learns Torah from his rebbi absorbs the flow of wisdom that Hakadosh Baruch Hu channels to him, which is why at that moment, his fear of his rebbi must be akin to his fear of Heaven.

Punishment Is Meted to Those Who Do Not Serve Talmidei Chachamim

The Gemara relates (*Sanhedrin* 68a): "When R' Eliezer fell ill, R' Akiva and his colleagues entered to visit him ... When the Sages realized that his mind was settled, they entered and sat before him ... R' Akiva said to him: 'What will be my death?' R' Eliezer replied: 'Yours will be worse than theirs.'" Rashi elaborates: "Yours will be worse than theirs — for your heart is as broad as the entrance to the Sanctuary, and had you served me, you would have learned a great deal of Torah."

These words of Chazal are chilling — especially considering the following account of the Gemara (*Menachos* 29b). When Moshe Rabbeinu ascended to Heaven, he saw Hakadosh Baruch Hu adding crowns to letters in the Torah. He asked Him why He was doing this, and Hakadosh Baruch Hu replied, "There is a man who is destined to live after several generations, and his name is Akiva ben Yosef. He will expound upon each and every point heaps and heaps of halachos."

"Ribbono Shel Olam!" cried Moshe. "If You have a man like this, why are You giving Torah through me?"

To this, Hashem replied, "Silence! This is what I have determined."

So exalted was R' Akiva's spiritual stature that he was worthy of receiving Torah on Har Sinai and delivering it to Klal Yisrael! Moshe Rabbeinu himself couldn't fathom why Hashem had chosen him over R' Akiva. How, then, could R' Akiva be condemned to the gruesome death of having his skin flayed with iron combs (*Berachos* 61b) due to the seemingly minor omission of not serving R' Eliezer as he should have?

R' Chaim explains that this Gemara highlights the profound loss resulting from a failure to properly serve *talmidei chachamim*. Had R' Akiva served R' Eliezer, he would have acquired an even higher level of Torah, which he would then have transmitted to future generations. Since he failed to do so, he forfeited that Torah, and the entire world suffers the loss of this priceless Torah until this very day. Since R' Akiva was so outstandingly righteous, Hashem subjected him to strict judgment, and he was punished with an excruciating death.

Based on this, we can understand the Be'er Heitev's statement regarding the value of shedding tears on Yom Kippur over the loss of Nadav and Avihu. The grief we are meant to feel over the deaths of these *tzaddikim* relates not to them personally, but to the crushing, permanent loss that befell the world due to their deaths. Had Aharon's sons not perished before their time, they would have surely continued serving Moshe Rabbeinu for many years and acquired an immeasurable amount of Torah wisdom and *derech halimud*, which would have been bequeathed to future generations until this very day! Their premature deaths caused the entire world to forfeit untold Torah treasures.

Everyone Is Obliged to Increase Shimush Chachamim

Shimush chachamim is an integral aspect of Kabbalas HaTorah, and without it, it is impossible to truly grasp the wisdom of Torah. One who is negligent in *shimush chachamim* triggers a grave loss — not only to himself, but to the entire world for generations to come. This obligates each one of us, for no one can say, "I'm okay as I am. I possess enough Torah knowledge." Rather, we must constantly strive for more, aspiring to learn without interruption or distraction.

A genuine *mevakesh* thirsts to toil in Torah without limits, just as a person walking through a hot desert craves even a drop of water. The Midrash states: "Just as these fish grow in the water, yet when a drop falls from above, they receive it thirstily as if they have never tasted water, so, too, Yisrael flourishes in the water of Torah. When they hear something new from the Torah, they accept it thirstily, like someone who has never heard a word of Torah" (*Bereishis Rabbah* 97:3). This lesson is obvious to anyone who has ever seen *talmidei chachamim* and *gedolei Yisrael*. The more they fill their minds and hearts with Shas and Poskim, the more they crave to learn Torah.

Each day in Maariv, we recite the words, כִּי הֵם חַיֵּינוּ וְאֹרֶךְ יָמֵינוּ, וּבָהֶם נֶהְגֶּה יוֹמָם וָלָיְלָה, *For they are our lives and the length of our days, and in them we shall engage day and night*. Every one of us must aspire to regard Torah as life itself, and to feel and know that without Torah, we have neither purpose nor existence in this world, as the Mishnah teaches: "These are the things that have no fixed amount. *Pe'ah* and *bikkurim* and being seen [in the Beis HaMikdash on Yom Tov] and performing loving-kindness and learning Torah ... and learning Torah is equivalent to them all" (*Pe'ah* 1:1). There is no limit, fixed time, or designated place for Torah study, and one is obliged to devote every hour and day of life to toiling in Torah, because *talmud Torah k'neged kulam*!

Make Yourself a Rav

An additional lesson that we derive from the Gemara's statement about *shimush talmidei chachamim* is that every person — even the greatest *talmid chacham* in the world — is required to find someone greater than he whom he can establish as his rav who will teach him Torah. Since a rav is the spiritual channel through which Torah streams from Hakadosh Baruch Hu into the heart and mind of the *talmid chacham*, every person needs a rav to serve, in order to receive that bounty of Torah. This obligation is set forth clearly by Chazal who instruct, עֲשֵׂה לְךָ רַב, *Make for yourself a rav* (*Avos* 1:6).

This conduct was modeled by the Rosh Yeshivah R' Eliezer Yehudah Finkel, who, even before the age of bar mitzvah, ran away from home in order to seclude himself in a *makom Torah* — and we cannot forget the kind of home where he was raised! He was the son of the Alter of Slabodka, and of a righteous mother who descended from seventeen or nineteen generations of rabbanim! Notwithstanding the *kedushah* and Torah permeating his home, he fled because he felt that his family was being supported by the yeshivah, and he did not wish to benefit from these sacred funds. He wandered from place to place, aspiring to learn Torah from all *gedolei Yisrael*. In Telshe, he learned Torah under the tutelage of R' Eliezer Gordon; and during another period, he journeyed to the court of the Avnei Nezer in Sochachov. While the Avnei Nezer was a chassidishe Rebbe, and R' Eliezer Yehudah was a staunch Litvak, he saw no harm in learning Torah from the *tzaddik*. Apparently, however, he did not understand the Polish-chassidish dialect spoken in the town, and when he approached the Avnei Nezer to ask him what to do, the Avnei Nezer instructed him to continue his travels, while showering him with effusive *berachos*, and he left.

He spent the next year learning in Radin, during which time he mastered two *sedarim* in Shas — *Moed and Kodashim*, supporting himself by teaching young children, serving as *gabbai* in the local shul, and arranging places in the shul. With his meager income, he also supported five *talmidei chachamim*, so they would be able to learn in peace. Among these five *talmidei chachamim* were R' Naftali Tropp; R' Alter Stuchiner, father of R' Chaim Shmulevitz; and another three individuals, all of whom blossomed into *gedolei Yisrael*.

Most significantly, however, he studied under R' Chaim Brisker, who became his *rebbi muvhak*. He once shared that his father-in-law, the Rosh Yeshivah R' Eliyahu Baruch Kamai, had once remarked that if he would merit entering Olam Haba and could learn *b'chavrusa* with anyone of his choice, he would choose R' Akiva Eiger. R' Eliezer Yehudah then replied that if the choice was presented to him, he would choose to learn in Olam Haba with R' Chaim Brisker.

When my rebbi, R' Chaim Kamil, received the offer to serve as rosh yeshivah in Ofakim, he traveled to the southern town and spent two Shabbosim in the yeshivah before announcing that he would accept the position. When a close *talmid* asked him why he was accepting the post, R' Chaim answered that he had seen that the *talmidim* in the yeshivah in Ofakim were *mevakshim* who yearned for a rav from whom they could learn and absorb Torah. This spurred R' Chaim to accept the position of rosh yeshivah in Ofakim, despite the distance from Yerushalayim.

One should never say that it is too difficult to find a rav. We can learn this from the *pasuk*, וַיָּבֹאוּ כָּל אִישׁ אֲשֶׁר נְשָׂאוֹ לִבּוֹ, *Every man whose heart inspired him came* (*Shemos* 35:21), regarding which the Ramban teaches: "None among them had studied these crafts from an artisan or was trained to perform these skilled labors. Yet they discovered the inherent capacity to do it, *and his heart was elevated in the ways of Hashem* (*II Divrei HaYamim* 17:6), to come before Moshe and tell him, 'I will do all that my master says.'"

These *chachmei lev* did not despair because they lacked the skills or professional training to perform the tasks required to craft the Mishkan and its vessels. Rather, because their hearts were elevated, they longed to do the work. They refused to succumb to indolence or lethargy and persistently asked Moshe Rabbeinu exactly what to do.

If the building of the Mishkan, which required the finest precision and artisanry, could be performed by those who possessed wise, elevated hearts, then certainly we must never shirk our spiritual obligations on the grounds that we are incapable. On the contrary, we must elevate our hearts in the ways of Hashem and gather our strength, and then, with Hashem's help, we will witness great success in all our endeavors.

פרשת קדושים
Parashas Kedoshim

◆§ *Striving for Sanctity*

דַּבֵּר אֶל כָּל עֲדַת בְּנֵי יִשְׂרָאֵל וְאָמַרְתָּ אֲלֵהֶם קְדֹשִׁים תִּהְיוּ כִּי קָדוֹשׁ אֲנִי ה׳ אֱלֹהֵיכֶם.

Speak to the entire assembly of the Children of Israel and say to them: You shall be holy, for I, Hashem, your God, am holy (*Vayikra* 19:2).

The mitzvah of קְדֹשִׁים תִּהְיוּ, *you shall be holy,* obligates Klal Yisrael to sanctify ourselves in all our ways, and the Torah seems to give a reason for this mitzvah: כִּי קָדוֹשׁ אֲנִי ה׳ אֱלֹהֵיכֶם, *for I, Hashem, your God, am holy*.

The Ohr HaChaim is puzzled by this reason. Is it possible, he wonders, to obligate a creation to be like its creator? Besides, he adds, Hashem possesses many qualities that are not relevant to us.

If indeed the reason we are commanded to sanctify ourselves is that Hashem is holy, then it follows that we are obligated to attain the same level of sanctity. Clearly, this is impossible for a human being, as a person formed of flesh and blood can never achieve Hashem's consummate level of *kedushah*.

The Ohr HaChaim explains that this question prompted Chazal to explain the *pasuk* as follows: "This means, if you sanctify yourselves, I regard it as if you sanctified Me; and if you do not sanctify yourselves, I regard it as if you did not sanctify Me" (*Toras Kohanim, Kedoshim* Ch. 1). The underlying premise of the commandment of *kedoshim tihyu* is that Hakadosh Baruch Hu's own *kedushah* is dependent, so to speak, on Bnei Yisrael's *kedushah.* When Bnei Yisrael sanctify themselves and conduct themselves in a holy manner, Hashem rewards us as if His supreme holiness in this world was brought about by us! Yet if, *chas v'shalom*, Bnei Yisrael do not sanctify themselves, they are accountable for the lack of *kiddush Hashem* in this world.

Kedushah Engenders More Kedushah

My rebbi, R' Chaim Kamil, taught[5] that the mitzvah of *kedoshim tihyu* reveals a new approach to *avodas Hashem.* There are times when, due to a person's circumstances or spiritual level, he cannot attain the desired level of *kedushah.* Yet he must nevertheless begin serving Hashem and engaging in the process of acquiring greater levels of *kedushah,* and then Hakadosh Baruch Hu will confer sanctity upon him and help him to improve in this area.

This concept is reflected in Chazal's interpretation of the *pasuk:* וְהִתְקַדִּשְׁתֶּם וִהְיִיתֶם קְדֹשִׁים, *You are to sanctify yourselves and you shall be holy* (*Vayikra* 11:44). Chazal expound (*Yoma* 39a): "If a person sanctifies himself a little, he is sanctified a great deal; if he sanctifies himself down below, he is sanctified above; if he sanctifies himself in this world, he is sanctified in the World to Come."

In this *pasuk,* the Torah juxtaposes a mitzvah with a promise. A person is obliged to work hard and strive with all his might, but he is then assured that *you shall be holy,* meaning that he will receive the *siyata diShmaya* that will enable him to purify himself even more and soar to loftier heights of *avodas Hashem.*

The Torah commands us *you shall be holy* and then immediately adds *for I, Hashem, your God, am holy,* in order to allay our concerns and reinforce the lesson that one should never be deterred or discouraged from aspiring to attain a higher level of *kedushah.* Sanctity is a gift from Hakadosh Baruch Hu, and His hand is large

---

5. *Imrei Chaim, Aliyah B'Maalos HaTorah V'HaKedushah.*

enough to rain blessing down upon all of Klal Yisrael, yet it is still incumbent upon each individual to strive to climb the ladder of *kedushah*.

Kedushah Generates Miracles

The Malbim (*Vayikra* 19:2) presents another explanation of the above statement of the Midrash, "If you sanctify yourselves, I regard it as if you sanctified Me; and if you do not sanctify yourselves, I regard it as if you did not sanctify Me."

Hakadosh Baruch Hu programmed the world to function according to man's conduct. When man is drawn after material pursuits, then Hakadosh Baruch Hu likewise runs the world according to the laws of nature. When man sanctifies himself, however, elevating himself beyond base materialism and empowering his intellect to dominate his physical desires, then Hakadosh Baruch Hu directs the world in a supernatural way. This is reflected in Chazal's words, "if you sanctify yourselves," meaning that if Klal Yisrael transcend their physical inclinations and give primacy to spiritual pursuits, then Hakadosh Baruch Hu will also run His world supernaturally, performing miracles for our benefit. Hashem then "regards it as if we sanctified Him," since our behavior prompted supernatural conduct on His part, engendering great *kiddush Hashem* in the world.

The *Zohar* relates that when R' Shimon bar Yochai's *talmidim* reached this *parashah,* they rejoiced upon the secrets that he revealed (*Kedoshim* 81a). In light of the above, we can explain that their *simchah* emanated from their recognition of the tremendous levels that a Yid is capable of attaining, as this *parashah* conveys. One who continually aims for higher spiritual levels will experience boundless *siyata diShmaya* in his life that will spur his ascent to an exalted level of *avodas Hashem*.

Just Start Learning

This approach relates to *limud Torah,* as well. One of the marvelous benefits of *limud Torah* is that one who toils in learning is guaranteed *siyata diShmaya* that will boost his efforts and propel him forward in his learning. Even — and especially! — when one feels that learning is a challenge, if he only overcomes the urge to desist and begins learning, he will be rewarded with Heavenly assistance that will empower him to attain great levels in Torah and mitzvos, beyond his physical capacities.

R' Chaim Kamil added[6] that one who toils and delves deeply in Torah will merit to fulfill all the mitzvos in the most optimal manner. Examining the mitzvos objectively, we find that many are beyond human capability and are extremely difficult to fulfill, such as the mitzvah of וְאָהַבְתָּ לְרֵעֲךָ כָּמוֹךָ — for how can we genuinely love another person as we love ourselves? Nevertheless, we find that *gedolei Yisrael* throughout the generations excelled in even the toughest mitzvos and fulfilled them in an awe-inspiring manner, as the Chazon Ish attests in one of his letters, "I am rich in my love of my fellow" (*Igros* Vol. 1, Torah, 14).

His secret is revealed in another one of his letters (ibid. 3), where he writes: "The words of Torah endure only in one who kills himself over it. The death [referred to] here is veering from a simple existence to a profound existence — to the innermost depths of life."

One who learns Torah superficially, without toil, and does not innovate *chiddushim* is living a "simple existence," and will never acquire lofty levels of Torah or manage to fulfill the most challenging mitzvos. In contrast, one who toils to learn Torah, invests blood, sweat, and tears into his learning, and works to develop *chiddushim* is living a "profound existence." Such a person elevates himself beyond physicality and makes spirituality the dominant force in his life, which enables him to attain lofty spiritual heights and fulfill all of the mitzvos — even those that are difficult to do.

Gedolei Yisrael, who elevated themselves from simple living to the innermost depths of life, and who invested their maximal efforts into toiling in Torah, ultimately achieved exalted levels of spiritual sanctity and were privileged to fulfill even the hardest mitzvos optimally.

---

6. *Imrei Chaim, Chiddushei Torah.*

May Hashem help us to redouble our efforts in *limud Torah,* to give primacy to spiritual pursuits, and to sanctify ourselves in every respect, so that we will be worthy of infinite spiritual bounty.

פרשת אמור
Parashas Emor

☙ *Forty-Eight Kinyanim of Torah*

וּסְפַרְתֶּם לָכֶם מִמָּחֳרַת הַשַּׁבָּת ... שֶׁבַע שַׁבָּתוֹת תְּמִימֹת תִּהְיֶינָה: עַד מִמָּחֳרַת הַשַּׁבָּת הַשְּׁבִיעִת תִּסְפְּרוּ חֲמִשִּׁים יוֹם.
You shall count for yourselves — from the morrow of the rest day ... seven weeks, they shall be complete. Until the morrow of the seventh week you shall count, fifty days (*Vayikra* 23:15-16).

The festival marking the culmination of Sefiras HaOmer, as well as Kabbalas HaTorah, is called Shavuos, as we say in the *Shemoneh Esrei* of this Yom Tov: חַג הַשָּׁבֻעוֹת הַזֶּה זְמַן מַתַּן תּוֹרָתֵנוּ, *this Festival of Shavuos, the time of the giving of our Torah.*

The essence of this Yom Tov, and what we commemorate for all generations, is, undoubtedly, the Torah that Klal Yisrael received on this day. Why, then, isn't the Yom Tov referred to chiefly as "Zman Mattan Torah"? What is the significance of the name "Shavuos," and why is this name given precedence, in our *tefillos*, over the giving of Torah? Finally, what is the connection between the mitzvah of Sefiras HaOmer and Mattan Torah?

R' Eliyahu Lopian teaches[7] that although the name "Shavuos"

7. *Lev Eliyahu, Vayikra, Chag HaShavuos – Mattan Torah.*

relates to the culmination of the mitzvah of Sefiras HaOmer, it also alludes to the fact that this day is "Zman Mattan Toraseinu."

The forty-nine days of Sefiras HaOmer are a time of intensive preparations and purification in anticipation of Kabbalas HaTorah, as described at length in the *Zohar*. The reason we mention Shavuos together with Mattan Torah in davening is that the counting of these weeks is, indeed, a preparation for Mattan Torah.

The Mishnah teaches: "Torah is greater than priesthood and royalty, for royalty is acquired with thirty attributes, and priesthood is acquired with twenty-four; but the Torah is acquired with forty-eight things: learning, listening ... and crediting something to the one who said it" (*Avos* 6:6).

The *talmidim* of R' Yisrael Salanter would work on one *kinyan* of the forty-eight *kinyanim* of Torah every day of Sefiras HaOmer, and on the forty-ninth day, they would work on all the *kinyanim* collectively. The days of Sefiras HaOmer, they explained, are the means with which to reach the goal of Mattan Torah. This is why the number of days between Pesach and Shavuos equals the number of attributes through which we acquire Torah, with each day symbolizing another aspect of growth that enables a Yid to reach Mattan Torah in a state of spiritual purity. Without these vital weeks of spiritual development, one cannot reach the unique time known as Zman Mattan Toraseinu.

The example set by the *talmidim* of R' Yisrael Salanter indicates that there are two methods of acquiring the forty-eight *kinyanim* of Torah. The first is by toiling to acquire one *kinyan* each day, and the second is by instilling all the *kinyanim* in our hearts at once. A person who attempts this latter method must already possess a profound connection to all the *kinyanim*; only then can he acquire them all in a single day.

Kinyan Leads to Ownership

One who learns Torah without working to acquire its *kinyanim* may still succeed in his learning, yet only one who strives and toils genuinely to acquire all the *kinyanim* and incorporate them into his learning truly acquires the Torah and makes it part of himself. Dovid HaMelech expresses in *Tehillim* (1:2): כִּי אִם בְּתוֹרַת ה׳ חֶפְצוֹ וּבְתוֹרָתוֹ יֶהְגֶּה יוֹמָם וָלָיְלָה, *But his desire is in the Torah of Hashem, and in His Torah he meditates day and night*, and the Gemara expounds: "At the outset [the Torah] is ascribed to the Holy One, Blessed is He, but eventually it is ascribed to *him*" (*Avodah Zarah* 19a). The Torah that a person learns is not transient or fleeting, but evolves into an actual entity that endures within him until it is genuinely *his* Torah! This level of *limud Torah* can be attained only by one who strived to acquire all forty-eight *kinyanei haTorah*.

This can be compared to a wealthy man who owns multiple properties and estates and hires a property manager to attend to all household maintenance. A stranger could easily mistake the property manager for the owner, as he is involved in and aware of all the details of each property. Yet one who is conscious of their business relationship appreciates the fundamental difference between the homeowner and the hired manager. The manager may be familiar with each estate, but the owner paid for them and owns them. At any time, the manager can resign or be fired, in which case he would instantly sever his connection to the properties. While managers come and go, however, the owner maintains possession of the properties, and they are exclusively his.

One who learns Torah must endeavor not only to be *familiar* with Torah and amass knowledge of it, but also to *master* it and acquire it as his own, so that the Torah belongs to him. This level of possession of Torah can only be attained, step by step, through its *kinyanim*. The forty-eight *kinyanim* are more than just ways to learn Torah comprehensively and know it well; they are the tried-and-true method of mastering Torah, to the extent that one owns it.

Another significant point — which was presumably the intention of R' Yisrael Salanter's *talmidim* in toiling throughout the first forty-eight days of Sefirah to acquire forty-eight *kinyanim* of Torah, and then working to improve them all collectively on the forty-ninth day — is that if a person acquires all the forty-eight *kinyanim* except one, then all the rest of his *kinyanim* of Torah are lacking as well. When the Mishnah teaches that Torah is acquired with forty-eight things, it indicates that all forty-eight *kinyanim* are prerequisites to acquiring Torah. To ensure that they did not miss even a single *kinyan*, R' Yisrael Salanter's *talmidim* reviewed all forty-eight on the last day of Sefiras HaOmer and worked on them at once. This is analogous to one who purchases a house and, before moving in, ensures that he has attended to every aspect of the transaction — signing a legally binding contract before a lawyer, transferring the payment, and arranging all the relevant deeds and registrations — in order to guarantee his legal status as the property owner. One who skips even a single stage of the purchase and registration process risks forfeiting his legal right to the property.

No Deception

The first *kinyan* presented in the Mishnah as a means of acquiring Torah is *talmud,* learning. Considering that the entire concept of Torah revolves around learning, why did the Mishnah include this most obvious method in its list?

R' Eliyahu Lopian (ibid.) presents a beautiful answer, explaining that the Mishnah is not referring to the act of learning, but to knowledge of the entire Talmud. The parameter of this specific *kinyan* is that a person should do his utmost, relative to his ability, to expand his knowledge of Torah Shebe'al Peh, including Mishnah, Gemara, Rishonim, and the leading Acharonim.

He relates that he once spent a Shabbos in the home of the Chofetz Chaim. When the Chofetz Chaim recited *Eishes Chayil,* and reached the *pasuk,* נוֹדָע בַּשְּׁעָרִים בַּעְלָהּ בְּשִׁבְתּוֹ עִם זִקְנֵי אָרֶץ, *Her husband is distinctive in the councils, when he sits with the elders of the land* (*Mishlei* 31:23), he paused and translated the words to Yiddish.

He explained that Chazal teach that "*Eishes Chayil*" refers to the Torah (*Midrash Mishlei* ibid.), and the *baal* — the "husband" — of Torah is the *talmid chacham* who learns it. Shlomo HaMelech is teaching us that in this world, a person can deceive others. He can answer a question on *Tosafos* in *Seder Nezikin* without clear knowledge of *Tosafos,* but by quoting the *Ketzos HaChoshen* or *Nesivos HaMishpat* that discusses that *Tosafos;* he can even resolve a query on *Seder Nashim* based on a Gemara that he remembers quoted in the *Pnei Yehoshua* or *Avnei Miluim*. I would add that nowadays, many people don't even know the Gemara's words from the *Ketzos* or the *Nesivos*, or even from the *Kehillos Yaakov* — they know them from one of the myriad *marei mekomos sefarim*!

After a person expires from this world — at the time "when he sits with the elders of the land," rejoicing in the Olam HaEmes with the angels and *neshamos* of the *tzaddikim* of his generation — he is asked to repeat what he has learned, *masechta* by *masechta*. Only then will the true extent of the Torah he has learned and acquired be revealed to all, as indicated by the words נוֹדָע בַּשְּׁעָרִים בַּעְלָהּ, which can be understood as a reference to the gates of halachah. In Olam Haba, there can be no deception, so how ashamed a person might be!

The Chofetz Chaim concluded in a voice laden in emotion. "Why do the yeshivah *bachurim* '*kvetch*' in their learning? How can any *bachur* leave yeshivah without mastering at least two *Sidrei Gemara*?"

When one who acquired all forty-eight *kinyanim* of Torah learns, he feels ownership over the *sugya*. He has mastered it, and it is his! He doesn't read or skim it as he would read a list, but toils and labors over it in order to plumb its depths. When a *lomed Torah* feels ownership over his learning, it is a sign that he has acquired all the *kinyanim* of Torah.

This past week, I sat in the Friedman *beis midrash*, and I experienced great *nachas* and pleasure from watching the *dibbuk chaveirim* and *rischa d'Oraisa* prevailing there. Yet at the same time, I was also disappointed to see a smattering of *lomdim* learning the *sugya* from *marei mekomos sefarim*. Do the *avreichim* learning from these *sefarim* believe that this is the way they can truly acquire Torah? This is for *am haaratzim*! We can never attain genuine mastery over a *sugya* if we haven't opened the real *sefer* and learned it inside — just as no seasoned businessman would ever sign a deal without examining every single aspect of the purchase to verify its credibility and profitability. Learning from *marei mekomos sefarim* is not the way to grow and attain *gadlus baTorah*.

In the past, a *talmid chacham* was one who could describe the *tzuras hadaf* of the *Ketzos*, whereas today, the *tzuras hadaf* changes from one *sefer marei mekomos* to the next. People see the section of the page that was copied in the *sefer marei mekomos* they are learning, and that's all they ever see when learning the *sugya*! Some assume that when they learn *bekius*, it's enough to open a *sefer* here and there, but they are sorely mistaken. The foundation of *limud* is *havanah*, understanding, which compels the *lomed* to learn the *sugya* properly, from beginning to end. Only once he has learned the entire *sugya* and clarified any difficulties can he formulate his own *chiddushim*. It's impossible for a person to start making a *kvetch* here or there without first learning the entire *sugya* properly, and one who does will remain with neither the *sugya* nor his *chiddushim*.

"Listening, learning with the lips, understanding in the heart, trepidation, fear, humility, joy" — the *kinyanim* listed in the Mishnah are the ultimate "*seder halimud*" that we must follow in order to acquire Torah.

Obviously, one who works to acquire all these *kinyanim*, but does not actually learn, will be left only with the *kinyanim*, but without Torah. The *kinyanei haTorah* must all be utilized for learning, and this will elevate the learner to the optimal level of *limud Torah*. The Torah he learns will become indistinguishable from his own character, for he has gained ownership over his Torah.

Years ago, only the greatest *lamdanim* learned *Chiddushei R' Shmuel*. Who would dare open a R' Shmuel without first learning the *sugya* thoroughly? Only the most brilliant and talented *lamdanim* who had already plumbed the depths of the *sugya* would then open the *sefer* to see R' Shmuel's *chiddushim*.

Today, every *bachur* who enters *yeshivah gedolah* has already opened *Chiddushei R' Shmuel*. Young *bachurim* in *yeshivah ketanah* skim Rav Shmuel as if it were a novel! It's disastrous! R' Shmuel's prestige is sinking year by year ... How have we fallen so low? Instead of opening *sifrei chiddushim* like *Chiddushei R' Shmuel* after learning and clarifying the *sugya*, many will open it immediately so they can learn the Rishonim and Acharonim straight from there, without ever opening another *sefer*. There are others who aim even lower, skipping R' Shmuel and heading directly to all the *marei mekomos sefarim*.

Owning Torah Means Constant Connection

In the past, objects were assessed based on their intrinsic value, and people appreciated things that carried innate worth. Today, value is gauged by the transient pleasure that can be extracted from an item. A *bachur* can exit a *shiur* and ask his friend, "Did you like it?" as if it were ice cream! Is it only possible to acquire *kinyanei haTorah* if we enjoy the process? On the contrary, to truly merit Torah, we must fulfill the words of the Mishnah: "This is the way of Torah: Eat bread in salt, and drink water in measure" (*Avos* 6:4).

Nevertheless, one who learns Torah the right way enjoys pleasure in both this world and the next, as the Mishnah continues: אִם אַתָּה עֹשֶׂה כֵּן, אַשְׁרֶיךָ וְטוֹב לָךְ, אַשְׁרֶיךָ בָּעוֹלָם הַזֶּה, וְטוֹב לָךְ לָעוֹלָם הַבָּא, *If you do this, you are fortunate and it is good for you. You are fortunate in this world, and it is good for you in the World to Come.*

R' Eliyahu Lopian notes that the Mishnah's words, "It is good for you in the World to Come," are understandable; even if one toiled and struggled in Olam Hazeh to learn, he will be rewarded in Olam Haba. Yet how could the Mishnah also state, "Fortunate are you in this world"? How can one who subsists on bread and salt and sleeps on the rough earth be called fortunate?

This is why the Mishnah added the phrase, "if you do this." The only way that a person can truly feel that despite the harsh conditions of his life, he is "fortunate in this world" is if he actually lives such a life. One who did not attempt to live that life can never understand or appreciate it, regardless of how many times it is explained to him.

This can be compared to one who never drank wine in his life but wants to know what it tastes like. His friend tries explaining that he should imagine a combination of a certain percent of sourness and a certain percentage of sweetness, declaring that "this is what wine tastes like." Obviously, this description in no way satisfies the person's desire to know how wine tastes. Yet if someone would just pour him a glass of wine, and he would taste it, he would not require these long-winded, ineffective explanations, because he'll have experienced the taste himself.

The Mishnah teaches that there are many who wonder why they never experienced the Mishnah's promise of *ashrecha v'tov lach*. Therefore, it adds, "if you do this." Only if one actually follows the Mishnah's advice will he reach the level of *ashrecha*, by attaining the *kinyanei haTorah* and achieving ownership over Torah.

These days of Sefiras HaOmer are designated for acquiring *kinyanei haTorah* and advancing spiritually every day, until one is truly worthy of Kabbalas HaTorah, as the *Sefer HaChinuch* (Mitzvah 306) so aptly expresses:

> We are commanded to count from the day after the Yom Tov of Pesach until the day of the giving of the Torah so that we internalize the great desire for that honored day, which is longed for in our hearts. We are thus like "a slave who awaits the [evening] shade" (*Iyov* 7:2), who continuously counts, wondering when the time for which he longs — the time at which he will go free — shall arrive. The act of counting indicates to the person that his entire yearning and his entire desire is to reach that time. The fact that we count from the [bringing of the] *Omer*, that is, we say, "such-and-such days of the count have passed," and we do not count down by saying, "such-and-such days are left to the time [of Shavuos]," is because all of this shows our strong desire to reach that time.

פרשת בהר
Parashas Behar

◆§ *Shemittah Inspires Bitachon*

דַּבֵּר אֶל בְּנֵי יִשְׂרָאֵל וְאָמַרְתָּ אֲלֵהֶם כִּי תָבֹאוּ אֶל הָאָרֶץ אֲשֶׁר אֲנִי נֹתֵן לָכֶם וְשָׁבְתָה הָאָרֶץ שַׁבָּת לַה׳. שֵׁשׁ שָׁנִים תִּזְרַע שָׂדֶךָ וְשֵׁשׁ שָׁנִים תִּזְמֹר כַּרְמֶךָ וְאָסַפְתָּ אֶת תְּבוּאָתָהּ. וּבַשָּׁנָה הַשְּׁבִיעִת שַׁבַּת שַׁבָּתוֹן יִהְיֶה לָאָרֶץ שַׁבָּת לַה׳ שָׂדְךָ לֹא תִזְרָע וְכַרְמְךָ לֹא תִזְמֹר.

Speak to the Children of Israel and say to them: When you come into the land that I give you, the land shall observe a Sabbath rest for Hashem. For six years you may sow your field and for six years you may prune your vineyard; and you may gather in its crop. But the seventh year shall be a complete rest for the land, a Sabbath for Hashem; your field you shall not sow and your vineyard you shall not prune (*Vayikra* 25:2-4).

The *Sefer HaChinuch* teaches (Mitzvah 84) that the purpose of the mitzvah of Shemittah is that "man should increase his trust in Hashem." When a Yid abandons his fields for a full year and allows them to lie fallow, without working or cultivating them as he did throughout the previous six years, he is compelled to stop and think about where his sustenance will come from, as expressed in the words, וְכִי תֹאמְרוּ מַה נֹּאכַל בַּשָּׁנָה הַשְּׁבִיעִת הֵן לֹא נִזְרָע וְלֹא נֶאֱסֹף אֶת תְּבוּאָתֵנוּ, *If you will say: What will we eat in the seventh year? — behold! we will not sow and not gather in our crops* (*Vayikra* 25:20). These reflections empower him to place his trust wholeheartedly in Hakadosh Baruch Hu and rely exclusively on Him to provide for his needs.

When a Yid attains this lofty level of *bitachon*, Hakadosh Baruch Hu showers him with goodness and blessing, as the *pasuk* states: וְצִוִּיתִי אֶת בִּרְכָתִי לָכֶם בַּשָּׁנָה הַשִּׁשִּׁית וְעָשָׂת אֶת הַתְּבוּאָה לִשְׁלֹשׁ הַשָּׁנִים, *I will ordain My blessing for you in the sixth year and it will yield a crop sufficient for the three-year period* (ibid. v. 21). This blessing and relationship with Hakadosh Baruch Hu are not limited to the year of Shemittah alone, but exist any time a Yid casts his burden upon Hashem and trusts in Him to provide for his needs.

This principle is reflected, as well, in Rashi's explanation of the function of the jar of *mahn* that was placed in the *Aron* (*Shemos* 16:32): "In the days of Yirmiyah, when Yirmiyah would rebuke them for failing to toil in Torah, and they would say, 'If we abandon our work and engage in Torah, how will we support ourselves,' he removed the jar of *mahn* and said to them, *You! See the word of Hashem* (*Yirmiyah* 2:31). It does not say 'hear,' but rather 'see' [for Yirmiyah was saying] 'With this, your ancestors were sustained. Hashem has many messengers and means of preparing sustenance for those who fear Him.'"

Hakadosh Baruch Hu's promise endures throughout the generations until this very day, and one who trusts implicitly in Him will find that He provides for all his needs. Often, when people discuss their prodigious efforts to earn a livelihood, they explain that they must engage in this extensive *hishtadlus,* for without it, they will not be able to provide for themselves or their families. The above, however, is evidence to the contrary, indicating that one who trusts wholeheartedly in Hashem and learns Torah is promised that Hashem will provide for his needs.

The *nisayon* of *bitachon,* which means trusting that Hashem will provide for us constantly, is not limited to the year of Shemittah alone, but is a supreme challenge that we Yidden face every day of life. We all endure ups and downs, yet if we place our absolute faith in Hakadosh Baruch Hu, then we will surmount these hurdles with tranquility and genuine joy, without faltering or despairing. A person is at risk of plummeting to despondency only when he believes that he is in control of life, for when things don't go his way, he feels powerless, weak, and immobilized, which quickly spirals into despair. If, however, he would only remember that Hakadosh Baruch Hu runs the world, and that everything in life is from Him and for the good, he will feel safe and secure, like an infant cradled in the arms of its mother.

Bitachon — Emunah Peshutah in Practice

The Rosh Yeshivah R' Chaim Shmulevitz teaches[8] that the primary method of strengthening and reinforcing *bitachon* is to live with simple, tangible *emunah*, as opposed to deep, intellectual understanding. Even if one attains a high level of *bitachon* through brilliant scholarship and logic, this is not sustainable, and will ultimately fade with time. But if one grows accustomed to living and feeling plain, simple *emunah* in his regular day-to-day activities, then he will eventually acquire complete *bitachon* in Hashem and soar to an exalted level that will remain with him permanently.

R' Chaim quoted R' Yerucham Levovitz, who taught that when we discuss *bitachon* publicly, it's important to focus on the simple things and events in life that touch our hearts, as opposed to profound, esoteric concepts. He explained that *bitachon* is contingent not on intellectual understanding, but on a person's emotions. The more a person experiences *emunah* and *bitachon* palpably, to the point that he can practically touch it, the more it will become an intrinsic part of him.

Chazal present numerous examples of how lofty levels of *bitachon* were demanded of even simple people. One example is this statement of the Gemara (*Bava Metzia* 42a): "One who is about to measure the pile of grain in his silo recites the following prayer:

---

8. *Sichos Mussar, Bitachon* 2.

'May it be Your will, Hashem, our God, that You bestow blessing upon the work of our hands.' When he begins to measure the pile of grain, he says: 'Blessed is the One Who bestows blessing upon this pile.'" From here we see that even a simple farmer can achieve an exalted level of *bitachon* and draw blessing upon his produce through his simple but genuine belief that Hashem is the One Who showers bounty upon him.

Sustainable Bitachon

We recite daily in *Shemoneh Esrei*: וְתֵן שָׂכָר טוֹב לְכָל הַבּוֹטְחִים בְּשִׁמְךָ בֶּאֱמֶת, וְשִׂים חֶלְקֵנוּ עִמָּהֶם, וּלְעוֹלָם לֹא נֵבוֹשׁ כִּי בְךָ בָּטָחְנוּ, *And give goodly reward to all who sincerely believe in Your Name. Put our lot with them forever, and may we not feel ashamed, for we trust in You*. This *berachah* implies that there are people who are "*botei'ach b'emes*," who truly trust in Hashem, and also those who do not genuinely trust in Him, but are still considered to possess *bitachon*.

One who professes trust in Hashem, but does not genuinely feel it in his heart, is not a *baal bitachon*, but rather an impostor and a liar. Who, then, are the people who are considered to have *bitachon* even though they are not *botei'ach b'emes*?

Those who are *botei'ach b'emes* trust in Hakadosh Baruch Hu with simple, concrete *emunah*. Because their faith is rock-solid, it is able to weather the challenges and storms of life. In contrast, those whose trust in Hashem is based only on intellectual knowledge cannot maintain that faith in the long run. As soon as they face challenges, the *yetzer hara* worms its way into their hearts, presenting compelling reasoning that sways them and causes them to abandon their faith. They are therefore considered not *botei'ach b'emes*.

This is why we daven to Hashem to "put our lot forever" with those who are *botei'ach b'emes*, and to fill our hearts with simple, concrete faith. There are many who profess to have *bitachon*, yet their trust in Hashem is not based on *emunah peshutah*, which makes it insincere.

Acquiring *emunah peshutah* does not compel us to struggle or exert much effort. All we have to do is survey the magnificent world around us, and feast our eyes upon the spectacular beauty of creation — trees and flowers, animals and birds, and, above all, human beings. The very fact that a person wakes up every morning and stands on his two feet is a marvel! The faculty of speech, the ability to daven, eat, and learn — these are all incredible miracles! One who contemplates the splendor of it all will recognize that all of creation proclaims the wonders of its Creator, and this will fill his heart with simple, palpable *emunah*.

Recently, I was approached by a righteous woman whose husband had passed away. Her son learned in the yeshivah for several years, and since then, she has consulted with me frequently about various issues. She recently asked me if I think it is worthwhile for her to consider remarriage. I did not reply immediately, although I did eventually tell her that it depends primarily on her feelings. I noticed her loneliness and melancholy, and I advised her that whenever these sentiments rise in her heart, she should recite *Perek* 103 of *Tehillim* and focus specifically on this *pasuk* (v. 20): בָּרְכוּ ה' מַלְאָכָיו גִּבֹּרֵי כֹחַ עֹשֵׂי דְבָרוֹ לִשְׁמֹעַ בְּקוֹל דְּבָרוֹ, *Bless Hashem, O His angels; the strong warriors who do His bidding, to obey the voice of His word.* These words convey that even human beings can acquire a phenomenal level of strength that mirrors that of the angels, by living and feeling *emunah* and *bitachon* tangibly. One who strengthens his trust in Hashem will never feel alone or abandoned, nor will he ever have reason to feel sad. *Baruch Hashem*, my answer comforted her, and she left my house with a smile.

People often approach me to discuss personal issues, and I tell them all, first and foremost, that our duty is to strengthen ourselves in the qualities of *emunah* and *bitachon*, as this is the primary solution to every challenge!

What Is Emunah Peshutah?

The following incident illustrates what *emunah peshutah* is. A critically ill patient lay on his deathbed, and his friend came to visit him. In the course of their conversation, the friend posed a question to him: How is it that a rich man earns a livelihood? A pauper feels the need to beseech Hashem for *parnassah*, but the wealthy person does not, so how does he make money? The patient replied that in truth, the rich man is not deserving of great wealth. Yet because Hashem bestows good upon everyone — as it is written, טוֹב ה׳ לַכֹּל וְרַחֲמָיו עַל כָּל מַעֲשָׂיו, *Hashem is good to all; His mercies are on all His works* (*Tehillim* 145:9) — He has mercy even upon the undeserving.

This patient was *botei'ach b'emes*, as his answer reflected pure, concrete, and simple faith. Most people have no problem understanding how a wealthy man can eat his bread with confidence, but those who live with *emunah peshutah* realize that it is actually the pauper who can be assured of sustenance; since he raises his eyes to Heaven, Hashem accepts his prayer and provides him with bread, for he deserves it! The wealthy man, in contrast, is supported only because of Hakadosh Baruch Hu's boundless compassion on all His creations.

Bitachon in Avodas Hashem

It is natural for people to assume that *bitachon* relates to material needs, and that when one trusts implicitly in Hashem, He fills all his needs. Yet *bitachon* applies equally to spiritual needs and desires. Furthermore, *emunah* is an essential facet of *bitachon*, because a person who does not fully believe that everything in this world is a result of Hashem's mighty hand cannot feel confident that he is being carried in the arms of Hashem, as a mother carries her infant.

Two *bachurim* once approached me with a request that I give *shiurim* on the topic of *emunah* and *bitachon*. I asked the rebbetzin what she thought, and she suggested that I learn from the *sefer Mofes Hador* on R' Yechezkel Levenstein, who was a living paradigm of these attributes. Anyone who just gazed at R' Chatzkel — a *tzaddik* whose life was one long expression of *emunah* and *bitachon* — was inspired by him to grow in these qualities. I opened the *sefer* and read the following, in the first chapter. While the *mashgiach* lived these words, I merely read them:

> Just as we are compelled to utilize the *middah* of *bitachon* and *emunah* in our hope for *parnassah* and the like, the same applies to spiritual matters. One who *walked in darkness with no light for himself* (*Yeshayah* 50:10), not succeeding in his learning or prayer, *let him trust in the Name of Hashem, and rely upon his God* (ibid.), and then he will surely emerge from the darkness into light, and in one fleeting moment he can acquire Gan Eden. Hakadosh Baruch Hu showers bounty endlessly from His open, generous hand.

With these words, the *mashgiach* teaches that just as when it comes to *parnassah, bitachon* is indispensable, since a person should never feel that his own efforts earn him his sustenance, the same applies to spiritual matters. One who thinks that he does not require *siyata diShmaya* to succeed in his learning will not succeed, no matter how much he learns and davens. Only one who is keenly aware that his spiritual success is a result of Hakadosh Baruch Hu's absolute *chessed*, and who trusts that He will lead him out of darkness into light because He is Good and His kindness is everlasting, will merit success.

R' Chatzkel continues: "*It is not in the heavens* (*Devarim* 30:12). That anyone can merit it is not natural, and this bounty is supernatural. The smallest person can attain the level of a great person, if he only toils and draws himself near to the Creator. *Open your mouth, and I shall fill it* (*Tehillim* 81:11), for Hakadosh Baruch Hu gives and gives."

From the *pasuk* he quotes, we learn that everyone is capable of achieving greatness in Torah, even the simplest person who lacks money, talent, and *yichus*. All he must do is internalize that Hashem runs the world in supernatural ways and trust in Him, and then he will surely attain *gadlus*. Even though habit and routine tend to weaken our *emunah* and *bitachon*, it is still incumbent upon us to examine the world around us and appreciate that everything in it operates according to the miraculous workings of His hands, and that there is nothing natural in the world at all. Although we have not yet merited attaining this exalted level, we must know that it is possible to achieve it.

R′ Chatzkel writes further:

> *It is not hidden from you and it is not distant* (*Devarim* 30:11). Man is the one who creates the distance between himself and his Creator and who foolishly forfeits the greatness that is so close and ready for him to grasp … From the above, we can derive how mistaken it is to become neglectful or to despair when we do not succeed in *limud Torah* and *tefillah*. There is a miraculous system in the world that enables every individual, even one who lacks talents, to grow and ascend endlessly, as long as he toils to eliminate the distance between himself and his Creator. Wisdom is a Heavenly gift, and it is delivered to the one who primes himself to receive it, and the same is true of *tefillah* and character traits — every individual can succeed and grow.

To succeed in our spiritual *avodah*, we must ingrain in our hearts *emunah* and *bitachon* in Hakadosh Baruch Hu, along with the knowledge that all our success is in His hands. In addition, we must strive with all our might to abolish the distance between ourselves and Hakadosh Baruch Hu, and draw close to Him.

פרשת בחקותי
Parashas Bechukosai

The Ameilus Imperative

אִם בְּחֻקֹּתַי תֵּלֵכוּ וְאֶת מִצְוֹתַי תִּשְׁמְרוּ וַעֲשִׂיתֶם אֹתָם.
If you will follow My decrees and observe My commandments and perform them (*Vayikra* 26:3).

"This teaches that Hashem desires that Yisrael should toil in Torah" (*Toras Kohanim, Bechukosai* Ch. 1).

The Midrash clarifies that "walking in the laws of Hakadosh Baruch Hu" refers to *amal,* toiling in Torah, and that this is what Hashem desires of us. The *pasuk* adds, וְאֶת מִצְוֹתַי תִּשְׁמְרוּ, *and observe My commandments,* to teach that the purpose of toiling in Torah is "to keep and fulfill" (Rashi).

Lack of Yegiah Expresses Contempt

The ensuing *pesukim* follow in this vein: Rashi interprets the words, וְאִם לֹא תִשְׁמְעוּ לִי, *but if you will not listen to Me* (ibid. v. 14), as referring to failure to toil in Torah. Similarly, regarding the words, וְאִם בְּחֻקֹּתַי תִּמְאָסוּ, *If you consider My decrees loathsome* (ibid. v. 15), the Chizkuni writes, "To contrast with אִם בְּחֻקֹּתַי תֵּלֵכוּ."

This teaches that if one learns Torah but does not toil in it, he demonstrates blatant disregard of Hashem's command and eschews His laws. This statement is both very strong and very surprising, for even if *amal* is a lofty quality, the Torah itself possesses infinite value. Why is a person who learns Torah without *amal* regarded so negatively that he is condemned as one who rejects Hashem's laws? After all, he's still learning!

Here, the Torah refers to *ameilus* as a *chok,* and the Ohr HaChaim (ibid. 3) explains that the Torah wanted the mitzvah of *ameilus baTorah* to remain a *chok,* for even if one learned something many times and is well versed in it, it is still a mitzvah for him to toil in it and relearn it. Chazal say that Hakadosh Baruch Hu even decreed that people would forget what they learn, in order to facilitate the process of learning Torah with enthusiasm and desire, because one who never forgets what he learns will feel frustrated and bored when he learns it again and again (*Koheles Rabbah* 3:10-11).

Amal is not just added value or a commendable addition to *limud Torah,* similar to *hiddur mitzvah,* but is an indistinguishable and intrinsic part of it. Therefore, one who learns Torah without *amal* is regarded as if he didn't learn at all.

Why is this?

More Beloved Than a Korban Olah

Avos D'Rabbi Nosson (Ch. 4) states:

> It says, כִּי חֶסֶד חָפַצְתִּי וְלֹא זָבַח וְדַעַת אֱלֹהִים מֵעֹלוֹת, *For I desire kindness, not sacrifice; and knowledge of God more than burnt-offering* (*Hoshea* 6:6). From here we see that a *korban olah* is more precious than *shelamim,* for the *olah* is burned in its entirety, as it is written, וְהִקְטִיר הַכֹּהֵן אֶת הַכֹּל הַמִּזְבֵּחָה, *and the Kohen shall cause it all to go up in smoke on the Altar* (*Vayikra* 1:9); and learning Torah is more precious to Hashem than a *korban olah,* because if a person learns Torah, he acquires Hashem's knowledge, as it is written, אָז תָּבִין יִרְאַת ה׳ וְדַעַת אֱלֹהִים תִּמְצָא, *then you will understand the fear of Hashem, and discover the knowledge of God* (*Mishlei* 2:5).

One who toils in Torah is greatly praised, and his *amal* is more precious to Hashem than had he offered a *korban olah*, but what is the connection between *amal* and *korbanos*?

The simple explanation is that a *korban olah* is a purer offering than other *korbanos* because it is כָּלִיל לַה׳, burned entirely on the Mizbei'ach, with no parts designated for man to eat and enjoy in this world. Similarly, a Yid who toils in Torah dedicates himself exclusively to Hakadosh Baruch Hu, and his thoughts are entirely directed toward *avodas Hashem*, without any intention of reaping benefits in Olam Hazeh.

When a Yid dedicates himself entirely to Hashem and immerses himself in his learning to the point that he can attain the pinnacle of *dveikus* — וְדַעַת אֱלֹהִים תִּמְצָא, that is "more precious to Hashem than a *korban olah*." This does not come easily, yet it is possible to achieve when one genuinely invests all of his efforts to toil in Torah!

No Learning Without Ameilus

At the time when Yehoshua laid siege to Yericho, a *malach* appeared to him, as the *pasuk* relates (*Yehoshua* 5:13): וַיִּשָּׂא עֵינָיו וַיַּרְא וְהִנֵּה אִישׁ עֹמֵד לְנֶגְדּוֹ וְחַרְבּוֹ שְׁלוּפָה בְּיָדוֹ וַיֵּלֶךְ יְהוֹשֻׁעַ אֵלָיו וַיֹּאמֶר לוֹ הֲלָנוּ אַתָּה אִם לְצָרֵינוּ, *He raised his eyes and saw, and behold! — a man was standing opposite him with his sword drawn in his hand. Yehoshua went toward him and said to him, "Are you with us or with our enemies?"* The Gemara (*Megillah* 3a) teaches that the angel rebuked Yehoshua, saying, "This afternoon, you neglected to offer the daily afternoon sacrifice, and now you have neglected the study of Torah." Yehoshua responded, "For which of these [misdeeds] did you come?" The *malach* replied, עַתָּה בָאתִי, *I have come now* (v. 14). *Tosafos*, citing the Rivan, explain that the angel meant, "I came because of Torah study." Indeed, later, during the war with Ai, the *pasuk* states, וַיֵּלֶךְ יְהוֹשֻׁעַ בַּלַּיְלָה הַהוּא בְּתוֹךְ הָעֵמֶק, *Yehoshua lodged that night ... in the valley* (ibid. 8:13), and the Gemara expounds: "R' Yochanan said: This teaches that he delved into the profundities of Torah law."

The Gemara implies that the *malach's* grievance was not that

Yehoshua and Bnei Yisrael had entirely neglected Torah study, for they must have devoted at least some time from their day to learn Torah even during the trying days of the siege. His criticism focused on their failure to delve deeply into it, an omission that Yehoshua subsequently rectified by "delving into the profundities of Torah law."

Why did the *malach* descend from heaven at this time to rebuke Yehoshua for insufficient toiling in Torah? Klal Yisrael were at war! How could they be expected to simultaneously fight for their lives and still plumb the depths of Torah?

The only possible explanation is that *limud Torah* without *amal* is simply not *limud Torah*, as Chazal teach, "If a person tells you ... 'I did not toil, and I found,' do not believe him; 'I toiled and I found,' believe him!" (*Megillah* 6b). *Amal* is an intrinsic, fundamental aspect of *limud Torah*, so without *amal* and *yegiah*, there is no *limud Torah* at all! Therefore, if a person professes that he did not toil in Torah and still achieved knowledge, one should not believe him, because it is impossible.

Limud Torah is akin to offering a *korban olah*, which is a symbol of cleaving to Torah with all one's might and with one's very being, without interruption or distraction. *Limud Torah*, like the *korban olah*, is כָּלִיל לַה׳, entirely for Hashem!

The obligation of *ameilus baTorah* applies constantly, in every time and place — even in times of war! — because *limud Torah* without *amal* is defined as *bittul Torah*, and this is why Yehoshua set about rectifying this flaw by "delving into the profundities of Torah law."

It follows that one who does not toil in Torah projects contempt for Torah, because *amal* is not just an added value, but an essential aspect of man's *avodah* in this world — to cleave to Hashem at all times, which is the ultimate purpose of Creation. A person who is deficient in this area is lacking in his entire *avodah*!

Throughout the generations, *amal baTorah* was always the hallmark of *gedolei Yisrael*. Some of us were privileged to see in the last generation how the Chazon Ish did not partake of any pleasures of this world, but devoted his very being to toiling in Torah, to the point that at the end of the day, he would collapse onto his bed utterly spent.

At All Times, in Every Generation

The Ohr HaChaim (*Vayikra* 26:3) calls attention to the word בְּחֻקֹּתַי, which is written in the plural form, rather than the singular form, בְּחֻקָּתִי, explaining that this conveys that a person must establish fixed times for Torah study both by day and by night, in keeping with the *pasuk*, וְהָגִיתָ בּוֹ יוֹמָם וָלַיְלָה, *you should contemplate it day and night* (*Yehoshua* 1:8). Here, the Torah teaches that the obligation of *ameilus baTorah* is renewed every day and night.

The Ohr HaChaim offers a second explanation: A person must learn himself, and also teach others, as the Torah states: וְלִמַּדְתֶּם אֹתָם אֶת בְּנֵיכֶם, *You shall teach them to your children* (*Devarim* 11:19). The use of the plural form, בְּחֻקֹּתַי, implies that one should learn and teach, and keep and fulfill.

The Torah is informing us, then, that an integral aspect of a father's obligation to teach his sons Torah is to teach them to toil in Torah. *Amal haTorah* is a crucial element of man's obligation in this world, and therefore, every Yid must toil in Torah at all times, night and day — and he must teach his children to do the same.

Walking: The True Test

The Torah uses the word תֵּלֵכוּ, which literally means "you shall walk," to connote the obligation of *amal*: אִם בְּחֻקֹּתַי תֵּלֵכוּ. What connection is there, wonders the Ohr HaChaim, between walking and toiling in Torah?

Imagine that a person enters a house and sees people dressed in their finest, sitting around beautifully set tables laden with delicacies. At first glance, it appears that the guests are enjoying all the pleasures of life, and he is about to feel envious — but then, when they start to move from their places, he notices that all of these people are physically disabled and unable to walk. Indeed, only when a person starts to move from his place can his true abilities be discerned.

Similarly, the only way to truly measure a person's spiritual greatness and the extent of his *amal baTorah* is when he "walks" — when he is outside the *beis midrash*. As long as he is sitting and learning in the pure atmosphere of the *beis midrash*, he is encased in holiness. Even one who is usually controlled by his *yetzer hara* can behave properly in the sacred environment of the *beis midrash*, as Chazal teach, "If this revolting one [the *yetzer hara*] engages you, draw him to the *beis midrash*. If he is like a stone, he will dissolve; and if he is like iron, he will shatter" (*Succah* 52b). Yet when a person walks in the street, where his eyes and heart threaten to trip him, he can easily fall prey to the *yetzer hara*. It is on the street, the place where we walk, where we demonstrate where our minds and hearts truly lie, and whether they are immersed in *amal haTorah*.

More Desires, More Achievement

A person cannot acquire any positive attribute without aspiring and working toward it first — and the more he aspires and strives, the more he will attain. One who yearns to become a *talmid chacham* will eventually merit reaching a level that is at least close to that of a *talmid chacham*; and one who strives to become a *gadol baTorah* will at least become a great *talmid chacham*! Yet one who contents himself with the bare minimum spiritually will achieve no more than that.

Torah giants of previous generations were fluent in Talmud Bavli at a young age, while the majority of us do not achieve this even in our later years, even though knowledge of Shas is the primary qualification for success in *limud Torah*. How many of us are well-versed in the *Ketzos HaChoshen* or the *Mishnah Berurah*? Why not? It is our obligation to know these *sefarim* comprehensively, and not just partially.

The cause of this spiritual degeneration is that people's aspiration for knowledge of Torah has dwindled, and while it was once obvious to every young *bachur* that he must know Shas, today we are complacent and content ourselves with much less.

A person should never think that because his intellectual powers are limited, he cannot grow or achieve beyond what he is naturally capable of, for one can always turn to Hashem and beseech Him for wisdom that surpasses the laws of nature. On a personal note, there was a period when I was delivering a daily *iyun shiur* to the yeshivah's *chaburas hadaf*, which learns a *blatt Gemara* a day, and until today, I can't understand how I did it! Moreover, if you would have asked the members of this *chaburah* if they could write *chaburos* on these *sugyos*, they would surely have answered that they can't do it, for lack of time. But the fact is that they are writing *chaburos*! How? Because a *lomed Torah* receives energies and *siyata diShmaya* that transcend his natural capabilities!

Some may argue that focusing on amassing comprehensive knowledge of Torah negatively impacts the quality of one's learning. They support this contention by noting that the Gemara (*Kiddushin* 30a) interprets the word וְשִׁנַּנְתָּם, *and you shall teach them thoroughly* (*Devarim* 6:7), to mean, שֶׁיִּהְוּ דִּבְרֵי תוֹרָה מְחוּדָּדִים בְּפִיךָ, *that the words of Torah should be sharply honed in your mouth* (*Kiddushin* 30a). Yet this is an utter misconception. Comprehensive knowledge of Torah does not affect the quality of one's learning, and every Yid is actually *required* to amass this comprehensive knowledge.

Ameilus Protects From the Yetzer Hara

We have spoken many times about the obligation to toil and cleave to Torah with our entire being, but frankly, I am bewildered. Just yesterday, I was approached by a delegation of prominent rabbanim who claimed that there are still *bachurim* in various yeshivos who own non-kosher phones, despite the blanket prohibition against them. Even using a kosher phone can involve *bittul Torah*, and there is no cellular device that is deserving of the description "kosher," but how can *bnei Torah* own a not-kosher phone? It's a catastrophe! The *yetzer hara* is still managing to vanquish us! Each one of us must rebuke our friend if we are aware that he owns a non-kosher device. Furthermore, under no circumstances may anyone ever use even a kosher device in the *beis midrash*!

Amal haTorah is the only thing that protects a person from the *yetzer hara*, and the greatest proof of this is the fact that Hashem obligates a Yid to toil with all his strength in Torah.

No one is spared from the wiles of the *yetzer hara*, even a *bachur* or *avreich* who sits and toils in the *beis midrash* day and night. As soon as he exits the *beis midrash*, the *yetzer hara* is there waiting to trip him up with prohibited sights. How can we protect ourselves from transgressing?

The only answer is *amal haTorah*! *Amal* is the ammunition that Hashem granted us to combat the *yetzer hara*, as Hashem declares, "I created the *yetzer hara*; I created the Torah as its antidote, and if you engage in Torah, you are not delivered into his hands" (*Kiddushin* 30b). Therefore, even when one leaves the *beis midrash*, he must try to keep his mind focused on his learning, so that he can withstand the ye*tzer hara*.

Rabbosai! Moshe Rabbeinu called to Bnei Yisrael, מִי לַה׳ אֵלָי, *Whoever is for Hashem, join me* (*Shemos* 32:26), and the *pasuk* immediately continues, וַיֵּאָסְפוּ אֵלָיו כָּל בְּנֵי לֵוִי, *and all the Levites gathered around him*. Now, I'm calling upon each member of our *tzibbur* of *bnei Torah*, and beseeching each and every one of you! If you see your friend faltering in *ruchniyus*, don't abandon him! Rebuke him pleasantly, and don't wait to do this, because "Thus is the craft of the *yetzer hara*: today he tells him, 'Do this,' and tomorrow, it tells him, 'Do that,' until it tells him, 'Perform idolatry,' and he goes and performs it" (*Kiddushin* 30b). This is especially applicable today, when the force of the Satan is so powerful that it doesn't even attempt this roundabout route, but immediately sets about shoving a Yid into the abyss. Therefore, if you see your friend veering from the proper path, you should do everything in your power to lead him back to his rightful place.

We are now in the days of Sefiras HaOmer, which is the time of preparation for Kabbalas HaTorah. *Baruch Hashem*, the *tzibbur* is immersed in *limud Torah*, and we are seeing the fruits of our labor. Still, the *yetzer hara* lingers right outside the door of the *beis midrash*, waiting to ensnare us. It's up to us to toil in Torah even outside the *beis midrash* and stop ourselves and our friends from falling into the *yetzer hara's* trap.

Chazal promise us, "One who accepts the burden of Torah upon himself, the burden of the government and the burden of a livelihood are removed from him" (*Avos* 3:5). Our acceptance of the burden of Torah is through learning Torah with *amal* and *yegiah*, without interruption or distraction, and with *mesirus nefesh*! Hakadosh Baruch Hu should help that we should all merit to toil in Torah *lishmah*, so that we can truly fulfill the precept of וְהָגִיתָ בּוֹ יוֹמָם וָלַיְלָה.

ספר במדבר
Sefer Bamidbar

פרשת במדבר
Parashas Bamidbar

◆§ *The Force of Willpower*

וּפְקֻדַּת אֶלְעָזָר בֶּן אַהֲרֹן הַכֹּהֵן שֶׁמֶן הַמָּאוֹר וּקְטֹרֶת הַסַּמִּים וּמִנְחַת הַתָּמִיד וְשֶׁמֶן הַמִּשְׁחָה פְּקֻדַּת כָּל הַמִּשְׁכָּן וְכָל אֲשֶׁר בּוֹ בְּקֹדֶשׁ וּבְכֵלָיו.

The charge of Elazar son of Aharon the Kohen is the oil of illumination, the incense spices, the meal-offering of the continual offering, and the anointment oil — the charge of the entire Tabernacle and everything in it — of the Sanctuary and its utensils (*Bamidbar* 4:16).

"The oil of illumination in his right; the incense spices in his left; and the meal-offering of the continual offering of the day hanging on his arm" (*Yerushalmi Shabbos* 10:3).

The *Yerushalmi* teaches that Elazar ben Aharon carried all these items on his body, yet the Ramban (*Bamidbar* 4:16) points out that the weight of the *ketores* for one year was 365 *maneh* (as stated in *Kereisos* 6a) and the volume of the *shemen hamaor* for one year was 183 *lugin*; and that was besides the weight of the *korban minchah*. How could Elazar bear this enormous weight wherever he walked?

The Ramban explains that Elazar was physically strong and robust, similar to Yaakov Avinu, Moshe Rabbeinu, and Aharon

HaKohen; he applies to this the verse: וְקֹוֵי ה׳ יַחֲלִיפוּ כֹחַ, *But those whose hope is in Hashem will have renewed strength* (*Yeshayah* 40:31).

These words reveal a marvelous lesson for life. It is clear that Yaakov Avinu was very strong, as the Torah states that he rolled the stone off the mouth of the well (*Bereishis* 29:10), and Rashi elaborates: "Like one who removes a cover from a bottle, to inform you that his strength was great."

Yet the Ramban implies that this was the function not of physical prowess but rather of spiritual strength, as expressed by the *pasuk*, וְקֹוֵי ה׳ יַחֲלִיפוּ כֹחַ. Yaakov possessed a fervent desire to fulfill the will of Hashem, and this is what infused him with the physical capacity to do what he needed to do.

This was also the secret of how Elazar was able to carry all the articles required to perform the daily *avodah* in the Mishkan. Since his role required him to carry all these items, and he strived to fulfill his duty to perfection, he was granted the prodigious strength necessary to accomplish this.

From here, we learn that a person's capabilities are a direct outgrowth of his aspirations! Even if Elazar was physically incapable of carrying such a heavy burden, his desire to serve Hashem and fulfill His will was so compelling that Hakadosh Baruch Hu endowed him with supernatural strength. I remember that R' Chaim Kamil would always *bentch* me with the *pasuk*, וְקֹוֵי ה׳ יַחֲלִיפוּ כֹחַ — because those who strive to grow close to Hashem merit superhuman strengths. R' Chaim also frequently repeated that "everything is dependent on a person's will and his aspirations."

R' Zelmaleh of Volozhin, a brother of R' Chaim of Volozhin, was a Torah giant and genius whom the greatest scholars in his generation extolled with the rare praise that had he not passed away in his youth, he would have likely reached the level of the Vilna Gaon. It is related that once, while learning, he wished to reference a certain *sefer*, but in order to reach it, he needed to move a very heavy, cumbersome box. R' Zelmaleh, who was weak and small, was unable to move the box on his own, yet his desire to learn was so intense that he refused to surrender to the physical obstacles in his path.

He began repeating to himself the words of Chazal regarding the *pasuk*, לֹא בַשָּׁמַיִם הִוא ... וְלֹא מֵעֵבֶר לַיָּם הִוא, *It is not in heaven ... nor is it across the sea* (*Devarim* 30:12-13): "For if it were in the heavens, you would be compelled to ascend after it; and it if were across the sea, you would have to cross it" (*Eruvin* 55a). As he said these words again and again, his heart ignited with fervor, and he reflected that a Yid must exert himself beyond his physical capacity in order to learn — even if it means climbing to the heavens or crossing the ocean! Thus inspired, he grasped the box and, in one swift motion, heaved it aside to expose the *sefer*.

It is clear that R' Zelmaleh's stunning physical achievement was not a miracle, for Chazal teach that we may not rely on a miracle (*Yerushalmi Yoma* 1:4), and he should have not attempted to lift the box if doing so would have been dangerous. Rather, R' Zelmaleh yearned so intensely to learn Torah that he received a surge of strength that allowed him to transcend his human limitations and perform a supernatural feat. In this vein, Chazal teach that if Torah were in the heavens, a person would be obliged to climb to the heavens in order to learn it — because he would be able to! There is nothing that can stand in the way of a Yid's fervent desire to learn and achieve greatness in Torah.

We see occasional examples of this phenomenon in regular life as well, such as when a fire breaks out and people perform the impossible in order to rescue their loved ones. The only explanation for this is that a person's willpower can infuse him with strength he never dreamed he had.

Aspirations Lead to Spiritual Attainment

This lesson was actually revealed to us already at the time of Mattan Torah, when Hakadosh Baruch Hu spoke to Bnei Yisrael face to face, as the *pasuk* describes: פָּנִים בְּפָנִים דִּבֶּר ה׳ עִמָּכֶם בָּהָר מִתּוֹךְ הָאֵשׁ, *Face to face did Hashem speak with you on the mountain, from amid the fire* (*Devarim* 5:4).

The Alshich wonders (*Shemos* 19:2) how it is possible that a nation comprising 600,000 men was worthy that each person, without exception, should merit the exalted level of "face-to-face" prophecy. He answers that man is created on the level of prophetic communication, and from the time he is born, his soul is lofty and pure enough to merit speaking with Hakadosh Baruch Hu directly and having Him teach him His Torah and His holy ways.

The serpent's venom, which entered our bodies at the time of Adam HaRishon's sin, caused us to forfeit this lofty level of *nevuah*. Only during Mattan Torah, when Bnei Yisrael soared to the apex of spirituality, did this venom finally dissipate (*Avodah Zarah* 22b), and for a brief time, we reclaimed the glorious spiritual level of Adam and Chavah prior to the sin. Just as Adam and Chavah were privileged to speak face- to-face with Hakadosh Baruch Hu in Gan Eden, so, too, Hashem spoke directly to Klal Yisrael at Har Sinai.

The Ohr HaChaim (*Shemos* 20:17) understands this differently, explaining that the venom dissipated when Klal Yisrael stood around Har Sinai due to the intensity of Hashem's voice, not because they soared to the lofty spiritual height of Adam HaRishon at Creation.

If this is the case, then we return to the Alshich's question of how all of Klal Yisrael, men and women, young and old, were worthy of direct prophecy. The Alshich's explanation that Bnei Yisrael reclaimed the exalted spiritual level of Adam HaRishon before the *cheit* is insufficient, because according to the Ohr HaChaim, Bnei Yisrael reclaimed that ideal state of perfection only after Hashem spoke to them, so in what merit did they receive that first prophetic communication?

The answer is that when a person aspires to reach the loftiest heights, he receives the requisite strength to achieve his goals. When Bnei Yisrael proclaimed "*Naaseh* v'*nishma*" at Har Sinai, and beseeched Hakadosh Baruch Hu to speak to them directly instead of through a messenger, they revealed their profound yearning for *kirvas Elokim* and were therefore catapulted to the exceptional level at which they were worthy of receiving direct *nevuah*. Even though, as the Ohr HaChaim writes, they still retained traces of the serpent's venom, their intense desire for *kirvas Elokim* enabled them to attain the lofty level at which they could receive prophecy.

This concept is reflected in the words of the *Chovos HaLevavos* (*Shaar* 8, Ch. 3, *Cheshbon* 21):

> One should make a spiritual accounting regarding what he is capable of achieving in *avodas Hashem*, and accustom himself and work consistently on this, running and resolving to accomplish this until it becomes natural for him. Then, he should endeavor to add all that he is capable of adding, and he should desire in his heart and reflect frequently and entreat Hashem to help him and strengthen him in that which is beyond his mental and physical ability, in his heart and faithful conscience. And when he does this consistently, Hashem will fulfill his requests and open for him the gates of His knowledge and strengthen his mind and limbs to fulfill His mitzvos beyond his physical capacity, level by level ... until it almost resembles a prophecy from Hashem.

When a person strives to grow limitlessly, beyond his natural capabilities, and entreats Hashem to help him, Hakadosh Baruch Hu fulfills his request and facilitates his spiritual climb, helping him to rise step by step, slowly but surely, until he reaches a level close to prophecy. We also find that the more a Yid yearns and strives to reach exalted spiritual heights, the greater the *siyata diShmaya* he receives.

The *Chovos HaLevavos*, however, imparts another important lesson regarding spiritual growth, writing that initially, a person should not strive for the pinnacle of spiritual greatness that is beyond his ability; rather, he should aim for "what he is capable of achieving in *avodas Hashem*." One who reaches too high too quickly is likely to stumble, fall, and despair, as Chazal teach, תָּפַסְתָּ מְרֻבָּה לֹא תָּפַסְתָּ, *When you seize a large amount, you have not seized [anything]* (*Yoma* 80a).

The proper way for a person to aspire and strive for spiritual success is to first achieve what is in one's power to achieve, and only then to strive for more. When he sees that he has accomplished his first set of goals, he will feel satisfied with himself, and his heart will fill with greater desire and yearning to go further.

Striving for Greatness

Tanna D'Vei Eliyahu Rabbah (Ch. 25) teaches: "Each and every Jew is obligated to ask, when will my actions reach the actions of my forefathers Avraham, Yitzchak, and Yaakov?" But how can a simple person be expected to attain the exalted levels of Avraham, Yitzchak, and Yaakov?

Obviously, one will not be punished for failing to achieve the greatness of our nation's forefathers, yet one who does not even *aspire* to attain their spiritual greatness and to reach as far as he can will surely be punished. A Yid is obligated to yearn for the greatest of spiritual heights — even those as lofty as those of our *Avos*, as it is these aspirations that draw *siyata diShmaya* upon him and enable him to attain far greater heights than he is capable of reaching with his innate abilities.

A Yid's willpower is his very life force! Only with willpower can he grow and advance in life, transcending his natural limitations. At times, we see *bachurim* or *avreichim* who are not *shteiging* in learning as they should be, and it's not for lack of intellect or ability, but just because they lack the willpower to achieve. Conversely, we see clearly that one who sincerely longs to grow and achieve, and is willing to work hard, can accomplish astounding feats.

One of the greatest failings in our generation is the lack of *she'ifos*. In previous generations, people possessed enormous aspirations, and even simple *baalebatim* knew Shas inside and out. In our generation, sadly, we are *mistapek b'muat,* contenting ourselves with the bare minimum spiritually and lacking the aspiration to know *kol haTorah kulah.* We're content with our humble accomplishments, satisfied with knowing the *sugya* that we're currently learning. But the truth is that each and every one of us must adopt a mindset that if we *really* want to accomplish, we will succeed, and nothing will hinder our success!

When R' Chaim Kamil discussed this topic,[1] he quoted one of the *talmidim* of the Brisker Rav as saying that whenever the Brisker Rav would learn the Netziv's *sefarim,* he would marvel at

1. *Imrei Chaim, Koach HaRatzon.*

how the Netziv had attained such awe-inspiring *chochmas haTorah*. Indeed, one who peruses the Netziv's *sefarim* can't help but notice the mind-boggling scope of knowledge contained in every *sefer*.

R' Isser Zalman Meltzer revealed how the Netziv attained this level, in line with what we have discussed above. He explained that just as a person who sees a raging fire consuming his home acquires a burst of energy that enables him to leap through the flames to rescue his prized possessions, so, too, the Netziv's willpower enabled him to acquired his profound knowledge of Torah. When the Netziv sat and learned Torah, he resembled a man rushing into flames to save his valuables, and this passion was rewarded with incredible *siyata diShmaya* that propelled him to an exalted spiritual level.

This demonstrates that a Yid who struggles and toils in Torah out of a fervent yearning for connection to Hashem succeeds in the most marvelous way! One who seeks the easy life, however, will never succeed, and there is no one more suited to share this message than R' Chaim Kamil, whose life epitomized *she'ifos* and *yegiah* in Torah.

There was once a *bachur* in the yeshivah who was not particularly bright or talented, yet he possessed unmatched determination and willpower to *shteig* in Torah. And *shteig* he did! He connected with a group of *bachurim* who took turns giving weekly *chaburos* on the *sugya* being learned that week in yeshivah. Week after week, the *bachur's* heart twisted in envy — *kinas sofrim* — of his friends' ability to effortlessly formulate and relay impressive *chaburos*, when he was incapable of such a thing. Yet he refused to give up, and with dogged persistence, he sat and sweated over the *sugya* day by day, week by week, until he finally began to notice a change. He was still far from being able to weave together stunning *chaburos*, but at least he was able to talk to his friends in learning.

Today, many years later, this same *bachur*, who displayed incredible determination and perseverance, is a distinguished *maggid shiur* and *marbitz Torah* in Klal Yisrael and has raised children who are likewise prominent *talmidei chachamim*. This is a clear demonstration of how far the willpower that a young man displays in his youth can carry him in life!

Another vital point to highlight is that when the Brisker Rav learned the Netziv's *sefarim*, he would repeatedly marvel and delight in the wisdom therein, but when we sit down to learn the Netziv, most of us don't blink an eye! We don't express awe or wonderment at the greatness of the *gedolim* of yesteryear, and we don't even see this lack of admiration as a problem.

It's easy to rationalize and say that we can't fathom the greatness of these *gedolim*, and that we can never attain a level even close to theirs, but this thinking is fundamentally flawed! It's wrong! Each and every one of us is capable of astounding achievement in Torah, and all it takes is genuine *she'ifos*!

I believe that we need to follow the example of the holy yeshivos of previous generations and create *chaburos* of five to ten *bachurim* and *avreichim* who gather from time to time to brainstorm how to intensify their aspirations, passion, and determination to grow in Torah. Such *chaburos* are very effective and breed wonderful results, because when someone sees his friend aspiring for *gadlus*, he receives the *cheishek* to work harder too, as the Gemara states that "envy of scholars increases wisdom" (*Bava Basra* 21a).

One of the fundamental tenets of Kabbalas HaTorah is that a person's willpower can propel him to unimaginable heights, far beyond the limits of his natural abilities. When we internalize this, we simultaneously recognize our obligation to intensify our own willpower, so that we can merit the *siyata diShmaya* that will enable us to grow and achieve great heights in *limud Torah*!

פרשת נשא
Parashas Nasso

◆§ *The Obligation of Continuous Growth*

אִישׁ אוֹ אִשָּׁה כִּי יַפְלִא לִנְדֹּר נֶדֶר נָזִיר לְהַזִּיר לַה׳.
A man or woman who shall dissociate himself by taking a Nazirite vow of abstinence for the sake of Hashem (*Bamidbar* 6:2).

The Mishnah teaches (*Nedarim* 9a) that if one who wishes to undertake *nezirus* or a vow says, "Like the *nedarim* of the wicked," he has effected a vow, since the wicked are in the habit of making *nedarim*. Yet if he said, "Like the *nedarim* of the virtuous," he has not said anything, since it is not the way of the virtuous to make *nedarim*. If, however, he said, "Like their [the virtuous ones'] *nedavos*," he has effected a vow, for it is the way of the virtuous to offer gifts.

The Gemara (ibid. 9b) explains that when someone vows to offer a *korban*, there is always the chance that he will be delayed in fulfilling it until after three festivals have passed, which is why those who are righteous avoid making vows and, instead, follow the example of Hillel, who would bring his animal to the entrance of the *Azarah*, sanctify it, and slaughter it immediately.

The Gemara adds that there is a marked difference in the way that *tzaddikim* and *reshaim* approach their commitment to *nezirus*, as Shimon HaTzaddik expressed:

> In my life, I have never eaten of the *asham* offering of a *nazir* who became impure, except for one. Once, a *nazir* came from the south, and I saw that he had beautiful eyes and was handsome, and his locks were arranged in curls. I said to him, "My son, why did you see fit to destroy your beautiful hair?"
>
> He answered me, "I was a shepherd for my father in my town, and I went to fetch water from the river, and I gazed at my reflection. My evil inclination rushed over me and sought to banish me from the world [by inciting me to sin]. I told him: 'Wicked one! Why are you conceited in a world that is not yours, with one who is destined to be reduced to worms and maggots? I swear that I shall shave you for the sake of Heaven.'"
>
> I immediately arose and kissed him on the head, and I told him, "My son, may there be many more *nezirim* like you in Israel!"

The Gemara explains that typically, individuals would undertake *nezirus* for thirty days due to their spiritual yearning. If, however, the *nazir* became impure at any point during the month, then the previous days of his *nezirus* would be invalidated, and he would be required to begin his thirty-day count again. This could lead him to regret his original pledge, since it had extended longer than he originally intended.

Shimon HaTzaddik was concerned that even though such a *nazir* had not sought to annul his vow, since he had regretted his *nezirus* his intentions could no longer be regarded as pure, and his *korban* would not be accepted on high. A rare exception was this *nazir* from the south of Eretz Yisrael, whose intentions were obviously *l'shem Shamayim.*

This is a compelling lesson for life. Although *reshaim* do occasionally regret their evil ways, and are even willing to accept *nezirus* upon themselves in their quest for atonement, their intentions are usually impure. They do not accept the yoke of Heaven upon themselves wholeheartedly, but rather seek occasionally to rectify their misdeeds in order to quiet their burning conscience. In contrast, it is easy to discern a person who repents genuinely and wholeheartedly, like the young *nazir* who came to Yerushalayim to express his genuine yearning to serve Hashem, which prompted Shimon HaTzaddik to partake of his *korban*.

The Kedushah of a Nazir

When the period of his *nezirus* ends, a *nazir* is commanded, בְּיוֹם מְלֹאת יְמֵי נִזְרוֹ יָבִיא אֹתוֹ אֶל פֶּתַח אֹהֶל מוֹעֵד. וְהִקְרִיב אֶת קָרְבָּנוֹ לַיהֹוָה כֶּבֶשׂ בֶּן שְׁנָתוֹ תָמִים אֶחָד לְעֹלָה וְכַבְשָׂה אַחַת בַּת שְׁנָתָהּ תְּמִימָה לְחַטָּאת וְאַיִל אֶחָד תָּמִים לִשְׁלָמִים, *On the day his abstinence is completed, he shall bring himself to the entrance of the Tent of Meeting. He shall bring his offering to Hashem: one unblemished sheep in its first year as a burnt-offering, one unblemished ewe in its first year as a sin-offering, and one unblemished ram as a peace-offering* (*Bamidbar* 6:13-14).

Why is a *nazir* obligated to bring a *korban chatas* at the end of his *nezirus* period, even though he has not sinned?

The Ramban (ibid. v. 11) explains:

> The simple reason is that this man is considered a sinner at the culmination of the period of his *nezirus*, because he is now removed from his [previous] sanctity and service of Hashem, and it would have been worthwhile for him to commit to *nezirus* forever and remain for the rest of his life a *nazir* who is holy to Hashem his God, as it is written, וָאָקִים מִבְּנֵיכֶם לִנְבִיאִים וּמִבַּחוּרֵיכֶם לִנְזִרִים, *I established some of your sons as prophets and some of your young men as nazirites* (*Amos* 2:11). Here, the *pasuk* compares [the *nazir*] to a prophet … He requires atonement when he returns to defiling himself with the pleasures of the world.

The Ramban explains that undertaking *nezirus* is not a sin but actually a great mitzvah, as it draws enormous sanctity upon the *nazir*, who separates himself from the material, base pursuits of the world and draws close to Hashem, almost like a prophet. This extra dose of spirituality, however, is what turns him into a sinner when he resumes regular life and activities at the end of his *nezirus* period, instead of striving to perpetually maintain the extra level of *kedushah* that he acquired.

Even so, why does this require him to bring a *korban chatas*? No one is obligated to become a *nazir*, and one who chooses *nezirus* does so of his own volition. Furthermore, when he pledges to become a *nazir*, he clearly stipulates a thirty-day timeframe, so why would he be expected to retain the state of *nezirus* forever? Finally, what of the one who never pledges to become a *nazir* and never attains the extra *kedushah* achieved by the *nazir*? Is he also regarded as a sinner and obligated to bring a *korban chatas*?

Keep Climbing

A *nazir* who sanctifies himself for a period of thirty days ascends to a higher plane of spirituality and asceticism than he ever experienced, which invites a powerful accusation against him: How can you forfeit the lofty level of *kirvas Elokim* that you gained?

One who forges a close bond with the Ribbono Shel Olam must maintain that bond as long as he lives. At the end of the *nezirus* period, however, a *nazir* heartlessly surrenders that *kirvas Elokim* and falls back into his simple, mundane life filled with material pursuits, proving that he sorely lacks appreciation of the exalted level of *kedushah* and *kirvas Elokim* that he was privileged to acquire and experience.

The Torah demands from Klal Yisrael constant, unflagging pursuit of spiritual elevation and holiness, and the *nazir's* willful abandonment of all this renders him a sinner. The Ramban conveys that while there is nothing wrong with living a simple, normal existence in line with Torah, if a person has already begun ascending a special path of *avodas Hashem* and *yiras Shamayim*, he may not cease his efforts, for stopping along the way is regarded as a sin.

Moreover, a person who interrupts his spiritual ascent is liable to slip and fall even lower than the starting point from where he originally began his *nezirus*. Therefore, one who pledges to become a *nazir* must introspect honestly in order to ensure that undertaking this mitzvah won't ultimately lead him to sink spiritually.

This principle is also reflected in the following teaching of the Gemara: "Why in these times are converts afflicted with pain, and hardships are visited upon them? Because they held themselves back from entering under the wings of the *Shechinah*" (*Yevamos* 48b). This Gemara implies that even if the converts observed the seven Noahide commandments and did not sin, they are punished for procrastinating conversion.

Why, asks the Yaavetz (ibid.), is a convert punished, when he has absolutely no obligation to become Jewish and undertake the 613 mitzvos? He explains that their eventual wholehearted acceptance of mitzvos and desire to enter beneath the wings of the *Shechinah* are regarded as similar to an oath to give *tzedakah*, and they are thus obliged to fulfill their oath and convert. A convert who unnecessarily delays acting on his desire to join the Jewish nation is effectively a sinner and is punished for this.

The Yaavetz's explanation leaves many unresolved questions, as the laws of *nedarim* obligate Bnei Yisrael, not gentiles, and gentiles are not bound by the prohibition to delay the fulfillment of a vow, as we learn from *Tosafos* (*Nazir* 61b, s.v. *Hanicha*). If so, why is a gentile deserving of punishment for delaying his conversion?

The answer is in line with what we have explained above: Even a gentile who attains a superior level of sanctity is expected to maintain that close relationship with Hashem, just as a *nazir* is expected to maintain his *nezirus* throughout his life. A gentile who independently arrives at the recognition of Hashem's existence and of Klal Yisrael's status as the Chosen Nation, which inspires him to cleave to the *Shechinah* and link his destiny with Klal Yisrael, has attained a spiritual plane lofty enough to compel him to hurry to accept the yoke of Torah and mitzvos.

Increasing Kedushah

The Ibn Ezra (*Bamidbar* 6:7) adds another point that sheds light on why ending *nezirus* is considered a sin. The word "*nazir*," he explains, draws from the word *nezer*, crown, as the *pasuk* states, לְאָבִיו וּלְאִמּוֹ לְאָחִיו וּלְאַחֹתוֹ לֹא יִטַּמָּא לָהֶם בְּמֹתָם כִּי **נֵזֶר** אֱלֹהָיו עַל רֹאשׁוֹ, *To* *his father or to his mother, to his brother or to his sister — he shall not contaminate himself to them upon their death, for the* ***crown*** *of his God is upon his head* (ibid.). While most people in the world are slaves to their inclinations, a *nazir* is liberated of physical desires. Moreover, since he is not enslaved to physicality, but is master over his impulses, he is regarded as a king bedecked in a royal crown. This indicates that a *nazir* reaches such an exalted level of *ruchniyus* that he is compared to royalty!

The Baal HaTurim derives another lesson regarding the sanctity of a *nazir*, from the prohibition for the *nazir* to come into contact with a *meis*. There are three basic halachos that apply to the *nazir*: (1) the prohibition of drinking wine; (2) the prohibition of cutting hair, which is followed by the requirement of shaving after the *nezirus* has ended; (3) the prohibition of coming into contact with a *meis*.

The Rosh Yeshivah R' Chaim Shmulevitz notes[2] that the prohibition of drinking wine is understandable, since it represents abstention from physical pleasures, as the Gemara instructs: "One who glimpses a *sotah* in her disgrace shall abstain from wine" (*Sotah* 2a). The prohibition of cutting hair is likewise logical, since it involves shunning physical beauty. But why does the Torah prohibit the *nazir* from coming into contact with a dead body? This is no special expression of *perishus*. Moreover, recalling one's impending death is an excellent means of increasing *yiras Shamayim* and prompting oneself to *teshuvah*, as Shlomo HaMelech states, טוֹב לָלֶכֶת אֶל בֵּית אֵבֶל מִלֶּכֶת אֶל בֵּית מִשְׁתֶּה בַּאֲשֶׁר הוּא סוֹף כָּל הָאָדָם, *It is better to go to the house of mourning than to go to a house of feasting, for that is the end of all man* (*Koheles* 7:2). The *pasuk* concludes, וְהַחַי יִתֵּן אֶל לִבּוֹ, *and the living should take it to heart*, about which the Midrash teaches, "These are the *tzaddikim* who place their deaths opposite their hearts" (*Koheles Rabbah* 7:5). Contemplating the day of death is an excellent spiritual tool, so why would the Torah prohibit a *nazir* from having contact with a *meis?*

R' Chaim, citing the Baal HaTurim (*Bamidbar* 6:6), explains that

2. *Sichos Mussar, Kedushas HaNazir.*

the Torah was concerned that the *nazir* would attain such elevated spiritual heights that the *Shechinah* would rest on him, leading people to suspect that it was because he sought out the dead. Therefore, the Torah barred the *nazir* from any contact at all with the dead.

Since one who pledged *nezirus* is worthy of having the *Shechinah* rest on him, he is called a *nazir,* from the word *nezer,* a crown of glory. This also clarifies why a *nazir* — who saw with his own eyes what he is capable of achieving — is judged so harshly for terminating his *nezirus*.

The Cornerstone of Nezirus: Sincerity

The Mishnah teaches (*Nedarim* 20b) that "motivational *nedarim*" do not have the status of *nedarim*, and it brings the example of one who is selling an item to a customer and says, "I vow that I will not sell it for less than four dinars," to which the customer replies, "I vow that I will not raise my offer to more than two dinars." It is clear that both merchant and customer intend to compromise on three dinars, and the vow is just a figure of speech to persuade the other person to relent. The Rosh (ibid., s.v. *Shneihem*) explains that this is not considered a vow because their intentions do not match their words.

Nezirus, in contrast, requires absolute sincerity, and that is why a *nazir* is condemned for halting his spiritual ascent mid-stride at the end of his *nezirus*. Since the pledge of *nezirus* requires wholehearted commitment, the *nazir* should have contemplated ahead of time whether he would be capable of maintaining the lofty level of *nezirus*; and since he did not, he is censured.

A parallel can be drawn to Klal Yisrael's declaration of "*naaseh*" before "*nishma*" at the time of Kabbalas HaTorah. Declaring that they accept the yoke of Heaven would have been meaningless had the words been spoken insincerely. Indeed, we find that a "*shanah u'piresh*" — someone who studied Torah but then abandoned it — loses more than one who did not study at all, as the Gemara states, "One who learns and abandons is worse than all of them"

(*Pesachim* 49b). Similarly, one who verbally commits to accept the yoke of Torah but does not mean it sincerely is like one who began learning and then stopped; it would have been better if he hadn't started at all. This idea is reflected in the verse, טוֹב אֲשֶׁר לֹא תִדֹּר מִשֶּׁתִּדּוֹר וְלֹא תְשַׁלֵּם, *Better that you do not vow at all than that you vow and not pay* (*Koheles* 5:4).

The Gemara relates: "On the day of Atzeres (Shavuos), Rav Yosef would say, 'Prepare for me a third-born calf.' He said, 'If not for this day, how many Yosefs are there in the marketplace!' " (*Pesachim* 68b). Rav Yosef was expressing that he had once been a regular person, but after he learned Torah, he became spiritually elevated, which distinguished him from the many other "Yosefs" in the marketplace.

We see, then, that Klal Yisrael's sincere *kabbalas ol malchus Shamayim* — in which their mouth and their heart were aligned — propelled them to lofty levels of *kedushah*, similar to the *nazir's* spiritual ascent.

The Midrash teaches (*Devarim Rabbah* 8:2):

> "Hakadosh Baruch Hu says: "If you recited a blessing on the Torah, you are blessing yourself.' From where do we know this? It says, כִּי בִי יִרְבּוּ יָמֶיךָ וְיוֹסִיפוּ לְּךָ שְׁנוֹת חַיִּים, *For through me your days will be increased, and they will increase years of life for you* (*Mishlei* 9:11). "And if you will say that I gave the Torah to harm you — I gave it to you for your benefit, as the ministering angels desired it, and it disappeared from them ... My children, it is beyond the capacity of the ministering angels, yet it is not beyond your capacity."

How, asks the *Miluei Even*,[3] could anyone think that the Torah was given in order to harm us? Why would Hakadosh Baruch Hu, Who is purely good and does only good, give the Torah for any reason other than to benefit us?

He explains that one might assume that the Torah was given only as an antidote to the *yetzer hara*, but lacks any intrinsic value or worth. Accordingly, there would be no reason to recite a blessing

---

3. *Eil HaMiluim, Parashas Nitzavim*, p. 86.

upon it — just as one who drinks water to take medicine does not recite a *berachah*, since he does not enjoy the water.

Hakadosh Baruch Hu answers that this is not the case. Aside from the Torah serving as an antidote to the *yetzer hara*, it also provides wonderful benefits, as evidenced by the fact that the angels desired it for themselves even though they have no *yetzer hara* and are not tempted by sin. Torah possesses infinite intrinsic value, and this is why we are commanded to recite a *berachah* upon it.

Chazal teach that the Torah is so powerful that it elevates the learner and imbues him with extra *kedushah*. Therefore, if one is lax in *limud Torah*, then aside from being guilty of *bittul Torah*, he also hinders his own spiritual growth, to the point that he actually decimates his own potential for sanctity.

Continuing the Ascent After Shavuos

This lesson is particularly relevant to Shavuos, and we must strive to incorporate it in our lives even after Yom Tov has passed. As we prepare to receive the Torah, we should give thought to the importance of heartfelt acceptance, which elevates a person and leads him to acquire life in both this world and the next. Then, once we have experienced the elevation of Mattan Torah, we must ensure that we do not revert to our regular daily routine, but draw from the holiness and bounty of the Yom Tov to keep striving higher.

Every Yom Tov has its distinct spiritual bounty. Pesach is the time to remember Yetzias Mitzrayim; Succos is the time for *simchah*; Shavuos is the time of Mattan Torah. Each festival affords us a wondrous opportunity to inspire ourselves through the spiritual gifts of that Yom Tov, and it is incumbent upon us to grasp onto those gifts and use them to elevate ourselves throughout the year. Only *limud Torah* elevates a person, as we learn from Rav Yosef, so we must continue striving and toiling to discover new *chiddushim* in Torah.

Just as a *nazir* is obligated to bring a *korban chatas* because he is not maintaining the *kedushah* that he attained, one who does not continue drawing upon the inspiration and spiritual elevation that he received at the time of Mattan Torah can also be regarded, to an extent, as a sinner. This applies not only to the spiritual elevation that follows Shavuos, but also to the spiritual heights that we acquire every time we learn well or share a *shtickel Torah.*

We learn in *Nedarim* (3a) that a *nazir* who postpones the start of his *nezirus* transgresses the prohibition of *bal te'acher*, because one who experiences a surge of purity must act upon it without delay, so that he can grow spiritually.

Indeed, Chazal exhort us to capitalize on mitzvah opportunities immediately, as they say, מִצְוָה הַבָּאָה לְיָדְךָ אַל תַּחְמִיצֶנָּה, *If a mitzvah comes to your hand, do not allow it to become "leavened"* (*Mechilta, Bo* 9:63). This requirement applies also to one who accepts the yoke of Torah. One who has already begun the process of spiritual growth must never falter or delay, but should redouble his energies to keep on climbing. This is our *avodah* during these days. As *bnei Torah* who have already merited to elevate ourselves, we must continue to grow!

Affected by Sight

The Gemara teaches: "Why was the topic of *nazir* juxtaposed with the topic of *sotah*? To teach you that one who sees a *sotah* at the time of her disgrace should abstain from wine" (*Sotah* 2b). The simple explanation is that one who had the rare experience of glimpsing the miraculous eradication of *tumah* must take the lesson to heart and spur himself to grow in *avodas Hashem,* for otherwise, he will be left with nothing from the experience.

Another explanation offered by many *mefarshim* is that when a person witnesses the disgrace of a *sotah,* whose infidelity was revealed through the waters, he is exposed to licentiousness and impurity, and is liable to be affected by what he saw and be drawn after it. Therefore, he must build extra spiritual safeguards around himself to avoid stumbling similarly.

The juxtaposition of these two topics illustrates just how devastating the impact of a single glance can be, and how it can cause a person to fall headlong into a downward spiral that ends in spiritual catastrophe. It also underscores how much effort we must make to strengthen our *shemiras einayim,* by avoiding forbidden sights and gazing only upon that which is pure and holy. In merit of our efforts to guard our eyes, may Hashem grant us *siyata diShmaya* in all our endeavors!

פרשת בהעלותך
Parashas Beha'aloscha

Lashon Hara — Harming the Essence of Life

וַתְּדַבֵּר מִרְיָם וְאַהֲרֹן בְּמֹשֶׁה עַל אֹדוֹת הָאִשָּׁה הַכֻּשִׁית אֲשֶׁר לָקָח כִּי אִשָּׁה כֻשִׁית לָקָח. וַיֹּאמְרוּ הֲרַק אַךְ בְּמֹשֶׁה דִּבֶּר ה׳ הֲלֹא גַּם בָּנוּ דִבֵּר וַיִּשְׁמַע ה׳.

Miriam and Aharon spoke against Moshe regarding the Cushite woman he had married, for he had married a Cushite woman. They said, "Was it only to Moshe that Hashem spoke? Did He not speak to us, as well?" And Hashem heard.
(*Bamidbar* 12:1-2).

Rashi comments: "If Miriam, who did not intend to malign, was punished so severely, how much more so for one who intends to malign his friend."

Chazal teach (*Yalkut Shimoni, Bamidbar* 737):

It is a *kal vachomer*. Miriam did not intend to speak negatively of her brother, but rather in his praise; her intentions were not [that Moshe intended] to diminish from [the mitzvah of] procreation, but to add; and [she spoke only] of her younger brother, and spoke quietly, as it is written, "And Hashem heard," and she was [still] punished [so severely]. One who intends to speak negatively of his friend and not to praise, and to minimize procreation and not to add to it, and [speaks] of those greater than him and before others — how much more so [shall he be punished].

We see from this *parashah* how severely the Torah regards one who speaks *lashon hara* about his fellow Jew, and how harshly he is punished. Miriam's words could have been excused on several counts instead of being deemed *lashon hara*, for not only was her intention for the sake of a mitzvah, but she also took care to speak privately where she would not be heard. And yet, Miriam was punished with leprosy! If this is the punishment meted out for such innocuous words, we surely cannot fathom the grave punishment awaiting one who intentionally speaks *lashon hara* about a fellow Jew or humiliates him publicly.

The Prohibition of Lashon Hara

Immediately after this incident with Miriam, Hashem commands Moshe Rabbeinu: שְׁלַח לְךָ אֲנָשִׁים וְיָתֻרוּ אֶת אֶרֶץ כְּנַעַן, *Send forth men, if you please, and let them spy out the land of Canaan* (*Bamidbar* 13:2).

Rashi comments: "Why were the topics of the *meraglim* and Miriam juxtaposed? Because she was punished for her words against her brother, yet these wicked ones saw and did not take heed." The *meraglim* were held accountable for speaking negatively of Eretz Yisrael specifically after bearing witness to the terrible punishment that befell Miriam HaNeviah when she spoke *lashon hara* about Moshe Rabbeinu, as they did not learn from her mistake or take the lesson to heart.

On the other hand, there is a marked difference between the *lashon hara* spoken by Miriam and the *meraglim*. Miriam criticized Moshe Rabbeinu, while the *meraglim* did not malign a person; they spoke contemptuously only of inanimate objects, rocks, and trees. Why should they have drawn a lesson from Miriam, who spoke *lashon hara* not only about a fellow Jew, but about Klal Yisrael's spiritual leader? Their negative report about the land in no way compares to Miriam's disparaging statement about Moshe Rabbeinu.

From here we learn that the prohibition of *lashon hara* is regarding the evil speech itself, and not necessarily the collateral damage, which is why there is no practical difference between speaking *lashon hara* about a person or an object. A Yid must guard his tongue from negative speech regardless of the outcome, and this is why the *meraglim*, who did not learn a lesson from Miriam, were punished so severely for their sin.

The Chofetz Chaim wrote a landmark *sefer* on the laws of *lashon hara* and *rechilus*, but why did he choose this, out of the 365 prohibitions in the Torah? What is unique about the sin of *lashon hara*?

Other *aveiros*, such as theft, adultery, and murder, are obvious crimes whose consequences are seen and felt by the sinner. A person who murdered his fellow man instantly witnesses the devastation that he has wrought, as the victim lies dead before his eyes, and he recognizes that he is now a *murderer.* Similarly, when a person steals, he feels the stolen item burning a hole in his pocket and immediately sees the grievous results of his crime.

Lashon hara is different. Even when one's disparaging words have no impact upon the subject, they are still strictly forbidden, because the prohibition relates to the negative words themselves, as evidenced by the *meraglim*.

The Chofetz Chaim saw fit to devote a *sefer* specifically to the halachos of *lashon hara* in order to raise awareness of the severity of this sin, which many people do not sufficiently recognize.

Measure for Measure

This *parashah* also teaches that one who sins by speaking *lashon hara* is punished with *tzaraas* and forced to sit outside the camp, as it is written: וַתִּסָּגֵר מִרְיָם מִחוּץ לַמַּחֲנֶה שִׁבְעַת יָמִים, *So Miriam was quarantined outside the camp for seven days* (*Bamidbar* 12:15).

Why is *tzaraas* the punishment for the sin of *lashon hara*?

The answer is found in the Torah's words: אַל נָא תְהִי כַּמֵּת, *Let her not be like a corpse* (ibid. v. 12), on which Rashi comments that "a *metzora* is regarded as dead." The *mefarshim* explain that one who speaks *lashon hara* is really deserving of death, and since a *metzora* is compared to a dead man, the *lashon hara* speaker suffers a form of death through his *tzaraas*.

The Rosh Yeshivah R' Chaim Shmulevitz explained[4] that a *metzora* is forced to sit outside the camp, completely alone and disconnected from society, and is therefore unable to give to others or help them. Olam Hazeh is built upon connection and interpersonal relationships, and one of the ultimate elements of life is the capacity to coexist and share with others. One who is unable to benefit another is no more significant than a corpse.

The Gemara conveys this lesson when it says, "Four are regarded as dead — a pauper, a *metzora*, a blind person, and one who has no children" (*Nedarim* 64b). The common denominator among these four is that they are unable to give to others: A blind person cannot give because he cannot see; a pauper possesses nothing to give; one who is childless does not have to whom to give; and a *metzora*, who is forced to sit alone outside the camp, likewise has no one to accept his bequest.[5]

One who is capable of reaching out and giving to others is considered alive, whereas one who lives for himself and keeps everything for himself lacks the quality of giving, and is no better than one who is dead.

With this, we can understand how the punishment of the *lashon hara* speaker is *middah k'neged middah*. Someone who speaks negatively about his fellow man demonstrates that he does not recognize, and certainly does not appreciate, the other person's positive attributes. He does not desire what is best for him, and therefore sees no reason to avoid speaking negatively of him. This disparaging attitude toward a fellow Jew is what makes him deserving of *tzaraas*, which compels him to sit outside the camp for seven days, where he cannot give to others and is as good as dead.

Speaking *lashon hara* indicates an inadequate appreciation for the essence of human life. The greatest attribute of a living person is his capacity to give to others; without this, he is no better than a lifeless, inanimate object or a corpse. Even if he did not harm his

---

4. *Sichos Mussar, Yeshev Badad.*

5. See *Parashas Tazria*, "Outside the Camp."

friend with his forbidden speech, the very fact that he is capable of denigrating him proves that he does not respect him, and does not regard him as a human being who has value and would not want others to speak disparagingly of him. One who speaks *lashon hara* shows that he lacks the ability to give to others and empathize with them. This itself is a reason that he should be punished with *tzaraas*, a punishment akin to death that renders the person useless.

Banishing Negative Character Traits

Now that we understand how terrible *lashon hara* is, we must ask ourselves, how can a person plummet to such a deplorable level that he would dare to speak *lashon hara* about his fellow Yid?

The simple answer is that this is the result of bad *middos*. The Torah wants us to appreciate and respect others and draw close to them, and one who lives this way will not come to speak *lashon hara*. If, however, a person feels superior to others and believes that he does not need anyone else, or if he is jealous or angry, then he loses control over himself and is incapable of noticing the other person's good qualities. Chazal say, regarding an arrogant person, "Hakadosh Baruch Hu said, 'I and he cannot coexist in the world'" (*Sotah* 5a), and regarding an angry person, "Even the *Shechinah* is not important to him" (*Nedarim* 22b). Because such people are so self-absorbed, and do not reflect upon the needs and feelings of those around them, they can fall to the level of speaking ill of others.

How does a Yid develop such poor *middos*, which cause him to degenerate to the level of a *meis?* The Torah answers: וַיִּשְׁמַן יְשֻׁרוּן וַיִּבְעָט, *Yeshurun became fat and kicked* (*Devarim* 32:15), revealing that the source of bad *middos* is excessive good. Many people have so much blessing in their lives, yet unfortunately they do not appreciate it. They fail to recognize that everything they have is a gift from Hashem and from those who love them, and they selfishly reject — "kick" — their parents, teachers, and benefactors.

The evil trait of ingratitude is highlighted by the Torah in the episode of the *misonenim*, as it states, וַיְהִי הָעָם כְּמִתְאֹנְנִים רַע בְּאָזְנֵי ה׳

וגו׳ וְהָאסַפְסֻף אֲשֶׁר בְּקִרְבּוֹ הִתְאַוּוּ תַּאֲוָה וַיָּשֻׁבוּ וַיִּבְכּוּ גַּם בְּנֵי יִשְׂרָאֵל וַיֹּאמְרוּ מִי יַאֲכִלֵנוּ בָּשָׂר וגו׳ וַיִּשְׁמַע מֹשֶׁה אֶת הָעָם בֹּכֶה לְמִשְׁפְּחֹתָיו אִישׁ לְפֶתַח אָהֳלוֹ, *The people took to seeking complaints; it was evil in the ears of Hashem ... The rabble that was among them cultivated a craving, and the Children of Israel also wept once more, and said, "Who will feed us meat?" ... Moshe heard the people weeping in their family groups, each one at the entrance of his tent* (*Bamidbar* 11:1,4,10).

This episode is truly mind-boggling. Hakadosh Baruch Hu had just performed unprecedented miracles for Bnei Yisrael and was sustaining them with the *mahn*, a miraculous food that could taste like anything they desired. This liberated Bnei Yisrael from the burden of supporting themselves, and they did not have to worry about tomorrow's bread. How did they stoop so low as to complain that they desired meat and cry over the prohibitions of adultery they had been commanded at Har Sinai?

Human nature is such that a person never feels satisfied with his material circumstances, as Chazal teach, "He who has one hundred wants two hundred; he who has two hundred wants four hundred" (*Koheles Rabbah* 3:13). This was true when Bnei Yisrael were in the Midbar eating the *mahn*, and it remains true until today, when our world is flooded with material pleasures. Humans are rarely happy with their lot and are constantly inclined to complain about what they lack, and this is what breeds bad *middos*.

We have the choice of whether we want to be among those who "kick," or whether we want to focus on the incredible gifts and *chassadim* that Hakadosh Baruch Hu constantly bestows upon the world and upon each individual. One who genuinely ponders the goodness in his life will realize that his success and assets are not due to his wisdom, talents, or even efforts, but are purely a function of *siyata diShmaya*. Moreover, one who makes the effort to appreciate Hashem's gifts will naturally rejoice with his lot, because it is impossible not to! It's enough to merely contemplate the basic kindness that Hashem performs for us each moment by giving us air to breathe. If the oxygen in the world would deplete for even a few moments, we would all perish! And oxygen is but one of the innumerable kindnesses that He performs for us every second. How much more so should we feel joyous and grateful to Him for giving us food, clothing, our families, and all the wonderful bounty that surrounds us always!

Yishuv Hadaas Breeds Joy

One of the main reasons why a person finds it challenging to be happy with his lot is that he lacks *yishuv hadaas*, which prevents him from taking the time to stop and reflect upon all the goodness and gifts in his life. The Rashbam (*Bamidbar* 11:1) explains that the *misonenim* were "distressed by the hardship of their travels." With these words, he reveals that Bnei Yisrael complained because they were upset by their wearying travels, and lacked the peace of mind to examine things clearly. He implies that had they possessed *yishuv hadaas*, they would have surely been able to see how irrational and imprudent their complaints were.

Achieving *yishuv hadaas* is part of our lifelong labor of *tikkun hamiddos*, which is the basis of all *avodas Hashem*. The Vilna Gaon writes: "All *avodas Hashem* is dependent on rectifying *middos*, which are like garments for the mitzvos and the precepts of the Torah; and all sins are rooted in *middos*" (*Even Sheleimah* 1:1). He adds, "A person lives primarily to strengthen himself constantly in breaking his *middos*, for if not, what is the purpose of his life?"

If we constantly recall the kindnesses that Hakadosh Baruch Hu bestows upon us — morning and night, individually and collectively — we will automatically stop complaining and instead find happiness in our lot in life. Man's natural dissatisfaction with his life circumstances is an outgrowth of self-absorption, but when he stops to examine his life and all that he possesses, he will recognize Hashem's kindness, which will lead him to rectify his character traits, in both *bein adam lachaveiro* and *bein adam laMakom*.

פרשת שלח
Parashas Shelach

◆§ *Humility — A Prerequisite to Transmitting the Mesorah*

וַיִּלֹּנוּ עַל מֹשֶׁה וְעַל אַהֲרֹן כֹּל בְּנֵי יִשְׂרָאֵל וַיֹּאמְרוּ אֲלֵהֶם כָּל הָעֵדָה לוּ מַתְנוּ בְּאֶרֶץ מִצְרַיִם אוֹ בַּמִּדְבָּר הַזֶּה לוּ מָתְנוּ וגו׳ וַיְדַבֵּר ה׳ אֶל מֹשֶׁה וְאֶל אַהֲרֹן לֵאמֹר עַד מָתַי לָעֵדָה הָרָעָה הַזֹּאת וגו׳ אֱמֹר אֲלֵהֶם חַי אָנִי נְאֻם ה׳ אִם לֹא כַּאֲשֶׁר דִּבַּרְתֶּם בְּאָזְנָי כֵּן אֶעֱשֶׂה לָכֶם.

All the Children of Israel murmured against Moshe and Aharon, and the entire assembly said to them, "If only we had died in the land of Egypt, or if only we had died in this Wilderness!" ... Hashem spoke to Moshe and Aharon, saying, "How long for this evil assembly ... Say to them: As I live — the word of Hashem — if I shall not do to you as you have spoken in My ears' (*Bamidbar* 14:2, 26-28).

Regarding the words כַּאֲשֶׁר דִּבַּרְתֶּם, *as you have spoken*, Rashi comments, "For you asked of Me, *or if only we had died in this Wilderness*." This implies that Bnei Yisrael were punished for the sin of the *meraglim* not because they spoke *lashon hara* about Eretz Yisrael or believed the *lashon hara* of the *meraglim*, but because they lamented, "If only we had died."

Midrash Tanchuma (*Shelach* 22) gives the parable of one who came before a king for judgment and incriminated himself with his own words. "I judge you based on the words that emerged from your lips," said the king, "and you shall be punished as you said." Similarly, in response to Bnei Yisrael's own wish of "if only we had died in this Wilderness," Hakadosh Baruch Hu told them, בַּמִּדְבָּר הַזֶּה יִפְּלוּ פִגְרֵיכֶם, *In this Wilderness shall your carcasses drop* (ibid. v. 29).

Let us examine Bnei Yisrael's grievance against Moshe and Aharon for wanting to lead them into Eretz Yisrael, as expressed in the declaration, "If only we had died in this Wilderness."

Even if the generation of the Midbar had truly believed the *meraglim's* false claim that Eretz Yisrael was a land that consumed its inhabitants, it would still have behooved them to enter Eretz Yisrael and attempt to conquer and settle the country rather than perish senselessly in the Midbar or return to Mitzrayim. Languishing in the Midbar, where they possessed no means of survival, was a clear death sentence, whereas if they would attempt to enter Eretz Yisrael and conquer it, there was at least a chance that they would triumph over their enemies and endure as a nation. What could they possibly gain by remaining in the Midbar?

After experiencing the many miracles in Mitzrayim, at the Yam Suf, and in the Midbar, Bnei Yisrael had grown so accustomed to their supernatural existence that they believed that this was the natural way of the world. Hakadosh Baruch Hu enveloped them with so many wonders — the *mahn*, the well of Miriam, the Clouds of Glory, and other miracles large and small — that they were certain they could prolong this existence forever. Therefore, they preferred to remain in the Midbar than to enter Eretz Yisrael, which the *meraglim* had maligned as a country that consumes its inhabitants.

Why were Bnei Yisrael convinced that they could continue this supernatural existence? Even if they had grown accustomed to this way of life, they were surely aware that it was not in keeping with the laws of nature and could not continue forever. Moreover, even if they believed that they were permitted to rely on miracles and trusted implicitly that Hakadosh Baruch Hu would not deprive them of their needs, people are naturally inclined to favor a normal way of life over relying on miracles every day. All this leads us back to our original question: Even if Bnei Yisrael believed the *meraglim's* claim that Eretz Yisrael was a land that consumed its people, the *meraglim* themselves had also described the country as a "land flowing with milk and honey," so why wouldn't Bnei Yisrael prefer entering a country rich in natural resources over perishing in the Midbar?

The Sin of Wanting to Live Supernaturally

The root of Klal Yisrael's flawed conduct was a desire to perpetuate their supernatural existence and continue relying exclusively on miracles instead of resuming a normal existence in line with the laws of nature. This yearning was so powerful that they were even willing to sacrifice the opportunity to enter Eretz Yisrael, and remain in the Midbar until they expired. This was because they believed that they were worthy of the miracles Hashem bestowed upon them in the Midbar, and therefore, He would surely allow them to prolong this supernatural existence.

The erroneous belief that they deserved these myriad gifts from Hakadosh Baruch Hu was rooted in arrogance. Indeed, the *middah* of *gaavah* causes a person to get so carried away that he comes to believe that Hashem Himself is duty-bound to fulfill his desires! Having experienced so many miracles, Bnei Yisrael demanded more and more, to the point that they felt justified in their craving to live a supernatural existence eternally. It was this deep character flaw that caused them to fall to the lowly level of speaking negatively of the land promised to them by Hakadosh Baruch Hu, which brought death and calamity upon the entire generation and caused them to lose the privilege of entering Eretz Yisrael.

A Humble Person Perpetuates the Transmission of Torah

We may still wonder, however, why Bnei Yisrael's desire to live a supernatural existence was so terrible that it caused them to be deserving of death.

A person who appreciates Hashem's kindness, and recognizes that everything that happens is an expression of Hashem's love and compassion for him, automatically embraces the *middah* of *anavah*. This quality of genuine humility leads him to realize that nothing is truly his and that anything he seemingly possesses is only a gift from Hashem. Such a person is capable of plumbing the depths of Torah and discovering its truths, and he is, moreover, worthy of transmitting the *mesorah* onward.

In contrast, one who insists that the many gifts bestowed upon him are his entitlement, and that his positive qualities make him deserving of all the goodness Hashem grants him, is so trapped in the morass of *gaavah* and *kavod* that he can never arrive at the truth of Torah and will never have the capacity to relay the *mesorah* to future generations. The reason that the generation of the Midbar was punished with death was that they were unworthy of perpetuating Torah and transmitting it to the next generation.

A Yid who instills within himself the *middah* of *anavah* merits to grasp the truth of Torah and live his life in accordance with *daas Torah*. This empowers him to ingrain these vital values and lessons in his *talmidim* and impart them to future generations, perpetuating the holy *mesorah* that began with Moshe Rabbeinu at Har Sinai and continues until this very day. It is no coincidence that Moshe Rabbeinu, who was chosen to transmit the Torah to Klal Yisrael, was also the humblest of men, as the *pasuk* attests, וְהָאִישׁ מֹשֶׁה עָנָו מְאֹד מִכֹּל הָאָדָם אֲשֶׁר עַל פְּנֵי הָאֲדָמָה, *Now the man Moshe was exceedingly humble, more than any person on the face of the earth* (*Bamidbar* 12:3). The Torah itself is called *"Toras Moshe,"* after him!

Moshe also testified about himself, לֹא חֲמוֹר אֶחָד מֵהֶם נָשָׂאתִי, *I have not taken even a single donkey of theirs* (ibid. 16:15), which Rashi interprets as, "I did not take the donkey of even one of them, even when I traveled from Midian to Mitzrayim and let my wife and children ride upon the donkey. I should have taken a donkey from them, but I took my own."

Despite his lifelong efforts and self-sacrifice on behalf of the nation, Moshe Rabbeinu, in his unparalleled humility, did not feel that Bnei Yisrael were obligated to honor or repay him in any way, even with the minimal gesture of affording him the use of a single donkey. Similar words were expressed by Shmuel HaNavi, who, in his later years, fearing that he might have benefited from the people, asked them to tell him, אֶת שׁוֹר מִי לָקַחְתִּי וַחֲמוֹר מִי לָקַחְתִּי וְאֶת מִי עָשַׁקְתִּי אֶת מִי רַצּוֹתִי וגו׳ וְאָשִׁיב לָכֶם, *Whose ox have I taken? Whose donkey have I taken? Whom have I robbed? Whom have I coerced? ... And I shall make restitution to you* (*I Shmuel* 12:3). In their supreme humility, both Moshe Rabbeinu and Shmuel HaNavi felt undeserving of any recompense from Bnei Yisrael, which is precisely why both were worthy of teaching Torah.

A Yid must acknowledge that all his needs are provided by Hashem, in His infinite kindness and compassion, and not because he himself is deserving of it. When entreating Hashem in prayer at any time, we must do so with the perspective that we are nothing but dust and ashes, and are unworthy of miracles. Then, we can hope that Hashem will grant us *siyata diShmaya* and success in all our endeavors.

פרשת קרח
Parashas Korach

◆ *Separate From the Whole*

וַיִּקַּח קֹרַח בֶּן יִצְהָר בֶּן קְהָת בֶּן לֵוִי וְדָתָן וַאֲבִירָם בְּנֵי אֱלִיאָב וְאוֹן בֶּן פֶּלֶת בְּנֵי רְאוּבֵן.
Korach son of Yitzhar son of Kehas son of Levi separated himself, with Dasan and Aviram, sons of Eliav, and On son of Peles, the offspring of Reuven (*Bamidbar* 16:1).

The Satan's Power in Disunity

Regarding the words וַיִּקַּח קֹרַח, *Korach took,* Rashi comments: "He took himself to one side to separate himself from the congregation, to argue about the Kehunah."

Rashi's explanation implies that Korach's power to generate *machlokes* drew from the fact that he separated himself from the congregation, and it was this departure that enabled him to contest the Kehunah. As long as Bnei Yisrael were united, as one man with one heart, Korach lacked the power to sow conflict in the nation, yet when he took a stand to actively separate himself from the *tzibbur*, he was able to influence others to join him and introduce dissension and hostility among the people.

This episode highlights the immense power of the *klal*. Even if a person harbors a personal grievance or has a reason to enter a conflict, as long as he does not actively remove himself from the community, he lacks the power to propagate the *machlokes* and influence others to join his camp. As soon as he chooses to separate himself from the community, however, he is able to cement the *machlokes* by virtue of the fact that he is no longer part of the *tzibbur*.

This is the *koach* of the *tzibbur*! As long as the *tzibbur* is unified, it has the capacity to protect itself from calamity. Had Korach not taken that fateful step of separating himself from the congregation, Klal Yisrael would have been spared terrible destruction.

Why is the *achdus* of a *tzibbur* is powerful?

The Gemara relates: "There were two men whom the Satan provoked to argue every Erev Shabbos. R' Meir intervened and stayed with them for three consecutive Fridays, until they made peace. Rabbi Meir [then] heard the Satan say, 'Woe unto me that R' Meir banished me from my home'" (*Gittin* 52a).

The Satan dwells amid discord and strife, whereas in a place where peace and harmony prevail, there is no room for him. Shabbos is a time of *menuchah*, as the Torah says, וַיָּנַח בַּיּוֹם הַשְּׁבִיעִי, *and He rested on the seventh day* (*Shemos* 20:11), and as we recite in Minchah of Shabbos: מְנוּחַת שָׁלוֹם וְשַׁלְוָה וְהַשְׁקֵט וָבֶטַח, *a rest of peace and serenity and tranquility and security*. Furthermore, the *Zohar* interprets the *pasuk*, לֹא תְבַעֲרוּ אֵשׁ בְּכֹל מֹשְׁבֹתֵיכֶם בְּיוֹם הַשַּׁבָּת, *You shall not kindle fire in any of your dwellings on the Sabbath day* (*Shemos* 35:3), as an allusion to the fire of *machlokes*. Since Shabbos is a time dedicated to peace, harmony, and rest, which are the diametric opposite of animosity, discord, and strife, a Yid is warned against allowing the flames of dissent to penetrate his home on Shabbos Kodesh.

In his perpetual attempts to cause Bnei Yisrael to stumble, the Satan cunningly approaches on Erev Shabbos and plants seeds of discord in order to cause Yidden to enter Shabbos upset, angry, and singed with *machlokes*. In this way, he disrupts the peaceful atmosphere in the house, introduces tension and strife, and thus ignites conflagration in the home, which is similar to a desecration of Shabbos. A Yid must therefore take extra precautions, especially on Erev Shabbos, to avoid being dragged into arguments or conflict, which open the door for the Satan to destroy his *shalom bayis.*

Quarrels and dissension are the building blocks of the Satan's dominion, and once we afford him entry into our homes, he becomes the master and does as he pleases. Accordingly, only when Korach separated himself from the congregation to create an opposing camp did his scheme succeed, for then he was empowered to confuse and rip the nation apart with his grievances and derision.

The Benefits of Shalom

In striking contrast to the destruction wrought by *machlokes* are the wonderful advantages and gifts engendered by *shalom*. Indeed, Bnei Yisrael were worthy of receiving Torah only in the merit of the *shalom* that prevailed among them, as the Torah states, וַיִּחַן שָׁם יִשְׂרָאֵל נֶגֶד הָהָר, *And Israel encamped there, opposite the mountain* (*Shemos* 19:2), about which Rashi famously comments, כְּאִישׁ אֶחָד בְּלֵב אֶחָד, *like one man with one heart*. Only when the nation achieved a state of absolute peace and unity were they worthy of receiving Torah.

We conclude several *masechtos* in Shas and a number of *tefillos* with the words, תַּלְמִידֵי חֲכָמִים מַרְבִּים שָׁלוֹם בָּעוֹלָם, *Torah scholars increase peace in the world,* underscoring that Torah study and prayer serve to enhance *shalom* in the world and create peace between Bnei Yisrael and our Father in heaven.

Beyond this, we also find that Hashem's Kingship is manifest at a time when Bnei Yisrael are in a state of peace and unity, as the Torah states, וַיְהִי בִישֻׁרוּן מֶלֶךְ בְּהִתְאַסֵּף רָאשֵׁי עָם יַחַד שִׁבְטֵי יִשְׂרָאֵל, *He became King over Yeshurun when the numbers of the nation gathered — the tribes of Israel in unity* (*Devarim* 33:5). The *Daas Zekeinim MiBaalei HaTosafos* explain, "This means that when the Jewish people are together in brotherhood and friendship, then Hakadosh Baruch Hu is King over them; but during times of strife, they act as if Hakadosh Baruch Hu is not King over them."

This is a chilling statement! When we are embroiled in strife, we annul Hakadosh Baruch Hu's dominion upon the world, as it were, acting "as if Hakadosh Baruch Hu is not King" over us! Of course, the converse is true as well, and when we dwell harmoniously together, we merit drawing Hashem's Kingship upon us and coming close to Him as His children and servants.

Shalom is such a lofty value that Chazal point out that if peace reigns among them, Bnei Yisrael are not punished even if they worship idols! As the Midrash states (*Yalkut Shimoni, Bamidbar* 711):

> R' Eliezer the son of R' Elazar HaKappar says: Great is peace, for even if the Jewish people worship idols, but there is peace among them, Hakadosh Baruch Hu says, as it were, "The Satan shall not touch them," as it is written, חֲבוּר עֲצַבִּים אֶפְרָיִם הַנַּח לוֹ, *Ephraim is attached to idols; let him be* (*Hoshea* 4:17). When they are divided, however, what does it say of them? חָלַק לִבָּם עַתָּה יֶאְשָׁמוּ, *Their hearts have become detached; now they will become desolate* (ibid. 10:2). Here [we see] that peace is great and discord is despised.

Similarly, despite their grave sin, the Dor HaHaflagah — which is described by the Torah as speaking one language (*Bereishis* 11:1), and excelled in the quality of unity — was not annihilated, but rather scattered throughout the world, as the *pasuk* says: הֱפִיצָם ה' עַל פְּנֵי כָּל הָאָרֶץ, *Hashem scattered them over the face of the whole earth* (ibid. v. 9).

Rashi asks: Whose sin was worse? That of the Dor HaMabul or that of the Dor HaHaflagah? The Dor HaMabul did not rebel against Hashem, while the Dor HaHaflagah rebelled against Him, as if to fight against Him. Yet the Dor HaMabul was annihilated, while the Dor HaHaflagah was not! Rashi explains that the Dor HaMabul were shameless thieves who were enmeshed in arguments and strife, and Hashem therefore destroyed them. Yet the Dor HaHaflagah spoke a shared language and treated one another with compassion and friendship, so they were allowed to remain in this world. This proves, says Rashi, that "Discord is hated, and peace is great" (ibid.).

Similarly, we find that in the times of Dovid HaMelech, Klal

Yisrael were renowned as great *tzaddikim*, and yet whenever they set out to war, many soldiers fell in battle. The *Yerushalmi* (*Peah* 1:1) explains that this was due to the friction among them: "Everyone in Dovid's generation was righteous, yet because there was conflict among them, they would head out to war and fail. Yet in Achav's generation, when [the nation] served idols, because there was no conflict in their midst, whenever they would go to battle, they would triumph."

These examples all illustrate the destructive nature of *machlokes*, and, conversely, the protective power of *shalom*.

The power of *shalom* is readily apparent on happy occasions, when everyone sings and dances joyously, and friendship, camaraderie, and *achdus* prevail. During these elevated moments, we are enveloped with spiritual ecstasy, and we merit a bounty of Torah wisdom, as we collectively crown Hashem as King upon us. At such times, there is no room for the Satan in our midst. Yet if we allow ourselves to fall prey to *machlokes*, the opposite can occur.

Korach's power to influence the *tzibbur* and sow destruction in Klal Yisrael derived from that one fateful step he took to separate himself from the congregation. Through that, he managed to mislead people and bring calamity upon them, because the force of divisiveness and discord can ensnare even the wisest and most righteous among us.

A *ben Torah* must embrace the path of love and brotherhood toward his fellow man, and must constantly seek to foster peace and harmony in his environment. May our heartfelt pursuit of *shalom* lead us to reveal Hashem's Kingship in the world, so that everyone can wholeheartedly receive the Torah in all its splendor.

פרשת חקת
Parashas Chukas

◆§ *By Order of the King*

זֹאת חֻקַּת הַתּוֹרָה.
This is the decree of the Torah (*Bamidbar* 19:2).

No Reason at All

Rashi comments: "Because the Satan and the nations of the world aggrieve Israel by saying, 'What is this commandment?' and 'What reason is there to it?' therefore [the Torah] wrote of it 'decree.' It is a decree from before Me; you do not have the right to question it."

The *Sifsei Chachamim* explains that Rashi's question is why the Torah wrote both "*chukas*" and "*Torah*," which seems redundant. In other places, the Torah uses only one of these words to introduce a mitzvah; for instance, זֹאת חֻקַּת הַפָּסַח, *This is the decree of the pesach-offering* (*Shemos* 12:43); or זֹאת הַתּוֹרָה לָעֹלָה לַמִּנְחָה וְלַחַטָּאת, *This is the law of the burnt-offering, the meal-offering, and the sin-offering* (*Vayikra* 7:37). Why, in this case, did the Torah use both words?

Clearly, this is meant to emphasize that the mitzvah of *parah adumah* is a *chok*, a decree that has no underlying reason at all. While all mitzvos in the Torah are regarded as a "decree of the king" that we cannot fathom, the mitzvah of *parah adumah* is even more extreme in this regard, since it is both a *chok* and also paradoxical, for it purifies the impure while defiling the pure. Yet despite all this, we may not doubt or challenge it.

In a similar vein, the Gemara teaches (*Nedarim* 16b) that the mitzvos were not given to us so we could enjoy them. We are meant to fulfill Hashem's commandments not for our own pleasure, but because they are the King's word.

Nevertheless, we find that *lomdei Torah* derive profound enjoyment from toiling in Torah, and one is hard-pressed to find a deeper or more fulfilling pleasure than speaking in learning with a *chavrusa*! We must therefore conclude that *limud Torah* is different, and deriving pleasure from learning is an integral aspect of Torah study, as the *Eglei Tal* writes in his preface, "The essence of the mitzvah of *limud Torah* is to rejoice and delight in one's learning, and then the words of Torah are absorbed in his blood. Because he enjoys the words of Torah, he cleaves to Torah."

It is said that R' Chaim Brisker once had a weighty personal question in halachah that he posed to the rav of Kovno, R' Yitzchak Elchanan Spektor. He requested that R' Yitzchak Elchanan deliver his ruling without any explanation or clarification, explaining that if he were to know the underlying reasoning behind R' Yitzchak Elchanan's conclusion, he might find a reason to argue, and then he would not feel at peace with the *psak*. If, however, he merely received a clear *psak halachah* without any explanation, he would not be able to contest it.

This story beautifully illustrates the precept of זֹאת חֻקַּת הַתּוֹרָה. Truly, all mitzvos in the Torah are *chukim* whose meaning we cannot fathom, and we must remember this prior to engaging in Torah study and the performance of mitzvos.

Tumah and Taharah Are Rooted in Kabbalas HaTorah

Why did the Torah choose to emphasize this lesson — that mitzvos are "decrees of the king" — specifically in the context of the mitzvah of *parah adumah*, when there are many other mitzvos that seemingly have no logical basis?

This can be explained based upon two halachic principles related to *tumas meis*: A gentile is not rendered impure through contact with a dead body (*Nazir* 61b), and only a Jewish body transmits *tumas ohel*, rendering as impure those inside the same house as the corpse, as opposed to a gentile's body, which does not transmit this impurity (*Yevamos* 61a).

Similarly, the Rambam rules: "A gentile who touched a corpse or carried it or covered it is like one who did not touch [a corpse]. To what can this be compared? To an animal that touches a corpse or covered a corpse" (*Tumas Meis* 1:13).

The Ohr HaChaim explains (*Bamidbar* 19:2) that ever since Bnei Yisrael received the Torah on Har Sinai and were elevated to exalted spiritual heights, the forces of impurity constantly seek to cleave to us — both during our lifetimes and afterward. This is why Bnei Yisrael require the ashes of the *parah adumah*, whose capacity to purify a person from *tumas meis* is a great *chiddush* that the Torah presented. The nations of the world, who did not accept the Torah and were neither sanctified nor elevated to spiritual heights, are not susceptible to forces of impurity, which do not seek to cleave to them as they do to Klal Yisrael. When the Torah states זֹאת חֻקַּת הַתּוֹרָה, *This is the decree of the Torah*, it conveys that the entire concept of impurity and purity are only a result of the Torah itself.

This can be compared to two barrels, one filled with honey and the other with refuse. When the barrels are emptied of their contents and placed outside, the majority of flies and insects flock to the residual sweetness in the barrel of honey as opposed to the stench of the refuse. The same is true of the body of a Yid. Even after his *neshamah* departs, residual *kedushah* remains in his body, and this attracts the forces of *tumah*, which descend upon it and leech all that remains from it, to the point that the entire room becomes saturated with *tumah*. The body of a gentile, in contrast, lacked this spiritual sanctity to begin with, and therefore does not attract the forces of *tumah* to the same extent.

We see, then, that the priceless gift of Torah that we received on Har Sinai and the exalted spiritual level that we achieved at that time are the basis for the many intricate laws of *tumah* and *taharah*. This may also be the reason why the Torah wrote זֹאת חֻקַּת הַתּוֹרָה specifically regarding *parah adumah* — to highlight that only because we were privileged to accept the Torah and soar to the pinnacle of spirituality are we bound by these laws of *tumah* and *taharah*, and we therefore require the mitzvah of *parah adumah* to purify ourselves.

When a Yid passes away, we generally say that he "was *niftar*," whereas when a gentile expires, we tend to say that he "died." This is not incidental, because even if a Yid is no longer among the living, he is not gone forever, but is simply *niftar* — "exempted" from the mitzvos that apply in Olam Hazeh, as the *pasuk* states, בַּמֵּתִים חָפְשִׁי, *among the dead who are free* (*Tehillim* 88:6). After his passing, a Yid is liberated from the obligations of this world, but can still continue cleaving to Hashem in Olam Haba according to his spiritual attainments. Evidence of this is the halachah barring one from entering a cemetery wearing *tefillin*, which is regarded as *lo'eg larash,* mocking the poor (*Berachos* 18a), since those who were laid to rest can no longer fulfill the mitzvos of this world. A gentile who has expired, in contrast, is called a *meis,* since he does not continue his lifelong pursuit of cleaving to the *Shechinah*. In this sense, he is similar to an animal, which is why he does not emit *tumah* after death.

Immortality of the Soul

Delving deeper, we discover that this *parashah* alludes to the eternal life of the soul after it expires from this world, and to *techiyas hameisim* by extension. *Baruch Hashem*, we are all *maaminim bnei maaminim*, and we all believe in the coming of the *geulah* and in *techiyas hameisim*. Yet this does not stop the *yetzer hara* from seeking to cool our spiritual fervor and confuse us until we begin to doubt these truths.

The solution to this is זֹאת חֻקַּת הַתּוֹרָה. By instilling in our hearts the belief that a Yid attains spiritual purity through the ashes of the *parah adumah,* we will simultaneously ingrain in ourselves faith in the immortality of the soul and the coming of Mashiach.

Obviously, this is not sufficient, and every Yid must still work to inculcate *emunah* into his very being by learning the holy *sefarim* that discuss it. One effective way that we can do this is by establishing a regular *seder* to learn the Chazon Ish's *sefer Emunah U'Bitachon*, which encompasses untold wisdom and has the power to inspire, encourage, and fortify us in these exalted matters.

Sometimes, it is also enough to hear simple words of *emunah* from others.

Just recently, an *avreich* from the yeshivah, who is a genuine *ben aliyah*, approached me and shared a personal tragedy that he just experienced, *lo aleinu*. Broken and weary, he expressed that he lacks *menuchas hanefesh*, and asked for advice to overcome his sorrow and difficult feelings. I asked if his wife also feels as shattered as he does, and he replied that she, unlike him, had managed to accept the judgment with love. I advised him to turn to his wife for *chizuk* and encouragement, because specifically her words — spoken from a place of both raw pain and acceptance — hold indescribable power to strengthen him.

The Rosh Yeshivah R' Chaim Shmulevitz, citing the Mashgiach R' Yerucham, expressed on many occasions that when we discuss concepts of *emunah*, there is no need to offer long, esoteric speeches or be drawn into complex philosophical debates. What's most effective are those simple, honest statements of *emunah* that radiate from the heart of every Yid.

When a person is happy and enjoying success in life, he sees Hashem's hand in every moment of life; he is enveloped in gratitude and able to fill his inner stores of *emunah*. Yet when challenges abound or tragedy strikes, *chas v'shalom*, and he sees his life crumbling before him, Hashem's hand — which was so clearly manifested earlier — suddenly seems blocked, and he feels alone and deflated. Our duty in life is to recognize, with *emunah peshutah*, that Hashem runs the world, and that all that transpires comes from Him. This will motivate us to repent before Him wholeheartedly.

Hashem should help that in the merit of strengthening ourselves in *emunah* and *bitachon*, we should all become genuine *ovdei Hashem*.

פרשת בלק
Parashas Balak

◆§ *Honoring Hashem's Creations*

וַיֹּאמֶר אֵלָיו מַלְאַךְ ה׳ עַל מָה הִכִּיתָ אֶת אֲתֹנְךָ זֶה שָׁלוֹשׁ רְגָלִים, הִנֵּה אָנֹכִי יָצָאתִי לְשָׂטָן כִּי יָרַט הַדֶּרֶךְ לְנֶגְדִּי וַתִּרְאַנִי הָאָתוֹן וַתֵּט לְפָנַי זֶה שָׁלֹשׁ רְגָלִים אוּלַי נָטְתָה מִפָּנַי כִּי עַתָּה גַּם אֹתְכָה הָרַגְתִּי וְאוֹתָהּ הֶחֱיֵיתִי.

The angel of Hashem said to him, "For what reason did you strike your she-donkey these three times? Behold! I went out to impede, for you hastened on a road to oppose me. The she-donkey saw me and turned away from me these three times. Had it not turned away from me, I would now even have killed you and let it live!" (*Bamidbar* 22:32-3).

Rashi comments: "Now that she has spoken and rebuked you, and you could not stand up to her rebuke, as it is written, *And he said, 'No,'* (ibid. 30), I killed her, so that [people] should not say, 'This is the one that dismissed Bilam with its rebuke, and he was not able to respond.' For Hashem takes pity on people's dignity."

No Limits

While the story of Bilam highlights how a person can fall to the depths of vulgarity and evil, it also teaches a fundamental lesson in how to honor Hashem's creations.

The *malach* took pity even on the wicked Bilam, killing his donkey so he would not suffer further shame. He did so even though every word the donkey spoke was true, and it was fitting that her words — along with the unprecedented miracle of a donkey opening its mouth and speaking — should be publicized to the world.

This incident reflects Hakadosh Baruch Hu's infinite mercy on His creations. Even a person as vile and contemptible as Bilam, who embodied impurity, immorality, and unbridled lust for honor, was accorded *kavod habriyos,* the basic respect due to every human being.

If someone were to ask any one of us if Bilam was deserving of such respect, surely the answer would be no. In our limited conception, someone like Bilam deserved to suffer eternal shame and degradation. The *malach,* however, acted differently, recognizing that there is no limit to the dignity that Hashem's creations deserve.

The Rosh Yeshivah R' Chaim Shmulevitz related[6] the following story that occurred in 1936, while he was a *bachur* learning in Yeshivas Mir in Poland. At the time, he had begun delivering a *shiur klali* in the yeshivah, yet because there were many *bachurim* his age in the yeshivah who were already outstanding *talmidei chachamim,* he felt shy and awkward addressing them in the audience.

Discerning his discomfort, the *mashgiach,* R' Yerucham, summoned these elite *bachurim* for a special *vaad* and read them a letter he had received from an alumnus of the yeshivah. The writer, who had traveled to America, sent the *mashgiach* a letter recounting the events in his life since he had departed Europe, and mentioned that he had publicly repeated a *shiur* that he heard from "Rav Chaim," which had delighted his audience. Upon mentioning the name "Rav Chaim," the *mashgiach* pointed to R' Chaim Shmulevitz, even though it was obvious to all that the letter was referring to R' Chaim Brisker. R' Chaim Shmulevitz added that although he

6. *Sichos Mussar, Taavas HaKavod.*

knew that the American *bachur* had not been referring to him at all, he experienced a powerful surge of pleasure that remained with him for a long time.

The whiff of *kavod* that R' Chaim felt at that moment was illusory, because no one attending the *vaad* harbored even a faint suspicion that the letter-writer had been referring to him. And yet the *mashgiach* deliberately accorded that extra show of honor to his *talmid* to teach how much we must all strive to honor one another and seek any opportunity to elevate another person's status among others. R' Chaim Shmulevitz was irrelevant to the letter-writer's account, but the saintly *mashgiach* still found a way to draw him into it, honoring him and making him feel good.

A person must make every attempt to eschew *kavod*, but only for himself! He should seek every opportunity to accord honor and respect to others, even if it's such a small gesture that the honor is only in the person's mind!

There was a righteous Yid who dwelled in Yerushalayim by the name of R' Dov Sokolovsky. R' Dov was a son-in-law of R' Avraham Tzvi Kamai, the Rosh Yeshivah and Rav of the town of Mir, who was "a very great man, a giant among giants," in the words of the Rosh Yeshivah R' Eliezer Yehudah Finkel. I once went to visit R' Dov in his home, and when he opened the door, he greeted me warmly and asked, "*Mah leyedidi b'veisi?* What brings my friend to my abode?"

His words were so simple and unassuming, yet they filled me with a wonderful sentiment of warmth, along with the knowledge that I was wanted and respected. R' Dov's wife, Rebbetzin Sokolovsky, was also a *tzaddeikes*, a paragon of *middos tovos*, and I named one of my daughters after her. These were two people who were experts at honoring others, and they likewise earned the esteem of all who knew them, as the Mishnah teaches: "Who is honored? One who honors others" (*Avos* 4:1).

The Egoist Removes Himself From the World

The above seems contradictory. On one hand, we regard *kavod* as a contemptible, destructive *middah*, one that "removes a person from this world" (ibid. 21). On the other hand, a person is bound to honor his friend limitlessly, and when he does, he automatically becomes honored.

How is this possible? And what is the purpose of rejecting honor for oneself, according it to others, and then receiving it anyway?

R' Chaim Shmulevitz explains that the sequence is actually the reverse. We are not expected to honor our friends because our friends crave honor and recognition; rather, because we are bound to honor others endlessly, Hakadosh Baruch Hu instilled within man a deep yearning for *kavod*, which serves as the vessel through which his friend can honor him — even with a minor gesture or false honor, as R' Yerucham accorded to R' Chaim.

A person who makes others his primary focus, by acknowledging their needs and seeking to honor them constantly, is ultimately rewarded, as others are naturally drawn to honor him. In contrast, one who is egocentric and sees only his own needs and desires degenerates spiritually and emotionally until he destroys himself and "removes himself from the world."

This was the case with Bilam HaRasha. When Balak's ministers approached him with the request that he curse Bnei Yisrael, even after Hakadosh Baruch Hu had already commanded him, לֹא תֵלֵךְ עִמָּהֶם, *You shall not go with them* (*Bamidbar* 22:12), and לֹא תָאֹר אֶת הָעָם, *You shall not curse the people* (ibid.), Bilam chose to share with them only the prohibition of accompanying them.

R' Chaim explains that Bilam's all-encompassing desire for honor prompted him to say that he was forbidden to accompany the ministers because they were not as distinguished as he was. Bilam did not even intend to lie, yet his deep character flaws and craving for honor caused him to distort Hashem's words to fit with his own desires.

We also find that Bilam caused Bnei Yisrael to sin with Baal Pe'or, which is the epitome of filth and repulsiveness, since his very being was one of breaking boundaries through abominable conduct (*Sanhedrin* 60b). Only a person who is so self-absorbed that he sees only his needs and immediate desires can sink so low.

The way to surmount the negative character traits that breed this desperate lust for honor is to focus on the needs of others and ingrain in oneself the value of giving to others and honoring them. Setting the spotlight on others automatically shifts one's thoughts away from one's own needs and desires, and, as the *Sefer HaChinuch* teaches (Mitzvah 16), the heart is drawn after the person's actions: אַחֲרֵי הַפְּעֻלּוֹת נִמְשָׁכִים הַלְּבָבוֹת.

Hakadosh Baruch Hu Honors His Creations

The importance of *kavod habriyos* is reflected in these words of Chazal: "Ten things were created on the first Shabbos evening at twilight, and they are: The mouth of the earth, the mouth of the well, and the mouth of the donkey..." (*Avos* 5:8).

Rashi notes that it was decreed from the time of the Six Days of Creation that Bilam's donkey would open its mouth and argue with him. Hakadosh Baruch Hu did not wish to alter the laws of nature, so He created the mouth of the donkey in advance, at the time of Creation, imbuing within it the capacity to speak to Bilam thousands of years before the actual event.

R' Chaim elaborates[7] that Bilam's donkey caused an extraordinary revelation of Hashem's honor in this world, as its very existence shouted *kiddush Hashem*! Imagine if this donkey were led through the streets, and everyone would point to it and excitedly declare, "This is Bilam's donkey, whose mouth was created during *Sheishes Yemei Bereishis*!" Surely, anyone who glimpsed this walking miracle of a talking donkey would attain higher levels of faith in Hakadosh Baruch Hu, as its very existence is concrete testimony to Hashem's creation and mighty hand. Just as we strive to strengthen our *yiras Hashem* and *emunah* by contemplating and imagining Krias Yam Suf and other miracles, seeing such a wonder with our own eyes would surely lead us to loftier planes of *emunah*. Nevertheless, Hakadosh Baruch Hu did not allow the donkey to endure, but killed it immediately — and why? To preserve Bilam HaRasha's dignity!

In this vein, the Midrash teaches (*Bamidbar Rabbah* 20:14):

---

7. *Sichos Mussar, Kevodo shel Adam.*

Hakadosh Baruch Hu took pity on the dignity of that *rasha*, so people would not say that this is the [donkey] that dismissed Bilam. And if Hakadosh Baruch Hu took pity on the dignity of a *rasha*, there is no need to describe [His mercy] on the dignity of a *tzaddik*. Similarly, it says, וְאִשָּׁה אֲשֶׁר תִּקְרַב אֶל כָּל בְּהֵמָה לְרִבְעָה אֹתָהּ וְהָרַגְתָּ אֶת הָאִשָּׁה וְאֶת הַבְּהֵמָה, *And a woman who approaches any animal for it to mate with her, you shall kill the woman and the animal* (*Vayikra* 20:16) — so people should not say, "This is the animal that caused that woman to be killed." This teaches that Hakadosh Baruch Hu takes pity on the dignity of His creations and knows their needs. He [therefore] closed the mouth of animals, for if they would speak, no one would be able to subjugate or withstand them. This [donkey], the least intelligent of all animals, and this [Bilam], who was the wisest of the wise — when she spoke, he could not withstand her.

How noble and compassionate are the ways of Hakadosh Baruch Hu, Who takes every precaution to preserve the honor even of the vilest of men! The Midrash implies that originally, Hashem was inclined to award the power of speech to all animals, yet He desisted in order to protect people's honor. *Kavod habriyos* is such an exalted value that it was worth limiting the qualities and potential of every living creature for this purpose.

Hashem Desires the Teshuvah of Reshaim

When the elders of Moav and Midian traveled to Bilam to convey Balak's message, Bilam replied, לִינוּ פֹה הַלַּיְלָה וַהֲשִׁבֹתִי אֶתְכֶם דָּבָר כַּאֲשֶׁר יְדַבֵּר ה׳ אֵלָי, *Spend the night here and I shall give you a response, as Hashem shall speak to me* (*Bamidbar* 22:8). Noting the emphasis on the word *here* — לִינוּ **פֹה** הַלַּיְלָה, *Spend the night* ***here*** — the Ohr HaChaim comments: "He was careful to add the word 'here,' as he may have intended to tell them that they should rest in his personal quarters ... so that as soon as Hashem would speak to him, he would immediately reply to them, which would not occur if they were lodging outside his personal quarters."

Accordingly, Hakadosh Baruch Hu turned to Bilam and asked, מִי הָאֲנָשִׁים הָאֵלֶּה עִמָּךְ, *Who are these men with you?* (ibid. v. 9). The Ohr HaChaim explains: "This was a derogatory response, as if Hashem were saying, 'Who are these people that you brought into the special place that is reserved for your dialogue with the angel of Hashem?' For Hashem defended the honor of Bilam before the nations, since he was their prophet, and as we find that He killed the donkey for the sake of Bilam's dignity."

Hashem further instructed him, לֹא תֵלֵךְ עִמָּהֶם, *You shall not go with them* (ibid. v. 12), which the Ohr HaChaim interprets as, "They are not worthy of going with [Bilam], due to his prominence; Hashem was showing Bilam that Balak demeaned [Bilam's] honor when he did not send him a delegation of honored ministers." This is another example of Hashem going to extra lengths to defend Bilam's honor and show him respect despite his reprehensible conduct.

Similarly, the Sforno writes, regarding the *pasuk*, וַיִּפְתַּח ה' אֶת פִּי הָאָתוֹן, *Hashem opened the mouth of the she-donkey* (ibid. v. 28): "All this was so Bilam would be spurred to repent when he would recognize that the ability to speak comes from Hashem, even if it is unnatural; He can certainly take that power from someone who has it. All this was so a man like him should not be destroyed."

This is an awe-inspiring statement! It is surely justifiable that "a man like him" — a *rasha* like Bilam — would be obliterated from this world. Bilam, who possessed exceptional powers, exploited the forces of evil for his benefit and engaged in the most depraved sins, which even the lowest of humanity would not commit. Bilam was the epitome of decadence and corruption, and yet Hakadosh Baruch Hu manipulated the laws of creation and molded world events to ensure that a man of his caliber, with unrivaled spiritual potential, would not be lost and would have the opportunity for *teshuvah*.

What emerges, then, is that a person with spiritual potential is desired by Hakadosh Baruch Hu even after he plummets to a spiritual abyss. Even if there is but a slim chance that he will repent, Hashem still yearns for his *teshuvah*. Therefore, it is incumbent upon us to take every effort to do *teshuvah* and inspire others to do *teshuvah*, as well.

This principle reveals the profundity of Chazal's words, חָבִיב אָדָם שֶׁנִּבְרָא בְצֶלֶם, *Man is beloved for he was created in the form [of Hashem]* (*Avos* 3:18), which apply even to one as wicked and depraved as Bilam HaRasha. Hashem loves every one of His creations; He guards their honor staunchly, and eagerly awaits their *teshuvah*. If Hakadosh Baruch Hu can act so kindly with a person as contemptible as the wicked Bilam, how much more does He display His infinite love and compassion toward His children, Bnei Yisrael! And all the more so toward *bnei Torah*!

We must seek to emulate Hashem's ways by acting compassionately toward one another — and especially toward *bnei Torah*! We must reach out to others, draw them near, and at every opportunity assist them to realize their vast spiritual potential so that, as the Sforno teaches, "a man like him will not be lost," *chas v'shalom*.

This value is reflected in the prohibition of *lashon hara*, which forbids one from speaking negatively of his friend. Indeed, if one were to honor his friend properly and accord him the respect that he deserves just by virtue of his status as a human being, he would not be able to bear his shame or pain and would therefore never be able to utter a negative word about him.

Since we are unfortunately unaccustomed to honoring our friends as we should, we fail to recognize the terrible injustice in speaking negatively about them. If we would only esteem and honor our fellow Jews as we should, we would never come to speak *lashon hara* about them, because who could shamelessly inflict harm or humiliation upon a person who is precious and beloved to him — a fellow Yid who was created *b'tzelem Elokim* — and remain aloof and untouched by the pain and destruction that he caused?

Playing With Fire

R' Chaim often said[8] that one who inflicts pain upon a fellow Jew is punished not only for the actual misdeed, as is the case with

---

8. See *Sichos Mussar*, *Zechiras Maaseh Miriam* and *Bein Adam LaChaveiro*.

other *aveiros*. Even if there was no actual sin involved, he would still be punished because a fellow Jew suffered because of him. He presents several examples, from Tanach and Chazal, of individuals who caused another person pain without actually committing any sin, one of whom is Peninah. Peninah did not sin, yet her words and conduct caused deep, cutting pain to Chanah, and she was punished harshly, as eight of her ten sons perished (*Bava Basra* 16a).

Hurting a fellow Jew can be compared to placing one's hand in a fire. Whether or not the person placed his hand in the fire intentionally, his hand is burned, because the burn is not a punishment, but a consequence. Similarly, the pain that one Jew causes another brings punishment, whether or not he transgressed an actual prohibition.

How cautious we must be in our interactions with others, and especially with a wife. The Gemara teaches: "One who loves his wife as himself and honors her more than himself, about him the *pasuk* says, וְיָדַעְתָּ כִּי שָׁלוֹם אָהֳלֶךָ וּפָקַדְתָּ נָוְךָ וְלֹא תֶחֱטָא, *You will know that your tent is at peace, and you will visit your home and find nothing amiss* (*Iyov* 5:24)."

The Rambam also rules: "The Sages commanded that a man must honor his wife more than himself and love her as he loves himself" (*Hilchos Ishus* 15:19). In this case, we are not even discussing the prohibition of hurting or humiliating another person; we are discussing the obligation upon every husband to honor his wife more than he honors himself — which is a clear-cut halachah. Is there any one of us who can attest that he fulfills this dictum as he should?

Hakadosh Baruch Hu should help us internalize the lesson of how to honor one another properly, so that we should never hurt or humiliate a fellow Yid, and so that we should honor our wives as the Torah expects.

פרשת פינחס
Parashas Pinchas

◆§ *Zealousness Born of Love*

וַיַּרְא פִּינְחָס בֶּן אֶלְעָזָר בֶּן אַהֲרֹן הַכֹּהֵן וַיָּקָם מִתּוֹךְ הָעֵדָה וַיִּקַּח רֹמַח בְּיָדוֹ.

Pinchas son of Elazar son of Aaron the Kohen saw, and he stood up from amid the assembly and took a spear in his hand (*Bamidbar* 25:7).

Rooted in Love

Rashi comments: "Pinchas saw the incident and was reminded of the [relevant] halachah. He said to Moshe, 'I have received from you that one who has relations with a non-Jewish woman, zealots may kill him.' [Moshe] said to him, 'The one who reads the letter, let him be the messenger [to carry out its contents].' Thereupon, 'and he took a spear in his hand.'"

Regarding the halachah that "zealots may kill him," the Gemara (*Sanhedrin* 82a) teaches that if one comes to *beis din* while such a transgression is being committed to take counsel as to whether he should kill the sinner, the *dayanim* do not instruct him to do so.

The Rambam elaborates (*Issurei Biah* Ch. 12:4-5): "One who has relations with a gentile woman, if the zealous strike him and kill him, then they are praiseworthy [for their] alacrity; and this was a halachah [told] to Moshe at Sinai. Evidence to this is Pinchas [who killed] Zimri. The zealot is not entitled to strike them, except during the moment of sin. And if a zealous one appeals for permission from *beis din* to kill him, they do not instruct him to do so, even if it is at the time of the action."

If the halachah explicitly states that a *kana'i* is commended for killing one who sins with a gentile woman, why doesn't *beis din* instruct him to proceed when he is in doubt?

The Rosh Yeshivah R' Chaim Shmulevitz explains[9] that the above halachah was not directed to every person, but only to one who acts with genuine zealousness to guard Hashem's honor and who harbors no personal ill will toward the sinner. Moreover, not only must he be free of any negative feelings toward the sinner, his heart must also be overflowing with *ahavas Yisrael,* to the extent that he would never harm the sinner at all if not for the zealousness inflaming him to take action and defend Hashem's honor at any cost. This halachah, therefore, does not apply at all to one who has not attained an exalted level of *kana'us,* and anyone else who dares to commit an action like this under the guise of zealousness is guilty of murder.

There is an exceedingly fine line between *"kana'in pogin bo"* and murder. One whose focus and intention are exclusively *l'shem Shamayim* is privileged to fulfill a very rare and lofty mitzvah, and is, moreover, obligated to do so. However, one who acts out of his personal inclinations and ulterior motives is a murderer. Therefore, if a person approaches *beis din* to request permission to fulfill this halachah, it is impossible for the *dayanim* to discern on which side of this fine line his true motives lie, so they do not grant their consent.

R' Chaim adds that there are many who erroneously interpret the term *"kana'us"* to mean anger or wild antagonism that triggers uncouth behavior — shouting and actions that are contrary to the gentle ways of our holy Torah. True *kana'us* is a fervor that rises

---

9. *Sichos Mussar, Ohev es HaBrios U'Mekarvan LaTorah*

and bursts forth from the heart of one who is completely pure and wholesome and cannot tolerate *chillul Hashem* or actions that transgress our holy Torah. As he so pithily expressed in Yiddish, "*Nisht di vus varfen shteiner zeinen kana'im* — those who throw stones are not *kana'im*."

This is why the halachah of *kana'in pogin bo* applies only to one whose heart burns with *ahavas Hashem* and *ahavas Yisrael* to the exclusion of all else, and whose irrepressible *kana'us* impels him to terminate the sinner.

Illustrious Lineage

The *pasuk* says: וַיַּרְא פִּינְחָס בֶּן אֶלְעָזָר בֶּן אַהֲרֹן הַכֹּהֵן, *Pinchas son of Elazar son of Aaron the Kohen saw* (ibid.). Why did the Torah recount Pinchas's illustrious lineage when describing his alacrity in lifting the spear and killing Zimri in the midst of his sin?

Several *pesukim* later, Hakadosh Baruch Hu proclaims: פִּינְחָס בֶּן אֶלְעָזָר בֶּן אַהֲרֹן הַכֹּהֵן הֵשִׁיב אֶת חֲמָתִי, *Pinchas son of Elazar son of Aaron the Kohen, turned back My wrath* (ibid. 11), once again calling attention to Pinchas's lineage. The Gemara notes that Hashem did so in order to honor Pinchas after the other *shevatim* began disparaging him, saying, "Did you see this son of 'Puti' whose mother's father fattened calves for idol worship, and yet he murdered a *nasi* from Yisrael?" (*Sanhedrin* 82a). Even if the Gemara's explanation of the second mention of Pinchas's lineage is understandable, why did the Torah also trace Pinchas back to Aharon HaKohen at the beginning of the *parashah*?

The Mishnah famously describes Aharon HaKohen with the words, אוֹהֵב שָׁלוֹם וְרוֹדֵף שָׁלוֹם, אוֹהֵב אֶת הַבְּרִיּוֹת וּמְקָרְבָן לַתּוֹרָה, *he loves peace and pursues peace; he loves people and draws them close to Torah* (*Avos* 1:12). R' Ovadiah of Bartenura elaborates:

> How was Aharon a lover of peace? Whenever he would see two people fighting, he would go to each one, without the other's knowledge, and tell him, "See how much your friend regrets and is berating himself for hurting you. He asked me to come to you [to request] your forgiveness." When they would meet each other, they would kiss one

> another [and reconcile]. How did he draw people close to Torah? When he knew of a person who had sinned, he would connect to him and show him a smiling face. The man would be ashamed and say, "If this *tzaddik* would know of my evil deeds, he would surely distance himself from me." This would spur him to repent.

The Torah's description of Pinchas as a descendant of Aharon HaKohen implies that Pinchas attained the level of *kana'i* specifically because he emulated his grandfather's quality of loving and pursuing peace, and loving people and drawing them close to Torah. Pinchas's distinguishing characteristic was his unbridled *ahavas Yisrael,* which is the prerequisite to *kana'us,* for even a minor lack of *ahavas habriyos* renders *kana'us* insincere and can, *chas v'shalom,* lead one to act upon personal leanings as opposed to genuine pursuit of *emes* and desire to defend Hashem's honor.

Murder vs. Halachah

When a father wishes to teach his child, he is sometimes compelled to *potch* him in order to get him back on track, yet a *potch* is effective only when delivered lovingly, with the intention to draw the child back to the proper path. If it is given because the father feels angry or offended, it not only loses its power, but can actually have the opposite effect and push the child farther away. Only when the child feels his father's love together with the strike of his hand can the *potch* have its desired effect.

Just this week, a couple visited me from America and shared that their fourteen-year-old son has no interest in learning. When they asked me how to deal with this, I inquired if he usually acts with *derech eretz.* They replied that he only listens to them when they deal with him strictly, and otherwise he ignores them completely. I advised the couple to be firm with their son, but to make sure to clearly show him love, because if their conduct appears to be motivated by distress, anger, or frustration, they will not achieve their goal in *chinuch.*

This underscores why a *kana'i*—whose heart overflows with *ahavas Yisrael,* and whose behavior is motivated only by the halachah of *kana'im pogin bo,* not by any personal leanings — is not guilty of murder at all, but is simply fulfilling halachah. In contrast, one who does not excel in *ahavas Yisrael* and sets out to harm a sinner is not fulfilling halachah, but is guilty of murder! This is emphasized in the words, תַּחַת אֲשֶׁר קִנֵּא לֵאלֹהָיו, *because he took vengeance for his God* (*Bamidbar* 25:13), which indicate that Pinchas's zealous act was performed exclusively *l'shem Shamayim,* with no ulterior motive.

Chazal further state: "How great is peace, for Hakadosh Baruch Hu is called 'Shalom,' as it is written, *And he called him 'Hashem Shalom'* (*Shoftim* 6:24)" (*Sifri, Bamidbar* Ch. 42).

If Hashem's Name is "Shalom," then a genuine act of *kana'us l'shem Shamayim* can be carried out only by one whose heart is aflame with *kana'us,* who excels in the *middos* of *shalom* and *ahavas habriyos,* and who passionately aspires to cleave to the ways of Hakadosh Baruch Hu. One who does not embody peace and *ahavas habriyos* cannot achieve a level of authentic *kana'us* or act exclusively *l'shem Shamayim,* because he is simultaneously driven by ulterior motives.

Sadly, there are times when a *bachur* acts improperly, and there is no choice but to ask him to leave the yeshivah. Before we reach this agonizing decision, however, we must make every attempt to help him mend his ways. If we find that there is truly no choice but to distance him from the yeshivah, it is still incumbent upon us to carry out this task with love and with genuine concern for his well-being, while using the right words. Every situation must be handled vigilantly, with profound awareness of the gravity of each word and action, as these are *dinei nefashos*! Only then can this process be regarded as an authentic act of *chinuch* and not just a means of throwing a *bachur* out of yeshivah, which places him at severe risk of spiritual degeneration.

Measure for Measure

The Torah teaches that Pinchas received an extraordinary reward for his action: לָכֵן אֱמֹר הִנְנִי נֹתֵן לוֹ אֶת בְּרִיתִי שָׁלוֹם וְהָיְתָה לּוֹ וּלְזַרְעוֹ אַחֲרָיו בְּרִית כְּהֻנַּת עוֹלָם תַּחַת אֲשֶׁר קִנֵּא לֵאלֹהָיו, *Therefore, say: Behold! I give him*

My covenant of peace. And it shall be for him and his offspring after him a covenant of eternal priesthood, because he took vengeance for his God (*Bamidbar* 25:12-13).

Targum Yonasan ben Uziel interprets this as, "Hashem promised him: 'From My Name I am decreeing My covenant of peace for him, and I shall make him into a living angel, and he shall live forever, to proclaim the Final Redemption at the End of Days." This is in keeping with Chazal's revelation that Eliyahu HaNavi is Pinchas (*Pirkei D'Rabbi Eliezer* Ch. 46). Hashem gave Pinchas His "covenant of peace," just as *malachim* harbor no jealousy or hatred, and are characterized by peace, and just as Hashem's own Name is "Shalom."

We see, then, that Pinchas received his reward *middah k'neged middah,* as he avenged Hashem's honor with pure zealousness and without any self-interest. In return, he was elevated to the status of a *malach,* which is devoid of envy and exists in a state of absolute *shalom* — a lofty spiritual level over which death has no power.

Ahavas Habriyos — A Prerequisite for Kabbalas HaTorah

The Mishnah in *Avos* that describes the virtues of Aharon HaKohen does not culminate with his *ahavas habriyos,* but adds that he drew people close to Torah: אוֹהֵב אֶת הַבְּרִיּוֹת וּמְקָרְבָן לַתּוֹרָה. The sequence implies that teaching a person Torah is contingent upon loving him, and conversely, one who is lacking in *ahavas habriyos* is unable to teach and draw others close to Torah.

R' Chaim explained this based on the Rambam's interpretation of the Mishnah: "When Aharon *alav hashalom* sensed that a person was evil, or when he was told that someone was evil and a sinner, he would engage him in a pleasant [relationship], until he became liked by him, and he would speak to him often. The person would then feel ashamed and say, "Woe unto me! If Aharon only knew the secrets of my heart and the wickedness of my actions, he would not allow himself to look at me, let alone speak to me. Since he considers me an upstanding individual, I will prove his words and thoughts correct, and repent." Then, he would join the group of disciples learning from Aharon."

The Rambam's description indicates that Aharon invested effort to cultivate a warm relationship with such a person, leading him to regard Aharon as his rebbi. Since a *tzaddik* like Aharon HaKohen couldn't simply tolerate a sinner, who had defied the will of Hakadosh Baruch Hu, he first needed to exercise his overriding *middah* of *ahavas habriyos* in order to connect with the person and draw him close to Torah.

Regarding the *pasuk*, וַיִּחַן שָׁם יִשְׂרָאֵל נֶגֶד הָהָר, *And Israel encamped there, opposite the mountain* (*Shemos* 19:2), Rashi comments, "like one man with one heart." The Ohr HaChaim notes that this verse is phrased in the singular form, as Klal Yisrael were unified like one person, and only then did they become worthy of receiving the Torah.

Similarly, Chazal say, "Hakadosh Baruch Hu said: Since Yisrael despised conflict and loved peace, and they encamped as one, behold, this is the time when I will give them My Torah'" (*Derech Eretz Zuta, Perek HaShalom*). Only when a Yid attaches himself to the attribute of peace does he become worthy of receiving Torah, and with this in mind we can understand the Mishnah's description: "He loves people and draws them close to Torah."

A Yid who possesses *ahavas habriyos* and cleaves to *shalom*, which is one of the holy Names of Hakadosh Baruch Hu, is empowered to draw Yidden close to Torah. This is reflected in the Gemara's dictum: "R' Elazar said in the name of R' Chanina: *Talmidei chachamim* increase peace in the world" (*Berachos* 64a). A Yid who achieves the level of a *talmid chacham* naturally excels in the *middah* of *shalom*, which is the prerequisite to Kabbalas HaTorah, and causes Torah to spread throughout the world.

פרשת מטות
Parashas Mattos

✎*The Power of Prayer*

וַיְדַבֵּר ה׳ אֶל מֹשֶׁה לֵּאמֹר נְקֹם נִקְמַת בְּנֵי יִשְׂרָאֵל מֵאֵת הַמִּדְיָנִים אַחַר תֵּאָסֵף אֶל עַמֶּיךָ וַיְדַבֵּר מֹשֶׁה אֶל הָעָם לֵאמֹר הֵחָלְצוּ מֵאִתְּכֶם אֲנָשִׁים לַצָּבָא וגו׳ לָתֵת נִקְמַת ה׳ בְּמִדְיָן.

Hashem spoke to Moshe, saying. "Take vengeance for Bnei Yisrael against the Midianites; afterward you will be gathered unto your people." Moshe spoke to the people, saying, "Arm men from among yourselves for the legion ... to inflict Hashem's vengeance against Midian" (Bamidbar 31:1-3).

The Tzaddik's Wish: To Increase Kevod Shamayim

Hakadosh Baruch Hu commands Moshe Rabbeinu: נְקֹם נִקְמַת בְּנֵי יִשְׂרָאֵל, *Take vengeance for Bnei Yisrael,* which Moshe rephrases as לָתֵת נִקְמַת ה׳ בְּמִדְיָן, *to inflict Hashem's vengeance against Midian.* What message did Moshe convey in changing Hashem's words?[10]

---

10. *Midrash Tanchuma* (*Mattos* 3) already discusses this question: "Hakadosh Baruch Hu said נִקְמַת בְּנֵי יִשְׂרָאֵל and Moshe said נִקְמַת ה׳. Hakadosh Baruch Hu said to them: 'My humiliation and yours demand [vengeance], for they caused Me to harm [punish] you.' Moshe said: "Master of the world, if we were gentiles or idol-worshippers or apostates, they would not despise us or persecute us; [they do so] only because of the Torah that You gave us. Therefore it is only Your

R' Aryeh Finkel, in *Sefer Har Yera'eh*,[11] explains this based on the *Meshech Chochmah* (*Bamidbar* ibid. 3). A *tzaddik's* core desire and aspiration is to increase Hashem's honor and prevent *chillul Hashem* in the world. Therefore, while Hakadosh Baruch Hu may prefer to punish a *tzaddik* in Olam Hazeh and reserve his reward for Olam Haba, where he can bask in eternal pleasure, the *tzaddik* himself requests his reward in Olam Hazeh in order to avert the *chillul Hashem* that results from his suffering in Olam Hazeh.

When Hakadosh Baruch Hu said נְקֹם נִקְמַת בְּנֵי יִשְׂרָאֵל, Moshe Rabbeinu modified His words, saying נִקְמַת ה׳ בְּמִדְיָן. This implies that while Hashem wished to avenge Bnei Yisrael's honor, out of His compassion for them, and was not concerned with the crimes of the Midianim, who had sinned blatantly against Him, Moshe Rabbeinu's thoughts and worries were focused only on averting the desecration of Hashem's Name and honor, which led him to declare, נִקְמַת ה׳ בְּמִדְיָן.

The preface to *Shaarei Yosher* presents a similar explanation of the *pasuk*, קְדֹשִׁים תִּהְיוּ כִּי קָדוֹשׁ אֲנִי ה׳ אֱלֹהֵיכֶם, *You shall be holy, for holy am I, Hashem, your G-d* (*Vayikra* 19:2), about which the Midrash teaches: "You shall be holy — lest you think [that you are obligated to] be as [holy] as Me, the *pasuk* says, 'Because I am Holy.' My Holiness is loftier than your holiness'" (*Vayikra Rabbah* 24:9).

This Midrash implies that there is but a slight difference between Hashem's *kedushah* and the *kedushah* required of Bnei Yisrael, and that Hakadosh Baruch Hu's *kedushah* is greater only because it is infinite and all-encompassing. Yet how can the sanctity that we mere mortals are meant to attain compare to Hashem's *kedushah*, which is immeasurable and limitless?

The concept of *kedushah* requires that our efforts and life's mission be dedicated exclusively to the *klal*, and in this way, we acquire an infinitesimal aspect of Hakadosh Baruch Hu's *kedushah*. Just as His way of relating to His creations is by bestowing goodness

---

vengeance. One who stands against Yisrael is actually standing against Hakadosh Baruch Hu, which is why Moshe altered [Hashem's] words and said, לָתֵת נִקְמַת ה׳ בְּמִדְיָן."

11. Essay entitled *L'maancha Elokim Chayim*.

upon them, so too our actions mirror His when we direct them to benefit the *klal*.

Hashem's desire to do good for His creations is the reason why He commanded, נְקֹם נִקְמַת בְּנֵי יִשְׂרָאֵל. Our duty is to emulate Hakadosh Baruch Hu by benefiting others as much as we can, and thereby enhance His honor in the world.

Tefillah Enhances Kevod Shamayim

R' Aryeh adds that the essence of *tefillah* is also to increase Hashem's honor in the world, and a *tzaddik's* ultimate aspiration with his prayers is to ask that Hashem's honor intensify. Since the entire universe was created in order to proclaim and exalt Hashem's holy Name, any desecration of His Name causes irreparable damage to creation, which is why every *tefillah* must be uttered with the intention of increasing Hashem's honor in the world.

In this vein, Chazal instituted in *Shemoneh Esrei* of *Aseres Yemei Teshuvah* the addition of זָכְרֵנוּ לְחַיִּים, מֶלֶךְ חָפֵץ בַּחַיִּים, וְכָתְבֵנוּ בְּסֵפֶר הַחַיִּים, לְמַעַנְךָ אֱלֹהִים חַיִּים. The ultimate purpose of man's life in this world is לְמַעַנְךָ, for Hashem's sake — to serve Him and increase *kevod Shamayim*. We daven for life specifically during the Yamim Noraim, when we crown Hashem as King upon the world, in order to prevent His holy Name from being desecrated. When the gentiles see Hashem's nation downtrodden, suffering, and persecuted, they scorn Hashem as unable to rescue the Jewish people from devastation and ruin, and we request life and prosperity in order to avert that gross *chillul Hashem*. We likewise ask in our *tefillos*, עָזְרֵנוּ אֱלֹהֵי יִשְׁעֵנוּ עַל דְּבַר כְּבוֹד שְׁמֶךָ, *Help us, God of our salvation, for the sake of the honor of Your Name*, meaning that the primary goal of all that we receive is to increase Hashem's honor in the world.

The prayers that we offer to succeed in learning are also a *tefillah* to elevate Hashem's honor in the world, as every additional word of Torah increases *kevod Shamayim*. There is no limit to the *hatzlachah* that a Yid can request in Torah or any realm, because when he lives his life guided by Torah principles and ensures that his every word and action is *l'shem Shamayim*, his requests are not personal, but are merely a means of increasing Hashem's honor in the world.

Tefillah — A Prerequisite to Torah

Not only does prayer for *hatzlachah* in Torah increase Hashem's honor in the world, it is also vital for the one who wishes to merit Torah wisdom, for without *tefillah*, one will not be able to attain it.

The Gemara (*Niddah* 70b) relates that the residents of Alexandria once asked R' Yehoshua ben Chananyah, "What can a person do to become wise?"

R' Yehoshua answered: "He should spend more time learning, and spend less time engaged in business."

"Many have done this, and it did not help them," they objected.

R' Yehoshua replied: "Let them request mercy from the One to Whom all wisdom belongs, as it is written, כִּי ה׳ יִתֵּן חָכְמָה מִפִּיו דַּעַת וּתְבוּנָה, *For Hashem grants wisdom; from His mouth knowledge and understanding* (*Mishlei* 2:6).

If the attainment of wisdom depends upon prayer, wonders the Gemara, what is R' Yehoshua teaching us by saying that a person should spend more time learning? The Gemara answers that neither is sufficient on its own. Without *amal,* one cannot be successful in learning, but *amal* itself is not enough, and one also requires tremendous *siyata diShmaya* in order to be able to grow in Torah. The way to merit this *siyata diShmaya* is *tefillah,* for only fervent, intense prayer will enable a person to attain the wisdom he desires.

Without *tefillah,* one cannot attain wisdom at all. Even if one toils in Torah day and night, if he does not plead for mercy from the One Who owns all wisdom, then his efforts will not bear fruit.

The Vilna Gaon, in his commentary on *Mishlei,* writes regarding the *pasuk,*אָז יִקְרָאֻנְנִי וְלֹא אֶעֱנֶה יְשַׁחֲרֻנְנִי וְלֹא יִמְצָאֻנְנִי, *Then they will call Me, but I will not answer; they will search for Me, but they will not find Me* (*Mishlei* 1:28), that there are two prerequisites to *kinyan haTorah:* The first is *yegiah* and *amal* in learning, and the second is *tefillah* for *siyata diShmaya*, as the *pasuk* says, דִּרְשׁוּ ה׳ וְעֻזּוֹ בַּקְּשׁוּ פָנָיו תָּמִיד, *Search out Hashem and His might, seek his presence always* (*Tehillim*

105:4). The words דִּרְשׁוּ ה׳ refer to learning with *yegiah* and with one's whole self, and the words בַּקְּשׁוּ פָנָיו connote *tefillah*, as it is written, וּבִקַּשְׁתֶּם מִשָּׁם אֶת ה׳ אֱלֹהֶיךָ וּמָצָאתָ כִּי תִדְרְשֶׁנּוּ בְּכָל לְבָבְךָ. *From there you will seek Hashem, your God, and you will find Him, if you search for Him with all your heart* (*Devarim* 4:29). This implies that a Yid is obligated to beseech Hashem for the *siyata diShmaya* to delve into Torah until it penetrates and fills his heart.

Know Before Whom You Stand

The precondition to genuine *tefillah* is awareness of *Malchus Hashem*. Before rising to pray, a Yid must pause, reflect upon Whom he is about to approach, and prepare himself to address the King of all kings. Only once he has reached this recognition of שִׁוִּיתִי ה׳ לְנֶגְדִּי תָמִיד can he stand before Hashem and face Him in prayer.

The Rosh Yeshivah R' Chaim Shmulevitz posited that if someone hears a thought and does not respond or add to it, it is a sign that he did not hear properly and definitely missed a key point in the message. Therefore, I ask you all to truly listen, so we can add two fundamental points to this lesson on *tefillah*.

The first point is that *tefillah* must involve deep contemplation and careful attention, for we know that רַחֲמָנָא לִיבָּא בָּעֵי, *Hashem desires our hearts*; indeed, the *navi* states, כִּי הָאָדָם יִרְאֶה לַעֵינַיִם וַה׳ יִרְאֶה לַלֵּבָב, *Man sees what his eyes behold, but Hashem sees into the heart* (*I Shmuel* 16:7). Furthermore, the Mishnah teaches (*Menachos* 13:11) that whether one does more or one does less, the main thing is that he should direct his thoughts to Heaven. In this vein, the *Shulchan Aruch* rules, "Better less … with *kavanah*, than more without *kavanah*" (*Orach Chaim* 1:4).

The first prerequisite to *tefillah* is to truly feel what we ask, as prayers that emanate from the heart are reliably effective.

In this regard, Chazal taught: "One who requests mercy for his friend, and he needs the same thing — he is answered first" (*Bava Kamma* 92a). One reason for this is that when a person genuinely feels and shares his friend's pain, his prayer emanates from his heart, and he is therefore answered sooner. Even if he is anguished more by his personal troubles — which is only natural, since a person always feels his own pain more deeply — I still believe that as long as he genuinely sympathizes with his friend, his *tefillah* is regarded as "words that emerge from the heart," which draw him close to Hakadosh Baruch Hu. This closeness is what causes his *tefillah* to be accepted, and he is answered first.

This past week, I was approached by several people — some from within the yeshivah and others who are not affiliated with it — each with his own set of troubles: one was struggling with a health issue, another with *parnassah,* a third with *shidduchim.* After they all left, I reflected that they hadn't actually come to seek advice, as there are many greater and wiser people from whom they could have sought counsel. Nor did they come for *berachos,* because there are also many *tzaddikim* greater than I. Perhaps this may sound arrogant, but I believe that the reason they came to me was that they knew that there was a person who was open to hearing their troubles and would allay some of their pain.

We must remember how crucial it is to feel a person's pain and listen to him! In addition, when we stand in prayer before the King of kings, we must take the time to reflect on all our requests in advance, so they will be desirable to Hashem.

Trusting in Our Tefillos

The second point I wish to highlight is that when we daven, we must not only hope, but also believe wholeheartedly, that the *tefillah* is heard on high and answered. This unequivocal faith in *koach hatefillah* has two advantages: The first is that it strongly impacts the *tefillah* itself, because one who believes that prayer can effect a change and generate *yeshuos* automatically davens with greater intensity and fervor. And the second is that it augments the *koach hatefillah,* because the complete faith that a prayer will be answered leads Hashem to answer it.

On a personal note, just this week I davened for a particular need, and I had a very strong feeling that my *tefillah* was going to be accepted and fulfilled. This sentiment fortified my resolve, and

I found myself davening with extra *kavanah*. A person's confidence in his *tefillah* and belief that it has the power to effect a change strengthens his *tefillah* and impels him to daven from a place deep within his heart. This stimulates a positive cycle that allows the *tefillah* to hit its mark.

Tefillos of Our Avos

To incorporate these positive qualities into our *tefillos*, we must seek to emulate the *tefillos* offered by our *Avos*, who instituted the three daily *tefillos*, as the Gemara relates: "The prayers were instituted by our forefathers. Avraham instituted the Shacharis prayer, Yitzchak instituted the Minchah prayer, and Yaakov instituted the Maariv prayer" (*Berachos* 26b).

Chazal glean the above from three *pesukim* in the Torah:

Regarding Avraham Avinu, the Torah recounts: וַיַּשְׁכֵּם אַבְרָהָם בַּבֹּקֶר אֶל הַמָּקוֹם אֲשֶׁר עָמַד שָׁם, *Avraham arose early in the morning to the place where he had stood* (*Bereishis* 19:27), and Chazal elaborate: "*Standing* refers to nothing other than prayer." This *pasuk* refers to Avraham's davening to Hashem to avert the destruction of Sedom, and with regard to that *tefillah*, the *pasuk* states: וַיִּגַּשׁ אַבְרָהָם וַיֹּאמַר הַאַף תִּסְפֶּה צַדִּיק עִם רָשָׁע, *Avraham came forward and said, "Will you also stamp out the righteous along with the wicked?"* (ibid. 18:23). Rashi comments that the term וַיִּגַּשׁ, *approaching*, is used in the context of approaching for war, approaching to appease, and approaching in prayer, and explains that Avraham Avinu approached Hashem in all these ways: to speaking strongly, to appease, and to pray. We see, then, that both וַיַּשְׁכֵּם and וַיִּגַּשׁ are terms of *tefillah*.

The term וַיַּשְׁכֵּם is also used in connection with Avraham Avinu's preparation for the Akeidah: וַיַּשְׁכֵּם אַבְרָהָם בַּבֹּקֶר וַיַּחֲבֹשׁ אֶת חֲמֹרוֹ, *So Avraham woke up early in the morning and he saddled his donkey* (ibid. 22:3). The Gemara expounds (*Pesachim* 4a): זְרִיזִין מַקְדִּימִים לְמִצְוֹת, *The zealous are early to [perform] mitzvos*, which implies that the word וַיַּשְׁכֵּם connotes the *middah* of *zerizus*, alacrity. Furthermore, since *zerizus* in regard to *tefillah* is commendable, a person should muster alacrity to pray with full concentration, as a son before his father.

The term וַיִּגַּשׁ, when used in respect to *tefillah*, connotes *hachanah*, preparation. This underscores that every prayer requires ample *hachanah*, and without it, the *tefillah* is deficient. The Gemara relates that "the early pious ones would wait one hour and then daven, to direct their hearts to their Father in heaven" (*Berachos* 30b).

One who begins davening without preparing himself sufficiently to approach Hashem is only chanting the words meaninglessly, and his *tefillah* is vacant. *Tefillah* is not just words; its essence is supplication before Hashem, like a pauper beseeching at the doorstep. Regarding this Chazal say, "R' Yochanan said: 'At the beginning one says, ה' שְׂפָתַי תִּפְתָּח, *Hashem, open my lips*'" (*Berachos* 4b). These opening words to *Shemoneh Esrei* are a preliminary prayer to Hashem to open our lips and hearts to focus on our *tefillah*, which in and of itself is a preparation for davening.

We are not on the level of the early chassidim and, therefore, do not require extensive preparations before davening. For us, it is sufficient to devote several brief moments to reflect upon the magnitude of the impending task of approaching Hashem in prayer. As we stand solemnly and take three steps backward, we should contemplate the imminent *tefillah* and utilize those seconds to prepare ourselves to greet our King properly. Obviously, one who does come early to davening and prepares himself in advance, following the example of the early chassidim, achieves a higher level of prayer, and the emotions that he stirs in his heart enable him to approach Hashem with the confidence that his *tefillah* will be answered.

Tefillah requires constant *chizuk*, because people quickly grow accustomed to davening, which is probably the spiritual activity that people perform most frequently throughout their day. On the other hand, it is also the activity that enables us to achieve unsurpassed closeness to Hashem. This is why it is so vital that we do not grow jaded in *tefillah*, *chas v'shalom*, and that we constantly remind ourselves that our very lives are contingent upon the prayers that we offer our Creator.

One should not think that only a genuine *ben aliyah* who davens every day with intense fervor and *kavanah* is capable of attaining lofty heights in *tefillah*. Regarding the *pasuk*, וְאֵל זֹעֵם בְּכָל יוֹם, *God is angered every day* (*Tehillim* 7:12), the Gemara teaches (*Avodah Zarah* 4a):

> How long does His anger last? A moment. And how long is this moment? One fifty-three thousand eight hundred and forty-eighth part of an hour. This is a moment. And no creature could precisely compute when this moment occurs, except the wicked Bilam … who knew how to ascertain the exact moment at which the Holy One, Blessed is He, becomes angry … R' Elazar said: The Holy One, Blessed is He, said to Israel: "My nation! Observe how many benevolences I performed for you in that I did not become angry in all those days [when Bilam was seeking to curse you], for had I become angry with you, no remnant whatsoever would have remained (from the idolaters) from the enemies of Israel [i.e., the Jews themselves] . . . And how long is a moment? … A moment is equal to the time it takes to say the word "*rega*."

If Bilam could exploit the precise moment of Hashem's anger to curse and annihilate all of Klal Yisrael, then surely the reverse is true as well, and a *tefillah* that emerges from deep within the heart has even greater power than his curse, as we know that Hashem's kindness is five hundred times more substantial than the punishment He metes out. If even a single *tefillah* is uttered with the right emotions, with proper concentration, and with the desire to increase Hashem's honor in this world, surely it will bring vast blessing to the world — to each individual and Klal Yisrael collectively.

Hashem should help us to daven with the proper preparations and *kavanah*, so that all our *tefillos* should be accepted.

פרשת מסעי
Parashas Masei

◆§ *The Essence of the Two Batei Mikdash*

וְלֹא תְטַמֵּא אֶת הָאָרֶץ אֲשֶׁר אַתֶּם יֹשְׁבִים בָּהּ אֲשֶׁר אֲנִי שֹׁכֵן בְּתוֹכָהּ כִּי אֲנִי ה׳ שֹׁכֵן בְּתוֹךְ בְּנֵי יִשְׂרָאֵל.

You shall not contaminate the Land in which you dwell, in whose midst I rest, for I am Hashem Who rests among the Children of Israel (*Bamidbar* 35:34).

Chazal expound: "This teaches that bloodshed contaminates the land and banishes the Divine Presence" (*Sifri, Masei* 3).

In this vein, the Gemara teaches (*Yoma* 9b): "Why was the first Beis HaMikdash destroyed? Because of three [sins] that occurred there: idol worship, immorality, and bloodshed ... But the Second Beis HaMikdash — when the people occupied themselves with Torah, mitzvos, and acts of kindness — why was it destroyed? Because of the gratuitous hatred that existed there. This teaches you that gratuitous hatred is tantamount to the three cardinal sins of idolatry, immorality, and bloodshed."

What is the significance of the fact that the first Beis HaMikdash was destroyed due to the nation's transgression of the three cardinal sins, while the second Beis HaMikdash was destroyed due to their baseless hatred? Furthermore, it is surely not by chance that the three sins that led to the first destruction are sins for which a Yid must sacrifice his life rather than commit (*Sanhedrin* 74a).

Three Cardinal Sins Versus Kedushah

The Maharal[12] explains that Bnei Yisrael's lofty spiritual level during the era of the first Beis HaMikdash was due to the *Shechinah* that dwelled in their midst, as the *navi* describes: לֹא יָכְלוּ הַכֹּהֲנִים לַעֲמֹד לְשָׁרֵת מִפְּנֵי הֶעָנָן כִּי מָלֵא כְבוֹד ה׳ אֶת בֵּית ה׳, *The Kohanim could not stand and minister because of the cloud, for the glory of Hashem filled the Temple of Hashem* (*I Melachim* 8:11). However, when Bnei Yisrael became unworthy of the *Shechinah*, the essence of the Beis HaMikdash was negated, which left it susceptible to destruction. When Bnei Yisrael transgressed the three cardinal sins, defiling both themselves and the Beis HaMikdash, they forfeited the privilege of having the Beis HaMikdash, since Hashem's *Shechinah* does not dwell amidst impurity. Thus, it was destroyed.

Each of the three cardinal sins is referred to as *tumah*, impurity, as the Gemara teaches (*Shevuos* 7b):

> The Sages taught: וְכִפֶּר עַל הַקֹּדֶשׁ מִטֻּמְאֹת בְּנֵי יִשְׂרָאֵל, *Thus shall he provide atonement upon the Sanctuary for the contaminations of Bnei Yisrael* (*Vayikra* 16:16). This includes the impurity of idol worship, the impurity of immorality, and the impurity of bloodshed. Regarding idol worship, it says, לְמַעַן טַמֵּא אֶת מִקְדָּשִׁי, *in order to defile My Sanctuary* (ibid. 20:3); regarding immorality, it says, וּשְׁמַרְתֶּם אֶת מִשְׁמַרְתִּי לְבִלְתִּי עֲשׂוֹת מֵחֻקּוֹת הַתּוֹעֵבֹת וגו׳ וְלֹא תִטַּמְּאוּ בָּהֶם, *You shall safeguard My charge not to do any of the abominable traditions etc. and not contaminate yourselves through them* (ibid. 18:30); and regarding murder it says, וְלֹא תְטַמֵּא אֶת הָאָרֶץ, *You shall not contaminate the Land* (*Bamidbar* 35:34).

Baseless Hatred Versus Unity

The second Beis HaMikdash did not house the *Shechinah*, yet this era was characterized by *achdus* and *chessed*, and the Beis HaMikdash unified the nation. During this period, Bnei Yisrael were forbidden to sacrifice on *bamos*, so the Beis HaMikdash brought the

12. *Netzach Yisrael* Ch. 4.

nation together in a single location, under the sole spiritual authority of the Kohen Gadol. But when baseless hatred infiltrated their hearts, and the nation became riddled with conflict and strife that counteracted this remarkable unity, they no longer deserved to have a Beis HaMikdash in their midst.

In the Zechus of the Avos

The Maharal explains that the first Beis HaMikdash existed in the merit of the *Avos*, who distinguished themselves in these three realms: Avraham Avinu excelled in sanctity and abstention from immorality, as evident from his words to Sarah, הִנֵּה נָא יָדַעְתִּי כִּי אִשָּׁה יְפַת מַרְאֶה אָתְּ, *See now, I have known that you are a woman of beautiful appearance* (*Bereishis* 12:11). The Gemara interprets this to mean that Avraham never gazed at Sarah (*Bava Basra* 16a). Yitzchak Avinu, who willfully sacrificed himself as a *korban* to Hashem, symbolizes the diametric opposite of idol worship; and Yaakov Avinu embodied the sanctification of life and the avoidance of bloodshed.

Yaakov's essence and actions countered those of the wicked Eisav, who was called אַדְמוֹנִי, *red*)*Bereishis* 25:25) and personified murder (Rashi ibid.). In a similar vein, Chazal teach that "Yaakov Avinu did not die" (*Taanis* 5b) and that "he never saw *keri* in his life" (*Yevamos* 76a). Discharging *keri* is regarded as a form of murder since it is a loss of the potential to form human life.

When Bnei Yisrael transgressed these three cardinal sins, they forfeited the privilege of having the *Shechinah* in their midst.

Chazal teach that *zechus Avos* was gone before the era of the second Beis HaMikdash (*Shabbos* 55a), and this Beis HaMikdash was distinguished, instead, by the concept of *Knesses Yisrael*, the assembly of the nation, which represents unity and connection — the opposite of baseless hatred. Consequently, when dissent and loathing crept into the hearts of the people, they began a process of spiritual degeneration that made them unworthy of a Beis HaMikdash, and it was destroyed.

The *Yerushalmi* states: "Any generation in which the [Beis HaMikdash] is not rebuilt in its days is regarded as if they destroyed it"

(*Yoma* 1:5). Each and every generation harbors the potential to rebuild the Beis HaMikdash through mitzvos and good deeds. Therefore, if we have not yet accomplished this, it is considered that we have destroyed the Beis HaMikdash with our own hands.

Clearly, our generation is also held accountable for transgressing the three cardinal sins and for stumbling in baseless hatred — but how can this be? Are we guilty of idolatry, immorality, and murder?

Unfortunately, if we venture outside to the streets, we will see that we are surrounded by the three cardinal sins, *Rachmana litzlan,* and we must be exceedingly vigilant to avoid them. The same is true of *sinas chinam,* for if the third Beis HaMikdash has not yet been rebuilt, it is a clear sign that even we *bnei Torah* are guilty of this *aveirah.*

In the times of the Beis HaMikdash, if a Yid sensed even a slight flaw in his *avodas Hashem,* he would immediately journey to the Beis HaMikdash to repent and purify himself in that realm. Today, however, when the Beis HaMikdash lies in ruins, a Yid who aspires to cleave to Hashem must toil intensely to attain any spiritual goal, and this in and of itself is a reason for us to yearn for the coming of Mashiach!

Let's all take the time to introspect and contemplate whether we are genuinely awaiting Mashiach and anticipating *techiyas hameisim.* To instill this yearning deep in our hearts, we must repeatedly proclaim and internalize the belief in the coming of Mashiach and await his arrival every day, even if he delays.

May Hakadosh Baruch Hu accept all our *tefillos* with love, and may we merit seeing the Beis HaMikdash rebuilt speedily in our days. Amen!

ספר דברים
Sefer Devarim

פרשת דברים
Parashas Devarim

⊰§ *Fences Against Heresy*

אֵיכָה אֶשָּׂא לְבַדִּי טָרְחֲכֶם וּמַשַּׂאֲכֶם וְרִיבְכֶם.
How can I carry alone your contentiousness, your burdens, and your quarrels? (*Devarim* 1:12).

Rashi comments: "*And your burdens* — this teaches that they were heretics."

No Limits

Rashi explains that the burden that weighed so heavily upon Moshe Rabbeinu's shoulders was the spiritual decline that swept through the nation, leading many to degenerate to the level of *apikorsus,* heresy.

Moshe Rabbeinu expressed in anguish: אֵיכָה אֶשָּׂא לְבַדִּי, *How can I carry alone?* Yet what did the nation's *apikorsus* have to do with his leading them alone? Had he been assisted by deputies or officers, would he have better controlled or handled a sin as grave as *apikorsus*?

Moshe's other grievances are better understood: "טָרְחֲכֶם, *your contentiousness* — that Bnei Yisrael were troublesome [in matters of judgment]; וְרִיבְכֶם, *your quarrels* — that they were petulant" (Rashi). A leader can guide his people more effectively when others help bear the brunt of the people's arguments and complaints, yet *apikorsus* is not mitigated by the support of others, since it is a flaw that must be uprooted at its source. Why, then, did Moshe lament his having to carry this burden alone?

To understand Moshe's words, we must first define the concept of *apikorsus*. The *Sifsei Chachamim* explains that *apikorsim* are rebels, and the word *apikorsus* is a contraction of two words: אַפּוּק רֶסֶן, which translate literally as "*remove muzzle*." This means that *apikorsim* are those whose constraints have been removed, so they rebel like a horse that walks without a muzzle.

The root of *apikorsus*, then, is not flawed philosophies, heretical notions, or even the negative influences of those with wrongful beliefs, but simply the act of removing one's "muzzle," which is symbolic of rules and limits.

One who proceeds without inhibition, unfettered by authority, is like a wild horse with no muzzle. Such a person, who rebels against his environment, contravening the rules and values that serve as protective fences, is regarded as an *apikorus*, since the road from wanton behavior to heresy is short and slippery.

Moshe Rabbeinu's lament of "how can I carry alone" conveyed that Klal Yisrael require extra protection, guidance, and constraints, since they were acting without inhibition, and his exalted spiritual leadership was inadequate to counter their profligate behavior. The nation therefore also required tribal leaders, along with officers of thousands, hundreds, and tens, as well as judges and officers to ramp up their spiritual protection, preserve the holy, pure character of the nation, and prevent them from acting like an unmuzzled horse on the run.

Root of Destruction

The rampant *hefkerus* in a society lacking boundaries and spiritual fences was one of the fundamental flaws that caused the destruction of the Beis HaMikdash.

The Gemara states (*Shabbos* 119b):

> Abaye said: Yerushalayim was destroyed only because they desecrated Shabbos in it ... R' Hamnuna said: Yerushalayim was destroyed only because they diverted the schoolchildren in it from their Torah studies ... Ulla said: Yerushalayim was destroyed because they had no shame for each other ... R' Yitzchak said: Yerushalayim was destroyed only because they equated young and old ... R' Amram the son of R' Shimon bar Abba said in the name of R' Shimon bar Abba, who said in the name of R' Chanina: Yerushalayim was destroyed only because they did not admonish one another ... R' Yehudah said: Yerushalayim was destroyed only because they demeaned Torah scholars in it.

This Gemara implies that Bnei Yisrael in the generation preceding the *Churban* were deficient in all these areas: They desecrated Shabbos, equated young and old, and had no shame of one another. The Amoraim do not argue whether these wrongdoings were perpetrated, but merely debate which one prompted the destruction of Yerushalayim and the Beis HaMikdash.

Examining the list of flaws, we see that each one is an expression of a careless, unrestrained attitude, reflecting an approach to life that lacks boundaries and inhibitions. This *hefkerus* leads to *apikorsus* and, ultimately, the destruction of the Beis HaMikdash.

Bnei Yisrael in the era of the *Churban* were guilty of desecrating Shabbos, whose essence is cessation of labor, as defined by its many laws and prohibitions. To the outsider, Shabbos sounds restrictive, and indeed, one who routinely behaves without restraint cannot bear the thought of these boundaries and will surely come to desecrate Shabbos; he will also not conduct himself properly *bein adam lachaveiro.* Similarly, the spiritual failings of shamelessness and equating young and old demonstrate both chutzpah and a breaching of barriers and hierarchies, while demeaning Torah scholars is likewise born of impudence and brazenness.

Shame and fear are correlated, as the Maharsha writes (ibid., s.v. *V'amar Ula*): "Shame is fear, as it is written, וּבַעֲבוּר תִּהְיֶה יִרְאָתוֹ עַל פְּנֵיכֶם, *so that the awe of Him shall be upon your faces* (*Shemos* 20:17)

— [Chazal say,] 'This refers to shame' (*Nedarim* 20a). They also stated: 'May it be the will of God that the fear of heaven be upon you like the fear of flesh and blood' (*Berachos* 28b), as there are numerous sins from which man refrains when he is in the presence of others."

One who has no *bushah* does as he pleases, when he pleases. He has no sense of responsibility, fear of Heaven, or even fear of his fellow man. It is this *apikorsus* — the reckless removal of limits — that banished the *Shechinah* from Bnei Yisrael's midst and instigated the *Churban*.

Seeing that Bnei Yisrael could not endure without constraints and restrictions, Moshe Rabbeinu appointed ministers and judges upon them to enforce laws and limitations. When *hefkerus* again became rampant in the era of the first Beis HaMikdash, as Bnei Yisrael flagrantly breached all boundaries, the *Shechinah* could no longer dwell in their midst, and the Beis HaMikdash was destroyed.

We are now approaching *bein hazmanim*, a time that poses great physical and spiritual peril, for it is all too easy to shake off our usual restraints. The Rosh Yeshivah R' Chaim Shmulevitz would regularly express in his *shmuessen* that he cannot fathom the grounds for permitting *bein hazmanim*, yet since this system was instituted by previous generations, we are not authorized to annul it.

Still, we must guard ourselves with supreme caution during these days and establish clear boundaries to ensure appropriate behavior in every realm of life, so that we will not, *chas v'shalom*, behave in a way that smacks of *apikorsus*.

I have emphasized on numerous occasions that a true *ben Torah* is distinguished by his conduct during *bein hazmanim* — his *tefillos*, his learning, and his comportment wherever he may be.

Hashem should grant us the wisdom to guard ourselves properly and preserve the spiritual acquisitions that we attained over this past *zman*. Let us utilize these coming days productively, as we rest and recoup our energies in preparation for the upcoming *zman*, so that we can sanctify the Name of Hashem in His world.

פרשת ואתחנן
Parashas Va'eschanan

◆§ *Kirvas Elokim — The Core of Tefillah*

וָאֶתְחַנַּן אֶל ה׳ בָּעֵת הַהִוא לֵאמֹר.
I implored Hashem at that time, saying (*Devarim* 3:23).

Regarding the word וָאֶתְחַנַּן, Rashi comments: "Forms of the word חַנּוּן, *imploring,* in all places mean nothing but a gift for free. Although the righteous could make [their requests] dependent on their good deeds, they seek from the Omnipresent nothing but a gift without payment. Because [Hashem] told [Moshe], וְחַנֹּתִי אֶת אֲשֶׁר אָחֹן, *I shall show favor when I choose to show favor* (*Shemos* 33:19), Moshe spoke to Him with the word וָאֶתְחַנַּן."

Chazal teach: "From where do we know that Moshe prayed at that time 515 prayers? It is written, וָאֶתְחַנַּן אֶל ה׳ בָּעֵת הַהִוא לֵאמֹר — *I implored Hashem at that time, saying*. The word וָאֶתְחַנַּן has the numerical value of [515]" (*Devarim Rabbah* 11:10).

Moshe beseeched Hashem with 515 separate prayers, yet his request was not fulfilled. Had he offered even one more entreaty, however, he would have been answered and permitted to enter Eretz Yisrael.[1] Hashem stopped him from adding that one prayer,

1. See *Pnei Yehoshua* (*Berachos* 32a s.v. *Darash*), who writes that the verse, רַב לָךְ אַל תּוֹסֶף דַּבֵּר אֵלַי עוֹד בַּדָּבָר הַזֶּה, *It is too much for you! Do not continue to speak to Me further about this matter,* implies that had Moshe prayed even one more prayer

as He told him, רַב לָךְ אַל תּוֹסֶף דַּבֵּר אֵלַי עוֹד בַּדָּבָר הַזֶּה, *It is too much for you! Do not continue to speak to Me further about this matter* (*Devarim* 3:26). Prayer is so potent that had Moshe uttered even one more prayer, his efforts would have, so to speak, compelled Hashem to capitulate to his request.

A Symbol of Closeness

Rashi notes that Moshe Rabbeinu entreated Hashem using the expression וָאֶתְחַנַּן, *I implored,* which connotes beseeching for *matnas chinam,* a free gift, as opposed to demanding to receive his due. Although *tzaddikim* are surely entitled to link their requests to their virtues — especially Moshe Rabbeinu, whose illustrious character and spiritual attainments surpassed those of every living being — they refrain from relying on their own merits but rather beseech Hashem like a person requesting a free gift.

The Sfas Emes (*Va'eschanan* 5646) wonders how the example of Moshe entreating Hashem proves that *tzaddikim* in general appeal to Hashem for *matnas chinam,* as opposed to attributing their requests to their righteous actions, when ultimately, Moshe Rabbeinu's request was refused. On the contrary, had Moshe Rabbeinu enumerated his righteous deeds in his prayers, perhaps Hashem would have forgiven him and afforded him entry into Eretz Yisrael!

R' Chaim Kamil explains[2] that Moshe Rabbeinu's objective in his intensive prayers was not to enter Eretz Yisrael, but simply to implore Hashem in the manner of one seeking a *matnas chinam,* since this type of supplication leads to *kirvas Elokim.* Without a doubt, Moshe Rabbeinu longed for Hashem to accept his *tefillos* and permit his entrance into Eretz Yisrael, yet his primary motive was to draw close to Hashem regardless of the outcome of his prayer.

— for a total of 516 prayers, which is six times the numerical value of 86 (אֱלֹהִים), he would have sweetened the six judgments mentioned in *Perek Bemah Beheimah,* and his prayer would have been answered. See also *Derashos Chasam Sofer* Vol. II, *Derush* 7 Av 5573.

2. *Imrei Chaim, Avodas HaTefillah.*

The *tzaddik* views *tefillah* as an opportunity to attain *kirvas Elokim* by standing before Hashem and requesting a free gift. *Tzaddikim* refrain from linking their requests to their meritorious deeds, because while this is effective in bringing about the fulfillment of their wishes, it does not satisfy their primary desire and yearning for *kirvas Elokim*, which is achieved by appealing to Hashem like a destitute pauper beseeching for life.

The Gemara relates that R' Yitzchak ben Elyashiv was approached by two disciples who entreated him to pray that they should merit wisdom, to which he replied, "I once had it, and I banished it" (*Taanis* 23b).

Rashi explains that R' Yitzchak was saying, "This was [formerly] in my power, that everything I requested, I was granted; but now my prayers are not accepted as much." The *mefarshim* note that R' Yitzchak's power of prayer was so potent that every request he uttered was immediately fulfilled, yet he willfully surrendered this gift.

How could R' Yitzchak, or anyone, deliberately forfeit this incredible power? Furthermore, these *talmidim* did not ask him to petition for material wealth, but for wisdom so they could succeed in Torah. By exercising his power of prayer, R' Yitzchak could have easily fulfilled their request, yet he refused.

R' Yitzchak's baffling choice teaches a profound lesson in *tefillah*. The principal *avodah* of *tefillah* is to attain *kirvas Hashem* by beseeching like a pauper for *matnas chinam*. One whose prayers are instantly answered is liable to lose the feeling of standing helplessly before Hashem, and the diminished intensity of his *tefillos* will then result in his achieving less *kirvas Elokim*. While a *tzaddik* surely desires the fulfillment of his wishes and prayers, his chief objective is to attain *kirvas Elokim* through intense *tefillah*, and he will therefore reject anything that diverts him from this goal. This message is beautifully expressed in Moshe Rabbeinu's words, *And I implored Hashem*, which connote that the goal itself is to entreat Hashem.

Approaching *tefillah* as a medium to attain *kirvas Elokim* is so important that R' Yitzchak bar Elyashiv was willing to sacrifice his power to have all his requests fulfilled for the privilege of cleaving to Hashem through brokenhearted, desperate supplications, like a pauper. The capacity to draw immediate salvation upon himself and others was worthless to him if it diminished even slightly from the sentiment of dire need he felt when facing Hashem in *tefillah*.

The *pasuk* states, כִּי מִי גוֹי גָּדוֹל אֲשֶׁר לוֹ אֱלֹקִים קְרֹבִים אֵלָיו כַּה' אֱלֹקֵינוּ בְּכָל קָרְאֵנוּ אֵלָיו, *For which is a great nation that has a God Who is close to it, as is Hashem, our God, whenever we call to Him?* (*Devarim* 4:7).

Onkelos translates, "Whose God is close to them to accept their prayers at any time like Hashem our God [Who is close to us] at any time that we pray before Him."

Targum Onkelos and *Targum Yonasan ben Uziel* concur that this *pasuk* refers to the *tefillos* of Bnei Yisrael, which are heard and accepted by Hakadosh Baruch Hu at every opportunity. Yet how does their translation dovetail with the reality, in which we pray consistently and earnestly for our heart's desires, yet at times our prayers are rejected?

Compounding this question, the Gemara teaches, regarding the *pasuk*, וְחָרָה אַפִּי בוֹ בַיּוֹם הַהוּא וַעֲזַבְתִּים וְהִסְתַּרְתִּי פָנַי מֵהֶם, *My anger will flare against it on that day and I will forsake them; and I will conceal My face from them* (*Devarim* 31:17): "Rav Bardela bar Tavyomi said in the name of Rav: Anyone who is not subject to 'concealment of the face' is not one of them" (*Chagigah* 5a). Rashi explains that a person who does not experience *hester panim* is not from the Jewish people, about whom Hashem says, *I shall hide My face from them,* meaning that a Jew cries out due to the troubles that befall him, but he is not answered.

Every Yid has times when he cries out to Hashem to ease his suffering, but his prayers go unanswered. How, then, can both Onkelos and Yonasan ben Uziel translate the *pasuk* to mean that Bnei Yisrael's *tefillos* are always heard and accepted on high?

The answer is that the *pasuk*, כִּי מִי גוֹי גָּדוֹל אֲשֶׁר לוֹ אֱלֹקִים קְרֹבִים אֵלָיו כַּה' אֱלֹקֵינוּ בְּכָל קָרְאֵנוּ אֵלָיו, *For which is a great nation that has a God Who is close to it, as is Hashem, our God, whenever we call to Him,* does not necessarily refer to Bnei Yisrael's power to generate salvation through their *tefillos*, nor does it guarantee that every *tefillah* will be heard and immediately fulfilled. Rather, it refers to the promise that a Yid can achieve closeness to Hashem at any time through genuine, fervent prayer. A *tefillah* that generates that closeness is a *tefillah* that is truly accepted and beloved in *Shamayim*, as illustrated by the paradigm of R' Yitzchak bar Elyashiv, who favored *kirvas Hashem* over the fulfillment of his desires.

Hashem Runs the World Based on Man's Closeness

On the sixth day of Creation, the world is described in these terms: וְכֹל שִׂיחַ הַשָּׂדֶה טֶרֶם יִהְיֶה בָאָרֶץ, וְכָל עֵשֶׂב הַשָּׂדֶה טֶרֶם יִצְמָח, כִּי לֹא הִמְטִיר ה׳ אֱלֹקִים עַל הָאָרֶץ וְאָדָם אַיִן לַעֲבֹד אֶת הָאֲדָמָה, *Now all the trees of the field were not yet on the earth and all the herb of the field had not yet sprouted, for Hashem God had not sent rain upon the earth and there was no man to work the soil* (*Bereishis* 2:5).

The Gemara wonders how it is possible that by the sixth day there was no growth of vegetation on the earth, considering that plant life was created on the third day of Creation, as the Torah states, וַתּוֹצֵא הָאָרֶץ דֶּשֶׁא עֵשֶׂב מַזְרִיעַ זֶרַע לְמִינֵהוּ, *And the earth brought forth vegetation: herbage yielding seed after its kind* (ibid. 1:12).

Chazal answer (*Chullin* 60b) that "blades of grass emerged and waited at the level of the earth until Adam HaRishon came and prayed for them, and then it rained, and they grew. This teaches that Hakadosh Baruch Hu desires the prayers of *tzaddikim*."

Regarding the words כִּי לֹא הִמְטִיר, *for He had not sent rain*, Rashi comments: "Why did He not let down the rain? For there was no man to work the earth and recognize the goodness of rain. When Adam came and he knew that [rain] was vital for the world, he prayed for it, and it rained, and the trees and grasses grew." It wasn't until there was a person in the world to appreciate his utter dependence on Hashem's infinite goodness, and to daven and achieve *kirvas Elokim*, that Hashem was prepared to release His gift of rain upon the world. Indeed, from here we derive the awe-inspiring lesson that Hakadosh Baruch Hu actually runs His world based on the *kirvas Elokim* attained by man.

A Paradigm of Tefillah

Moshe Rabbeinu's conduct sheds light on both the colossal power of *tefillah* and the ideal manner of prayer. Even after Hashem decreed, כִּי לֹא תַעֲבֹר אֶת הַיַּרְדֵּן הַזֶּה, *for you shall not cross this Yarden* (*Devarim* 3:27), Moshe did not despair but rather beseeched Hashem with 515 compelling *tefillos*. Ultimately, Moshe did not achieve his deepest desire, yet Hashem did acquiesce partially when He instructed him: עֲלֵה רֹאשׁ הַפִּסְגָּה וְשָׂא עֵינֶיךָ יָמָּה וְצָפֹנָה וְתֵימָנָה וּמִזְרָחָה וּרְאֵה בְעֵינֶיךָ, *Ascend to the top of the cliff and raise your eyes westward, northward, southward, and eastward and see with your eyes* (ibid.).

Regarding the words וּרְאֵה בְעֵינֶיךָ, *and see with your eyes*, Rashi comments: "You asked of Me, וְאֶרְאֶה אֶת הָאָרֶץ הַטּוֹבָה, *and [let me] see the good Land* (ibid. v. 25), and I am showing you the whole [Land]."

Tefillah is so potent that it can tear through all heavenly barriers. When Moshe Rabbeinu entreated for mercy on behalf of Klal Yisrael at the time of the *cheit ha'eigel,* he did so with *mesirus nefesh,* as alluded by the *pasuk,* וַיְחַל מֹשֶׁה אֶת פְּנֵי ה׳ אֱלֹקָיו, *Moshe pleaded before Hashem, his God* (*Shemos* 32:11). The Gemara expounds (*Berachos* 32a): "Shmuel said: It teaches that [Moshe] risked his life for their sake ... R' Eliezer the Great says: This teaches that Moshe stood in prayer before Hakadosh Baruch Hu until he was seized by *achilu.* What is *achilu*? R' Elazar said: Fire of the bones [i.e., infection]."

The paradigm of Moshe Rabbeinu's *tefillah* conveys that we must never despair of Hashem's compassion; instead, we should intensify our prayers for salvation.

A similar lesson is derived from the case of Chizkiyahu HaMelech, who was censured for his failure to engage in the mitzvah of procreation. Yeshayah HaNavi told him: כֹּה אָמַר ה׳ צַו לְבֵיתֶךָ כִּי מֵת אַתָּה וְלֹא תִחְיֶה, *Thus said Hashem: Instruct your household, for you shall die; and you shall not live* (*Yeshayah* 38:1). Chizkiyahu, who had foreseen that he would bear a sinful child, deliberately abstained from the mitzvah, yet Yeshayah HaNavi rebuked him for this, on the grounds that a person may not intervene in Hashem's ways, which are hidden (*Berachos* 10a).

Upon hearing this rebuke, Chizkiyahu immediately began to pray, as it is written, וַיַּסֵּב חִזְקִיָּהוּ פָּנָיו אֶל הַקִּיר וַיִּתְפַּלֵּל אֶל ה׳ וכו׳ וַיֵּבְךְּ חִזְקִיָּהוּ בְּכִי גָדוֹל, *Chizkiyahu then turned his face to the wall and prayed to Hashem ... And Chizkiyahu wept an intense weeping* (*Yeshayah* 38:2-3). His prayers were answered, as Hashem told Yeshayah, הָלוֹךְ וְאָמַרְתָּ אֶל חִזְקִיָּהוּ וכו׳ שָׁמַעְתִּי אֶת תְּפִלָּתֶךָ, רָאִיתִי אֶת דִּמְעָתֶךָ, הִנְנִי יוֹסִף עַל יָמֶיךָ חֲמֵשׁ עֶשְׂרֵה שָׁנָה, *Go and tell Chizkiyahu ... "I have heard your prayer; I have seen your tears. Behold, I am going to add fifteen years to your days"* (ibid. v. 5). The Gemara (*Berachos* ibid.) reveals that before Chizkiyahu poured out his heart in prayer, Yeshayah informed him, "The verdict has already been sealed," to which Chizkiyahu replied, "Son of Amotz, end your prophecy and exit! I was taught by my ancestors that even if a sharp sword rests on man's throat, he should not desist from begging for mercy."

Tefillos of the Tzibbur

The Gemara states (ibid. 8a): "Hakadosh Baruch Hu does not spurn the prayers of a multitude," and the *mefarshim* explain that although a prayer offered by an individual carries enormous strength, the collective *tefillos* of many is far more powerful. Had Bnei Yisrael united in prayer on behalf of Moshe Rabbeinu and beseeched that he be allowed to enter Eretz Yisrael, their collective *tefillah* would have been effective.

The Midrash relates (*Devarim Rabbah* 7:10) that Moshe called Bnei Yisrael to task for failing to daven for him, adding that had they prayed for him, they would have been answered: "R' Shmuel bar Yitzchak said: When Moshe was on the brink of death, and [Bnei Yisrael] did not pray that he should enter Eretz Yisrael, he assembled them and began to admonish them. He told them: 'One man saved 600,000 at the time of the *cheit ha'eigel*, and 600,000 could not save one man?' "

The *Sefer HaIkrim* (Ch. 21, *Maamar* 4) elaborates that Moshe was telling Klal Yisrael: "You should not think that just as my prayer was not answered, if you sin today or tomorrow, then your prayer will not be accepted either. Do not think that the prayer of the community and the individual are equal in this regard, for it is not so. Despite my spiritual stature, because I am an individual, my prayer on my own behalf was not accepted, whereas although you are idolaters who bowed to Baal Pe'or — and there is nothing as loathsome before Hashem as *avodah zarah* — my prayer on your behalf was accepted, and Hakadosh Baruch Hu forgave you, even though my prayer on my behalf was not accepted." With these words, Moshe Rabbeinu revealed that a *tefillah* for the public is ever more powerful than a *tefillah* for an individual.

With the words וָאֶתְחַנַּן אֶל ה׳, Moshe Rabbeinu revealed the fundamental precept that the paramount objective of *tefillah* is *kirvas Elokim. Kirvas Elokim* is attained through heartfelt supplications, notwithstanding the outcome of the prayer. Moshe also taught that a person should daven with feelings of *mesirus nefesh,* never faltering or despairing of Hashem's compassion and salvation, as Chizkiyahu taught that "even if a sharp sword rests on man's throat, he should not desist from begging for mercy." Furthermore, we learn from Moshe's example that if a person sees that Hashem has not answered his prayer, he should ask others to daven for him, since the power of collective prayer is infinitely more potent.

Rabbosai! This lesson is particularly relevant to us, both as individuals and as a *tzibbur.* We are living in extremely difficult times, when "outside, the sword slays, and inside, fear prevails." The war rages on, and the danger rises with each passing day. During these ominous times, each and every one of us is assigned a special *tafkid,* and we must be aware of the precise nature of that role.

During the war between Bnei Yisrael and Midian, Hashem commanded Moshe Rabbeinu, אֶלֶף לַמַּטֶּה אֶלֶף לַמַּטֶּה לְכֹל מַטּוֹת יִשְׂרָאֵל תִּשְׁלְחוּ לַצָּבָא. וַיִּמָּסְרוּ מֵאַלְפֵי יִשְׂרָאֵל אֶלֶף לַמַּטֶּה שְׁנֵים עָשָׂר אֶלֶף, *"A thousand from a tribe, a thousand from a tribe for all the tribes of Yisrael shall you send to the legion." So there were delivered from the thousands of Bnei Yisrael, a thousand from each tribe, twelve thousand* (*Bamidbar* 31:4-5).

The Midrash elaborates (*Bamidbar Rabbah* 22:2):

> Some say that he sent two thousand from each tribe, and some say three thousand from each tribe. Twelve thousand to guard their weapons [i.e., fight], and twelve thousand to

pray. From where do we learn this? It says, אֶלֶף לַמַּטֶּה אֶלֶף לַמַּטֶּה, *A thousand from a tribe, a thousand from a tribe,* which totals twenty-four thousand; and וַיִּמָּסְרוּ מֵאַלְפֵי יִשְׂרָאֵל אֶלֶף לַמַּטֶּה, *there were delivered from the thousands of Bnei Yisrael, a thousand from each tribe,* which adds another twelve thousand. What is the meaning of וַיִּמָּסְרוּ מֵאַלְפֵי יִשְׂרָאֵל אֶלֶף לַמַּטֶּה, *there were delivered from the thousands of Bnei Yisrael, a thousand from each tribe*? That they were delivered as partners for one another.

The Midrash teaches that for every Jewish warrior who set out to battle the Midianites, there was a Jew davening to Hashem to safeguard him in battle. During these treacherous times, we must intensify our Torah study, toiling with all our might, and daven with *mesirus nefesh,* as a *tzibbur*, thereby attaining *kirvas Elokim.*

We must also take extreme precautions to avoid *bittul Torah,* which can cause a person to forfeit the tremendous benefits of *limud Torah.* Above all, we should never despair of the power of *tefillah,* for Hakadosh Baruch Hu eagerly awaits our heartfelt prayers, so that He can shower us with His infinite bounty and *siyata diShmaya.*

May Hashem help us to stand before Him in *tefillah* with appreciation of its massive potential. We should all daven with sincerity, entreating Hashem like a person who has nothing and is begging for dear life, so we can merit the fulfillment of the *pasuk,* וַאֲנִי קִרְבַת אֱלֹהִים לִי טוֹב, *But as for me, God's nearness is my good* (*Tehillim* 73:28).

פרשת שופטים
Parashas Shoftim

◆§ *Sifrei Mussar — Our Contemporary Officers*

שֹׁפְטִים וְשֹׁטְרִים תִּתֶּן לְךָ בְּכָל שְׁעָרֶיךָ.
Judges and officers shall you appoint in all your cities (*Devarim* 16:18).

Rashi comments: "The word שֹׁפְטִים means *judges* who pass judgment, and the word שֹׁטְרִים means *officers* who impose authority over the people following the order of [the judges] with stick and with strap, until one accepts upon himself the verdict of the judge."

We Can't Trust Ourselves

With the command to appoint officers to enforce law and judgment, the Torah imparts a profound lesson for life. A Yid knows that he must fulfill all the mitzvos in the Torah and uphold any verdict or directive issued by the nation's *dayanim*. Why, then, does Klal Yisrael require officers to enforce these laws and verdicts using physical aggression and corporal punishment? Could the Torah not have relied on people's awareness and understanding of their moral obligations?

The answer is, a person cannot trust himself! Humans are naturally inclined to evade responsibility, and even if one is aware of his obligations, in the absence of fear of authority and retribution, he will be tempted to ignore his responsibilities and indulge his desires. The role of officers, then, is to enforce laws and mitzvos by compelling the masses to adhere to them, lest they face the consequences of their imprudent actions and omissions.

Appointing officers serves another purpose as well. At times, a Yid is inspired to enhance his *avodas Hashem*, and undertakes *kabbalos* to improve his character and his fulfillment of mitzvos. While he may initially approach the task enthusiastically, human nature is such that, with the passage of time, his passion will fade, and he will begin to falter spiritually. This phenomenon is particularly apparent at the start of a new *zman*, when the *tzibbur* flocks to the *beis midrash* with fervor, burning with zeal and motivation. Yet as the months pass, there is a conspicuous drop in the energy and vibrancy of the learning atmosphere. Preventing such lapses is enough of a reason to appoint officers.

Sefer HaChinuch (Mitzvah 491) explains that this mitzvah to appoint judges and officers ensures that all religious laws are upheld. When leaders and officers are appointed to enforce the laws, the people regard these leaders with awe and fear, which spurs the masses to act with integrity. This proper behavior ultimately becomes second nature to them.

These words of the *Sefer HaChinuch* convey a third reason for appointing *shotrim*. He writes that the force exercised by the officers elevates a Yid to the level at which performing mitzvos becomes second nature! From this, we learn that performing all the Torah's mitzvos as second nature is a fulfillment of this mitzvah of שֹׁטְרִים תִּתֶּן לְךָ בְּכָל שְׁעָרֶיךָ, *Officers shall you appoint in all your cities.*

Even today, we are still privileged to have *shoftim*, distinguished *dayanim* among us who are appointed to resolve disputes and render their verdict in *beis din*. Yet we sorely lack שֹׁטְרִים — officers with the authority to enforce the fulfillment of Torah and mitzvos. Given that people are naturally inclined to shirk responsibility, how can we remain firm in our commitment to Torah, and guard ourselves from *aveiros,* without *shotrim* to remind us of our obligations? What binds us to halachah and mitzvos, and what infuses our hearts with newfound spiritual vigor during moments of weakness? Above all, how can we acquire positive habits that become second nature and guarantee our unflagging dedication to Torah and mitzvos?

Contemporary Shotrim

In recent generations, *gedolei Yisrael* and the venerable *baalei mussar* bequeathed to us a new form of *shotrim* — the study of *mussar*! Through *mussar* study, we reap both benefits that Bnei Yisrael drew from the *shotrim* of yesteryear. The first is the "stick and strap," which forcefully inculcate us with fear of Hashem and alert us to the dangers of living a life of permissiveness.

The second benefit of *mussar* is that it counteracts spiritual stagnation by imbuing the learner with aspirations, fervor, and desire to continually grow and strive in *avodas Hashem.* The study of *mussar* also encourages regular *hisbonenus,* contemplation and introspection, which has the power to rouse a person from his spiritual slumber and spur him to grow. Finally, the consistent study of *mussar* cements positive behaviors, attitudes, and emotions into habit, embedding them in the person's character until they become second nature.

Mussar study is thus a fulfillment of Hashem's command to appoint *shotrim* to safeguard ourselves from faltering spiritually. Moreover, it has the added value of infusing fervor and vitality into our *limud Torah* and fulfillment of mitzvos, and turning these qualities into intrinsic parts of our character.

Learning Torah with *hasmadah* also spurs a person to *hisbonenus,* yet the only way to perform consistent *hisbonenus* without distractions or lapses is through the regular study of *mussar.* But *mussar* study is effective only when conducted in the proper way — with flaming lips, a sweet melody, deliberation, and, above all, a broken heart. Only in this way does *mussar* function like a guard or officer who stimulates constant spiritual growth and ascent.

Baruch Hashem, the *beis midrash* is full of outstanding *lomdei Torah*. Beyond the regular *sedarim* and *tefillos*, the yeshivah's schedule includes a daily *mussar seder*, and every *ben yeshivah* should commit to maintaining all the yeshivah's *sedarim*, so that the sound of *mussar* study should prevail during this brief *seder* and inspire us to repent.

Sifrei mussar are our personal *shotrim*, which unlock our minds and hearts to serve Hashem and cleave to Him. Every individual is personally responsible for the *klal*, as Chazal say that all Yidden are guarantors for one another. Therefore, if even one person abandons his seat and is not present in the *beis midrash* during *mussar seder*, he is held accountable for the collective weakening that ensues, and he is destined to face judgment for this in *Shamayim*.

Shotrim for the Month of Elul

The obligation of appointing *shotrim* is particularly germane during the month of Elul, when we must seek ways to prepare for the imminent Yom Hadin. This day is not a day of judgment for Klal Yisrael only, but a day of judgment for all of humanity and for the universe itself, yet only we — as *bnei Torah* who fathom the profundities and secrets of the Yom Hadin — are in a position to perform the requisite preparations for this day.

Every day in the month of Elul compels change. Primarily, we must recognize that we are approaching the formidable day when Hakadosh Baruch Hu judges each and every individual. This awareness leads a Yid to fathom the enormity of this day, palpably feel the terror of the impending judgment, and consequently make the requisite spiritual preparations.

In previous generations, the very mention of Elul was sufficient to instill dread in the hearts of men, as R' Yisrael Salanter wrote: "In the past ... every man was gripped by terror from the sound of the voice heralding '*Chodesh Elul*'" (*Ohr Yisrael, Iggeres* 14), as this is the time when we approach the Day of Judgment. In that era of spiritual giants, the month of Elul itself served as the *shotrim*, embedding awe and fear in people's hearts. Unfortunately, our generation is distant from the exalted spiritual level of R' Yisrael Salanter and his *talmidim,* and without extra spiritual inspiration, we are liable to arrive at the Yom Hadin devoid of awe and fear. It therefore behooves us to seek ways to instill in ourselves the emotions befitting these Days of Awe.

The study of *mussar,* and learning Torah with *hasmadah,* are the ingredients that lead a Yid to *hisbonenus.* Primarily, then, we must fortify ourselves in Torah and *yiras Shamayim* and ensure that we are present in the *beis midrash* from the beginning of *seder* until its very end. Elul is not the time to fritter away any opportunity for learning, as it is a time when we must prepare to face judgment! During these days between Rosh Chodesh Elul and Yom Kippur, days of supreme closeness to Hashem, we must engage in frequent, consistent *hisbonenus,* introspecting and seeking additional opportunities for growth. While extra *hasmadah* can inspire *hisbonenus,* consistent *hisbonenus* results only from regular *mussar* study; and with the combined strength of *mussar* and *hasmadah,* we should all merit complete atonement on the Day of Judgment and a blessed, good year for Klal Yisrael.

פרשת כי תצא
Parashas Ki Seitzei

◆§ *The Perpetual War Against the Yetzer Hara*

כִּי תֵצֵא לַמִּלְחָמָה עַל אֹיְבֶיךָ וּנְתָנוֹ ה׳ אֱלֹקֶיךָ בְּיָדֶךָ וְשָׁבִיתָ שִׁבְיוֹ.
When you go out to war against your enemies, and Hashem your God will deliver them into your hand, and you will capture its captivity (*Devarim* 21:10).

Parashas Ki Seitzei is read during the month of Elul, and it behooves us to delve into this *parashah* and discover the *avodah* required of us throughout the year, and particularly during these days of love, repentance, and closeness to Hashem.

Battle of Wills

The Chofetz Chaim wrote that the theme of *eishes yefas to'ar* can be interpreted as a metaphor for Bnei Yisrael's perpetual war against the *yetzer hara.* Man's greatest enemy is his evil inclination, which resorts to every possible tactic in its quest to cause him to stumble and plummet into a spiritual abyss. It is therefore up to us to wage a mighty war against him every hour of every day.

Chazal teach, "Man should always incite his *yetzer tov* against his *yetzer hara*" (*Berachos* 5a). Even if one fears that he will lose the war against his *yetzer hara*, he must still strengthen himself to rise and do battle. The constant struggle with the *yetzer hara* can be compared to a clash between two business partners, one of whom embezzled funds from the company. Although the innocent partner is aware that he will never see the stolen money again, that does not stop him from calling his partner to task for his offense, in order to protect himself from future losses. Furthermore, if the embezzler develops more conniving methods, the wronged partner will certainly devise clever strategies in response, and will monitor the thief's activities carefully. Similarly, every Yid must engage his *yetzer hara* in constant combat, for even if this cannot repair the past, it will surely help for the future, by preventing the *yetzer hara* from tempting him again to sin.

At times, the *yetzer hara* cunningly convinces the person to do mitzvos, when his true intention is to lure him to sin. The solution for this is to engage in fervent Torah study, so that the *zechus* of *limud Torah* will protect the person from the wiles of the *yetzer hara*.

The Torah says, כִּי תֵצֵא לַמִּלְחָמָה עַל אֹיְבֶיךָ, *When you go out to war against your enemies*, conveying that if you take a stand to battle the *yetzer hara* and his cunning tactics, you will merit *siyata diShmaya* and prevail over him, as the *pasuk* concludes, וּנְתָנוֹ ה׳ אֱלֹקֶיךָ בְּיָדֶךָ וְשָׁבִיתָ שִׁבְיוֹ, *and Hashem your God will deliver them into your hand, and you will capture its captivity.*

Until Your Dying Day

The Torah continues: וְרָאִיתָ בַּשִּׁבְיָה אֵשֶׁת יְפַת תֹּאַר וְחָשַׁקְתָּ בָהּ וְלָקַחְתָּ לְךָ לְאִשָּׁה, *And you will see among its captivity a woman who is beautiful of form, and you will desire her, you may take her to yourself for a wife* (*Devarim* 21: 11). The *Meshech Chochmah* (ibid. v. 10) explains that the Torah permitted an *eishes yefas to'ar* only when Bnei Yisrael win a total victory, as reflected in the words, וּנְתָנוֹ ה׳ אֱלֹקֶיךָ בְּיָדֶךָ, *and Hashem your God will deliver them into your hand*. If, however, the enemy is not completely vanquished, and both sides merely agree to a ceasefire and prisoner swap, the *yefas to'ar* is forbidden to the Jewish soldier, lest the gentile army keep even one Jewish woman in exchange for the *yefas to'ar* who remained in Jewish hands.

If Bnei Yisrael set out to war and vanquished their enemies entirely, it is clear that Hashem was with them, and that they received tremendous *siyata diShmaya* due to the unshakeable faith of each and every soldier. If this is the case, how could the *yetzer hara* succeed in enticing these *tzaddikim* with an *eishes yefas to'ar*?

The Torah is informing us that even one who has attained supreme spiritual heights should not trust himself to withstand the *yetzer hara*, as Chazal exhort, וְאַל תַּאֲמִין בְּעַצְמְךָ עַד יוֹם מוֹתְךָ, *Do not trust yourself until the day you die* (*Avos* 2:5). Even in a case of unilateral victory due to Klal Yisrael's exalted spiritual stature, a Yid is always susceptible to the schemes of the *yetzer hara* and can easily fall prey to him. Chazal's warning of "until the day you die" implies that the war against the *yetzer hara* is a perpetual, lifelong battle.

Elul — A Time of Introspection

The *eishes yefas to'ar* is permitted after the process of וּבָכְתָה אֶת אָבִיהָ וְאֶת אִמָּהּ יֶרַח יָמִים, *She shall weep for her father and her mother for a full month* (*Devarim* 21:13), about which Chazal say, "This is the month of Elul" (*Zohar Chadash, Ki Seitzei*).

Chazal draw a parallel between Elul and the *eishes yefas to'ar*: Just as the Jewish warrior is required to wait thirty days, while his captive sits in disgrace and grieves her loss, so that he can reflect upon his behavior and change his mind, so too a person must introspect throughout the year, and especially during the month of Elul, in order to spur himself to repent.

Just yesterday, a *mashgiach* shared with me that he had consulted a great *talmid chacham* regarding which topics of *mussar* he should address during the month of Elul. The *talmid chacham* replied that it is vital to focus on *emunah* during this time, so that people will palpably feel that in a matter of days, they will be standing before the King of kings, Who will judge each person for his actions and decree upon him life or death, prosperity or hunger, health or illness.

Do we really believe this? Throughout the month of Elul, the *yetzer hara* does everything in his power to dampen our fervor and cool our quest for spiritual growth, with deceptive reminders that there is still a full month ahead until the Yom Hadin, and we have no cause for concern. We must counter his devious ways and remove the blindfold that he places on our eyes by recalling that "the time is short, and there is much work to be done." Indeed, in but a few days, each and every one of us will stand before the Heavenly Court to be judged, in both the material and spiritual realms.

Often, a person wakes up in the middle of the night and recalls that he must repent for a specific matter, but then he falls back asleep. By the time he reawakens the next morning, the thought has vanished.

Yet this week, I experienced a miracle! I awoke in the middle of the night, and while lying in bed introspecting, I recalled a particular matter that required *teshuvah*. The next morning, when I awoke, Hashem granted me *siyata diShmaya,* and I remembered my thoughts from the previous night and set about rectifying the issue immediately.

Every day requires a burst of renewal, as the *yetzer hara* does not relinquish its hold on man for even a moment, which is why we must engage in a perpetual battle against the *yetzer hara*. I am hardly the one worthy of delivering *mussar*, but during the month of Elul, it is incumbent upon us all to rouse ourselves from our spiritual slumber and perform careful introspection.

Hashem should grant us all *siyata diShmaya* to repent wholeheartedly to Him, and we should all be *zocheh* to a *kesivah v'chasimah tovah.*

פרשת כי תבוא
Parashas Ki Savo

◆§ *An Expression of Gratitude*

וְלָקַחְתָּ מֵרֵאשִׁית כָּל פְּרִי הָאֲדָמָה אֲשֶׁר תָּבִיא מֵאַרְצְךָ אֲשֶׁר ה׳ אֱלֹקֶיךָ נֹתֵן לָךְ.

You shall take of the first of every fruit of the ground that you bring in from your Land that Hashem, your God, gives you (*Devarim* 26:2).

Recognizing the Good

The foundation of the mitzvah of *bikkurim* is expressing gratitude to Hashem. When a person carries that precious first fruit of his crop to the Beis HaMikdash, he recalls that these fruits — along with all other delights of Olam Hazeh — are gifts of his Creator, and this insight fills him with profound sentiments of gratitude to Hashem. The mitzvah of *bikkurim* thus illustrates the overriding imperative of *hakaras hatov* to Hakadosh Baruch Hu for the countless miracles and wonders that He performs for us every moment of every day, and conversely, the gravity of spurning His everlasting kindness. Moreover, just as the mitzvah of *bikkurim* highlights our obligation to feel and express gratitude to Hashem, it likewise points to our moral duty to express appreciation to our fellow man.

Some believe that *hakaras hatov* means repaying a kindness to another, yet its true definition is actually discerning the kindness that someone did on your behalf, and this recognition is truly the greatest recompense that the giver can receive from the recipient. The same applies to the *hakaras hatov* that we owe Hakadosh Baruch Hu; the very recognition of the kindness that He performs for us every hour of every day is the ultimate manifestation of *hakaras hatov*.

Gratitude for Teshuvah

We are currently at the height of the days of mercy and atonement, when Hakadosh Baruch Hu showers Klal Yisrael with love and closeness and grants us the process of *teshuvah*.

Rabbeinu Yonah writes (*Shaarei Teshuvah* 1:1): "Among the great kindnesses that Hashem bestows upon His creations is preparing for them a path to rise from their lowly actions and flee the abyss of sin ... And if they sinned greatly and rebelled against Him, He still does not close the doors of repentance to them."

Teshuvah is an unparalleled gift from Hakadosh Baruch Hu. *Kovetz He'aros* (*Yevamos* Ch. 21 §24) notes that whereas the repentance of a gentile takes effect at the time that he repents and impacts his future so that he will not be punished in Olam Hazeh, the repentance of a Yid works retroactively as well, erasing his misdeeds as if he never sinned at all.

This is an incredible idea, as logic dictates that a person who sinned and rebelled against Hakadosh Baruch Hu should be undeserving of any clemency. Yet Hakadosh Baruch Hu, Who is a loving and compassionate Father, bequeathed to His children the priceless gift of *teshuvah*, which uproots sins retroactively at their source, and we must value this deeply.

Let us examine why Hashem saw fit to create the power of *teshuvah* and what we can learn from His ways.

Man experiences many ups and downs throughout life, and can be considered "alive" during his good periods and "dead" during his difficult periods. His temperament and feelings shift constantly, especially since the *yetzer hara* baits him day and night. Yet man's duty is to choose life — וּבָחַרְתָּ בַּחַיִּים — and this is a recurring choice that presents itself every day anew. It's a choice we face every morning as we recite *Modeh Ani,* and a choice we face before every *tefillah,* and during every moment of life.

The novelty of *teshuvah* is not that a sinner can erase his sins, as this is but a consequence of *teshuvah.* Rather, it is the fact that a person who sinned previously, but now faces new choices at each and every juncture, can still choose the proper path. And it is this choice and yearning for spiritual life that bring about the erasure of his sins.

Had the world been created for life in Olam Hazeh alone, there would have been no purpose in the concept of *teshuvah.* Yet man's purpose in this world is to prepare for Olam Haba, as Chazal teach that this world is compared to a corridor to Olam Haba (*Avos* 4:16). Life in this world is about choosing between good and evil: If man chooses good, then he merits to enter Olam Haba — which is the ultimate objective of *teshuvah.*

The Chofetz Chaim, we know, was once visited by a wealthy man who was appalled by his humble abode and meager furniture, which consisted of little save for a table, some chairs, a bed, and bookshelves.

"Rabbi," asked the man, "where are all your furniture and belongings?"

The Chofetz Chaim responded with a question of his own. "And where are yours?"

"I am traveling," the guest answered, "and I brought along only my bare necessities. At home, I have everything."

The Chofetz Chaim answered, "I am also a guest in Olam Hazeh, and my treasure houses await me in Olam Haba."

This is the embodiment of "choosing life," and for this we were granted the power of *teshuvah,* for which we must express our gratitude to Hakadosh Baruch Hu.

Gratitude for Spiritual Bounty

The common assumption is that we owe Hashem gratitude for material blessings only. People can easily appreciate health, livelihood, and the children Hashem gave them, but they tend to think that their spiritual acquisitions — namely, Torah and mitzvos — are their own, and that they have no obligation of *hakaras hatov* for this. Some people actually feel that *they're* owed a debt of gratitude for waking up every morning to daven!

A little thought can go a long way in helping to develop *hakaras hatov* for spiritual matters. If we thank Hashem for the countless material gifts that He showers upon us constantly, then certainly we must contemplate and identify His kindness in granting us opportunities to easily acquire eternal life. All it takes for a person to achieve this level of genuine gratitude is some thought and reflection.

The privilege of numbering among those who learn Torah and toil in the word of Hashem is a gift of epic value, and our obligation of *hakaras hatov* is even more pronounced because Hashem simultaneously grants us health, *parnassah,* and children. Especially during these days of Elul when we can so easily draw additional bounty to the world, how can we not open our hearts to repent to Hashem and express our gratitude to Him for the gift of these days?

Candle-lighting in the Mishkan

The theme of *hakaras hatov* is also evident at the start of *Parashas Beha'aloscha,* which follows the description of the generous *korbanos* offered by the *nesi'im*. Rashi, citing Chazal, asks (*Bamidbar* 8:2): "Why was the topic of the Menorah juxtaposed with the topic of the *nesi'im*? Because when Aharon saw the inauguration of the *nesi'im,* he felt badly about it, for neither he nor his *shevet* was with them in the inauguration. Hakadosh Baruch Hu said to him: 'I swear [that] your [role] is greater than theirs, for you kindle and prepare the lamps.'"

The Ramban (ibid.) is puzzled by this, as he writes:

> It is not clear to me why [Hashem] consoled [Aharon] with candle-lighting, and did not console him with the *ketores,* [which is offered] every morning and night ... or with all

korbanos, the *minchas chavitin*, or the *avodah* of Yom Kippur, which is permissible only [when performed] by the [Kohen Gadol] who enters the Holy of Holies when he is completely sanctified, stands in His sanctuary to serve Him, and recites a blessing with His Holy Name; [and the fact that] his entire tribe [are privileged to] serve Hashem.

He answers that this *pasuk* alludes to the Chanukah lights kindled by Aharon HaKohen's descendants, the Chashmonaim.

Yet Rashi implies that the lighting of the Menorah in the Mishkan features a unique element that is not found in the *ketores* or any other *avodah* in the Beis HaMikdash, which is why Hashem consoled Aharon HaKohen by telling him, "Your role is greater than theirs."

What was so remarkable about lighting and preparing the lights of the Menorah?

The Rosh Yeshivah R' Chaim Shmulevitz[3] explains that lighting the Menorah was an expression of Bnei Yisrael's *hakaras hatov* to Hakadosh Baruch Hu. This quality was exclusive to the *avodah* of lighting and preparing the flames of the Menorah, as we do not find that the purpose of any other *avodah* was to show gratitude to Hashem. The Midrash below explains that when the Kohen lit the Menorah, Bnei Yisrael repaid Hashem, so to speak, for illuminating their path for forty years in the Wilderness, and it was this privilege of serving as Bnei Yisrael's emissary in expressing gratitude to Hakadosh Baruch Hu that soothed Aharon.

The Midrash states (*Bamidbar Rabbah* 15:5):

> The Jewish people said to Hakadosh Baruch Hu: "Ribbono Shel Olam, You tell us to illuminate before You; [but] You are the Light of the world" ... Hakadosh Baruch Hu said to them: "Not that I need you[r light], but you should illuminate for Me just as I illuminated for you. Why? To elevate you before the nations, so they should say, 'See how Yisrael illuminates for the One Who illuminates the world.'"
>
> To what can this be compared? To a seeing person who

3. *Sichos Mussar, Hakaras Hatov.*

> walks on the road together with a blind man. When they enter the house, the seeing person tells the blind one, "Light a candle for me to illuminate for me." Says the blind man, "In your kindness, when we walked along the way, you supported me; until we entered the house, you were the one escorting me. And now you tell me, 'Light a candle for me and illuminate for me?'"
>
> Replied the seeing man: "So you would not be indebted to me for escorting you along the way, I told you, 'Illuminate [the room] for me.'"
>
> The seeing man is Hakadosh Baruch Hu, and the blind man is Yisrael ... Hakadosh Baruch Hu led [Bnei Yisrael] and illuminated their path for them [in the Wilderness], as it is written, וַה׳ הֹלֵךְ לִפְנֵיהֶם יוֹמָם וגו׳, *Hashem went before them by day* (*Shemos* 13:21). When the Mishkan was complete, Hakadosh Baruch Hu called to Moshe and told him, "Illuminate for Me," as it is written, בְּהַעֲלֹתְךָ אֶת הַנֵּרֹת, *When you kindle the lamps* (*Bamidbar* 8:2), in order to elevate you.

This Midrash teaches that the mitzvah of lighting the Menorah was, in fact, an expression of Bnei Yisrael's *hakaras hatov* to Hashem for illuminating their path in the Midbar. Hashem promised Aharon HaKohen, "Your role is greater than theirs, for you kindle and prepare the lamps," as the special *avodah* of preparing the Menorah's lights represented Bnei Yisrael's recognition of Hashem's everlasting kindness and symbolized a form of repayment for it. Moreover, this mitzvah endures forever, in the form of the Chanukah of the Chashmonaim, even though all other aspects of the *avodah* have ceased. This is why the lighting of the Menorah in the Mishkan surpassed the *ketores* and other forms of *avodah* in the Beis HaMikdash.

Another lesson we can glean from the words of Chazal is that *hakaras hatov* is so essential that a person must express gratitude even when the benefactor derives no pleasure or benefit from it. Indeed, Hashem has nothing to gain from Bnei Yisrael's appreciation, yet He still commands us to light the Menorah, because the gratitude expressed by the beneficiary to the benefactor is an end in and of itself.

This concept of *hakaras hatov* is one of the core foundations of the *avodah* in the Beis HaMikdash, as reflected in both the mitzvah of *bikkurim* and the lighting of the Menorah, and it is likewise an essential aspect of man's personal *avodah* each and every day of life. When a Yid rises in the morning, he proclaims, מוֹדֶה אֲנִי לְפָנֶיךָ מֶלֶךְ חַי וְקַיָּם, *I thank You, Hashem, a Living and Existing King,* even though he is still lying in bed and has not even washed his hands! Chazal instituted this brief *tefillah* apart from the regular order of prayer to instill within us the importance of *hakaras hatov* — for as soon as a person opens his eyes in the morning, he must express gratitude to Hashem for His limitless kindness in restoring his *neshamah* to his body.

Hashem should help us to appreciate the kindnesses that others do for us, and to recognize the infinite gifts that He showers upon us every moment of every day, especially during these days of mercy and atonement.

פרשת נצבים
Parashas Nitzavim

◆§ *The Danger of Habit*

כִּי הַמִּצְוָה הַזֹּאת אֲשֶׁר אָנֹכִי מְצַוְּךָ הַיּוֹם לֹא נִפְלֵאת הִוא מִמְּךָ וְלֹא רְחֹקָה הִוא וגו׳ כִּי קָרוֹב אֵלֶיךָ הַדָּבָר מְאֹד בְּפִיךָ וּבִלְבָבְךָ לַעֲשֹׂתוֹ.
For this commandment that I command you today — it is not hidden from you and it is not distant ... Rather, the matter is very near to you — in your mouth and in your heart — to perform it (*Devarim* 30:11-14).

The Ramban writes that the words הַמִּצְוָה הַזֹּאת, *this commandment,* can be interpreted in two ways.

The first is as a reference to the entire Torah, as the *pasuk* emphasizes that Torah is neither concealed nor distant from man. The second interpretation is that these words refer to the mitzvah of *teshuvah*, repentance, which the *pasuk* also describes as neither concealed nor distant from man, but rather close to his heart and accessible at any time and place.

If the mitzvah of *teshuvah* is so natural and close to a person's heart, and can be easily grasped, why do we find so few people taking advantage of it? If all it takes is a genuine feeling and expression of regret, why don't we all do *teshuvah*?

The Comfort of Complacency

The Rosh Yeshivah R' Chaim Shmulevitz[4] decried the force of habit as the greatest catastrophe in man's world. Despite knowing that his ways are misguided or sinful, man all too often falls into complacency and does not repent. Habit wears away at his sentiments of dismay and remorse, and he becomes so accustomed to his wrongful ways that he eventually sees no need to repent.

Therefore, although the potential for *teshuvah* is, indeed, close to a person's heart, the buildup of habit silences the soul's yearning and deflects the possibility of repentance until it appears entirely inaccessible to man — as distant as the heavens or the other end of the ocean.

Suppose that every time a person committed a sin, he would instantly sense the spiritual plunge he'd taken and the deleterious effects on his soul. This awareness would shock him and spur him to immediate repentance. This can be compared to a person who is unaware of the concept of death, until one day he learns that every person is bound to die at some point. This realization would surely shake him up and cause him to mend his ways and return wholeheartedly to Hashem. Unfortunately, though, just as people have become accustomed to the concept of death and are therefore not shaken by the thought, most people do not take to heart the severity of their sins, and they are not open to inspiration, which prevents them from repenting.

The force of habit is so toxic that Chazal teach (*Yoma* 86b), "Once a person commits a sin and repeats it, it becomes permitted to him. Can it even enter your mind that [the sin] becomes permitted to him? Rather, say that it becomes to him as though it were permissible." The more times a person repeats an offense, the less significant he considers it, until he all but forgets that it is a sin.

Rabbeinu Yonah elaborates (*Shaarei Teshuvah* 1:38) that when someone repeats a sin to the extent that it becomes permissible in his eyes, he is considered to have thrown off the yoke of this commandment and enters the category of a *mumar l'davar echad* (an apostate regarding this specific mitzvah).

---

4. *Sichos Mussar, Tardemas HaHergel.*

Moments of Inspiration

A person's closeness to the mitzvah of *teshuvah* is conditional, then, upon his eliminating the force of negative habit and opening his eyes to the gravity of his sin. This can be compared to a chicken that wallows in the mud and becomes encrusted in filth. If the farmer attempts to clean the chicken, it will take him hours to scrub it feather by feather. Yet if the chicken merely flaps its wings, all the mud will fly off, and its feathers will be instantly cleaned.

The same is true of a person who does *teshuvah*: If he endeavors to repent by rectifying each and every action separately, it will take him a frustratingly long time. Yet if he simply awakens in an instant, like a chicken flapping its wings, then he can repent immediately, as the *pasuk* says, כִּי קָרוֹב אֵלֶיךָ הַדָּבָר מְאֹד, *rather, the matter is very near to you.*

Born of Indolence

Habit is rooted in the *middah* of *atzlus,* indolence. One who is indolent grows lethargic and sleepy, whereas one who is active and refuses to sit back and relax does not slumber, but remains constantly alert to what is required of him, and does not succumb to the force of habit.

Shlomo HaMelech cautions us against *atzlus* with the words: לֵךְ אֶל נְמָלָה עָצֵל רְאֵה דְרָכֶיהָ וַחֲכָם, *Go to the ant, you sluggard; see its ways and grow wise* (*Mishlei* 6:6). The ant works industriously without pausing to rest for a moment, and a person who observes this minuscule creature in action can draw great wisdom from its ways. Several weeks ago, I glanced down at the floor and noticed an ant heaving a granule as large as its entire body across the room. The ant was clearly struggling, dropping the granule again and again, yet it kept obdurately to its goal, continuing to drag its load to its destination. Shlomo HaMelech exhorts us to watch the ant, observe its diligence in laboring toward its goal, and absorb the lesson of consistent effort — because this is the only way to avoid falling prey to the pernicious force of habit.

Preserving Inspiration

Chazal relate (*Sotah* 13a) that when Yaakov Avinu was carried to Me'aras HaMachpeilah for burial, the wicked Eisav attempted to halt the funeral procession by claiming that the burial plot was rightfully his. The *shevatim* responded that their father had purchased the plot from Eisav, whereupon Eisav demanded to see the deed of sale. The *shevatim* replied that the deed had remained behind in Egypt, but sent Naftali, who was swift as a deer, to sprint to Egypt and retrieve it.

Chushim ben Dan, who was deaf and unable to follow the dialogue between his uncles and Eisav, did not understand the cause of the unseemly delay. When he asked what was happening and was told that Eisav was holding off the burial until Naftali's return, Chushim was appalled by the disgrace to his grandfather Yaakov, and he grabbed a stick and beheaded Eisav.

What motivated Chushim ben Dan to zealously defend Yaakov Avinu's honor? Why was he more offended by the disgrace to his grandfather than the others, including the *shevatim*, who were Yaakov's own sons? Finally, what connection was there between his zealous act on Yaakov's behalf and his impaired hearing?

As soon as the *shevatim* began arguing and negotiating with Eisav HaRasha, they accepted — *and grew accustomed* — to the temporary slight to Yaakov Avinu's honor that resulted from the delay in his burial, and they did not even protest it. Only Chushim, who was unable to hear the discussion between the *shevatim* and Eisav and whose feelings of horror were not dulled due to complacency, observed the disgrace to Yaakov in mounting horror, until he grew so distraught that he zealously grabbed a stick and killed Eisav. This indicates how destructive the force of habit can be, for people can be lulled into complacency even in the face of something as severe as an affront to *kavod hameis*, and even when the person in question is Yaakov Avinu!

Outward Action Breeds Inspiration

Even mere outward actions have the power to influence a person and rouse his emotions. Chazal teach, regarding the mitzvah of retelling the story of Yetzias Mitzrayim (*Pesachim* 116a): "The Rabbis taught: If his son is intelligent [enough to ask the *Mah Nishtanah* questions], he asks him. But if [the son] is not intelligent enough, his wife asks him. And if not, then he asks them to himself. And even two Torah scholars who are proficient in the laws of Pesach must ask one another."

The mitzvah of remembering Yetzias Mitzrayim is a perpetual obligation, so a person can easily feel jaded and uninspired by the story. To ensure that each individual will feel that he personally departed Egypt, Chazal instituted the halachah that the story should be related in question-and-answer form, as questions inevitably awaken a person and provoke inspiration.

The power of an outward action to spur a person to repentance is evident in the following teaching of Chazal as well. The Gemara states (*Kiddushin* 49b) that if a man tells a woman, "Become betrothed to me on condition that I am a *tzaddik*," the halachah is that even if he is a complete *rasha*, she is betrothed to him, for it is possible that thoughts of repentance came to his mind. How can a wicked person be transformed into a *tzaddik* through a fleeting thought of *teshuvah*?

The *mefarshim* answer that the man's very declaration, "on condition that I am a *tzaddik*," prompts thoughts of *teshuvah* and inspires him to repent. This external action can spur him to such potent *teshuvah* that he can become a complete *tzaddik*.

Bridging the Distance

Regarding this mitzvah, the *pasuk* continues (*Devarim* 30:12-13): לֹא בַשָּׁמַיִם הִוא לֵאמֹר מִי יַעֲלֶה לָּנוּ הַשָּׁמַיְמָה וְיִקָּחֶהָ לָּנוּ וְיַשְׁמִעֵנוּ אֹתָהּ וְנַעֲשֶׂנָּה, וְלֹא מֵעֵבֶר לַיָּם הִוא לֵאמֹר מִי יַעֲבָר לָנוּ אֶל עֵבֶר הַיָּם וְיִקָּחֶהָ לָּנוּ וְיַשְׁמִעֵנוּ אֹתָהּ וְנַעֲשֶׂנָּה, *It is not in heaven, [for you] to say, "Who can ascend to the heaven for us and take it for us, so that we can listen to it and perform it?" Nor is it across the sea, [for you] to say, "Who can cross to the other side of the sea for us and take it for us, so that we can listen to it and perform it?"*

R' Leib Chasman notes[5] that it is logical to tell a person that he

---

5. *Ohr Yahel, Lo Nifleis Hi, V'im Nifleis — Mimcha.*

shouldn't make the mistake of thinking that something is miles and miles away when it is really only a single mile away. But what sense is there in telling a person that something isn't far away in the heavens, but is actually so close to him that it is right there in his mouth? Can a person make such a fundamental error as to think that something is so far away when it is actually right inside him?

Furthermore, the *Targum Yerushalmi* (ibid. 12) interprets the *pasuk* to mean that the Torah is not in the heavens so that we must be as exalted as Moshe Rabbeinu, who was capable of ascending to heaven to bring it down, nor is it hidden in the depths of the ocean so that we must be as exalted as Yonah HaNavi, who was able to descend to the depths of the sea. If there is any reason to believe that Torah could be attained only by righteous individuals the likes of Moshe Rabbeinu and Yonah HaNavi, then how could simple people like ourselves ever be expected to fulfill the Torah?

R' Leib Chasman explains that there are two opposing forces in man's soul: the physical force that results from man's being created from the earth, as the Torah says, וַיִּיצֶר ה׳ אֱלֹקִים אֶת הָאָדָם עָפָר מִן הָאֲדָמָה, *And Hashem God formed the man of dust from the ground* (*Bereishis* 2:7); and the spiritual force produced by Hashem's "blowing a spirit of life" into our bodies.

A person who gives his spiritual powers dominance over his physical abilities can soar to heights of spirituality that surpass even those of the heavenly angels. If, however, a person allows his physical abilities to rule over his spiritual powers, then he will live a life of physicality and materialism, similar to an animal.

Every human being encompasses both of these poles, which are as distant from each other as heaven and earth.

When the Torah states, לֹא בַשָּׁמַיִם הִיא, *it is not in heaven*, it conveys that after one has made his spirit sovereign over his corporeal body, the Torah becomes קָרוֹב אֵלֶיךָ ... מְאֹד בְּפִיךָ וּבִלְבָבְךָ לַעֲשֹׂתוֹ, *very near to you — in your mouth and in your heart — to perform it.* But if he allows his physicality to overwhelm his spiritual strength, then the Torah will be as distant from him as if it were high in the heavens or across the sea.

There is but a minute difference between making one's spirituality dominant over his physicality and the opposite. In the split second that it takes a person to wholeheartedly accept the yoke of Torah, he can catapult from the earth all the way to the heavens and emerge from darkness into light. Although Torah and the mitzvah of *teshuvah* are truly remote from a person, it is still possible to bridge this distance through a single moment of deep inspiration and introspection.

Indeed, Chazal (*Devarim Rabbah* 8:3) expound the words לֹא נִפְלֵאת הִיא מִמְּךָ, *it is not hidden from you,* to mean, "It is not hidden; and if it is hidden, it is מִמְּךָ, because of you, since you are not occupied with it." We see, then, that neglecting Torah is what causes a person to be distant from it.

This same principle can be applied to *teshuvah.* In a single moment of spiritual awakening, a person can repent wholeheartedly to Hashem and elevate himself from the abyss of darkness to the heights of spirituality.

From Introspection to Inspiration

A person is capable of committing sin after sin without fear or remorse, despite knowing that he will one day be forced to account for his actions before the Heavenly Tribunal. How can this be? Why aren't we terrified of sin?

Hashem exhorts, רְאֵה נָתַתִּי לְפָנֶיךָ הַיּוֹם אֶת הַחַיִּים וְאֶת הַטּוֹב וְאֶת הַמָּוֶת וְאֶת הָרָע, *See — I have placed before you today the life and the good, and the death and the evil* (*Devarim* 30:15), and Rashi comments: "*The life and the good* — one is dependent on the other. If you will do good, see now, you have life; and if you will do evil, see now, you have death. The Torah goes on to explain how."

The Torah prefaces the choice between good and evil with the command of רְאֵה, *see!* The first thing we are required to do is to look and see — to reflect, introspect, and awaken ourselves from our spiritual slumber. We are bound to choose good not only because it is an alternative to choosing evil, but because we have reflected, introspected, and concluded that this is the correct and beneficial path. And the only way to achieve this level of introspection is by learning *mussar*!

Only if a person engages in the study of *mussar* and reflects upon the will of Hashem and what truly leads to אֶת הַחַיִּים וְאֶת הַטּוֹב, *the life and the good,* will he be inspired to feel awe and fear and set himself upon the proper path in life. The way to experience a spiritual awakening that will empower us to subjugate our physical nature to our spiritual powers is by learning *mussar*!

May we merit to repent sincerely before Hashem, and may we all be blessed with a sweet new year.

פרשת וילך
Parashas Vayeilech

☙ *Choosing Good*

וַיֵּלֶךְ מֹשֶׁה וַיְדַבֵּר אֶת הַדְּבָרִים הָאֵלֶּה אֶל כָּל יִשְׂרָאֵל, וַיֹּאמֶר אֲלֵהֶם בֶּן מֵאָה וְעֶשְׂרִים שָׁנָה אָנֹכִי הַיּוֹם, לֹא אוּכַל עוֹד לָצֵאת וְלָבוֹא, וַה׳ אָמַר אֵלַי לֹא תַעֲבֹר אֶת הַיַּרְדֵּן הַזֶּה.

Moshe went and spoke these words to all of Yisrael. He said to them, "I am a hundred and twenty years old today; I can no longer go out and come in, for Hashem has said to me, 'You shall not cross this Yarden'" (*Devarim* 31:1-2).

Rashi comments: "Can it be that his strength failed him? The *pasuk* says, לֹא כָהֲתָה עֵינוֹ וְלֹא נָס לֵחֹה, *His eyes had not dimmed, and his vigor had not diminished* (*Devarim* 34:7). What is [the meaning of] לֹא אוּכַל, *I can no [longer]*? I am not allowed, for authorization was taken from me and given to Yehoshua."

Because Hashem Asks

By saying אֵינִי רַשַּׁאי, *I am not allowed,* Moshe Rabbeinu imparts a profound lesson, as he expresses that the only thing stopping him from entering Eretz Yisrael is that he is unauthorized to do so. Nothing stops a person from doing something, except that he is "not allowed." A Yid cannot say, "I can't," because as long as the Torah does not exempt him from a mitzvah, he is obligated to fulfill it, and he may not evade it even due to age or frailty.

On the other hand, a Yid who does everything required of him must know that his accomplishments are not the product of his own willpower or abilities, but are simply a function of Hakadosh Baruch Hu's command to him. Mitzvos are not elective; they were given as dictates to perform the will of Hashem. Even if he would have performed a particular action without being commanded, a Yid must still do the mitzvah only because he was commanded to do so.

Strong and Courageous

Moshe Rabbeinu continues: חִזְקוּ וְאִמְצוּ אַל תִּירְאוּ וְאַל תַּעַרְצוּ מִפְּנֵיהֶם כִּי ה׳ אֱלֹקֶיךָ הוּא הַהֹלֵךְ עִמָּךְ לֹא יַרְפְּךָ וְלֹא יַעַזְבֶךָּ, *Be strong and courageous, do not be afraid and do not be broken before them, for Hashem your God — it is He Who goes before you, He will not release you nor will He forsake you* (*Devarim* 31:6).

The *mefarshim* note that Moshe Rabbeinu was the greatest man in the world, a man so exalted that the *Shechinah* spoke through his mouth. The Torah itself attests, וְלֹא קָם נָבִיא עוֹד בְּיִשְׂרָאֵל כְּמֹשֶׁה אֲשֶׁר יְדָעוֹ ה׳ פָּנִים אֶל פָּנִים, *Never again has there arisen in Yisrael a prophet like Moshe, whom Hashem had known face to face* (*Devarim* 34:10). On the very last day of his life, before passing from the material world into a world of utter spirituality, Moshe Rabbeinu faced the people of his generation — the Dor Dei'ah, who had borne witness to the miracles and wonders in Egypt and at the Yam Suf and had received the Torah on Har Sinai — and offered them two words of *chizuk:* חִזְקוּ וְאִמְצוּ, *Be strong and courageous.*

Moshe did not elaborate which realms or qualities Bnei Yisrael should seek to strengthen, for he knew that every individual, even the greatest, requires *chizuk* every moment of every day, and not only under extenuating circumstances.

Indeed, Moshe's final call of חִזְקוּ וְאִמְצוּ was not directed exclusively to the nation that was about to enter Eretz Yisrael, nor was he offering Bnei Yisrael encouragement for all future generations.

Rather, it was an overarching directive obligating every Jew, young and old, at every juncture in life. Every person is liable to stumble and fall spiritually, yet he must gather strength and courage from within time and again, under every circumstance, so that he can overcome his fears and doubts and remember that Hakadosh Baruch Hu is always helping and supporting him.

If these words of *chizuk* were told to the people who received the Torah on Har Sinai, how much more so does our spiritually bereft generation require *chizuk* in our *avodas Hashem.* Therefore, each one of us must take heed of Moshe Rabbeinu's exhortation to Bnei Yisrael to strengthen ourselves continuously.

This spiritual strengthening does not occur in a single step or action, but requires intense, repetitive effort and the choosing of the proper path each day anew. This message is illustrated by the Gemara's statement: "R' Yitzchak said: Man's evil inclination renews its [battle] against him every day ... R' Shimon ben Levi said: Man's evil inclination strengthens itself against him every day and endeavors to kill him ... and if not for Hakadosh Baruch Hu aiding him, [man] could not prevail over him" (*Kiddushin* 30b).

Had Moshe Rabbeinu's *chizuk* sufficed to inspire Klal Yisrael for all generations to choose the proper path in life, there would have been no purpose in Hashem creating the concept of *teshuvah*. The existence of this gift of *teshuvah* indicates that a Yid must reinforce this message in his heart every day, so that he should not fall prey to the *yetzer hara.*

Furthermore, since no person is immune to sin — as the *pasuk* states, כִּי אָדָם אֵין צַדִּיק בָּאָרֶץ אֲשֶׁר יַעֲשֶׂה טּוֹב וְלֹא יֶחֱטָא, *For there is no man so wholly righteous on earth that he [always] does good and never sins* (*Koheles* 7:20) — Hakadosh Baruch Hu, in His kindness, created *teshuvah,* to allow one who slips and falls to rise again, strengthen himself, and repent from his evil ways.

In order to strengthen oneself constantly, a person must first choose the proper path in life. Hakadosh Baruch Hu imbued man with unfathomable physical and spiritual capabilities, and man is given the constant choice of whether to utilize these strengths to serve Him, or, *chas v'shalom,* to use them for the opposite.

Under a century ago, the whole world witnessed the mass destruction that one man wrought by abusing the vast strengths that Hashem imbued within him. Hitler, *yimach shemo*, possessed extraordinary talents and capabilities, but instead of using them to benefit humanity, he employed them to devastate the world. How much strength does every individual possess to accomplish good or evil! The choice is in our hands.

Rosh Hashanah — Judging the Future

During these days, we are judged for the choices we made throughout the last year, both good and bad. It seems puzzling, however, that Rosh Hashanah, the day of judgment, marks the first day of the new year as opposed to the final days of the year that just ended.

Logic dictates that a person be judged after he has acted, and not before. Why, then, does the Yom Hadin coincide with the dawn of a new year? Furthermore, why is this Yom Tov referred to as Rosh Hashanah — "the head of the year" — when it is essentially a day of judgment on the past year?

The judgment of this day focuses primarily on a person's *future*, not on his past actions. On Rosh Hashanah, a person is assigned his *tafkid* for the coming year, which encompasses what he must accomplish in order to bring this world to its final *tikkun*. But since a person can only be assigned a role that he is capable of fulfilling, he is also judged regarding his past actions, and how he fulfilled his mission throughout the past year. If he did not carry out his role faithfully, his spiritual stature sinks, and he is designated a less prestigious role and given inferior tools and capabilities relative to his true potential.

Rosh Hashanah, then, is not a day when man's actions are judged so that he can be punished for his sins. Rather, it is a day when he is allocated the tools and abilities that he will require throughout the coming year in order to serve Hashem and optimally fulfill the role that he was assigned. This is the primary reason why this day is called Rosh Hashanah, as it is the starting point of the new year and the day when a person receives all the tools he will need in order to serve Hashem and accomplish his mission in the world.

During these days of *teshuvah* and atonement, we must strive to fulfill the directive of חִזְקוּ וְאִמְצוּ more than ever. This is a time when we stand at a spiritual crossroads, trembling in awe as we await, on one hand, the weighty verdict regarding how we fulfilled our mission throughout the past year, and, on the other hand, our assignment for the next year. The heights that we will achieve in Torah and *yiras Shamayim* and the growth that we will experience in *avodas Hashem* are all determined on this momentous day.

During these auspicious moments, we can still muster the courage to strengthen ourselves to choose our paths anew, and to opt for good by repenting and pledging to fulfill Hashem's will in the future. Moreover, the very fact that we possess the ability to choose good and thus impact our yearlong spiritual ascent and mission means that it is surely incumbent upon us to do so!

When a Yid stands in prayer before Hashem, recites *Vidui,* and *klaps Al Cheit,* his focus should not be directed to his past actions, but to his future deeds. His yearning, moreover, should reflect that of a *ben aliyah* who is striving courageously to succeed in *avodas Hashem.*

On a simplistic level, it would seem that man's *bechirah* is a question of good and evil, black and white; yet this is far from the truth. Every mitzvah opportunity compels a Yid to choose not only *whether* to fulfill the mitzvah, but also *how* to fulfill it, and whether to adhere to each halachic detail. It is for these fine choices that man is judged. Did he recite a *berachah* with more *kavanah* or less *kavanah*? Did he observe Shabbos with all its requirements? Was he cautious with other people's money, and was he careful to avoid humiliating a fellow Yid? He is likewise judged for his *middos*: Is he arrogant? Is he angered easily?

One who examines every nuance of his conduct and every detail of his mitzvah observance will achieve an exalted level of *teshuvah*!

A person who appreciates the significance of this period and recognizes his obligations during these days can approach Rosh Hashanah and Yom Kippur with the sentiment of וְגִילוּ בִּרְעָדָה,

and rejoice when there is trembling (*Tehillim* 2:11). On one hand, he trembles in fear of the impending judgment for last year's sins and the ensuing verdict for the coming year. Yet, on the other hand, he rejoices over the vast potential embedded in these days, when he can easily choose to change direction, return to Hashem, and within a remarkably short time transform his entire life into one of joyous *avodas Hashem.*

We must remember, though, that these days are numbered and pass far too quickly. Woe unto one who idles and thereby forfeits the incredible potential of this time.

Hashem should help us redouble our efforts in *avodas Hashem,* Torah, *tefillah,* and *bein adam lachaveiro.* May we all find the strength inside us to reinforce each other's commitment to Torah and *teshuvah,* and in the merit of this unity, may we emerge from darkness to spiritual light and radiance.

פרשת האזינו
Parashas Haazinu

⁂ *Testimony of the Heavens and Earth*

הַאֲזִינוּ הַשָּׁמַיִם וַאֲדַבֵּרָה וְתִשְׁמַע הָאָרֶץ אִמְרֵי פִי.
Give ear, O heavens, and I will speak; and may the earth hear the words of my mouth (*Devarim* 32:1).

Rashi comments: "*Give ear, O heavens* — that I am giving warning to Yisrael, and be witnesses to the matter, for thus did I tell Yisrael, that you shall be witnesses. And similarly, [this is the meaning of] *and may the earth hear*. Why did [Moshe] call the heavens and the earth as witnesses? Moshe said, 'I am flesh and blood; tomorrow I will be dead. If Yisrael were to say, "We did not accept the covenant upon ourselves," who could refute them?' Therefore, He called the heavens and earth as witnesses against them, witnesses who last forever."

Moshe Rabbeinu calls upon the heavens and earth to serve as witnesses that Bnei Yisrael accepted the Torah at Har Sinai. The halachah states that if two witnesses can give testimony, it is a mitzvah for them to approach *beis din* and testify. The Gemara (*Bava Kamma* 56a) adds that if two witnesses are capable of testifying but do not, they transgress the Torah's precept, אִם לוֹא יַגִּיד וְנָשָׂא עֲוֹנוֹ, *if he does not testify, he shall bear his iniquity* (*Vayikra* 5:1).

The testimony rendered by the heavens and earth takes the form of the bounty that they deliver to the world, as it is written, הַגֶּפֶן תִּתֵּן פִּרְיָהּ וְהָאָרֶץ תִּתֵּן אֶת יְבוּלָהּ וְהַשָּׁמַיִם יִתְּנוּ טַלָּם, *The vine gives forth its fruit, the land gives forth its produce, and the heavens give forth their dew* (*Zechariah* 8:12). If Bnei Yisrael observe Torah and mitzvos, the heavens will attest to their righteous deeds by showering them with rain and dew, and the earth will give plentiful produce. If, however, they do not fulfill their part of their covenant with Hashem, then both heaven and earth will unite in testimony against them by fulfilling the words of the *pasuk*: וְעָצַר אֶת הַשָּׁמַיִם וְלֹא יִהְיֶה מָטָר וְהָאֲדָמָה לֹא תִתֵּן אֶת יְבוּלָהּ, *He will restrain the heaven so there will be no rain, and the ground will not yield its produce* (*Devarim* 11:17).

Sustaining the World

The world's continuity is contingent upon Bnei Yisrael's fulfillment of Torah and mitzvos. If Bnei Yisrael are negligent in their commitment to Torah, the world as we know it will cease to exist. Hashem's witnesses will render their testimony and cause the world to revert to nothingness.

The Gemara states (*Shabbos* 88a): "Reish Lakish said: What is the meaning of the *pasuk* וַיְהִי עֶרֶב וַיְהִי בֹקֶר יוֹם הַשִּׁשִּׁי, *And there was evening and there was morning, the sixth day* (*Bereishis* 1:31)? Why is there an extra ה [in הַשִּׁשִּׁי]? It teaches that Hakadosh Baruch Hu stipulated with the works of the creation, saying to them, 'If the Jewish people accept the Torah, you will endure. But if they do not accept the Torah, I will return you to astonishing emptiness!'"

This Gemara underscores that all of Creation was dependent upon that momentous *yom hashishi*, the sixth day of Sivan when Bnei Yisrael accepted the Torah at Har Sinai. The giving of the Torah was the singular purpose of Creation and without it, there is no justification for the existence of the world. This is expressed by the *navi's* words: אִם לֹא בְרִיתִי יוֹמָם וָלָיְלָה, חֻקּוֹת שָׁמַיִם וָאָרֶץ לֹא שָׂמְתִּי, *If my covenant with the night and with the day would not be; had I not set up the laws of heaven and earth* (*Yirmiyah* 33:25).

By upholding our covenant with Hashem and observing Torah and mitzvos, we actually sustain the world! Conversely, if we fail to fulfill our duties, the world will cease to exist. On a practical level, if the world exists right now, that is incontrovertible proof that the *kol haTorah* resounds in the world and has not ceased for even a moment throughout history.

This is the compelling lesson gleaned from this week's *parashah, Parashas Haazinu,* which is read on Shabbos Shuvah, the Shabbos before Yom Kippur. In this *parashah,* Moshe Rabbeinu calls the heavens and earth to testify on Bnei Yisrael's behalf, revealing that the world's very existence is conditional upon Bnei Yisrael's fulfillment of Torah and mitzvos. What better preparation is there for the imminent Yom Hadin?

Reflecting Upon Judgment Breeds Yiras Hashem

Later in the *shirah* of *Haazinu,* Moshe expresses, הַצּוּר תָּמִים פָּעֳלוֹ כִּי כָל דְּרָכָיו מִשְׁפָּט קֵל אֱמוּנָה וְאֵין עָוֶל צַדִּיק וְיָשָׁר הוּא, *The Rock! — perfect is His work, for all His paths are justice; a God of faith without iniquity, righteous and fair is He* (*Devarim* 32:4). Hashem's judgment is eminently fair, and is actually a gift to us, for our benefit, just as the suffering that *tzaddikim* endure in Olam Hazeh enables them to receive their true reward in Olam Haba.

Do we really appreciate and feel the judgment? Are we conscious of the profound consequences of the verdict hovering ominously over us? I doubt that we do, because if we were properly aware of the implications of these Days of Awe, we — and our lives — would look very different. I believe, however, that by delving deeply into these *pesukim* in Haazinu, we can attain the sentiments required of us during these days.

Learning With Chiyus, Without Distraction

Just yesterday, I heard a story about R' Yosef Shalom Elyashiv, and I feel that it is a mitzvah to publicize it. A distinguished *avreich* once approached him to ask how a person can overcome the tendency to forget the Torah he has learned.

R' Elyashiv replied with a question of his own: "Do you review your learning well?" The *avreich* replied affirmatively.

"That is not enough," said the *gadol hador*. "Every time you learn a *sugya*, you should feel that the learning is brand new and fresh, as if you never learned it before. If you learn like this, you will not forget your learning."

Torah that is learned with *cheishek* and pleasure becomes embedded deep in the person's heart and remains there permanently, never to be forgotten. When a person learns a new *sugya*, he approaches it with passion and desire. The content is unfamiliar and intriguing, so he toils assiduously to understand it and plumb its depths. One who reviews an "old" *sugya*, in contrast, approaches his learning with the feeling that he already knows the material, and he is therefore less inclined to analyze every argument, word, and nuance. This attitude leads to forgetfulness, because the learning is not absorbed in the person's heart. In this regard, Chazal teach: "It is harder for a person to return and learn a *sugya* that he has already forgotten than to learn a *sugya* that he has never before learned" (*Yoma* 21a).

It is said that when the Vilna Gaon wished to test a young man who wanted to join his *beis midrash*, he would ask him to review a topic several times in succession. As the *bachur* learned and reviewed the *sugya*, the Gaon would scrutinize him to see whether he was learning the Gemara with the same desire and passion as he had learned it the very first time. Only if the *bachur* exhibited that vital *cheishek* did the Vilna Gaon deem him worthy of becoming his *talmid*.[6]

I, too, was privileged to know a Yid who embodied this quality — my rebbi, R' Chaim Kamil. R' Chaim could sit and learn a *sugya* with immense *cheishek* even after he'd already learned and mastered it thoroughly dozens of times! Every time he reviewed his *limud*, he would come alive as if he were experiencing the words and tasting their sweetness for the very first time. This, indeed, is the key to acquiring and internalizing Torah!

Returning to the previous story, the *avreich* then asked R' Elyashiv if he had any other advice for how to learn Torah without

---

6. *Menuchah U'Kedushah, Shaar HaTorah* 1:4.

forgetting it, to which Rav Elyashiv replied, "Yes! Learn without *hesech hadaas* — without distraction!"

"How much time is considered *hesech hadaas*?" the *avreich* inquired.

R' Elyashiv gave an astounding reply: "The amount of time it takes to blink. That's *hesech hadaas*."

The very thought is chilling! Torah learned with *hesech hadaas* is reduced to "tatters" (*Sanhedrin* 71a). Rashi (ibid.) explains that this means that the person forgets his learning, and recalls it only alternately. Only Torah that is learned with *retzifus*, and without distraction, cements itself in the mind and memory of the learner.

R' Elyashiv taught us two fundamental lessons that enable us to succeed in *limud Torah*. The first is to approach every *sugya* as if it is the very first time we are learning it, and the second is to avoid even fleeting distractions while learning.

Not only did R' Elyashiv teach these lessons, but anyone who ever observed the *posek hador* in action recognized that he truly personified them. An *avreich* once wanted to ask him a question in halachah. Loath to interrupt the *gadol* in the middle of his learning, he waited until he would become available. Waiting behind the closed door, he listened, enraptured, as R' Elyashiv spoke animatedly with his *chavrusa*, analyzing every aspect of the *sugya*. Only later did the *avreich* realize that R' Elyashiv was learning *alone*, but in the traditional style of *shakla v'tarya*, as if learning with a *chavrusa*. For indeed, only by learning the *sugya* with *chiyus*, as if for the first time, does a person merit to remember what he has learned.

The Rosh Yeshivah R' Eliezer Yehuda Finkel once designated a group of ten *bnei aliyah* who committed to learn no less than twelve hours a day. I was privileged to number among those ten *avreichim*. Once, circumstances prevented me from meeting my quota of learning hours, and I actually escorted my *chavrusa* home on foot in order to make up the lost learning time by walking and talking in learning.

Standing now on the brink of the Yom Hadin, we must remember that Hashem's judgment is an act of kindness, and is purely for our benefit. When we undertake *kabbalos* for the new year, we must direct our focus to our holy Torah, for only by learning with *chiyus* and without distraction will we merit to acquire Torah. In this *zechus,* we can approach the Yom Hadin with confidence that we will surely merit a *g'mar chasimah tovah.*